EXPERIMENTAL HEART

SURRENDERED

BOOK 5

SHANNON PEMRICK

Surrendered
Experimental Heart | Book Five

Copyright © 2019 Shannon Pemrick
www.shannonpemrick.com

Cover Illustration by Jackson Tjota
Cover Typography by Amalia Chitulescu
Editing by Sandra Nguyen and Cody Anne Arko-Omori

ISBN 978-0-9984464-9-3 (paperback)
ISBN 978-0-9984464-8-6 (hardcover)
ISBN 978-0-9984464-6-2 (e-book)

For my eternal dragon
For, well, eveything.

BOOKS BY SHANNON PEMRICK

EXPERIMENTAL HEART
Destiny
Pieces
Secrets
Exposed
Surrendered

ORACLE'S PATH
Prophecy of Convergence

Prophecy Tested
Prophecy Chosen

LOOKING FOR GROUP
Spellbinding His Ranger
Protecting His Priestess
Summoning Their Elementalist

Light from the full moon filtered in through the barred window of the cell. I sat in my corner, as always, contemplating my fate—remembering all the mistakes I'd made leading up to this point. I didn't wallow in self-pity—it wouldn't change a thing. Fighting the inevitable hadn't helped me, either. I wasn't meant to have any other life.

I looked to my friends who slept nearby. I just wished my mistakes hadn't dragged them into this.

My eyes grew heavy, my weakened state not allowing me to stay awake long when I wasn't dealing with torture. I allowed slumber to come. The remaining memories waited for me.

CHAPTER 1

Phyre held up his arms and announced, *"Ambassador Laz'shika!"* Orange light flickered across the forest clearing, casting tall shadows of people onto the trees. The night sky, while dulled by the air pollution of the city beyond the forest, twinkled with stars. People in decorative costumes danced around the fire, while others mingled about in the clearing.

As I expected, everyone wanted to talk to me. Some just wanted to congratulate me on my passing the test and my official Ambassador title, while others wanted to chat. I knew I was going to have to get used to it since I was now the Ambassador, but that wasn't going to be easy for me. I wasn't a people person. And on top of that, I had limited knowledge of rituals and customs for the tribes beyond the West Tribe. *There are many people far more qualified than me.*

The ever-present voice in my head, one not belonging to me, spoke, *"Oh, stop it. You're plenty qualified."*

One good thing that had come of it was my reconnection with Arnia and Jaybird. They apologized for missing the test, but were happy for my end result. After speaking with them for a bit, they went to join a group of North Tribe shamans. The two had really hit it off with the tribe, and it made me wonder about their future after we were free. They could benefit from a teacher, and the North Tribe was the only one I knew of to have any metal shamans or metal elementalists in the area.

A relieved sigh left my lips when I was finally allowed to sit down and relax for a moment. Raikidan sat down next to me, and my friends took their seats around us. They had stayed with me while I had endured all the greetings, and I was grateful. Their support made it easier to deal with, and Raikidan had also done his job by pulling me away when I became too overwhelmed.

My brow rose in surprise when a stout, blond dwarven man with a large septum piercing came up to us and handed me a mug, his braided beard with metal rings and clasps with large decorative plates bouncing in front of him. I hadn't seen him since the competition in his city of Azrok, several months ago. "Vorn?"

"Aye, lass." He smiled and shifted his hammer as it leaned on his shoulder. "Ye dun think I be missin' this ol' party ye be havin', did ye?"

I chuckled and took the mug of ale. "Good to see you, too, but did you really have to bring your hammer with you?"

He laughed, his eyes shining bright. "Lass, ye know I dun go any-where without it."

"All right, you got me there."

I went to take a swig of my drink as he walked away, when I noticed a woman looking like a near spitting image of Ryoko, frantically searching for… something. A dark-skinned elven man with tattoos, piercings, and a partially shaved head followed her, attempting to calm her down. *Peacekeeper Ryoko and Varro? Why would two of the Peacekeepers be here?* I had been quite surprised to see Peacekeeper Ryoko show up during my test, so seeing her here at my party was quite the perplexing sight.

Looking around, I found Peacekeeper Pyralis mingling with his clan, along with a green-haired, golden-eyed woman. I guessed her to be Peacekeeper Reiki. Pyralis' presence with his clan didn't surprise me, due to the strong connection he had to them when I visited the clan over the summer.

Mingling with some shamans, and now Vorn, were Peacekeepers Assar and Raynn, the latter throwing me off briefly since the Raynn we knew looked eerily identical.

"Where is she?" Peacekeeper Ryoko mumbled.

"Calm down," Varro said. "We'll find her. We have all night."

I shook my head. *Peacekeeper Ryoko, you're going to make this night very interesting.* "Ryoko, Varro, over here."

Ryoko looked at me, her brow twisted, and then squeaked when Peacekeeper Ryoko appeared suddenly in front of her. Peacekeeper Ryoko tilted her head and assessed Ryoko. Ryoko stared back at the woman with uncertainty.

After she was done looking Ryoko over, Peacekeeper Ryoko laced her fingers into Ryoko's hair. "Your hair is so silky. I could never get my hair like this. How do you do it?"

Ryoko shrugged. "Conditioner. I can only imagine the beauty products we have now are a lot different from what you had."

Peacekeeper Ryoko thought this over and Varro chuckled. "After years of war, hygiene wasn't a priority to put resources into."

Peacekeeper Ryoko nodded. "That's true."

Ryoko touched Peacekeeper Ryoko's hair. "Yours is really soft, though—more so than mine, if you want my opinion. Consider yourself lucky to have such naturally soft hair."

Peacekeeper Ryoko smiled widely and the two began talking about similarities and differences between them. Amused, I listened in while paying attention to the dances the Southern and Northern Tribes performed around the fires.

The two women had quite a bit in common, but they also had many differences, and I could tell this talk with Peacekeeper Ryoko made Ryoko feel a lot better about herself. She had always thought less of herself because she was a clone, feeling that marked her as unable to be her own person.

"I just hope they don't try to dress the same. Then we'll have a problem," the voice said.

"Oh, don't even suggest that. I don't want to deal with that again."

"Those twin assassins you trained?"

"Yeah, that was the stuff of nightmares." Psychic assassins—the first of their kind. I was glad the project ended and they resumed standard psychic training.

Ryoko's ears twitched as the two went back and forth. "Off topic, but I'm going to forget if I don't ask now. Peacekeeper Ryoko, did you actually end up dying alone? That ending to your life always seemed a bit fishy to me."

Peacekeeper Ryoko giggled. "No, I didn't. Whoever made up that story is dumb. I had my pack." She gestured to Varro. "And I also had him."

My interested gaze swept to Varro. He laughed. "Surprise!"

"Surprise, indeed."

"Life is full of them! You're in for a bumpy ride in the next coming weeks."

"What's that supposed to mean?"

The voice chuckled but refrained from giving an answer.

"Raynn and Assar were the only ones who really liked all the attention we received after the war, so the rest of us hid in the shadows," Varro explained. "No one really knew what we were doing with our lives, and that was how we liked it. It was peaceful."

"Explains the theory about Ryoko, though," Rylan said. "If people didn't know what happened to her, or about her relationship with Varro and the others, they'd theorize she went off to be alone."

I nodded. "That makes a lot of sense."

"You and Varro, really?" Ryoko questioned.

Peacekeeper Ryoko shrugged. "He grew on me."

"We had known each other for some time prior to everyone getting together," Varro explained. "Wasn't really a spur-of-the-moment situation."

Peacekeeper Ryoko rolled her eyes. "He's leaving out the part where I hated him during that time."

"You hated everyone in the village," he shot back.

"No, I just didn't trust them. I actually hated you."

"That's a lie, and you know it."

Ryoko giggled. "You two sound like Laz and Raikidan."

"We do not act like that," Raikidan and I objected.

"Oh, boy. Now you're on the same wavelength."

The others laughed at the two of us. My eyes narrowed and I finished off my mug of ale. My attention turned when someone approached us. I smiled at the man dressed in thick robes with various chains, pouches, books of different sizes, quills, and parchments hanging off it. Standard scholar garb, though to this day, I still didn't understand why they insisted on using quill and ink instead of pens. "Me'kunar."

He pulled down his hood with an intricately painted hand, revealing his weathered mocha-tan skin and long black hair smattered with bits of gray. Elven ears poked out of his dark tresses. His forest green eyes sparkled with a youth that contrasted with his age. He smiled and sat down in front of me. "It's been a while, Eira."

I sighed contently. "Thank you for not addressing me by my new title."

"I suspected you'd be more comfortable if I didn't."

I smiled my thanks. "So, did you come over here to congratulate me, or just chat?"

He smiled. "A little bit of both. I do want to congratulate you on both your shaman status and your new job with us. Being appointed as our Ambassador is nothing to sneeze at, and is a highly desired position. But I also want to thank you for the information you sent to me about the find in Larkren."

I grinned, remembering the trip to the seaside town several months back and the chance find. "I can only imagine it was of some help, yes?"

His face lit up. "It was the best find of the decade! There has been so much information in that area, I've had to make several trips to make sure I got it all."

The image of him grumbling to himself about the long trek, while also being excited about collecting new information, crossed my mind and I laughed a bit. "I'm glad I could be of some use."

"I'm hoping you can be of more use soon, if you're willing. While translating it is no problem, I need help piecing it all together, as a lot of it is only fragments. You've always been helpful when it came to piecing together fragment stories."

"You should help."

"I can try to help. I've got a book that can access the Library, so if you publish it in there, I can take a look at any time."

Me'kunar cocked and eyebrow. "You have a book? How did you gain possession of one?"

Shva'sika waved her fingers. "I gave it to her."

Me'kunar laughed. "Shva'sika, of course. I shouldn't be surprised in the least you gave her your family book."

"She's my family, so I see no reason to keep it from her."

Me'kunar nodded. "Of course, of course."

The two fell into conversation on the Eternal Library, my elven friend telling him of the new entrance find, and the book discovery on the Makers, getting Me'kunar excited.

"No way!" Peacekeeper Ryoko suddenly screeched, pulling my attention back to her and Ryoko. "You get a tail?"

Ryoko blinked, her face strained with shock and surprise. "Yeah. It shows up before I have to shift, because of the full moon. I guess you didn't?"

Peacekeeper Ryoko groaned. "That's not fair! I wanted a tail. Even if it was only for a few days."

I chuckled at her childish behavior. The two definitely acted alike.

"You don't need one," Varro insisted.

"But I always wanted one," Peacekeeper Ryoko said.

"You're fine just as you are."

Peacekeeper Ryoko pouted. "But I wanted one…"

Ryoko grunted. "Well, if I could, I'd give it to you. I can't stand it. I had to cut some of my clothes to accommodate it."

"It's not like it put a dent in your stock of clothes," Rylan said.

She poked him in the chest. "You be quiet."

I chuckled and kept my voice low before speaking to Peacekeeper Ryoko. "He's got a tail fetish."

Rylan's eyes narrowed at me. "Shut up, I do not."

"Yeah, you do," Blaze argued. "You get all weird when she has her tail."

Argus smirked. "Weird is an understatement."

The two laughed, and Rylan glared at them with flushed cheeks. "I need another drink."

A capped bottle of beer was tossed to him, but before he could take a sip, Ryoko stole it and took a few gulps. Rylan gave her a scolding look, and she laughed before handing it back to him. I looked at my empty bottle and decided I needed more. As I was about to get up, Ne'kall and Tla'lli approached. They were helping each other carry something covered in feathers.

I cocked my head with a raised brow. "What is that?"

Ne'kall let go of his end and smiled. "A headdress."

"Okay…"

Tla'lli giggled and held it out. "It's for you. It belonged to the last Ambassador. She fashioned it from a skull that has been inherited by each subsequent appointed Ambassador since the first." She smiled. "We'll hold onto it for you until Zarda is dealt with, but I wanted to present it to you now, so you knew it'd be coming your way eventually."

I smiled and took the heavy headdress from them. Red and orange feathers of various lengths splayed out across my legs, going all the way to the ground, as I did my best to look over the headpiece. A large bird-like skull, about a foot long, sat as the centerpiece, with two golden medallions on either side. Etched into the metal was the same symbol as on my cloak. *That's interesting…* I thought the symbol was unique to Raikidan and me. I made a mental note to investigate it at a later time.

Looking over how it was worn, the skull would rest directly on the person's head, the feathers arching out behind it and flowing down the back of the person. The feathers had yellow, blue, and white accents. The arch and placement of the colored accents reminded me of sun-rays, or fire. "Thank you. What kind of skull is it?"

Ne'kall chuckled. "What, you've never seen a bird skull before?"

"No way that's from a bird," Ryoko said. "That thing is huge!"

Tla'lli laughed. "That's because it's a phoenix skull."

Everyone stared at her.

"Our first Ambassador cared for the last living phoenix a long time ago. Even though the creature went through several rebirth cycles, its life did eventually end. She kept its skull and many of its feathers as a memento, and we have passed it along to the next Ambassadors in her honor."

Ryoko scratched her head. "There aren't even any records of when those creatures officially went extinct. Most believe them to be crea-tures in myths and legends, to spice up stories. When was the first Ambassador picked?"

Tla'lli shrugged. "The exact timing isn't known, due to all the wars, and information was lost as a result. She was the first shaman, and started what we are today. It's said that happened at least six millennia ago, but that's the best we know."

Ryoko cocked her head to the side. "Why not go find her in the afterlife and ask?"

"No one can find her," Ne'kall said.

Rylan's brow furrowed. "What?"

Tla'lli nodded. "No one can find any of the Ambassadors."

"So they just stopped existing?" Rylan asked.

"Well, no. Just 'cause you can't find someone doesn't mean they don't exist. They could have been reincarnated, or they just don't want to show up."

"Interesting." Rylan went to thinking. "You also mentioned the first Ambassador was a woman. How many have been women and how many have been men?"

"They're all women," I answered. "And their official Guards all happen to have been men as well." I turned my eyes to Tla'lli. "At least that's what I've been able to find on that topic in my most recent searches with the Eternal Library, since the shamans had appointed me the position as a farce for Zarda."

Me'kunar spoke in her stead. "That would be correct. The gods choose both the Ambassador and her official Guard, but not much else is known beyond those few texts. We scholars are looking for any information we can find about the Ambassadors. Due to the War of End, knowledge about the second and third Ambassadors was lost, and what's available for the first is incomplete. The only Ambassador with a substantial historical listing is the one who came before Laz'shika, and even those entries have unusual holes in them. The Ambassadors are as hot a topic as the Makers."

I found this fascinating. In my readings, the Ambassador traditionally held an important position of keeping peace between the tribes, no easy task sometimes with their differences. Due to the importance, it surprised me the title wasn't often given, and for so much history to be lost, that was a big deal. I would have thought the Eternal Library had all possible information. *Maybe it does, but it's hidden somewhere.* The Eternal Library did have a mind of its own when it came to allowing you to find certain entries.

"She's a mischievous entity."

"She? What, is she like a god or something?"

"Maybe."

Some of the things this voice knew or said confused me. How could this special library that stretched across all of Lumaraeon be a god? *Wait, maybe that's how she can be...*

"Bingo!"

I'd have to look into that more. But at this moment, I needed to focus on the party in my honor. I chose to try the headdress on. The skull fit well on the top of my head, its heavy weight counterbalanced by the plumage in the back. I pulled the skull down over my face and found I could look through the eye sockets, though not perfectly.

Ryoko giggled. "You look silly."

I frowned. "Really? I thought I might look good in it."

"I think you do," Tla'lli said. Several of the others around me agreed with her, which made me feel good.

With a grateful smile to Tla'lli, I removed it from my head and handed it back. "Thank you for presenting it to me. I'll let you take it back so it's not damaged."

Tla'lli nodded, and she and Ne'kall carried the headdress away. I scanned the clearing, and a young woman with long, platinum blonde hair standing away from the party on the opposite side of the clearing caught my attention. *Iana?*

I got up and headed that way. "I'll be right back."

2

CHAPTER

(RYOKO)

I watched Laz get up and head off somewhere, saying something about being right back. *Where could she be going?*

Peacekeeper Ryoko tapped my shoulder, trying to keep my attention on her. "So, when do you get your tail?"

I wanted to laugh. I couldn't believe she was still hung up on that. "It's never consistent. Sometimes it's a day before the full moon, and sometimes it's a few days."

"Do you have it after the forced shift?"

I shook my head. "No, just before."

One of her eyes squinted, while the other opened more as her brow lifted, as if she didn't believe me. "No other time?"

I couldn't help but laugh. "Nope."

Today had been interesting, to say the least. Never in a million years would I have imagined I'd see half of what I had. Laz showing off her power—gods fighting mortals in honor-like combat, without the to-the-death part, of course—and now meeting the woman I'd been cloned from. All my life, I'd walked in her shadow, thinking I was just a living memory of the woman she was. I thought that I couldn't be my own person, and that if anyone found out my origins, they'd either expect me to be her, or shun me.

Sitting here with her, though, made me realize how wrong I was, in respect to our likeness, at least. Sure, there were a lot of similarities, but we were each our own person, too.

I smiled at my ancient… *I guess she's my sister, if you really think about it.* As a clone, that made me a twin of hers, just separated by hundreds of years. I didn't have any blood siblings that I knew of; it made me a bit jealous of some of the others. But then, I had a type of surrogate family, if a little bit messed up. *I mean, seriously, Ryoko, what kind of sane family starts dating each other?*

But thinking of Peacekeeper Ryoko as my sister made me happy.

Peacekeeper Ryoko tilted her head. "So, you don't get your tail before you shift voluntarily?"

My ears drooped. "I can't do that, actually."

Peacekeeper Ryoko blinked. "Really? That should be a natural process by now, at your age."

I held up a finger. "Well, I was on anti-transformation pills up until a few months ago. Once I came off them, my transformations were random, and slowly became most consistent with the moon's phases each passing month. I've been so focused on that, I didn't think an unforced shift was possible."

She thought about this. "Sounds like it altered the natural flow of the wogron blood, and is causing your body to go through a change similar to that of young wogrons when they start adolescence."

I tilted my head. "Huh?"

Peacekeeper Ryoko snapped her fingers. "That's right. We've been so secretive, even you wouldn't know much about us. You obviously know how we half-wogrons shift into the wogron form on the night of the full moon? Well, full wogrons shift into humans on the full moon."

My brow rose. "Really?"

She nodded vigorously. "Yeah. It happened several generations after the curse mutated and forced them to keep the wogron shape permanently. So, when wogron pups hit adolescence, they start experiencing the change, and it takes a few years for it to regulate to the normal cycle of once every full moon. As a half-wogron, it was thought I'd go through something similar when I hit adolescence, but I didn't. I only changed for the full moon. Being the only half-wogron until your existence, we believed it'd be the same for any other half-wogrons."

I rubbed my chin. "Interesting." I turned to Laz's scholar friend. "Did you know that, Me'kunar?"

He shook his head. "No. I haven't done much study on the wogrons. But my sister has, so I wouldn't doubt she knows."

My brow twisted. "You and your sister are scholars? Is this a sibling hobby, or do you have other family members who are curious brainiacs too?"

"No, this is a family affair. Few of our family members have chosen other paths."

I laughed. I hadn't actually expected that answer from him.

"So, Peacekeeper Ryoko," Rylan began, "when the curse mutated, was that when bites and scratches from a wogron also become toxic to non-wogrons?"

Peacekeeper Ryoko nodded. "Yes. Those walked hand in hand."

I held my chin and thought. "Interesting. I wonder what caused the curse to change."

She shrugged. "No one knows. How the curse even came to be is still a mystery. There are only scattered records and stories of people having it, but nothing about how it started."

I chuckled. "I guess the search for answers continues."

Me'kunar held up a finger. "And that's where I come in. We'll find all the knowledge some day, I'm sure of it."

Peacekeeper Ryoko turned her attention to where Laz had disappeared to. "Who is that she's talking to?"

A few of us turned our attention in the same direction to see Laz conversing with a fair-skinned, lithe woman with long platinum blonde hair and crystal blue eyes. "Oh, that's Iana. She's an old military comrade of ours. It's been some time since any of us have seen her."

"She's the first Eira has personally approached," she observed. "Why is that?"

"She and Laz have a unique relationship due to an ability Iana has. Laz is the only person who knows much about the ability, but from what the rest of us do know, it comes from her hands and she sometimes struggles to keep it in check, hence the gloves she wears."

Peacekeeper Ryoko tapped her lips with a finger. "You've never seen the ability?"

I shook my head. "I've never even seen her in battle. She's always been a shy thing, so when you ask her about it, she shuts down. It's why Laz got her out of the military and underground once she could."

Rylan leaned forward. "It's rumored she's not even tank-born."

Peacekeeper Ryoko's brow rose. "You're saying she was forced into service?"

He nodded. "Something to do with her ability and that she refuses to use it. That's the rumor, at least."

A portal opened up near them, and three men came through. All three looked as though they'd come right off of some ranch outside the city. One man, with brown hair and blue eyes, carried a young lamb, maybe no older than a week or two, in his arms, and a long-haired shepherd dog with a spotted coat stood by his feet.

Peacekeeper Ryoko's brow rose. "Who are they?"

Blaze chuckled. "She's as nosey as our Ryoko."

I tossed an empty bottle at him and he ducked. Me'kunar chuckled. "That would be Alistair and a few of his ranch hands. They're notoriously late to parties."

The three joined a group of North and East Tribe shaman. I noticed Arnia and Jaybird had mingled in with the group, the former sitting with the shaman who saved them from certain death, Ven'lar. The two had really hit it off with the shamans. It made me wonder if they'd relocate to one of those towns after our fight with Zarda. That got me wondering what others would do. I hadn't even thought about what I wanted. *Would everyone leave the house, too?*

We all had lived together for so long, the thought of us living elsewhere sent a prickle of pain through my chest. *I guess that's all part of change, though.*

This got me looking around at everyone, acting all nostalgic and taking in each of their faces and the memories that came with them. *I'm ridiculous.*

My gazing stopped when I noticed a translucent woman sitting near Blaze, watching him. He acted as if she weren't there, but I could tell, by the glances from the others, I wasn't the only one seeing her.

Telar swiveled his head my way. *"Don't say anything to him."*

My brow furrowed. *"Why?"*

"She's made it clear she doesn't want him to see her."

"Who is she?"

"I'm not sure. Zane and Argus said it's best to leave it be."

I found this rather strange. In all my years of knowing the guy, I couldn't think of a woman who would have reason to follow him around in secret. *What secret is he hiding?*

Movement in the forest caught my eyes. Looking in that direction, I spotted a muscular, bronze-skinned man standing in the shadows of a tree. *Zeek…*

He motioned me to come over. My ears twitched and I swallowed, but complied. *It's fine, Ryoko. There's nothing wrong with speaking with him alone. Even if he is a past lover…* "I'll be right back, guys."

"Hm, who is that guy?" Peacekeeper Ryoko asked, her words carrying all the way over to my sensitive ears.

"Zeek," Blaze said. "Past boyfriend, I think."

"How do you not know?"

"Look, she and I aren't particularly close. I didn't even know she had a boyfriend before, until she freaked out at me several months ago when I made an assumption."

"You're just going to let your mate talk to him?" I guessed she was asking Rylan this.

"Yeah, that's a lot of trust you have in her," Blaze said.

"It's not a matter of trust or commitment, neither of which I expect you to understand, Blaze." Rylan's sharp words surprised me. "I will let her get the closure she needs—however that needs to happen."

My heart fluttered. I didn't know what would happen with Zeek and me alone. I didn't want to do anything that would tarnish the relationship I had with Rylan, but I appreciated his words and his trust. *Whatever happens, I'll tell him when we're alone so there are no secrets. It's the right thing to do.*

Zeek smiled at me and grabbed my hand, pulling me farther away from the gathering. The warmth of his hand sent a rush of familiarity through my body. *I remember this touch.*

He faced me when we'd gone far enough. His usual cocky and carefree demeanor had been replaced by an unusually serious one, and before I could think to ask what he wanted from me, his large arms wrapped around me and pulled me tight against him. My heart raced, and also ached at the same time. I remembered this embrace, burned so deep into my memory I'd never forget. It was like he'd never died.

"I'm sorry," he whispered. "I'm sorry for making a mistake and leaving you alone. I'm sorry… for causing you so much pain."

I buried my face into his chest, a small smile spreading across my lips. "Thank you, but an apology isn't needed. I don't blame you for what happened. It was a hazard of the life we had to live. It's a hazard of my current life, still."

I gazed up at him. "Losing you still hurts, but I've had time to cope. Sometimes I wonder what life would be like if you'd lived, but I know that's not something I can dwell on. It's allowed me to move on enough to find new happiness."

My eyes fell away as the guilt crept into my chest. "I feel awful, because as much as I love Rylan, there's a part of me that still loves you. So much so, time will never be able to remove that from my heart."

Zeek cupped my chin. "Loving someone new after loss isn't easy. You know about Alsaira, I didn't hide that past relationship from you. I may not have stopped loving her, even long after I lost her, but that didn't mean my love for you was any weaker. Just as your love for Rylan isn't weak." He wiped away a tear welling up in my eye. "I'm happy for you. Admittedly jealous of him, but happy nonetheless."

I smiled. "Thank you."

"I shouldn't keep you any longer than I have. But…" His hand still holding my face, he crashed his lips into mine. The passion in this kiss set my blood ablaze, sending my heart into overdrive. Memories of a time spent with him came flooding back to me, each one pleasant and not unwelcomed. The memories—the familiarity of this embrace—I abandoned all logic and reasoning and embraced the feelings of this lost love.

Zeek pulled away, leaving me breathless. "You're still as tempting as ever; I envy Rylan's claim over you. A part of me wishes he'd kept his head up his ass for just a while longer."

He started to fade, and my sight became blurry as tears welled up in my eyes. "Know that I will love you until the end of time, and will be here when we are reunited once again. Until that time, my little she-wolf."

He disappeared, and the tears streamed down my cheeks. My legs gave out and I collapsed into the snow, holding myself as I sobbed. The pain of losing him again, mixed with my feeling that I'd betrayed Rylan, took over me.

Feet crunched in the snow behind me, but I couldn't compose

myself. A soft hand rested on my shoulders, and before I knew it, I was pulled against a female form, tendrils of her brown hair spilling over my shoulders. Peacekeeper Ryoko's scent wafted into my nose. She held me close, stroking my hair and murmuring quiet words.

Minutes passed before the tears dried up. I pulled away from her, sniffling and wiping the remaining wet streaks away. "Thank you."

"Are you all right?" she asked.

I nodded. "Yeah. It hurt to see him go again, but weirdly enough, I feel better than I have in a long time. Though I do feel guilty, too."

She smiled at me. "Your mate won't hold it against you, as he shouldn't. Most are allowed to move on after losing those they love. But what you've experienced is what Eira and those who are touched by the spiritual plane experience. Moving on is difficult for them, as the reminders are always there."

I frowned. "I never thought about that. Laz doesn't talk about that ability."

"She's strong and handles it better than most." Peacekeeper Ryoko continued to smile. "Just like you have. My father had a mate prior to my mother. He told me what it was like being in your shoes. I do not envy that struggle, but I do admire you and him for facing it as well as you do."

I cocked my head. "I'm curious, how did things work out with your parents?"

She rubbed the back of her neck. "That's an interesting situation. Um, well, my mother was the last of the A'shi people."

"A'shi?"

"They were a nation of humans who had the ability to suppress shifting abilities. The ability manifested as either an aura or an activated ability, like elemental control. My mother so happened to have an aura, and it suppressed the curse of the wogrons."

My eyes grew wide. "That's cool."

She nodded. "It could be dangerous, too, but the pack made it work."

"How did they meet?"

She half laughed, her face contorting as if she were nervous or embarrassed. *Maybe both?* "Well… she tried to kill our Alpha, thinking he was another wogron."

I stared at her. "What?"

"Yeah… one merciful event led to another, and my father claimed her as his mate." She scratched her face. "Told you it was an interesting situation."

I nodded, unable to find the right answer to that.

Peacekeeper Ryoko rose to her feet and held her hand out to me. "Should we head back?"

"Yeah." I took her offered hand and got to my feet. "Why did you follow me out here?"

She smiled. "Sick curiosity. I wanted to know what you'd do. It ended up far tamer than I expected."

Heat rushed to my face. "I wouldn't betray Rylan like that."

Her eyes softened. "He wouldn't have seen it as a betrayal. I can tell by the way he acted. While uncomfortable, he would have understood. I'm sure he'd struggle with this type of situation himself."

I looked away. "Yeah, well, I don't even think what I did was right."

I headed back for the party, but she stopped me.

"Wait." Looking back, I found her eyes dancing with mischief. "I want to do something fun first."

My brow rose. *What evil plan has she concocted?*

3
CHAPTER

(EIRA)

My chat with Iana had been pleasant, if a bit disappointing. She hadn't progressed any with her ability. She still had little control over it, and it still caused her a great deal of pain. I really had hoped she'd had gotten over her fear. She didn't believe me when I'd told her this reluctance to use her ability caused this pain. *Maybe if I find out more about this ability of hers, that would help her believe me.*

"You do have more resources to pull. It would be wise to utilize them. Her ability shouldn't cause these problems."

The voice had a point. Even if I failed to find anything, at least I tried to utilize the extra resources. *Maybe the shamans can encourage her.* Arnia had called Iana over to join their group, and she complied after some encouragement from me. I'd stayed to monitor her for a few minutes. She, while shy, hit it off with those three newcomers, the dog they brought attaching himself to her hip almost immediately.

As I made my way back to the others, I noticed our little group had changed a little bit. My mother and Jasmine, who had disappeared while I had been greeting people, returned and sat with Ryder, who had also disappeared during that time. Azriel, who had gone off to chat with some friends when we had arrived, was with them, and Peacekeeper Ryoko and Ryoko were nowhere to be seen. There was also a new person sitting with everyone whom I didn't know, although she didn't appear to be one of the living.

The woman, translucent but visible enough to see a little color in her form, sat near Blaze and watched him and his interactions with the others. Blaze and the others paid her no mind as if she wasn't even there, making me curious. *She's obviously a spirit, but why isn't she taking on a physical form like the other spirits here so she can interact with everyone? I could tell she knew Blaze by how she watched and reacted to his actions, but what was their relationship?*

"Sometimes, it's not good to poke at old wounds."

Seda looked my way. *"Laz, do not mention the woman sitting with Blaze. He's not to know she's there, unless you want to cause him distress."*

"Should I know the history between them, just in case?"

"No. It'd be best to just let this one be."

"Very well. Thank you for letting me know."

I sat down between Ryder and my mother. "So where did Ryoko run off to?" I peered around and noticed Peacekeeper Ryoko truly was missing. "Both of them."

"Zeek wanted to talk to Ryoko privately," Rylan said.

"And my Ryoko decided to be nosey and follow," Varro said.

"I still don't get you letting her go with him," Blaze said to Rylan.

"I told you, I have my reasons, and someone like you would never understand, so drop it," Rylan muttered.

I studied Rylan as he sipped his beer. I, too, was curious about his decision to be okay with it, although I could see the rigidness of his posture, which told me it did bother him.

"If I had to guess, he wants Ryoko to get the closure she deserved. No matter how that needs to happen."

"That would make sense."

Blaze stretched. "Speaking of those two, this double-Ryoko thing is getting a little hard for my head to handle."

Varro chuckled. "You're not alone, trust me."

"Maybe we should give them new names while they're together?" Telar suggested.

I snickered when the two Ryokos calmly came out of woods. "Well you're more than welcome to run the idea by the two of them. They're back." The two acted quite normal as they walked back into the clearing. *Too normal. Something is up.* "Everything okay, Ryo?"

She nodded. "Yep. Zeek and I are good."

I eyed Peacekeeper Ryoko. "And you followed because?"

"Because I'm nosey and wanted to understand the dynamic of her relationship with this man and her actual partner."

Ryoko rolled her eyes. "And she wanted to bother me about the tail thing some more."

Peacekeeper Ryoko crossed her arms and pouted once more. "It's not fair you get a tail."

Ryoko shook her head with a sigh and sat down next to Rylan. "So, as we were coming back, I heard you say had an idea you wanted to run by us?"

"Yeah, this whole Ryoko, Ryoko name thing is really confusing," Blaze told her. "We're thinking of giving you guys nicknames for the duration of the night."

Peacekeeper Ryoko giggled as she sat down next to Varro. "That's stupid."

"Maybe to you," Blaze muttered. "But not to us."

Peacekeeper Ryoko faced Varro. "You don't like their idea, do you?"

He shrugged. "It's a little confusing, and it'd be helpful, but I'm not going to push the issue."

Eyes wide, Ryoko looked at Rylan. "Ry, you're not in on this idea, are you?"

Rylan nodded. "Actually, I kinda am." Her eyes narrowed and he held up his hands. "It wouldn't be that bad. Just little nicknames." He smirked. "She can be Grandma Ryoko and you can be Little Ryoko."

Ryoko stole his drink. "I'm not little, jerk."

Peacekeeper Ryoko pointed at him, exclaiming, "And I'm not that old!"

I turned my gazed to Valene when she sat down next to me suddenly. "Hey there."

She smiled. "Hi. It looked like you guys were having fun over here, so I figured I'd join."

I chuckled. "You could join us even if we weren't having fun."

Valene's smile grew wider. "So, what was I missing?"

"The guys are being jerks," Ryoko muttered.

Valene blinked. "How so?"

"They want to give us nicknames because they suck at dealing with our names."

Valene chuckled. "Maybe they should get bigger brains."

My mother laughed and gave Valene a tight hug. "Oh, I really love this girl. Eira, dear, you picked a good girl to adopt."

I smiled. "I don't regret it."

Valene beamed with happiness. "Mom says hi, by the way. She's spending some time with Daren right now, but said she'd try to spend some time with us before the night is over."

"That'd be nice." It was nice knowing Valene was taking her mother's passing so much easier now. When I noticed Rylan looking at Peacekeeper Ryoko and Ryoko in an odd way, I became curious. "Something the matter, Ry?"

"Yeah, you've been looking at me funny for a while now," Ryoko said.

Rylan released an exasperated breath. "You two really tried to pull this on us?"

Everyone focused on him, confused, and I burst out laughing, slapping my hand on my knee. "I knew the two of you were up to something!"

Ryoko blinked. "What are you two talking about?"

Blaze, realizing what we had figured out, laughed. "They pulled the old identical twin switch!"

"I should have known... So predictable."

Ryoko blinked. "Really, guys? You seriously think we did that?"

I continued to chuckle. "We know you did."

Ryoko shook her head. "You guys ar—"

"Peacekeeper Ryoko, give it up," Ryoko, disguised as her predecessor, said. "They know, and you can't convince them otherwise. I told you it wouldn't work." Varro, who had his hand resting on Ryoko's hip, retracted his touch, and Ryoko shot him an apologetic look. "Sorry, it was her idea."

He chuckled. "No need to apologize. I should have expected that from her."

Peacekeeper Ryoko crossed her arms, her lower lips sticking out into a pout. "None of you are any fun."

Ryoko chuckled and stood. "Now, I'd like to sit next to Rylan again, if you don't mind."

Peacekeeper Ryoko grumbled and reluctantly swapped places. When Ryoko was seated next to Rylan, she looked at him apologetically, but he only smiled back. It didn't surprise me in the least that he had figured it out. I suspected their scent difference gave them away, even with attempts to fix that, knowing the better-than-average sense of smell Rylan had.

"I can keep these clothes, right?" Ryoko asked Peacekeeper Ryoko. "I like them."

"Yeah, I don't mind," Ryoko said. She turned her eyes to Rylan. "What do you think?"

Rylan grinned. "I think they're fitting."

Peacekeeper Ryoko looked at Varro. "Do you like the clothes she let me use?"

Varro's face reddened. "Y—yeah. They're nice."

Peacekeeper Ryoko peered up at him through her lashes, her shoulders slouching and her arms pulling in close to make herself look bustier. "Just nice?"

I laughed. "Easy, Ryoko. You're going to give the poor man a nosebleed."

She grinned wickedly. "That was the plan."

I glanced at Ryoko. "If she could bring clothes with her into the spiritual, I'd suggest you let her raid your closet."

Peacekeeper Ryoko held up a finger. "Actually, due to the fact that we have our physical form tonight, I can swap clothes. I'll just keep the new ones until another day like this arrives."

Ryoko rubbed her hands together, a mischievous smile on her face. "Then I think we need to make a trip to the Iron Hawk Mall before the night is over."

Peacekeeper Ryoko's eyes lit up and Varro swallowed, clearly terrified of these two's ability to plot against him.

Valene waved her hand to grab Varro's attention. "Um, I'd like to ask you something. I hope it's not overstepping any bounds, but it's been on my mind since I spotted you. The statues that honor your group depict you differently than—"

He held up his hand to stop her. "I know what you're getting at. Unfortunately, I was hit with a bit of prejudice, even after everything we did for Lumaraeon. The people had a hard time wrapping their minds around my appearance, mixed with the knowledge I was a healer. Because of this, they chose to portray me in a way they thought was better suited for an elven healer."

Ryoko glowered. "Not cool."

Varro shrugged. "I honestly could care less. It's just a statue."

Ryoko crossed her arms. "Well, I'm going to have it changed after this."

"You really don't need to do that."

I chuckled as the two squabbled and sipped my drink, taking the time to look about. People of various walks laughed and mingled. The South Tribe kept up their music, the North Tribe sometimes changing it up with their own. Dancers still performed by the fires, taking a break now and then to allow elementalists to show off their prowess in the form of dances. Overall, I couldn't find a single person who wasn't having fun. It brought a smile to my face.

A small group of children scurried over to Me'kunar, catching my attention. They sat down in front of him and he chuckled, knowing what they were looking for. "What can I do for you little ones tonight?"

"Can you tell us a story?" one of the older children asked.

Me'kunar chuckled again. "I could." He looked at me. "But I think Eira might be able to tell you a better story."

The children turned their bright and exited eye on me. I gave Me'kunar a pointed look. "You know better stories than me."

"But yours are so exciting!" a child chirped. I recognized him as one of the children from the West Tribe, who had witnessed many of my stories. "Please tell us a story!"

I blew out a breath while smiling. "Okay, okay, I'll tell you a story." The children squealed with excitement and scooted closer to me. "What kind of story do you want to hear?"

"One about princesses!" a young girl said quietly.

"No, that's lame!" a boy argued. "Tells us a story about Old Knights!"

"No, one with dragons in it!" another child insisted.

I chuckled. "All right, all right, calm down. Let me think…"

I could tell a story that incorporated all three ideas, since the three topics were commonly put together in stories, but with the dragons here, I was siding against it. Our human stories weren't all that kind to them most of the time. But taking the dragons out made it difficult to use the princess and knight idea. I sighed mentally. *Why me?*

"Just make us the bad guy," Ebon called out from where he was mingling. "We know your stories aren't always nice to us. We get it. We won't hold it against you."

"Well, some of us won't," Corliss said.

I narrowed my eyes at him and he laughed. Rolling my eyes, I chose to just go with making the dragons the bad guys. It would get this story telling over with. I motioned for the children to turn around, and they listened. "All right, watch carefully."

I took a deep breath as I thought up the details of the story before raising my hands and taking control of one of the bonfires. Slowly, I manipulated the flames as I let the details of the story run through my head and out to my fingertips, speaking it aloud as it played out.

The fire morphed until it took the shape of a knight riding through the woods on horseback, at an incredible pace. He jumped over every obstacle, rode over every mountain, and fought all enemies that stood in his path, but none of it would stop him from getting to his destination.

He traveled for many days before he came to a large abandoned castle, except he knew it wasn't abandoned. The knight dismounted his horse and carefully made his way inside. He searched the castle room by room, but didn't find what he was looking for. He headed for some stairs that led to the tower, but stopped when something caught his attention.

The children watched eagerly as the knight ventured away from the stairs and into the courtyard, and then gasped when I manipulated the fire into a large dragon. The knight drew his sword and fought valiantly against his mighty foe. The two battled until only one came out victorious.

The knight struck the killing blow to the dragon, the enormous creature falling into a crumpled heap, and then rushed back inside the castle. He ran up the stairs to the tower, and broke down the locked door at the top. Inside, in the tiny room, sat a princess, held captive until the day a valiant knight could defeat the dragon charged to guard her and rescue her from her unfortunate situation. The knight took the princess, and they rode away from the castle together.

"She should have just befriended the dragon. Would have been less of a hassle."

"Just enjoy the story."

The children cheered with delight when the story ended and then gazed at me eagerly. "What, one wasn't enough?"

"Never enough!" they shouted. "Tell another!"

I chuckled. "Okay, okay, give me a minute to think."

"Tell one about dragons!" a child told me. "Good ones!"

"No, tell one about the gods!" another called out.

"How about you tell one about us?" Peacekeeper Ryoko suggested. "Those are fun stories."

The children's eyes lit up and I thought about the idea. I smiled when something came to mind. "Sure, I can do that, but I'll need a little help with this story."

I shifted my gaze to Valene and she blinked. "Me? What can I do?"

I reached into my satchel and pulled out my pan flute. "I need you to sing."

Her eyes lit up. "We're going to tell that story?"

I nodded and she squealed with delight.

Rylan chuckled. "Looks like we're going to hear a good one, from her reaction."

Amused chuckles rumbled through the crowd of people.

I glanced over at Seda and Telar. *"If you two would like to help, I think it would enhance this story."*

"I'll pass," Telar said. *"Seda will do a better job than me."*

Seda smiled. *"I'd love to. I've also let Talon know, since I know how much he likes this story, too."*

I smiled when I noticed Talon getting ready by a pair of bass drums. This story was quite old, and not many knew it anymore, but Talon was one, and it had to be his favorite story. And since it was designed to be sung instead of spoken like other stories, it wasn't told often.

Once everyone appeared to be ready, I played my pan flute and the fire responded to my will. Someone began playing a piano and Valene sang. As she did, the flames formed into a large picture of a battlefield, the entire clearing used as the setup.

The battle was chaotic—no single side to be seen as each fiery figure attacked anyone in sight until they were taken down themselves. Dragons fell from the sky from powerful gunfire; humans shot wogrons and elves before being taken down themselves by the rare grekeleon race, and sorcerers ripped their enemies asunder with powerful magics. Every time someone fell, three more of the same race would take their place, and the death toll rose.

"Such an awful time for the mortal races," the voice murmured, her voice strained.

I glanced at Seda to find her lifting her hands up for her part. Her short hair stood on end a little, and soon, images of real people began to mix in with my fiery ones. Working together, we increased the depth of the story by making it feel as if the fighting was going on right here, as if we had been temporarily teleported into the past.

Then, Seda added in a new twist. Out of the sky, a red and a green dragon dove into the battle, and from their backs, three figures jumped down into the center of the battlefield. Ryoko, with the strength of the earth on her side, divided the land and pushed the battle back. Varro, Raynn, and Assar kept her safe from any retaliating attacks, while Reiki and Pyralis used their strong wings to create wind strong enough to push the fighters into submission. Pyralis used a bit of smoke to subdue some of the more resilient fighters, but he, like everyone else, was careful not to hurt them.

When the fighting had slowed, Ryoko spoke to them, insistent about something. After a few moments, the people around her looked at each other. As she kept speaking to them, they lowered their weapons and the fighting finally stopped. The battling had finally ended, and so could the pain.

I pulled the flute away and let out a quiet breath while everyone took in the song.

"Look at your brothers and tell me how the two of you are the exact same," Varro murmured.

"Look at your enemy and tell me how they are different." Pyralis continued.

"Look at me, and tell me why I have to be your enemy when we are all different and yet all the same," Reiki said.

Assar nodded slowly from where he drank with Vorn. "Aye, no truer words were spoken from ye, lass, than those words that day."

Peacekeeper Ryoko ducked her head, her cheeks turning several shades of red. I watched as everyone around me took in the story. When the amazement had finally filtered through their brains, the children squealed with excitement and piled on me.

I laughed and held my flute away. "Easy there guys, you're going to break my pan flute!"

"That was so amazing!" one of the children squealed.

"You're the best!" another said.

I chuckled. "I don't know about the best."

"Yes, you are!" they insisted.

I laughed and continued to as they climbed on me more.

"Show us your neat flute!" one of the children begged.

"I will if you stop climbing on me, you little monkeys!"

They didn't climb off me right away, but when I still didn't show them the flute, they reluctantly let go. Happy for my freedom, I held the pan flute out for them to look at. One of the girls went to touch it but stopped and gazed up at me apprehensively.

"You can touch it, if you're careful. It's really old," I said.

The girl smiled and she touched it. Her smile grew as she traced the symbols on each pipe. "What do these say?"

"Love. Peace. Spirit. Loyalty. Serenity. Strength. Wisdom."

"So it's a spiritual pan flute then," Varro said.

My brow rose. "A what?"

"It's a type of flute that aids with drawing out spiritual and elemental aspects of a being when played." He regarded me for a moment. "I'm guessing you don't know whether it is or not, then?"

"It was a gift." I jerked my head in my mother's direction. "From her."

Varro turned to my mother. She shrugged. "I found it on one of my travels."

I looked over the flute as she spoke. She murmured that lie so easily now. Had she finally gotten over him, or was it easy for her to tell others a lie because I was around?

"Let go of that pain."

"That pain keeps me from making the wrong choices."

"No, it keeps you from finding happiness."

Pyralis crouched down in front of me all of a sudden and held out his hand. "May I take a look at that for a moment?"

"Uh, sure."

He took it carefully from me and inspected the instrument. "I thought this looked familiar. This belonged to my daughter."

My eyes widened. "Really?"

He nodded. "I had it made special for her. It went missing some time after her passing. I never expected it to last this long."

"What was her name?"

"Velsara…" her name came out strained and quiet. It was obvious that her loss, even after his own death, still hurt him. *She must have died before him. That's really tough on a parent.* It also sounded like he didn't know where she was in the spiritual plane. *I wonder why…*

"You know that answer."

"What?"

"Look deep inside yourself."

"The box this came in has someone else's name on it," I said, ignoring the voice's odd choice in words. "So who ever ended up with it, took excellent care of it before it landed in my hands."

Pyralis nodded. "The box I had made for the flute was still in my possession after the instrument went missing, so I'm not surprised a new one was fashioned."

"So, was my guess right?" Varro asked. "Is it a spiritual flute?"

Pyralis nodded. "Yes. She had shaman abilities."

I cocked my head. This sounded interesting. "Shaman?"

He nodded again. "It's not unheard of for dragons to manifest special gifts. Some are shamanistic, while others are psychic." He quickly glanced at Raikidan and it didn't surprise me. Raikidan had once said it was believed his mother had psychic abilities, but I never thought much about it. "They're rare occurrences among our kind, and they don't manifest the same way as they do in humans and elves. Sometimes they need objects to help them release their ability, while the other can only access it at certain times. Or in the case of some psychics, they can only see fragments of what needs to be known. My daughter used this flute to help her. It wasn't necessary for her to do so, since she had a better connection with her gift than thought possible, but she felt most comfortable using it."

"Sounds like dwarves." I peered over to where several dwarves were mingling and having a grand old time. "Right, Vorn?"

Vorn laughed. "Aye, we be makers, lass, but sometimes we can be somethin' else an it ain't like what ye humans can be. Rare, o' course."

Pyralis handed the pan flute back to me. "Thank you. I trust you'll take good care of it now."

"Of course I will," I assured.

I started putting my pan flute away when Pyralis spoke, "So, what do you say to a friendly match against me?"

I regarded him for a moment. "Against you? Are you sure?"

"Yeah, no harm in it, right?"

"Do it," an eager voice whispered. I'd never heard this voice before, but it came to me much like the ever-present one in my mind, as well as the one that spoke to me while I had been by the lighthouse in Larkren.

"Listen to her. This will be good."

I tried not to make any obvious expression in reaction to the strange situation going on in my head, and shrugged. "Sure, why not?"

Pyralis made his way over to the fires, and I followed. When I was in position, I readied myself and waited for Pyralis. I had no clue what was in store for me, but I was a little excited. I didn't get to spar with the dragons at home since they got all weird about it, so this was a good opportunity to take.

Far too predictably, Pyralis attacked with a hot blast of fire from his mouth. Dissipating the flame with ease, I readied myself for another attack, which was another blast of fire. This continued several times and I began to become a little disappointed. None of his flames became any stronger like I was hoping for from this ancient dragon. His flames weren't nearly as strong as Zaith's or Raikidan's, and they barely rivaled the flame of a new elementalist or shaman.

Then, Pyralis threw in a curve when I least expected it. Just as I blocked his fire, he bolted around to my side and tried to knock me down. Unfortunately for him, I was a little more flexible and agile than he would have liked, and I was able to duck around him. He tried to swing an attack backward at me, but I was still too quick for him to land a blow.

He cursed and exhaled another flame on me, but I retaliated with my own instead of dissipating his flame, anticipating that would leave me open for another attack. Pyralis was forced back, and I took the opportunity to make my move. Acrobatically maneuvering around our dissipating flames, I attempted to land a few swift kicks on him, but he managed to block with his superior strength.

The two of us went at it like this for some time, neither willing to give an inch. I couldn't fully explain it, but I felt a strong need to win against him. With our battle strength obviously in far different categories, winning against him shouldn't have been such a big deal to me, but it was.

"Keep going. You'll get him this time," the new voice said.

Then, before I knew it, it was all over. Pyralis lowered his guard and I followed suit, knowing his action was not out of weakness. Neither of us had really won or lost, but it had still been a good, satisfying fight. There was no need for it to continue.

"Oh, c'mon. you both can do better than that!"

"Hush now, and leave Eira be."

"What in Phyre's name is going on in my mind right now?"

My inquiry was met with silence. *Figures.*

Pyralis bowed his head and retreated to visit with his clan some more, but just as I went to head back to my spot with my friends, Ne'kall stepped up.

I grunted. "Please don't tell me you want another match with me."

He chuckled. "Just a friendly one."

"Do you like getting beat up or something?" I shook my head. "Or are you just stupid?"

"I'm not sure if I should answer that."

I chuckled and readied myself. "Let's get this over with."

Ne'kall, reckless as ever, charged right in without prepping himself. Rolling my eyes, I dodged his attack and beat on him until he was flat on his back and not showing signs of trying to get back up immediately.

I loomed over him. "Had enough?"

Ne'kall coughed. "Yeah…"

"Dad, you suck," one of his kids yelled. Laugher echoed through the crowd.

He sighed. "Great…"

I chuckled and helped him up. "Your fault."

"Yeah, I know." He gave me a high five. "Good fight, regardless."

I nodded and caught the sound of a few shamans telling some others not to challenge me as well. They were concerned for my health, since I'd gone through a rigorous test, and these two fights were special occasions.

"Yeah, Ne'kall's challenge was special, all right."

I appreciated their concern, though I'd had plenty of time to rest and refuel. But it was probably for the best. We didn't need to cause any issues with unnecessary fights. *I'll have to come up with a day where others Shamans of the Rising Sun can test their skills against me.* I didn't see harm in that. It'd keep my skills from going rusty, and it built strong bonds with others, aiding me with my new position.

"That's a wonderful way to see it. You're going to do great as their Ambassador."

"Yeah… still not convinced."

Sitting down next to Raikidan, I relaxed and observed the party around me some more. Raikidan nudged me after a moment and then stood, jerking his head slightly in a silent request for me to follow him. Curious, I followed him and the two of us slipped into the woods unnoticed, or so we thought.

I accompanied him farther and farther away from the party, and couldn't help but laugh when he seemed to be leading me nowhere. "Raikidan, where are we going?"

He stopped walking and gazed around. "This should be far enough, I guess."

I laughed some more. "What are you talking about?"

"I figured you could use some time away from all the partying to takes a few breaths of fresh air."

I smiled. I honestly had been fine, but it really was thoughtful of him. "Thank you." I shivered. "But did we really need to go so far? I'm not really clothed appropriately for winter without a large fire around, and I don't like having to trudge through this snow with these new boots."

He smirked. "There's music playing. You could dance to warm up."

My gaze fell away. "I don't know any dances for a beat like this."

Raikidan's eyes scanned me, making me hyperaware of my appearance. *Why is he staring?*

"You mean besides the fact that you are one good-looking woman?"

"Knock it off."

"I don't know," Raikidan said. "You look dressed for those dances you've done at shaman parties. Beat sounds the same." He grinned again. "I wouldn't mind seeing you dance like that again."

My winter-bit cheeks warmed as the memory of his reaction last time I belly danced flashed through my mind. "These boots aren't great for that. They're pretty heavy."

Raikidan drew up next to me and positioned his hand in the air as if about to dance. "Then dance with me. I watched those performers long enough to get the idea of it."

A grin spread across my lips. This could get interesting. Accepting the offer, the two of us *attempted* to dance. Raikidan's movements were sloppy, but trying to coordinate with him made me no better. The two of us laughed until we gave up. At least we tried, and the silliness of our behavior put me in an even better mood.

Before I had the chance to think about returning to the party, Raikidan moved behind me, wrapping his arms around my waist, and nestling his face into the crook of my neck. The gesture sent a wave of calmness and heart-quickening warmth through me. "I want you to stay out here with me for a little bit longer."

My whole body warmed. "O–okay."

The voice chuckled but refrained from commenting.

The two of us remained like this for several more moments, the warmth and peacefulness flowing over me, so enticing I didn't want to be anywhere else.

I looked up when an owl hooted. It peered down at us, and I realized it was best not to indulge in this kind of closeness any longer. I took in a deep breath and pulled away from Raikidan. "I think we should head back."

He frowned, but then smiled and nodded. "All right." Just as he turned to lead the way back, he stopped. "Oh, and"—his lips met mine briefly—"congratulations. Your hard work paid off. You deserve all this."

I stared with shock as warmth mixed with a fluttering joy welled up in my chest. Recovering, I quickly pushed the feeling away. *It's not right to feel that… It's not like that…*

"I don't know about that. Why kiss you like that if it was a mere congratulations?"

"I don't need false encouragement." I forced a smile. "Thanks."

He smirked back before leading the way, but we didn't make it far before we ran into two people.

I tilted my head. *Xaneth? Anahak?*

Xaneth smiled. "You can keep going, Eira. We just need to talk to Raikidan real quick."

I looked at her and then Raikidan before nodding. "Okay…"

Slipping past them, I continued on, but found myself glancing back several times. I frowned when I noticed how defensive Raikidan seemed to be acting. *I hope they're not causing him too much trouble…*

"Hey, Laz!" Ryoko called. "Where have you been?"

I smiled as I approached, trying to shove away the nerves. "Just needed to get away from everything for a few minutes."

She smirked with a sly grin. "With Raikidan?"

I scowled. "Don't even start."

She laughed and held up a bottle of beer and a plate of food. "You should eat something."

I nodded and gratefully took her offering before sitting down and refueling myself. As I ate, I went back to observing the party guests. Just as before, overall, everyone forgot about their problems for a night.

I gazed at Raikidan curiously when he finally showed back up and sat down next to me. He wasn't smiling, and I was a little worried. "Everything okay?"

"Yeah, everything is fine," he said, though his tight tone said otherwise.

"Okay. Do you want anything to eat?"

"No."

"Okay…" I went back to eating, but I wasn't able to enjoy it as much. Raikidan hadn't eaten all night, and I knew he wasn't fine.

"Just be patient. He'll talk when he's ready."

"Sure he will…"

I stopped eating when a dark-skinned, blue-eyed man from the west desert region of Lumaraeon approached us. "Hey, Ken'ichi. Need something?"

Ken'ichi smiled. "Not from you. We need Raikidan. Some of us Guards would like to challenge him."

My brow rose. "What's the catch?"

He grinned. "If he loses, he forfeits his title as your Guard to the winner."

Raikidan glanced at me and I shrugged. "I don't care what you do. It's your choice."

He climbed to his feet. "Sure. Gives me something to do at least."

"Someone sounds confident," Amara teased.

When the two left, I went back to eating, keeping an eye on the event. I wasn't worried Raikidan would lose, but I also didn't need him getting carried away.

I closed my eyes to listen as the music playing changed. The South

Tribe knew how to craft music, and with this sparring going on, they were sure to accommodate a better atmosphere.

My eyes snapped open when Jasmine gasped, and I caught the tail end of Ken'ichi slamming his head into Raikidan's. Raikidan rammed his head into Ken'ichi's in retaliation, and then pummeled him before picking Ken'ichi up and throwing him in my direction, careful not to step out of the circle they had made.

Ken'ichi bounced and then rolled to a stop by my feet. He coughed a few times and then groaned before I spoke to him. "You okay?"

He chuckled with a small cough. "Yeah. I'll be fine."

I held out a bottle of beer. "Want one?"

"Sure." He took it before standing up and heading off. I didn't miss the exchange between him and Raikidan, but to my relief, it was a good one.

I watched as another Guard challenged Raikidan, and concern flared up in me. *Rai, please don't go overboard… if pummeling Ken'ichi isn't considered going overboard…* The way he acted—it wasn't like him. He didn't act that way at all when he was sparring with the guys. Had Ken'ichi said something to upset him? Or had it been because of that weird mood he was in when he had come back?

"I'm going to vote the first option."

"I'm thinking it might be a mix of the two."

"Fair."

When this fight had finished and nothing bad happened, I relaxed and figured it had to be something Ken'ichi had said. He was a nice guy and all, but that didn't mean he wasn't capable of saying something that could upset someone.

Raikidan brawled it out with several more Guards, but none of them were able to put up enough of a fight to make me worry. Each fight that passed, I found myself more engaged in watching… him. Every punch and throw—each ripple of muscle—the light of excitement in his eyes growing with each win.

I rested my cheek on my hand. He glanced back at me, smirked, and took on another challenger.

"He's perfect."

"Yeah…" I perked up a bit, realizing what I'd done. *"I mean…"*

The voice chuckled. *"Your honesty is accepted here. No need to pull back on my account."*

"I still don't understand why you're encouraging this. Do you get enjoyment out of my misery? Or do you like the prospect of me attempting to be a homewrecker?"

"Neither. I think… no, I know, you're missing a very important piece of information on this situation. You shouldn't hide your desires and should go for what you want. He's proven to me he is a good pick. I no longer doubt his ability—desire—to protect you."

Raikidan beat his opponent and I sat upright when Ir'esh approached. *What is he up to?*

The tribe leader held up his hands. "I'm not here to challenge you. You've proven yourself more than worthy of your position." He pointed in our direction. "I want to spar against you."

Ryoko pointed to herself. "Me?"

"Yep." He waved her over. "Get on over here."

Ryoko's eyes lit up and she jumped to her feet. "All right!"

"No earthquakes!" I warned them both. "We want to save the city, not demolish it."

Ir'esh laughed and waved me off. "Fine, fine. Bare-knuckle brawl it is."

My brows rose and I took a swig of my drink. "Gods have mercy on you."

His brow and head twisted in confusion, and it grew when someone called out, "Ryoko, don't break him!"

The crowd roared with laugher and Tla'lli shouted, "Yeah, he's old. Don't be too rough."

Ryoko cranked her shoulder, a wicked grin on her lips. "No promises."

"She's going to win."

"I don't doubt it. I just hope she doesn't go overboard."

"You know she will."

The two squared off, Raikidan returning to my side, and then they went at it, although as I expected, it didn't last too long. Ryoko made two good fist strikes to the chest and got a little carried away, throwing Ir'esh a good fifteen or so feet. He landed with a *thud* and rolled in pain. Several people jumped to their feet to help him out, but he stubbornly refused and pulled himself to a standing position.

Ryoko outclassed most people I'd ever met. Not even Raikidan could get her to break a sweat the few times I managed to convince him to spar with her, and he was a dragon.

Ir'esh pointed to Ryoko while holding his ribs. "I want to talk to you more later. After I get these ribs fixed."

Ryoko recoiled a little, her eyes stricken with remorse. "Sorry. I tried to hold back but got carried away."

Ir'esh let out a boisterous laugh. "Yeah, I really want to talk to you later."

Peacekeeper Ryoko held up a hand. "I'll help."

He pointed at her. "Excellent."

We all watched him hobble away, trying to hide the amount of pain he was in.

Ryoko headed back to her spot, clearly disappointed she it had ended so soon. I scanned the area and caught a glimpse of an assassin hiding in the shadows of a tree. *He looks familiar…* the man was too far away to identity, but when he noticed me looking his way, he beckoned me. I approached him, curious about what he wanted.

When I made it behind the tree, I was met with more than one assassin—four in total, three men, and one woman. I had to resist the instinct to defend myself from a possible attack when I recognized all of them. They were past disciples of mine—the best of all the assassins I had ever trained.

Helkin, lankiest of the four men, had white hair and pale eyes, and had an ability to turn himself, and anyone he touched, into a mist-like substance, giving him the codename Mist. Greeve, a clean shaven blue-eyed man, who rarely knew when to take things seriously, utilized his abilities of stealth, just like me, to take out his targets, making him the easiest of my disciples to teach. The only difficulty with him, besides his inability to focus, was his unique ability to utilize shadows to blind his targets, giving him the codename Shadoweye. The last two, Sendara and Zelmen, were fraternal twins, with completely different ways of working. Sendara, a beautiful and irresistible woman, used her looks to her advantage to seduce her targets. And when that tactic failed, she'd just take them down with her dual chained sickles, giving her the codename Dark Angel. Zelmen, having dark hair and dark eyes, was codenamed Reaper, and for good reason. He preferred to use stealth to sneak up on his targets and take them out with his large scythe.

I chuckled. "Well, this is certainly a surprise."

Helkin ducked his head respectfully. "Shadow Phoenix."

I shook my head. "Just call me Eira now."

"We'd still prefer to call you that. It's your rightful name."

"I'm not really an assassin anymore, so I have no use for it," I objected. "But if you insist, go for it. I don't really care either way."

Helkin snickered. "You haven't changed."

My lips twisted in thought. "I wouldn't say that's entirely true. Though I'm making a huge assumption and saying all four of you have. I never thought you'd join our cause."

"At first, we couldn't understand why you'd leave," Greeve admitted. "Or how you could have been marked as a failed experiment."

"Then one day everything became clear to us," Sendara explained. "It just hit us out of the blue and we couldn't just sit still and watch you do what was right while we hid in our fears."

My eyes flicked over their faces. "But I can see not all of my best found this clarity."

Zelmen chuckled. "Salis is here, if that's who you're referring to. Per his nature, he's just analyzing everything going on right now."

"He was the one who prompted us to see so clearly," Sendara admitted. "He refused to believe you'd leave without a good reason, and couldn't be convinced otherwise."

"But I can't take all the credit." I spun around at the sound of the strong masculine voice behind me to see a tall, pale skinned, muscular man. He had lavender eyes and blond hair, and in his hands he carried a pair of three-bladed claws uniquely styled to be optimal for assassins. He looked nothing like an assassin, but that was part of what made him my best disciple. He knew how to use his size against stronger targets, but utilized the assassin ways to get the sneak attack in before his opponent knew what hit them.

I smiled. "It's good to see you, Salis."

He held his arm out and I reached over and gave him the half hug he was looking for. "You too, Commander."

I pulled away. "So you said you can't take all the credit. Care to elaborate?"

He smiled and then gazed beyond me. Before I could turn to investigate, a new male voice spoke, this one deep and raspy. "He had a bit of help from someone else who has gone just as soft as you, Sweetheart."

My heart stopped. *It can't be.* I whirled, stunned silence falling over me at the sight of the tall man with short salt-and-pepper hair and well-kept beard, dressed in black leather. A leather eye patch covered his right eye—his good golden eye, clearly visible in the low glow of the firelight.

"Well, look what the cat dragged in."

"Shyden…" I finally managed to say. "You're… alive?"

He laughed heartily. "Last I checked." He held out his arms. "Come here."

I ran over to him and wrapped my arms tightly around his neck. "You have gone soft."

"I blame you," he teased as he pulled away. "No matter how much I tried, there was no way for me to get you to embrace your design to its fullest. And that got me to question what we were doing. The day I disappeared, I'd gone to search for our meaning. By the time I figured things out and came back, you had been long gone, leaving me to work with Salis."

"Why didn't you tell me you were back?" I asked. "Why didn't any of you let me know you were on our side now?"

"Well…" Greeve rubbed the back of his neck. "We're not technically part of the rebellion. We work separately."

I chuckled. "I should have known. None of you would do well under the structure of the rebellion. I barely do."

Sendara nudged me. "Helps that you have a reason to stay."

I rolled my eyes when I recognized the look in her eye. "Don't start that."

She snickered. "You're so stubborn. You should be happy a guy like that follows you around like a faithful puppy."

My brow furrowed. "Have you been spying on me?"

"Every now and then," she replied, a smirk on her lips.

"We should let you go back to the party," Shyden said. "It's not a good idea to keep the guest of honor away too long."

I smiled. "You're probably right. It was good seeing you all. Don't be strangers, okay?"

Shyden placed his hand on my head. "We'll see how the shadows fall."

"Stay out of sight," I said.

Helkin placed his hands on Sendara and Zelmen's shoulder and their forms distorted and then disappeared into a mist. Shyden touched Salis and Greeve, and by stepping into my shadow, used his signature ability to become one with it, and ultimately disappearing inside—Salis and Greeve gone with him.

"It was nice seeing them all again."

"Yeah, it was."

As I went to sit down, a portal appeared a little ways off, catching my attention. An elven woman with umber skin and ash brown hair decorated with colorful feathers exited the mystical gateway. While lithe in form, she had a bit of weight on her, though the squirming, cooing bundle in her arms explained it all. *Alena.*

CHAPTER 4

Everyone quieted down when an olive-skinned elven man with black-and-red mohawk and various tribal-like tattoos, piercings, and gauged ears with feather earring attachments, my mentor Del'karo, also came through the portal. In Alena's arms, a tiny bundle squirmed and cooed. She smiled warmly and scanned the party. Valene ran over to me and grabbed my wrist. Alena's face glowed when she spotted us. She patiently waited while we picked our way over to her.

"How are you feeling, Alena?" Valene asked.

"Tired," Alena admitted.

Valene gazed at the small child in Alena's arms. "How is she doing?"

"Demanding." Alena laughed. "But all our children were, so it's nothing I can't handle."

I looked at the child carefully. She had brilliant blue eyes and auburn hair. "She has your eyes."

Alena's eyes sparkled with delight as she stepped closer to me. "Here, hold her."

"Alena, I don't think that's a goo—oh, ok." I carefully held the small child Alena had shoved into my arms. All I could do was stare at her, and she stared right back.

"*She's so cute,*" the voice said.

"What's her name?"

"She doesn't have one yet." Alena admitted.

I stared at her, my mouth agape. "She was born a few weeks ago and she still doesn't have a name?"

Del'karo placed his hands on Alena's shoulders. The two exchanged a look before Del'karo spoke. "We want you to name her."

I took a step back. "W—what?"

"Oh wow…"

Alena nodded. "We'd be honored if you did."

I shook my head. "Del'karo, Alena… I… I can't…"

This wasn't something they wanted me to do. Becoming the shaman Ambassador was one thing to take on as a responsibility, but naming a child, that was not something I could do. What if I chose the wrong name? This child would have to live with the name I chose. I didn't even choose Ryder's name. I wouldn't have been able to come up with such a good name for him.

But above all that, names were important to elves. Most believed the name they carried gave them their strengths. Not only that, to be asked to name someone else's child was a great honor because they believed you carried qualities that would also be passed onto the child through the name you chose.

Del'karo's voice from a few weeks back echoed through my head. *"We're hoping she'll be just like you."*

I knew he was proud to be my mentor, and I got along with him and Alena and their entire family really well, but what qualities could I possibly possess that they would want passed to their precious little girl?

"A lot."

Alena gazed at me with pleading eyes. I let out a reluctant sigh. "All right… But I think you're making a mistake."

I peered at the small child, hoping a name would pop into my head quickly, but that didn't happen. I was at a loss as to where to start. *How do you pick out a name? Doesn't it require time and planning? Why did they have to choose me to do this?*

The girl started to squirm, until she managed to wriggle her arms free of her blanket. She reached out at nothing. I touched her hand with a finger and her hand clamped down on my finger tightly. I smiled. *For someone so small, she has a strong grip.*

I moved around as I thought, but it wasn't long before I sat down on a stone seat an earth shaman created for me because I was struggling to hold the girl. As strong as I was, she was several pounds of helpless dead weight, and difficult to hold after a while. *I don't know how Alena has done this with thirteen kids…*

Rimu and his siblings came over to investigate the tiny bundle in my arms. They were careful around her, as if aware of how small and fragile she was, and were just genuinely curious about her. I doubted they had seen such a young elf before, so it didn't surprise me.

My mother came over to sit next to me and look at the child. She didn't say anything, or give me hints that she was there to help, and I wanted to sigh. If she wasn't going to help me, then no one would.

"Nope, it's all you, girl. Good luck!"

"Thanks, you're a boatload of help."

"Happy to oblige."

I bit my lip as I tried desperately to come up with a name. All the ones I picked out seemed stupid to me, and nothing her parents would be proud of having their precious little girl being called. Sighing, I gave up trying so hard. I wasn't getting anywhere pressuring myself, although the stress of everyone watching with eager anticipation wasn't helping me much, either. Instead I just watched the child with soft eyes. *She's so tiny. So fragile… precious… beautiful…* I blinked slowly. That was it.

"Vanya." I smiled as the name rolled so sweetly off my tongue. "Her name will be Vanya."

My hopeful eyes turned to Del'karo and Alena for their approval, and their reaction was better than I could have imagined. Del'karo looked so proud, and I swore Alena was about to explode with joy. This girl's parents couldn't have been any happier if they tried.

Everyone around me erupted in loud cheering and excitement, but unfortunately this scared poor little Vanya, and she began to wail. I desperately tried to hush her, and glared at everyone as I failed to calm her down. When slight bouncing and more cooing hushes didn't work, I did the one thing that came to mind. I began to hum.

Vanya didn't respond right away, but I continued, and when my mother joined in, she finally began to calm down. We continued to hum even after she was done fussing. It relaxed her, and if we were lucky, she'd fall asleep and Alena could get some much-needed rest as well. The gods knew how much she needed it.

When Rimu and his siblings began to relax, and some even fell asleep, I became more interested. I knew Raikidan knew this tune, but I had never really found out if it belonged to the dragons or what its real purpose was. My mother had always used it as a tool to calm me down or relax me, and from the looks of the dragonlings, that may have been its true purpose.

My gaze swept over the gathering when several female dragons began to hum with us. They all hummed on a different pitch, creating a beautiful, harmonized song.

"What type of song is this?" I heard someone ask. I almost stopped humming to chuckle when I realized it was Me'kunar. He and his endless curious mind would want to know about this song.

"It's a lullaby," Xaneth explained.

"I never imagined dragons coming up with such a lovely song," he stated.

"It's one of the few." Xaneth chuckled. "Though, as you can hear, the human vocal cords are better at it than our natural dragon ones."

"I somehow doubt that," Me'kunar tried to argue.

Xaneth chuckled again. "You haven't heard us try to sing it yet."

Just then she began to sing and I closed my eyes. It was in her tongue but it came out so smooth, a stark contrast to their standard guttural-sounding speech. I had to agree with Me'kunar, it didn't sound bad at all in the natural tongue, but that could have been because of the human form Xaneth had taken. I had no idea how her voice sounded in her natural state.

It wasn't long before more female dragons joined in, and then, to my surprise, male dragons. I kept up my humming as best I could, even though I was tempted to stop and listen to the dragons carrying this song. *It's just so… beautiful.*

As the song ended, my gaze lowered to Vanya, who was sound asleep. I smiled. She was so innocent and pure. *It's a shame they can't stay this way forever.*

Standing up, careful not to disturb the sleeping dragonlings around me, which wasn't easy in the least, I picked my way over to Del'karo and Alena.

Alena held out her arms to take Vanya back, but I shook my head and kept my voice low. "You go sleep. I'll put her in the crib."

She chuckled softly. "Thank you."

I nodded and followed them through the portal. When we came through on the other side, I looked around the nursery. It was cozy and warm, and full of different types of toys and stuffed animals to occupy her as she grew up.

Del'karo, the sweet husband he was, picked Alena up and cradled her in his arms, carrying her to their room while I went to put Vanya in her old, but beautifully hand crafted crib. Once I was sure she'd be fine, I went through the portal without waiting to see if Del'karo would be coming back. I couldn't stay in that nursery anymore. As much as I tried to not let if affect me, knowing I never had such a life with my mother or with Ryder made it difficult to be in there.

When I came out of the portal I made my way over to the stone seat that had been created for me earlier and just watched everyone as they enjoyed themselves. It was nice seeing everyone getting along and act like everything was right in the world. Why couldn't it always be like this? Why couldn't Lumaraeon be at peace when beings of such different backgrounds could get along right now, right in front of me?

As I watched everyone I realized I was watching certain groups of people. *No, groups isn't right.* More likes pairs. People who seemed quite close and were enjoying this time together. *Pairs...* A sharp pain ran through my chest and I wish it hadn't. It threatened to bring back memories I didn't want to remember. As I tried not to remember, and try to seem invisible so no one would notice the turmoil inside me and start asking questions, I noticed an acoustic guitar lying on the ground by me.

"Hey, Chickadee, if you're not too busy, can you help me with this?"

I wanted to ignore it lying there, but I couldn't. I couldn't stop myself from picking it up.

"Don't worry, you don't have to sing. I just want you to play the guitar while I try the lyrics we finally fleshed out so I can see if it's ready for the competition."

Slowly, I began to strum. As I did, I let the memories flood into my mind and felt a familiar presence sit behind me. The presence was faint, as if they weren't fully there, but I knew it was. I knew this presence and, on queue with the music, he began to sing. My chest swelled with pain at the sound of his voice, and the pain grew when Rylan and the boys picked up their instruments and joined in right on cue just like old times.

I strummed on, even though my mind screamed at me to stop and repress all the pain. I strummed on because the song was stronger, and it spoke how I felt. It released my pain and the pain others also felt when they'd failed someone and wished they had done everything differently to fix it. I couldn't repress this pain any longer. I needed someone to see through the wall for once and understand how I felt.

My strumming came to a stop when the song ended, but I didn't move. I let my broken emotions swell inside me as I tried to sort them out. As I did, I could feel him sit up straight and rest his back against mine. *Tannek...*

Slowly, I lifted my arm up and leaned my hand back. I needed to touch him. I needed to know he was really there. He seemed to mimic my gesture, but just as it felt like the back of my hand was going to contact his, I pulled away and leaned over my guitar as if I was going to start playing another song. I couldn't touch him. It wasn't right. As if he were aware of my thoughts, his presence disappeared and I felt a deep emptiness crawl in my heart from his absence. *Tannek...*

To take my mind off it all, I went to play another song, but a child ran up to me and grabbed my hand. I blinked in confusion as he tugged. When I didn't move like he wanted, he yanked me off my seat. The guitar crashed to the ground and I tried to pick it back up, but the boy wasn't having it.

He pulled me along and every time I tried to resist, he'd yank on me to keep me following. It wasn't long before I found it pointless to resist, and just followed the boy as he picked his way through everyone until we reached a small group of children sitting with an elderly elven woman. The boy pushed me down to sit in front of the woman, then sat with the other children.

I glanced at the woman, then the boy, and then at the woman again. "Okay..."

The woman chuckled. "I'm sorry, dearie. I'm blind, and Alson is mute, so I had no idea whether he had brought you over yet."

I smiled. "It's fine. How can I help you?"

"I was but a young girl when we lost our last Ambassador. She had been so kind and helpful, and it was hard losing her." The woman smiled. "I just wanted to meet you as well, even if I can't see you."

I looked over at Seda, who was already making her way over to us. I took the woman's hands in mine. "Yes, you can."

She shook her head. "Dear, I'm, well, ancient, and I've been blind now for many, many years. I've tried to see with my hands, but because I could see once, it doesn't do me any good. How do you expect me to see?"

Seda sat down next to us. "With my help."

The old woman held out a hand and Seda took it in hers. She then pressed the woman's hand against her eye covering, to show her what abilities she could offer.

The woman smiled. "You're the young psychic helping the twins. I thought I recognized your voice."

Seda smiled. "Yes. And I have the ability to give you back your sight temporarily."

The woman shook her head. "That's impossible. How do you plan to pull off something like that?"

"By temporarily taking my sight away," I said.

The woman's blind eyes widened with surprise. "Is that really possible?"

Seda smiled. "Yes. I don't have many hours of practice in this technique, but I have enough to give you sight for a few minutes."

"Would you… really do that for me?" the woman asked.

"Of course." The woman's eyes welled up with tears and I giggled. "Don't start crying yet. You'll want to save that for when you can see."

The woman nodded. "How do we do this?"

"You'll need to close your eyes to begin with." Seda instructed. "Then I'll do the rest. Make sure you keep your hand connected to me at all times. If you let go, there will be problems for both of you."

The woman nodded before closing her eyes. "I understand."

I closed my eyes when Seda looked at me, and waited. Nothing seemed to happen, but when Seda told us it was safe to open our eyes, I did as I was told. I had to stop my body from panicking when my open eyes were met with nothing. I realized it was more than just dark, as if I'd just had my eyes closed. I had never done this before, just knew that Seda was capable of doing it. I had my ideas of what it would be like, but I had never thought this was how it would feel to go blind.

The old woman's grip on my hand tightened as she gazed around, and I couldn't help but smile. I could tell how happy this made her.

"Nana, can you really see?" one of the children asked excitedly.

"Yes…" The woman began to sob. "Yes, I can." The children clapped and cheered, and the elderly woman held my hands up to her forehead. "Thank you. Thank you so much. I've been blessed in this life. I've seen and experienced many things. But not many have been given the chance to meet an Ambassador, let alone two in their lifetime. You have given this to me, and for that, I am so grateful."

I just smiled at her. There really weren't any words for me to say.

"I'm afraid I can't hold this connection for any longer." Seda said. "I need both of you to close your eyes once again."

I nodded and did my best to make sure my eyes were shut tight.

"All right, it's safe to open your eyes," Seda informed us.

I slowly opened my eyes and had to blink a few times to adjust to my renewed sight. When everything was all set, I noticed the elderly woman was smiling, and I couldn't help but smile back. To most, my gesture would have seemed small, but to this woman, it was something huge.

I blinked when I noticed a dwarven woman with pulled back braided blonde hair and bright blue eyes kneeling behind the woman with her hands on the woman's shoulders. *Gina, the goddess of health and healing.* Her presence made me aware this elderly woman used to be a healer and I could only imagine how happy she had been to see Gina. *This was kind of you, goddess. I know at least you appreciate the service this woman performed on your behalf.*

"Many gods do. They're just limited on showing how."

"I'm sure."

Then, suddenly, the elderly woman threw herself at me, tears streaming down her cheeks. I held her and let her express her gratitude as she saw fit. As I embraced the woman, Phyre, the god of fire, appeared in a puff of smoke and sat down with the children, picking up Alson so he could sit on his lap. Alson, excited he was chosen, grinned from ear to ear.

"You're a kind woman, Ambassador Laz'shika." The elderly woman said through her sobbing. "Kind and beautiful. I'm so glad I was given the chance meet you."

I chuckled. "You sound like you're not going to make it much longer here."

She hummed, calming herself and wiping tears away from her flushed cheeks. "This is life. We never know when our last days are, young or old."

I nodded. "This is true."

"I also got a good look at that man you call a Guard." Her voice was low and almost sounded devious. "And I have to say, you picked a good looking man. Good husband material, for sure."

I pinched my nose, though not out of irritation. The way she said that, it actually had me embarrassed, and a blush threatened to rise up on my face.

"Don't be embarrassed. You want that."

"Ma'am, please don't start teasing like everyone else. It's not… like that."

She giggled. "You young kids and your embarrassment about feelings."

I shook my head, and everyone around me laughed. There was no convincing these people nothing could come of my friendship with Raikidan. *He's not mine to have…*

"Not true."

I grunted when a child crashed into me. "Eira, tell us a story!"

I laughed when I recognized her voice. It was one of Ne'kall's daughters, Ellie. "Tell you a story? Haven't you gotten enough stories tonight?"

"Not enough from you!" she exclaimed as she held onto my arm. "You tell the best stories."

"Hey, I thought you said I tell the best stories!" Ne'kall called out.

"You tell the second best stories, Papa," Ellie mumbled.

Ne'kall sighed. "Now I'm losing my kids to her. What's next, my wife?"

"Careful what you say," his wife teased.

Ne'kall grumbled and everyone laughed at him but me. I was too busy being piled on by the children as they now begged for a story.

"Hey, don't pile on me!" I protested with a laugh. "You'll crush whoever's Nana this is."

The girl with her arms securely around my neck giggled. "She's my Nana and she's not that old. She won't get crushed."

The old woman and I laughed and those around us joined in but my laughter was cut short when I heard a strange noise in the canopy of the forest. Others began to notice as I became increasingly agitated.

"Watch your back."

"Laz," Seda warned.

"Kid, go back to your parents," I ordered as I tried to hand off the elderly woman to Seda.

"But—"

"Now!" I stood and scanned the canopy.

The children scrambled away and several soldiers drew their guns. A whistling noise caught my attention, and I jumped out of the way when a large claw-like object attached to a chain came flying at me from the canopy. As I readied myself for another attack from above, several people jumped down from the trees and surrounded me. One look at their uniforms and weapons told me they were assassins from the capture unit, and I wasn't stupid—they were after me.

"Don't resist us, Commander," one ordered. "Just come with us quietly, and we'll act as if we didn't see the others working with you."

I drew my dagger in response and shaped it into my favored reverse blade. There was no way I'd believe that. When Talon and several other rebel soldiers readied their guns to give me a hand, I shook my head. "Stay out of this."

Talon furrowed his brow. "But—"

"Stay back," I ordered.

He sucked air through his teeth and lowered his gun a little, though remained ready just in case I changed my mind.

An assassin chuckled. "As we would expect from you, Commander Eira. Too bad your stubbornness will cost you."

"Now," I hissed.

Events happened quickly. Salis appeared from the shadow of the assassin before me and skewered him with his clawed blades. Helkin misted in with Greeve, the former immediately misting out an attacking assassin, though not himself, dispersing the man to the wind, and the later blinding a female assassin and silencing her in quick succession.

I ducked instinctively when the sound of a scythe swinging caught my ear, and Zelmen lopped the head off of another assassin while Sendara attempted to distract another male assassin. Her tactics failed due to his training, and so she resorted to slicing into him with her sickles after he made an attack on her.

Two assassins remained, though not for long. They both came at me, hoping to complete their assignment, but a hand reached out of the shadows of one, and pulled the unsuspecting man in, his form swallowed into darkness. I ducked under the attack of the last assassin and thrust my blade into his throat, careful to move out of the way of the blood spray as much as possible when I pulled away. The man choked and gasped, but still tried to fight back by blindly swinging a blade toward me. His attempt didn't come close to hitting me, and I plunged my dagger into his back. He choked and then fell limp on the ground.

I took a deep breath, the blood in the air teasing me, but unlike in the past, where the voice would get excited and I'd lose control, it remained calm, and spoke, *'It's okay. You're okay. You don't have to fight anything. Everything is okay."*

Shyden came up through Salis' shadow. "Are you all right, Eira?"

I nodded. "Yeah, I'm fine." He gave me a look to indicate he meant my mental state more than my physical one. "Really, Shyden. I'm fine."

"She's more capable than you give her credit for," Phyre said. "It's why I didn't step in."

"You're a god, you can't step in," I shot.

He held up a finger. "Depends on who you ask." He winked. "I'm not good with authority."

I shook my head, a smile on lips. *This man.*

"Yeah, he's something else."

Shyden nodded. "Very well. I'm not foolish enough to argue with a god."

"Laz would be!" Ryoko shouted.

The crowd roared with laughter, including Phyre and myself.

Greeve nudged me. "Good thing we decided to stick around."

I snorted. "It would have been handled with, or without your help."

Talon sat down begrudgingly. "Yeah, thanks a lot."

I snickered and then surveyed the bodies around us. "We need to get rid of—"

Shyden's shadow distorted and then connected with the bodies. We all watched as the shadow consumed them and then receded back to its normal place by Shyden. "All taken care of."

"Very well." I peered past the friendly assassin to the group of shamans I had been conversing with before the attack. "Are you guys all right?"

"Everyone is fine, don't worry," Seda said.

"Good." I turned away and began walking for the woods. "I'm going for a walk."

"Laz, you sure?" Ryoko called out.

I waved her off. "I'm fine."

"Okay, just making sure…"

"She's being honest," Rylan said to her quietly. "Don't worry."

I trudged through the snow with no aim to my path. With the warmth of the bonfire gone, I grew cold quickly, but used my fire to heat myself up. I knew it wasn't a great idea to use my fire so openly without a cloak to hide my identity, but I had too much on my mind to care. My past—the voice and its change over these past months—the woman I had seen in the mirror—being chosen by the gods as worthy enough to be the shaman Ambassador. Nothing added up. What was I missing?

I came to a halt and scanned my surroundings. I had made my way to the lake. The full moon cast a silver light over the park and illuminated my puffs of breath. At this time of night, civilians were nowhere to be found, and the city, while still rather busy, sounded quieter than usual. The sounds of the party were even deafened in the cold night.

Breathing in deep, the crisp air stinging my lungs, I sat down in the snow and stared out at the frozen water—my mind still stuck on the same topics. That was, until I sensed I wasn't alone. "Helkin, I don't appreciate you spying on me."

A mist formed next to me and then transformed into a male body. "I'm sorry. Shyden wanted to make sure you were okay."

"Well you can tell him I'm fine. I just needed to be alone to think."

He knelt. "Do you need someone to listen?"

I shook my head. "I just need time to sort out my thoughts."

"Very well. I'll leave you to it, then." He then disappeared in a mist.

Several minutes passed before footsteps crunching in the snow caught my attention. Before I had the chance to look back, a heavy fur pelt was draped over my shoulders. "You're going to get hypothermia if you keep coming out here without proper winter protection."

My eyes flicked to Raikidan when he sat next to me. "You're one to talk, Mister Hibernation."

He grinned and nudged me before gazing out at the lake. The two of us sat there in a comfortable silence for quite some time. After a while, I did notice his attempt to hide his shivering, so I scooted closer and draped part of the fur pelt over him.

Raikidan smiled. "Thanks."

I nodded. "It won't warm up your ass, but it'll help."

He chuckled and then reached out and slipped his arm behind me. A pathetic squeak came out of my mouth when he hauled me into his lap. Raikidan's strong musky-ashen scent wrapped around me and teased my nose. He then adjusted the pelt so that it easily covered us both, and then rested his head against mine. "This should make it easier for us both to keep warm."

"Oh, good boy."

My cheeks warmed. "Yeah, I–I guess."

"Would you rather go back to the party?"

I shook my head. "I don't think I want to go back. I know the party is for me, but…"

"Then we'll go home." He moved from under me, resulting in me being plopped down into the snow again. "I'll get our cloaks so we can go home without issue."

He draped the fur pelt over me again and walked off. I looked at the pelt and felt it before watching him walk off. *Why didn't he insist we stay?* This party was happening because of me, and my mind was uncharacteristically clear. Even if I wanted to leave, I knew I should stay. So why hadn't he insisted I stick around for a bit longer?

"Because, stupid, he's looking out for your well-being. You're not a huge people person."

"Can't argue that."

"And he wants to spend time with just you."

My cheeks warmed again. *"Shut up, no he doesn't."*

I gazed across the lake when Raikidan disappeared into the trees. With him gone, my mind went back to the many questions still buzzing in my head. The icy surface of the lake sparkled in the light of the moon. The pelt fell to the ground when I stood. Taking a slow and steady pace across the slippery surface, I made it several feet before looking around the park and then up at the moon, bathing in its silver glow. *Lunaria, what am I? My life used to be black and white. I knew what I was and what I was made to do. Now, I don't understand what I am or if my purpose really is my purpose at all. If not to kill, what is my real purpose? What do you and the gods expect of me?*

The light of the moon remained consistent, and no whispering voice came to show that she was reaching out to me. The only sound came from the crunching of snow under foot. I suspected Raikidan was back, but I had one last plea.

Please, tell me something. I'll even take a sign that needs to be deciphered at this point.

The moon remained quiet, but that no longer mattered. I placed my hand on my chest when I felt an unusual warmth where my heart was. The warmth pulsed, much like a heart, but with a different beat than my own. *What in Lumaraeon?*

The sound of Raikidan yelling in pain brought me out of my thoughts and my gaze went over to him. My eyes widened at the sight of him collapsed on the ground, his hand pressing against his chest. As quickly as I could on the slick surface, I skated to the shore and ran through the snow over to him.

"Raikidan, what's wrong?" I asked, keeling down and placing my hands on his shoulder.

"I don't know," he said. "I went to say something to you to get your attention, and I briefly felt a burning sensation in my chest—and then pain." He took a deep breath and then removed his hand. "I'm good now."

He felt something in his chest? Is… it connected to what I experience? I decided to not make him aware of what happened to me. Not yet, when I wasn't sure of what I'd experienced myself. "It was all that fighting you did with the younger Guards. Your age is getting the better of you."

He nudged me. "Shut up. I'm young, for a dragon. You're the old one."

"Excuse you. If I was an ordinary human, sure, I'd be an old lady, but I'm nu-human, and I'm still young." I stuck my tongue out at him. "So there."

He snorted. "Well, those Guards had nothing on me. That's why I'm still yours."

I smiled. "Which I'm glad for."

He smiled back and held my gaze. The world around us slipped away for a minute before Raikidan broke it by looking at the cloaks he had dropped. He retrieved them, and that's when I noticed the blue and black orb resting in the snow. "What's with the portal?"

"It was given to me so we wouldn't have to walk home," Raikidan said. "With the portal ban temporarily lifted, seemed like a good idea to take advantage of it."

"Who gave it to you?" I asked. "I want to be able to return it when we're done. I already have some I don't use. Doesn't make sense to hoard more."

He shrugged. "I don't know. It was thrown to me as I left the gathering with the cloaks."

"Okay. I'll figure it out eventually."

Raikidan handed me my cloak as he stood, and clasped his around his neck before retrieving the fur pelt I had abandoned when going to stand on the lake. When we were both ready, I thought of my bedroom, squeezed the orb, and then tossed it on the ground. The orb distorted, and grew until it became a tall, black and blue swirling mass.

Glancing at Raikidan to make sure he really was okay, I led the way into the swirling vortex. It shrunk down into its inactive orb form once the two of us made it to the other side in my room, and I picked it up to store it away for safe keeping. Raikidan left my room, and I took the opportunity to change into my nightclothes in peace.

"Hey, Voice."

"I have a name."

"Yeah, but you can't tell me what it is."

"True."

"Tell me something. Do you know what happened to me when I spoke out to Lunaria?"

"I… cannot say."

"Okay…" I chewed on my lip to figure out how to word myself. There had to be an answer here. I just had to ask the right questions. *"Did it have something to do with Raikidan?"*

The voice was quiet for a moment. *"Yes."*

I knew it… "Are you connected to any of it?"

Again the voice remained quiet for a moment. *"Yes."*

Shock rippled through me. *"How?"*

Silence.

"Eira, you okay in there?" Raikidan asked. "Need any help?"

"I'm fine," I muttered, realizing I'd stopped changing to speak with this presence. "You stay out there."

"Just trying to help…"

"Aw, he's so disappointed. You should just let him help you."

My face flushed. *"No."*

I slipped into a cotton camisole and flannel pants. Once my new shaman attire was safely stored, I left my closet and found Raikidan sitting in his usual spot on the windowsill, now in a men's tank and flannel pants.

I sat down on my bed and went about removing my necklace, but before I could remove my ring, Raikidan jumped onto my bed and latched onto me. The two of us fell over and he curled into me, crushing his hard form against my softer one. His powerful scent overwhelmed me again.

"Raikidan, what are you doing?" I tried to squirm out of his grip and laughed when the attempt failed.

"Stay still. You need to be warmed up after all that time you spent in the cold without something to protect you."

"I'm fine," I said.

"No, you're being warmed up."

An exasperated sigh left my lips. "Can you at least ease up on your grip? You don't need to hold on so tightly."

His grip tightened in response and he rested his forehead on the top of my head. He inhaled deep, as if taking in the scent of my hair to calm himself. My brow creased, confusion and concern flooding through me. Something wasn't right about this, and not in the *inappropriate for friends* kind of way. It wasn't just his tight grip I noticed. *His entire body is tense.*

"Raikidan, what's wrong?" I asked.

"I was so scared," he whispered. "I'm happy you passed your test, but not just because you deserved to. Ken'ichi told me if you failed the test, your fire would be taken away. He said you'd change because of it. That you might die…"

"He told you about his brother, didn't he?"

Raikidan nodded.

"He never told me how his brother lost his fire, but he warned me what can happen to someone when their element is taken. Warned me those people can't cope with the loss… I wasn't going to end up like that. I can live without my fire."

"His brother thought so, too."

I snuggled in close, the ring he gave me grazing my cheek. "Well, I didn't fail, so you're stuck with my weird freakish self."

He rubbed his forehead on me. "I'm glad. I like you as you are. I don't want you any different."

I smiled and listened to the beating of his heart. *Strong, just like him.* My smile faded and I glanced at the ring on my finger, pain twinging in my chest. *It's funny how someone who isn't human can do everything so right, but be so wrong for you.* I closed my eyes. *But, that's my life. The nice things are always just out of my reach.*

5
CHAPTER

Loud banging echoed through Zane's shop, sending pulses of pain through my head. I cringed. Even with the noise-canceling earplugs Argus gave me, the different projects the others worked on couldn't be silenced.

I'd woken up this morning with a splitting headache. I suspected it was due to dehydration from my eventful night, but even after watering myself and filling my belly with food, I felt no better. Shva'sika guessed it to be a side effect of exhaustion, and advised I rest for the day, but Zane needed extra help at the shop, so of course I volunteered.

I glanced up from my schematic and watched Ryoko, Rylan, and Raikidan head out of the shop, keys in hand. Brow raised, I removed the earbuds and turned Zane's way. "Where are they going?"

He looked up from some papers. "Getting some special parts that came in early. Truck can't get to us due to an accident, so I set up a way for us to do a pick up elsewhere."

I nodded and when back to my task. Well, I tried to. Argus' schematic didn't make sense in the least. Usually I could figure them out without any help, even though he'd written notes in Common in case someone outside our circle found them. But this revamped communication schematic for the helmets were just a bunch of lines, scribbles, and gibberish.

Someone tapped on my shoulder and I jumped. Whirling around, I came face-to-face with a startled Zo, his hands up defensively. *Great, you would show up today.*

General of some Dalatrend army company that I never thought to inquire about, even from Ryder, who reported to him, Zo wasn't a horrible man to deal with. But his strange and unwanted, interest in me, and his poor dating skills, made him a pain to work with.

"It'd be nice if the creep would leave you alone," the voice said. *"You'd think he'd take a hint."*

"Well, it doesn't help that up until recently Genesis made me go on those dates with him. And at least he's not bad to look at when I have to put up with him."

"That's… one way to put a positive spin on it."

I pulled my earbuds out. "Sorry, I can't hear with these things in."

He rubbed his head. "Well, I'm glad there's a reason. I didn't mean to startle you."

I smiled at him. "Don't worry about it. How can I help you?"

He tossed his thumb in the direction of where the others were working. "Zane is retrieving a progress report for me, so I thought I'd see what you're working on. You looked deep in thought—or confused."

I laughed and turned my gaze back down at my work. "Confused is an understatement." I raised my voice. "Because someone doesn't know how to make a schematic."

"I can, too!" Argus shouted from his end of the shop.

The two of us chuckled. Zo peered at my paper. "Mind if I take a look?"

I took notice of his uniform helmet sitting on my workbench. *I wonder…*

"Oh, not a bad idea. Give it a shot."

I shrugged. "Have at it. No secrets here."

The voice snorted. Zo's eyes glittered with amusement and he took a look at the schematic. His brow furrowed. "This is that helmet design you and Argus were working on months ago. I thought the two of you had finished this by now."

"We'd make progress, and then backtrack every time we added something new to the design. After a while, though, we were breaking it more than getting things working right. And then the worst happened…" I sighed, the real memory vivid in my mind. "Zane's girlfriend tried to give us a hand one day, opting to clean the office since no one else does, and ended up shredding all the paperwork on the design by mistake. Then, while we were trying to reverse engineer what we'd accomplished, Ryoko had an accident that destroyed the prototype."

I rested my forehead in the palm of my hand. "We had to start from scratch."

Zo held up his hand. "Wait, back up, Zane has a lovely lady on his arm now? Since when?"

"Since she started making it up." The two of us glanced up. Zane stood in the doorway of the office, his arms crossed. "I don't have a girlfriend."

I grinned. "Don't lie. You're completely smitten with Elarinya."

"Only smitten?" Argus laughed as he came over from his side of the shop. "He almost asked her out on a date the other day, but chickened out."

My brow rose. I didn't even know that. Zane grumbled to himself, his cheeks tinting a light shade of pink, and went back into the office instead of fighting us.

When he started trying to learn Shva'sika's elven name, I began to suspect he had a growing interest in my friend. And as the weeks passed, he'd paid more attention to her, more than he'd ever done for any women he'd met; I confirmed it with the guys, and that confirmation made them aware of Zane's actions. And well… let's say he hasn't been able to get us off his back since.

Shva'sika was a good pick, and I could confirm the interest wasn't one-sided. She hadn't been subtle with her growing interest in the man as of late.

Hence the reason she'd tried to help clean up. Shva'sika had shown up with lunch as a surprise, and offered to clean the office, unprompted. It wasn't her fault the helmet schematics had been in there. It'd been mine. Luckily no other important documents had met the same fate.

Zo looked down at my work schematic. "Well, I'm going to agree with you, Sweetcheeks. These make no sense."

The voice scoffed. *"You'd think he'd come up with a more appealing name for you by now."*

I snickered when Argus grumbled about it making sense to him and walked off. "It'd be helpful if we had something to go off of, but since only the military have anything like it, it's a difficult process."

My eyes flicked to the paperwork and I drew a red X on a hookup I suspected wouldn't work. Zo watched me.

After a few moments, he reached for his helmet and offered it to me. "Here. Just don't break it."

My brow rose. *No way that worked.* "You sure?"

"You're just looking at it to get an idea, right?"

"Well, yeah."

He grinned. "Then it's no trouble."

I smiled and took the offered safety device. On the exterior, it didn't appear much different than the ones used when I'd been in the military. Upon checking the functions, I noted the similarities of my past experience and civilian helmets.

"There's not much difference, if you ask me."

"I suspect the big difference is the bulletproof design and the advanced features. Now to come up with a way to check those without raising an alarm."

"Just play innocent civilian. Worst he can do is scold you."

She had a point. I glanced Zo's way, the man still watching me. "Can I put it on?"

He nodded. "All confidential lines are shut off."

I placed the helmet on my head and left out an *oof* sound, when it slid around due to all the gaps between the padding and my head. "You have a big head."

"I do not."

Blaze approached, a grin on his lips. "I'd be taking that as a compliment if I were you." Knowing exactly what that gutter mind of his meant, I flipped him my middle finger and he held up his hands. "Hey, if you want to—I'm game."

"Not even if you were the last man in Lumaraeon."

He shrugged. "Your loss. Plenty of smarter ladies would take me."

I stuck my finger into my open mouth and made a fake wrenching noise. "More like dumber."

Blaze scowled, and I went about playing with the helmet until the dark visor slid down over my eyes and displayed an absurd number of digital functions. "Oh wow, this is disorienting. Argus, I like yours better. There's less on here."

Argus came over. "Well that's because the military has more things to monitor."

I narrowed my eyes. "I know that. I'm just saying, be careful what you decide to display with yours. You do tend to get some crazy ideas."

His brow rose. "Yes, and it seems I'm the first to think of a one-way visor."

My brow furrowed. *It's not one-way?*

Zo took interest in the comment. "You can do that?"

I turned my head toward him. *Seriously?*

"Yeah, that's pretty bad on the military's part."

Argus crossed his arms. "It's easy. But then again, I wasn't putting so much on the visor display."

"I'll have to see what reason we have for not using such an idea. You might be hearing from me about it," Zo said.

Argus nodded. "As long as you pay well enough for something like that, I'll do the work."

"I wouldn't expect a different response."

"Hey, Zo," I said, looking at all the different displays. "How do you do anything with all this stuff in your face?"

He chuckled. "We can turn it off. We don't walk around with all that running."

"Well, that's good."

Zane strolled out of the office with some paperwork in his hands. "I agree. Now Eira won't try to walk around with that on her head." I pointed at him with narrowed eyes and he laughed. "Zo, if you can pull yourself away, I found those plans."

Zo nodded and joined Zane by the office. With Zo's attention pulled away, I focused on checking this out based on our tactical needs. Genesis made me aware the other day the Council had been looking for ways to spy on the military in a more direct way that didn't involve the moles. This would ensure quicker intel and less risk to individuals.

A few proposed wiretapping military helmets, but thanks to the moles, we knew of a new helmet in the testing phase. If it passed, new ones would be manufactured, so tapping now would only be useful for a short window. The Council chose to tap a few mole helmets for now, until we had more information on the new rollout.

Thanks to my connection with Ryder, I did know what to look for with these few test helmets. I couldn't be sure Zo had one, but to pass up the chance to check would be foolish.

I noticed Zo's attention coming back to me as he spoke with Zane. It concerned me. If I didn't play this innocent civilian card right, he'd get too suspicious of me. So, I played with the visor a few times, and make it look like it enthralled me. Zo chuckled and continued to work with Zane, but his attention didn't stray from me.

"You need to be more creative."

"I just need him to think my interest is innocent as I look about for the right signs on this stupid display."

"But why stop there?"

My brow rose and I peeked at an interesting display on the corner of the visor. *"Wait, you mean to see if I can convince him to leave the helmet with me?"*

"You could give the rebellion the opportunity to learn more about the helmet and plant a bug."

"Do you really think I could pull that off? That'd be a suspicious request."

"I know you're smart enough to come up with a plan."

I thought about this, pulling the helmet off and looking at my schematic to create an illusion of me thinking about the project at hand. What could I do to further this opportunity? Argus and Blaze had gone off to work on their projects some more, so it'd be hard to utilize them. *But not impossible.*

I marked a few changes on the schematic, pretending they actually meant something, and focused on the helmet again. My face reflected against the armored body. *Wait, Ryder reports up to him. Maybe…* "Hey, Argus, did the others say if they were going to pick up dinner while they were out?"

"I don't think so—why, you hungry?"

"Yeah. I'm going to try that code sending to Rai, so I can keep practicing. Can you look over my shoulder to make sure I'm doing it right?"

"Sure."

He joined me at the table as I pulled out my communicator. I was aware of the extra attention Zo now placed on me, but did my best to look innocent in my task. I created the basic code message the communicators had the capability of creating.

Ryder, help get Zo out of shop.

I showed it to Argus and he nodded, though his eyes gave away his curiosity. "That's right. Now you can send it and wait for a response."

With a nod, I sent the message off and placed the communicator on the workbench. Argus examined the schematic as I picked the helmet back up.

He pointed to one of my markings. "Why did you do that?"

I didn't look at him as I spoke. "Because it won't work."

"Yes it will."

"Nope." My communicator went off and I took a look at the message.

Outside shop waiting. Will see what can do.

My brow rose. Zo made him stand outside? How many others were there waiting, and why?

"Argus, does this say he already got me food?"

He took a look and nodded. "Yes."

I scrunched my nose. "He'd better have not gotten me a salad again."

Argus chuckled as I made it look like that was my response.

Thank you.

I showed Argus to keep up the act and then sent when he nodded. "Thanks for the help, Argus."

He patted me on the shoulder. "You're getting better. Next time try to do it without me. I'm confident you'll do fine." He made a mark over one of my markings on the schematic and left my side. "And that will work."

I let out an exasperated sigh and went back to playing with Zo's helmet, aware of Zo's gaze on me. My eyes met his. He smiled and then he focused on Zane. *That was weird.*

Turning the helmet upside-down, I searched for any physical markings indicating the type of helmet it was. *There!*

"*Nice job.*"

All attention went to the entrance of the shop when the door flew open and Ryder rushed in. "General, we have a situation you need to look at."

Zo left Zane's side and pulled Ryder away from us. "What it is?"

Ryder kept his voice low to indicate that it was something non-military shouldn't know. "The incident we were recently assigned to help with—there's been some development around it. It's worse than we thought. We need to report back to get more information."

"Shit." Zo looked to Zane. "I'll be back another time to finish discussing those plans. We have an emergency to handle."

Without waiting for Zane to respond, or to make sure Ryder followed, Zo rushed out of the building. Ryder flicked his eyes my way. I mouthed "thank you" to him and he winked before rushing after his commanding officer.

When the door slammed shut, the guys focused on me and pointed to the helmet, but I raised my hand to keep them from talking. I continued to stare at the door, thinking Zo would remember he'd left the helmet behind, but the door remained shut.

Blaze wandered over and peered out a window, even going as far to venture outside, only to come back in and shake his head. "They're gone."

I doubled over in laughter. "I can't believe it worked!"

"You shouldn't doubt yourself so much."

Zane placed his hand on his head. "You were trying to get his helmet?"

Argus crossed his arms. "I could have just asked to borrow it, if that was the case. He did want me to possibly work on the one-way visor."

"I'm still convinced you could have asked real nice and he would have done it in a heartbeat."

I leaned on workbench, my fingers laced together, a mad grin on my lips. "Yeah, but that'd raise too much suspicion. They'd check the helmet for tampering, and we don't want that if we want to learn about these new helmets."

His eyes widened and his shoulders relaxed. "Seriously?"

I held up the helmet. "Here you go, genius. Your time to play."

Quicker than I'd seen him move before, he closed the distance and snatched the helmet from my hands, his eyes bright with excitement. Zane's grumbling caught my attention and I laughed when I caught him fighting with the plans he pulled out. He tugged on the papers, but they wouldn't leave his hand.

My eyes turned up as they narrowed. "Having trouble with those spines, Uncle?"

He snorted. "That's an understatement. I don't know how you don't get this issue."

"Oh, I do. I'm just better at getting unstuck and am more discreet about it." I'd never told anyone that Zane and I shared the same ability. It was always more fun seeing other's reactions when they found out, due to the fact my mother and Jasmine didn't have the trait. My uncle lucked out, though. He only had them in his hands, where I had them in both my hands and my feet. They were useful when climbing, but also made for some interesting situations when I got stuck to something.

Zane exhaled a relieved breath when he freed himself and headed into the office once again to store the papers. I looked to Argus and Blaze. "You two hungry?"

Blaze threw his fist into the air. "I'll never turn down food."

Argus nodded. "I could use something, too."

"Uncle, what about you? I was thinking of hitting up a sandwich shop close by so I wouldn't have to walk far. It's not freezing, but it's not exactly spring yet."

"Sounds good, you know what I like," he called back.

Argus and Blaze wrote down their preferred order as I slipped a jacket on. But just as I took the note from Argus, my communicator went off. Brow raised, I answered. "Hello?"

"Eira, its Genesis," came the voice on the other end. "I need you to come home to handle something."

I sighed. "Okay. All the cars are gone, so it's going to take me a bit to get home. And I was just about to go grab some dinner, so I'd like the chance to pick something up to hold me over."

"That's fine. Just get here as soon as you can." She hung up, leaving me irritated.

I turned my attention to the others. "Sorry guys, guess I'm not getting food."

Argus waved me off. "Not your fault. I'll give Ryoko a call so the others can grab something for us. Good luck with whatever you're being assigned to do."

I nodded my thanks and headed out, taking a path to the closest sandwich shop.

A light breeze ruffled my hair and brought with it the promise of spring—the one season I couldn't wait for. Not only because winter would end, but because the Council aimed for spring to be the last season we'd see under Zarda's rule. Some days I struggled to believe that would happen, but I needed to stay strong and keep pushing forward. We couldn't let him win.

Movement caught my periphery, and I snapped my head over my shoulder to find nothing.

"Watch yourself."

My brow rose but I kept walking. *"What do you sense?"*

"Something sinister."

I unzipped my jacket and drew a dagger from my arm. Ryoko had a habit of making fun of me for carrying them around, but I didn't like taking chances. You never knew when you'd need them, and I'd followed all of the applicable laws to be allowed to carry them in public. After almost losing a few in that first house inspection the first week of my return to the city last spring, I made sure that wouldn't happen again.

Holding the weapon close to my chest, I continued on, keeping an ear open and my eyes peeled for danger. Pebbles clattered behind me.

"Watch out!"

I was already spinning around by the time the voice shouted her warning. My blade clashed with another, and I used all the strength I could muster to keep my attacker's blade from slicing into me. My eyes narrowed at the sight of my assailant—dark hair and blue-veined ashen skin. A black shield with a red teardrop was tattooed on his neck. *Him.* The nu-human man who'd orchestrated the Crimson Sanctuary's attack on Dalatrend. The voice also snarled without uttering a word.

My assailant tried to overpower me. "How many times do I have to kill you for you to stay dead?"

Narrowing my eyes, I forced him away and readied myself in a defensive stance. I had no idea what he meant, but this wasn't the time to ask questions. "You underestimate me if you think such a poorly executed attack could take me by surprise."

The ashen skinned man readied his blade. "No matter. I've chased you for several millennia. I will succeed in destroying your soul and eradicating your filth from this land."

"Over my dead body!"

His muscles tensed and I readied myself. But before it could happen, a bright light blinded us from the periphery. The man cringed and backed away. Eyes half-closed, I took the opportunity to slice my dagger into him. He howled in pain and swung a sword at me, but his blinded state reduced his accuracy, and he swung too wide.

The searing light disappeared, and a figure rushed us. My eyes widened at the white-haired woman clad in ancient swordsman attire. *Arcadia?* She drew one of her many katanas and sliced the sharp blade through the air at him. The man staggered, avoiding the attack, and reached his hand into a pocket. He pulled out a small, round object and tossed it on the ground. A bright light flashed and I shielded myself, sensing Arcadia placing her body between me the mysterious man.

When my sight returned, my head snapped in several directions only to find the man gone. Arcadia swore in what I thought was Old Tongue, and sheathed her weapons.

"Thank you for the assistance, Arcadia," I said. "I'm not sure the reason, but I won't take it for granted."

She turned my way, her plate crystal eyes staring into me. "You're welcome. I'm sorry I didn't get here sooner. He threw me a false trail to follow, and I got to you the instant I realized my mistake." She looked around. "He's always one step ahead of me these days."

"Who is he?" I asked.

The goddess shook her head. "Don't worry about it. You just head on your way."

"Don't let this go."

My eyes narrowed. "Oh, no. This is not the first time he's tried to take my life. I deserve to know who he is—and why you're hunting him."

She held my gaze for a moment and sighed. "You won't let this go otherwise, so very well." Her eyes scanned our surroundings again. "It's not safe to discuss this here. Accompany me to the Plane of Between."

I nodded and followed her into a spiraling portal she created with the wave of her hand. Just as I did, I heard my name called out. *Raikidan?* But before I could turn back to be sure, the portal closed behind us. *Oops.*

"He'll live. Panic a bit, but he'll live."

"That won't be fun to deal with when I get back."

"You'll live, too."

I refrained the urge to roll my eyes and continued to follow Arcadia through the portal. She glanced my way a few times, but never uttered a word. The swirling portal brightened as we neared the exit, and then we walked out onto a stone path surrounded by fire and ice flowers. Tall metal and stone half arches towered over us as we walked toward the large tree in the clearing. As I gazed around, I still couldn't believe I'd caused such a beautiful reshaping of this this area.

Arcadia stopped when we made it to the tree and stared at it. The longer she did, the more curious I became about it. "Arcadia, can I ask you something about this tree?"

Her gaze shifted to me, her usual solemn expression twisting to a small smile. "You want to know what it is, yes?"

I nodded. "I saw it react to the lava Phyre spread to its roots. I watched as all of you gods created this reshaping around it. And it looks like the tree you showed me in Hell."

Arcadia turned to face me. "It's called the Birth Heart. It's a direct line to Lumaraeon herself." My eyes widened, but she continued. "One exists on this plane, as well as the plane we gods reside on. There is one on the mortal living plane as well, though that one is well-hidden, and guarded for its safety."

My brow furrowed. I'd never heard of such a thing existing before. Not even shamans talked about it. "What about the one in Hell?"

She nodded, her eyes closed. "A mere replica. Another reminder to the souls regarding what they've given up."

I gazed up at the towering tree. "So, how is it connected to Lumaraeon?"

"It's how one can contact her directly." I looked at Arcadia, surprised, and she smiled. "Upon touching the tree, if she so wishes, she will communicate with the individual. She can be quite chatty, but that's to be expected from a primordial god."

My brow furrowed. "What?"

Arcadia chuckled. "Lumaraeon is a goddess, Eira. The first ever— the only primordial god. The land we call Lumaraeon, the place we call home, is she."

I let this all sink in.

"She's telling the truth."

Arcadia smiled. "But we didn't come here to discuss that, now did we?"

I composed myself. "Right. I want to understand who this man is who has made an attempt on my life twice now."

Arcadia closed her eyes and took a moment before opening them and speaking. "His name is Kir and he is a revenant. He founded the Crimson Sanctuary."

My blood ran cold. *No… it can't be…*

The voice snarled. *"I knew he was familiar."*

I shook myself. "Are you sure he's a revenant?"

Arcadia nodded. "I've chased his soul since he died in battle during the first war his Crimson Sanctuary caused. I have not imagined the millennia that have passed. I've not overlooked the power he has accumulated in his undeath—the faces he's taken to bring others to his vile cause—the pain and suffering he's brought unto others for his own selfish, dark ideals." Her fists clenched and I noticed the rage building up in her. "I don't know how he does it, but I can't allow him to achieve his ultimate goal."

"What goal is that?"

"Ascension."

My eyes widened. "Can that happen to the dead?"

Arcadia shook her head. "I'm not sure, and I don't want to find out. That type of power in such a man's hands would be catastrophic for all of Lumaraeon."

I steeled myself. "I'll help wherever I can. It's a shaman's duty to handle revenants when they come about, as rare as they are now. And I can't allow myself to let a man like this cause more pain to those who have a right to live."

"Don't worry, young Ambassador. You already are." My brow rose and she continued. "You are a target because he knows your nature. As long as I keep an eye on you, more than I already do, that helps me to know where he may be."

"Press her more on this."

I regarded the goddess for a moment. "How does he know my nature?" Arcadia didn't answer, and my eyes narrowed. "He wanted to know how many times he has to kill me before I stayed dead. He said he'd chased me for several millennia. This revenant knows my nature beyond just being a halfling, doesn't he? What does he know that I don't?"

Arcadia's jaw tightened.

"What do you know that you won't tell me?"

The goddess still refused to speak. My fists tightened, but I didn't let my irritation get the better of me. It wouldn't help.

"Keep pressing."

"There's no point." I turned away from Arcadia. "Very well. There is no need for me to remain here any longer. Please provide me passage back so I can continue with my original task prior to this interruption."

Arcadia reached out for me. "Eira, please don't be angry. Tru—"

"I have a revenant targeting me and you won't tell me anything about him." I tossed a scowl over my shoulder. "I don't care what you want. You posture and try to pretend you care, but none of you really do."

"That's not true, little firefly." I turned to find Phyre approaching. "We do care."

I opened my mouth to reply, but he held up his hand and contin-ued. "We hear you when you curse us—when you pin blame for your circumstance on us, and we don't fault you. This is not the life that had been laid out for you." His eyes darkened. "But someone stuck their hands into the timelines and caused all sorts of problems. You were also affected by this."

Phyre's eyes softened. "We may be gods, but we aren't perfect. We have limitations. We try our best to fix events within the cosmic laws as ordained, but sometimes it's not enough and we can only hope mortals are able to succeed where we have failed."

I crossed my arms. "Then tell me what I should know."

Phyre opened his mouth but Arcadia spoke. "Stop it, Brother. You've already gone against the rules and said more than you should have."

My lip curled and Phyre addressed his sister. "I'm not good with rules, Sister. Especially rules I find stupid. Like this one."

"He's got you there, Arcadia."

Her jaw set and her eyes narrowed, but unlike her, I appreciated his words. "Since you're willing to speak, Phyre, can you answer my questions?"

He frowned. "I'm afraid not."

I crossed my arms. "Why?"

"Believe me, I wish I could tell you everything. You deserve to know. But there's a law in place that is so strong, even the most rebellious can't go against it. Every time we call up the answer, it leaves us, as if we never knew. When the question is dropped, the answer returns."

I thought about this for a moment. This happened to the voice every time I asked her certain questions.

"Yes, it's strange, and obnoxious."

"Any tips on how to get around it?"

"Not at the moment, sorry."

I sighed. "So, how am I supposed to help, and figure out who this Kir is, if no one can tell me anything?"

Phyre reached out and placed my hand on my chest, my heart beating beneath. "The answers lie within. You'll have to rely on your own wit to find them."

I frowned, but at this point, it was all I'd get. Arcadia waved her hand, and a portal returning to the living plane appeared. I bid them a good day and left. The moment I exited the portal, I spotted Raikidan sitting on the ground next to the wall of a building.

He jumped to his feet and rushed over to me. "Are you all right?"

I smiled, touched by his concern. "I'm fine. I just had a situation that required me to speak with Phyre and Arcadia."

His eyes widened. "So that was her with you. What happened?"

"You remember that creepy guy that tried to kill me when the Crimson Sanctuary attacked?" He nodded. "He showed up and attacked me again."

My hands flew up to Raikidan's chest when panic flooded his eyes. "Easy, he didn't hurt me. He's about as quiet as a warthog and fights with all the skill of a monkey."

Raikidan's head jerked and his brow furrowed. "You say the weirdest things sometimes."

I chuckled. "But it's true."

"So, Arcadia gave you a hand dealing with him, then?" He asked. I nodded. "Any particular reason why?"

"Because he's not a living man." Raikidan's brow furrowed and I continued. "He's a vengeful spirit called a revenant. They're rare these days due to the vigilance of shamans, but they do appear."

"Why did he attack you specifically?"

I frowned. "He somehow knows of my halfling blood, and since he founded the Crimson Sanctuary, it's logical for him to target me."

Raikidan cupped my cheek. "I won't let him get you."

I placed my hand on his and smiled. "I know. You should know, that it'll be my duty to deal with him in time. My main focus will need to remain the major conflict at hand, but I'll be letting the shamans know of what I've learned and will work with them to deal with this revenant. He can't be allowed to wander and cause problems anymore."

He nodded. "I'll help you where I can."

"Good, now let's get home."

He tossed his thumb behind him. "I have the car. I also have dinner for you."

I smiled. "You're the best."

He chuckled and headed for the vehicle. "I'll let Rylan and Azriel know."

I shook my head, a smirk on my lips, and followed him. Hopping into the car, he handed me food. By the time we reached the house, I'd finished and relaxed in my seat, prepping myself for whatever assignment Genesis had cooked up.

Upon opening the door to the basement and entering the living room, I was met with an unusual sight. We had a guest, speaking with Seda and Shva'sika. But one look at the fair-haired, fair-skinned woman with a dark blindfold over her eyes, I knew exactly who she was. "It seems today is a day of gods gracing us mortals with their presence."

The woman turned my way. I dipped my head respectfully, and my eyes darted around the room for any more guests. "Good evening, Sela."

"Hello, Eira," she said, her voice hollow, like Seda. "Don't worry. My brother isn't here waiting to pull some prank on the next person to step into the house."

Sela was said to have the usual calm personality of most Seers, hence the inspiration for their name. Her twin brother, Tyro, on the other hand, was known to be a bit of a fun-loving trickster, unlike the serious or cocky nature of Battle Psychics. Seda told me once that psychics who fit the profile for Battle Psychic but managed to evade the mandatory military conscription in most cities had similar personalities as Tyro. But so few were around these days, no one could be sure except for the oddball Battle Psychic who crossed people's paths. *Like Telar.*

"I'm glad you've made it home safe." Her lips spread into a smirk. It made me think of Seda for some reason. "Not that I doubted Arcadia's ability to aid you, of course."

She looked at Seda. "I should be going now. I quite like this more open communication, unlike in the past. So, my granddaughter, I will catch up with you again soon. And hopefully with your brother and your new sisters as well."

Seda smiled at her. "I'd like that. Thank you for stopping by."

The psychic goddess nodded once and left, exiting down the stairs to the front door, but the door never opened or closed. Curious, Rai-kidan followed a moment later and confirmed she had disappeared.

I turned to Seda. "That was interesting to walk into. And to hear you're her granddaughter? I think an explanation is in order."

Seda rubbed the back of her neck. "Well… Sela doesn't like to stay on the immortal realm. She finds it boring, so she likes to stretch her legs and mingle from time to time. That's how she met a man that caught her eye. One thing led to another, and they were married with a child on the way. My mother."

My eyes widened, and Seda chewed on her lower lip. "And before you ask, no, my brother and I aren't tank-born. We were raised in a small town south of here—at least, for a little while. Our powers grew at such a rapid rate that neither my parents, Sela, nor Tyro could understand or combat. After some discussion with Lord Taric, it was decided that we'd be brought here and taught in a more stringent manner how to control our gifts. Unfortunately, that still didn't help, so it was agreed we'd be placed in a stasis until our powers could normalize."

Her gaze lowered. "The stasis lasted twelve years—longer than they'd anticipated, but it couldn't be helped. They didn't want to release us until they were sure our abnormally high power wouldn't cause us any harm. It wasn't until later that we determined our unusually high power came because of our close ties with Sela and Tyro. The psychic gene skipped my mother, but not us, so it's believed it doubled in power. Celestial blood is a potent material."

"Is this how that geneticist got the idea there was a psychic gene?" I asked.

Seda nodded. "Yes. I'm surprised they waited so long to test the theory, though. It's not like I'm all that young, especially for a born nu-human."

"So, if you were born, and not made, how is it your sisters exist?" Raikidan asked.

"When non-tank-borns are conscripted into the military, they hand over DNA. This is used to help heal them or save their life if a situation requires it. Unfortunately, this also gave Zarda extra DNA to test once he came into power."

"How come you never told us?" I asked. "It's not like we'd judge you for it. It's pretty cool, to be honest."

Seda scratched her cheek. "My brother and I got used to hiding it. There are plenty of awful people out there who would love to get their hands on a demi-god or descendant of a god. It's why I offered to stay by Genesis' side. I knew the type of struggles she was going through."

"Sela said she liked the open communication now. Does that mean you had contact with her before?"

Seda nodded. "I saw her all the time when Lord Taric ruled. But When Zarda took power, we decided it would be best to limit our interaction for safety reasons. We never thought to change it once I started living here."

I hesitated on my next question but asked anyways. "Is your mother around?"

Seda frowned. "No. While she was a demi-god, giving her an extended life, she contracted an aggressive disease, and couldn't be saved. That happened after my long stasis, so I got to spend quite a bit of time with her before her passing."

I nodded, glad Seda'd had that time with her mother. Footsteps echoed down the hall. I turned to find Genesis approaching. "I'm here now. Sorry for the delay."

She shook her head. "Don't worry about it. I was just informing the Council we had to pass. Sela let us know you were dealing with a far more important issue."

I smiled my thanks. "I still am, technically." I looked to Shva'sika. "We need to contact the other shamans and have a meeting. There's a revenant on the loose."

Shva'sika's eyes widened. "Are you sure?"

I nodded. "His name is Kir. I'll explain more when we have everyone gathered, but know that he has ties to the Crimson Sanctuary."

Her eyes darkened and her jaw set. "I'll inform them right away."

I headed for my room to change. I didn't have a lot to give them, but they may have more to share with me. It may help me get closer to these unanswered questions.

"I'll try to help."

"I won't bank on it."

"I understand. This force that prevents me from telling you everything may be an obstacle, but it's not impossible to get around. I will find a way."

I almost chuckled. *"Good luck with that. In the meantime, I'll continue to look for clues, like always."*

I threw on my shaman clothes and waited for Shva'sika to let me know where we'd meet the others to formulate a plan.

6
CHAPTER

My eyes fluttered open, the sensation of sleep gone. I stared up at my ceiling lying in bed, unable to find any tiredness in me. *Something's not right.* I wiped my violet hair from my face and sat up, only to find the room cold and almost distant. Even Raikidan seemed far away as he slept quietly.

As I watched him, a new presence appeared beside me. I turned to look and nearly jumped out of my skin when I noticed the young woman standing beside my bed. It appeared to be the same woman who had been sitting beside Blaze at my celebration.

I went to say something, but she spoke instead. "Save him."

My brow furrowed. "What?"

Her eyes pleaded with me. "Please, save him."

My head tilted. Who was she talking about? Who was she for that matter? She had been following Blaze during my celebration a few days ago, though I'd left her alone as requested. Now I wasn't so sure that was such a good idea. "Who are you?"

"Please, there's not much time. Please save him!"

She then faded away. My eyes closed involuntarily, and when they opened again, my sight was met with the ceiling. I blinked to make sure I wasn't seeing things, and when my view didn't change I sat up. The room was normal now, and Raikidan sounded as if he was snoring.

What was that woman trying to tell me? I didn't understand. If she really was the woman who had been following Blaze around, then it was possible she was referring to him, but why did she need me to save him? Sighing, I climbed out of bed. I figured it wouldn't hurt to just go and check on him.

Squeezing past Raikidan and through the door, I headed for Blaze's room. As I did, a cold breeze rushed through the living room. I noticed the door to the roof was slightly ajar. Rolling my eyes, I shut it and continued on. *I don't know what's so difficult about closing doors, especially during the winter.*

I made my way through the house. Rounding a corner by the music room, I was knocked off my feet. "Ow…"

Argus helped me back up. "Sorry. I wasn't expecting anyone else up."

"Mind telling me what the rush is?" I questioned.

"I'm looking for Blaze. He was acting strange earlier today, and then was making weird noises a few hours ago. I went to check on him just now to make sure he was okay, and he's gone."

My brow furrowed in thought. It was too late for him to go out. All the clubs would be closed by now.

"Please save him."

An image of the open door came flooding back into my mind. "The roof…"

Horror flickered over Argus' face, and I rushed back to the living room—my heart thundering in my chest. Whatever he was doing on the roof, it wasn't good. Almost ripping the door off its hinges, I bolted up the stairs. Making it to the top of the winding stairs, I found the door leading to the outside wide open, pushing me to move faster. I burst into the open, brisk air. To my horror, I found Blaze standing on the parapet of the roof in front of me.

"Blaze, what are you doing?" I shouted. He stood there, unresponsive. "Blaze?"

Argus finally made it to my side and took a few breaths. "What is he doing?"

I didn't have a chance to respond. Blaze made the move to walk off the ledge and I lunged for him. Grabbing onto his arm, I pulled him back and he fell to the ground. He jerked and swiveled his head back and forth. "What the hell? How did I get out here?"

My brow furrowed. "You walked out here, of course."

He continued to look around. "I what?"

I shifted my focus to Argus for answers, to find him holding his chin with his fingers, his face scrunched in thought. "Argus?"

It took him a moment to respond. "I think he was sleepwalking."

My brow rose and I refocused on Blaze. "You sleepwalk?"

His gaze turned away. "I used to. I fixed that issue, though."

"Apparently not." I rubbed my arms when a cold breeze blew. "We need to get back inside. We'll all catch a cold at this rate."

Blaze held up his hand. "Wait, what was I doing that made you come up here? I can't imagine you were awake and in the greenhouse at this hour."

"She saved you from walking off the roof," Argus said.

Blaze's eyes widened. "I was doing… what?"

I shivered again. "You're welcome. I'm going inside now."

Neither stopped me from leaving, but they didn't follow either, piquing my interest. I closed the door behind me, but stopped there, listening close to their conversation.

"We need to discuss your sleepwalking," Argus said. "You said you fixed it."

"I did… That's the first time in years."

"No it was the second in the last few months." There was a pause before Argus spoke again. "You dreamt about her again, didn't you?"

"What? No." Blaze sounded taken aback by the accusation. *Who could they be talking about?*

"Don't lie to me, Blaze. You would only sleepwalk when you dreamt about her."

"I wasn't dreaming about her!"

Argus sighed. "Fine, whatever. Let's just get back inside. It's freezing out here."

Quietly, I headed down the stairs. I didn't need them catching me eavesdropping, and I really needed to get back to bed.

I took my steps with purpose as I headed down the hall. I wasn't planning on confronting Blaze about this morning's event so soon, but a few things about the situation ate at me.

I stopped when Blaze came around the corner. He looked at me and I stared back.

"You just going to stand in the middle of the hall or can I get past?" he asked.

"Who is she?" I wanted to kick myself after speaking. Not the way I wanted to start this conversation.

His face scrunched. "What are you talking about?"

"A spirit came to me this morning and told me to stop you from walking off the house. I saw her following you around at my celebration. Who is she?"

He shrugged, his eyes relaxed, showing he didn't care much for this conversation. "I don't know."

"Don't lie to me, Blaze."

"How am I supposed to know who this spirit is? You just said it was a woman and gave no description. She could be a sister I didn't know I had."

I crossed my arms. "She had long chestnut hair with blonde highlights, and dark blue eyes. She was maybe an inch or two taller than Ryoko and had soft, kind features, as if she could never be mad."

He stiffened and didn't respond. He almost seemed afraid of what I had just told him.

I stepped closer to him and kept my eyes soft. "Who is she, Blaze?"

He crossed his arms and shifted his gaze away. "Aiva. Her name is Aiva."

"How do you know her?"

"She's… she was… my girlfriend."

I eyed him. "You don't stay with one person for more than a night."

He sighed. "No… not since her."

His eyes gave away the pain aching inside. Whatever caused her fate, it had really changed him. "What happened to her, Blaze?"

"She died." His voice carried good a measure of anger, and pain on top of it.

My lips twisted as I bit back a snarky retort. Now wasn't the time with him. "I'm aware of that. She wouldn't be a spirit otherwise. I want you to tell me what happened."

His hands clenched into a fist. I knew this was going to be hard on him, but I needed him to tell me, for his sake. There was a reason she was still following him around.

"It was late. We had just seen a movie and were going to dinner. She hated having dinner before a movie, because she didn't like feeling rushed while eating. It didn't bother me, because it worked well with what I had planned.

"The light was green, so I didn't see a reason to worry as I drove through the intersection. That's when the drunk idiot drove through the intersection and slammed into us…"

His whole body shook. *Blaze…* He had kept this bottled up for the goddess knew how long, and it had been slowly eating away at him. This was why he was sleepwalking. This was why he had nearly walked off the roof. *It's not your fault…*

"I couldn't feel that kind of pain again," he admitted. "I couldn't allow myself to be close to anyone after that…"

That's when I noticed her. Aiva stood behind him, sadness and pain clear on her face. She had to watch him endure this. This was why she couldn't move on. He couldn't let her go, so she couldn't move on knowing he carried such a weight on his chest.

Blaze stiffened when I wrapped my arms around him. "You need to let go, Blaze. You're not doing yourself any good by living this way. You're making it worse. You're hurting yourself more than you would if you just let it all go."

He rested his hands on my shoulders as if he was planning on pushing me away. "I can't…"

"She wants you to." He locked up again. "She doesn't want you to keep blaming yourself for what happened. She doesn't want to keep seeing you in so much pain. She wants you to live your life for the both of you. Aiva… Aiva wants to see you be happy again, even if that means you end up with someone else."

Blaze wrapped his arms around me tightly, his body shaking. I could tell he was trying not to cry. I stood there and let him hold onto me as it all burst forth—years of pain and anguish poured from his soul in waves of anguish. Over his shoulder, Aiva watched on with keen sympathy.

When his tears finally died down, she gazed up at me. A silent "thank you" left her lips, then she faded from sight.

CHAPTER 7

ool, dark water lapped at my feet, and a gentle breeze blew. Puffy white clouds floated in the blue sky above. I stared out across the vast lake before me, the stone building in its center still intriguing me.

This was the calmest I'd seen the lake, and the first time I'd gotten such a clear view of the building, a temple of some sort. But what did it contain? Why was it here? *How do I get to it?*

Time and time again I'd revisit this place, always between dreams. But not once could I find a way there. I couldn't even swim there. It frustrated me.

I turned when the soft sand shifted behind me, and smiled at the sight of Raikidan approaching. He returned the gesture with one of interest. "You're aware of my presence."

My brow rose. "I guess this means you're walking my dreams."

He chuckled and stood beside me. "Just wanted to check on you. You weren't yourself today."

I returned my gaze out to the lake. "A lot on my mind."

"Is that why you're standing here looking at that building?"

I nodded. "I don't know what it is. I have this dream a lot, but each time, I can't get to it. There are no boats, no bridges or paths, and no way to swim there."

"I don't have an explanation for that, but this isn't a dream, Eira."

My brow rose in question. "Excuse you?"

"This is a place in your mind, between dreams. Your mind comes here to rest before falling into a dream state again. Most aren't aware of this state of mind. It's why your recognition of my presence surprised me."

I thought about this. Jasmine had taught me about sleep patterns, mostly because I never got enough of it, and it made her concerned for my health. REM sleep was where we experienced our dreams, and non-REM sleep came in stages through the night—a type of ebb and flow, with each cycle lasting longer or shorter in certain areas during the course of a night. But where did this rest state fall into all that? Was it all of non-REM, or was it a specific stage?

Raikidan cocked his head and leaned closer. "Something wrong?"

I looked at him with a wan smile. "Sorry. I was trying to figure out how this matches with the scientific study of sleep. I'm not understanding that, so I'll leave it to the sleep doctor to talk to a Dreamwalker."

Raikidan chuckled and gazed out at the temple. "So you really have no idea what that is?" I shook my head. "Nothing happens with it?"

"No. The weather here changes, but lately it's been good weather. Today has been the best."

Raikidan scratched his chin. "Do you have any memories that are patchy, or it feels like you're forgetting something important? And I mean critical-knowledge-type of important."

My back straightened. "The second one."

He nodded. "I thought that might be the case. Because this is a link to your mind, I'm going to guess you have something important locked away in there, and that building is the result."

I grabbed my chin with my thumb and index finger as I thought about this. Could this have something to do with my bloodline? Something never felt complete about that knowledge. Or maybe the voice? My posture straightened as I stared out at the lake. *Are they connected in some way?*

The trees in the surrounding forest swayed, and then shook when a gale shot past us from the direction of the building. I pulled my arms up to protect myself from the flying sand, and Raikidan wrapped his body around me to act as a shield. When the wind died, we scanned our surroundings. Everything had gone back to normal. "That was weird…"

Raikidan's brow furrowed. "Did you by chance have a significant thought just before that happened?"

I bit my lip. "I was thinking of a few things. Nothing stands out as a cause, though."

He latched onto my hand and invaded my space. "Are you sure, or are you lying to me?"

My brow furrowed. *What should I tell him?*

"Eira, I want to help. I get this feeling it's important—whatever is hidden away. But I can't help unless you trust me."

Dammit… I rubbed the back of my neck. "It's not that I don't trust you…"

He let go. "So you are keeping something from me."

"Raikidan… it's… complicated."

Raikidan's face turned serious and displeased. My gaze lowered. "I know, I know, I tell you not to say that to me, but… I don't know how to tell you this. I don't understand it myself. So if I don't understand, how can I explain it to someone else?"

He stroked my cheek with the back of his finger. "Something, even if confusing, is better than nothing. Please try."

My heart hammered in my chest. Could I tell him? Could I trust him to know my bloodline? Could I tell him I've got this crazy voice talking to me in my head that doesn't belong to me? Would he understand? *Would he…* I sighed, unable to keep eye contact, and my shoulders sagged. *What should I do?*

Raikidan lifted my chin, making me look at him, but just as he opened his mouth to speak, the ground beneath us shook. The lake water splashed around in its agitated state. Then, the tremors stopped. I scanned our surroundings, trying to figure out what happened. When my eyes flicked to Raikidan, I found him gazing at me expectantly.

I held up my hands. "I don't know. I was only thinking about how I should tell you if I don't understand, and then you touched me and the ground started shaking."

His brow furrowed, he reached out and caressed my cheek, making my heart skip a beat and the hair on the back of my neck rise. The ground shook again. He retracted his touch, the quake stopping. "It's reacting to me." He faced out to the lake. "What if… this temple has something to do with me, too?"

I crossed my arms. "That doesn't make sense. I've known you for a little less than a year. I don't have any forgotten or hidden memories of you."

"I know it sounds crazy, but…" He ran his hand through his hair, his tongue dragging tongue over his lower lip. My eyes followed the motion for brief moment before I caught myself. "Since I met and got to know you, I always wondered what the odds were of us crossing paths. Then Phyre said it wasn't a coincidence when he made our shaman statuses official. If these area effects are happening in relation to you and me, then it could be assumed that temple is connected to it all"—he faced me again and grabbed my hand—"I don't know how, but I want to find out."

My gaze lowered when water splashed over my feet. The dark lake water lapped over my skin again, this time a bit higher, and I backed up. "Watch it. This water has a bit of a mind of its own. Likes to grab at you when you least expect it."

Raikidan's face contorted with confusion and interest, but followed me anyways. As he did, I noticed something. "That's interesting."

Raikidan halted. "What is?"

"Move around in the water some more."

He cocked an eyebrow, but did as asked. As he shifted about, the dark water dispersed, leaving a trail of crystal clear liquid. The darkness quickly consumed the purified water when his presence didn't return.

The two of us exchanged a glance, and I pointed down the shoreline. "You want to go take a walk with me? An extra pair of eyes for a way over would be helpful."

A smile on his lips, Raikidan grasped my hand and tugged me to follow, setting the pace. "Let's go."

I didn't know if he'd be able to help, or if he was connected to this temple, but I couldn't push anything away right now. And then there was the part about telling him the truth. The more we worked together on this, the harder it would be to keep all of that a secret from him. Did I want to run that risk?

Raikidan glanced back at me, smiled, and then set a quicker pace, forcing me to run. Our hands remained entwined. Occasionally the ground shook or the water lapped over our feet, but it didn't separate us.

If I told him, would he accept me? Or would he leave as well?

CHAPTER 8

My eyes closed, I inhaled and exhaled deep through my nose, embracing a warm breeze blowing in through the open living room window. According to the newscast, it wasn't looking like it'd get much colder any time soon, meaning spring had finally returned. That helped my mood.

Genesis sat on the couch, allowing me to process the information she and our guest relayed. I turned and focused on the Hunter. He leaned against a wall on the far end of the room, keeping an eye on everyone. There weren't many Hunters who were part of the rebellion. Their extreme modifications made them loyal to their creator. Those who did join struggled to fit in or trust anyone.

"You're sure he believed the body was me?" I struggled to trust all they'd told me.

The Hunter nodded. "We even looped in some scientists to run fake tests to 'prove' it."

"That doesn't mean he believes it. And if he doesn't, he'll keep searching for me."

"We're as sure as possible. Even the psychics were convinced and talk spread quickly in the ranks. Soon everyone will believe the infamous assassin traitor is dead."

I turned my attention to Genesis. "And you said the body is real?"

She nodded. "One of our own was dying of an illness. She hadn't been able to contribute for years as she deteriorated. She volunteered her body be modified to look like you as a final act."

"Shva'sika, you confirmed this?" I didn't want to be *that* person who questioned the moral standing of others around me, but messing with the dead wasn't smart.

She nodded. "Yes. She was happy to help in such a way. She said it was just a body that would eventually rot into dust. This was a better use for it in her eyes."

"You don't know when to take a good thing for what it's worth, do you?" the Hunter said.

My eyes narrowed at him. "Forgive me for knowing Zarda. I'm not so foolish as to believe this is so easy to pull off."

Seda raised a hand. "Easy, both of you. There's no need to go at each other. Laz, we're going to keep an eye on things to make sure the plan doesn't fall apart. If we catch wind he's suspicious, we'll be ready."

"And the Hunter, who is the martyr of this reveal? What of him if Zarda figures out the ruse?"

"We already have a plan in place," the Hunter said. "We know how to keep our own from tracking us. It's how we keep all of your scents off us."

I let out a breath, my shoulders relaxing. "Alright. Nothing I can really do now that it's done, but let's hope it works. It'd be nice to not worry so much.

Seda's attention turned to the outside for a moment, and then she focused on the Hunter. "We have some soldiers on their way—a small, non-aggressive squad. You should leave."

He nodded and left through the basement without another word. Not long after, someone knocked on the front door. Shva'sika put her book down and went to greet our visitors. When I heard Zo's voice greet Shva'sika, I took her book to pretend I was reading it. Shva'sika returned, leading Zo and other soldiers up into the living room.

"What can we do you boys for?" Zane asked. "Another inspection?"

Zo shook his head. "Not this time. We're actually here on business."

Ryoko's eyes turned up as she smirked. "I didn't realize inspections were done on leisure time."

Zo chuckled and shook his head. "Don't twist my words now, Ryoko."

She giggled.

"All right, so spill it," Zane said. He was being uncharacteristically impatient. "What is this business you have with us?"

Zo shook his head. "Not all of you, just Eira. We require your assistance with something."

I pursed my lips. "Why me?"

"I'm afraid, due to the classified nature, I can't tell you here."

A muscle in my neck twitched. After the talk with the Hunter, I didn't like where this secrecy was going. *However…*

Raikidan grunted as he crossed his arms. "You say you need her help but won't tell her what it's about. You really expect her to agree to that?"

Zo's eyes narrowed at Raikidan. "I didn't say I wasn't going to tell her at all. I'm just unable to until we get to the compound."

"I'll agree to come with you, on the terms that the others can come as well," I said. Zo wasn't acting out of sorts. If this was related to the false body situation, none of the soldiers would be this calm. And even if this was a legit thing, I wasn't going to go with them alone, just in case. "Also, in the event I don't agree with the task I'm needed for, I require the freedom to decline to help."

Zo's brow wrinkled as he thought about my terms, the soldiers behind him looking at each other warily. *Apparently my request is a loaded one.* Zo finally nodded. "I can agree to your terms."

I smiled and rose to my feet. "Thank you. I'll go get a light jacket so we can leave."

As I rummaged through the jackets in my closet, someone knocked on the frame of closet entrance. I turned around and blinked. "What's up, Rai?"

"Are you sure about this?" he asked.

I nodded. "I might as well see what they want with me. To be honest, I'm rather curious. As far as they know, I don't have any abilities that could be of any use to them." I eyed him slyly. "I am just a civilian, after all."

He smirked. "All right, if you say so."

"Do you want a jacket?" I asked as I finally found one for me that was light enough.

"No, I'll be fine. I can handle cold better than you."

I pushed him as I exited my closet and headed for the living room. "Jerk."

Raikidan chuckled. "You'd worry if I wasn't at least sometimes."

I laughed as I entered the living room and then smiled at Zo to indicate I was ready. It only took a few more moments for the others to assemble, and then he led us out of the house. The soldiers ushered us into several military vehicles, and the convoy rolled away from the house toward our destination.

I stared out the window, watching the city fly by. Nothing in particular caught my eye, but I figured it best to not draw attention to myself around all these soldiers.

I became alert when the vehicle slowed to a stop and the driver rolled down his window. When he chatted casually with someone outside the vehicle, I looked around more to find we had arrived at the compound already. The soldiers finished their conversation and we were given clearance to enter. I took in the details of the compound to get a feel for the place.

It was large, though not as big as some of the ones we had infiltrated in the past, and was constructed much better than the ones around in my day. Then again, there were also a lot more compounds scattered around the city than when I had been under Zarda's orders.

I sat up when we came to another stop, and the soldiers hopped out of their vehicles. Not wanting to do anything wrong, I waited until Zo opened my door and ushered me out. He motioned for us to follow him into a small building, and no one argued. Several men and women inside took interest in us, but then went about their usual business when some of the soldiers escorting us gave them a few dirty looks.

We were led down a hall and into a small room, with dim lights and a large glass pane and an adjacent door on a single wall. Taking a quick close look, there was another room on the other side of the glass with two facing chairs standing in the center. A knot grew in my stomach. *This is an interrogation room.* My concerns from earlier resurfaced.

"Stay calm. It may not be as bad as it looks."

Zane crossed his arms. "You planned to bring Eira here? What reason do you have to interrogate her?"

Zo held up his hands. "Easy, she's not here to be interrogated. I would have arrested her and brought her by force if that was the case."

"See."

He had a point. I did my best at my innocent act. "So, why am I here?"

"Eira, how can you be so calm?" Zane demanded.

I shrugged. "I'm not really seeing a reason to freak out. I've done nothing wrong, unless you can think of something, Zane."

He grunted but accepted my argument. I chuckled and then looked at Zo expectantly, who seemed to be deep in thought now.

After a few moments he finally spoke. "Do you remember the attack on the city a few weeks ago?"

I placed my hands on my hips. "How could I not? I was taken hostage."

He nodded. "That's true. And do you remember the soldiers who infiltrated the building you'd been held in?"

I held my chin as I thought.

Large double doors to the room burst open, and two muscular men rushed in. Another man, of a slighter athletic build, came in behind them. The first two men, while both burly, had about a two-inch height difference. They both had light skin and blue and red hair. The leaner man was a few inches shorter than them and also had light skin, but had violet hair.

He's talking about my clones. I nodded. "Yeah, I remember them. Strange trio they were."

"I was given a report that you got them to listen to you without much effort—is that correct?"

Ah, shit, that would come back to bite me. I nodded. "They weren't doing much help in all the panic, so I took charge of the situation." I held a clamped fist up to my mouth, pretending to be timid and unsure. "Was that bad?"

Zo rubbed his chin. "No, not exactly. It's just…"

A soldier chuckled and stepped forward. "I'll explain. The three experiments you came in contact with are part of a group of experiments that are unpredictable and aggressive. During training, they destroy everything, even civilian dummies we've told them to leave be. They have even lashed out at other soldiers. There are few who can be near them and safe, and even fewer who have the ability to order them around. We didn't want to send them into the city due to these flaws, but the demands they made during the hostage situation forced our hands."

He gazed at me with kind eyes. "The reason we asked you to come here is to help us understand why any of the civilians there came out of that situation alive. And to help us understand what made you able to control them, especially when you'd never worked with them before."

I nodded. "I'm willing to try my best. I didn't know they were deadly people. It's made me even more curious about them now."

Rylan held up a hand. "Wait, hold on, Eira. Don't go agreeing to this just yet. He makes it sound like he wants you to interact with these people again."

The soldier nodded. "That's exactly what we want. Well, one of them for now."

"Are you insane?" Raikidan shouted. "We don't know if the way they reacted to Eira was some sort of fl—"

I placed my hand on his arm. "Rai, stop. I want to help them. I'm pretty sure I'll be okay." I peered past the soldier. "And even if something did come up, I think I'm covered."

The psychic I focused on chuckled in my head. *I'm on your side one-hundred percent.*

"He's telling you the truth, Eira," Seda messaged.

There seemed to be a lot more psychics on our side these days. It was a bit strange.

Raikidan tossed his thumb toward the door. "Can I talk to you outside, Eira?"

My brow ticked up, but I nodded and followed him out, closing the door behind me.

Raikidan took a deep breath. "Are you sure about this? I mean really sure—if something goes wrong…"

A pained expression crossed his face, as if his imagination were going wild on him. I reached out and brushed the back of my fingers across his cheek. "Do you trust me?"

He grasped my hand, his eyes locking with mine. "Of course."

Smiling, I pulled my hand from his and pushed on his forehead with two fingers. A rush of familiarity came with the action, though I wasn't sure why. I didn't do this to him often, but it felt as though I did, or should be. "Then trust me with this decision. I can protect myself if needed. There are two psychics in the adjacent room. And there's only a door holding you back. When you are determined, not even that could stop you. But I have a good feeling about this; I'm going to be fine."

Raikidan remained hesitant, but relented in the end. "I'm busting down the door if he even twitches in a way I don't like."

"Aww, how sweet."

I chuckled. "I wouldn't be able to stop you."

"You could promise a reward, if he does behave. A kiss perhaps?" She chuckled. *"Or something more."*

"Shut up."

I pulled away from him, and when he had no other protests to give, I reentered the room. I addressed Zo. "So, what do you want me to do?"

Zo hesitated for a moment, as if my forwardness threw him, and then pointed to the window. "Head into the interrogation room and take a seat at one of the chairs. We'll let the man in an adjacent door and monitor your interaction with him. Be yourself, but try not to make any sudden movements or show aggression."

I nodded. "I will do my best."

A soldier opened the door to the interrogation room for me, and I strolled in. I took in the dimly lit interior, noting the window now appeared like a mirror from this side. I sat down at one of the prepared chairs to wait.

"Eira, you're free to speak as you please," the psychic soldier messaged. *"Seda and I will be altering what they're capable of hearing. This will allow you to get to know your brother as you should."* He chuckled. *"And I get to have my fun."*

I snickered. *"You won't hear me complaining."*

The door in front of me opened and a young man, no older than twenty, with violet hair cautiously made his way inside.

I smiled when he noticed me. He stared at me in response, obviously confused about what was going on. "I–it's you."

"Hi again," I greeted. My clone's eyes darted around, as if he were suspicious of something. I smiled. "The room isn't booby trapped."

He eyed me. "You sure?"

"Well, if it is, and they sent me in here, there's going to be a few dead bodies in the other room"—I chuckled—"and a few new faces would appear on a *Most Wanted* poster."

He thought about this for a moment, his green eyes never leaving me, and then made his way over to the chair before me. His mouth remained shut as he sat there looking me over. I remained silent and still, to allow him to process this on his terms. I understood the position he was in. When I came out of my tank, it took me a long time to adjust to new situations. It took me some time to learn to sort things out quicker.

Slowly, he lifted his hand up and waited. Understanding his gesture, I rested my hand against his, making him smile.

I smiled back. "What's your name?"

"Bone." I giggled, and he glared at me. "Don't make fun of my name."

I shook my head. "I'm not. I'm amused at how fitting it seems to be. You look like someone who could pull off that name."

He blinked and then grinned. "What's your name?"

"Eira."

He nodded. "Pretty name. Like you."

I avoided eye contact and felt my cheeks and ears burn. Bone took my hand and looked at it curiously, even going as far as to trace some of the lines on my palm. When he was done with that hand, he took the other one to look at before allowing me to do the same. I then touched his face, and he closed his eyes as if to tell me he trusted me. His was so tuned in to his primal instincts, connecting with him like this felt so easy. But that wasn't a surprise to me in the least. We shared the same blood. His primal instincts explained why he was unable to control himself. He had a similar monster as mine living inside him.

"You're not a monster," the voice said.

I stopped touching his face, and his eyes opened slowly before he reached for mine. I closed my eyes and let him do what he wanted.

My eyes snapped open when his hand migrated to my breast and my hand struck him, the other wrapping around myself protectively. "How dare you!"

He held his face in shock for a moment and then his face down-turned. "Sorry. I guess that's one of the inappropriate things I was told not to do."

I crossed my arms. "You think?"

His gaze dropped. "I didn't mean to upset you."

My eyes softened. "I know. You're just curious. I was the same way once."

"Is it safe for you to say such things?"

"I have connections."

The remaining tension drained from his body and he smiled. "Then I can tell you how glad I am to see you again, Sister?"

I smiled back. "I'm glad to be able to see you, too."

"Are you here just to see me?"

I rocked my head side to side. "Sorta. I came here because Zo was being cryptic about why they needed my help. I agreed to enter this room because they told me I'd be seeing you again."

"Why are we here?"

My brows rose as I took a deep breath. "Well, it's because you and our two brothers listened to me and didn't kill any of the civilians."

Bone's brow furrowed. "We're not supposed to kill civilians."

I nodded. "I know, but I guess with the way you've acted behind the fortress walls, they thought you would."

His eyes glittered and his lip curled. "Who made you think we were horrible people?"

I rested my hands on his balled-up fists, and kept my gaze soft. "Easy, Brother. I understand it hurts. I wasn't treated well back in the day, either. I had different problems than you, but I understand that you have some. Some of what they said is true, though, isn't it? You've attacked people without reason before, haven't you."

He started to relax, but also looked away from me. "Yes…"

"I want to help you, Brother." He lifted his gaze back up at me. "I don't care that you're a modified clone of me. You're still family. I want to understand what makes you tick so we can work on it. I want you to be able to be integrated into the city—to have a happy life eventually."

His gaze lowered once again and his voice came out much quieter than I expected. "I want us to be a family. All of us."

"How many are left?" I had seen over two dozen on the paperwork Arnia had given me last spring. I highly doubted they were all still alive.

"Including me, only ten out of the thirty-five. Zarda executed some because they were so wild and uncontrollable, and there were many who didn't make it back from the raid."

"I see…"

"All of them wanted to meet you. Especially Trigon and Rhaec. The way you pursued after that enemy, and then came back and took charge of the situation—you even had the resolve to boss us around—you really impressed them."

He held up a finger. "Oh, and Yára wants to meet you, too. I think she's the most excited, though she may not show it when you see her."

"Zarda made a female clone of me?" I held my chin and went into thought. "I didn't see that in the papers…"

His shoulders sagged, as did his brow. "Are you not happy about that?"

I gasped. "No, of course I am! I'm just… confused. The things Zarda does, it confuses me a lot. He never seems to make sense."

"Well, when you meet Yára, you may have an easier time figuring it out. When I first saw you, I mistook you for her for a brief moment."

I thought this over. Maybe I did know what Zarda was thinking. I was pulled from my thoughts when the door I had entered from opened. Seda walked in and carried a chair with her. Bone became immediately interested and attempted to stand up, but I motioned him to stay put. He complied, though with reluctance, and waited as Seda set down her chair and took a seat. His leg bounced, showing his impatience.

Seda smiled. "Hi."

He dipped his head. "Hello."

I smiled. "Bone, this is Seda. She's a close friend of mine. Seda, this is my brother Bone."

Seda kept up her friendly energy. "It's nice to finally meet you."

"You're psychic." Bone's eyes narrowed. "I'm not a fan of most psychics. They're unkind."

Seda smiled and held up her hand. "I'm a Seer. We're a bit nicer than the Battle Psychics."

Bone didn't return the gesture, but Seda kept up the gesture.

I watched him. I was trying to wrap my hand around the fact he picked up her psychic nature when she was using the cloaking watch. "Bone, how did you know she was psychic?"

"I just do."

Thanks, Bone, that was real helpful.

"Well, he is your brother."

"Oh, shut up."

"How do you make your face look like that?" Bone asked Seda. "It doesn't look like the psychic face I saw."

She pointed to the cloaking watch on her wrist. "This disguises me. I'm curious. How did you see a psychic's face? We do our best to keep that obstructed, for personal reasons."

He frowned. "I saw a male psychic torturing a female one in a hall one day, and he ended up taking off her veil."

Seda nodded. "I can only presume it was a Battle Psychic tormenting his Seer twin. I've seen that all too often in the past…"

"So, what did you do, Bone?" I asked.

He crossed his arms. "I attacked him, of course! As well as a few of our brothers who were with me. Yára stayed back to help the female psychic and make sure she was okay."

Seda tilted her head as she examined him. "All of you attacked him without a moment's hesitation, but I suspect none of you killed him."

Bone snorted. "Rhaec was about to crush his skull when the female psychic asked us to let him go. She told us there wasn't a need to kill him, though I didn't see why we shouldn't. Even if he was her brother, he shouldn't have gotten away with what he did."

Seda shook her head. "He didn't get away with it. The group effort you made to overpower him was punishment enough. He must now live with knowing he was beaten and nearly killed for what he did. He'll remember that memory quite well. And you gained an ally in the process. By saving the Seer and listening to her request, you gained her respect. She will be more than willing to help you in the future."

Bone grinned. "Well, since you put it that way, I guess I'm fine with letting him live."

"And you would have likely killed her as well," I said. "The psychic bond creates that strong of a connection."

"I think she would have been fine," Seda said. "Due to his treatment of her, the bond would have entered a weakened state. The connection is funny like that."

Bone's brow creased. "I didn't know any of that. I will keep that in mind as I interact with psychics."

He moved his chair to sit in front of her and rested his hand against the one she still held in the air. I smiled at his acceptance of her. At least we were getting somewhere with him.

I looked at Seda. "So, Seda, why are you in here? Did the soldiers ask you to come in?"

She dropped her hand and shook her head. "No, I figured I'd confuse them more."

My mouth curved into a half-smile as I snickered. "Is that possible?"

"With the way they're talking, I doubt it, but I knew it couldn't hurt to try."

I laughed. "That reminds me. I still haven't done what they wanted me to do."

Seda held up a finger. "Technically, you have. All they wanted you to do was come in here and see if Bone would react well with you again. You've passed that test with flying colors, putting them in a world of confusion. With some psychic help, of course."

"Well, that's true. But there is something else they want me to do, besides interact with Bone. They want me to figure out why he and the others are so aggressive." I looked at Bone. "And I'd like to know as well. Bone, why do you attack everything? Is there something specific driving you?"

Bone averted his gaze. "Can we not talk about this, Sister?"

"We need to talk about this, Bone. It's important."

He sighed and stayed quiet for a moment. "For me, smells are my trigger. If I don't like the smell, I have the urge to kill it. Women don't have that bad smell. They have a pleasant smell that makes me want to protect them."

"Zo said there are a few soldiers who have gained your trust. How many of them are men?" I asked.

"One. He doesn't give off a strange smell. It's not a nice smell like women, but it wasn't bad either. I gave him a chance because of it."

Seda tapped her finger on her lips. "So there are neutral scents to him."

I thought about this. If what he said is true, then the soldiers weren't looking at this as carefully as they should be.

"It's the same smell that lingers on you, Sister." Bone said. "It's strong, like he's around you all the time."

Seda looked at me. "Sounds like he's talking about Raikidan."

Bone stared at me. "I want to meet him."

I watched him carefully. He may be my brother, but I didn't want him attempting to kill Raikidan if they got off on the wrong foot. "I'll consider it. Right now, I want you to tell me about the others. What are their triggers?"

Bone shook his head. "I don't know. They don't talk about it. Now let me meet this man you trust."

I exhaled a hard breath through my lips and Seda laughed. "He's stubborn and persistent—like you."

"Stubborn doesn't begin to describe you."

I laughed and Bone smiled. "I like hearing you laugh, Sister. It reminds me of the song birds in the morning."

My brow twisted. "What?"

"You'd love to hear her sing, then," Seda said.

Bone nodded. "I'd like to sometime. From what I've heard, it's not something I want to miss out on in this lifetime."

My face flushed. "I'm really not that good. I don't know why everyone makes such a big deal about it."

He chuckled and stood. "Now, I'd like to meet this Raikidan person."

I worked my jaw. "Only if you give me your word you won't hurt him."

His brow spiked. "Is he special to you?"

The question gave me pause—he was treading on a dangerous subject. I hesitated a moment, then nonchalantly shrugged. "He's… a good friend."

Seda nudged me. "A good friend who knows you better than anyone else you've known longer."

My ears burned and I glared at her. "Don't you start, too. Dealing with Ryoko on this subject is difficult enough."

She just giggled and headed for the door.

I smiled at Bone. "I'm glad I could see you again and get to know you a little better."

"I hope to see you again," he said.

"Me too. And promise me you'll start trying to get this killing issue under control? I really don't want to lose anymore of you."

He nodded. "I'll do my best. For you."

I smiled and left the room. The soldiers watched me. "He wants to speak with Rai now."

Raikidan's brow rose. "Why?"

I shrugged. "He caught your scent on me or something like that and demanded to see you."

Zo shook his head. "I can't agree to that. Not until we can understand this situation more."

"Rai will be fine," I insisted. "Bone gave me his word."

"And you're just going to believe it?" a soldier said.

I rested my hands on my hips. "Do I look dead to you?" The soldier stared with a blank face. "Yeah, that's what I thought. Seda and I are both very much alive, much to your surprise. Bone was quite pleasant to be around, much more than I can say for about half of you here. I'll take his word because I'm pretty sure I can trust it over any of yours."

Another soldier snickered. "You just got told."

"Shut up," the first soldier muttered.

Zo sighed. "I still can't—Kid, where you going?"

Raikidan opened the door for the interrogation room and enter without responding to Zo's question. Zo's lip curled, but didn't go in to stop the interaction that was about to transpire.

I forced myself to breathe as I watch Bone stalk over to Raikidan. The two stared at each other for several moments before Bone spoke. It appeared as if Bone was threatening him.

I shifted my gaze to Zo. "Why can't we hear anything?"

He and several soldiers fussed with the speakers and other electronics. "I'm not sure."

I glanced at the psychic, who smirked. What was he up to?

I focused back on Raikidan and my brother. Bone continued to threaten Raikidan, and then suddenly stopped, as if waiting for Raikidan to respond. He did, by grinning and offering his hand for a handshake. This took my brother by surprise.

After a few moments, Bone returned the gesture, and the two shook hands as if their exchange had been some "manly" diplomatic interaction.

"There, that should fix it, I think," a soldier said.

We could hear them breathing now, but the interaction was done. Bone turned and headed for the door he had come from earlier while Raikidan did the same.

"What did the two of you discuss, Kid?" Zo demanded when Raikidan was back inside the room. "We had technical glitches here."

Raikidan shrugged. "Nothing important."

"Everything that happens in that room is important. Especially since he didn't kill you when everything we have says he should have." Zo turned to the psychic working against him. "What did you hear?"

The psychic gestured to Raikidan. "What he's about to tell you."

Raikidan sighed. "Bone just wanted to make sure I treated Eira well."

Zo gave him a dumbfounded look. "What?"

"He's taken a liking to her, and his enhanced sense of smell made him aware I'm around her a lot, so he felt the need to threaten me." Raikidan chuckled. "Although he never expected me to be okay with his threat."

"That's it?" Zo asked.

"That's it."

Zo looked at the psychic, who nodded to confirm Raikidan's words as truth.

A different soldier stepped up. "What about you, Eira? Your discussions with him were rather basic, and a little unconventional with your lengthy explaination about landscapes you've seen in your years." *Wow, Seda and that psychic really went all out.* "And then we had technical glitches much like with your friend's case. Did Bone say anything that gave you any hints on how we can better understand them? I'm involved directly with their integration issue, so anything would be helpful."

I rubbed my chin to make it look like I was thinking. "Two things, actually. He mentioned a woman by the name of Yára. Said I looked a lot like her."

The soldier who had given me the information about my brother prior to going in the room spoke up. "She's another soldier design like him. She has an uncanny resemblance to you. It would make sense if that were a trigger to why he listens to you. She bosses them around a lot, and they don't complain."

I shot a questioning glance to Zo. "Another person who looks like me?"

Zo rubbed the back of his head. "I'm not at liberty to discuss the nature of that situation, but know that you're still free and clear."

My eyes narrowed. *Was it because of what I was told earlier today?*

"I believe it might be."

I shrugged. "I hope not. I don't want to be compared to some troublemaker."

"What was this other point?" the soldier asked.

I scratched my cheek. "Bone said I smelled nice, and then mumbled to himself about how he thought all women smelled nice. When I asked him about his sense of smell, he also said a man he's friends with had a neutral smell. I think that is a clue to his actions. I mean, if I didn't like the smell of something, I'd want to eliminate it."

Zo chuckled. "You have a good point. We'll keep this in mind as we monitor them more. Thank you for assisting us."

I nodded with a smile. "Bone seems nice, and just needs someone to believe in him. I'm happy to be that person."

Blaze ran his fingers through his hair. "Since Eira is done playing peacemaker, can we go home now?"

My eyes squinted as my lips curled into a half smile. "What, you bored?"

He crossed his arms as he leaned against the wall. "I had to stand here and watch you chat with a stranger. And the topics you picked were less than stimulating. I think I have the right to be bored."

I snorted. "No one made you come."

"You'd call me an inconsiderate jerk for the rest of the week if I stayed home!"

Ryoko placed her hands on her hips. "And that's different from any other week?"

Blaze's eyes narrowed. "Shut up, Ryoko…"

She laughed at him and I shook my head. "We should get going."

"We'll escort you back home," Zo stated.

"Just to the outside of the compound will be fine."

"You can walk if you want, Chickadee, but I'm not," Zane said.

I poked him in the stomach. "You could use the exercise, tubby."

"I'm not fat!"

"Yeah, yeah, you keep thinking that," I said as I headed out.

"Eira, get back here!"

I laughed and took off running, with him and the others close behind. I ducked around soldiers when they got in my way and finally made it outside without any of the others catching me, though I did trip Zane when he made it out the door creating a good laugh for everyone. He grumbled as he climbed to his feet and went to come after me but we both stopped when we heard a little girl crying.

Looking behind Zane, I found a little girl sitting on the ground and a soldier desperately trying to get her to calm down. Not caring whether it was my place or not, I strolled over and crouched in front of her with a smile. "Hey there."

The little girls crying slowed to a sniffle. "H–hi."

"My name is Eira, what's yours?"

She sniffled again. "Nikki."

I smiled more. "That's a really nice name."

She smiled a little. "Thank you."

"So, Nikki, why are you crying? A pretty little girl like you shouldn't be crying."

"Because… because I'm in trouble." She began trying again. "D–Daddy said if I was bad, t–then the military would take me away!"

I smiled sympathetically. "Why do you think you're in trouble, Nikki?"

"C–cause I lost my daddy, and went and told a soldier I couldn't find him… They took me here after…"

I giggled. "Oh, Nikki, you're not in trouble. They just brought you here so they can contact your dad."

She sniffled. "Are you sure?"

"Well, I'm here. Do I look like a troublemaker?"

She shook her head. "No."

"See? Just because we're here doesn't mean we're in trouble. The military wanted you to be safe while they located your dad, so they just brought you here."

Mana knelt beside me. "She's right."

Seda crouched on the other side of me. "So cheer up. You'll be back with your dad soon."

I grunted when someone slammed their hand down on my shoulders to lean over me. "Of course, we could all be wrong and be in trouble without knowing it."

"Ryoko!" I shouted.

Instead of crying, Nikki giggled, which became contagious to all the women around her.

"Nikki?" a masculine voice called.

"Daddy!" Nikki shrieked with joy.

She jumped to her feet and rushed over to a man who stood by a military vehicle. The man, obviously happy to see her, picked her up and held her close. "Nikki… I'm so glad you're safe."

"I'm sorry I worried you, Daddy. Am I in trouble?" she asked.

"No. It was my fault we were separated," he told her. "And you did the right thing and looked for help. Me, on the other hand, I'm going to be in big trouble with your mother."

Nikki giggled. "I'll make sure she goes easy on you, Daddy."

Her father chuckled and started walking toward the compound gates. "That's kind of you, hon. Now let's go home."

"Okay!" She then looked back at us and waved.

The four of us waved back, and Seda giggled. "I think it might be time for us to head home, too."

I nodded and headed for the gate with them. "C'mon boys, let's go!"

Today had been a bit more eventful than I had expected, not that I was complaining. I just hoped I'd be able to see Bone again.

9

CHAPTER

Cars roared, honked, and screeched in the distance. The darkness of night concealed me as I sat in the shadows of a building, waiting. I had no idea why the Council had told me to wait here for my partner for tonight's assignment, but I wasn't in a position to question. The details were quite serious, so any further delays would hinder my success.

The echo of footsteps caught my ears. I cast a glance out to the world around me and spotted a lone person strolling my way. So as to not blow my cover, I leaned against the wall of the alley and brought a lit cigarette my lips, only pretending to inhale. The nauseating smell bothered my senses, but I sucked it up. Someone smoking a butt was less conspicuous than some woman hanging around doing nothing.

The passerby gave me a curious glance, but continued on his way without incident. After a moment, I checked my communicator for the time. Just after ten p.m. My partner in crime would be showing up any moment. I was told he had to deal with another assignment prior to joining me; hopefully the second part of our assignment wasn't time sensitive. We weren't entirely sure if our information was accurate or not to begin with, though I didn't see that as a reason to stall.

I jumped when a presence suddenly appeared behind me and spun around ready to defend myself. The young man with short multicolored hair behind me sticking out of the wall of the building held up his hands, his kaleidoscopic eyes going wide. His skin rippled with several shades of color as he moved. *Chameleon.* "Easy, it's just me."

I let out a deep sigh, my shoulders slumping. "You really need to be more careful when you pop out near people."

"Sorry. I can't tell which way someone is facing as I move through mass."

"It's fine." I put out my cigarette. "I'm just glad I don't have to deal with this nasty thing anymore."

Once I was sure the cigarette had been sufficiently smothered, I stored it away in a bag and deactivated my cloaking watch, going from unruly delinquent to your average day Eira. "I wasn't sure who I'd be working with, but if we can get along long enough, the assignment should go smoothly."

"I have every intention of working with you without issues." He held out his hand to me. "Now, we should get to our target location."

I nodded and accepted the gesture. Pulling me close, he instructed me to hold my breath and close my eyes like the last time we had done this, before pulling us both into the wall. My body's molecular structure changed and moved through several types of materials. The sensation wasn't anymore pleasant than the last time the two of us did this.

When I thought I couldn't hold my breath any longer, we popped out on a roof. I inhaled deeply, relishing the ability to breathe, and looked around. We stood on top of a tower overlooking a compound. If he'd brought us to the right place, we'd be right in the middle of the Hala Street base.

Chameleon pulled a canteen of water out of a satchel he carried and took several big gulps. "So, just to be sure we're on the same page of the assignment, I'm to get you inside, where you're supposed to plant a bug of some sort, right?"

I nodded. "Argus called it keylogging. I have a portable computer with me that will plant the bug and also search for important data up front. That'll be the easy part."

His brow rose, and he took in some more water. "It seems I wasn't informed of a task beyond the keylogging. What else are we to do?"

"We received information that they're holding someone here. We don't know the affiliation of the individual, but if the military is holding them, we want them."

Chameleon nodded. "That explains why I'm here. It'd be fairly easy for you to infiltrate a place like this on your own, if a bit slow going. But with me, I can get you both out easy."

I had also suspected this when he first showed up. "One hiccup. I don't know where they're holding this person of interest. And since we don't know their current condition, I would prefer to look for them first. Even if it's just to locate them."

"I was going to suggest that as well, so I'm glad we're on the same page."

It was weird interacting with him in such a civil manner. After all the years of dealing with such nasty attitudes, it wasn't something I was going to get used to overnight. *It's almost like the old days.*

Chameleon put away his water and approached. "Before we head in and do any looking, I want to apologize. I've acted beyond poorly to you, for no good reason. I fell for Raynn's bull when I knew better. You're the only reason Aliyah wasn't put to death and was able to live a normal life. You risked so much for someone you didn't know well, and you did it without hesitation. I'll never be able to repay you for that act."

He looked away, his face a little red. "I know you didn't do it for me, but she meant everything to me."

"Looks like she still does." I smiled at him when he glanced my way, his face growing a shade darker. "Though who knows what kind of person she's become in all these years."

He nodded, his expression becoming subdued. "That's true. It'll be nice to finally end this war and go see her. Just to see how she's been doing."

I patted him on the shoulder. "Not much longer. Now, let's get this assignment moving so we can ensure we get closer to that goal."

Chameleon took up position next to me, and after preparing myself, the two of us were moving through the compound again. We popped out periodically, so I could take a breath and get a feel for where we were. But the longer we searched, the more it felt like our information had been wrong.

Just when I thought it would be good to give up the search, we came upon a locked room, currently unguarded, but from a quick peek through window, I knew it wouldn't be long before someone returned.

Inside, strapped to a chair, was a woman of darker complexion. Her head was slumped forward on her chest, long chestnut hair obscuring her face. She sat there unmoving, and I feared the worst.

Chameleon brought us through the wall into the room; the sensation was such a quick transition that it was disorienting but bearable. I rushed over to the woman to check on her condition, quickly discerning that she wasn't conscious, and I already knew her identity. "Aliyah?"

Astonishment and fear both registered on Chameleon's face, and he immediately lifted her chin. It was her, a little older looking since the last time I'd laid eyes on her, but neither of us could forget her face.

"What is she doing here?" I mumbled aloud as I looked around the room.

Chameleon fiddled with her bindings. "What does it matter? We need to get her out of here."

He was right, although as much as we needed to get her out, we also needed to understand why the military had her. How did they find her? Why did they capture her after all of these years, when I had made it look as though she were dead? I'd even brought back a false body dressed as her to throw Zarda off.

I look for papers, tools, any obvious sign that would throw me a hint. But I found nothing. Not willing to give up, I pulled out my communicator and dialed up Argus. It didn't take him long to answer.

"Need help?"

"We found the mysterious captive, but she's not in good shape. I want to use the computers in this room to find out why they have her. Would we be able to also throw in a keylog here, or should it be done in the original target room?"

"Both would be ideal, if you can manage it."

"I think I can. I'd like your assistance to speed things up."

"Of course, whatever you need."

I plugged the portable computer in to the nearest station, and Argus and I went to work. I kept an eye on Chameleon as he took great care in freeing Aliyah. He only used his molecular ability on her if he really had to, as if afraid he'd harm her further.

"I think I found the information," Argus said.

"Good. We're going to want to grab all the data. I believe it's important."

Argus went to work downloading the information just as Chameleon pulled Aliyah into his arms and cradled her gently. "I need to get her medical attention immediately."

I nodded. "Get her out of here. Argus and I will finish this."

"I'll return for you, don't worry."

A chuckle escaped my lips. "Worry about your girlfriend there, before you worry about me."

Chameleon's face tinted a shade of pink and then the two of them disappeared into the floor.

"Everything is downloaded and transferred to the Council for them to look over, and the bug is planted," Argus said. He then chuckled. "Also, since your mode of transportation just left without you"—the sound of something sliding open behind me caught my ears—"you're welcome."

I spun on my heels to find the door to the room had opened.

"Normally a keycard is needed to open that, but opening it manually is nothing for a genius like me."

That's rather advanced for a compound. Most doors of that nature were only located in the fortress. *I guess they really are rolling out the new tech, like Genesis said.* That wasn't a comforting sign.

The side of my mouth upturned slightly. "Thanks, genius."

I heard a short chuckle. "I'll disconnect now. Call me if you need me again."

"Sure."

I poked my head out into the hallway and peered around, finding myself alone. *So strange.*

"Be careful."

"Wow, you spoke."

"I didn't want to distract you."

I slipped down the hall. *"Sure, sure."*

"I don't have to talk if I don't want to, just like you."

"But this is you. You normally have something to say in any situation."

"Maybe I'm taking cues from you."

"I highly doubt that."

I continued down the expansive hallway, following the directions on my computer until I made it to my destination. I didn't run into a single soul and that didn't sit right with me. *What, is everyone getting a midnight snack?*

"I want one."

"You don't eat."

"Doesn't mean I don't want one."

I rolled my eyes and looked for a way to open the door. *Shit.* It was another one of those keypads. I called Argus. "Problem. This place has another keypad. Why didn't our intel warn us of this?"

"Maybe it's new? Either way, if this keypad is like the ones in the fortress, it'll be easy to get around with that device. There should be a tiny port for you to plug in and hack remotely."

I searched the scanner box and found it on the side. Plugging in, I ran the decoder program, and within seconds I had the door sliding open. "Bingo. Thanks. We're going to need to keep this in mind for future infiltrations."

"Seda already has the Council informed. They'll do some more digging about the tech rollouts. In the meantime, this keylog will help. The bug will infect their system quickly, without them knowing, and jump to any device that gets hooked into it. Hitting up a few more bases would be ideal in the end, as it'll speed up the process."

I slipped into the room and the door shut behind me. "And this is your program?"

"I designed the base, and others helped with the development."

"Good thing you play well with others." I plugged in the portable computer, and Argus helped me complete this assignment.

Numbers and letters flashed across the screen of the handheld device. I may not have known what it said, but since Argus showed no signs of worry, I stayed relaxed, assuming it was all going well.

In less than three minutes, the bug had been planted, and Argus did a personal check to ensure it was working correctly. "Okay, you're good to get out of here."

Just then, an ear-shattering alarm went off, and lights flashed. "Shit, what happened?"

"It's not us. It's possible the missing captive was noticed."

"Shit." I unplugged the computer and ran for the door when it slid open and three armed soldiers entered. *Fuck.*

"Hold it right there," one said as they readied their weapons.

I took a deep breath and held up my hands. One approached. I counted his steps and gauged potential reaction time. *I might be able to pull this off without getting killed.*

"Be careful."

When the soldier came into range, I made quick strikes to the gun and his arms, disarming him, and then used his body against the others by pushing him into them. One of them had poor reaction time and wasn't able to get out of the way, dropping his weapon from the impact of his buddy. The other was another story.

She moved out of the way and took aim at me, but before she pulled the trigger, her body spasmed and fell to the ground. I glanced at the other soldiers to find them jerking as well. It stopped and they lay unmoving, though still breathing.

Argus chuckled through my earpiece. "You're welcome."

I inspected the fallen soldiers. "What did you do?"

"I tapped into their helmets and forced a high energy short. The design doesn't keep the wearer safe when that happens. It's always been a major flaw no one wanted to admit could be exploited."

"Well, I'm thankful for it now. And thank you for the assistance. That could have turned out bad."

"I'd like it if you came home."

I jumped and readied for a fight when a presence suddenly appeared next to me. Chameleon held up his hands. "You really like to attack me, don't you?"

I blew out a breath. "You need to stop popping in like that. Especially when I'm dealing with a compound on high alert."

He noticed the three bodies then. "Oh, that explains a lot. I can't hear all that well when I'm moving about. Let's get you out of here."

"Bring us just out of the danger range. I want to discuss a few things with you."

He nodded and then grabbed hold of me, barely giving me a moment to prepare.

We sped through a number of different substances and objects before we popped out somewhere in the city. I peered around, finding us in some alley. "Where are we?"

"About three miles from the base."

My brow rose. "You can move fast."

Chameleon leaned against a wall and drank some water. "When I need to. Takes a lot out of me, though."

"Well, I'm grateful you were willing to expend the extra energy." I gave him a warm smile. "Now, how is Aliyah doing? Argus got her capture data down to the Council for them to look at."

"She wasn't conscious by the time I left, but a couple medics are tending to her. I was told you may be able to help us source a healing shaman quickly, though."

I nodded. "I was just thinking that actually. Shva'sika can heal, so once you're up to returning me home, we can talk to her."

He stored his water canteen and approached me. I prepared myself to go through the discomfort of his ability one last time, when he reached out and pulled me into a strong hug. "Thank you." His grip tightened. "Thank you…"

I reached out, and patted him on the back, my lips curving into a smile. "You're welcome."

"Deep down, he's still the little softie you once knew."

"It's nice he's still there."

"Okay. Let's get your friend," Chameleon said just before sending us through the ground to the house.

10
CHAPTER

*P*uffy clouds floated by lazily above me like they always did. Time passed slowly when I wasn't being ordered around. It was nice, and it gave me the chance to be alone. My gazing didn't last much longer once I heard someone approaching. I looked down to see a young man with olive-tan skin, deep brown eyes, and dark, crew-cut hair coming my way.

He peered up at me and smiled. "You know, I'm starting to think you're part cat with how many times I catch you in trees, Chickadee."

My eyes narrowed. "You know, thanks to you, Tannek, both my uncle and Telar have started calling me that."

He grinned. "You're welcome."

I rolled my eyes. He climbed up into the tree and stood on a branch just below me. "Of all the things you could be doing on your time off, you're watching the clouds."

"Of all the things you could be doing on your time off, you've chosen to not care about keeping your face clean."

He rubbed his chin. "I'm growing it out a bit. I want to try something different."

"It looks like you just got lazy."

"You think it looks that bad?"

"You look funny."

He chuckled. "Gee, thanks. Truth is, I ran out of razors and I can't get my new supply until tomorrow."

"Sucks to be you, then."

He chuckled again as I went back to watching the clouds. "Hmm, I'm starting to see why you do this."

I peered over to see him staring up at the sky. "Tannek, why don't you think I'm weird like everyone else?"

He shifted his gaze toward me. "I've told you before, you're not weird."

"Why are you the only one who thinks that?"

He half smiled. "Maybe because they're the weird ones?"

A small smile crept across my face; it was a strange gesture to me. Not many were able to pull one out of me, but Tannek could. He didn't seem to see me as strange, which was weird in its own right.

Ever since the incident those many years ago when I blacked out and murdered everyone in the gladiatorial pit, no one wanted to be near me—no one except Ryoko, Rylan, Telar, and now Tannek. I didn't mind having him around. He was always nice and careful when I had an injury, as rare as that was.

He frowned and turned his attention elsewhere when someone called my name. "Looks like Amara needs you."

I nodded. "Guess so."

"Be safe if you're sent out somewhere."

"Sure." I jumped down from the tree.

I thought I heard him sigh as I walked away, but shrugged it off as nothing. Amara didn't smile when I approached her, and I knew my little time off had ended.

I followed her, but stopped and cranked my neck back to Tannek. He waved. A small smile crept on my face again as I waved back with my fingers.

I stared up at the blue sky, my back to the roof. Puffy clouds lazily floated by above me like they always did, the light breeze teasing my bangs. *Just like that day in my dream last night.*

Spring was starting to show itself, and it wasn't just the plants and animals being affected. Anyone who had someone to share their life with was getting all lovey-dovey, and those who didn't went looking for some sort of companionship. This yearly phenomenon drove me to seclude myself where no one would come looking for me. I didn't want anything to do with that.

"Your dragon-man would make for a nice cuddle buddy."

"Drop it."

The door to the roof opened, and Azriel walked out. "Hey, Az, what are you doing here? Shouldn't you be hunting down a new cuddle partner? We both know how much you love doing that, and this day gives you all the excuses in the world."

He chuckled and sat down next to me. "I plan to later. I wanted to check on you, since I know how much you hate this time of year."

I shrugged and stared up at the sky again. "I'll be fine. Rylan's raging hormones are bombarding me thanks to our mind bond, but it's nothing I can't handle." I chuckled. "As long as I don't have to deal with the other zombies in this house."

Azriel brushed my bangs out of my face. "You can have that again, you know. It's not a crime."

My eyes narrowed at him. "I don't know what you're talking about."

His eyes remained soft. "Don't try to pull that with me. Tannek was my brother. I knew all about your secret relationship with him."

I looked away. I didn't like him bringing this topic up.

"I know his loss hurt you, but there's nothing wrong with trying again. You deserve to be happy."

My lips turned down. "Why do I have to be with someone to be happy? What is wrong with being alone?"

"That's not what I'm saying. There's nothing wrong with being happy on your own. Plenty of people are, and that's great. But I know you. I see how much happier you are when you're around him."

My upper lip curled as I glowered at him. "Don't you start with that. I'm so sick of it! There's nothing between Raikidan and me." Pain pulled in my chest and I tore my gaze away from Azriel so he wouldn't notice. "I wish everyone would just accept that and leave us alone."

"It's because we all see what's going on!"

"Stuff it."

"Chickadee, we see how the two of you look at each other. You need to stop being so stubborn about this."

I winced. *He called me Chickadee… just like…*

Azriel rested his forehead on his palm and sighed. "I'm sorry. I promised I'd never call you that. I know how much I sound like him when I do."

"It's… fine…"

He placed a hand on my shoulder. "I get that you don't want to feel that kind of pain again. Love is not a word you like because of what you've gone through. Just know it does exist. It's not fleeting or a lie. And when it clings to you, it's worth everything in Lumaraeon."

My shoulders sagged. I really didn't like this conversation. Azriel had become someone to confide in over the years. He'd listen and only give input when asked, and I never had to worry about him telling others. Of course, that came at the cost of being a double edge sword. Him knowing everything, down to my anger toward my father, my opinions of other people, and my position with "love," he tended to try to push topics when others would let it go.

Azriel patted my shoulder and stood. "Just think about giving it one more chance." He waved as he walked away. "And take good care of those plants. It took me forever to find them."

My brow furrowed and I set my eyes on the spot where he had been sitting. In his place were two potted plants. One pot had an amazing, tiny bush of dark pink plumeria. The other plant was a vine of bleeding hearts that had pink outer petals and purple inner petals. *Ironic.*

These two plants were hard to find, and the plumeria wasn't easy to grow. It could only thrive in conditions the south region of Lumaraeon could produce—conditions only advanced greenhouses like mine could replicate.

I picked up the plants and headed for the greenhouse. Only Azriel had the means to get these, and he knew I could care for them or he wouldn't have given them to me. I could see Valene's face now. *She'd be so jealous.*

I placed the pots down near my messenger hawk's perch and chuckled. "For a gay man, he sure is a ladies' man."

The hawk tilted his head in response.

I threw my hands up. "And ballzy! He had the nerve to bring Tannek up and act like my choice to be alone is a result of me losing him." I blew out a breath and leaned on the table. "Unfortunately, he's not wrong…"

"Do you want to talk about it?" the voice asked.

"No, I don't want to talk about it."

"You said that out loud, you know that, right?"

I searched for two larger pots to transplant the new flowers. "And your point? I was just talking to a bird and there's no one around to find out how screwed up in the head I am."

"You're not screwed up."

I grunted. "I'm talking to you aren't I?"

"It's not like I'm some figment of your imagination."

"Then what are you?" She didn't respond. I placed two pots on a bench. "Surprise, surprise, you can't answer."

"Don't be testy with me just because you're in a foul mood."

"Then stop talking to me." I opened a bag of potting soil. "I didn't ask you to strike up conversation."

She remained quiet, and I mixed the soil into the clay pots.

"I just want you to be happy."

I snorted. "Great, so you also think I can't be happy alone. Thanks."

"No, I just know how miserable you were when he was gone."

"Yeah, well, it doesn't matter. That spot in his life isn't made for me. That's the reality no one wants to see. A human can't live as long as a dragon. A human can't make a dragon happy like another dragon could. Someone still trying to piece together their life after shattering a few too many times can't be…" I leaned on the bench, my head hanging. "I'm just not good enough."

"Eira, don't be like this…"

A light tapping on glass caught my attention. Looking around a bunch of flowers, I spotted Raikidan peering in through the door. I noticed he held one of his hands behind his back as if he were hiding something, intriguing me. I headed over to the door.

Raikidan smiled when he spotted me and entered. "What are you doing in here?"

"Talking to myself."

"You are not!"

Raikidan chuckled. "That's it?"

"And tending to some plants." I looked him over, noting he still held something behind his back. "What are you doing here? You said you were going to be out for a while."

"I wanted to get away from the crazies in this house, but out in the city is just as bad."

I chuckled and headed back for my plants. "Does that really surprise you?"

"Well, I'd hoped to find one sane person. I guess I should have stuck with you."

The voice snorted and I lifted my brow. "I did just say I was talking to myself."

He smirked. "I'll take that over other people today." He noticed the plants I received. "Looks like someone has an admirer."

I moved the plumeria from its small transporting pot to a larger one. "If you can call Azriel an admirer, then yes, as a matter of fact, I do."

"Damn, I guess I have some tough competition."

I whirled around, my eyes wide. "What?"

Raikidan threw back his head as he laughed. "Your reaction was priceless!"

My eyes narrowed and I punched him in the arm. "Not funny."

I then went back to finishing off my transplanting of the plumeria. *"What, no snarky comment?"*

"No, I actually didn't like that joke."

Raikidan sighed. "Someone made a comment, didn't they?"

I hesitated on starting my next plant pot for a moment. "Azriel and I got into a small argument. It's why I came in here to talk to myself like a pathetic lunatic."

"Stop it, you are not."

He grabbed my hand. "Don't talk about yourself like that. You're not pathetic, or a lunatic."

"See? Listen to your sexy bodyguard."

"Shut up."

"What, not going to talk to me out loud now?"

Raikidan squeezed my hand. "Will a gift make up for it?"

My gaze snapped to him. "Gift? Is that what you've been hiding behind your back this whole time?"

He let go of me to rub the back of his neck. "Yeah, though I'm not sure it'll top Azriel's gift. It's no—"

"Let me see it!" Normally, a gift wouldn't excite me, but Raikidan had never given me a bad gift before.

He pulled his hand out from behind his back and I gasped. In his hand was a tiny clay pot containing a plant with six linear leaves and three racemes of orange flowers. "Where did you get this?"

"I just found them on display at small flower shop I passed by."

"Raikidan, do you know how hard it is to find orange hyacinths?"

He shrugged again. "Not really. I just thought you might like it, so I picked it up."

I stared at him. "These are the rarest color of hyacinth in all of Lumaraeon!"

"So I picked the right plant? You like it?"

"Are you kidding? I love it! I never dreamed I'd ever get the chance to ever have a bulb of them in my greenhouse."

Raikidan rubbed the back of his neck again. "So, are they better than the two flowers Azriel gave you?"

I threw my arms around his neck and hugged him. "Yes!"

"Not pulling my leg?"

I pulled away. "Azriel gave them to me because he's Azriel. It's what he does. You gave them to me because… well…"

"They made me think of you?"

I shifted my gaze away, warmth spreading across my face. "Yeah…"

Raikidan held the plant out to me and I took it, the two of us smiling at each other. Several moments passed with neither of us breaking the contact, until my messenger hawk screeched, causing us to jump. Raikidan cleared his throat as he scratched his head, and I glared at the bird.

"Damned avian creature. It was about to get good."

"You have an overactive imagination."

Raikidan examined the bench I worked on. "So, uh, need any help with your project here?"

I raised an eyebrow. "You want to help me replant flowers?"

He shrugged. "Sure. It's a lot better than being in the house with the others."

I chuckled. "I can't disagree there. Here, I'll show you how to mix the soil and then we'll do the replanting."

Raikidan placed his full attention on me as I taught him about the soils. I couldn't help but smile as I gave him his lesson. He would be the first to want to do something so mundane with me and enjoy it. It was nice… comforting, even. Made me feel a little less… alone.

"He makes you happy."

"It doesn't matter…"

The hours ticked by and the two of us migrated from transplanting to standard maintenance of the other inflorescence. Raikidan asked all kinds of questions and it elated me. Not just because he wanted to be around me, but because he wasn't hesitating. It'd taken a long time for him to allow his curiosity to show through, but to see the fruit of that labor made me happy.

Raikidan looked back at the house and frowned. "Seda says I'm needed for something. I won't be back until tonight."

"Oh, okay…" My eyes lowered as disappointment flooded over me. "Good luck."

"If I need help, I'll give you a call."

He bent closer and pecked me on the cheek. My eyes widened and my hand flew up to my warming cheek as he walked off.

"For someone who 'isn't meant for you' he kisses you an awful lot. And boy, is he good at it. You should aim to get more. I know you like them."

Shock numbed me to her words. *Why did he do that?*

11
CHAPTER

Argus traced some lines on a circuit plan with his finger and then repeated the action with a circuit board on the bench the two of us sat at. My acquisition of Zo's helmet had been one heck of a steal, and it was the Council's number one priority to replicate so I could return the armor before suspicion could arise. Especially since I'd run into Zo enough times since the incident and I kept my mouth shut.

Satisfied with whatever he'd been checking, Argus installed the circuit board back into Zo's helmet and held it out to me. "Everything is a go. We can return it."

My brow rose. "Are you sure? I doubt I'm going to get this thing back if your plans turn out wrong."

He chuckled. "Yes, I'm sure. And even if I wasn't, the bug I planted will help me find the missing pieces."

"Okay, if you say so." I pulled out my communicator and sent a coded message to Ryder.

Are you with Zo?

It took several minutes to get a response.

I am, why?

He left something at the shop.

We can come by.

Out getting lunch. Can drop it off.

Okay. Patrolling Syben St.

I put the communicator away. "I know where he is, so I'll deliver it."

"Don't forget lunch!" Ryoko called out from under a car.

I chuckled and made sure I had the list in my pocket. "Don't worry, I got it."

Raikidan approached, wiping his hands on a rag. "Do you want me to come with you?"

"Say yes. He'll get grumpy if you don't."

I thought about it and then shook my head. "Since I'm dealing with Zo, I think I'll have better success keeping suspicion down if it's just me. We know how well the two of you get along."

Raikidan scowled as snickers echoed through the shop. I gave a half smile and then left. Hopping into the car, I set a course to Syben Street, keeping an eye out for a roaming band of soldiers.

When I made it half way down the street, I began to wonder if I'd either missed them, or they'd moved on for some reason. Then I spotted six soldiers speaking with an elderly woman walking a small white dog. One of them had the dark armor of a general rank. *This has to be them.*

I pulled into a parking spot close by and hopped out. One soldier, who had turned when I pulled up, waved two fingers to me. *That's got to be Ryder.* At least I'd found the right group.

Ryder spoke to the general I suspected was Zo, who then turned his focus to me as I strolled up. He excused himself, leaving his men to continue dealing with the problem at hand.

"Time to put on the charm."

His helmet visor slid up as we met. "Eira."

"Hey, Zo."

Zo peered over his shoulder for a moment and then placed his hands on his hips as he turned back to me. "Ryder says you needed to give something to me."

I smirked and held up his helmet. "I'm returning this, though I see you've gotten a replacement already."

He stared at the offered object and then took it. "Should I ask?"

"You left it at the shop, and the boys stored it in the office for safe keeping." I chuckled. "It was so safe, they forgot about it until I found it looking for some paperwork."

Zo snickered. "Well, I'm grateful. I can stop being in trouble for misplacing it."

The thought of how easy this was made me smile, adding to my faux friendliness. "Glad to help." I peered past him to the others speaking with the old woman. "Something the matter with her?"

Zo shook his head. "No. Her dog broke off his leash, and we were assisting in its recapture. Apparently she'd gotten the leash pre-owned, as she's on a fixed income, and it wasn't in as good a condition as she was led to believe."

I pursed my lips. "Let me check my car. I should have an extra in there."

Before he could respond, I jogged back to my car and opened the passenger door. I leaned into the back and rummaged, quickly discovering that someone had been throwing trash back there without me knowing and not cleaning up. *I could have sworn I'd left one in here the last time Raid and I had done an assignment together.*

"You boys need to be taught some manners!"

"Oh boy."

I halted my rummaging for a moment when the woman yelled. What had they done? I shook the thought and kept searching. *Ah, there it is.*

I retrieved the dual-colored rope leash and pulled out of the car, only to find the old woman hitting one of the soldiers with an umbrella. My brow rose as I rejoined Zo, who was watching the event instead of stopping it.

"Leering at a young woman like that is undignified and unbecoming of young men." She continued to hit the three men.

Ryder sat on the front stoop of a home, along with the only woman in the squad, both finding amusement in the reprimanding.

"Based on what's she's saying, I don't think I need to ask," I said to Zo.

"No, they did deserve it," he replied.

The woman's attention fell to him, and her eyes narrowed. Zo straightened as she approached him, her dog padding along with his tail wagging and tongue lolling out. Zo then curled into himself when she began hitting him as well. "Don't think I didn't see you leer at this pretty young lady as well. You were the worst."

"Oh, I like this woman."

Had I not already expected such behavior from him, I would have found this situation uncomfortable. Instead, I enjoyed watching him get beaten by an old lady.

"Only that young man over there sitting down behaved himself like a real gentleman. Honestly, your mothers would be ashamed of you," she chided.

"Uh, we're experiments, ma'am," one of the soldiers said, rubbing his arm where he'd been smacked several times. "We don't have mothers."

"Well, except Ryder there," the soldier next to him said.

The woman straightened her blouse and set the tip of her umbrella on the ground. "Well, that explains it, then." She then looked at me. "Now, dear, what do you have there?"

My lips pressed into a thin line as I tried to keep my laughter under control. I liked this woman. "Zo here told me you were having leash trouble. I happened to have a quality one in my car you can have."

"Oh, dearie, you don't have to do that."

I smiled and held it out to her. "It's one of my many extras. It's also made of a durable but soft material, so it'll be good for your hands."

She took the handled end and a smile spread across her wrinkled face. "This is a fine leash indeed. Are you sure you wish to give it to me?"

I nodded and then crouched down to pet her dog that was now sniffing my shoes. He wagged his tailed as he enjoyed the attention. I then unhooked him from his previous leash and attached him to the new one. "There we go."

"You're a kind young lady," the woman said. "Unlike this man here."

She hit Zo again with her umbrella for some reason, and this time I couldn't stop the bit of laughter as he complained.

"Ma'am, please stop or I'll have to cite you," he warned.

"Oh, you'd cite an old woman, would you? I see how it is." She hit him a few more times.

"Yes, I really like this woman."

I backed away slowly. "I should get going now. If I don't pick up lunch soon, the guys will be calling me about how their bottomless pits still require sustenance."

"You drive safe, sweetie," the old woman said as she waved. "And get yourself a nice man. Unlike these uncultured barbarians."

I laughed. This woman was beyond amusing.

"She's already got one," Ryder said from his safe place on the stoop. "Sort of. He pads after her like a faithful companion enough that we think so, at least."

I narrowed my eyes as I pointed at him. "Don't you start with that."

He held up his hands. "Hey, I just call it like I see it."

"He has a point."

"Shut up."

The female soldier next to him chuckled. "He calls it like a lot of us see it."

This confused me. I knew Ryder was teasing me about Raikidan, but was this woman thinking he meant Zo? Most soldiers that knew Zo had an interest in me, but they also knew of my lack of interest in him. And I seriously doubted just any soldier paid any attention to my close friendship with Raikidan.

The woman lifted her visor and winked a light blue eye. *Ariela—of course.* She was another mole we had stationed in Zo's company. That explained everything.

I rolled my eyes. "Anyway, I'll see some of you around, I guess."

Zo lifted the helmet in his hand. "Thanks again for returning this."

I shrugged and walked off. "Sure."

I opened my car door and spotted the old woman hitting Zo, reprimanding him for leering again. Chuckling, I drove off in the direction of the café everyone wanted their lunch from.

It didn't take me long to arrive, but parking was an issue. I found myself having to park in a lot three blocks down. Luckily, today was a good day for a stroll.

When I arrived at the café, I regretted not coming at a different time. Workers ran about, trying to fill orders as quickly as they could while a line that looked a mile long waited to be serviced. *Did everyone really need food from this place?* I resigned to my fate and stood in line, now wishing I'd accepted Raikidan's offer. Even if his presence would have caused tension with Zo, at least then I wouldn't be standing in a crowded place alone.

"I'm sure he'd be capable of keeping you company in a more private area, if you'd rather. As Ryder said, he does go out of his way to please you."

"Stop it."

The line moved slowly, the voice making snide comments every now and then, trying to get a rise out of me.

"Are you bored or something?"

"Always."

Eventually, I made it to the counter and placed my order. I did my best to be pleasant, even when the woman taking my order copped some attitude when I had to fix the order after realizing I'd read something wrong on my order notes. Luckily another employee set her straight before I lost my temper.

Once I had the food in hand, I made a hasty retreat back to the car. I didn't know why, but something put me on edge while in there. As much as I didn't like being around people, I could put up with it well enough. But today, I wasn't able to feel like I was invisible standing in line, even though I was the least conspicuous person in that building. *And why can't I shake the feeling now that I'm not alone?*

"Eira," the voice warned. *"Something isn't right."*

"So, my intuition is correct?"

"Yes. Keep your eyes peeled and get to the car quickly."

My pace picked up as I turned a corner. It wasn't a straight path to the car, but this street was less crowded, and if there was something I needed to spot, it'd be easy to do so with fewer distractions around. Unfortunately, the uneasy feeling didn't go away—in fact, it heightened.

I took another turn down an empty street, my pace quickening to a near jog. The unease of being watched followed me.

"I found you," an ethereal voice said.

"Eira, behind you!"

I pivoted in time to narrowly evade an ashen-skinned hand reaching for me. Using my momentum, I shifted my weight and swung my leg up, nailing my assailant in the side. He cried out and stumbled, allowing me to back away to keep distance between us. Now able to get a good look at him, it wasn't hard to understand why I felt watched. *Kir.*

He chuckled as he righted himself. "Not too shabby, Girl. I knew you'd be a fighter in this life, but I believe I underestimated how well you were trained."

I snorted and took a step back. "I'm an experiment trained for battle. What do you think they taught us, how to plant daisies?"

"No, I'm well aware they taught you how to make sure others were pushing up daisies. I'd merely assumed you'd have lost your edge in these years of sulking around in the underbelly of this city."

"Shows how much you really know."

Kir's eyes glittered. "I will end you."

"No, you won't," a masculine voice said from nowhere.

"That voice."

She was right; it was familiar-sounding, even to me. *But from where?*

Then suddenly, out of nowhere, a fist slammed into the unsuspecting revenant before me. Kir stumbled, and I took in the sight of the new-comer. Broad-shouldered, muscular bronzed skin, and multi-colored hair. *It's that shapeshifter guy I keep spotting and losing simultaneously.*

Kir righted himself, but as he aimed to retaliate, my mysterious shifter threw out his hand and suddenly Kir froze. Not a single muscle moved, not even a twitch of the eyes.

The mystery man then faced me, and I pulled myself into a defensive stance. He came at me, and I readied to defend myself when the voice spoke. *"Don't do that. He's okay."*

Her lack of concern over this man caught me off guard, enough so that my guard lowered and the man grabbed my wrist.

He yanked me as he ran past. "C'mon, that won't hold him for long."

"What did you do to him?" I asked as I was forced to follow. *He has a strong grip.*

"I froze him. But he's too strong for me to hold for long. We need to get you out of here."

"Who the hell are you?"

"Doesn't matter right now. Just keep running."

My eyes narrowed and I dug my heels into the ground. "Oh no. I'm not putting up with that bullshit. I'm not going anywhere with you until you give me answers, buddy."

His head snapped back to face me as he continued to drag me along. *Damn he's really strong. Too strong for any non-Brute nu-human.* "I came in

Arcadia's place. She wasn't going to get here in time, and if you fought Kir, you would have died."

My upper lip curled. "Don't underestimate my—"

"I saw it happen." A ripple of shock went through me. He saw me lose? "I don't doubt your abilities at all. But I know what I saw. Is that enough information to make you stop being a pain in the ass for a moment and keep moving?"

The voice chuckled. *"Cute."*

I half laughed. "You really know how to talk to a woman, don't you?"

My mysterious rescuer chuckled. "I just know how to talk to you."

We rounded a corner, and my car came into view. "You act as if you know me, and yet I only know you to show up at convenient times to save my ass, or appear and disappear randomly, making me think I imagined you."

He glanced back at me, a wry smile on his lips, and winked. "What else is there to know?"

My eyes narrowed, but I wasn't going to get the chance to continue figuring this out on the go. We made it to my car and he shoved me into the driver's seat before I could get the door fully open, my food almost spilling out all over the floor.

"Rude."

"Sorry for being pushy, but that freeze is breaking. You need to go, now," he said. "Don't look back; just get to your friends where you'll be safe."

He went to shut the door on me, but I managed to stop him. "Wait. Tell me your name. I deserve that much."

He blew out a reluctant breath, conflict flashing across his eyes. "Nal."

My brow rose. "Don't tell me that's just a nick name."

He winked and then shut the door on me. *Ass.*

"Cheeky, isn't he?"

That was one way to describe him. Nal tapped the hood of my car and motioned for me to get going. I turned the key in the ignition, the engine roaring to life, and ripped out of the parking spot. Making it down the street several yards before coming up to the intersection to the main street, I did what I was told not to do, and looked back in the mirror. He was gone. *The hell?*

I didn't wait to see if Kir would show up though. I wasn't that stupid.

I merged into traffic and made it four blocks before I relaxed in my seat. *Why can't my life be simple?*

"Because life never is."

"Thanks, Captain Obvious."

"You're welcome."

I took a deep breath and thought about what just went down. Kir was definitely following me, but he didn't attack until I was alone. That was strange. If he wanted to kill hybrids, why not do so where others could see? That would send a better message.

"His actions are perplexing."

And who was this "Nal" person? What was up with his ability to not only shapeshift, but also freeze Kir? I definitely hadn't imagined those two abilities. And furthermore, where did he disappear to? It was like he appeared and disappeared into thin air, like every other time I'd met him.

"Library."

"You really think the answer is in there?"

"It's possible. If not there, in some book somewhere."

"Jeez, that's helpful. Let me just put the entire rebellion on hold so I can search the entirety of Lumaraeon for a book."

The voice chuckled. *"You're so funny."*

I rolled my eyes and focused on driving. One thing I did know was that no one would know about today's events. Telling them would only cause unnecessary concern that wouldn't change anything. I already knew Kir was after me before this incident. So now, it was only a matter of when he'd pop up next.

CHAPTER 12

Shrugging on a light jacket and waterproof boots, I headed out the front door without a word. Blaze waited outside, a small bouquet of roses in hand. Neither of us spoke as we made our way down the waterlogged street. *Spring really knows how to make its presence known.*

The city bustled with life. Ten minutes in, I stopped at a small flower stall to purchase a bouquet of flowers. Blaze waited without making a peep. The lack of conversation between us didn't faze me. I knew this was going to be hard on him, but he asked me to be here while he did, making me feel good that he had that amount of trust in me. He needed someone to help him through this.

I peered up at the metal arch positioned on top of the stone wall of the graveyard as we entered. It was run down, and well overdue for a fixing. I made a mental note to get a formal complaint written up, hoping it wouldn't fall on deaf ears.

Blaze led me down a dirt path that led to the back end of the graveyard. As I took in all the gravestones, I realized this was the end where some of the wealthier civilians were buried. It made me wonder if Aiva had come from a family that had that kind of money, or if a few people had pooled in the money to get a nicer plot.

Instead of wracking my brain on it, I studied Blaze. He appeared so devoid of emotion it was disturbing. No person could try hard enough to look this emotionless. Not even I could.

"Be prepared for the worst."

"Already made that mental note."

After the incident on the roof and my discussion with Blaze the day after, I'd made sure Argus and Seda kept tabs on him. We didn't need him doing something devastating. And after today, who knew what his mental state would be like.

Blaze came to an abrupt halt and stared at the tall, well-crafted gravestone before us. *Impressive.* He knelt and removed an old, withered bouquet of flowers, and placed the new bouquet of roses in its place. I waited for him to say or do something, but he just stared at the stone and clenched the old bouquet in a death grip.

Being careful not to startle or upset him, I put my flowers down and out of the way, and I carefully took the withered flowers from Blaze. He didn't react; it was as if he were lost in another world. Taking out two small, ornate vases from my jacket pocket, I split the bouquet in half and placed them in the vases. Placing one vase down on one side of the stone, I pulled out a lighter and lit the dried foliage. When it started to smolder, I moved around Blaze and did the same with the other vase.

Once I was done, I went back to where I had been watching. Not a moment after, Blaze bent over and began to cry. I listened as he cried and begged for her forgiveness; I watched as he apologized over and over for what happened. I didn't say anything—didn't try to correct him as far as where he should be placing the blame—I just let him release all his pain.

The smoldering flowers died in the vases just as Blaze calmed down. He sniffled and wiped his face with his sleeve incessantly before looking back at me as he climbed to his feet. "Thank you. I'm sorry you had to see that."

"You don't have to apologize for having emotions." The phrase left a tingle on my tongue.

"Neither do you."

Blaze spread the ashes of the flowers around her grave and then handed me the vases. "I'm ready to go now."

"You sure?" He nodded. "All right. I have my own respects to pay elsewhere before we head back to the house."

He bent down and picked up the bouquet of flowers I had purchased. "I figured as much when you bought this."

I gave a weak smile and led the way out of the graveyard and through the city. I didn't let him lead until we were close to the destination. Since I had been labeled an immigrant civilian, we needed it to look like it was him doing the visiting and I was just here for the moral support.

Two soldiers took great interest in us as we approached the entrance of the military graveyard. It should be an honor to stand guard for the fallen, but one of them appeared bored and uninterested. It sickened me. They'd shown compassion and loyalty to their comrades in life, but couldn't muster up the energy to continue doing so once they were buried.

"Blaze," the bored soldiers greeted.

Blaze nodded curtly. "Len."

"Been a long time since you've made a visit."

Blaze nodded. "I know. That's why I'm here. I should have come by a few times by now."

Len eyed me. "Civilians aren't usually permitted to enter."

I frowned and Blaze grunted. "Since when?"

"Since Len is being a pain in the ass," the other soldier said. "Just let them by, Len, and let them pay their respects."

I smiled gratefully at the soldier. At least one of them wasn't miserable doing this job.

Len's mistrust in my presence remained, but he didn't say anything as he stepped aside. "Make sure your friend doesn't cause any trouble."

I smiled as Blaze led me in. "I promise I won't."

"What's your problem, Len?" The other soldier hissed when he seemed to think we were out of earshot.

"Something isn't right about that woman."

My brow twisted. *What had I done to make him think that?*

"Why, because she was quiet?"

"She was too quiet for a civilian. She didn't even look around with curiosity like most civilians."

"Did it cross your mind she was trying to show she wasn't going to be an issue? Not all civilians are troublemakers."

"Just ignore them," Blaze said. "Len doesn't trust anyone he doesn't know personally, and isn't afraid to make it clear. He's been known to give other civilians issues as well."

I chuckled. "Noted."

He handed me the flowers. "I suspect you want these now."

I smiled my thanks and took them. We moved through the cemetery in silence until we came to the row of weathered graves we were looking for.

I removed the old flowers I had placed on my mother's grave the last time I'd visited and replaced the bouquet with four new ones. I took out a special vase and put the old flowers in it and then lit them with my lighter until they smoldered.

I didn't try to talk to her. I didn't try to tell her how much I wished she were here, or how I wished I could have made better choices to save her. I didn't say anything at all. I just stared at her grave and felt the emptiness of my heart constrict my chest.

Seeing her at my celebration had been hard. Seeing her with the false physical form that only lasted for those few hours had hurt beyond what words could describe. I wanted her back, but I knew that wasn't possible. The type of wound, the way she died, she couldn't fake that. This grave held what was left of her decaying body, and that was the reality of this life I had been forcibly given.

When the flowers turned to ash and the smoldering died, I picked up the vase and emptied the ashes on the ground around the grave before storing the vase in my pocket. I retrieved the three flowers I kept out. "I have two more graves to visit."

Blaze nodded, letting me lead the way. It didn't take long to find it, tucked away near a dormant tree and some other headstones, though my finding out it existed was another story. Since Jasmine had helped us escape, I'd assumed Zarda hadn't allowed for her to be properly buried. But somehow, a few managed to sneak her out and into a proper place of rest. I wished she'd been placed next to my mother, her sister, but I knew this was the best way to keep Zarda unaware, just in case he chose to stop by for one reason or another.

I performed the same ritual as with my mother's grave. Seeing her, as well, hadn't been easy, especially since I was partially responsible for her death. She didn't blame me, that much she'd made clear to me, but that didn't erase the guilt.

Once I'd finished paying my respects here, I led Blaze to the last destination. The path toward this grave wasn't as easy, but we managed.

Under a dormant tree lay a weathered tombstone. Wilting flowers rested before it—I guessed them to be maybe a few days old, as well as spread ashes from the last visitor.

I knelt before this headstone and set up for another ceremonial burn, using the wilting flowers as fuel and resting the new ones in their place. I left the ashes undisturbed and then stared at the stone. *Tannek…*

I felt I should say something. Apologize for avoiding this for so long. Tell him I was sorry I'd done exactly what he didn't want me to do, and shut down. Him showing up at the party, and then subsequent dreams and discussions about him with Azriel, I couldn't keep his memory at bay. *The least you could do is apologize for what you did to him, stupid…*

But the words lodged in my throat as I knelt in the mud, my hands gripping my pants. I lowered my head. I had no right to beg for forgiveness. I deserved this pain—this loneliness.

"Please don't—never mind. This isn't a good time to argue with you."

Her words rolled off me as emotions slipped away. All but one—sorrow.

The burning flowers turned to ash and smoldered out, yet I remained still. Blaze knelt next to me, and still I stared at the ground in front of the headstone, my pain locking me into place.

"I forgive you," an ethereal voice whispered.

My heart stopped. *Tannek?*

"Because I never once blamed you. And neither should you, Chickadee."

Then, suddenly, it all disappeared. The pain—the sorrow. Calmness washed over me in a wave and I didn't know how to handle it. Was that the truth? *He's never lied to me before.*

"It's not in him to lie to you, of all people," the voice said.

I needed time to process this. I spread the ashes of the burnt flora and rose. "I'm ready to leave now."

Blaze got to his feet. "Are you sure?"

I nodded and headed for the entrance.

"Hey, Eira," Blaze called out as he caught up. "Are you okay?"

"I'm fine."

His gaze fell to his feet. "I thought for a moment I may have to deal with tears, and coming from you, I wouldn't know how to handle it."

I chuckled. "Don't worry, that would never happen. I'm incapable of producing enough tear fluid to do more than keep my eyes from drying out."

His brow furrowed. "Ryoko said she saw you cry once, when the both of you were younger."

I shook my head. "She's mistaken. I've never been able to… as much… as much as I've wanted to sometimes."

He gazed at me, but didn't respond.

We made it through the cemetery and past the two soldiers before he spoke. "Hey, Eira?"

"Yes?"

"Would you mind… uh, letting me see Aiva one last time?"

I nodded. "If she'll let me."

He gave a weak smile and nodded.

Blaze sat on the floor of his room as I centered myself. I told him that due to my inexperience, I needed a moment to prepare so that nothing bad would happen during this process, and he didn't argue. He was actually rather quiet, as if he weren't sure he really wanted to do this.

I took a deep breath and held out my hands. "All right, I'm ready. When you are, place your hands on mine."

He nodded but didn't grasp my hands right away. He stared at them, as if reluctant to go through with this.

"Blaze, if you don't feel you're ready, you don't have to do this. We can do this another time."

He shook his head. "No, I need to do this."

"Then why are you hesitating?"

"I'm just making sure I have the right action plan when I see her. I don't need to freak out and look stupid."

I chuckled and held my hands out further. "You'll do fine."

He nodded slowly and then closed his eyes as he placed his hands on mine. I closed mine over his and then pulled us through to the Plane of Between. Once sure we were there and stable, I opened my eyes and pulled my hands away so I could stand.

Blaze opened his eyes as well and mirrored my movements before looking around at the gray, lifeless world. "So, where is she?"

"I have to call her." A pulse of spiritual energy left me as I called out, "Aiva. Aiva, can you hear me? I have someone here who would like to speak to you."

We waited a few moments with no response and Blaze began to fidget. "How long do we have to wait?"

"We'll know if she wants to talk in a few more moments."

"If?"

"She may not want to talk with you right now. It's her right to say no, and if she doesn't show up in a few more moments, we'll know she doesn't want to talk."

My look changed to a sympathetic one when his expression dropped. I understood his desire to see her, but I couldn't make her appear, and if she didn't think he was ready to see her, she wouldn't show.

My attention pulled away when I sensed a presence approaching. I smiled when Aiva slowly appeared before us. I then looked at Blaze. "I'll just be over there if you need me. You'll only have about ten minutes before I have to bring you back. That's all I can handle right now."

He nodded his thanks and approached Aiva. I did my best to not listen in on their conversation by trying to find interest in something in this lifeless world, but some of their conversation would slip through every now and then.

Blaze was apologizing again, and Aiva wasn't having it. She was trying to get him to stop feeling sorry, and to my surprise, asking him to move on and find someone else. I had always been told that people who died and had been in love had a hard time accepting their partner moving on and taking someone new into their life, but Aiva didn't appear to be that way. The way she was trying to convince Blaze that there was someone new out there for him to share his life with, it was obvious his moving on was her greatest wish.

"Hey, Eira."

I jumped at the new voice right next to me. Turning around I was surprised to see the tall, blue-silver haired man standing there. "Xye?"

He smiled. "Sorry for startling you. I swear it wasn't my intention."

I chuckled. "I'm sure. Is there something I can help you with, or are you just here to chat?"

"A little bit of both actually. I was hoping you could deliver this note to my sister for me."

I blinked when he handed me a folded piece of paper. "Since when do spirits write notes to the living?"

"When the person we're trying to contact is too busy to talk to us."

He laughed. "There are a lot of things we can do that are a bit strange. You should know that by now."

I grunted and took the note. "You have a point. And I'll make sure she gets it."

He smiled. "Thank you."

"Xye, can I ask you something?"

"Of course."

"Why'd you do it? Why didn't you listen to me?"

He ran his fingers through his hair. "Because all I was thinking about was your safety. I figured, even if I couldn't stop all of them, if I could just stop even one, you'd be better off."

Is that why Tannek— I crossed my arms. "I wish you hadn't…"

"I know, but I hadn't thought about what you wanted in that moment. It's probably for the best anyway. I really wanted to be part of your life, Eira. But I knew, even if I didn't want to fully admit it, you didn't want that, and it would have been difficult for me to live with that kind of reality."

"You would have figured it out, and you would have found someone better. It's one of the perks of being you."

"There isn't anyone better." He gazed at me with so much sincerity it made me a bit uncomfortable. *He's wrong.*

"But, what's done is done. I made that choice fully knowing this might happen. I'm sorry to have hurt you with that decision."

"It's fine. You were always too stubborn for your own good anyway."

He chuckled. "Look who's talking. But I shouldn't keep you any longer. You'll be running out of energy soon, and your friend just finished up his conversation."

"It was nice seeing you again, Xye."

"Likewise, Eira."

I turned and headed back to Blaze, who willingly met me halfway. "Ready?"

He nodded and held out his hand. "Thank you for doing this."

I smiled and took his hand. "Sure."

CHAPTER 13

Raikidan took yet another box from my arms and handed it over to a shaman for me. I lifted another, and Telar stole it from me, using his abilities to add to the two he already carried, though being careful enough to not draw attention to himself.

I sighed. We'd been helping this caravan unload goods for thirty minutes, and neither Raikidan nor Telar had let me hand off a single box. Figuring it was pointless to pull another box of supplies, I hopped out of the wagon and searched for Shva'sika in hopes of helping her instead.

I stopped dead in my tracks and braced myself against a stack of crates when the ground shook violently. A few crates stacked a little too high crashed to the ground, their contents spilling out everywhere, and then the trembling stopped as suddenly as it started.

All the shamans turned to me for an explanation, but I just shook my head. "I don't know what that was about. Dalatrend isn't located near any fault lines."

"So, it's nothing to worry about?" Ken'ichi asked.

"I don't know."

"Something is wrong," the voice said.

He nodded and went back to working, as did everyone else. I turned my attention to Telar. He stood still as if using his ability to search for information, and that got me thinking.

North of Dalatrend were the Mountains of Jin. They were known to be a plentiful source of metals and the birthplace of Jin, the goddess of refined earth. But there was one other thing the mountains had that not many thought about, and that was a huge lake. No lake in Lumaraeon could compare to the magnitude of this one, and the only thing keeping it there was an ancient dam. This dam was closely monitored, due to the risk it posed if it ever failed, and that tremor made me worry about the effect it'd have on it.

"Laz!"

I perked up. *"Seda?"*

"There's no time to explain. You need to get everyone moving."

"Moving? Why? To where?"

Just then, another tremor began. My heart raced when a loud siren went off. Everyone looked around in a panic, as if expecting another raid, but this wasn't a raid siren. This was much worse.

"Get moving," the voice said.

"Everyone needs to get out of here!" I shouted.

"What's going on?" Ken'ichi asked.

"Are we under attack again?" someone else asked.

"No," Telar said, not yet out of his trance. "The dam above the city in the Mountains of Jin has burst."

It was just as I feared. "We need to forget about this cargo and get moving."

Instead of moving, they just stared at me. "Didn't you guys hear me? It's not safe!"

"Yeah, we heard you," Ken'ichi confirmed. "But what about the lives of the people in this city?"

"Why do you think I'm telling you all to move? There's a ton of water heading our way, and we have little time to get people to a safer location."

"Is there even a safer location?" Shva'sika asked as she made her way over.

I licked my lips. "I don't know…"

"Don't stall, Eira. You must move quickly. You're all in grave danger," the voice said

"I'm aware of that, thanks."

"Then why not stop the water instead?" Raikidan suggested. "It'd be easier than moving thousands of people to a new location that may not even be safer, if anyone made it there anyway."

"Do we even have that kind of man power?" I took in the shamans assembled. "This isn't just a job one or two shamans could take on alone. We'd need an army."

"The military is an army," Telar said. "They're already mobilizing what elementalists and psychics they have. Working with them is our best option."

"He's right. It's risky, but there are few safe options beyond fleeing and hoping for the best."

I gave a slow nod. "That's a good idea. It'll also eliminate most conspiracies of shamans sabotaging the dam. That's what we'll do. Screw the laws—use the portals and get moving. We need two groups. One will go to plug up the dam and control the water just under the mountain, and the other will stay here and keep the water from destroying the city, diverting it in any way we can."

"The military is gathering at the park," Telar said. "That's where we'll go to assist them."

"The first team can spread out to help with dispersing the water as best as they can to help those here," another shaman suggested. "I've seen that lake. It's not going to be easy."

"That would be wise to do." I pulled out a portal. "I'll be part of the group that stays here. Those shamans who don't have an element that can help with the water issue will have to work with the soldiers to get the civilians out of the city in case we fail."

"Wouldn't it be best to just split the groups now?" someone asked.

I shook my head. "No. Since we will be working with the military, we need to know how many people will go in what groups to be effective."

The others nodded as they pulled out portals, and we abandoned the caravan without a second though. Lives were more important than money.

I rushed through the portal with Raikidan beside me, and Shva'sika and Telar close behind.

"Why is this city below a dam?" Raikidan asked. "That doesn't sound too smart."

"This city began as a trading town centuries ago. At the time, they didn't know the dam was up there. It wasn't until the town expanded into a small city that they discovered it. Since the city had already been established, they didn't want to move it. We now just keep checks on it to make sure it's in good condition, and that allows us to set up a warning signal just in case it does break."

"Obviously they needed a better method. This doesn't give anyone any time."

I sighed with annoyed agreement and rushed out the other end of the portal. When we came out, we were greeted with chaos. Soldiers ran around trying to herd civilians to the city gates; shamans who'd arrived before me attempted to work out plans with the soldiers, and Ken'ichi seemed to be the only one who was getting anywhere with a general.

I ran over to them and the general saluted me quickly. "Ambassador."

I bowed my head respectfully. "General."

Most of the ranking officers knew my cloak pattern by now, thanks to a few parties I'd had to attend. My coronation, as we were calling it, had been announced, and the military put on a big three-part spectacular to show their supposed support. Raikidan and I'd had to attend them all, but, luckily, I was given space when I had asked for it, so it had been bearable.

"We're glad for your help," he said. "We were lucky to have two psychics up at the dam for monitoring when the cracking began. They were so focused on keeping it as stable as possible, they barely managed to get a message off to us to sound the alarm. At this time, we're unable to determine what caused the problem to begin with."

I nodded and watched as others gathered around us to hear what needed to be planned. "I doubt they'll be able to keep it at bay for long, if they're already struggling with what little has happened."

"I suspect you have a plan to propose?" the general asked.

"We plan to send out shamans to help with the fix, as well as spreading out on the land to divert the water if the dam bursts despite our efforts. That should help lessen the water that rushes toward the city."

"What about the town between the mountains and here?" a soldier asked.

"I wasn't aware there was a town there."

The general I had been speaking with nodded. "It was built several years ago."

"That's inconvenient," the voice muttered.

"Then they'll need to be evacuated as well. I won't accept saving lives here and not attempt to spare a town. If you can spare any elementalists or psychics to help, it would be greatly appreciated."

The general nodded. "I can see what is possible. What do you propose if the water isn't able to be diverted from the city?"

I took a deep breath. "I need a map to show you the plan we've discussed. I have high doubts, even with the skills of those going outside the city walls, that they'll be able to keep the water from hitting the city."

The general pulled out a hologram map and I showed them the plan.

"We plan to set up three diversion points in the city, spanning the length of the walls, or in the case of fire shamans, evaporate it as much as possible." I pointed to the three locations. "As you can see, they are all in the North side of the city, but spread out enough to, in theory, stop the water from destroying most of the city. Whatever elementalists and psychics you can't spare to leave the city, it would be best to have them join one of these lines."

The general nodded as he tried to picture the plan. "I can't hate this plan. What shamans are planned to be part of all this?"

"Technically all shamans will be involved, but water, ice, fire, earth, and the few wind shamans we have will be the ones taking care of the water, while the others will be helping to get the citizens out by whatever means they can, hopefully easing that burden for your soldiers as they also try to do this task."

He scowled. "You will be using portals, then."

"Really? He's going to be like this?"

"It seems so." I steeled myself. "I could care less about your laws in a time like this, General. You tell us where the citizens have to go, and that's where we will bring them."

The general held his gaze with me, but I refused to back down. This was too important to argue, and even if he said no, we'd still use them.

"Sir," a soldier address quietly. "We can't ignore their help. The lives of the people in this city depend on it. Allow the portal use."

"It's the only way to minimize civilian loss, sir," another soldier put in. "We're running out of time."

"Fine," came the general's terse reply. "The consequences of breaking our laws, though, will fall on you, Ambassador."

I held my head high. "I take full responsibility for that. Now, if you'll excuse me, I must take my place at the first line of defense inside this city."

"Ambassador Laz'shika, please reconsider that choice," Ken'ichi begged.

I shook my head. "We Shamans of the Rising Sun will be useless when it comes to diverting the water before it reaches the city, Ken'ichi. Because of this, I will take up the first line of defense inside the city to evaporate what I can."

"We'd prefer if you'd take the last line," another shaman said. "We don't want you to get hurt."

I sighed. "My life is no more important than anyone else's."

"I beg to differ."

"If the first two lines fail, you will be needed to make the final attempt to save this city," Raikidan pressed. "We are needed there."

I clenched my fists and refrained from yelling at him. I knew that wasn't the reason he was siding against me. He didn't want me to risk getting hurt, and while I understood his job made him responsible for putting my safety first, but this wasn't the time to worry about that. Other lives were at stake, and those lives were not more important than mine.

Shva'sika called for a vote. "All in favor of the Ambassador holding the last line, raise your hand."

I watched with a mix of anger, annoyance, and horror as all the shamans around me raised their hands and even many of the soldiers, including the general I had been arguing with. Telar also raised his hand.

"If I had a hand to raise, I'd be with them."

"Stay out of this."

"No."

I was outvoted, and time was of the essence. I let out a slow exhale as irritation gripped me. "Very well. I will lead the last line of defense."

I heard several sighs of relief from shamans around me, including Raikidan, Telar, and the voice. I could only assume both men had prepared to argue with me had I chosen to be stubborn about this.

When no more shamans showed up through portals, I began to

worry. Our current count was much lower than I had anticipated, and I wasn't sure if it would be enough to accomplish anything if more didn't show up. I went to address the shamans in the vicinity when a psychic flew over to us. "General, the dam's condition has just worsened. We must to act now."

Just then, several portals opened around us and shamans flooded the street, sending a wave of relief through me. *We might be able to pull this off after all.* One shaman in particular caught my eye as he approached. "Del'karo."

He grinned. "Good to see you again, Ambassador."

"Likewise." I couldn't help but smile. "Please don't tell me you were looking for me once again when trouble popped up."

His grin didn't leave his face. "Guilty as charged."

I chuckled. "Just our luck." I surveyed the gathering shamans. "Is this all we have?"

Del'karo nodded slowly. "Afraid so. After your coronation, most left to go about their usual business, and there isn't enough time to gather more."

I took a deep breath and hoped my disappointment wasn't showing. "It'll have to do, but…" I looked at the map the general was still holding. "We're going to have to modify the plan."

Del'karo came closer. "What's the plan, then?"

I pointed to the map where the middle line of city defense would have gathered. "All those staying inside the city will have to gather here, and span out until we make one unbreakable line, wall to wall."

"Are you sure we can't do at least two lines?" the general asked. "You have my men."

"And civilian psychics," the psychic above us informed. The general tilted his head, as if urging her to explain. "They insisted on putting their skills to good use instead of running."

"Of course we'd all help, we're not chickens," Telar projected into my mind. *"Even my sister would put up a fight against this water in her state."*

I almost laughed. *"Did you mean to send that to me?"*

"Oops."

"Very well." The general turned his attention to me. "Won't that be enough for two lines?"

I shook my head. "No. We still need people to leave the city to take care of the dam, evacuate the town near the dam, and take positions between the dam and this city to put away as much water as possible before it reaches the city. I've chosen the middle position, to form a line to make sure those in the city defense group will have time to prepare, and to minimize as much city property damage as possible."

I gasped when the ground shook, and would have fallen over had Raikidan not caught me.

"Time is up," Del'karo said.

I nodded. "We move now. Those going out of the city, do so. Those staying to stop the water, follow me. Those going to get civilians out, move quickly. May the gods light our paths."

"Be careful."

Portals appeared en masse, and the area around us cleared out quickly. I looked to Telar. *"I want you to go to the dam."*

He turned his head toward me. *"I'm staying here with you."*

"Telar, I trust your abilities more than most. We need someone as strong as you to help keep as much water at bay as possible. That will lessen the burden on us down here."

He hesitated, then placed a hand on my shoulder. *"Please be careful, then."*

I smiled. *"I can't promise anything."*

He sighed and then went to join the group headed to help with the dam. I tossed a portal on the ground and rushed through, with Raikidan and Del'karo close behind, while Shva'sika went to assist with the civilian evacuation.

Adrenaline pumped through my veins as we drew close to the other end of the portal. The reality that we might not make it, even with our combined efforts, plagued the back of my mind.

Everything we were striving for, everything we had wanted in our fight, could be destroyed in this one moment, and I didn't doubt that Zarda was putting many of his psychics to use protecting his castle, in order to ensure he continued to rule regardless of what happened, not caring whether his own people lived or died.

I forced those thoughts out of my head as we exited the portal. I needed to believe we could do this and that we'd do it with minimal casualties. I needed to focus on doing this right.

"Everyone spread out in one line," I ordered, as more shamans flooded out of the portal.

It wasn't easy for us, seeing as there were civilians running aimlessly in a panic, but we managed to get our line set up in the end. Raikidan stood to my left while Del'karo stood to my right, each of them showing no signs of fear, and I was vaguely aware of soldiers working with the civilians, particularly one general who I didn't want around—ever—and really wished he wasn't in the vicinity.

"You sure you want to do this?" I asked Del'karo. "If things go bad, Alena—"

"Yes, I'm sure," he said with unwavering conviction. "I have no doubts about the outcome of this. Alena won't be left alone with the children."

"You act as if you can see the future."

He grinned. "Maybe I've glimpsed something that makes me optimistic."

I eyed him, curious what crazy things were going on in the head of my mentor, but didn't get the chance to ask anything further. The ground shook and then rumbled, and my heart began to pound.

"Brace yourself," Seda messaged.

"Everyone stand ready!" I shouted.

The rumbling grew louder as we waited in anticipation, and soon, stray pebbles on the ground began to jump around from the force of the impending wave that rushed toward the city. I lit fires in my hands and braced myself. As aware as I was that breathing my fire would give me more powerful flames, I needed to make sure I kept up as steady of a stream as possible. With Raikidan only able to breathe fire, I was going to need to be able to cover for him when he needed to take a breath of air.

When the large wave crashed over the walls of the city and came rushing toward us, I sent a silent prayer. I couldn't be sure it'd help in the least, but it wouldn't hurt to try. When the water came closer, we unleashed our defenses, and the hood of my cloak fell down from the wind created from the collision. I didn't care, though. Right now, it didn't matter that my identity was exposed. I'd deal with it later. Saving the city was my priority.

We put everything we had into pushing the water away, but it seemed to do nothing but stall the inevitable. I knew we were close to the mountains, but this amount of water was more than I had ever predicted. *What are they doing up there? Making it worse?* It did feel that way, especially when I saw shamans dropping quickly from expending so much energy. That, of course, made things worse. Shamans and psychics had to stretch their abilities more, and that made our defense weaker.

"I'm sorry," Del'karo whispered before he fell to his knees and failed to muster up any more fire, or strength for that matter.

I didn't fault him. There was only so much someone could give, no matter their skill level. Instead, I took position in front of him and stretched my fire thinner. I even exerted more power in hopes it would help, but it just tired me more.

"Take this energy from me." A familiar rush of power, the same from when I'd had my test, coursed through me and my fire power intensified. But I knew that even that wasn't enough, and it wasn't going to hold out forever.

"They're almost done fixing the dam," Seda message. *"Just hang in there."*

Unfortunately, I wasn't sure if we could hold out much longer. We were dropping like flies. Even the psychics were failing to keep rank, and this water kept coming as if someone had left a huge faucet running.

My strength continued to ebb out of me, the borrowed power completely gone at this point, but I refused to give up. I refused to fail these people. I may not matter to them; they may hate me. But that didn't mean they deserved to die—not like this.

"Keep going. You have this," the voice said. *"I believe in you."*

"They're almost done!" Seda insisted.

I sighed inwardly. It didn't matter if the dam was fixed in moments. This still needed to be taken care of, and we were losing too much manpower to hold on that long. I knew what needed to be done. Not many would care. Not many would bat an eye at the sacrifice, but it didn't matter. That never mattered to me. It was why I liked being part of the rebellion. I had the camaraderie I loved, and I wasn't exposed to any fame or given much attention.

"No, don't do that. Anything but that," the voice said.

"I must." I took a deep breath and pulled energy from deep within myself.

"Eira?" Del'karo whispered. "What are you doing?"

I continued to pull energy instead of replying. He wouldn't agree with what I was about to do.

Raikidan halted his defense, ignoring the shouts of protests from the psychics above him, and stared me down. "Eira?"

"I'm doing what needs to be done." I felt my body pulse with energy and accepted my fate.

"No!" Del'karo shouted. "Don't do it. There's another way. There's always another way than that!"

"Listen to him. Don't do this. There are other ways."

This is the only way… I watched as my skin started to glow, and I felt the power I had summoned transform within me. Closing my eyes, I took one final breath and then unleashed the power. It shot out of my body through my hands, in the form of fire, and collided with the wall of water, but the water didn't stop it. The moment the two forces touched, the flame transformed into a fiery bird and forced its way through, spreading as far as the water did. The water hissed angrily as my fire burned it away. I felt the power of the fire consume every drop it touched, but I also felt the life within me fade at the same rate.

I staggered when the water disappeared, and the fire died along with it. Stinging cold crept over my skin. Overwhelming weakness consumed me. I collapsed.

"Eira!" Raikidan roared.

"No… you shouldn't have done that. I can't save you like this, not in my current state. Why couldn't you have just waited a moment longer?"

"I made my choice." My vision faded in and out as I fell. My breath came shallower and shallower as the seconds passed. *"Everyone is safe because of my sacrifice."*

A new voice crossed my ears, in the way a memory would. *"Now they'll stop fighting. They can all be happy again…"*

"Eira!" Del'karo cried.

"Eira…"

My vision faded, and when it came back I was in Raikidan's arms. He looked desperate and at a loss as to what to do.

"Rai…ki…dan." It hurt to breathe, let alone speak, and I could feel my life force slipping away, but I reached up to him all the same. *I just want to say goodbye…* Then, my vision and my body failed me simultaneously.

Darkness surrounded me, and numbness clung to my body. Was this what it felt like to die?

Then something unexpected happened. My eyes cracked open, and I found myself being carried in a hurry by Raikidan, his brow creased with determination and concern. *Am I seeing my final moments?*

I heard a muffled voice calling out to me, but I couldn't tell where it came from.

I wanted to grab Raikidan's attention, but my body wouldn't listen, and my eyes were so heavy it was hard to keep them open. They closed, and when I managed to open them again, my vision was blurry. I was no longer in Raikidan's arms. I knew because I could feel the sheets of a bed around me, and I could make out blurry figures hovering over me. It almost sounded as if one or two of them were attempting to speak to me, but I couldn't respond. *Is this the end?*

My heavy eyes closed again.

When I finally had the strength to open my eyes, they were clear and no one was hovering over me. It was as if I had imagined them, which was entirely possible. *I'm not dead.*

Beyond all logical reason, I was alive. I was in a strange bed, with no idea where I was.

The voice let out a long, relief filled exhale. *"You're finally awake. You had me so worried."*

"Well, if I wasn't sure about my living state, I've got my proof now."

She chuckled. *"Fresh out of a coma, and you have all the bite in your tongue already. I missed it."*

A coma? *"How long have I been out?"*

"A while."

That didn't help me in the least. I made an attempt to sit up, but it hurt to do so. A fair hand touched my shoulder and I looked up, only to smile. "Shva'sika."

My voice was hoarse, but at least I was able to say something.

"You need to lie down," she said in a soft tone. "You put your body through a lot; it's going to need a lot of time to rest."

"Can I at least be propped up?" I smiled. "I'd rather not have to see the ceiling all the time while I'm here."

She coaxed me to lie flat on my back. "Rest some more, and I'll find out if you're well enough to sit up."

"Where am I?"

"The home Ken'ichi has been staying in with some other shamans. It was the first place he could think of when he put down the portal."

My gaze wandered until it fell on my hand. Panic welled up in me—it was bonier than my normal hand, and my nails were more talon-like. My skin also wasn't as smooth anymore. Some patches were leathery and showed signs of previously having had designs to them, and possibly being more than just leathery skin prior to me waking up. It looked so similar to the time I had lost control at the range.

I reached up to touch my face, ignoring my body's protests of pain. The moment my fingers came in contact with my skin, my heart stopped. My face also had the same designs as my hands.

"It's okay. There's no need to panic."

Shva'sika rested her hands on mine. "Take it easy. Not many know."

I eyed her warily. "How many do?"

She took in a sharp inhale. "Besides Rylan and Zane, who already knew, just the few shamans who helped bring you back from the brink of death, and Ryoko and Ryder. Telar found out, too. Your skin didn't change until after your life force was stable again, and Rylan made sure your visitations were limited to him, Zane, Ryder, and Ryoko. But he had thought Ryder and Ryoko had already known when he okayed it. And Telar… well, he'd been monitoring your state without anyone knowing for a while."

I pressed my lips together. "What about… Raikidan? Does he know?"

Shva'sika made an odd wide-eyed expression; one that told me what she was about to say would be interesting. "No, but I don't think I've ever seen anyone so distressed before. When we brought you in, he tried his hardest to remain in the room. He wouldn't listen to words, and fought against Ryoko, Ken'ichi, and Telar when they tried to forcibly remove him. Corliss even had to step in, and I thought we were going to have a dragon fight to deal with as well."

She shook her head. "He's done nothing but pace, when his attempts to force his way in haven't worked." She smiled. "It's heartwarming in a way."

That sounded like him. Though I would call it stubborn and annoying, rather than heartwarming.

"Cut him a little slack. As unusual as it is, it's his way of showing he cares."

"What happened when he found out Telar was keeping tabs on me?"

Shva'sika shook her head. "He pitched a giant fit and then demanded to see you, only to be denied again."

"It was amusing to hear."

At least they were able to keep him out. I touched my hand. *I don't need him seeing… this.* "How are Zane and Ryder doing?"

"Restless. Ryder has only been able to stop by twice, and each time he's been reluctant to leave you. I'll be sending him a message to let him know you've finally woken up. As for Zane, he was in here more than anyone." She smiled. "He'd talk to you in hopes you'd hear him or that it'd convince you to wake up. He was afraid he'd lost you, too."

"It was sweet to see."

I smiled. "Well, do me a favor and tell him not to worry for me? Let everyone know to stop worrying."

"Are you sure you don't want to tell them yourself?"

I shook my head, a feat that happened to be more difficult than I'd hoped. "I don't want any visitors right now. Not until I'm feeling much better."

"Even Raikidan?" she asked. "After everything I told you? It'd calm him down."

I glanced at my hands. "Yeah, I'm sure."

"There's only so long you can keep your secrets from him, Laz. He's going to find out the truth sooner or later."

"I agree with her. And it wouldn't be a bad thing for him to know."

"Yeah, we'll see." I closed my eyes briefly, but when I opened them again, the room was darker and I was no longer flat on my back. I was propped up a little, as I wanted to be. *I must have fallen back asleep. That was really rude of me to do to Shva'sika.* I knew she wouldn't take it personally considering my state, but it didn't make me feel any better about it.

"Don't feel guilty. You need your strength to recover. I'm just glad you woke up again."

"Me too."

I shifted my focus to my arms and hands. I let out a relieved breath. They were back to normal, and when I slowly reached up to touch my face, I relaxed when I felt smooth skin. My body wasn't acting up anymore, which made me happy.

"It wasn't acting up to begin with."

"I don't want to talk about it."

"About time you woke up," a familiar masculine voice said.

I glanced to my right, to find Raikidan sitting on a desk with a teasing smile on his face. "How did you get in here?"

He pointed to the open window letting in a warm gentle breeze. "Shva'sika is too diligent for her own good, let me tell you. Not even Mana could persuade Shva'sika to let her in. She even used that face you call the puppy eyes, or something like that. Even Telar couldn't physically enter, with her standing guard."

"And with good reason. I told her I didn't want visitors."

He shrugged and came closer. "I don't care. I wanted to make sure you're actually okay. Verbal confirmations don't cut it, either."

"Aww. What a good boy."

"Stop it."

"Well I am. Now you can"—I noticed the bundle in his hands—"What's that?"

He sat down on the edge of my bed. "Food, for you. There's only so much life energy your body will take for sustenance before it needs real food to function."

"My body can feed off life energy for a few days," I said.

"You've been out for ten."

My eyes widened, shock rippling through me. "Have I really been out for that long?"

He nodded. I couldn't believe I had been unconscious for ten days. It felt like I had only been out for a few hours, maybe a day or two at most.

"I told you it had been a while."

I smiled weakly. "Well, thanks for the thought, but I don't have the energy to chew anything right now. Talking is running me low as it is."

"I can fix that." He grinned as I eyed him skeptically. "I could feed you fire."

"I'll retreat now so you two can have some alone time."

"Stop it."

No response. My eyes narrowed at Raikidan. "Yeah, I don't think so."

"Consider it a favor for when you saved me when I was shot."

"Favor or payback?"

He chuckled. "You pick."

My gaze faltered. "I'd rather you not…"

"I'd rather see you better." He wasn't going to take no for an answer, and before I could come up with another way to say no, he leaned closer.

I sighed with reluctance but didn't fight him—not that I had the energy to do so. Raikidan bent close, his strong fingers curling under my chin. His hot breath brushed my lips and traveled down my neck, making my shiver.

He was gentle, as if he were worried I'd break easily, and to my relief, he went easy on the fire. He only gave it to me in small breaths, making it easier for me to absorb it. My body amazed me with its ability to adapt to the treatment. Even though I could eat fire and convert it, he was the first to be capable of directly performing this task with me.

Raikidan pulled away, and I let out a slow exhale as my body converted the fire into energy. "That should do it for now."

I closed my eyes and relished the feeling. When I opened them, I was surprised to still see him there.

He chuckled. "You didn't fall asleep this time."

"Well, that answers that question." I glanced at the window. "How are things out there?"

"Progressing. Both walls were destroyed, and several plantations and homes were wrecked. Casualties were minimal, and everything should be back to normal soon. Zarda made it out safe, as everyone expected. That whole fortress had managed to be turned into a 'safe haven' for the ruler and the people lucky enough to make it there, thanks to the psychics."

He shrugged. "At least, that's what the military and news claim. I've been more concerned about you than the state of the city, or Zarda's status. Nothing bad happened to any shamans that I'm aware of, in case you were wondering."

I nodded. "Yes, that was on my mind. Anyone know why the dam broke?"

"There was some discussion; there is evidence that the Crimson Sanctuary had something to do with it. But I don't know if anyone proved it or not."

The voice hissed, but said nothing more, sticking to her claim to leave the two of us alone *unsupervised.*

My eyes darkened. "I wouldn't doubt they were behind it. Leveling an entire city and any towns between isn't beneath them."

Raikidan ripped opened the wrapping of the meat he had and tore into it. "Enough about that. It's time for you to eat something."

"Raikidan, I can't," I protested. "I may be gaining strength from the fire you fed me, but I can't eat solids yet. I'm too weak."

He grinned deviously. "Who said I was going to let you eat it in chunks?"

My eyes widened. "Oh, no. You are not feeding me."

"Consider it *payback* for when you did it for me." He chuckled. "And I won't allow you to say no, because you need this."

The voice chuckled, but again, left it at that.

I crossed my arms and looked away. He chuckled again and chewed up the meat. When the meat was mashed enough, I reluctantly held out my hand, but he pushed it away. I knew exactly what he had planned, and it was definitely payback.

Once he had force-fed me the meat, I chewed it briefly and then swallowed, not relishing it in the least. Raikidan bit into the meat again and we repeated this process several times, holding light conversation to distract me before someone burst into the room.

Raikidan, seemingly uninterested, continued to chew the meat in his mouth, but I was in slight shock. "Del'karo?"

It wasn't like him to disobey a no-entry placed by both a healing shaman and a patient, and it was definitely out of character for him to barge into a room. He didn't say anything as he watched us, as if he were trying to process the scene before him. Raikidan finished his chewing and handed the food off to me by hand. I reluctantly took it, even if I was grateful he wasn't feeding me by mouth in front of Del'karo.

It wasn't until I managed to swallow my food did Del'karo react. He moved quickly and I was sent into shock, and a little bit of pain, when he scooped my upper body into his arms and embraced me in a tight hug. "Del'karo?"

"I thought I lost you…" It sounded like he wasn't going to be able to hold himself together. "Don't you ever do that to me again…"

I rested my hand on his back. "I can't promise anything."

"You must."

"Del'karo, I do what must be done, even if that means my life is forfeit."

He released my slowly, being mindful when resting me against the soft surface of my pillows. "And what about your promise to Ryder?"

My gaze fell to my lap. "I suppose there's that."

I looked up when my door opened again, and I smiled at Ryoko standing in the doorway. Tears rolled down her cheeks and she rushed over to me, giving Del'karo little time to move before she threw herself on me. I cringed in pain as she held on, but didn't complain. Instead, I chose to stroke her back and let her sob.

Glancing up, I found the others gathering in the open doorway and nodded to let them know it was okay for them to come in. Might as well let them all visit before I became too tired. Even with the fire and the food I had managed to consume, I knew I'd be resting for some time yet.

"How are you feeling?" Rylan asked.

"I've been better," I said. "But I've also been worse."

"You really scared us, Chickadee," Zane said.

I smiled. "Well you can stop worrying. I'm not going anywhere."

"You'd better not," Ryoko muttered.

Ken'ichi chuckled. "She was ready to drag your spirit back to your body if needed, the gods be damned."

I rubbed Ryoko's head. "That doesn't surprise me one bit."

"You look tired," Shva'sika said. "We should let you rest more."

I nodded. "If you say so."

Ryoko shook her head. "I'm not leaving."

"Ryoko, I'm not going anywhere." She tightened her grip and I sighed. "I'm just going to rest some more, and then I'll wake up again. I promise."

She let go hesitantly and held my gaze before nodding. One by one they left, until Telar remained. He looked… sad.

"I'm going to be okay, Telar," I mentally thought to him.

"I thought I lost you, Sweet Thing."

My eyes remained soft. *"I didn't send you away just so I could pull this."*

"I know. That doesn't make me feel any better."

"Telar, I did what I had to to save people. We were overwhelmed and dropping left and right, spreading ourselves thinner and thinner by the second. I couldn't think of another way."

"I know that!"

I flinched. He'd never yelled at me before. Raikidan rose to his feet, a dark look directed at Telar. I placed a hand on Raikidan's arm. "Stay out of it."

Raikidan tensed as he stared Telar down. "What did he say to make you react that way?"

"I'm sorry," Telar said out loud. "I shouldn't have yelled."

I tugged Raikidan's arm and he sat back down, though reluctantly.

Telar shoved his hands into his pockets and turned his head away. *"I was so focused on my job up at the dam, I didn't know what was going on down in the city. I didn't know what you did until after. I've sat outside your room for ten days, unable to do more than monitor you."* His shoulder moved, as if trying to point with it. *"Even he's able to help you more than I can."*

"Telar, you did exactly what I asked you to do. Had you not been up there helping, I'd be dead for sure, whether I pulled that drastic move or not. You did save me."

He stared at me and silence filled the air for a moment. *"I won't tell anyone what I saw. Your secret is safe until you want to reveal it."*

I smiled. *"I know, I trust you. Now go get some rest."*

"Someone should stay and keep an eye on you."

I glanced Raikidan's way, finding him tearing into the meat again. *"I'm not going to be able to convince him to leave for a bit, so someone will be here for a little while."*

Telar frowned. *"All right, if that's what you want."*

His gaze lingered on me a moment longer and then he left, closing the door behind him. This allowed me to focus on Raikidan, who was ready to feed me again. *Great.*

"He does it because he cares."

After feeding me several more times, he finally allowed me to relax. But instead of leaving the room to do so, he went back to sitting on the desk.

My eyebrow rose. "You're really going to watch me sleep?"

"Someone has to keep an eye on you."

I snorted and made myself a bit more comfortable. "You're such a creep."

"If it were anyone else, I'd agree. But with him, it's sweet."

"I don't have the strength to argue with you right now."

She chuckled. *"I know. That's why I'm getting this in now."*

"Just go to bed so you can get better," Raikidan said.

I chuckled before closing my eyes. I cracked them open when I felt his presence grow. He sat on the floor by my bed and rested his head and arms on the mattress. I couldn't stop myself from reaching out and resting my hand on his head. His worry was touching even if he should be putting that energy into other things.

Allowing a warm feeling to fall over me, I closed my eyes and fell into a deep sleep.

CHAPTER 14

I did my best to ignore the whispers as I cleaned the bar. I knew there would be talk. Thanks to my "heroic" act two weeks ago, I hadn't found a single person who didn't recognize me now, and I'd only been off bed rest for two days. Since everyone knew, I chose to wear several accessories that many would associate with a shaman, like feathers and natural jewelry. I didn't see a reason to hide.

I suspected the military would force both Raikidan and me to quit this job anyway, and fine us for taking up work when we weren't allowed to. It was a big reason I convinced Shva'sika to let me work tonight. She didn't want me exerting myself, but I owed it to Azriel to work for him one last time.

Azriel threw a fit when I told him. He had scolded me yet again for my reckless heroics, and then cursed Zarda for the rule set in place. He didn't want to replace Raikidan and me.

I suppressed a sigh when Zo approached the bar. *Looks like my time is up.*

"Great, him of all people. I'll let you handle this on your own."

"Gee, thanks." I held my head high. "Here to make me quit?"

"No." He sat down at the bar. "I'm here for a drink—and the truth." My brow rose. "You give me the truth about you, and I'll waive the fine and allow you to continue working here."

I regarded him with skepticism for a moment and then leaned on the bar. "Where do you want me to start?"

"Who are you, really?"

"My common name is Eira. But my shaman name is Laz'shika."

He blinked with surprise. "You're the—"

I nodded as I poured him a glass of scotch. "Yes. And that's to stay between the two of us, you hear? My identity is to remain a secret as much as possible. Not for the other shamans' sakes, but for mine."

He nodded. "Very well. Tell me where you come from, why you chose an amnesia story, and how you were able to get the others to go along with it. Tell me how you met them while you're at it."

I chuckled and place the glass on the bar. "You're a bit pushy today."

He sipped his scotch. "You're the one breaking the law."

I smirked. "You already know where I come from. I didn't lie about that. Same with my amnesia. Though, I did exaggerate how much memory I lost."

"Was your amnesia really caused by you getting caught in a fire?"

I nodded. "Yes. And I did lose my family from it. While I left home to train as a shaman at a fairly young age, I returned many times for visits." I let my gaze falter to sell the story. "It just so happened, I was visiting home when events played out as they did."

"Okay, how did you meet the others?"

"I met Zane some time ago, thanks to my parents. He's a good family friend of ours, and I came to see him as a distant relative—an uncle, if you would. When I lost my memory, I tried my best to relearn everything, but I was having difficulties, so Zane offered to allow us to come live with him and the others. It just ended up working out in my favor, and I was able to attempt a double life that let me have what I had missed."

Zo turned his head. "What do you mean?"

"While I've only recently gone through official coronation, I've had my job within the shamans for some time. It's not a position you just pick up or offer to take. You're chosen, and I was chosen young. Because of it, I didn't have the normal life most people had at my age. I thought living this double life could give me some of that."

"Did it?"

I nodded, a smile spreading across my lips. "It gave me more than I was hoping for."

"I see." He gazed at his glass. "Explain to me who Ray really is."

I crossed my arms. "Our agreement was only for me to talk about myself."

"But he is a part of this story." He looked up at me without moving his head. "And he does work here."

I exhaled a reluctant breath. "Most of what you know is the truth. He doesn't like lying. We have known each other since we were children and are quite close. His common name really is Ray, and his Shaman name is Raikidan. It was chosen because of the name I've called him since childhood."

"Rai."

I nodded. "Yes. My inability to say his name properly as a child was true."

"What role does he play in your life?"

"He's my Guard."

He looked down at his glass. "So, that story… the engagement…"

I tilted my head as I played dumb. "Engagement? What are you talking about?"

His eyes flicked up. "That story he told me… you don't know about it?"

My brow twisted. "Story? What are you blabbing about, Zo?"

Zo shook his head. "Nothing. Forget I said anything." He sighed as he stared at his glass. "The two of you… are you two a thing?"

Taken aback by his question, I wasn't sure how to respond, nor was I able to suppress the warmth spreading across my face. *No, Eira, don't start going there.*

"The way the two of you act." He still didn't look at me. "The closeness you two share…"

I smiled at him. "Rai is my Guard, Zo, and my best friend. Of course, we're close. But there's nothing really between us… right now." I fussed with my hair as if I were embarrassed, deciding to sell the thought he had.

"Yeah, sure it's all him."

"Why, does it seem like there is?"

Zo shook his head. "I had just heard something, that's all. I guess it was typical gossip." He grinned slyly. "But since it's just gossip, you wouldn't say no to going out on another date with me, would you?"

I blinked, pretending to play dumb. "What did you just ask?"

He smiled. "Look, if you're worried I'm going to go back on my word, you don't have to. I'm letting you stay employed here."

The patrons listening in cheered with approval, which surprised me a little. I didn't think I was that well liked here. "Zo, I'm not worried about anything. I knew you'd keep your word. You're a man of honor."

He smiled more. "Then go out with me."

My stomach turned. No way was that happening. "I'm sorry, Zo, but I'm going to decline. I—"

He frowned. "Why?"

I chuckled. "Well, if you'd let me finish, I'd tell you."

Zo nodded, a curve to his mouth, and waved so I'd explain myself.

"The truth is, I'm still recovering from my near-death experience, and I'm not even supposed to be working. I'm only here because Azriel had to step out and he trusts me to keep this place in one piece. Once he's back, I'm going home to rest some more."

"All right, I can't really argue with that. I'll just have to catch you when you're all better, then."

"You say that like it'll be easy."

He grinned and went to say something, but was stopped when Azriel showed up. "Well, looks like your knight has come to relieve you of your post duty."

"You say the weirdest things sometimes, Zo."

The two of us laughed and Azriel just smiled. "Seems like everything is in order."

I nodded. "No problems so far."

He continued to smile. "Well that's a relief. And speaking of relief, you can go home to rest."

I nodded again. "Thanks. See you around, Zo."

He sipped on his scotch. "You sure will."

As I walked away, I listened in on his and Azriel's conversation.

"She does a good job acting as your replacement," Zo said.

"I was hoping to promote her to a manager's position soon," Azriel replied. "She's really shaped this place up with methods I never believed in a million years would work."

Zo chuckled and rose to his feet. "Well you don't have to worry about giving that position to anyone less deserving. I'm waiving the fine and allowing her to stay."

"You could get into a lot of trouble for this," Azriel said. "How noble of you. Or maybe it's not nobility. Maybe it's something else."

Zo grunted and placed some money on the bar. "Make sure she gets the tip."

"Pretty generous tip for one drink."

"She gave me more than a drink, trust me."

I headed through the back to collect my things. The gods only knew what he meant by that. I'd never understand that man, or any man for that matter. Then again, I couldn't understand myself sometimes.

15
CHAPTER

I tapped my fingers on my arm as Ryoko, Rylan, Raikidan and I waited for our ride outside Zane's shop. Raikidan, impatient, paced about, adding to my already-high stress. Wearing a military uniform did that to me. It threatened to send my mind back to times that should have been forgotten. Our assignment should be the reason my nerves stood on end, but I was confident we'd accomplish our goal.

By tapping Zo's helmet, we'd successfully obtained enough data for the Council to have Team Six plus Argus and any other intelligent outlier mass produce any necessary components. After that, they assigned seven teams to infiltrate their delivery and supply chain to slip the bugged component into the manufacturing warehouses, routing with moles to reduce suspicion.

Our team had been selected, due to the convenience of drop-off and pickup for the truck and equipment. No one would question why a military driver was stopping here. We just had to wait for our truck to show up.

"Raikidan's pacing is starting to wear on me now," the voice said.

"Asking him to stop won't do any good."

"I know, but that doesn't make it any less annoying."

The rumble of an engine caught our attention, and then the bright lights of a truck pulled into the road, heading directly for us. Raikidan finally stopped his pacing at the vehicle's arrival. When the truck came to a halt, the driver cut the engine and two women jumped out. I recognized the light-skinned blonde with high cheekbones. "Niccola?"

Niccola was an assassin I trained back in the day. She and Zena had worked with us briefly for an assignment dealing with some gang led by a creep who'd tried to abduct me.

She gave a sly grin and waved her fingers. "Hey, Eira."

"What are you doing here? No longer working for that creep Ergren?"

"Oh, no, Zena and I are still stuck with him for a while yet. There's been some traction on the black market information, particularly in human trafficking, so we've chosen to keep going with the charade."

I nodded. "Good reason to stay, though I wish it weren't with him."

She smiled. "Don't worry, we can handle him. We got him back for what he tried to do to you, for example."

I appreciated that.

She glanced Raikidan's way. "It added to the hit to his ego when 'Big Boss' over there decided to stop working with him, due to the obvious threat Ergren posed." She smirked. "And because he wasn't thrilled Ergren would so brazenly try and steal his prize woman."

Raikidan snorted and said nothing more.

I looked to the dark-haired, bronze-skinned woman who accompanied Niccola. I didn't recognize her, so I suspected she was the mole we were to work with.

The woman gave a curt nod. "My name is Avez. I'm on the roster for delivering this truck. Stick to my lead, and the cargo will be delivered without any issues."

Ryoko shifted her weight to one side as she crossed her arms. "Where are the others? We were told we'd be swapping places temporarily with them."

Niccola grinned. "There was a roster change up, and Avez was ordered to deliver with some loyals, so Zena is keeping them occupied."

I grunted. "One thing she enjoys doing."

The smile remained on Niccola's red lips. "If we get a move on here, she won't be the only one getting all the fun."

I shook my head. "I don't want to hear about the fantasies you play out."

She shrugged. "Suit yourself. More for me, then."

Avez threw her thumb out in the direction of the truck. "We'll need to do a quick unload before we get the new units in."

I nodded, and the six of us went about unloading the truck. Once that was done, Niccola and I worked on moving the cargo to be disposed of hidden in the shop while the others focused on loading up the bugged cargo.

"So, I hear you had a run-in with death recently," Niccola said as we entered the shop with our first crates.

I nodded. "Yeah, I took a few extra risks that almost didn't work out so well."

"You hadn't planned it to work out the way it did."

"She doesn't need to know that."

A sly grin spread across Niccola's face. "The success have anything to do with that sexy friend of yours?"

"Yes."

I sighed and set my box down. "No, so drop that topic right there."

"Don't be like that."

"You stay out of this."

"I've heard the rumors, Commander."

"And rumors are just that. People get bored and make things up for their own entertainment."

"Except it's not made up with you two."

"Stop…"

Niccola invaded my personal space, looking up at me with devious intent. "Are you sure you're not finally digging out some rusty seduction techniques to wrangle up a pair of strong arms to keep you warm at night?"

A few different techniques flashed through my mind, each one having Raikidan as my intended target. I snuffed them out as quickly as I could, doing my best not to react to such ridiculous and improper actions.

"Oh, don't be like that. You'd have a lot of fun if you used one or two of those."

"It's not like that."

"Oh, yes it is, and you know it."

The grin on Niccola's lips deepened. "I see the shade of red you're trying to hide. There is something there."

I centered myself and pressed on for the door. "No, there isn't, Niccola."

Just as I cracked the door open, she placed her hand on it, keeping it shut. "I'm not letting you get away like that, Eira. I came here specifically to talk to you about this, instead of staying with Zena to help her keep those soldiers busy."

"Well, I'm sorry I ruined your fun night, because now you've gotten your answers. There's nothing between Raikidan and me. Everyone wishes to believe there is, because they don't think a person can be happy on their own, and because it's fun to imagine little ol' Eira finally acting like someone they believe she should be."

"Wow, a bit harsh."

Niccola frowned and leaned against the door. "That's not why I think the way I do."

I crossed my arms. "Then enlighten me."

"We all fight for freedom, but freedom comes in different forms. I want to see you free from Zarda's grasp, Eira. I hate the woman he forced you to become for the sake of his own amusement, instead of the woman you wanted to be."

"So you think me being in love means I'm free?"

"I believe you allowing yourself to fall in love means he has no control over you anymore."

I looked out the window, seeing Raikidan help Ryoko stack up some extra boxes to reduce their trips. "Well, I'm not in love."

Niccola smiled, her eyes going soft, before opening the door. "Yes, you are."

"See. You can't keep lying to everyone. It's way too obvious."

I watched Niccola head to the pile of crates. *"It doesn't matter. The reality is, he'll never be mine."*

"He can be."

"No, he can't."

I left the shop and helped Niccola with the task at hand. She'd look at me funny from time to time, but I ignored it. Raikidan and the others finished before we did, and gave us an assist to speed the process up; I was grateful. I found myself slowing with each pass, my energy stores running far too low for my liking.

When Raikidan took crates from me so I'd have less to carry, like he always did, I caught Niccola grinning ear to ear. Ryoko did the same, and the two exchanged looks. *Great, they're conspiring against me.*

"If you'd just be forthright with your feelings, they wouldn't conspire."

"I can't be honest about all that. And you know it."

"I do? Are you sure? Because I think I've been telling you the exact opposite."

"Why are you so insistent on this?"

"I have my reasons."

"Tell me."

"The block is not allowing me to."

Frustration burned inside me. This was getting far more than ridiculous. *"Well, unless you can, butt out of my personal decisions. They're not yours to make."*

"Eira, I'm just… trying to help."

Pain pulsed in my chest as I lifted a crate. *"Yeah, that's what everyone else tries to claim, too. But you're all only looking out for what you want, not what I want. Now leave me alone."*

Raikidan tried to take the box from me, but I pulled it out of his reach and kept going. "Eira, I can help."

"I'm more than capable of carrying my own crate," I snapped.

Raikidan recoiled, his face flickering between concern and regret. *Great, now my irritation is projecting onto him.*

I entered the building, picking up Rylan's attempt to find out what the two women had done. When I turned around after depositing the box, I found Raikidan entering, only one box in his hand.

"What did they say to you?" he asked.

I shook my head. "Don't worry about it. And I'm sorry for snapping. You didn't deserve it."

He placed a hand on the doorframe to prevent me from passing. "I want to know what they said to you, not an apology."

"Same shit, different day." I ducked under his arm and went to grab one of the remaining boxes.

Avez gave me a sympathetic smile as we passed each other, but I didn't respond, nor did I pass either Ryoko or Niccola a glance of acknowledgement as they walked by.

I lifted a larger crate over my shoulder and Rylan tried to stop me to talk, but I brushed him off. "Leave it be. I don't need you rescuing me like some damsel."

"That's not…" He exhaled. "I'll drop it."

The last of the old cargo was locked up into the shop and we took up our positions, activating cloaking watches while we were at it. Avez would drive, to reduce any suspicion, Ryoko and I would sit up in the cab with her, and the boys would hole up in the back, acting as hidden protection for the cargo. According to Avez, this was the most common setup for transporting these types of goods.

Niccola wished us luck before heading off, and Avez drove away. Things were quiet in the cab of the truck. I had no desire to talk, and focused on the city passing us by.

After ten minutes, Ryoko checked in on the boys through a sliding window on the back of the cab. They were doing all right for having to share the space with a bunch of cargo.

Another five minutes passed before Ryoko tried to speak to me. "Are you still mad at me?"

I refused to answer and continued monitoring the outside world.

"Really? You're that petty you're going to give me the silent treatment?"

I refused to acknowledge her insult. If she really thought me being mad at her for her obnoxious meddling was petty, then yeah, I was.

Ryoko let out an aggravated sigh. "Avez. Give me a hand here."

"You don't want to hear what I have to say," Avez said.

This grabbed my interest.

"Well, since everyone has either gotten on my case or is ignoring me, might as well give me your two cents," Ryoko said.

"I think you need to stop trying to control other people's personal lives. They're personal for a reason."

"I'm not—"

"Yes, you are. You are trying to dictate what is best for Eira. You're trying to tell her what to do because *you* think that would make her happy. What you're doing, while kinder, is no better than Zarda."

"I am not like him." Ryoko's tone had a dark edge to it.

Avez kept her eyes fixed to the road and didn't flinch. "Then stop trying to dictate what others do. Let them decide what will make them happy, even if you don't agree with it."

Ryoko sat back in her seat and remained quiet. I could only assume she was stewing. I gave Avez a grateful glance. It wouldn't stop Ryoko, she was stubborn like that, but I appreciated the support from someone who didn't know me all that well.

"I hope you don't expect me to change my mind," the voice said.

"No, you're just as stubborn."

"I know what I'm doing when I encourage this."

"Clearly."

The truck came up to a guarded fence, and Avez pulled to a stop at the gate. She rolled down her window and smiled at a man on the other side of the door. "Hey, Elren."

A half-smile spread across his face. "Good to see you, Avez."

"Oh, hottie, ten o'clock," Ryoko said as she nosily looked over in their direction.

I snorted, and Avez and Elren chuckled. Avez then handed Elren some paperwork. Other soldiers went about inspecting the truck, even opening the back to speak to the men and do a brief visual check on the cargo—all typical behavior for a security checkpoint at a place like this.

I glanced behind me when Ryoko started flirting with one of the guys doing checks on our side. He had no qualms conversing with her instead of sticking to his job. *Another soldier distracted enough not to give us any potential issues.*

"What do you mean my shipment isn't right?" Avez said, pulling my attention.

Elren showed her a planner, the digital display listing something. "According to this, your truck should be carrying a completely different set of cargo."

"That's ludicrous!" Her upper lip curled. "This is the cargo loaded into my truck right from the facility, and I know I'm at the right location."

"Avez, I know you're upset, but I can't—" He placed a hand on his ear, making me aware of the small communication device he carried, one we still couldn't get our hands on for some reason. I made a mental note to talk to the Council about that. "Hold on, my paperwork may be wrong."

Avez snorted. "I'll say."

Elren spoke to someone on the other end of his discreet communicator. I found tension building in my shoulders. If this didn't work out, we were screwed. *Why is this even a problem?* Everything should have been situated before we rendezvoused at the shop.

"Stay calm. It'll work out."

Elren nodded before looking up at Avez. "Sorry, our data was out of date. Your shipment was a last-minute change."

Avez let out a short breath. "Of course it was."

He flashed her a brilliant smile. "I'll treat you to dinner to make up for it."

She pondered this for a moment. "I'll think about it. But now, I have to get this shipment delivered. Don't need the factory shutting down because of missing components."

He smirked at her and backed away. "Alright, raincheck it is. I'll see you later, Avez."

Her lips curved and her eyes twinkled, and when she spoke, a slight accent tinted her words. "Ciao, Elren."

We pulled into the compound, rolling up our windows. Ryoko leaned over the front seats from her perch in the back seat. "So, tell us about Elren."

I scoffed, and Avez laughed. "You're consistent, I'll give you that."

Ryoko winked. "I'm a fan of 'happily-ever-after.'"

Avez shook her head. "Right now, he's just a friend."

"But he's clearly interested."

"Yes, well, he's completely loyal to Zarda. I've never seen his devotion waver. So right now, it's not a good match."

Ryoko grinned. "Don't underestimate the power of feminine wiles. If he likes you enough, that will become his undoing."

"Perhaps."

I pulled my leg up onto the seat and rested my arm over my knee. "I noticed the accent in your voice. You're a tactician training in languages, aren't you?"

She nodded, taking a turn down a new road. "I'm not the best out there, but I've got Elvish, Grekeleon, some Dwarvish, and multiple common dialects and accents packed into this brain. I'm always learning more, too."

Ryoko grinned. "And Elren likes one in particular?"

Avez chuckled. "Yes."

Ryoko sat back in her seat, a satisfied smile on her face. "Then you, girl, need to get to work charming Zarda out of his pants so you can get in."

I groaned and slammed the palm of my fist on my forehead while Avez sputtered out a laugh. "Does this ever quit?"

"No," I said, shaking my head.

"Happily-ever-after," Ryoko said in a sing-song voice.

Avez chuckled some more and pulled up to a warehouse building. A few soldiers came out and assisted with unloading. This went smoother than earlier, and we were back on the road in less than thirty minutes. This time, Rylan and Raikidan were allowed to ride in the cab.

"Laz," Ryoko said. "Are you sure you don't want to sit back here? It's cozy."

I sprawled out a bit in my seat, aware of my even lower energy store. "I like my roomy seat."

"We can make room." She chuckled. "I doubt Rai would mind you sitting on his lap."

I wasn't going to entertain any thoughts she was trying to put in my head. "I'm good."

"Oh, don't—"

"Ryoko, drop it," Raikidan said, his tone stern.

Ryoko made a sound as if she was emotionally hurt or offended, and I choked on a laugh. Even Rylan chuckled.

Avez looked through the rearview mirror, a smile curving up one side of her face. "He's got no clue why we're amused."

I glanced back at Raikidan, confirming he was lost. I chuckled. "You say 'drop it' to dogs when they have something in their mouths."

Raikidan processed this and then snorted. "No need to revise, then."

Avez and I roared with laughter and Ryoko crossed her arms. "Jerk."

Our amusement came to an abrupt halt when Avez gasped and slammed on the brakes. We all braced ourselves and stared at Avez. Her hands clutched the steering wheel, her knuckles white, and she stared wide-eyed through the windshield. My gaze shifted to follow hers, and my blood ran cold. In the middle of the road, about four hundred feet in front of us, stood a man—a man with dark hair and ashen skin. *Kir.*

"Go."

"Go," I repeated the voice's words out loud, though I wasn't sure if they were in response to her voice or to command Avez. Numbness crept through me.

"What?" Avez said.

"Step on the gas and go."

"There's a guy standing in the road."

My eyes snapped to her. "I said go!"

She slammed her foot on the accelerator and we all braced ourselves, though my choice was to keep myself calm as I stared right at Kir. He wore a wicked grin as we closed the gap, his glowing red eyes focused right on me. Avez glanced at me, her eyes pleading to make her stop. I didn't.

Her eyes squeezed shut and Ryoko screamed as we "made contact" with him. Not surprising to me in the least, his body disappeared the moment the impact happened. I rolled down the window and looked behind us to find him back in the road, grinning at me. *Slimy son of a—* "Keep driving," I said to Avez, not pulling my eyes off Kir. "Whatever you do, keep driving."

"Okay…" Avez said in a shaky voice.

"Laz, what in the gods' name was that?" Ryoko asked.

I waited to answer until we'd driven a short distance away. Kir didn't follow. *What was his end game there?*

I pulled my head back into the truck and took a deep, calming breath. "Ryoko, you remember when you asked me once about bad spirits existing?"

"Yeah?"

"Well, that was one of them."

The air remained silent, the tension palpable.

After a moment, Avez spoke. "How bad is he?"

I chewed my lip, trying to figure out how much to reveal to them. "He's one of the worst at large right now."

"At large?" Rylan asked. "Doesn't that mean you should be dealing with him?"

I nodded. "We are. He's just too strong for any single person to handle on their own, and too slippery for us to plan a joint assault against him."

"So, that was Kir," Raikidan said.

I nodded again.

"You know this spirit, too?" Ryoko said.

"Yeah, he's got it out for Eira."

Her ears drooped. "Why?"

"It's not just me he's after," I said. "It's all halflings. Supporters, too. His hate for us is what keeps him connected to the living realm."

"How long has this been going on?" Ryoko asked. "Were you ever going to tell us?"

"It's a recent development, and I'd hoped to spare you from ever having to know."

"What are things like him called?" Rylan asked.

"Revenants."

"Like the evil spirits from stories?" Ryoko said.

I nodded. "Yes."

Avez glanced at me. "How do you fight something like that?"

I frowned. "With specialized training, utilizing spiritual energy."

"So, ordinary people like us are screwed." She nodded. "Cool, I like those odds."

"She's funny."

I chuckled. "Biggest bit of advice I can give—if you are faced with one, don't let it touch you, and run. It's the only way you have a chance of surviving. If one does manage to get you and you get away, seek out a shaman immediately. You won't have long before its abilities kill you."

She grimaced. "I'll keep that in mind."

I stared out the window. What did Kir want? He knew we were in a vehicle. Did he think he could make us crash? Or was he aware of my poor state? It was theorized he had something to do with the dam break. If he found out the condition I was in, he may have been looking for a chance to catch me when I couldn't defend myself properly.

Or was he just sending a message? Telling me he was out there and no matter where I'd go, he'd know.

I tried not to sigh. *As if this rebellion wasn't hard enough...*

Setting my messenger hawk down on his perch, I left my greenhouse and read Ryder's letter as I walked. Now that my shaman identity was known, it made it easier for me to get my hawk some exercise through my contact with him. There was no pushback from the military, either, much to my surprise. It may have had something to do with my influence over Zo, but after the news of my identity spread through the ranks, I expected a few issues, even if Zo told me things would be fine. But everyone accepted the news and acted as they always had. *Makes me wonder how much power Zarda really holds over the soldiers these days.*

I wasn't taking it for granted, though. I enjoyed the more regular and open contact with my son; and now that his concerns about my health were finally getting under control, that made me feel better. I hadn't realized how much my stunt had affected him until he came for his first visit once I had awakened after the incident. I had returned to the house by then, and I was already attempting to get back into my regular routine without pushing my body too much. It was hard to figure out if he was more upset that he had almost lost me, or that he wasn't able to be with me during my recovery.

"He's turned out to be such a good young man."

"Can't really take credit for it, though. It's not like I was part of his life for a good chunk of it."

"No, but you were there during the most crucial time, and that left a lasting effect on him. You should be proud."

"I am proud of him."

"I'm talking about you."

"Another note from Ryder?"

I looked up to find Raikidan sitting on the roof parapet.

"Yeah." I folded up the letter and sat down next to him. "Since you're waiting so patiently, I'm assuming you want to ask me something."

"Just wanted to make sure you're doing okay."

I snorted. "Don't give me that. You know I'm doing fine. I did that assignment last night without any problems."

"That's why I'm concerned. That was your first since the dam broke. You were exhausted after, and all we did was move cargo—and have a minor scare with Kir."

I wasn't buying it and he knew it. Had he been as concerned as he was trying to claim, he would have come right into the greenhouse to check on me.

Raikidan sighed. "All right. I've been thinking."

"That's dangerous."

He nudged me with a sly smile. "No more dangerous than you thinking."

I laughed and let him continue. He licked his lips in thought and then took a deep breath. "I just want to make sure of something. I know you offered, but it's been a long time since then. Do you really want to help me find my mate?"

I cocked my head. "Well, yeah. I wouldn't have offered to help otherwise."

He looked at me as if he expected something else from my mouth. "Why, though? Why do you want to help me with that?"

I stared at him, my brow furrowed. "Why not? If she's right for you, then why wouldn't I want to help you be happy? Besides, you're helping me with this big issue in my life. I don't see why I shouldn't try to return the favor in some way."

He nodded and then reached for something by his feet. I realized it was my pan flute box. "I'd like to know how you got this."

I chuckled when I took it from him. "You should know that by now. My mother, of course."

He eyed the carvings on the box. "It wasn't just from her, was it?"

I sighed. "I don't… I don't want to talk about it…"

"You can't keep running forever."

"All right," Raikidan said.

I ran my fingers over the top of the box. "Rai, do you know the name of your mate?"

"Excuse me?"

"Well, you said that the voice talks to you from time to time. Has it ever told you her name?"

He was quiet for a moment. "Yes."

"But you won't tell me, even if it'll help."

He shook his head. "That knowledge is for me and only me."

I nodded with understanding. "Okay."

"Do you mind playing me a song?" he asked quietly. "When you play, it reminds me of home."

"More like you feel like home."

"Stop it."

"Sure." I pulled the flute out of the box. Raikidan took the box to hold onto, and I played a quiet tune. When I was done, I let the gentle breeze carry the tune away before speaking. "Raikidan, are you afraid of finding her?"

He set his jaw. "I'm not afraid."

When I raised an eyebrow to indicate that I didn't believe him, he exhaled. "All right, maybe a little."

My eyes remained soft as I gazed at him. "Why?"

"I know what I want, and I don't know if I could accept her if she wasn't like that."

I tilted my head. "And what do you want her to be like?"

He chewed on his lower lip as if he was fighting himself over whether or not to answer the question. "I want her to be a lot like you."

"Like you? Like you? Why not actually you?"

Between his wording and the voice's offended reaction, I found myself confused, and my expression showed it.

Raikidan held up a hand. "Wait, before you freak out in some way, because that does sound weird, let me finish. You have a lot of qualities I admire and really want my mate to have. Particularly your independence, self sufficiency, and strong will. I don't want someone like Mana."

My brow rose. "Like Mana?"

"She's just a responsibility. She's so spacey and inattentive to everything around her, she can't be trusted to be on her own."

"Corliss doesn't see her as a responsibility. He enjoys every moment he has with her."

Raikidan grunted. "He likes dependent females. He likes having to worry about her all the time and making sure she's with him when he goes somewhere. I don't. I want to worry about my mate not because she can't take care of herself, but because it's the right thing to do, even though she doesn't need it."

As I studied his face during his explanation, something didn't connect. His words made sense, but there was something in his eyes that told me there was more to the truth than he was letting on. *Wait...* "It's not just her that you're worried about, though, is it?"

He didn't answer.

"This has to do with you, doesn't it?"

Raikidan pressed his lips together as if he weren't going to answer, but then he did. "What if... what if I'm not right for her? What if I can't... make her happy?"

I placed my hand on his arm. "What makes you question that?"

He hesitated. "My mother..."

"Raikidan, you mother loved y—"

"Yeah, I know. She loved me a lot and I made her happy, but..." He stared at his hands. "She tried to hide how unhappy she was with my father. She'd laugh and smile and act like everything was okay, but sometimes she'd slip up and I'd see just how miserable she really was. How inadequate he made her feel. How alone and misunderstood she really felt, and yet she still tried to love him, and it wasn't fair seeing that. Especially since my father seemed to either not notice or not care..."

His hands clenched. "I've been shunned by my kind because my scale color is mixed. My parents' relationship is all I've ever known to see. I don't know if I—"

"Rai..." My grip tightened on his arm. "You're an amazing dragon. You're loyal, protective, and caring. She'd be lucky to have you. You shouldn't think otherwise."

He held my gaze.

"If your mother was that unhappy, she would have left. I know you say you guys mate for life, but that doesn't mean you have to be miserable. She had free will and she chose to stay. Even if she was unhappy sometimes, that didn't mean she was all the time. I deny the existence of love, but that's because I'm jaded and spiteful. Your mother believed in love—believed in the wildness of the heart."

My eyes squinted as I smiled. "There's a reason our ribs are cages."

Raikidan continued to gaze at me, processing what I was saying.

I patted him on the arm. "She loved him, Rai, and unhappiness doesn't allow for that—trust me."

I put my flute away and headed for the greenhouse. He needed to think alone now, and I needed to get my head on straight as well. Setting my flute box down on a table, I ran my thumb over the carvings.

"Do you want to talk?"

"I'm not sure I want to talk to you about this."

"I won't tease you this time."

"You sure?"

"As sure as you're talking out loud to me as if no one could hear you."

I went over to my messenger hawk and refilled his bowl with meat from a cooler that rested nearby. "I can always play it off that I'm talking to him."

"Fair. How do you feel after that topic?"

"Don't you know what's going on in my head?"

"I'm not a mind reader."

I sputtered a laugh and she also chuckled. "I honestly don't know. I wish he'd stop being so hard on himself and realize he's his own person… dragon… male. You get it."

The voice snickered.

"He's not defined by his parents and the mistakes they may or may not have made."

"Are you sure you're talking about him and not you?"

"I told you, no snide comments."

"I'm not making one. It really does sound like you're talking about yourself."

"I guess that just shows how similar we are."

"But you're still under the belief you're not a good match?"

"He's got a destined mate. It's not me, and will never be me. That's how it is." I gave the hawk some more food. "He's been given an amazing gift to find this dragon that would be perfect for him—a gift most would kill to have."

"Would you?"

I thought about this for a moment. "In the past, maybe, but not anymore. I don't think there's anyone out there who could handle me at this point."

I leaned on the table next to the hawk's perch. "It's okay, though. Not everyone is meant to have another person by their side. It happens. I've accepted that."

"Have you?"

It was a good question. I could say the words, but did that mean I felt that way for sure? *Maybe I don't…* Even if I didn't, I knew what she wanted me to do. But I couldn't do it. Raikidan deserved to be happy. And I'd rather be friends with him than push him away because I had a fragile and desperate human heart.

Suddenly a sharp pain clutched my chest. I braced myself on the table and my hawk screeched in fright. My breath labored and then the pain subsided, allowing me to take quick calming breaths. "What the hell?"

That wasn't the first time I'd felt that sensation—the night of my Ambassador coronation, when I'd been out on the lake—the sensation was much like that.

"Are you okay?"

"Yes. I think it's just my defective heart acting up."

"It's not defective."

"Yes, it is. Defective and mangled. No one wants that."

"I'm not convinced, but you're too stubborn to listen to me, so I might as well not waste my breath."

"Are you mad at me?"

"No. Sometimes I am, but sometimes I'm happy or confused about you, too."

I tapped my fingers on the table. "Same. I wish I knew what you were."

"You do. The problem is, the truth is obscured."

"By what?"

"Meddling."

I sat there on the desk thinking about this. What was meddling with the truth? My brow knitted. Or was it a *who?*

CHAPTER 17

Sighing, I finished wiping down the bar and put the rag away. I was able to work again, but it was difficult to go at the pace that was needed. Even the warehouse assignment I had done a few days ago was easier than working here, and I had been dog tired after completing it.

My recovery from the dam break wasn't going as fast as I would have liked, but I couldn't be surprised. It took a long time for life fire to come back and I had almost used it all up. Shva'sika said I was lucky to be progressing as fast as I was, but I think it had to do with the fire Raikidan had been feeding me. Even now, on a nightly basis he'd give me a little to help.

I ground my teeth when I heard yet another waitress slap Andariel in the face. His club had been ruined by the floodwater and was in the process of being fixed. Because of this, he had felt the need to hang around here and claim he was visiting Azriel, although all he had done was bother all the waitresses as if they were his own workers.

"Andariel, leave them alone!" I hollered when he bothered yet another woman.

He made his way over to my side of the bar. "Aw, Eira, if you wanted some attention, you could have just said something."

I snorted and went back to cleaning my glasses. "Not even in your dreams."

"I'll make it worth your while, I promise."

I turned my back to him. "Get lost, Andariel."

He smirked in my ear and kept his voice low. "I could pretend to be my older brother for a night."

"How dare he," the voice growled.

My eyes grew wide and my body locked up. *He did not just say that. He did not just say such an awful thing to me.* Rage boiled up within me, releasing me from my state. I spun around and slammed my fist into his "pretty" face. He stumbled back into the shelves of glassware and liquor. Glasses and bottles crashed to the floor, and the commotion brought Raikidan and Rylan rushing over, but I didn't care. I was too furious.

Throwing the glass in my hand at Andariel, I stormed passed Azriel, who had also rushed over to figure out what was going on, and headed for the back before I really lost it.

I turned a corner and leaned against the wall when I felt I was far enough away from everything. I held myself tightly and held a hand over my mouth as I tried to cope with the chaotic feelings raging inside me. How could he do that to me? That wasn't fair at all.

"Eira?" I didn't look up when Raikidan called. "Eira, are you all right?"

"I'll be fine."

"Do you want to talk about it?"

I shook my head. "I just want to be alone to sort this all out."

"Don't bottle this up."

He placed a hand on my shoulder. "You sure?"

I nodded and it sounded like he was going to say something, but Azriel interrupted him. "Raikidan, you head back up front. I'll take care of this."

Raikidan sighed and walked off.

"Azriel, I don't want to talk about it," I said

"Tell me what he said to you. I've already kicked him out, so I might as well know why."

I looked away. I didn't want to talk about it…

He placed his hands on my shoulders and stood in front of me. "What did he say to you that upset you so much?"

I hesitated. "He… he told me he could pretend to be Tannek for a night…"

Azriel pulled me into a tight embrace. My body shook. It was such a cruel joke. It wasn't fair. "He won't be allowed back here. Not after that stunt. He had no right to say that to you."

I didn't respond. There was just too much pain.

After a minute or two, he pulled away. "I'm going to send you home."

"But I've only been here for two hours."

"And that took a lot out of you. I was planning on sending you home soon anyway, so I might as well now with all this crap going on."

I nodded and headed for the office. "Okay, I'll get my things."

"I'll let Rylan know so he can drive you home."

"Thanks…"

Rylan pulled the car up in front of the house and I climbed out. I didn't say anything to him before shutting the door, and I didn't say anything to anyone as I made my way through the house to my room. Ryoko attempted to ask me why I was home already, but I just shut my bedroom door and tossed myself face down on my bed.

I wanted to sleep, run away from everything, but I found myself turning my head and staring at my nightstand. I crawled over and opened the top drawer. Reaching into the far back, I pulled out an envelope and sat back on the bed before opening it up. I pulled out a handful of old pictures and a folded-up piece of paper. A knot formed in my throat. A man with olive-tan skin, dark hair, and dual set of ears appeared in them all. "Tannek…"

They were all of either him or him with me. We looked so… happy…

"Smile, will you?"

"It's not going to bite you."

"You're strange, but, so am I, so I guess that's why we work so well together."

Unfolding the piece of paper that was with the pictures, I scanned the symbols scribbled everywhere and the pain in my chest increased.

"What's that?"

"A song I'm attempting to write."

"Attempting?"

"I have the instrumentals down, but I can't seem to get the lyrics just right."

"Oh, well then I guess I'll leave you alone now."

"Wait, maybe you can help. Rylan said once you were good at this."

It was the original copy of the song we wrote together. The one he sang at my celebration…

"You can't read, can you?"

"You going to make fun of me too?"

"No, of course not."

"Why?"

"Why would I? It's definitely not the worst thing in the world."

"Well, I can't write either, so I can't help you."

"But I've seen you writing before. Well, writing some odd symbols, at least. Is that how you read and write?"

"Yes."

"How about you teach me it? Then we can do this together."

"You really want to learn?"

"Yeah. It could be like our own secret code."

"Others know it, Dingbat."

"Well then I'll just be part of this elite club of yours."

"You're stupid."

I went back to staring at the photos, which was a mistake. They brought back all the memories I had with him. It brought back everything…

"Eira, over here!"

"Chickadee, look at this."

"Hey, don't do that…"

"It's okay to tell me, Eira."

"I'm here for you."

"Look out!"

"Eira… I…"

The pain my chest tightened and I curled up with everything tucked in under me. "Tannek… you deserved better…"

18
CHAPTER

My dagger's blade slid across the whetstone with ease and I tested the sharpness, a smile spreading across my lips in approval. I didn't use them a lot, but it was good habit to keep them in tip-top shape in case the need changed. My head tilted when my communicator went off. *I wonder who that could be.*

Attaching it to my head, I answered without checking the number, "Hello?"

"Babe, I got something important for you," Aurora's voice came from the other end. "It's about that special dig you asked of me some time ago. Check your planner."

My brow furrowed and I retrieved my digital planner. Starting it up, I found a new file waiting for me. Tapping it, the file opened and I almost dropped the device in shock. "Aurora, is this really…"

"Yeah," she said. "When you asked me to look into it, I thought your request was a bit strange. I knew dragons had tough exteriors, but I figured any old gun could harm them. I didn't expect there to be an actual gun out there designed specifically for destroying them."

I stared at the plans. After Raikidan recovered from his near-death experience around the fall, I had Aurora look into what could have harmed him so badly. My experience with him and the other dragons told me a slashing weapon would have a harder time against their hardened scales, even the less protective underside ones. Back in the days when humans and dragons warred, humans used fine piercing-type weaponry or magic to take down their larger opponents. As it stood even now, basic bullets and rail gun ammunition couldn't hold up to their toughened exteriors. Because of this, I had always wondered how Zarda could force the dragons into cooperating with his demands, whatever they were.

"You know what that demand was."

"Not now."

I flipped through the data. This had to be how. Or some sort of threat around it. The damage done to Raikidan—the way the ammunition tore into him—it wasn't like any weapon I'd ever seen before.

"Thanks, Aurora. I'm going to need to speak to a few dragons in the Underground about this."

"I figured that would be the case, so I've already started to gather some."

"Appreciate it. I will be down once I collect the dragons here."

We cut the connection and I went searching for the dragons who resided in my home. I found Corliss and Mana speaking in the living room. Ryoko waited by the door. All three turned their attention to me.

"Corliss, I'm going to need you for a talk with the other dragons," I said. "It's an important development that concerns all of you."

He nodded, his expression growing serious. "All right."

Mana pointed to herself. "Do you need me there, too? I was going to go shopping with Ryoko."

I smiled. "You go have fun. I'm sure Corliss will fill you in after."

"Thanks!" She kissed Corliss on the cheek and then ran off with Ryoko.

Corliss looked my way. "If you need Raikidan, he's downstairs using the heavy bag."

"Good, we'll grab him on the way, then."

I led him down into the basement, where Raikidan's heavy breathing filled the air. We found him punching away on the weighted bag hanging from the ceiling, sweat glistening on his arms and bare chest.

"You're welcome to ogle. No one would blame you."

"Stop."

"How long have you been at this?" I asked him.

Raikidan jumped and whirled around. The heavy bag swung at him and he narrowly dodged. I stifled a laugh and he pointed at me with narrowed eyes. "You did that on purpose."

"No, but it was funny."

He grunted and stopped the bag from swinging. "I wasn't paying attention to how long. Thirty minutes, an hour? I don't know."

I shrugged. "Okay. Well I'm interrupting your workout to—"

"Strength training." Raikidan held up his arms, giving us a perfect view of his muscular physique. My eyes traveled along the corded muscles stretching and flexing along his sculpted body.

"Oh, the things you could do on that body."

I tried not to react to bits of mental images her words put into my head. *"I said stop it."*

"Oh don't be like that. I know what you're fighting."

Raikidan's arms dropped to his side. "I don't need to work out. I do need to keep my strength up to keep trouble away from you."

I rolled my eyes. "Sure, whatever. Doesn't change the fact I need you to put a shirt on and follow us to the Underground for an important meeting."

Raikidan looked at himself. "I don't see why I need a shirt for that, but okay."

Corliss chuckled. "It's so she won't be distracted."

My eyes narrowed and I punched him in the arm. "Don't start with that."

He smirked and went to open the secret door. "I'm just stating a fact."

"He's right."

My cheeks warmed. "Shut up."

"Was that for me or him?"

"What do you think?"

"Just him, good."

"I hate you."

Corliss chuckled some more, his eyes indicating he was taking my words as a lack of denial. I wanted to deny it, with every fiber of my being, but I couldn't, because he wasn't wrong. *That would be a bit of a distraction…*

The voice hummed a bit and I blocked her out. I didn't want to deal with her either on this.

Corliss led the way through the tunnel until we came to the sewers. He let me pass, and I set a brisk pace to the Underground. Upon arriving, Aurora jumped out of her computer station and led us to a meeting room where the dragons had gathered, handing me a small chip before leaving me to handle the complex situation.

Dragons of all colors sat in the room, including a few black dragons. Red Dragon and Velsara Clan leader, Zaith, along with Xaneth and her black dragon mate, Anahak, sat together. Raikidan and Corliss' full-black-scaled cousin, Rennek, even sat in the room. He and his mother, Salir, popped in on occasion, offering insight outside the city walls. The other dragons in the room I didn't know on a personal level, but those not from Zaith's clan had been recruited in some way.

Xaneth smiled at me as I approached. "It's good to see you, Eira."

"You too, Xaneth."

She frowned. "You look troubled. I suppose this meeting is that important?"

I placed the chip Aurora handed me into a receptacle on the table and turned on the hologram display. "Can one of you tell me how exactly Zarda managed to force all dragons into cooperating under a pact?"

Many of the dragons looked at each other, confused by my question. I guessed they didn't know the specifics, just that they were to follow the rules of the pact for their own safety. The dragons I was sure knew the answer were made obvious by their behavior. I watched Zaith's fingers curl on the table, and the jaws of Xaneth and Anahak set firm.

Holding eye contact with them, I activated the data on the chip and displayed a gun design, a three-dimensional construction of the weapon. "Does it have something to do with this?"

Xaneth's eyes went wide, but I received no response.

"Or, how about this?" I changed the data to a more advanced gun.

Corliss leaned on the table, as did a few other dragons. Raikidan stiffened next to me, and Zaith's eyes narrowed. "Where did you find these?"

"Due to a situation that transpired a few months ago, I had a technician do some digging for me in her free time. This was the last thing I thought we'd find, and it brings up more questions than answers. So, what do you know?"

Xaneth's shoulders sagged. "I'll explain. About ninety years ago,

Zarda approached many dragon colonies and tried to persuade us to swear allegiance to him. None of us wanted anything to do with his offer, so he resorted to threats. He spoke of a weapon that could pierce even the strongest dragon scales. Most of us brushed it off. No weapon like that had existed since the War of End. Then, eighty-six years ago, he proved it was no idle threat."

Xaneth's eyes filled with sorrow and Raikidan tensed beside me. "A dragon fell to the power of this weapon. It took her down so quickly, the other dragons around her couldn't think to save her. Due to our limited numbers after the War of End and Great War, we had no choice but to agree to the terms."

"What were the terms?" I asked.

Rennek shook his head. "Beyond going into hiding, no one knows. A dragon from the North Hyberia Clan took care of the specifics. The dragon killed had come from that clan, so it made sense."

My gaze focused on the displayed gun. *So that's how—*

Raikidan suddenly left my side and walked out of the room. My brow furrowed. "Raikidan?"

Xaneth's hands flew up to her mouth. "No…"

My heart stopped. *Wait, she can't mean…* My eyes snapped to Corliss, who stood now with his hands in his pockets, his expression subdued.

"It was Xephrya who died."

My blood ran cold. How could I have not realized? Raikidan told me she was killed by Dalatrend soldiers. *I should have—* I ran out after him.

Raikidan hadn't gone far, a few yards down the hall. He leaned against the wall, his arms crossed and his head down. I placed my hand on his arm, noting the tenseness of his muscles. "Rai?"

"I'm fine."

"No, you're not."

"I will be fine, how about that?"

I frowned. "I'm sorry… I didn't take the time to think this all out and put two-and-two together. I wouldn't have involved you in this, had I known." He didn't say anything so I retracted my touch, my eyes finding the floor as shame burned through me. "Why don't you go home and do something calming? I'll finish up here."

I turned to head back into the meeting room. Raikidan reached out and grabbed my hand. "Don't blame yourself. I didn't know this was all connected. I knew the soldiers had a gun that could kill her. I suspected it was the same gun that almost killed me. But I never thought there was a connection between her death and the pact. I didn't care much about it when my father told me of the pact's creation, to the point I forgot about it until you sent me away over the summer. I'm just not over her loss. She meant everything to me. I won't let you take blame for something that isn't your fault."

Except… it just might be…

"Don't go there."

"I can and will. Everything is connected."

"It's too coincidental."

"Maybe, but you heard what was said in there. It all matches up."

"Eira, please," Raikidan begged.

"You should go clear your head." I slipped out of his grip and headed back into the meeting room.

The other dragons gazed at me expectantly upon entering, but I didn't look at anyone in particular. I took up my position at the table and had the hologram display both weapons we had files on. I did notice how withdrawn Zaith had become all of a sudden. He appeared lost in his own mind.

Corliss leaned over to me and kept his voice low. "Will he be okay?"

I nodded. "He just needs some time. I've sent him home." Corliss nodded and pulled away, allowing me to continue the meeting. "We need to get back to the matter at hand. These two weapons are the only ones on file my technician found, and they're vastly different. Eighty-six years is a good amount of time for technology to improve, but the newer one is too advanced for that amount of time. Even with access to dragon DNA, there should have been some plans between the two designs. Or even data of some sort."

"Are you sure there's nothing?" Anahak asked. "Maybe your technician missed it."

I shook my head. "She's been looking into this for months, and she doesn't give me information without doing all the research she can."

Corliss leaned on the table. "I'm not sure knowing how they got to this newest model matters. They have it. And while I can guess the first design had power, if it could take Xephrya out without issues, we both know the destructive force this new design has."

Xaneth looked at us. "You've seen it used?"

Corliss and I glanced at each other and then I spoke, "It was used on Raikidan." Several dragons gasped. "We barely managed to save him. It's not a weapon we want to dance around lightly."

Someone new entering the room pulled my attention away from the hologram display. I took great interest in the well-dressed North Tribe shaman of dark complexion who now stood in the room. "Can we help you?"

She nodded. "Someone would like to speak with you."

Before I could say anything, a small crystal sailed through the air at me. I caught the clear quartzite, and my heart skipped a beat when the crystal pulsed in my hand, like a heartbeat. *A spiritual crystal?*

The shaman left without a word. Everyone in the room focused back on me. I wasn't sure what to do with it. I'd never used one before, though I'd learned a small bit about them over the past year. In my years spent with the West Tribe shamans, the large one in town had been the only one I'd seen, and only Maka'shi and a select few shamans had the okay to use it.

The crystal pulsed some more, and then a spiritual field exploded from it. It took me by surprise and others around me jumped back, even though they couldn't sense the field—only a trained shaman could feel that. Then, a new person appeared by my side. A familiar, older man with flame-red hair and green eyes. *Right, spiritual crystals can give spirits a temporary form, like that swordsman, Lazei, who protects that Library entrance.* "Hello, Pyralis."

He smiled at me. "Good afternoon, Eira. I thought you'd like some input on this weapon."

My brow rose with interest. "You can help with this?"

The older dragon touched the hologram, though it didn't react, and he huffed. I had to suppress a laugh. "This weapon was used on us dragons during the War of End."

My heart sank and eyes widened. "W—what? You mean this is similar to that ancient technology?"

"No." He turned his gaze on me. "I mean this is the same exact design."

I shook my head. "That's not possible. Weapon technology from that time has been lost since the war."

"No, he's telling the truth."

I caught the tension in the voice's words. *"How do you know?"*

No answer. *Of course.*

Pyralis shook his head. "Not everything is lost from that time. Artifacts thought lost to the ages are uncovered all the time. It's obvious by the sloppy design of the first, Zarda tried his first design prior to finding either a working weapon he managed to reverse engineer, or plans to create his own. We're lucky he isn't using plans based on a design that came about at the end of the war. With this one, there's a chance a dragon can be saved if action is taken quickly enough, but that design, there's no saving them." Pyralis' fist clenched. "I don't know how Zarda found this, but it doesn't bode well for anyone."

"You're right, though this shouldn't come as a surprise. Zarda will stop at nothing to have Lumaraeon. He'll even destroy her if it means no one else can have her." My fist slammed down on the table. "That slimy son of a—" I took a deep breath to calm myself. "Getting angry won't help. Thank you for the information, Pyralis. It's invaluable." I smirked. "Of course, for a dead dragon, you don't do well staying dead."

The dragons around me chuckled. Even he found my claim amusing, and held up his hands. "What can I say, I get bored."

"More like Aeryn is chewing his ear off even in the afterlife, so he needed to get away," a dragon from his clan mumbled.

Pyralis pointed at him with narrowed eyes, though the upturned corners of his lips gave him away, and I laughed. He then vanished, and the pulsing from the crystal died down to nothing. "No goodbye? Rude."

"Took the words right out of my mouth."

The dragons chuckled some more.

I deactivated the hologram. "I think we've beaten this horse enough. I don't have anything else to share, so you're all welcome to leave."

They all murmured their thanks and filed out of the room. I noticed Zaith's withdrawn demeanor remained—he hadn't reacted to Pyralis' presence or said anything before leaving. I flagged Xaneth down. I needed to know what was up.

"Nosey."

"Don't tell me you don't you want to know, too."

"Never said I didn't."

Corliss leaned over to me. "I'm going to go check on Raikidan to make sure he's okay."

I nodded. "Good luck. I'll return once I tie up loose ends."

He patted me on the shoulder and left, leaving Xaneth and me alone in the large room.

She smiled at me. "Need something from me?"

"I wanted to know if Zaith is okay," I said. "He's acting rather withdrawn since I asked about the pact."

Xaneth frowned and search for a place to sit, motioning me to follow when she located two chairs. She took a deep breath. "He would have been fine had we not realized it'd come about at the expense of Raikidan's mother. Zaith is… remembering his own mother's loss. Father, too. Well, adopted parents technically, but it was always easy to forget that part."

My eyes softened. "Adopted?"

She nodded. "She found him one day, newly hatched, maybe a few days old at most, wandering alone. None of the clutches at the time were missing eggs, so it was assumed he'd come from a pair not from to our clan. Possible egg abandon, assuming he'd never hatch."

I chewed my lips. "If I may ask, how did she die?"

Xaneth hesitated, her eyes giving away the pain she kept controlled. "She was a victim of the Purge." My blood ran cold. "Her mate was so torn by grief he rampaged through the wilds, killing any Crimson Sanctuary member he found, until his body gave out and he drew his last breath."

"The Purge happened six centuries ago. Zaith doesn't act much older than Raikidan. How old was he at that time?"

"Around a century. Stricken with grief at the loss of both parents, he fell into a deep slumber. A type of hibernation state we dragons can go into. It reduced his aging tremendously. He only woke up two centuries ago."

That explained a lot. "What were his parents' names?"

"You already know."

"What?"

"Taiegh and Velsara."

My eyes widened. "W—what was her name?"

Xaneth smiled. "Pyralis' daughter, Velsara. She was a remarkable female. We renamed the wilds to honor her."

I looked down at my lap. That explained why I'd seen so much pain in Pyralis' eyes when he spoke her name. I figured it was best to let Xaneth go now, but something stopped me. Something in the back of my mind nagged me about the information given to me.

"Think harder."

"Why?"

"Important answers lie deep within."

"Like?"

Silence. *Of course… Wait…* That nagging had to do with Velsara and her death. *The timing specifically…*

Xaneth tilted her head. "What's on your mind?"

I chewed my lip. "Sorry, Velsara's death has me—why did she die in the Purge?"

Xaneth held my gaze for a moment, her eyes soft. "You really don't know anything about her?"

My brow furrowed. "Should I?"

"Velsara was the last shaman Ambassador."

My posture straightened. Shva'sika told me the last Ambassador was a proud halfling. "That means…"

Xaneth nodded. "She wasn't full dragon—rare in their existence, but not impossible to exist, as some try to claim. Pyralis took a human mate—nu-human, to be exact. And that made her a target of the Crimson Sanctuary."

I leaned on my legs. This explained those two gravestones I saw by Pyralis' resting bones when I had visited the clan over the summer. And why the dragon clan had allied with the South Tribe.

"And Velsara took Zaith as her son because—"

"Because she had a kind heart." Xaneth frowned. "And she had two failed pregnancies prior to finding Zaith. She saw him as a sign from the gods and took him in as her own. Zaith couldn't have been more loved."

Her gazed lowered to the ground and she sighed. "It's why my heart aches to see Zaith so skeptical of human intentions now. That loss has changed him in ways… I wish I could go back in time and stop it all from happening."

I cringed when pain pulsed in my head.

"Where you going?"

"I have to do something!"

"No, Mother. They'll kill you."

"Zaith, I cannot allow them to continue to do this. I failed to stop them before. I cannot repeat that mistake."

I held my head. What was all this?

A gunshot ran in my ears—blood pooled on the ground.

"Velsara!"

"I... sorry, Taiegh. I failed. I'm sorry, Zaith. I ⌐—"

Xaneth placed her hand on my shoulder and I jumped. Her face creased with concern. "Are you okay?"

I shook my head. "Yeah, sorry. You were all okay with Pyralis' choice of mate?"

She nodded, a smile on her lips. "Some were unsure about it, but most of us didn't have any reason to see it as a bad thing. The two were happy."

I needed to change the subject a bit. This conversation wasn't making me feel good.

"Don't avoid this."

"Zaith doesn't speak like the rest of you. Did he pick that up from one of his parents?"

Xaneth regarded me for a moment and then nodded. "Taiegh came from the Sarget Morass, southwest of the clan's location. Velsara picked it up, and that's where Zaith got it from. We dragons are stubborn in our ways, so the rest of us didn't catch this, but Zaith also didn't lose it when he became the last one. I find it quite fitting for his personality."

I chuckled. "I'm going to agree with you on that. Another question. Velsara's adoption of Zaith... is that why he leads the clan now?"

She shook her head. "No. We remained leaderless after Pyralis passed. Most clans don't need a leader, as long as they worked well on keeping peace amongst themselves. Our clan has that cohesion, so it worked. When Zaith woke from his slumber and took the time to adjust, he needed a purpose, else we feared he'd sleep again. The clan decided to appoint him leader, and he took to it well, though he tried to refuse at first."

My brow rose. "Took to it well? Are we talking about the same dragon here?"

She grinned. "I didn't say he was perfect. He's young and learning."

"He should learn faster," I muttered.

Xaneth laughed. "He'll start to leave you alone, dear. Don't worry. You fit a profile of female he likes. He should wait for his destined mate instead of getting impatient, but most males his age are too bull-headed to listen to us wiser dragons."

"Bull-headed doesn't begin to cut it!"

I eyed her. "Not that I don't agree, but you sound convinced I'm not his, and he's hiding that truth."

She gave me a knowing smile. "I have my reasons to believe otherwise."

My eyes narrowed. "Don't even go there."

"Oh yes, please go there and convince our girl here how bull-headed she's being!"

"Shut up."

Xaneth's expression remained the same, her green eyes sparkling, her mischief clear, and she stood. "I should get going. I don't doubt Anahak is going crazy trying to corral the little ones."

My brow rose. "I haven't kept you long."

"You underestimate the power of seven whelps." Her eyes softened. "And Anahak struggles to be firm with them. It's one weakness I love to hate."

I snickered. "Go rescue him, then. Thank you for speaking with me."

"You're welcome." She hugged me. "And if you need anything, and I mean *anything*, just come to me. I'll do my best to help."

"Help her with her male suitor issue!"

"Knock it off!"

I smiled at Xaneth. "I'll try to remember that."

She patted me on the cheek and headed off, though she stopped in the doorway and glanced back at me. "Trust your heart, and *her* words, dear. Neither led you astray last time."

She left before I could question her farther. *What did she mean by* "her" *words?*

"You know the answer."

My brow furrowed. *"You?"*

No answer. I sighed and decided to head to Aurora's station to return the chip. I'd try to give back this spiritual crystal as well, and then check in on Raikidan. As I did, I attempted to process all the information thrown at me.

What did Xaneth mean by "her words?" Did she know about the voice? *No, she couldn't…* How would that even be possible?

My head began to ache. Things were getting more and more confusing by the minute.

"They wouldn't be if you'd just accept the truth."

"And what truth is that?"

Silence. *Of course.* I carried on, my mind cycling on with more questions than answers.

Words flashed through my mind, and an assigned voice whispered them in my ear as I touched the open Eternal Library access book beside me. The spiritual crystal handed to me earlier rubbed against my skin as I moved it between two fingers of my free hand. I'd attempted to return it, but the shaman who had handed it to me insisted I keep it. She even gave me a silk bag to carry it in, to keep it and anyone near it safe.

I decided it would be best to learn more about spiritual crystals. I knew those not experienced with spiritual energy could be harmed by them when they were active, and they helped spirits take on a corporeal form, with a few limitations, as well as allow shamans to communicate with spirits without requiring them to cross the plains, but that was the extent of my knowledge.

Upon arriving home, I'd planned to check on Raikidan, but found out from Corliss that he hadn't come home yet. Corliss decided to go searching for him, but I figured Raikidan needed time alone and chose not to join him. I came up to my greenhouse to get some quiet time to study the crystal.

I held the crystal up to my face. I'd learned quite a bit in my studying, and now thought I had enough knowledge to try to activate it. I just needed to link a spirit to it. *I hope Xephrya will be willing to assist.* I wanted to speak with her anyway, to possibly get some advice about helping Raikidan.

Taking a deep, controlled breath, I focused on the crystal and pushed my spiritual energy down through my hands and into the object. The gem glowed blue-white for a moment and then returned to its clear color. Then nothing. I pursed my lips and searched the entry again to figure out where I'd gone wrong.

I jumped when the crystal suddenly pulsed like a heartbeat, just as it was supposed to when a spirit attached, and a soft chuckle filled the air. "Give me a minute to respond to the call, would you?"

Before me, a sultry, red haired nu-human woman appeared. She had spectacular light green eyes and freckles scattered across her light skin. I smiled sheepishly. "Sorry. The book didn't say anything about a possible delay. Should have thought about that."

Her eyes twinkled and she sat down in front of me. "I know. I couldn't resist teasing you."

"Thank you for coming here. I figured you'd be okay with me trying this out on you."

She nodded. "I am. I wanted to speak to you anyway, so it works out for us both."

I took interest in this. "What can I help you with?"

She took a deep breath, showing certain physical habits didn't go away even when you were dead. "I needed to give you confirmation about how I died. It was at Zarda's hand, and it was by the prototype weapon."

She shook her head. "It wasn't nearly as powerful as the one he now has access to and almost killed my son with, but it had a more toxic bullet." She paused for a moment. "Pyralis mentioned a weapon Zarda hadn't found. I fear that even if that's not the case, he could make it. It's a weapon that's as powerful as the second design, but uses ammunition as toxic as the first." Her eyes fell to her lap and she started to shake. "I'm sorry. This is all my fault."

I reached out to her and lifted her chin. "Don't say that."

Her eyes welled up with tears. "I'm the reason Rizgar made the pact." *That name.* "I'm the reason my youngest son almost died the same way I had. I'm the reason y—"

I hushed her by placing my thumb over her lips. "No. I'm the reason Raikidan almost died. I brought him here. I'm the reason he fights these battles. His near death is my fault."

Xephrya removed my finger and cupped my cheek. "I'm the one who set this all in motion. *Everything.*" She held my gaze. "You know what I mean by everything."

I pulled away and averted my gaze. I didn't want to talk about that.

"Stop running from this. You won't find answers if you don't face everything."

Xephrya sighed. "I know this topic is difficult for you, Eira. But ignoring what we are does nothing for us. I know, I tried."

My eyes flicked back to her, but she was no longer looking at me.

"I'm a rare occurrence in dragons. I had some psychic abilities, of the Seer-sight variety. I had a twin sister, but she didn't make it past her first few hours after hatching with me. I was so small from sharing an egg, my parents didn't think I'd make it, either." She lifted her gaze. "I've seen things that others didn't believe. I tried to pretend I didn't have these abilities. I tried to run from the visions I had. But it didn't stop anything, and eventually I learned to embrace what I was, even if others didn't. My life improved once I did this."

My gaze faltered and she rested her hand on mine. "What you are isn't wrong. I don't know everything you've gone through in life, but I can see that whatever Zarda did when creating you, he made things more complicated and confusing. All the answers aren't right there in front of you like they should be."

Before I could say anything, the door to the house opened.

"That's Raikidan. I should go so he doesn't get upset. Please tell him the truth about you. I promise, you won't regret it." She began to fade. "And, when he is ready, I will speak with him."

Her form disappeared and the pulsing in the crystal ceased. I looked up from gazing at the quartzite when Raikidan's voice rang out, "Eira?"

He peered in, his head weaving.

"You can come in, Raikidan."

He entered, searching a bit more before spotting me, and approached. "The others said you were up here studying or something."

My gaze fell to my book and I nodded. "Something like that. How are you feeling?"

"Better, now that I've had time to think." He smiled as he sat down next to me. "Thank you for giving me that space. I wasn't thrilled Corliss came looking for me."

I shook my head. "Give him a break. He was concerned. You can't blame him too much."

He looked less than thrilled. "I'd still have rathered he not bother me."

I gave him a sly look. "And if I had come looking for you instead of him?"

"I still would have preferred no one come after me"—he avoided eye contact—"but I guess I wouldn't have minded if you came looking for me."

"Lying shit. He'd have loved it if you found him."

Raikidan pointed to the book. "What are you learning about?"

I smirked. I couldn't find it in me to disagree with the voice. "After you left, we discussed the weapon some more. Pyralis decided to get bored and pay us a visit using one of these spiritual crystals. He also had some valuable information to share, so it worked out, but it made me want to learn more about these. I didn't get the chance to learn much while staying at the West Tribe."

"How are you doing with that?"

"Great. Was a lot easier to learn than I expected. I even had the chance to use the crystal."

His brow rose. "On who?"

I hesitated on telling him the truth, but then decided it was best not to lie. "Your mother."

Raikidan's expression dropped. "Oh…"

"She wanted to talk to me as it was, so it worked out."

"What did you talk about?"

"Her. Me." I shrugged as I leaned back on my arm. "Simple stuff."

His brow rose. "Really? That's your answer?"

I laughed. "Well, what exactly do you want to know?"

He avoided my gaze. "I don't know…"

My head tilted. He did know, he just didn't want to say. I placed the crystal on the book. "You sure?"

Raikidan still wouldn't look at me. "I guess…" He sighed. "I would like to speak to her, too."

I reached out and touched his hand. "Are you sure you're ready?"

He finally met my gaze, determination burning in his eyes. "No, but I want to talk to her anyway."

"If that's what you want, then I'll bring you to see her." I went about positioning myself in front of him and took his hands in mine.

"We're not going to use the crystal?"

I shook my head. "No, not this time. Now take a deep breath, close your eyes, and relax. I'll do the rest."

He did as asked and I centered my mind and body. Projecting my spirit energy through my hands into him, I mingled the two energies and separated us from our bodies. The transition went seamlessly, and I waited a moment before giving Raikidan the okay to open his eyes.

He took in the grey version of our world. "Is this what the spiritual plane looks like?"

I stood. "This is the Plane of Between. It's the step before the spiritual plane. It's not ideal to bring the untrained over to the spiritual plane. I'm going to go out on a limb and say you didn't go to either when we almost lost you to that gunshot wound."

"Not that I remember." Raikidan also stood, looking around. "Where is she?"

"I have to call for her." A pulse of spiritual energy left me as I called out, "Xephrya, we'd like to speak with you, if that's okay."

The two of us stood there for a few moments. Raikidan started to fidget and I had to calm him. I understood his impatience and anxiety, but it wouldn't help.

I turned when footsteps approached behind us, and smiled at Xephrya. "Thank you for answering."

She smiled back. "I told you I would."

Raikidan remained motionless, his eyes wide and his jaw tight. His mother didn't give him time to process her presence. She reached out and touched both sides of his face. "Look at you. You've grown in these past few decades."

His eyes softened and he wrapped his arms around his mother so tightly I thought he might break her in half, if that were possible to do to a spirit. "I'm sorry... Forgive me..."

Xephrya patted Raikidan on the back, soothing him like any mother would in her position. "There's nothing to forgive. No one could have stopped what happened. I'm just glad you hadn't met the same fate."

I stepped away. Xephrya turned her gaze, her eyes pleading me to stay, but this conversation wasn't meant for me to be a part of. I found a spot to sit down and waited, though I didn't remain alone for long.

Someone sat down next to me and my brow rose when I turned my head their way. "Mom?"

She smiled, the corner of her green eyes crinkling. "Hello, dear."

"How can I help you?"

"What, I can't visit with you without needing anything?" I pursed my lips and raised an eyebrow. She laughed. "All right, I just wanted to make sure you're doing okay. A lot of information was thrown at you."

I shrugged. "I'm fine." She made the same expression as me just a moment ago and I in turn laughed. "Really, Mom, I'm fine."

She rested her hand on mine. "You've avoided a few topics. Ones you've avoided before—"

I sighed. "I don't want to talk about that."

"You can't keep running, Eira. It won't solve anything."

"Facing it won't, either."

My mother reached out and brushed my bangs out of my eyes. "You are special. I wish you'd see that."

My jaw set. "If I'm so special, why don't you explain to me how? Everyone keeps thinking I'm supposed to do something amazing, when I can't. I don't have some special power that brings peace. I'm not what everyone thinks I am."

Her eyes softened. "You have brought so many together for a common cause. You've brought hope to the hopeless. Y—"

"Anyone can do that. It's not hard to get others to work together if they have a common enemy. That's not some special power."

"If you'd trust in her, you'd see your power is much deeper than that."

My brow furrowed. "Her. Everyone keeps saying *she* can help. Who the hell is 'she?'" My mother's mouth remained shut. "Why is it no one answers that question? No one tells me anything. They expect me to know these answers, when I don't! What does everyone know that I don't?"

Tightness formed in my chest. I blew out a strained breath. My and Raikidan's time was up. I got to my feet. "To be honest, I think everyone has mistaken me for someone else. We may be the same type of person, but she clearly is the special one everyone is looking for."

"That's not true…" she said in a quiet voice.

I continued my way to Raikidan instead of arguing with her. I didn't have the time to. "Raikidan, I'm afraid we have to go back."

His eyes swept over me and his brow furrowed, his private words with his mother catching in his throat. "Eira, are you okay?"

"I'm fine."

His expression remained the same, but he didn't try to argue.

"I'm sorry that I can't keep us here longer."

"It's okay."

Xephrya grabbed my wrist and pulled me next to her son. "You two keep each other safe, you hear?"

We looked at each other, smiled, and then nodded at her. She smiled and then reached out for us both, entwining my hand with his. Her smile brightened and she pulled away. Raikidan and I peered at our hands and then each other. My cheeks warmed a bit as we pulled away, our eye contact going elsewhere. *She would try that.* Xephrya pouted.

Not wanting her to try again, and not having time to deal with such antics, I placed my hand on his shoulder and connected our spirits. "Take a deep breath, Raikidan, and close your eyes."

His gaze lingered on his mother before doing as I asked. Closing my own eyes, I brought us back the living plane, a fresh air filling my lungs the moment our spirits reconnected with our bodies. My eyes opened and I watched Raikidan. He'd opened his eyes before I gave him the okay, and he stared at his lap—his shoulders tense and his fists clenching his pants.

Water dripped down one side of his face and fell into his lap. He rubbed his face with his clenched fist, trying to not show any weakness. My eyes softened. I reached out and cupped his face with both hands, making him look at me. Various emotions plagued his eyes.

I wiped away another tear welling up in his eye with my thumb. "It's okay to grieve."

He tried to look away. "I need to be strong."

I scooted closer until I wormed my way into his lap and pulled his head into my shoulder. I rested mine in the crook of his neck, my voice low, "Showing emotion isn't a sign of weakness. You got me to see that."

Raikidan wrapped his arms around me and held me tight against him. His body shook as, for the first time since his mother's death, he allowed himself to feel everything. I laced my fingers into his hair and buried my face in his neck, showing him I was here for him. His strong scent teased my senses, tempting me to taking it in more.

"You're so perfect for him."

"Please don't start this right now. It's not an appropriate time."

"I think it's plenty appropriate. Since you don't believe you're special."

"Because I'm not. Everyone has mistaken me for someone else."

"I wouldn't be here if that were the case."

"Thank you," Raikidan mumbled into my shoulder, preventing me from getting any sort of clarification. "I won't ever be able to forgive myself for not being able to save her. I get no second chance there. But I've sworn to protect you." His grip on me tightened. "I never thought I'd have to do so from yourself, but now that I've almost lost you to even that, I won't make that mistake again."

"The path to healing requires you to forgive yourself. I learned this." I nuzzled my face in his neck. "Your mother doesn't blame you—I don't blame you—so neither should you. It's not easy, but you have to try."

"You should blame me."

I chuckled, noting how much he sounded like me. "You aren't responsible for things out of your control. But if you still insist on blaming yourself, I cannot stop you. I can, however, offer up repentance."

"I'm listening."

"Honor your mother's memory by keeping me safe."

"I don't know how that will honor her, but I will do that."

My eyes half closed. *Trust me, it does.*

The greenhouse door flew open, my messenger hawk screeched in fright, and Ryoko's voice boomed through the building. "Laz, Raikidan, you in here? I need some hel—"

The two of us looked at her when she came within eyesight of us and she stopped dead, then pointed behind her and turned around, heading back the way she came. "I'll just go find someone else to help me."

The two of us laughed, Raikidan being the first to speak when we calmed down. "She's not going to let us live that down."

I rested my head in the crook of his neck again. "I don't care."

He held me tighter and returned the gesture. "Same."

"Perfect for him."

I couldn't find the strength to fight her on it. A large part of me didn't want to. I liked the idea of being right for someone. That someone was right for me. But the other side of me, the logical side, couldn't allow me to give in to all of this. There was someone else more perfect for him. *She's probably the one everyone is confusing me with.*

"No one is confusing you with anyone. Now stop it!"

I couldn't find it in me to agree.

CHAPTER 19

With the help of my teeth, I tied off the string of sinew so the leather strips and beads made of bone and horns wouldn't slip off. Once I was sure the string was tightly knotted, I did the same for the other three strings part of the choker I made, and then secured a leather strip around them to hide the knotted ends.

My eyes flicked up at the sky quickly, before finishing off the choker by threading a thick leather string through the wide leather strap on both ends of the choker. It was getting late and I needed to finish this before it was too dark to see. I didn't have time to put this off any more, and I didn't want to work on it in my room at the risk of the recipient seeing it before it was time.

The door leading down into the house opened just as I finished. I tucked my project away and looked up to find Raikidan had poked his head around the door.

"What are you still doing up here?" he asked. "It's getting dark."

I shrugged. "Finishing something."

His head tilted. "What are you finishing?"

I grinned. "Come sit next to me and you'll find out."

An unsure look appeared on his face, but he then gave in to his curiosity and made his way over. Once he sat down, he watched me expectantly. "So, what is this little secret project you've been working on is?"

"First, close your eyes."

His brow knitted. "Why?"

"Because it's a surprise, duh."

He grunted but closed his eyes anyway. Smirking, I slipped in front of him and secured the choker to his neck. Before he could open his eyes, I headed into the house. I was glad Seda had given me such accurate measurements. I had worried it wouldn't fit him.

Closing the door behind me, I got ready for bed and pulled out my Eternal Library book to do some Old Tongue research before actually sleeping. Me'kunar really had found my discovery in Larkren helpful, like he had told me during my celebration. There was so much information to read through now.

I jumped out of my skin when Raikidan touched my shoulder, and he jumped back a little. "Sorry, I didn't mean to startle you."

I shook my head. "It's not your fault. I was so engrossed in my research I didn't realize you were here."

"You're not writing anything down. How can you be researching?"

I tapped my head. "It's all up here. I'm just taking in all the new information and then later I'll process it more and write down notes and such."

"You learning anything interesting?"

I nodded. "Oh yeah. Me'kunar found a lot of new things to translate from the Old Tongue find I had in Larkren. He's put the translations into the Library in hopes the rest of us can help piece together their meaning."

"Would this make you a scholar, too?"

I chuckled. "No. I'd have to dedicate my life to this to be considered one."

Raikidan sat down next to me. "Would you want to? When this war is over, that is."

I thought about this. "I'm not really sure what I want to do with my life. I honestly never thought I'd make it to that point."

"Think about it, right now. I highly doubt you want to be a waitress or bartender all your life."

I closed my book and thought carefully. "I don't know. All I've known is war and how to end people's lives. I never really thought I'd have a place in this world."

"Then why fight for this new world?"

"Because… it's the right thing to do. And, you never know, there could be some possibility I'd fit in somewhere."

He watched me carefully as I stared at the cover of my book, and then patted my shoulder. "Then think of something different. Think of something you're capable of doing that isn't part of your created design—something that you'd be happy doing for the rest of your life, however long that might be."

I leaned back into my pillows and held the book to my chest. "I guess… I guess I'd choose to go back to living with the West Tribe. I liked it there, and it was peaceful. I'm also the official Ambassador, so I have that obligation to uphold too." I glanced at the unfinished carving on my nightstand. "I could probably make a living off my woodworking. And I definitely don't want to be one of Azriel's waitresses for my entire life."

I sighed. "But it also depends on Ryder. I gave him my word we'd be together after all of this was over. If he wants to stay here, then I'll have to rethink what to do."

"You'd really do that? You'd change your life for him?"

I nodded. "I may not have chosen to have him as my son, but that doesn't mean I don't care about him. I care for him the best way that I can, and I want him to know what it's like to be part of a family. That's all I've wanted for him. I'd change everything in my life to give him that."

"That's very selfless of you." He smiled. "I don't think you'll have an issue finding your place in this new world we're trying to create."

I forced a smile back. *If only he knew the truth…*

"Now, to ask you about this necklace like I wanted to when you were distracted." He took the choker off and held it up. "Why'd you give this to me?"

Embarrassment ran through me and it made my responding smile seem weak. "Birthday gift."

He blinked. "Birthday?"

"Ebon told me your birthday, so I thought I'd make you something. I know it's a day early, but since you found out I was doing something,

I figured I'd give it to you now." I frowned. "Sorry if it's not all that great of a gift. I didn't really know what else to get you that wouldn't cost me an arm and a leg."

He shook his head. "Don't be sorry. I like it, really. I just didn't expect you to know about my birthday."

I smiled. "Promise?"

He chuckled. "It's nice—and even though it's jewelry, it's masculine enough not to feel weird wearing." He eyed me. "Though, I have a feeling it's not just because it's my birthday you made it."

I found myself unable to keep eye contact with him. "No, that's the reason…"

"Eira, don't be like that. It's okay to tell me."

My cheeks grew hot as I held my book close to my chest and continued to avoid eye contact. "Just… just 'cause I wanted to… I guess…"

He smiled and slid off my bed. "Well, thank you. I'll keep it on the dresser when I can't wear it so it doesn't get damaged."

I smiled back and watched him put the necklace down before shifting to his dragon shape. I had planned to go back to reading, but the way he was looking at me stopped me from doing so. I felt a strange compulsion to move closer and found myself unwilling to fight it.

I put down my book and crawled to the end of my bed. At the same time, Raikidan moved his head closer to me until I reached up and touched his snout.

He exhaled slowly and then closed his eyes as I stared at the spot of his nose I was touching. It wasn't often I was able to do this. My curiosity screamed at me to learn more about him, but logic tried to tell me I needed to go back to studying. Raikidan's eyes remained closed and I found logic changing its mind. *It's as if he wants me to do this.*

I allowed my hand to rub his nose. The scales felt stronger than Rimu's, and it made me curious about his body scales. Did those feel stronger and more durable, too? Or would they feel the same as Rimu's? Was it okay for me to ask these questions? Was it appropriate?

Before I could really answer, my body made its choice. My hands explored his face and kept it up until I ran out of exploration room. I slid off the bed and migrated to the side of his head. Raikidan opened his eyes but didn't stop me, watching me as I carefully touched the hard, plated scales above his eyes.

These scales felt much stronger than the basic ones on his face. I touched the plated scales that covered some of his horns—they had the same tough properties. It was as if these scales had a functional purpose on top of the visual appeal.

Apprehensively, I reached down and touched the large plated scales on his neck and chest. They, too, felt stronger, and as I ducked under him to touch the scales on his neck, I knew they were as well, though they didn't feel to have the same strength as the plated scales.

Even though I didn't reach down to double check, I could tell the scales on his belly were strong, but nowhere near as strong as his body scales, just as he had admitted to me once. They also weren't as polished as his body scales, as if he couldn't get them polished or didn't care to. *Maybe polishing them would draw unwanted attention.*

I looked at the scales on his front leg and noticed how much darker a few of them appeared. I realized it was roughly the same spot as the tattoo he now had, thanks to him being my full-time Guard. I had assumed Raikidan's black scales were as dark as they could possibly get, but apparently I was wrong.

This also posed a new question. Was this normal for dragons? If they got some sort of tattoo in their humanoid form, would it change the color of their scales in some way? It seemed logical, since it appeared their scale color had an effect on their skin tone, but Raikidan was really the only dragon I'd met that had a tattoo or tattoo-like mark on their body, so I couldn't be sure about my hypothesis.

My examination continued.

I gasped when I touched the side of Raikidan's belly and he shifted in response. His hands grabbed a hold of my waist and pulled me onto his lap, my legs straddling his hips. My hands rested on his chest as I failed to understand what was going on.

Raikidan held my gaze for several moments before speaking. "Which do you prefer?"

My brow furrowed. "What?"

"When you look at me, which side of me do you prefer looking at?"

I shook my head. He wasn't making much sense. "Are you asking me to choose between your dragon shape and human shifted shape?"

"Yes. Which side do you prefer?"

"I… I don't have a preference."

"Huh?"

"I don't know what brought this up"—I licked my lips—"but I can't just choose. It doesn't matter what form you take or what color you are. You're Raikidan either way."

He smiled and then pulled me in for a tight hug. "Thank you."

"Um, for what?"

"For accepting me as I am."

I hugged him back. "You're welcome."

He pulled away and looked me in the eye. "Now, I want to tell you something important."

An unsettling feeling fell over me. "Okay…"

"This is something I could get into a lot of trouble telling you if it's ever found out, but I trust you to keep it between us."

"Okay… What is it?"

"The real reason half-colors are so hated."

My brow rose. "Go on."

"Remember when we were at the temple and I told you the gods I worshipped?" I nodded. "Well, I left one out."

I pursed my lips. "Why?"

"Because this god is only known by dragons, and we like to keep it that way. His name is Zion, and he's a dragon.

Zion? I've heard that name before.

"He's a chromatic dragon, to be exact."

I stared at him. "Chromatic? Does that mean…"

Raikidan nodded. "His scales shimmer with the colors of all dragon colors, and he also has the abilities of all dragons. It's said he's the father of all the colors, and that's how we received our abilities."

"A chromatic dragon…" I tried to picture it as well as think on why they kept the knowledge of him so secret and what it had to do with Raikidan being a half-color. "So, how does this tell me why half-colors are so hated?"

"Zion is special to us. So special he has never shown himself to a non-dragon, which is the reason why we have never told any non-dragons about him. He's also the only chromatic dragon to ever exist, and with our kind, it's feared that if enough colored blood is mixed, a chromatic dragon can be created, meaning—"

"Sacrilege." I looked at him sympathetically. "It'd be a sacrilegious dragon color."

He nodded. "And powerful. It's believed this new chromatic dragon could have the same abilities as Zion."

"So there have never been any other chromatic dragons—ever?"

Raikidan shook his head. "No, though…"

He trailed off as he went into thought. I waited a few moments, but when he still didn't continue, I cleared my throat. "What are you thinking about?"

"I remember overhearing my mother talking to my father after she found and searched through an old abandoned library for things to take. She was telling him how she found an old book that was half in our language, and half in another she didn't know. It mentioned chromatic dragons, but since she couldn't decipher other language in the book, she wasn't sure what it was about exactly. I had always thought it was strange she couldn't read it, since she knew every language, but—"

His eyes widened as realization hit him. I spoke the words in his stead. "Except Old Tongue right?"

He nodded. "Yeah."

"Then that book is ancient, and it could have many answers hidden within it. Can you get the book?"

Raikidan sucked air through his teeth. "I'd have to face my father, and there's no guarantee he'd give it up."

I smiled. "Well, if you ever get your hands on it, I can see if I can help. Not sure if I can without Me'kunar's help, but it's worth a shot."

"You won't ask for his help on this?"

I shook my head. "This is between us. Unless you tell me it's okay to involve him, then it stays between us."

"Can he be trusted?"

"He's the only scholar I know who can keep his mouth shut if asked. Why?"

"Then I'll think about it."

I giggled. "You want to know now, don't you?"

His face reddened a little. "Is that a problem?"

"Of course not."

He smiled, and then it went away, his eyes saying he'd thought about something.

I tilted my head. "What is it?"

"Just a thought," he said. "You know some Old Tongue. If I said a word, would you be able to tell me the translation? If you did know it, of course."

"What's the word?"

"*Spekta.*"

"Yes, I know that word. Quite well, actually. It means *spectral*. Why did you think of it?"

"I just remembered that my mother had told my father the word and it had shown up in the book with the chromatic dragons a lot, more than most other words, so she thought it was important. My father brushed it off as her trying to make sense of a language she didn't understand."

I shook my head. "No, she's right to have considered it important. Old Tongue, while, well, old, is predictable. If a word is used often, typically it's important. If the book was talking about dragons, then it had to be related some way. I'm not sure how, but it's the only explainable reason it was there."

Raikidan nodded and went back to thinking, and I decided it was time to go back to the original topic he had brought up. "Raikidan, why did you tell me about Zion? Why didn't you keep it a secret like you were supposed to?"

Raikidan avoided eye contact. "I don't know… I guess… since you can accept me as I am, I thought I could trust you with knowing about him."

I smiled. "It's our secret, then."

He grinned and hugged me.

"Now, if this is some secret sharing time, I'm going to have to say sorry, no secrets from me."

Raikidan gazed at me for a moment. "You sure?"

I pursed my lips. "Well, had you not met Arcadia, I could tell you about her, but she's not really a secret. Just not as well known as other gods due to her sphere of influence."

Raikidan grasped my hand. "Are you positive there's nothing you want to share?"

My lips pressed together as my brow knitted. What did he want me to say?

His thumb slid over the top of my hand. "Show me."

"Show you what?"

"Show me the change."

Oh shit. My body threatened to lock up in its typical defensive response. "I–I don't know what you're trying to say, Rai."

His voice lowered. "Yes, you do. I've seen it before. Show me. Please."

I hesitated. He had to be baiting me. He didn't know anything. *There is no way he knows…* I sighed mentally. Who was I trying to fool? He knew. The way he held my hand—the way he waited so patiently. It was only a matter of time before he found out. I was a fool to think I could keep the truth from him.

My body heated as I let a part of my wall down and allow my hand to transform. Raikidan ran his thumb over my skin when I was done, and I avoided any eye contact. My body burned with uncontrollable shame and embarrassment.

"There's nothing wrong with being part grekeleon, Eira," he finally said.

I stared at him, surprised. With so few species out there with reptilian DNA, I would have expected him to assume I had some basic lizard DNA spliced in, much like Rylan and Raid and their canine DNA.

He held my gaze. "That's what you are, right?"

My gaze lowered. "Y–yes… How did you figure it out?"

"I caught a glimpse when you needed Rylan's help at the range, when you were angry at Zarda for fusing other's DNA with his body."

I waited for more to that answer. There had to be another reason he figured it out. A brief glimpse wouldn't tell him what I was. It would just make him curious.

"And I snuck into your recovery room while you slept after the ordeal with the dam to make sure you were really okay."

I worked my jaw. "How much did you see?"

"The way the skin on your hand is now, it was like that on parts of your face and arms. Your hands looked like this as well. That's how I knew it wasn't my imagination the first time."

I nodded. "Okay."

"You're upset."

"Just forget about it…"

"Eira, I know you didn't want anyone to come in while you were recovering, but I was worried about you. I'm sorry."

"I'm not angry with you, Rai."

"So, you're just upset because of what you are." I stared at the floor and stayed quiet. I really didn't want to talk about this. "Okay, instead of talking about you, tell me how this all worked for your mother. You said she claimed to have loved your father, but if he was grekeleon, he wouldn't have exactly looked human, right?"

I chuckled and shook my head. "You really are stupid."

He growled. "Eira, don't be mean."

I grinned. "Unlike the wogron, the condition that affects the grekeleon doesn't prevent them from shifting back to their human shape. He appeared human around my mom most of the time, instead of a lizard humanoid. Though, she did try to claim she didn't care how he looked either way."

"You didn't call it a curse."

"They don't think of it that way, so why should I?"

"Because it now affects you. You're ashamed of what you are, that's why you hide it."

"I want nothing to do with my father…"

"Just because you share his blood, doesn't mean you're like him." He lifted my chin with his finger. "You make the choices, not your blood. You don't want to be like him, then make choices to be you, without sacrificing any part of you." He smiled. "Besides, if you weren't grekeleon, you wouldn't be Eira, and we couldn't have that."

I smiled. "Thank you."

He shook his head. "No, thank you for being honest with me.

I did my best to keep my smile up. *If only you knew.* I couldn't find it within me to tell him the real truth. It was easier… safer, to let him think this way.

I squeaked when he turned me around suddenly and had me sit in his lap again. "What was that for?"

He grinned. "Because I can."

"You could have just told me to move."

He chuckled. "I didn't want you to move. I just wanted you to turn around."

"Why can't I just sit next to you?"

He wrapped his arms around me. "Because I don't want you to."

My face flushed several shades of red. "Raikidan, you feeling okay?"

He chuckled. "I'm fine. Just relax with me, okay?"

I nodded and the awkward feeling plaguing my body trickled away. It wasn't that bad. We were just sitting here. *There's nothing weird about this, right?*

"Raikidan?"

"Yes?"

"Do you really not mind that I'm a halfling?"

"Of course not. You could be part rabbit or"—he chuckled—"or even half-dragon instead of grekeleon, and I wouldn't care either way. You'd still be Eira."

A smile crept up my face. "Thank you…"

He rested his chin on my shoulder. "You're welcome."

We remained quiet for a few moments. I had a lot on my mind now. Was he really telling me the truth about how he felt? Did he really accept what I was, or at least, what he thought I was? *Can I trust him with knowing the real truth?*

"You're awfully quiet," I said to the voice. *"No input here?"*

"Oh, I have some, but I'm just enjoying this moment."

A strange noise escaped Raikidan's lips, pulling my attention. It was that odd growling purr he had done before. "Raikidan?"

"Hmm?"

For a second I wasn't sure if it was a good idea to ask. "What… what is that noise you make? I've heard a few times from you."

He smiled in my ear. "It's a dragon's sound of content. I'm just… happy."

I smiled a little. "Okay."

That meant every time I had heard it I had done something good for him. I had made him happy, even for just a moment. It was hard for me to do that. I never really seemed to do anything right with him. It was so funny how different we were. *And yet, how similar…*

I smiled when he began to hum. It was the dragon lullaby. The song my mother had always hummed to me when she wanted to cheer me up, and the times I had trouble sleeping, and when… I blinked slowly. She had sung it to me a lot, actually. No wonder I liked it so much.

I relaxed in Raikidan's arms and allowed my eyes to hood. I liked how he sang it. I smiled as my eyes closed more. *I really like the way he sings it.*

CHAPTER 20

I drummed my fingers on the coffee table, staring at my planner. A communicator sat on the table, a speaker plugged into it to allow Aurora to communicate with everyone in the room. I chewed my lower lip as I considered the data she'd sent us.

"Are you sure this is accurate?"

"I wouldn't have shared it with you and the Council if it weren't, Babe," she said, the sound of her clicking computer keys echoing through the call. "The Council is working the moles for clearer answers, but we're certain this human trafficking ring is just as bad as the data shows."

Rylan shifted on the couch. "It's a good thing we bugged those computers, then. No way would we have found out about this."

I tapped my lips. "I'm not so sure. The day I managed to steal Zo's helmet to tap it, Ryder said there was development with an incident they'd been watching. Later, he messaged me to tell me this incident was real, and a big deal. He promised me that once more developed about the situation, he'd relay it to me. I'm wondering if this is the same situation."

"I'll get someone in contact with him to find out," Aurora said.

"This is all well and good, but what does this have to do with us?" Blaze asked. "I mean, yeah, trafficking is bad, but we're fighting a war against Zarda. We're having a hard enough time with that, and now we want to spread our resources thinner to save stolen people we have no big leads on? It doesn't make sense."

Mana looked at him. "Helping people doesn't make sense? Isn't that part of your goal? Make sure *everyone* is free?"

Corliss rested his hand on her thigh. "Yes, but he has a point. We can't fight every battle. It'd be the same as trying to free the human slaves while fighting a war for a free land. Morally they're both right to do, but resources and time make it difficult to pull off both. It sucks we have to make these decisions, but sometimes they're unavoidable."

"It does affect us directly, though," I said, scrolling through the planner data. "We've had several operatives go missing over the course of the year. Two were found dead six months ago. We assumed the military got them and dumped the bodies, since they'd been found together. This data shows they were victims of this trafficking; drugs the cause of their deaths."

Ryoko tilted her head. "I remember those two, but they were a man and woman, neither close in age, either."

I nodded. "From the looks of it, whoever is running this ring is kidnapping people indiscriminately."

"So is this a problem we need to get involved with?" Raikidan asked.

I put the planner down and rubbed my face. "I'm not sure. It's a problem that needs to be dealt with, but Blaze is right. We don't have the resources to devote to this."

I shifted my gaze to Genesis. She'd remained quite this whole time. "What do you think?"

A frown rested on her lips. "I… don't know. This puts us in a precarious situation."

That's when I noticed Mocha pacing. I'd seen her do this every now and then, when her agitation got the better of her, or when she was bored. I suspected it was a result of her cat DNA. I wasn't even sure what type she had. "Mocha, do you have some input?"

She glanced up, realizing everyone was staring at her. "Sorry. This situation has me agitated. Don't mind me."

"I'd rather you talk about it than deal with it on your own."

I watched her hands clench and loosen several times, conflict raging in her eyes. Then she went back to pacing. I frowned.

"I've been given permission to tell you," Seda said. "She feels too worked up to put it into words. It seems the woman you mentioned was part of Mocha's former team."

Ryoko and Genesis gasped, and the others shared startled and concerned glances before staring at Mocha.

"What do you want to do, Mocha?" I asked. If she was this worked up, then she had a personal investment in it.

"I don't know…" She didn't stop moving. "I want to stop these people—to avenge Tel for what they did. But I can't do that on my own, and if we can't get anyone to help me, I'm stuck."

An ethereal figure blinked in behind Mocha for a moment—a woman. Then she disappeared. I glanced over to Shva'sika, who gave me a nod of acknowledgement. Tel wasn't at rest.

"What if," Shva'sika started, "we come up with a small group to look into this? A large-scale investigation wouldn't be doable, but we can't, in good conscience, leave this be. We could talk to the shamans and dragons to see if this is something we can utilize them for. The dragons and some South Tribe shamans, especially, will be useful with their shapeshifting abilities."

I nodded. "That is a good suggestion." I looked to Mocha. "If you want to be part of this, I have no issue with it."

She halted, processing my words, and then turned to Genesis for the approval.

Genesis nodded. "I'll permit it. That's if the rest of Council approves this plan."

Ryoko's ears drooped as she turned her eyes to Mocha. "You wouldn't do this on your own if they said no, right?"

Mocha shook her head. "I'm not that stupid."

I gave a curt nod. "Good. And that goes for the rest of us. This type of situation is too dangerous for one person to tackle. And from now on, I propose no one goes out on the streets alone if it can be helped. Not until we can find out more."

The others agreed. It may be an overkill precaution, but we didn't need anyone snagged due to carelessness.

"I'll relay this to the Council," Aurora said.

"Thank you, Aurora," Genesis said.

The line then cut, leaving us to think about things. Genesis requested that Mocha and Shva'sika follow her to discuss the potential of a small-scale search team. I headed for my room to put away my communicator and planner, as well as get back to carving figurines.

The one I'd nearly finished before this all went down sat on my bed waiting. It was a simple design, but eye-catching. This morning I'd received a tall order of carving requests for several caravans, more than I thought I'd be able to accomplish the way I chose to create. I needed to find a balance between intricate and time-consuming, and simple and quick.

Though, between working at the club, miscellaneous requests at the shop, and performing my duties as a rebel, I wasn't sure if I was going to be able to even do that. *Maybe I should listen to everyone and focus on this as my main source of income.* I did tell Raikidan I had thought about doing this for a living. And it brought in a nice, sizable chunk of income. *But I'd be putting Azriel in a pretty tough spot without me...* I was too nice for my own good sometimes.

I looked up when someone knocked on my door and came in. "Hey, Ryoko, what's up?"

"The military is here," she said. "They want to talk to you."

My brow knitted. "Do you know why?"

She shook her head. "No, they wouldn't say."

I shrugged and figured I'd find out. If I were in trouble, I'd know about it by now.

Entering the living room, I was met with a small squad of soldiers. Zo wasn't with them, like I half expected, but one soldier did stick out to me. He was one of the soldiers I had spoken with when they wanted me to interact with Bone.

"Ah, good, you found her," he said. "Eira, do you remember me?"

"You never told me your name, but, yes, I remember you," I said. "You were around when I was asked to help with a particular issue."

"I apologize. My name is Salin." He smiled. "And we're actually here about that again. We were hoping you could help us once again. You and the other ladies in this house."

"But you can't tell us exactly why, and what for, until we get to the compound, right?"

"It's as if you've done this drill before." He chuckled at his own joke. "And of course, like last time, your other housemates are welcome to come with you if you wish."

"And the recent revelation of my identity isn't a problem?" It was weird they'd ask for my help when they now knew I was a shaman. Honestly, the way the military didn't treat me any differently had crossed my mind many times. Especially when Zo continued to show interest in me and their lenience with my public relationship with Ryder. *Unless they're hoping I'll slip up and divulge some compromising information, it doesn't make much sense.*

Salin smiled. "Well, you've helped us in the past without protest, and we don't need you to be looking like your shaman self, so you tell me."

I chuckled. "Then I guess I can help you."

Ryoko, Shva'sika, Genesis, Mana, and Seda, who was using her cloaking watch to disguise herself, exchanged glances. All four nodded at each other. Ryoko then addressed Salin. "We'll try to help, too."

Salin smiled. "Excellent. Let us know when you're ready to head out."

I looked at Ryoko, who nodded. "We're ready now. It's warm today, so we don't need jackets."

Salin nodded. "Very well. Follow us."

We all filed down the stairs, men included, to the street and into the waiting vehicles. It didn't take us long to reach the compound they had brought us to last time, and right to the same building from our previous visit. Once inside the room that led to the interrogation room, we waited for Salin to brief us on what they needed us for.

He spoke in a low voice with someone, using a discreet communicator before addressing us. "As you've already figured out, we're hoping you ladies can help us with these experiments again. After reviewing Bone's interaction with Eira and Seda, we went back over the data recorded prior to the interaction. It seems Eira's suggestion about his reactions to women were on the right track. After reviewing, we found all issues that arose were with men.

He glanced out to the interrogation room before focusing on us again. "We also had one of Bone's favored female soldiers speak with him for a while. We gathered his reason for attacking all dummies was due to a lack of smell, making it harder for them to differentiate the different dummies like they were supposed to be doing. This has led us to believe they're more instinct-driven than we first thought."

"So what exactly do you want the girls to do?" Rylan asked.

"We'd like them to interact with every single one of these experiments, to see how they'll react to their presence," Salin said. "We believe we'll have similar results as the first time, even with more of them involved."

Raikidan crossed his arms. "How many experiments are we talking?"

"Ten."

Raikidan shook his head. "I don't like it."

"I don't either," Blaze said, surprising me. "That's far too many for them to deal with. I even doubt the one psychic you brought here will be able to hold them all off if something goes wrong."

"Don't doubt my ability," the psychic responded.

"Guys, don't worry," I said. "We're going to be fine. And if something does go wrong, Ryoko can just pummel them to the ground, right?"

Ryoko grinned and pounded her fists together.

"So will you help?" Salin asked.

I nodded. "Of course. I'd just like to make a suggestion on how this goes. I think it may be best if Seda and I are the first to sit in the room. While the interaction goes on, Ryoko, Xenna, Elarinya, and Jenna can be let in. This will make it so none of these experiments are overwhelmed with the number of us in there to begin with, and we can see how they react to the others coming into the room."

Salin nodded. "That's not a bad idea."

Ryoko smiled. "I think it's a smart one."

Mana nodded. "I agree."

"All right, we'll do that," Salin said. "If you and Seda would be kind enough to enter the room, we'll let the first experiment in."

We entered the room and each took a seat in the chairs that had been set up. It wasn't long before the door in front of us opened and a young man, no older than nineteen or twenty, with fair skin and blue-purple hair, cautiously walked into the room. I didn't recognize this one.

Seda and I smiled. He responded with a wary gaze, though I could see the interest in his eye every time he looked at me. It was as if he wanted to come over and investigate, but was too nervous to do so. I didn't doubt Bone had told them about his meeting with me last time, so it would only be natural for them to have growing curiosity over who I was.

The young man chose to lean against the wall instead of coming over, and the door opened again. Another man who looked similar to the first came out and reacted in the same manner as his brother. This continued until six men were in the room. They all kept their distance. Seda and I exchanged a glance.

"Any clue as to their behavior?" I asked mentally.

"Their thoughts indicate they're curious, but they're nervous. It's almost like they're unsure what to do without any direction."

This was indeed strange. Bone had been the complete opposite of them.

Just then, the door opened again, but instead of one person coming out, there were three, and one of them was Bone. The other two were much burlier than the other men in here. I'd met these two before, during the city attack.

Bone smiled wide at the sight of me and I gave him a small wave. Eager, he closed the distance and sat down. The others in the room reacted to his eagerness by relaxing. *Interesting.*

Bone rested his hand against mine when he sat down and then leaned over and rested his forehead on mine. "It's good to see you again, Eira."

I pulled away. "Same. You're looking well."

He smiled. "So are you."

"It's the same situation as last time. We can speak freely."

He leaned over on his arms. "Good."

The two men who had come in with Bone ventured over. One took a seat next to Bone, in front of Seda, and the other knelt next to me. I took in their presence. Unlike Bone and me, they didn't have any purple in their hair. Instead theirs were blue and red. This piqued my curiosity, and I assessed my other clones. They all had a different mix of these three colors, some even only had one of the three. *I wonder why.*

"They may be clones, but that doesn't mean mutations can't happen," the voice said. *"Your aunt would say that, at least."*

That made sense in some way. But I wasn't convinced that was the only possible reason.

The man next to me grinned. "It's good to see you again, Sister. When you're not bossing us around."

I laughed. "Well, someone had to. None of you were going to be useful otherwise."

My other burly brother snickered, but quieted when I gave him a look that told him he wasn't exempt from my claim.

The brother I conversed with lifted his large hand up and I rested mine against his in return. "My name is Rhaec." He gestured his head over to the man sitting next to Bone. "That's Trigon."

I held up my hand to Trigon and he returned the gesture. "It's nice to meet you two again." I looked around with a smile. "And finally meet all of you."

The unease remaining in my brothers disappeared, and they came over to greet Seda and me. They were all pleasant and curious, but, unlike Bone, they gave us our space. Rhaec, on the other hand, wasn't too familiar with keeping to personal space limits.

"Excuse you!" I slapped him across the face. "How dare you touch me like that? What is with you guys and grabbing my breasts?"

He rubbed his face where I'd left a red mark. "Sorry. I've never been able to touch a woman. Yára wouldn't let me, so I thought it'd be safe to do so with you, since you're our sister, too."

Seda snickered. "That doesn't make it safe. It just makes it weird."

Rhaec glanced at me apologetically, but I crossed my arms and nearly turned my nose up. "I'm sorry, Sis."

"Yeah, I'm sure."

"I promise I won't do it again."

"Maybe you should teach us how to behave," Trigon said. "Then we won't mess up as much."

I narrowed my eyes. "You should already know how to behave. Even I knew how to behave before I could control my more unwanted actions."

He looked down. "Sorry. This is all really hard for us."

I sighed. "I know. It's not easy being what we are. At least you have each other to give a hand. I had to do it on my own."

"But you had Mom," Bone said. "Almen told us you and she were really close."

I blinked. "Almen is still alive?"

Bone nodded. "Yeah, why?"

"Well, most scientists don't last more than a few decades."

Bone shrugged. "I guess he's just that good."

"What was Mom like?" Rhaec asked.

"She was kind." I chuckled. "And difficult."

"Don't forget stubborn," Seda added.

I laughed. "And forgetful. Man, could she make records with her forgetfulness."

"Wish we could have met her," one of my brothers said, sorrow laced into his words.

I frowned. "Me too… You would have liked her. Even though she couldn't help me as well as she liked, she did her best and never expected too much from me. Her goals were always attainable."

"Sister?" one of them asked.

"Yes?"

"How is it that you're able to walk around in the open like this? Almen said you were part of the rebellion. Are you not?"

"No, he's right. I am part of the rebellion. I just use cover stories to get myself to blend in."

"But you use your real name."

A nervous, awkward laugh escaped my lips. "That was a bit of an accident. I had left the city for some time, and when I came back, I didn't have time to make a cover name on the spot when some soldiers showed up. Luckily, I was able to convince them of my fake story and play off my name. Of course, Seda was a big help with that, too."

Seda giggled. "Had you thought to keep quiet and act like you were shy, we could have covered for you."

I snorted. "Yeah, I thought about that a little too late."

"Seda, what is your real name?" Trigon asked.

She smiled. "It's Seda. I use my real name when I use the cloaking device I carry to make me appear like a regular person. I use the name Crystal when in the form of a psychic."

Trigon nodded. "All right, we'll have to remember that."

"So, Sister," Bone began, "why is it that we're all here? What did we do? No one told us. They just said when we were supposed to come in."

I opened my mouth to speak, but closed it when the door to the viewing room opened. Ryoko poked her head inside and I waved her in. "I was just going to tell them about you guys."

My brothers stared for a moment as Ryoko, Mana, Genesis, and Shva'sika strolled in. When the four women were close enough, several of my brothers moved from the seats they had taken so the ladies could take them.

Rhaec leaned close to me and kept his voice low. "All of your friends are hot. Just saying."

I chuckled. "They're too old for you."

"So?"

I chuckled again. "And three of them are taken."

"Means I still have some sort of chance with the other two."

"And those two are way too old for you."

Shva'sika narrowed her eyes at me. "I heard that."

Ryoko nudged her. "I didn't realize you were a cougar."

Shva'sika winked. "I'm a rather adventurous woman."

I snorted and the other ladies laughed.

Bone chuckled. "As amusing as this is, can you tell us what's going on, Sister?"

"The soldiers just want to see how all of you would react to me and Seda and then to how well you could handle a group of us," I explained.

He blinked. "Why?"

"Because they're dumb."

"Fair enough."

"So I guess I'll start by introducing them to you." I gestured to Mana. "This is Mana. Her cover name is Xenna."

Mana smiled, and Bone nodded respectfully, as did a few of the others.

"This is Ryoko." I gestured to Ryoko, who waved, and then gestured to Shva'sika, who smiled. "And this is Shva'sika. She goes by her elven name, Elarinya, when the soldiers are around because she's a shaman, but you can call her Danika if that's too difficult to say."

Bone nodded. "And shamans aren't supposed to be a part of our cause."

"Our cause?" Ryoko's eyebrow ticked up. "Since when are you a part of all of this?"

"Since Eira is," Bone said. "We're on whatever side she's on."

Ryoko giggled. "Looks like you have an army on your side."

I shook my head. "Bone, you shouldn't choose to be on our side just because of me. You should do it because you believe what we're doing is right."

"You're family," he said. "We stick together."

"Besides, it's not like we like Zarda," Rhaec muttered.

I chuckled. "All right, I can take those answers. Now I have one more person for you to be introduced to." I gestured to Genesis. "This is Genesis. Her co—"

Bone's eyes widened with surprise. "You're Genesis? You're the one they're still looking for?"

Genesis blinked. "They're still searching for me? After all this time?"

"How long have they been looking for you?"

"For seven hundred years at least. It could be longer, though. I lost track after a while."

I scratched my chin. "I know we kept you secret as a precaution, but I never thought they'd actually still be looking for you. Why would they still be searching after all this time?"

"It doesn't matter," Bone said. "We will keep our mouths shut about her. But what is the name you go by?"

"I go by Jenna, and Genny when I use the cloaking device to appear like a child," Genesis said. "The child form is the safest form for me to use when soldiers are around."

He nodded. "We'll remember that."

I looked around. "So, where's Yára? I was told we'd be dealing with all of you, but I don't see her. Did they not let her come to this?"

Bone cranked his head over his shoulder in the direction of the door they'd all come through. "She's just waiting."

Some of my clones moved around and blocked the viewing room glass. I had to refrain from smirking. They weren't dumb. While the military did set up this meeting, and we had so far kept my fake death working, having Yára and me in the same room with prying eyes may set off a few signals if their view wasn't obstructed just enough. *That's if our psychics don't help with that as well.*

"We have it all covered," Seda messaged. *"Don't you worry."*

My gaze shot over my shoulder when the door to the viewing room flew open and Zo stormed in. Before I could think about why he was in here, or here at all for that matter, Rhaec jumped to his feet and pinned Zo to the wall, baring his teeth.

"Rhaec, let him go!" I said.

He ignored me and tightened his grip on Zo.

I ran up and placed my hand on his arm. "Please, Rhaec, let him go."

Either he was refusing to listen, or couldn't hear me in his rage. Ryoko rushed over and tried to pull him off Zo, but Rhaec shoved her away. She stumbled back, startled by the ease of the motion for him, and then turned her attention to me for permission to get rough.

I wasn't ready for that yet. I didn't want to incite any sort of violence unless necessary, just in case it'd cause the others to react.

I took a few steps back when I thought of something. "Ryoko, give me a boost."

Her brow cocked but she nodded, knowing time was of the essence. I took another step back, gauging my brother's height, and then sprinted up to Ryoko. She threaded her hands together and launched me into the air when my foot made contact with her.

I landed on Rhaec's shoulders, getting a good angle on the situation. Zo struggled against my brother, his face blue. I didn't have much time. I reached around Rhaec's head and pressed my thumb and index finger into two spots—under his chin and at the base of his skull. The moment I pressed into those points, Rhaec froze, his hands relaxing enough to allow Zo to breathe again. He gasped for air.

"Let him go, Rhaec." I kept my voice calm.

Rhaec, as if under a spell, let his arms fall to his side.

"Good. Now take four steps back." He did. My eyes flickered to Ryoko, and back to Zo. She nodded and went to check on him, though not allowing him to leave his spot until I gave the word.

I released Rhaec, and it took a moment for him to react. He reached up and rested his large hands on my thighs. "Eira?"

I jumped down and stared up at him, staying calm. "Go sit back down, Rhaec."

He opened his mouth and I repeated myself, my words still calm but punctuated. "Sit... back... down."

He swallowed, nodded, and then listened, taking his position next to Bone and keeping his head down. My attention drifted back to Ryoko and Zo. "Ryoko, I'll take of it from here."

She gulped and nodded, her eyes flicking to Zo for a moment before going back to her seat. Just like my brother, she also kept her head down.

I fixed my gaze on Zo and pointed to the door. "Out there, now."

Zo stared for a moment and then complied. Bone tried to talk to Rhaec and Ryoko, but she shushed him. I followed Zo into the other room and closed the door behind me.

"Care to explain what you were thinking?" My voice still came out calm and steady.

Zo hesitated, noticing the demeanor changes in my housemates as they almost shrunk back from me. "Um, why aren't you yelling at me?"

"Dude, answer her question," Blaze murmured. "She's so mad she's not yelling. That's when you know you really fucked up." His eyes drifted to me and then snapped away. "She's basically plotting your death while you sleep, and then will ensure you wake up just before."

Zo's eyes widened. "I–I'm sorry. I reacted to their behavior before thinking."

I placed my hands on my hips. "No, really? You're lucky I was able to stop him. Hell, you're lucky your approach didn't incite an even worse reaction. They react to aggression. They allow instinct to drive them when surprised."

Salin stepped forward. "How did you know how to stop him?" He gestured to the psychic in the room. "Rhaec's rage blocked the telepathy attempt until you calmed him. But by then, you had him so calm we didn't need it."

My posture relaxed and I crossed my arms, taking a more casual stance. "Ryoko taught me. She said it worked on most Brutes, and would be useful to know if I ever had a problem. I thought everyone in the military knew that."

Salin's brow creased. "You're right, we should know. I'll have to look into why that isn't common knowledge."

I nodded and pointed at Zo. "Don't do anything stupid again."

I spun on my heels and entered the interrogation room.

Rhaec glanced up at my approach and then returned his gaze to the floor. "I'm sorry for my behavior, Sister."

I sat down. "I want an explanation."

"I… I don't like him."

"So? That doesn't give you a right to kill him. That behavior isn't acceptable."

"I couldn't help it! He barged in and I couldn't stop myself."

"Then learn to. Learn to want to. If you don't, Zarda will have you killed like the others." My gaze softened. "And I don't want that."

"I'll try."

"Good."

He struggled to meet my gaze. "You know, you're really scary when you're mad. I thought you yelling would hurt, but you staying calm while mad hurts even worse. Not even Yára can get this scary."

Ryoko giggled. "You should have seen Amara. She put Laz to shame."

She had a point. Not many could rival the terror my mother could incite with one look.

"Sister, how do you know General Zo?" Bone asked.

"I met him because Ryoko and the others knew him and were dealing with him first," I said. "He's the reason I wasn't able to come up with a cover name in time, since he showed up uninvited."

"And now he won't leave her alone." Ryoko teased.

I twirled a finger in the air. "Lucky me."

"Don't tell me you've screwed that creep," Trigon said.

"Ew, gross!" I stuck my tongue out. "Don't even suggest that."

He chuckled. "Good. I'd have to question your sanity if you had."

I shook my head and then turned my focus on Bone. "Can I meet Yára now, before any more weird conversations pop up?"

He chuckled. "Sure."

Trigon rose and headed over to the door they had come through earlier. He knocked on it three times, and the door cracked open. He spoke with someone on the other side and the door closed again. Trigon waited and the door opened again after a moment, but this time someone came through. I peered around Bone to get a better look, but the person was wearing a cloak, obstructing my ability to get any identification on them. Bone moved to the seat Trigon had previously taken up, and the hooded figure sat down in Bone's former seat.

When she seemed to feel if was safe to show her face, she lifted up her delicate hands and pulled the hood of her cloak down. My eyes widened with surprise and awe at the young woman before me. Though younger, like my brothers, she looked eerily similar to me, right down to the hair color. She lacked freckles, like I figured she would, as all of my brothers were lacking them, and her hair was much longer and pulled to the side to keep it neat and together. But a few of her features were also different, making us a little less identical than I had initially thought we'd be.

I reached out and touched her face. She closed her eyes, and remained quiet and still while I delicately touched her. When I pulled away, she opened her eyes and then hesitantly reached out to do the same to me. I closed my eyes and stayed relaxed, to show her it was okay. When she pulled away, I opened my eyes and smiled at her. She smiled back.

"It's nice to finally meet you, Sister." Her voice was eerily similar-sounding to mine. "I've heard so much about you from Almen and Ryder, I couldn't wait to finally meet you."

"I'm glad to finally meet you, too." My smile changed to a curious look. "Though I'm surprised you know Ryder."

"Almen recently had us meet him," Bone said. "He said we were related somehow, but neither actually explained how."

"He's my son. So, therefore, your nephew."

Bone blinked. "That's not what I was expecting to hear."

"But that would explain why he has such similar features to her," Trigon said.

Rhaec nodded. "Agreed."

I cocked my head when I noticed Ryoko's awed facial expression. "What is it, Ryo?"

"I just can't get over how similar you and Yára are." Her eyes flicked between the two of us. "Freckles aside, as well as the obvious age gap, you're a near identical match."

"We're not that much alike," I stated.

Yára nodded. "I'm going to agree with my sister. Everyone said we looked pretty identical, but there's a bit of a difference."

Seda giggled. "That's because of the way the two of you see each other as opposed to everyone else. When you look at a reflected surface, what you're seeing is mirrored, and that's different from what everyone else sees."

Ryoko nodded. "So that's why we see you guys as nearly identical when you guys don't."

I tapped my lips with a finger. "Right, I forgot about that."

Yára nodded. "I guess that makes sense."

I rubbed my chin. "Not to get off topic, but this talk of similarities has actually got me wondering about something that's really important to know. What are all your positions in the military?"

Trigon blinked. "Positions? You mean what we're trained to do, right?"

I nodded. "That's exactly what I'm asking, though it's no secret you and Rhaec are Brutes."

Rhaec grinned and beat his chest. "You bet!"

"Anyone else a Brute?" I scanned my siblings. "I know looks can be deceiving, so I want to keep my assumptions to a minimum."

Trigon shook his head. "No, just us."

"The rest of us are assassins, just like you," Bone said.

I nodded. I suspected that might be the case.

"Well, everyone but Yára," Rhaec corrected.

I pursed my lips. She remained quiet, allowing me to study her for a moment. Her features were soft, and she held herself as if she were rather timid. She honestly looked like a civilian placed in a group of soldiers. *It's like she's had no training at all.* "So, what are you trained to do, Yára?"

Her eyes flicked to Bone, as if hoping he'd answer for her, but he didn't. She released a slow exhale. "I'm... I'm not."

My brow furrowed. "Huh?"

"I'm not trained to do anything. I just spend my day watching everyone."

I rubbed my chin as I thought about this. Something wasn't right about that.

"Is something the matter, Sister?" Bone asked. "I know Yára not having any training yet is a bit strange, but your thinking is unnerving."

"That's because we're war experiments," Ryoko said. "We're made to fight. That's our purpose. For Yára to not be given any training... well, you see what I'm getting at here."

"I have asked for training," Yára said. "I really have. It's just... every time I ask, I'm told no."

I steepled my hands. "I see..."

She tilted her head. "You see what?"

I set intense eyes on her. "Zarda didn't make you to be a war experiment. He made you to be a companion."

"What?" She reeled back. "Gross!"

"You sure, Eira?" Genesis asked.

I nodded. "By this point, she should have been given at least some training. And by the looks of it, she's nowhere near as aggressive as my brothers, am I right, Yára?"

She nodded. "I don't have any aggressive tendencies. I never have."

I worked my jaw. "Then Zarda did that on purpose. We all know about his twisted intention toward me; it only makes sense he would try again. Yára, how does he act around you?"

"How does he act?" She thought for a moment. "Well, he's actually nice and pays a lot of attention to me. Is that bad?"

I narrowed my eyes. "It's unsettling, to say the least. Now, I need to ask you a personal question, and I need an honest answer, okay?"

She nodded. "Of course, Sis."

"Has he made any overly friendly passes at you, or made you or anyone else think he was aiming for more than just a friendly request?"

She shook her head. "No."

I nodded. "Good. Bone, you and the others are to do everything in your power to keep Yára away from Zarda, you hear?"

He nodded. "Sure. Any particular reason why?"

"Just trust me when I say it's for the best. At any cost, she is not to be left alone with him."

He narrowed his eyes. "Sister, what happened between you two?"

I averted my gaze. "I… don't want to talk about it right now."

Rhaec grabbed my shoulder. "Tell us, Sis."

I sucked in a tight breath, my eyes closing. The memory, so vivid still to this day. "He tried to rape me."

They all stared at me, their shock and horror clear.

"Eira, I didn't even know that," Genesis whispered.

"Well, I don't exactly go throwing it around in casual conversation." I looked at my brothers. "So you keep Yára away from Zarda at all costs, you hear?"

"That bastard, I'll kill him!" Bone jumped to his feet, his rage rolling off him in waves.

"Bone, stop." I grabbed his hand. "Getting angry isn't going to help, and you can't take him out on your own. There are things you don't know about him. That's why we work in the rebellion. It's the most effective way."

He growled and plopped down in his seat. "You expect me to just accept what you just said and sit quietly?"

I nodded. "His time will come, but I don't want you recklessly throwing your life away because of one event."

He sighed again and nodded. "Okay."

I turned my head when someone knocked on the door to the viewing room. "It seems our time is up."

My siblings gazed at me sadly and I smiled. "Don't be like that. We'll see you again. Maybe I can get Ryder to convince them to let some of you come with him on visits to us."

Bone smiled. "We'd like that."

I stood and grabbed Yára's hand when she held it out to me. She smiled and then pulled her hood over her head before heading back to the door she came out of, along with a few of our brothers.

"Oh—Trigon, Rhaec, if either of you need any advice or training, talk with Ryoko," I told them. "She's the best Brute I know." I glanced at her. "And I doubt she'd be opposed to a good workout."

Trigon blinked. "You're a Brute?"

Ryoko giggled. "Yep!"

"There's no way you're a Brute," Rhaec said.

Ryoko grinned. "Wanna bet?"

I held up my hands. "Guys, don't start anything."

Rhaec grinned back. "Bring it on!"

"Guys, you're going to get us into trouble," I warned.

Ryoko and Rhaec moved so they'd have room to go at it.

"Hey, I could use some psychic help right now."

"I'm sorry, Eira, but I let them know what was about to happen, and they're okay with it. Because Ryoko is such a well-known and experienced former Brute class, they think she can handle this."

"You've got to be shitting me," I muttered.

"What?" Genesis said.

"Everyone move back," I said. "Those good-for-nothing soldiers in the other room are okay with what Rhaec and Ryoko are about to do."

Bone stared at me. "Are they insane?"

"I think you know the answer to that."

Trigon chuckled. "Chill out, guys. They're just having f—"

Rhaec went crashing into the wall. I turned my eyes to Ryoko and nearly laughed at her disappointment. "Something wrong, Ryoko?"

She grunted. "Yeah. I thought he'd be better than that. Even Raikidan could hold his ground longer."

I laughed, and Trigon stared at her in disbelief.

Rhaec moaned as he got up. "That… was embarrassing…"

"So, like I said, if you need any tips or training, ask to see Ryoko. I doubt after that display, there will be any issue with getting clearance to do so." I chuckled. "Looks like she could do you two some good anyway."

Trigon nodded. "I'll keep that in mind."

"Well, it's been great meeting with all of you." I waved goodbye before following the others into the viewing room.

I closed the door behind me and mentally prepared myself for the next event I was going to have to endure. "So, someone want to tell me why we've been called back in already?"

Salin blinked. "Well, we figured you had enough time, an—"

I snorted. "These things take time, and we didn't have enough to learn much that would be useful to you."

Zo crossed his arms. "You were in there for an hour."

Were we really in there that long? It felt so much shorter. The time just flew by with them. Like it does when spending time at the house with everyone... I crossed my arms in defiance. "Like I said, it takes time to gain their trust. You can't rush progress."

"Told you we should have let it continue," Salin muttered to Zo.

Zo only glared at him in response, and I had to restrain myself from outwardly sighing. His pride was obviously still recovering from the scolding I gave him.

Salin placed his attention back on me. "Were you at least able to learn something?"

I nodded. "I was able to do some decent observation. All of them seem to look to Bone for guidance, and he appears to be the one with the most control over his actions. The other experiments had decent control, but I could tell some were struggling after a while."

Salin scratched his chin. "I see. That would make sense since he was released first."

"Take this advice how you will, but I'd suggest putting Bone in charge of them. I believe they may benefit from his leadership. I'd also suggest giving Rhaec and Trigon better training. Ryoko has been retired for some time, and she was able to take Rhaec down with barely any effort. It's my understanding Brutes shouldn't be taken down that easily, even in the early stages of training."

Salin went into deep thought. "We'll have to think about it. I'm not sure we can trust them yet with any more training."

"Well, when you finally decide to, give me a shout," Ryoko chirped. "I'd be more than happy to help train them."

Salin look at her. "Are you sure, Miss Ryoko?"

Ryoko nodded. "I'm always looking for a good sparring partner."

"Is there anything else you can tell us about the experiments that might help us, Eira?" Salin asked.

"Bone is acting much better than last time, but he was doing pretty well then as it was." I shook my head. "Otherwise, I have nothing for you. The others were still learning to trust us."

Salin nodded. "Well, thank you for your help. The little bit of information we gathered from observing, and the information you shared, should help us with integrating them into the city soon. I hope to be able to ask for your assistance in the future if needed."

I smiled. "I'll see what I can do."

Escorting ourselves out, we headed out of the building and through the compound. I found my mind thinking about my siblings, and my eyes tried to wander back toward the building we had been in.

"You okay, Eira?" Raikidan asked.

I nodded with a small smile. "Yeah, I'm fine."

Raikidan looked at me as if he didn't believe me, but remained quiet, and I was grateful. The truth was, I wanted my siblings to come home with us. I wanted to know more about them and have that family I nearly lost… to have the family I always wanted.

But that wasn't the only thing on my mind. Salin had said they were going to try to integrate Bone and the others into the city soon. After speaking with the Council last summer, we had decided, no matter what, we were going to end this rebellion when Bone and the rest of them were released into the city. That time was coming. It was coming much faster than I was prepared for. But it couldn't be helped. This fight with Zarda was coming to an end, one way or another.

CHAPTER 21

A botched tune enveloped me as I hummed. I wasn't good at singing, but that didn't stop me when I was alone. Paper pieces fell onto my bed as I made snips into a larger piece, creating decorative designs. My eye wandered to a pile of crumpled balls of paper. Hopefully this design would look better than my last several attempts.

I didn't expect myself to be so picky about this idea, but I wanted it to be perfect. A memory book, or really *treasure* book, since the recipients were dragons. I liked having them here. It allowed me to learn so much beyond our walls, and they were fun to have around. They'd mixed into our dysfunctional little family so well, it really proved that the races of the land could get along if they didn't let their pride get in the way. Sure, it wasn't perfect, but nothing was.

I wiggled in excitement when my current cutout design came out how I wanted, and then glued it onto the page. *Now the photo.* I picked it up, smiling at the image of Laz up on Raikidan's back, pulling on his face. This was perfect for his book. I stuck the photo on the page and grabbed another, one of him and Laz yet again. I sorted through the photographs I'd picked out and realized she was the major subject of them all. I even had another copy of the two sleeping on the couch together.

Not that it was a huge deal. The two were practically glued at the hip. Every time they were in the same room, she was the object of his attention. They understood each other in a way no one else did. Everyone in this house was finally starting to see it like I did. I'd even caught the other dragons talking about it. It was so perfect, like their match couldn't have been more planned by the gods. But these two were just so damned stubborn.

I tapped the photo in my hand on my lips. They needed another push. I hadn't meddled in a while, listening to Rylan and letting it develop naturally. But it definitely had stalled. Something was in the way of these two getting over whatever issue they had. That something had overstayed its welcome and needed to go. *But how?*

A few items on the bed caught my eye. I'd picked them out because they represented his friends in some way, but some were so bulky I wasn't sure how I was going to manage it yet. *Wait.* I sifted through the items to find I never picked one out to represent Laz. I must have not with all the photos I'd selected.

A smirk curved up my face. I had my answer.

Slipping off my bed, I sauntered to Laz's room. That'd be the first place to find him. And find him I did, resting on the floor in his dragon form. I looked around to find Laz not in the room. *Perfect, she's not back from the assignment with Rylan.* Though I should have guessed. Rylan would have let me know he was back if they had returned.

For a moment I thought Raikidan may be taking a nap, with the way he breathed, but he lifted his head and turned a reptilian eye on me.

"Hey, I need your help."

He shifted, his body only clothed in pants that hung low on his hips, and crossed his arms. *Oh, girl, how do you resist all this yumminess?*

"What do you need?" Raikidan asked.

"I need you to give me something that reminds you of Laz. Or provide me something she gave you that you have kept for sentimental value."

His brow rose. "Any reason in particular?"

I smiled. "I've got a special project in the works. That's all I can tell you."

"Will it get ruined?"

I shook my head, my smile growing. It seemed he already had something in mind, but it was important to him. *Perfect.* "I'd never do that. I promise."

He eyed me for a moment and then nodded. I watched him lean under the bed and pull out a wooden box. Based on the beautiful craftsmanship, I guessed Laz had made it. *I hope he doesn't give me that. I wouldn't be able to use it for this project.*

To my relief, he opened it and sifted through the contents, many sparkly and shiny objects glistening within from the afternoon sun filtering in from the skylight. *Dragons do love expensive things. I wonder where he got all that.* Maybe Laz picked them up on some of her assignments. She'd been known to be a little klepto during those.

Or he could have gotten them himself, either by buying or stealing. I didn't like the thought of the latter, but that seemed to be an accepted behavior in dragon culture. *I wonder if Laz accepts this so readily as well, adding to her bond with Raikidan.*

Raikidan stopped his rummaging and pulled out something small and violet. Once he put the box back under the bed, he faced me, his hand outstretched but clamped tight around his momento. "I'll let you take this if you promise me you won't ruin it."

The strength of his gaze should have unsettled me, but instead it warmed my heart. "You have my word, Rai."

He took a deep breath and then opened his hand. I jerked back at the sight of the bound-up lock of hair. "Is that Laz's?"

"Yes." He had a straight face when he answered. "Is that a problem?"

"Well, no…" How should I word it to him? It was a bit… creepy that he had her hair.

Raikidan's brow furrowed. "Your response says otherwise. Eira didn't have an issue with it. When I asked for some, she just trimmed it off."

"Yeah, but it's hair."

He stared at me, still confused, and pulled his hand away, being sure to keep the lock safe in his grasp. "If this bothers you, I'm sorry."

Man, I was being insensitive. I held up my hands. "Let's back up, because for humans, this would be weird. For dragons, it's obviously not. Can you explain to me the meaning behind having her hair?"

"My hair isn't like yours. It doesn't grow."

My brow ticked up. That was news to me.

"On the other hand, your hair is much like our scales. It grows and falls off. You care for and treat it like it's important, so much so you've integrated its appearance into something important in your culture.

We do the same for our scales. Because they're so important, we give scales to those we hold close. Back when we didn't hide, armor and jewelry could be made with our scales, but most only had it if they were close to a dragon. Since Eira doesn't have scales, I was allowed to have some of her hair."

I placed my hands over my heart. It was so sweet. "Did you give her a scale?"

His gaze faltered. "She's… got many."

Oh, really? I grinned. "Would they perhaps be the ones used on the new shaman outfit she has?"

He stalled. "Some of them."

Oh, thank you for this, Raikidan. This is making it easy for me. "That's really sweet. And I'm sorry I acted so poorly at first. I'll be sure to be more open-minded next time."

I held out my hand so I could take the hair from him, but he didn't offer it. Instead he watched me carefully. I frowned. "Rai, I'm not going to ruin Eira's scale. I promise."

Hopefully that wording would get him to relax.

Raikidan stalled some more, but eventually held his hand out. I took the lock of hair. "I mean, why would I ruin a memento that reminds you of someone you care about so deeply?"

He narrowed his eyes. "Don't start."

I grinned wickedly. "Don't start what? Seeing how much you really care about her?"

"Ryoko."

"Oh, don't be like that, Rai. You admitted to giving her several scales. And you have her own type of scale right here. Do you have my hair?"

He frowned. "No."

"How about the hair of anyone else in this house?"

His eyes darted away. "No…"

"Would you say you're particularly close with anyone from this house besides her?"

"Maybe? I don't know." His lip twitched. "I've never thought about it."

"And you expect me, between all that, and how you're now acting, to not see what you're trying to hide, for the gods only know what reason?"

Raikidan shoved his hands in his pockets and refused to look at me.

"Well, if you change your mind, and want to admit how you feel, come and talk to me. I know ways to get even someone as stubborn as her to look your way." I turned around and headed out of the room.

"Ryoko, wait."

I stopped and grinned before throwing my head over my shoulder. He didn't meet my eyes, but I knew I'd won. "Yes?"

"What…" He took a few moments and then lifted his gaze to meet mine. "What's something she'd like to do that she hasn't had the opportunity to?"

I smirked, an idea already coming to mind. "I'm glad you asked. Because I know just the thing."

CHAPTER 22

(EIRA)

With an exhausted, annoyed sigh, I removed my shirt and tossed it on the floor. Last night's mission had taken its toll on me. I woke up late, just past noon, but my sleep hadn't been restful. Nightmares plagued my sleeping state, all related to the dragon-killing weapon Aurora discovered. Ever since the discovery, its ominous cloud haunted me. *I think one or two dreams were related to the human trafficking issue, too, but I'm not sure...*

The Council approved a small group to investigate the issue, and Mocha insisted on involving herself deeply. I worried for her, but needed to keep my faith in this group's success. And we always had at least one psychic working with them in case something happened.

I leaned on my dresser and looked myself over in a small mirror. I was surprised to not see bags under my eyes. One night wouldn't give me bad ones but I also hadn't been sleeping well lately. Last night's nightmare hadn't been the first in the past few weeks. Though it wasn't really bags I was looking at. My freckles held my attention.

"Disgusting."

I ran my fingers lightly over them, and noticed I had a lot more than I did a few years back.

"So there's no way to remove them."

"No, sir. They're permanent, and with exposures to the sun, there is a high likelihood of her obtaining more."

I licked my lips, exposing my canines.

"What's wrong with her teeth? They weren't like that before."

"Actually, sir, they were like this, they just weren't as pronounced. We believe it to be a late development manifestation from her type of DNA match up."

"Fix them. They look like they belong on an animal."

"Sir, I'm sorry, but that's not something we're capable of fixing. Either she has them as they are, or we remove the teeth permanently, and she's going to need them, so it's not advisable."

I took my hairclip out and let my hair fall before touching it.

"Such a strange coloring…"

I ran my fingers through my hair and rid it of the large tangles I found. I took in the conditions of the ends, and then assessed myself in the mirror again.

"You are to keep your hair long. Is that understood?"

"Eira," the voice warned. *"You need to get out of his cycle."*

I ignored her and reached down toward my sides, tracing the long, horizontal scars I never liked thinking about. Upon touching them, I remembered the pain I had gone through. The physical pain had been nothing compared to the mental.

"Eira, what happened?"

I gasped and spun around, to find Raikidan standing inside the room by the window. I held my arms around myself and shrunk back. "Raikidan, get out!"

"You're dressed," he said in a calm voice as he advanced.

"Hardly. Get the hell out!"

He lightly grabbed my wrist, preventing me from retreating into my closet. "Eira, I healed most of your scars, but the only two I couldn't take away were the one I gave you and these ones on your side. How did you get them?"

I avoided his gaze.

"Eira, please."

"Tell him, dear. It's okay."

I sighed. "I gave them to myself."

Raikidan's grip loosened enough for me to pull away and attempt to cover myself with my arms.

"Zarda prefers women with long hair. He never cared if long hair was practical for a particular profession or not. If he fancied a woman, he gave the order to never cut her hair. The only exception was when it became too long and unmanageable. Then we could trim it. I was given this order, and at the time, I hadn't been able to defy it. But there came a time when I finally despised him enough where I could defy his order, and I took a knife and cut my hair."

"But there was a price," Raikidan said, understanding where this was going.

I nodded. "Defying that order was the hardest thing I had ever done. It caused me immense mental pain. I refused to give in to it, and my body reacted by inflicting physical pain to teach me to never do it again. But in doing so, something changed in my mind. It was as if doing that one act broke the bonds of that embedded design."

Raikidan nodded. "And then you used that to break away from him, until orders no longer affected you."

"Yes."

He reached out and brushed his fingers against my cheek. I jerked my head away. "The order you defied wasn't the only thing you were thinking about, was it?"

I tried to move away, knowing full well where this conversation would end up going, but Raikidan cupped my chin. "He's wrong, Eira. Whatever he said, whatever negative thoughts he had about your physical appearance, he's wrong. He doesn't know your true worth."

"I'm not worth anything to anyone." I pushed past him and headed into the bath, grabbing the folded towel I had laid out from the dresser.

"Eira, don—" I slammed the door and locked it behind me. I took slow, deep breaths and did my best to not react when Raikidan pounded on the door. "Eira, don't be like this! Please…"

"Eira, listen to him. He's right."

"Shut up."

I peeled off the clothes I still had on and slipped into the bath. The water sloshed around from my quick entrance, but I didn't care. I was so overwhelmed by the thoughts swimming in my mind that my head nearly spun. I squeezed my eyes shut and attempted to count backward. It didn't help. It never did, but it didn't hurt to try.

I sighed with aggravation and washed up. I knew Raikidan meant well, but he had to be just as bad as me when it came to making someone feel better about a difficult situation. I couldn't understand why he continued to insist I was worth something. No one had ever put value on me. I wasn't worth anything to anyone. *At least not to anyone alive...*

Unable to use my bath time to relax, I climbed out and wrapped my towel around myself. When I entered my room, to my relief, Raikidan had left, but there was a folded pile of clothes on the dresser. Curious, I went over to look them over, but was more intrigued by the folded note placed on top when I noticed it.

> *Eira,*
>
> *I picked this out for you. I'm confident you'll look great in it. When you're dressed, meet me at the park. I have something for you.*
>
> *Raikidan*

My brow furrowed and I flipped the note over in hopes to find a second part answering why he picked out these clothes or why he wanted me to go to the park, but no dice. I looked over the outfit. There was a pair of denim pants, lacey tank top, denim jacket, socks, silk and lace bra with matching panties, and knee-high boots on the floor. I wasn't sure if I should have been more concerned he had picked out clothes that made a complete outfit, or that he went through my underwear drawer.

"Concerned, or excited?"

"Stop."

I chewed on my lower lip. *Should I wear it?* I took a deep breath. Of course I should. There was nothing odd about this. Logically, Raikidan picked clothes because I wasn't in a great mood, and knew I hated worrying about fashion choices.

I checked myself over in my full-body mirror once I was clothed, and ran fire-infused fingers through my hair until it was dry enough to be put up. I huffed when I found myself fussing. *There's no need for me to fuss...*

"I wouldn't say that. He took the time to pick out quite the nice outfit. Not just any guy would do that."

I headed for the door, but turned around and found a new pair of earrings to wear.

"See, even you are seeing it the way things are."
"Shut up, it's not like that."
"Can't keep lying to yourself forever."
When I finally stopped fussing, I headed for the front door. It would be quicker to drive, but it was a beautiful day out, so a walk would be a nicer option. It wasn't like Raikidan would die from waiting a little longer to show me this sudden surprise he cooked up.

I peered around as I wandered through the park. Raikidan hadn't been waiting for me at the front gate, and after waiting for him for a little while, I figured I'd look for him. I had yet to find him. I was actually a little annoyed. It felt more like a practical joke, and I wasn't amused.

"Lookin' for someone, or just takin' a leisurely stroll?"

I spun around to find Zaith leaning against a tree. "What are you doing here?"

"Observin' to understand nu-humans better," he admitted as he strolled over to me.

I grunted and turned to continue on my way. "I'm sure you are."

"Don't leave just yet."

An exasperated breath left my lips. "What do you want?"

He ran his fingers through his long hair. "To apologize."

My brow quirked up. He went to say more, but shut his mouth and sighed, unable to hold my gaze.

I jerked my head in a direction and headed that way. "Walk with me."

He followed, and the two of us strolled down the path in silence for several yards. I took the time to observe his behavior. He struggled to look at me, but also had no interest in anything around us.

"I may be irrational sometimes, but I'm not going to bite you," I said. "You can say what you need to."

He chuckled. "Thank you for wordin' yourself that way." My brow rose. "It reminds me of… someone important to me."

I understood his meaning. "Your mother, right?" I didn't miss the flicker of surprise in his eyes. "Xaneth told me a bit about her when I made an inquiry about your behavioral change during the meeting I'd called."

Zaith regarded me for a moment. "You didn't know about her before?"

"The Ambassador title is still new to me," I said. "I know very little about the past Ambassadors, as there aren't many records on them. And no one spoke of them around me during my time with the shamans."

"That's not what I meant." I looked at him, confused, and his brow rose. "You really don't know what I'm talkin' about, do you?"

"You've lost me."

He shook his head. "Never mind."

He went quiet again as we walked the cobblestone trail and I shook my head. "So, about that apology you mentioned…"

Zaith chuckled. "Yes, I do have one. It's for my behavior with you. You remind me a great deal of my mother—headstrong and independent in every sense of the words. I couldn't save her. I thought I'd never get the chance to make up for my failure. And then you came along." He glanced at me. "I thought if I could protect you, then she'd forgive me."

I went to say something, but he continued.

"My behavior, of course, didn't reflect that correctly. Your initial and subsequent dismissal angered me. It's why I couldn't stand your closeness with Raikidan. I'd proven I was stronger, higher in status, and had wealth to make you happy. It took time for me to realize first impressions were important." He chuckled. "And my approach that first day was not ideal, no?"

I eyed him. "You didn't refer to Raikidan's color when you spoke of him."

He nodded. "I don't care he is half-color. I have no ill will against any half-colors." He smirked at me. "After all, how could I be okay with you and my mother's existence, two halflings, and then turn around to say half-color is bad?"

A smirk tugged at the corner of my lips. "Wow, there is a brain inside there."

He laughed. "Sometimes it gets used."

I stopped us on a bridge and gazed out across the lake. "Zaith, why did you offer me a political proposal? If you just wanted to keep me safe, that's all you had to do."

He rubbed the back of his neck. "That is… uh, bit more complicated. You fit a type of female I prefer. Watchin' you, even when you were indifferent or hostile to my presence, made me want to be around you more."

His gaze shifted away from me. "I also know a bit about my destined mate. She sounds a lot like you, though acts a bit different and has a different name. As a halfling, I assumed you were goin' by a different name, since it's common for halflings to have two. Puttin' that all together, I thought it would be a good idea to offer, even with your constant rejection. I thought I could make you happy." He shook his head. "I know now I am not the male for that position."

I nodded and continued to look out at the sparkling water. "Why do you insist on protecting me? Besides reminding you of her, what makes me a target of your protection?"

Zaith's brow furrowed. "I don't understand your questions in regards to this. Rashta has told you everything, no?"

I slowly looked at him with bewilderment and confusion. "Huh?"

"I don't understand this reaction."

"And I don't understand what you're trying to get at, but I can confirm, from the other gods I've managed to speak with, Rashta is missing." My eyes narrowed. "And I don't know why you think, even if she weren't, a god of her caliber would come tell me anything personally."

Zaith stared at me, clearly perplexed. "She isn't missin'. She's stuck with you."

Stuck with me? Wait... I exhaled slowly and leaned against the bridge railing. "I know what's going on here. You've confused me with someone else. You wouldn't be the first, so don't feel bad."

Zaith leaned on the railing. "What do you mean?"

"My mother told me I was special. Said I'd have abilities no one else would ever be able to have. Other people have come to me, thinking the same, once they learned my origin. I believed it once, too." My gaze fell to the water flowing below the bridge. "But as I've learned more about what people expect me to be capable of, I realized they've all mistaken me for someone else like me. And now that you mention Rashta, it makes even more sense."

I drummed my nails on the railing. "If she's connected with this person, and the reason the gods told me Rashta is missing, then it all makes sense." I turned my gazed to him. "I'm not her. I'm just a halfling like her trying to survive."

Zaith stared at his hands. "We were certain it was you."

I frowned. "I'm sorry. It wasn't my intent to deceive any of you."

"Not your fault." He pushed away from the bridge railing. "I should go and discuss this with the others. We will still work with you, don't mistake that. You've been the first to shake things up in a long time. You may not be her, but that don't matter in this moment." He patted me on the shoulder and headed off. "Thanks for givin' me the chance to be civil with you finally."

"Zaith," I said. He fixed his gaze on me. "Your mother doesn't hold anything against you."

His eyes widened.

"I may not know her, but if she and I are similar in a way, I know she doesn't blame you. And neither should you." I pushed away from the railing. "Good luck finding this special person you seek. I'm sorry I'm not her."

I headed down the cobblestone path the way the two of us had come, my mind filled with questions.

"That was a true statement you told him. Velsara doesn't blame him."

"And how do you know that?"

"Because the true answer lies within, where you pulled your words. So natural an act, you didn't even realize the answer wasn't fully yours."

I mulled this over. *"Was Zaith correct about me? Are you Rashta?"*

Silence. *Dammit…*

I jumped and whirled around when a masculine hand landed on my shoulder. Raikidan stepped back, his hands up. "Just me."

Hand on my chest, I exhaled. "Don't do that."

"I called out to you three times," he said. "I didn't know how else to get your attention."

I rubbed the back of my neck, unable to keep eye contact. "Sorry. A lot of my mind."

"I can tell. Does it have anything to do with Zaith? I saw him a moment ago. He'd better not have bothered you."

I chuckled. "I did talk with him, but it was a pleasant chat. He won't be causing me issues anymore."

He gave me a dubious look, but then shook it off and grabbed my hand. "Come with me."

I cocked my head questioningly, and he chuckled. "Remember, I had a surprise for you."

"Yeah, what's up with that? And don't tell me it's some weird apology for what happened earlier. And it better not be a prank, either!"

Raikidan grinned. "No. I've been planning this for a few days. I planned to show you today, and the earlier events just so happened to transpire."

I pursed my lips. "Tell me what we're doing, then. You know I hate surprises."

"No, you'll have to wait."

I gave him my best pleading eyes. "Please?"

He hesitated, as if my look were working, and then shook his head. "No. You won't have to wait long anyway."

I huffed. Guess I sucked at that tactic, too. "How long is not long?"

"Couple seconds."

I scanned the park but didn't spot anything that screamed out at me. I squeaked when Raikidan let go of my hand and then covered my eyes. "Raikidan, what gives?"

He chuckled. "I don't want you seeing this surprise yet."

I tried to shake myself free of him, but it only made him laugh. "Quit it, or I'll have to carry you like some primitive human."

"I'm surprised you haven't done that already."

He snickered and then forced me to stop moving. He pulled his hands away and I blinked a few times to adjust to the bright, spring day.

I looked around. Nothing seemed to be overly special about the location we were in. It was just a little ways away from the lake, and a large oak tree shaded the particular spot I stood in.

Raikidan noticed my lack of understanding and snickered. "Look down."

Brow furrowed, I did, only to be more confused. At my feet sat a woven basket on top of a splayed-out blanket. "I'm still confused."

He chuckled and had me sit down on the blanket. "You've been so stressed out lately, I wanted to do something for you. I found out you'd never been on a picnic, so I thought that'd be the perfect thing to treat you to."

"Oh, how sweet."

A picnic? I opened the lid to the basket, finding several types of food, utensils, glasses and a bottle of some sort of drink.

"You haven't been on a picnic, right?"

I shook my head. "Not technically. I've eaten on the road before, but I wouldn't say they were picnics."

He gestured to the setup. "Well, now you can say you have."

I smiled at him. "Thank you."

I dug through the basket. "So what did you pack for us?"

"Um, food I thought was good for a picnic."

I laughed. "That question was set up for you to tell me exactly what's in here."

"Why would I do that? That would ruin the fun."

"You mean your fun."

He chuckled. "Okay, I can't argue that."

My eyes lit up when I noticed the selection of food as I sifted through the basket.

Raikidan smiled. "I tried to pick a few foods I know you preferred."

"A few? There's a lot of food I love in here!" A thought came to me as I pulled some out. "When did you learn to cook?"

His gaze faltered. "I picked most of these up at the store. I only made the sandwiches."

The voice snickered. *"He tried, at least."*

I unwrapped a sandwich and bit into one of the cut halves. My shoulders sagged and a quiet moan left my lips as the delicious flavors delighted my taste buds. "Yum."

His eyebrow arched. "Really?"

I nodded and ate some more. Raikidan, happy I wasn't pulling his leg, pulled food out onto the blanket. I felt inclined to help him, but not enough to put down my sandwich, so I did my best with one hand. When everything was laid out, we ate and chatted.

A gentle breeze rustled the leaves above us, dapples of sunlight scattering across the grass. It felt nice to do something so… normal. It felt normal to hang out with Raikidan like this. I was going to hate to have to say goodbye to him when we won our battle, but it was inevitable. The shamans wouldn't be too happy since he was my official Guard, but after all the help he had given me, he deserved to be able to go back to his normal life. I could find another Guard. They wouldn't be as good, but I didn't need to be babied. Then again, that was if I made it out of this alive. *I can't forget what Seda told me all those years ago…*

"Why do you keep looking up at the sky?" Raikidan asked. "Don't tell me you think someone is going to jump down from the top of the tree and ruin our lunch."

I laughed. "No, of course not. I just like looking at it."

"Why? It's just big and blue with some clouds. Nothing out of the ordinary for a spring day."

I smiled at him. "It's because of the clouds actually." His brow rose in question and I giggled. "I guess you've never looked for shapes in the clouds?"

"Huh?"

I climbed to my feet, extending my hand to him. "C'mon, I'm going to introduce you to something I haven't done in some time."

He seemed unsure, but gave in to his curiosity, taking my offered hand and following me out from under the tree. Lying down on the sunny grass on my back, I peered up at the sky with a smile. Raikidan lay down next to me, but with his body facing the opposite direction.

He also stared up at the clouds. "So, what are we doing exactly?"

I pointed at a cloud. "What does that cloud look like to you?"

"Like a cloud?"

I laughed and shook my head. "No. That's not how you do this. You have to use your imagination. Like when I look at it, I can see a flower head."

"I don't see it."

"Watch." I traced the shape with my finger. "See? It has a similar shape to a flower."

"Okay… I think I can see it."

I decided to look at a different cloud. "What does that one look like to you?"

He thought for a moment. "A dragon."

I bit my lip and pointed to another one. "And that one?"

"Dragon."

"How about that one?"

"Dragon."

I laughed. "You're not even trying!"

"Oh yeah? Then tell me what you see," he challenged.

"That one looks like a rabbit. That one looks like a mountain. And that one… yeah that one looks like a dragon."

The two of us laughed. Raikidan rolled over, and I looked for more clouds. "You do this often?"

I stifled a laugh. It sounded like cheesy pickup line. I shook my head.

"Not anymore. I used to all the time with Mom. After a stressful day, she'd have me do this to calm me down. It was a lot of fun. Though, I always had a feeling she also had me do it to evaluate my mental state."

"You'd see bad things when you were low."

I nodded and rolled over. "As my life continued in the military, I found myself in that depressed state more often. I don't blame her for checking. I know that state concerned her." My gaze lifted to him. "And I liked doing something normal people could do."

Raikidan smiled and then stared at something on my face.

I blinked. "What?"

He reached out and brushed my bottom lip with his thumb. "You have a few freckles right there. I never noticed them before."

I picked at the grass, heat threatening to rise in my cheeks. "No one does."

"It's cute. Reminds me of the random one you have on your stomach."

I chewed on my lip and continue to pick at the grass. No one ever noticed that one, either.

"Why are you doing that? What has the grass done to you?"

I shrugged. "It's just something I've done for as long as I can remember. I guess it's now a habit."

"More like a nervous habit," he teased.

I pushed him. "Is not."

He pushed me back. "Is too."

I shoved him and then jumped to my feet. He was quick to chase after me. I weaved around trees and jumped over flowerbeds without caring about the food we abandoned or what people thought. I laughed when Raikidan nearly grabbed me but missed and fell. I hid behind large trees and let him search, but was always found because I couldn't stop myself from laughing.

I ran and found a new hiding spot, but I wasn't as stealthy this time, because Raikidan jumped around the tree and grabbed me. A surprised squeal escaped my mouth, but that's all I was able to do. Raikidan had a strong grip on me and before I could even attempt to struggle away, he was throwing me over his shoulder.

"Rai, put me down!"

"Nope." He chuckled. "I caught you fair and square." I groaned and wiggled until he finally put me down. "Brat."

I stuck my tongue out at him and he gave me a look that told me to behave or I was going back on his shoulder. "Caveman."

He chuckled. "You like it."

He looked up at the sky. The sun was now setting. It surprised me. I knew we had been out for a while, and it was just early enough into spring where the days weren't as long as summer, but I didn't think that much time had passed.

When Raikidan started leading me toward the entrance of the park, I became confused. "Raikidan, where are we going?"

"You'll see."

"But we have to take care of our food."

"It's taken care of. Don't worry."

I pursed my lips but followed him nonetheless. His confidence left little room for arguing. I also couldn't deny I was curious about what he had planned.

"Given earlier, I'm sure it'll be nice."

We walked down the street until he pulled me into a quiet alley. We only walked halfway down it before he had us stop. I looked around and was more confused than ever. "Raikidan, what gives?"

He chuckled. "Well, I can't just have people watch us shift now, can I?"

I stomped my foot. "Will you just tell me what's going on? You're not making any sense!"

Raikidan held out his hand. "All you need to do is trust me. And follow me. It won't do you any good to just sit here."

I huffed. I wanted to know exactly what was going on.

"Please, Eira. I promise you'll like this surprise."

I sighed and took his hand. With a brilliant smile, he pulled me closer and rested his head on mine. He mentioned shifting, so I knew to close my eyes and relax. What he changed us to was going to be a complete mystery—or not.

The shift was quick, and when I opened my eyes and moved a little, I knew he had changed me into a sparrow. Raikidan, who was also a sparrow, chirped at me and took to the skies. I flapped my wings gently to refamiliarize myself with this body, but when a cat jumped out of a trashcan, I took off as quickly as possible. I wasn't going to be some feline's snack.

My flying ability was still less than desired, but I managed to keep up with Raikidan all the same. We flew through the city at a spectacular pace. Having better control over this body made me aware of how fast this animal could fly. It was nice.

The temple came into view and my curiosity grew. Why did he want us to come over this way? When he increased our altitude my confusion only grew. I followed all the same. I wasn't sure how to communicate in this body. I wasn't even sure if Raikidan could. Even though his ability was known to me, I knew just about nothing about it, and I doubted my experiences were the same as his. I made a mental note to ask him about it sometime. Wouldn't hurt, right?

Raikidan flew right for the top of the temple and I followed as best as I could. I was having a hard time keeping up now, and I had a feeling the force shift was wearing off. The theory was proven correct when I reached the roof and I shifted back. Raikidan caught me just in case I lost balance and fell, and I didn't fight the help.

"So, you going to tell me why we're up here?" I asked as he led me farther up.

"No." He smiled and then sat down on the top of the roof. "But I'll show you."

He pointed and I followed the gesture. My eyes widened with awe. I could see beyond the walls of the city—miles beyond. I couldn't see the ocean, that was too far away, but I could see how the land rolled, how expansive the forest was, and how the setting sun cast its low orange rays over it, seemingly setting it on fire.

I sat down and watched the sun set. It was so beautiful. I never thought something like this could be seen from this awful place.

Raikidan scooted closer and kept his voice low. "What do you think?"

"It's amazing," I said, my voice breathy.

"I figured you'd like it."

I leaned on my knees. "So how did this idea come about?"

"I was scouting. Couldn't sleep one night, so I flew around to tire me out. I ended up here at some point and saw how spectacular the view was. I knew I needed you to see it, and not when we were working in some way. I figured it'd have a different effect if it wasn't for leisure."

"You were right. And thanks, I do like this surprise. I liked today. I liked being able to relax. No thoughts on the rebellion. No work. Just almost normal activities."

Raikidan's brow knitted. "Almost normal? I'm pretty sure I thought up a completely normal day for you."

I gave him a long look. "Because shapeshifting into a bird and watching a sun set on top of a temple is super normal."

He opened his mouth, and then closed it when he realized I had a point. Staring out at the sunset, he ran his fingers through his hair. The action drew my eyes to his face, the low sunlight illuminating his strong features just right. I also noticed the frown now tugging at his lips, as if my assessment of today's events upset him for some reason.

A sudden urge to lean and steal it a way hit me. Instead, I leaned against him, resting my head on his shoulder. "But that's okay. I don't think I'd like an absolutely normal day. Normal isn't really my thing."

Raikidan chuckled. "You sure?"

I nodded. "Yeah."

We quietly watched the remainder of the sunset. The silence was nice, comfortable even. Raikidan's arm slipped behind me, his hand resting on the curve of my hip. I didn't stop or question him. Even though I knew it should, nothing felt wrong about any of this. Nothing about today felt wrong and I liked that. I liked having a piece of normal, even if Raikidan and I were far from that.

When the moon sat high in the sky, Raikidan stood and extended his hand. "Ready to go home?"

I nodded with a smile. "Yeah."

Raikidan wrapped his arms around me and the two of us changed shape. When the transformation finished, Raikidan gave me a minute to get used to the small owl body he'd chosen for us, and then led the way back to the house.

Raikidan landed on the windowsill to my room as he shifted back to his human form. He jumped to the floor as I came in to land. My body shifted just as I touched the sill, and I accepted Raikidan's offered hand to use as leverage as I hopped to the floor. I smiled my thanks and he smiled back.

I found myself unable to let go of his hand as I gazed up at him. He dragged his tongue over his lower lip. My eyes followed the motion. "Thanks for today. It was nice."

The space between us lessened and Raikidan's lips met mine, his taste sending a *zing* down my spine. Shock rippled through me, but my eyes hooded and I found it difficult to find the desire to stop this.

"Damn, he makes these so nice."

Raikidan pulled away and stepped back toward the windowsill. "You're welcome."

He then shifted into the shape of an owl and flew out the window, leaving me in my confused state. *Why…*

"It's a shame you keep pushing him away. You'd be able to have more of those."

Someone knocked on my door then, but I didn't answer. They came in anyway.

"Laz?" Ryoko asked as she came in. I still didn't answer. "Hello, Laz?" She waved her hand in front of my face. "Lumaraeon to Laz, come in!"

I blinked and shook my head, finally coming to my senses, and then looked at her. "Hey."

A devious smile spread across her face. "Looks like someone had a nice day."

I shrugged and went to change into my nightclothes. "It was a nice, relaxing one."

"That look in your eye said it was more." She chuckled. "Or maybe I just barely missed something important."

I snorted. "We just hung out at the park."

"Right, so you had a date."

I sighed. "Ryoko, there's no romantic interest, so it can't be a date. We just hung out at the park as friends."

"Yes it was!"

I came out of my closet. "What makes you so sure?"

She grinned. "I helped him plan it."

My heart stopped. *He had all the details planned out, and roped Ryoko in on it all.*

"Told you so."

I crossed my arms when Ryoko nudged me. I knew what she wanted me to say, but I wasn't convinced she was right. It couldn't be a date… right?

"I don't know why you're trying to deny it. It's so obvious, even Blaze would see it."

Ryoko waited impatiently and I blew air through my lips. "Maybe it was…"

Her smile grew and she followed me as I headed for my bed. "Well, how was it?"

I sat down and smiled despite myself. "It was nice."

"See? Denying things doesn't make you feel better."

Ryoko climbed on the bed. "Well?"

"Well what?"

"What did you guys do?"

I shrugged. "Had a picnic for lunch, talked, and then watched the sun set. It was one of the most normal things I've ever done."

"But somehow still really enjoyable."

I nodded. "Yeah. It was thoughtful of him."

"So, anything else happen? Something after the date?" She raised and lowered her eyebrows a few times. "Something… surprising maybe?"

I scoffed, knowing what she wanted to know. "No."

"The far off look you had when I came in would beg to differ."

"I was just thinking about something he said."

"Right." She wasn't buying it and frankly I didn't blame her. I wasn't doing a great job lying to myself.

She slid off the bed. "You could have just spilled it now, but I'll find out eventually, and when I do, I'll make you regret not telling me sooner."

I snorted and curled up. "Good night, Ryoko."

"Night, liar pants."

"Yeah, liar pants."

I rolled my eyes and then allowed myself to fall asleep. I needed it.

CHAPTER 23

Gravel crunched under my shoes as I walked down the street. Citizens passed me by, some walking straight through me, as if I weren't really there. I wasn't. I knew it. I looked at my hands; there was a translucent appearance to them. Somehow, I was dead. A vision, or a dream, perhaps, but this was my current state. I knew, because I stood in front of my grave when I came to—start and end dates had been carved into the stone. Zarda was also gone, large signs in the cities spoke of the people's freedom.

I stopped in front of the house. I wondered what the others were up to. I passed through the door and trotted up the stairs until I stood in the living room. Everything appeared the same, just empty. I walked into my room. My bed was made, and clothes still hung in the closet. If I could open the drawers, I suspected I'd find all my belongings. Everything was untouched. I wondered why.

I wandered through the house, eventually finding life. Seda and Argus worked in his workshop on some invention. They appeared happy. I smiled. *Just as they should be.*

I thought about my uncle, wondering how he was, and suddenly, I wasn't in the house. I stood in the middle of the West Tribe. A wide smile spread across my face as I spotted him walking with Shva'sika. The two laughed and chatted as they carried some supplies through town. Valene ran up to them, beaming and happy.

Ryder came to mind, and suddenly, I was in the woods. Before me, three figures in scholar robes walked down a path. A young man and woman walked with them. The figures with the familiar white and long black hair were unmistakable. Ryder spoke with the scholars, Genesis listening in, swapping stories and discussing theories. They all laughed, so carefree it'd bring a tear to my eye if possible. I wanted this for him. For both of them. To be free and happy, regardless of what happened to me.

I thought about Ryoko and Rylan, wondering what they were doing, and suddenly I stood in a different forest. The trees around me were tall, thick, and ancient. *I think I'm in the Velsara Wilds.* Why was I here?

The sound of a wolf howling entered my ears. But it didn't sound quite like your typical wolf. *Wogron?* It made sense. It all made sense now. I walked straight for the sound, phasing through trees and brush. It should have unsettled me, but I accepted it.

A fort came into view. Two tall, bipedal wolf-like creatures stood on the battlements. I walked through the front gate, unseen by the sentries. Inside, a pack of wogrons ran about. Ryoko and Rylan stuck out to me easily, as they mingled and acted as if they belonged. They looked so happy. I smiled. My loss wasn't in vain. It didn't put the brakes on their lives, just like it shouldn't have. *Like I never believed it would.*

I appeared in a new forest all of a sudden. I wasn't sure why. I hadn't thought of anyone. The soft grass padded my feet as I walked. I wasn't sure where I was going, but I eventually I'd figure out where I was. Maybe.

An interesting sound got my attention. As I listened, I thought I recognized it as growling. *Dragons.* I ran toward the sound, and came to a small clearing. A large green dragon and green-black dragon lay near a cave. *Mana and Corliss!* Corliss had his tail in front of his face when a whelpling ran around him suddenly. He lifted his tail and then dropped it, the whelp squealing and running off. Mana watched, affection clear in her eyes. I noticed three other babies with her, snoozing away.

If they were here, then Raikidan could be nearby. I wanted to see how he was doing. I listened for a river, and took off into the woods. Finding it, I made my way upstream, eventually finding the waterfall of his cave. He wasn't outside, so maybe he was inside? I sprinted up the path and into the cave, but found no familiar black-red dragon. I frowned. Maybe he was out patrolling?

I gazed out at the falling water. Or maybe he'd finally gone out to find his mate. I ventured out of the cave and took in the beautiful scenery. I hoped he had. I wanted him to be happy, like everyone else.

They all deserved this. *Me being gone doesn't have an effect, and that's okay.* I wanted it that way.

"You're not seeing everything," a heavily accented masculine voice said. *"You're only seeing what you want to see."*

I found myself suddenly on top of Raikidan's cave. The ground shook, and trees in the adjacent treeline swayed. Corliss appeared and sat down next to me, as if he knew I was there. His head hung low, and a heartbreaking sound came out of his throat. Mana drew up next to him, and hung her neck over him, her eyes pained. I didn't understand. They were so happy a moment ago. Did something happen to Raikidan?

The pair disappeared in a blink of an eye, and I found myself in my room. Dark and dreary. Ryoko sat on my bed, sobbing, holding one of my shirts. Rylan was next to her, one hand on her back, trying to console her while holding himself together.

My brow knitted. *What's going on?*

I blinked and found myself on a hill with the scholars; Ryder and Genesis were sitting some ways off from them. I ventured over to find my son staring into a locket. The image inside was of him and me. Genesis rested her head on his shoulder. Ryder slid his thumb over the photograph, and then suddenly I appeared at the West Tribe's graveyard.

Shva'sika and my uncle stood in front of a statue depicting me, their smiles now gone. Valene sobbed on her knees in front of it. I didn't understand. Why was I seeing this? I understood they'd miss me. They cared enough to do that. But that didn't mean their lives stalled because I wasn't there.

"You're still not seeing it."

I found myself in a different graveyard. The military graveyard. I'd started here. But unlike last time, I wasn't alone. Before me, Raikidan sat with his arms hanging over his legs. My necklace hung from one hand and his other held my ring as he stared at my stone, unmoving. I walked around him and my breath caught. He looked horrible— dark rings around the eyes, unkempt, signs of emaciation—I couldn't believe what I was looking at.

I glanced up when the crunching of grass caught my ears. Ryoko and Rylan approached, with Corliss and Ebon behind.

Ryoko knelt next to him, holding up some food. "Raikidan, please eat."

He didn't acknowledge her.

She tried to shake his arms and he didn't move an inch. "Raikidan, please. We can't lose you, too."

He continued to stare, his eyes blank. It was as if he wasn't in there.

Tears welled up in her eyes. "Raikidan…"

Corliss came over to her and pulled her onto her feet. "There's nothing you can do, Ryoko. This is what happens when we dragons lose our mates. We can't live without them."

I didn't understand. What were they talking about? Raikidan and I weren't mates.

"Yes you are," said the masculine voice. *"Even if you don't believe it now."*

I whirled around to catch the source of this voice. Instead of that, I found myself now in front of a lake—the lake I always went to between dreams. Far out in the center stood the temple I could never reach.

"Beside you," said the voice, now no longer in my mind, but to my right.

My head turned, and before me stood a man with bright blue eyes, dark hair and facial hair, and dark skin typical of those from the western desert region. Lavish, colorful clothing and jewelry adorned his body.

I took a step back. "Raisu."

The god of dreams dipped his head, his eyes sparkling. "Good evening, Eira. I'm so glad I can finally meet you in person."

My brow twisted. "Why are you here? What do you want from me?"

Before I could get a response, a pair of strong arms wrapped around me—tight, but caring. I knew who owned these arms. *Raikidan.* Then two small hands grabbed mine. I looked down to see a little girl with violet and red hair, and a boy about the same age with violet and black hair holding onto me.

"What you perceive your destiny to be is not the right one, Eira," Raisu said. "Or more accurately, not the only one. You do not have to continue down this path. You are able to go the path of your choosing—to choose something like this."

Tightness formed in my chest, and I pulled myself from these images, dispersing them. "I once tried to make choices like that. All it did was lead me to more pain. I'm not meant to be happy."

"I hate to hear you say such things." He gazed at me with sorrow-filled eyes. "We've only ever wanted you to be happy. We wanted a much different life for you, but…"

He sighed. "I wish I was allowed to put it in words."

I turned away and headed down the sandy shore. "What we wish would happen and what truly is, are two completely different things. I've learned this painful lesson, time and time again."

"Your loss will hurt more than you wish to admit," Raisu called out. "Please consider this when the time comes to choose at the fork in your destiny."

I continued on, ignoring him. His words meant nothing. No matter how much I try, I could never escape the fate Seda warned me about.

"Eira!" a voice called out.

I turned to see Raikidan running down the beach after me. Raisu was nowhere to be seen.

Raikidan came to a halt next to me and took a deep breath, making me acutely aware this was the real him… for some reason. "Are you okay?"

I did my best to hide what I'd just gone through. "I'm fine, why do you ask?"

"I just had one hell of a time with your sentinel."

My brow arched. "Why? I gave you permission to be here."

He nodded. "That's true, but there are times when sentinels still cause us issues. It tends to be when your mind isn't being kind to you. I thought you might be having a nightmare, so I wanted to check on you."

My gaze fell. "Oh, that. Yeah, well, it's okay. Nothing I can't handle.

He reached out and held my hand. "Are you sure? I don't mind listening."

My eyes fell on our hands, and I was aware of the area around us reacting to the touch, just like last time we were both here. "Yeah, don't worry about it."

He gazed out to the temple. "Still can't get there, huh?"

I shook my head. "I'm stumped."

Raikidan rubbed his chin. "We can't walk or swim there, and you can't conjure up a boat or bridge…"

Raikidan had tried to teach me how to manipulate the area once. I managed a few things, but anything useful to get us closer to the temple wouldn't manifest.

"What if I fly us there?"

I shoved my hand into my pocket and stopped myself from biting my lip. I didn't like that idea. *Flying...*

"You'd have to allow me to shift," Raikidan said, his gaze darting to me. "It's the only way."

I thought about this hard. Did I dislike the thought of flying more than I desired to find out the secrets within that temple? It was a tough question.

Raikidan frowned. "Eira, are you okay?"

I wasn't sure how to answer that.

"The talk of flying has you out of sorts again. You refused to allow me to fly us close to the West Tribe when we first met. Does flying frighten you? I never thought to ask because you've been okay with flying as a bird."

He was right. I didn't have any issues with that. "I guess, for some reason, I never thought about that. Maybe because I was so preoccupied about getting somewhere, I never tried to take in what I was doing."

"So the concept of flying does frighten you?"

I nodded.

He squeezed my hand. "I promise it'll be okay."

I gazed up at him. He looked sincere enough. Why was I doubting his words? *Maybe it's because—* "How do I give you permission?"

"It has to be verbal, and you have to mean it. I promise this won't hurt you in any way."

"Do full black dragons need this permission?"

"We all do. Whenever we enter a dream or sleep consciousness, we are forced to take the form of the being's species. They then need to give us a verbal okay to be something else, forcing them to be aware of our presence in their mind."

"Interesting defense mechanism."

"We dragons don't know everything about the ability. We still don't know why Raisu bestowed it on us."

Raisu. Raikidan once told me he held the god of dreams to a high standard of importance. It was partially because of his dream ability that he did. Did he know about Raisu's visit to me? Or was that only for me to know?

I took a deep breath. "Okay. Raikidan, I give you permission to shift into another form so that we can try this theory out."

He chuckled. "So specific. But if that's what you wish, then that's how it will be."

I winced. *Shit, I did that wrong, then.* Of course I did. When did I ever do anything right with him?

Raikidan tried to lift one corner of my mouth. "I was only teasing."

He frowned when that didn't help banish these negative thoughts. *Great, now I'm making it worse.* What was wrong with me?

I squeaked when he suddenly pulled me into his hard body. He wrapped his arms around me and held me tight. "Uh, Rai?"

A moment passed and he let me go, but rested his forehead on mine. Warmth heated my face. "I needed some way to break you of that cycle. I hate seeing you withdraw inward. You're too harsh on yourself when you do."

I smiled as I closed my eyes. "Thank you."

He pulled away and stepped back a few paces. Within seconds he took his dragon form, unrestricted by the size of my room. I'd forgotten how large he was.

Raikidan extended a paw toward me. I hesitated and then placed a hand on one his enormous talon. He remained still as I took in the idea of how one of these talons could rip into another dragon's hide, and then how easily a soft human like myself could be torn apart.

I then hopped up into his paw and he closed it around me. I swallowed hard and took some calming breaths. I still had plenty of room, and could see the area around us. Raikidan flapped his enormous wings and then lifted off. I clung to Raikidan as best I could, trying hard to keep myself calm.

The ground turned to water, and the wind battered me. I surveyed the changing landscape, finding myself calming little by little. This wasn't so bad. It was different from flying. Safer, really.

"And he will teach you. That is how you'll know it's not a lie."

Raikidan cradled me so well, I didn't have to worry about falling out. He wanted me safe. He'd shared his shifting ability with me to allow me to experience that. He purposely picked a bird instead of a land creature. He taught me how to fly and not fear it. The fear of this situation disappeared as I gazed up at him.

Was everyone right? Even my mother? She told me the right one would teach me to fly. Was Raikidan the one she meant? Or had he just come along first and taken the time to help me?

Raikidan tilted his head down at me, his flying not faltering. "*Are you okay?*"

The Draconic words reverberated in my chest. I smiled and tried to speak, but the wind stole my words.

"*Speak my tongue.*"

My brow furrowed. How did I know the words he just spoke? He hadn't taught me them all, and yet I understood them as if I'd spoken the language my whole life.

"*Our consciousnesses are connected,*" he said, as if he knew my thoughts. "*Now speak.*"

I took a deep breath and tried. "*I am thinking.*"

My eyes widened. I did it. And it overpowered the wind. Was this the power of their language? It was so strong not even air travel could hinder them? It explained why their words carried so well when not flying. It made for an excellent adaptation.

"*What are you thinking?*"

"*How you freed me of my past. You gave me wings before I realized. This fear of flying does not belong. There is nothing scary about this.*"

"*I wish I could give you dragon wings. You would understand, then, why I love to fly.*"

"*Can you not transform me?*"

He went quiet for a moment as he focused on flying again. "*I am not sure. I did not think it possible, but now I wonder…*" He looked down at me. "*Would you allow me to try some day?*"

I thought about this and its possible implications. But I found very few. Even the ones that did rear up, weren't so bad. Raikidan got me to see a lot of things about myself I never wanted to face. But now, maybe it wasn't so bad.

I nodded. "*I want to know what it means to be a dragon.*"

He chuckled. "*No. You will experience a dragon body.*"

I frowned. "*I thought—*"

I sighed, my gaze dropping. This was more difficult to *explain* than I wanted. *Is it because—*

"*Eira.*" I lifted my gaze up, catching what appeared to be a smile on his toothy maw. "*You already know what it means to be dragon.*"

He stared at me so intensely, it scared me a bit. *Did he—*

"*To be dragon is to be yourself, Eira. You act dragon, you do not have to pretend.*" His large wings beat strongly against the air. "*We are selfish. We are proud. We are caring when we desire.*"

I grunted. "*You describe a human.*"

He nodded. "*As I have come to learn, humans and dragons are not much different. And where we are different, you are less so.*"

He said I acted like a dragon before. But did I really act that much like them?

Raikidan's gaze softened. "*You have changed me in many ways, Eira. It pleases me.*"

I found myself looking away, rubbing my arm. "*You have changed me, too. In a good way.*"

"*I want to always help you be the best you.*"

I tentatively returned my gaze to him. "*Always?*"

"*Always.*" He stared back with such intensity it sent heat into my face. It really didn't matter that he was in his dragon shape. He still made me react in ways I wasn't sure if I shouldn't anymore.

"*I want—*" I gasped when I noticed the temple. "*Raikidan, look!*"

His large head swiveled in the direction of the temple. It was now within reach. His idea worked!

Raikidan's wings beat harder and he picked up speed. A thrill ran through me. I stood and stuck my head out between his talons for a better look. Wind battered my face, but I didn't care. The temple drew closer, my excitement building. I was finally going to set foot here.

Raikidan swooped in for a landing, and I braced myself when he touched down. It was a little rough for me, but nothing I couldn't handle. He set me down and then shifted to his nu-human form.

I gazed up at the ancient building. High marble steps led up to it, braziers lighting the way. Tall pillars and arches carved from marble spanned around the building. On one side of the staircase stood an enormous statue depicting a valkyrie. She wore armor that appeared more ceremonial than practical, and wielded a large maul. *She looks... familiar.* On the other side of the stairs was an empty base. Something told me there should be another statue there.

My hand traced the smooth marble as I walked up the steps, gazing around. Raikidan followed, just as enthralled as me. We made it to the top and I strolled up to the giant doors. Chiseled into the marble were dragons, a valkyrie, gods, and individual people doing… something. I traced the etchings, trying to understand the story or meaning behind it. The more I studied, the more a sense of familiarity washed over me, and yet I couldn't figure it out.

Raikidan grasped one of the metal rings of the door and tried to pull it open, with no success. I gave him a hand, but I was no help. We walked around the temple, going opposite ways, and met up in the back. There were no other entrances.

"Well, this is frustrating," I said. I'd finally made it here, and I couldn't get in.

"Since this is most likely a secret locked up in your mind, it's not going to be easy to get inside," Raikidan said. "I mean, it took us this long to get here."

I frowned and went back to the front of the building, gazing at the carvings on the doors again. There was something important about it. The gods stood above all, then the valkyrie, that looked a lot like the statue at the bottom of the stairs. Below were dragons and people. My eyes narrowed. These people were women. I traced my fingers over one who appeared elven in nature and then one that had nu-human features. *What is the story?*

My hands stopped in an empty spot on the mural. The area was large enough for at least one other dragon and woman. Was it unfinished? If so, why?

Raikidan drew up next to me and gazed at the stone mural. He traced what parts of the dragons he could reach. I found myself watching him instead of trying to figure this all out. He looked awed by the etchings. His fingers dug into the carve marks as if he were trying to read something about them.

His hands stopped near mine, right in the empty spot. He blinked, as if he were in a trance. His gaze flicked to my hand, mere inches from his, and then me. His gaze sucked me in.

Warmth seeped into my hand when he placed his on mine. I continued to stare up at him. Raikidan reached up and cupped my cheek with his free hand. The warmth in my hand rushed to my face and a strong tingling sensation rippled through my body as he slid his thumb over my skin.

I gasped and jumped back when a warm pulse hit my hand through the door. Raikidan also jerked back and then focused on me. "What was that?"

I shook my head. "I don't know."

I rested my hand back on the door, but nothing happened. Raikidan placed his hand next to mine. Nothing. He moved his hand on top of mine, and still nothing.

I leaned against the door, pressing my ear to it. My lips twisted. Nothing. Raikidan rested his ear on the door as well, and the two of us continued to listen. Why, I wasn't sure. But I felt compelled to continue to stay put.

Then a feminine voice chuckled. "Almost."

Before I had a chance to process, everything around me disappeared in quick succession, including Raikidan. I plunged into darkness and my senses dulled. But only for a moment.

My senses returned little by little. I heard loud breathing, and felt the softness of blankets under me. Light hit my closed eyes and they fluttered open. I faced a wall, my arms under one of my many pillows. Crystal's brilliant blue eyes peered at me from where she lay, and she began to purr and knead the blankets.

I reached out and scratched her behind her feline ears, and then sat up. Raikidan was also awake, watching me.

I rubbed my eyes. "That was weird."

Raikidan shifted and jumped onto my bed. Crystal narrowed her eyes at him, but then purred when he reached out and pet her. Once he was done, he placed a hand on my forehead. "Are you feeling okay after that?"

I smiled and moved his hand. "Yes, I'm fine. Confused, but also happy. We made progress. It brought out more questions than answers, but at least we reached the temple."

I tucked some hair behind my ear. "I had imagined it'd be cool, but that… I don't know how to put it into words." I looked at him as excitement built in me. "And to speak your language so well. That was incredible! Will I ever be that good at it?"

He smiled. "At the rate you're going, I think so."

The etching on the door of the temple resurfaced in my mind. "I wonder what that mural was all about."

"It felt important," Raikidan said. "I sensed something from it for some reason. Did you?"

I nodded. "I can't place why, especially with the chosen subjects."

"You have no inklings at all? Dragons are an unusual subject."

I stared at my lap, chewing my lower lip. Did I? *Maybe...* I shook my head. "I'm sorry, I don't."

He lifted my chin. "It's okay. We have time to think about this. I give you my word I'll continue to help you. Whatever it takes, we're going to find out more about this temple, and that voice."

The voice... I knew it. I knew it well.

"Hey, voice. That was you, wasn't it?"

No answer. That was strange. At the rate she'd gone lately, she would have said at least something in response.

Raikidan tilted his head. "Are you okay, Eira?"

I smiled. "Yeah. Was just thinking about this some more. I wish I could go back to sleep and learn more right now."

"Allow your mind to rest. Being so active in that place instead of sleeping can be taxing. We'll get the answers." He leaned over, brushing my bangs to the side and planted a kiss on my forehead. My cheeks heated. "I promise. Now, I'll get you breakfast."

I tried to protest, but he left before anything could come out. What'd gotten into him all of a sudden?

CHAPTER 24

Slinking around in the shadows of the alley, I kept an eye out for patrolling soldiers while the others set up. We had been successful with keeping under the radar so far tonight, but I wasn't sure how long that'd last, especially since several dragons and shamans insisted on watching us on the rooftops. The dragons did a decent job at staying hidden, but the shamans were another story.

Argus came over to me and motioned for me to head over to the others. I nodded and let him take my post, making sure I didn't dawdle. Ryoko handed me a ventilation mask and then two paint cans when I was ready for them. I shook the cans as quietly as I could while approaching the alley wall. More cans were lined up along it to make my job a little easier, but my success fell on how quickly I could work—and luck. I glanced at Seda when I was ready, and she nodded. Taking a deep breath, I began spraying the wall with paint.

My spray strokes varied as I loosely painted down the base idea floating in my head. Seda would levitate a new paint can up to me when I needed it, and once my design span up farther than I could reach, she lent her gifts and lifted me in the air.

I worked with quick precision, but also with grace. I couldn't help but flourish my movements due to the levitation. It had been a long time since I'd worked with spray paint, but all those years of practice in the past rushed back to me as I'd worked tonight.

Just as I began to enjoy what I was doing and felt the mural was nearly complete, Argus ran back to us. "Soldiers. We need to get out of here."

I nodded and threw my cans of paint into a bag Ryoko held, while Seda levitated the cans on the ground into the same bag. When we heard the footsteps of the marching patrol, we hastened our cleanup and made it to the rooftops just in time. Keeping low, I peered over the edge and watched.

The patrol walked down the alley and then swore when they found my artwork. Ryoko growled when they insulted it, complaining about it being graffiti. Mocha quieted her down. It wasn't like we didn't know they'd see it as graffiti, since… well… it was, but we did have a purpose for it.

I was actually surprised the Council approved my request. Public defacing of property wasn't something they were okay with since it would be viewed so negatively on us, but Shva'sika and Raikidan managed to sway them… somehow.

"It's because they're outsiders. If they don't see it as poor taste, then the Council has a hard time arguing."

"That doesn't make any sense to me, but whatever."

When the soldiers made a call to report my work, we decided it was time to leave and head home. I didn't doubt the military had found some of the other paintings I had made, so making more would be tricky. Not to mention each one was time-consuming, and I wasn't sure I'd have enough time to complete another before the sun came up. It didn't matter. I had gotten quite a few done, and even managed to do two on main roads.

Hopefully they'd help us like I'd calculated. That is, if the military didn't figure out how to remove them before the citizens found them.

I wrapped a thin wire around a thicker one a few times before weaving them into the ring I was making. The largest order of jewelry I had ever received had been flown into by messenger hawk to me this morning while I was sleeping, and I wasn't sure how I was going to fill it. That, of course, wasn't even factoring in the carving order I received a few days ago, and the jewelry and carving order I had yet to fill from a few weeks ago.

Azriel is lucky I care about him so much. Had I not, I'd be making the decision to focus on this for my job. It only made sense at this point, with how popular my work had become.

I looked up when someone knocked on the front door, and Blaze went to find out who was here. When he returned, several soldiers followed him. Zo led the squad, and I was surprised to see Ryder, Bone, and Yára a part of the group.

"You have visitors," Blaze told me.

I nodded. "I see that."

Bone examined the room. "Nice place."

Yára came over to me and leaned on the back of the couch to see what I was doing. "These are pretty."

"Thanks." I handed her a necklace to look at. "It's my second job. Or at least, part of it. I make wood carvings and figurines as well."

"Wow," she breathed. She seemed to really like the necklace.

"Here." I lifted my head in time to see Ryder tossing me a bag. "I was on my way here to deliver these to you when I was dragged into this."

"Into what?" I asked as I opened the bag. Of course opening the bag only added to my confusion. "Ryder, I didn't make another gem order."

"Ray did," he said. "And it's already been paid for, so don't argue, please."

I huffed. "All right, fine. Now is someone going to tell me—Bone, what are you doing?"

He was in the kitchen now. "Just looking. Never seen a kitchen before. At least not a real one. I don't really consider the mess hall a kitchen."

I shook my head with a chuckle and turned my attention back to Zo. "All right, as I was asking, how can I help all of you?"

"We have orders to show these two around the city." Zo said. "Since you do well keeping them under control, or, at least, know when a situation will be overstimulating for them, we were hoping you'd join us."

My lips twisted. "From what I gathered, Yára wasn't someone to worry about, so why do you need me for just—"

"There are several others outside still," Zo interrupted. "We figured it'd be best to not crowd your home."

I nodded. "We appreciate that. This living room gets a bit crowded as it is when everyone from this house gathers into it all at once."

"So will you come with us?" Yára asked. When I didn't answer fast enough for her, she bent down closer to me. "I don't want to be the only woman in this group."

I laughed. "Well, when you put it that way, I can't really say no, not that I would anyway. I'd be happy to be of some help."

Yára smiled brightly.

"Just let me finish this piece."

They all agreed, and watched as I finished off the ring in my hands, Bone making a quiet comment to himself about how neat it was I could use my fire so precisely to solder the wires together where needed. When satisfied with the finished piece, I stacked my supplies on the table and headed for my room. As I grabbed a messenger bag from my closet, Raikidan folded up our shaman cloaks and handed them to me.

I cocked an eyebrow. "What's this for?"

"Seda said there's a possibility we might need them," he explained in a hushed voice.

I nodded and then stuffed them in the bag, annoying Raikidan since he actually tried to keep them neat for once. But I had done it for that sole purpose, because I was a jerk like that.

I put a box of finished jewelry in the bag just in case we ran into a caravan, and then went into the kitchen to snatch up a few bottles of water. When I was ready, Raikidan and I followed Zo and the other soldiers out. Several of my brothers were outside, and they greeted me with friendly but apprehensive smiles. There weren't as many here as I thought, and I was really surprised Rhaec and Trigon weren't a part of this group.

"The others are still going under evaluation," Zo let me know as we headed down the street.

I nodded. "Understandable. The two Brutes, Rhaec and Trigon, how are they doing?"

He shrugged. "Depends on who you ask."

"Meaning they're using their muscle more than their brains."

He chuckled. "Typical Brute behavior."

I grunted. "That's the truth."

"Ryoko?"

"Ryoko."

"She's been quite helpful," he praised. "I'd heard rumors of her skills, but never thought they were true. We could use more like her."

I nodded, not really knowing what to say that wouldn't possibly reveal my true past.

Yára squeezed herself between us and latched onto my arm. Her hair bounced on her shoulder, and as the sun caught it, I noticed something about it I hadn't in the poorly-lit interrogation room. Unlike my hair that had a more reddish tint to its color, she had a bluish tint to her violet. *Well, that's something to mark us as individuals.* It wasn't much, and most would miss that, but it made me feel a bit better.

"So where we going?" she asked.

I shrugged. "You'd best ask your ever-so-faithful general. I'm just tagging along."

Yára looked at Zo expectantly and he faltered. "I… don't have a mapped-out route just yet."

"It really was a sudden order," another soldier said.

"Sounds more like an excuse than a reason," Raikidan muttered.

Zo glared at him and I shook my head. "Why don't we go to Sector Six? It'll be fairly quiet around this time. Not too much stimuli to cause potential issues."

Zo's eyebrow lifted. "How do you know that?"

"The caravans go there to pass stock around to each other. It's hard to do that with tons of people around, so they figured out the safest but most quiet time and place to do it."

"But that's a popular shopping area," another soldier said.

I nodded. "Yes, but not in the afternoon on a day like today. Most people are at the outdoor centers in Sector Ten. I'm not trying to say Sector Six will be empty, it just won't be as crazy as Sector Ten."

Zo nodded thoughtfully. "Then we'll go there."

A wide smile spread across Yára's face. "Can we go shopping while we're there?"

I shrugged. "If you have money, I don't see why not."

"I'm not sure that's a good idea," Zo said. When Yára pouted, his tone changed rather quickly. "But we'll make a proper call when we arrive."

Pushover.

"You think he's smitten with her, too? You both do look a lot alike."

"Gods, I hope not. I don't know his age, but he's got to be around my age. Maybe a bit younger, since I never met him in the military."

"You didn't know everyone, though. And he looks older than you."

"That's true. Either way, I wouldn't allow it."

"I suspect she'd say the same."

Taking a corner on a main street, we were forced to stop due to a large crowd gathered on the sidewalk.

"I wonder what's going on," Yára said.

"Maybe we should find out?" Bone suggested.

I shook my head. "I wouldn't advise it."

"Why?" he asked. "Crowds are a sign of possible disorder, and our job is to keep things in order, right?"

"That would be part of a soldier's job," I agreed. "But that is not part of your job right now. You're just supposed to get used to city life and not kill anyone. C'mon, we'll walk around."

Bone sighed, clearly annoyed with my decision, but followed me as I stepped out onto the road to maneuver around the crowd. Zo, to my surprise, didn't voice an alternate opinion to mine. I could tell he wanted to know what was going on, though I wondered if his orders to deal with this task overruled his other duties.

As we walked around, the sight of some civilians taking pictures with their communicators flashed in my peripheral, pulling my attention. That's when I noticed the mural I had painted last night—one of the two I had painted on a main street. The sight of it made me stop and stare.

"What is it?" Zo asked.

"I think I know what's causing the crowd," I said before heading toward the mural.

People protested as I pushed my way through, but I didn't care. I wanted to see how it had turned out. For all I knew, it had come out to be a total mess. When I finally pushed to the front, I stared at the mural. It was a depiction of a large mountain, and the colors used were just as vibrant as I had hoped.

Yára made her way through the crowd soon after, with the others close behind, and gasped in awe. Zo took one look at the mural, grunted, and went to speak with some soldiers who were trying to get the crowd to leave.

"It's beautiful," Yára whispered. "But what is it of?"

"It's Mt. Azrok," I said. "The great mountain that houses one of the last dwarven cities."

"Dwarves? They really live there?"

I nodded.

She gasped. "Have you been there?"

I smiled at her. "Yes. Beautiful place. Pristine, and seemingly untouched by man. You can't even hear the bustling Dwarven city until you get close to the entrance."

"What are they like?"

"The dwarves?" I chuckled. "Loud, rowdy, half drunk most of the time, and an absolute blast to be around."

Yára laughed. "I don't know if hanging around half-drunk people is my idea of a blast."

I laughed with her. "You'd change your mind if you met them. Even when drunk, they can make great conversationalists. Well, when they're not yelling out some sort of far-fetched story, that is."

I went to walk up to the mural, but a soldier reached out to stop me. Before he touched me, though, Zo raised his hand. "It's alright, she's with me."

The soldier hesitated, but allowed me to continue. I ran my hand over the brick. "Whoever made this did a fantastic job."

Bone came up next to me. "Does it really look this nice?"

I shook my head. "No. It looks much better in person, but I suspect whoever made this did their best. Though it's a shame they didn't paint the city. That may even be a more impressive sight, if you ask me."

"It's just a bunch of junk graffiti some riffraff created," one soldier said.

I grinned as I turned to head down the street once more. "One man's trash is another's treasure."

One of my brothers looked around. "I wonder if there are any more."

Yára's eyes lit up. "We should find out!"

"No," Zo said, his tone authoritative. "Our orders are to show you around the city to become accustomed to it. We are not going to look for meaningless, fictional paintings."

"And who says they're fictional, or meaningless?" I asked him. "You sound more afraid than anything, Zo."

He faltered from my accusation. I continued to walk off without a care. "We won't go out of our way to find them, but there shouldn't be any harm in looking at more if they happen to cross our path."

Yára squealed, unable to contain her excitement. I wanted to see if the others were drawing the same attention. Between the excitement from the crowd and my ability to explain the mural to everyone, I was hopeful for the future.

It wasn't long before we came across another large crowd clustering by a wall, with soldiers trying to get them under control. Pushing through, we were met with the sight of a large lighthouse on the edge of a cliff facing the ocean. My siblings turned to me for an explanation for this painting.

"The lighthouse of Larkren." I smiled. "It's located at the highest point of the cliffs that brave the strong ocean waves."

I walked up to the wall and Yára followed. "The grass looks really tall."

"Based on the length of the grass, I'm going to guess whoever painted this saw this place during a healthy rain season." I ran my fingers over the dried paint.

I went to speak again, but a soldier rudely interrupted me. "It's nothing but rebel propaganda to confuse the citizens of this city. This place doesn't really exist."

I grinned. "Oh, but it does. I've been there during a time of plentiful rain. The grass grows so quickly the people of the town can't keep up. When I was there, I could easily hide in the grass while standing, and it's said it can grow even taller."

"That's one hard game of hide-and-seek," Ryder said as he gazed. Yára and I laughed.

"You shouldn't openly defend such evil people," a soldier warned.

"Are they?" I questioned. "Or are you?"

"Excuse me?" His eyes flashed, angered by the idea I might actually be siding with the vandals so openly.

"When one fights for a world they believe is more fair, how can they be truly evil? You may believe they are wrong, but they also believe you are wrong for what they believe is blind following. So, in the end, who is right? Who is truly good and who is truly evil, when both sides fight for what they claim to be right?"

Zo and the soldiers stared at me.

As I touched the mural, something stirred within me.

"Breathe on it." It was a voice, and in my head, but it wasn't the same as the one I normally heard. Or even the one I heard when I'd been at the lighthouse and told to call out to the birds flying above me. Or the one who wanted me to spar with Pyralis. *Great, I really am crazy.*

"Bring life to it."

I didn't know why she was telling me this, but I wasn't going to listen. For all I knew, I'd end up causing an accident.

"It's safe." When I still didn't listen, she spoke again. *"Trust that I will help."*

I took a deep breath. I couldn't believe I was going to actually listen to it. It'd be one thing to listen to the one voice I was used to, but this new one? I really was insane.

Leaning in close, I blew on the paint, my eyes half closing for an unknown reason. Nothing happened immediately, but just as my breath was about to run out, an unfamiliar energy pulsed within me and the paint moved in a way that sand would when blown around by wind. I pulled away as the painting came alive and surrounded us.

Before our eyes, tall grass sprouted up around our feet, swaying in the gentle, salty breeze. Gulls called overhead, and the waves of the ocean crashed against the cliff we stood on. The lighthouse now felt more real. It was as if we were actually at the location of the mural.

"What's going on?" Zo demanded.

"Memory magic," Raikidan murmured in awe.

"Magic is gone," a soldier said.

"Not all of it," Raikidan corrected. "Simple magic is still around, but it isn't shared outside of family lines anymore."

"But if a family line disappears, doesn't the knowledge of the magic go with them?" Yára asked.

He nodded. "Yes."

"Then why not share it?" a soldier asked. "Why selfishly keep it to themselves?"

"We live in a world where fear controls the hearts of men," I said, my voice soft. "We live in a world where men would rather lose valuable information than allow it to fall into the wrong hands."

The soldier snorted. "So, you feel that's enough justification?"

I nodded. "Yes. I am the last of my family line who knows of memory magic, and that's where it'll stay."

The soldier looked as though he was going to press the matter, but Bone shot him an ugly warning look that convinced him to back down. I was grateful. I wasn't even sure if this really was magic, or an illusion someone else created from an unseen place.

The magic ended then, and we were back on the street next to the painted mural. Civilians murmured and the soldiers frantically went about trying to calm them down, feeding them one lie or another. Me, on the other hand, I pushed through the crowd and continued down the street. The others caught up, and I watched as they took in the city.

They were handling everything a lot better than I predicted they would. Neither crowd had sent any of them into a murderous frenzy, nor were they showing any signs of strain. I wanted them to tell me how they were feeling, and find out if they had an easier time keeping themselves under control than I did at times, but I knew better.

I never thought I'd want to learn about them. I'd jumped to so many conclusions when I first saw their paperwork. I… allowed myself to do exactly what others had done to me—treat them like monsters when I didn't even know them. *How could I have fallen into that trap so easily?*

"Because you, like many others, have faults," the voice said. *"But what redeems you is that you are actively trying to fix your wrongs. That is what sets you apart from those who wronged you."*

I wasn't convinced. There was no justification for what I'd done.

I showed my family some shops to get them familiar with the idea of them, and the soldiers had them interact with civilians when the opportunity presented itself. They even allowed me to bring them into a pet store. Yára, of course, was as giddy as a schoolgirl as she pet all the animals and enjoyed herself. My brothers, on the other hand, were apprehensive, and many of the animals also acted a bit strange around them. No surprise, Raikidan had the same issue, but I already knew why.

As we walked down a new street, I kept an eye out for more murals and the caravans. There was one wagon in particular I was hoping to run into, since he was at the top of my list for my jewelry.

"Eira!"

I looked around and found a familiar shaman standing by a covered wagon, waving me down some ways off. Smiling, I checked to make sure it was safe to cross and set a quick pace over to meet with him. When I was on the other side of the road safely, I waved my fingers in greeting. "Hey, Ken'ichi."

He smiled wide. "Good to see you're walking around on your own."

"It's nice to not be half dead."

I smiled when Yára and the others joined me by my side. Yára's eyes lit up at the sight of the wares for sale and she couldn't resist checking them out.

As she did, a tall man poked his head out from inside. His black cloak with blue embroidery masked his face, but I'd recognize him even if he dyed it pink. "Eira, glad you're here. Do you have any pieces done for me to sell? I'm out."

Yára peered up at him and blinked before pointing at me. "I think you're looking for her."

The cloaked man turned my way and then back at Yára. When he looked at me again, I waved my fingers. "Hey, Ter'len."

He shook his head. "Should I even ask?"

I laughed. "No. I'm still not sure about it myself." I dug into my messenger bag. "But before you ask again, yes, I do have some jewelry for you. No carvings, though. I gave my last batch to Se'la's caravan."

He grunted. "Figures she'd get to you first."

I chuckled as I handed over the box of jewelry. "Her route asks for them the most. You always get first dibs on my jewelry stock, so don't complain."

"Fine, fine. Let's just see what you brought me."

He dug through the box and his smile grew wider and wider. "I don't know where you get these ideas of yours. Each are beautiful, and even repeated designs have a handmade uniqueness to them."

"Can I see them?" Yára asked.

"Of course." Ter'len handed them over. She sifted through the box.

The smile on Yára's face never left, and her eyes glittered. "These are so amazing." She pulled a necklace out of the box. "I like this one the most. Makes me think of that ring you made."

I came over and pulled out a ring. "You mean this one?"

She blinked. "How'd you do that?"

I chuckled. "I'm just that good. These two are actually meant to be a set—I do that from time to time. I thought about making a matching pair of earrings, but then sided against it."

Yára just smiled. "Well you're lucky to even have such talent."

I smiled, but it faded when a soldier decided to make a remark. "If you make money on this, why even work at Twilight? Another person from this city could use that job."

I grunted. "I don't work there for the money. I do it as a favor to Azriel. I knew him for a while before he offered me the job. He knew he could count on me."

"There are plenty of people capable of pulling a bartending and waitressing job."

"You really don't know anything. I'm his Assistant Manager."

Zo smiled. "So he did promote you."

I nodded. "Officially promoted me, anyway. I'd been doing most of those tasks prior to the paperwork filing."

"Well, good on you, Sweetcheeks."

Yára placed the necklace she liked back in the box. I handed it off to Ter'len after I put the ring back inside as well. He glanced at Yára and then ducked back inside his wagon. "Eira, do you mind coming in here? I have a question about one carving I can't seem to sell."

My brow ticked up. What was he up to? "Yeah, sure."

I hopped up in the back of the wagon, pushing my way through the packed store until I managed to get to him. He rifled through the jewelry box some more, a single carving of a mother bear and her two cubs sat on a chest next to him. At a glance, it looked fine, and the subject was usually popular, so I couldn't understand why he struggled with selling it.

"Use your head."

Tar'len glanced up at me, and then to the statue, and then the box in his hand. *Oh.* I should have known it was a ruse.

"Yeah, no kidding."

"Oh, shush you."

"So, is this the carving in question?" I didn't take my eyes off of him.

"It is." He pointed to my satchel and wordlessly beckoned for it. "Can you assess the quality again? I'm worried I didn't hear you right and priced it too high."

I handed him the satchel and then lifted the carving. "I'll see what I can assess."

While I examined the statue, Ter'len slipped two irregularly shaped items into the bag. I smirked. He was too nice a man sometimes. "Quality isn't the issue, your price is. You priced it too low, so people think there's something wrong with it."

He laughed. "Me and my old age!" He patted me on the shoulder and handed the bag back. "I'll fix that and watch it fly off my table."

I slung the satchel back over my shoulder and hopped out of the wagon. "If it still doesn't sell, maybe consider a trade with another caravan. Might just not be what your customers are looking for."

He nodded. "I'll consider your counsel. Thank you."

I smiled at him and waited for the others to be done with their window-shopping before heading off. My brothers asked a few questions about the shamans, though my answers were deliberately vague due to the military presence.

We stopped walking when something in an alley caught Bone's eye. Without a word, he ventured off and I ran after him. At the back end of the alley was another large mural, but it was simpler than the last two we looked at—not that I was surprised. This was the last one I had made, and, to my disappointment, you could tell it was a bit of a rushed job.

Yára, awed, gazed over the painting. "This is the best yet."

"You shouldn't be praising graffiti," a soldier chided.

"I don't think it's graffiti," she muttered.

I smirked. "One man's trash…"

"What is this place?" Yára asked.

"The Hyberia mountain range," I said as I ran my fingers over the wall. "It's the largest range of mountains in Lumaraeon, located in the North, and is the only mountain range in that area to have a small village nestled in it."

"You've been to this place, too?" Zo guessed.

I was quiet for a moment. "I lived there."

"What?"

"The village in this range is my home."

"Our home," Raikidan corrected.

"Is it nice there?" Yára asked.

I nodded. "It was beautiful there. Summers aren't too hot, and winters are snowy. The lake the village is built near was filled with fish, and the forest provided good hunting."

"You keep using past tense," one of my brothers observed. "What happened to the fish and forest?"

My skin scraped against the brick as my fist clenched. "Soldiers..."

"Excuse me?" Zo said.

"Soldiers from this city came and demanded submission and absolute obedience." I turned to look at them all, my lip curling. "But we wouldn't just blindly obey a man from some foreign part of Lumaraeon, so they destroyed the forests and poisoned the lake."

Zo stared in shock at the accusation.

"But that wasn't all they did." I continued. "Remember that fire I told you about? They were the cause of it. My family was to be an example of what happens when we resisted."

"Quit lying, woman!" a soldier ordered.

Raikidan's lip curled. "It's no lie. Check your death records, and you'll see we sent those soldiers back here in body bags. We weren't having any of your shit."

"But why would you be here if that was true?" Zo asked.

I stalked past them. "Because my job among the shamans comes before my personal feelings. They need me here to help keep order, and that's what I'm doing. Plus, I wanted to give you another chance. I wanted to see if redeeming changes could be made."

"Have they?" Zo asked.

"Unfortunately, no." I turned down the street and walked away from them. Their mixed emotions rolled off them and out of the alley, following me as I went. I smiled. I was getting a lot better at this acting stuff.

"You did well. Making them see the dark side of their actions will make them question what they're doing."

Raikidan ran to catch up to me and it wasn't long before the others were following as well. Even with the tension, they seemed to figure I'd at least finish this assignment with them.

I came to a halt when I felt something strange stir in my body. Focusing on it, I noted it was reacting to a type of heat source. It had done it once before when I was training as a shaman, but that had been so long ago I was surprised I remembered how that felt.

"What's wrong?" Raikidan asked.

"I'm not sure. It feels like I'm picking up an uncontained heat signature."

Bone pointed to something in the sky. "Could that be why?"

I tilted my head back to see dark smoke billowing into the sky.

"Looks like an out of control fire," Raikidan said.

"We need to get over there," Zo stated. "We may be needed."

"Are you sure we should come with you?" Yára asked.

Zo nodded. "I think you can handle it."

"We're going, too," I told Raikidan as I dug through my bag to grab my cloak.

"I don't think that's wise," Raikidan argued.

"Don't care." I tossed him his cloak and I clasped mine around my neck.

Before Raikidan could continue to argue, I ran off in the direction of the smoke, and I was pretty sure I heard him sigh in aggravation. Bone and my brothers were quick to follow, Yára catching up as well. Soon we rounded the corner where the fire was located.

Civilians had clustered to watch, while soldiers ran around trying to get the fire under control and keep the civilians as far back as possible. Breathing fire and an incantation into my hand, I voiced a message of help into the flame and let it go into the air. The fire took the shape of several butterflies and flew off.

Removing my bag from my shoulder, I tossed it to Yára and ran toward the commotion. Raikidan pushed past me, but stopped as he came to the crowd of people and knelt. I continued running, and when I reached him he gave me a lift.

My landing on the other side of the crowd startled the soldiers. One tried to get me to step back, but I couldn't have cared less what he wanted. Taking in a deep breath and walking toward the burning building, I reached out and felt the fire's strength. Grabbing hold of it, I merged its will with mine.

I was surprised by how large the fire was. The house looked so small from the outside. But that didn't matter. I took a deep breath and forced the fire to die. Raikidan and the others, along with a group of shamans I had called on for assistance via my fire butterflies, pushed through the crowd just as I killed any traces of fire.

The shamans went to work immediately at helping the civilians affected by the fire, while Raikidan came over to me. "You okay?"

I nodded. "Yeah. It was easy."

"You don't sound okay," he observed.

"I'm fine. I'm just feeling out for any more lingering fire."

"That was rather impressive," Zo complimented.

I shrugged. "Simple wild fire control. It's one the first techniques fire elementalists and shamans learn."

"You guys could make up a team of impressive fire fighters," Bone said.

I chuckled for a moment until a shaman flagged me down. She and Yára knelt next to a young boy with a fish bowl in his hands. From the looks of it, the water was murky, and I was pretty sure there was a fish floating in it.

"Ambassador, could you possibly help?" the shaman requested. I knelt in front of the boy and peered into the bowl. "The fish's spirit is still inside the body. I've never healed a fish, but I'm willing to give it a try if you can purify the water."

I smiled. "I'll do my best."

Raising my hands, I moved them in a fluid motion until I was able to feel out the water. Keeping my breath calm, I swirled the liquid until I had a good hold on it and then lifted the substance out of the bowl. I was careful not to harm the fish as I tried to separate the particles from the water, while also running fresh water through its gills in hopes that would stir it.

"Wait, I thought she was a fire shaman," Zo said.

"She is," Raikidan said. "She also has the rare ability to touch water, making her a water shaman as well. The Ambassador is the strongest and wisest of all the shamans. She has skills most will never be able to attain and knows how to use them wisely."

"I'll admit, I don't fully understand," Zo said.

I separated the purified water and the murky water. I tossed the tainted water away before placing the clean water back in the bowl and allowing the healing shaman to attempt to bring the fish back.

"There is much you don't know about us, Zo." I told him without looking back. "And most of it will remain that way. Not because we don't trust you, but because you aren't shamans."

The healer pulled her hands away from the fish when it twitched. The boy's eyes grew wide, and I smiled as the fish came back to life and swam around in the bowl as if nothing had happened.

The healing shaman patted the boy on the head. "All better now."

"Thank you!" A toothy smile spread across his sooty face and we couldn't help but smile back. This job was rewarding, that was for sure.

"Shaman Ambassador," a soldier called.

I rose and faced her. "Yes?"

"Thank you."

I smiled. "You're welcome. I should let you know—based on the feel of the fire, I believe some sort of gas was the catalyst. If you plan to go into the building, I'd advise caution."

She nodded. "Thank you. We appreciate it."

I nodded and then faced the shamans. "Thank you for helping."

Several of them bowed. "Of course, Ambassador. It's what we do."

Keni'chi approached. "Now that this has been taken care of, we do actually need your help with something."

I tilted my head. "If you needed me, why didn't you tell me when I was at the caravan?"

He stuck his hand in his hood and seemingly rubbed the back of his head. "I forgot."

I grunted. "Figures. But I can't help now. I'm already busy helping someone else."

"Oh, oka—"

"Actually, you can go with them now, Ambassador," Zo told me.

I turned to face him. At least he was being tactful about my name around the civilians. "Are you sure?"

He nodded. "You've helped a lot today. It's best we head back to the fortress to do some evaluations."

"All right then."

Raikidan joined me and we went to follow the group of shamans when Yára called out to me. "Wait, I still have your bag!"

I waved and smiled. "Keep it."

"Wow, really?" she asked.

"Yeah."

She smiled. "Thanks."

I watched as she crossed it over her shoulder and then headed off before she tried to stop me again when she found the gift inside.

"Looks good on you, Yára," Bone complimented.

"You think so?" she asked.

"Of course."

I heard her gasp and I smiled. "Wait, I think you forgot something in this bag!"

"Yára, I'm not so sure she forgot," Zo said.

"Huh?"

"Yeah, that looks like that necklace and ring you really liked," Bone pointed out. "I think she meant to leave it in the bag. I mean, last we saw it, it went into that box with jewelry. She had to have put it in the bag on purpose."

"He's right," Zo said. "And she doesn't do many things on accident. That's not her style."

"Wow… I'm going to have to find a way to thank her."

"You will. You're smart like that," Ryder said.

Zo's comment made me realize I hadn't finished my work with them as a rebel. The idea the shamans needed me for something had taken me off my mental track. I needed to see if I could still sway some of their opinions of us. Maybe even get some to join our cause. It was a long shot, but I needed to try. That was the point of the paintings, after all.

I stopped walking to turn back and gave Zo and the other soldiers some… advice. "Be wary of who you are told are allies and who are enemies, Zo. Blind following only leads to destruction."

A curious expression crossed his face. I continued on, allowing him to think on the words.

"Good call."

When we were out of earshot of the military, I turned my attention to Ken'ichi. "So, what did you need me for?"

He pointed to two cloaked figures from the East Tribe. "These two were asking for you at the caravan after you left. We got your help request just after."

The one closest to me dipped his head. "Ambassador. My name is Mar'nar and this is my sister Tel'les."

Tel'les dipped her head respectfully and I returned the gesture. "We were hoping you could help us discover the secret to your power."

My brow rose. "What?"

"The power you have is incredible," Mar'nar complimented. "And from what we've heard, you've only been practicing diligently for maybe a decade or so. Most shamans can't unlock even half the power you possess, and we believe there has to be a reason for it.

"It's because she's likely an old soul," Tel'les said.

Mar'nar shook his head. "Here we go again. Will you give that idea a rest? There's no way—"

"Wait," I said. "I want to hear what she has to say."

"Good call."

"I've done some reading," Tel'les said. "Well, a lot of reading, and I've come up with a theory on how we're chosen to be shamans. I believe we have to be a reincarnated soul."

I pressed my lips together as I thought about this. That was an interesting theory. It got me thinking…

"I believe because our souls have touched the spiritual plane, we are capable of accessing it when given another life."

"It's a farfetched theory," Mar'nar said.

"I don't think so," I argued. "I've met a spirit that called me 'Ancient Soul.' I couldn't make much sense of it until just now."

Tel'les' smile brightened.

"But that theory just talks about how to be a shaman," Raikidan said, killing Tel'les' mood. "It doesn't explain why Eira's abilities are so strong."

"I was going to get to that," Tel'les muttered. "If my theory is correct, when a soul is given another life, that soul becomes stronger, and thus abilities in their new life would also be stronger."

"So, you're saying, Laz'shika could have a soul that's been reincarnated several times?" Ken'ichi asked.

She nodded. "Yes. If her soul has had many lives, then her soul and her abilities would be that much stronger compared to an individual that was reincarnated once. I believe it's that strength that allows an elementalist and shaman to tap into their opposite element as well, like she has done."

"Seems valid, for a theory at least," Raikidan said.

I looked at Mar'nar when he continued to frown. "Since you don't agree with her idea, what's your theory?"

Mar'nar shook his head. "I don't have a concrete one yet. The Ambassadors all had amazing abilities. They've always been the best of all the shamans of their time, but have had different personalities and different abilities. If a person's soul is reincarnated, wouldn't each life they have produce that same personality, or, at the very least, the same abilities, just stronger?"

I thought about this. "I don't know. Everyone is rather unique, and are who they are based on how they're raised. If someone is born an elf with no money in one life, and then a human with all the riches in Lumaraeon, they'd act quite differently."

Mar'nar frowned. "I suppose that makes sense."

"But, you do have a point when it comes to abilities. I'm not sure how that would work."

Mar'nar took solace in that. I could tell there was a bit of a rivalry between them. This could get interesting pretty quickly with the two.

"So it seems you're onboard with helping, regardless of the outcome," Ken'ichi observed.

I nodded. "I'd like to see where this will lead us. Just tell me what I need to do."

"First, we're going to need to evaluate how far you can push yourself, and how much more you may be capable of unlocking." Tel'les told me. "Then we can proceed from there, but we'll have to do it from the safety of our own temporary homes here in the city."

I nodded in agreement. I wasn't sure if seeing my power was the right way to start, but this was their project and I'd do what I could to help. I, too, wanted to know why I was so different, or special in the eyes of these shamans. Why me?

Hopefully this would explain that, and this Ancient Soul business.

"You're on the right track."

This surprised me. *"You could tell me that?"*

"It appears that answer was vague enough."

I almost laughed out loud. *"Vague isn't something I'd call it, but I'll take it."*

This testing may also prove useful in explaining other things, like how I was able to use memory magic when I hadn't even known it still existed. And maybe, just maybe, it could tell me why the voice, well now voices, existed in my mind.

CHAPTER 25

Keeping low in the shadows, I adjusted the settings of the voice-changing device Argus had made, until I finally managed to get it just to the right setting—or as close to right as possible. They were still in the testing phase, and Seda insisted on joining us in case they malfunctioned so she could keep our voices hidden if needed, even for a little bit.

Raikidan fiddled with his changer and I tried to get him to stop. I knew he found it uncomfortable, but if he kept playing with it, he'd break it. When I finally managed to get him to stop fidgeting with the gadget, I looked at the time on my communicator. The Council had assigned us the *honor* of questioning a possible new recruit. We didn't have much to go on except it was a guy, he was a decently ranked soldier, and he was supposed to meet us in the alley below at ten sharp. He was five minutes late. *Some soldier.*

"This is a waste of time," Blaze whispered. "He's not going to show."

"Be patient," I said. "If he really is a soldier, he may have had a difficult time getting away."

"Or he's setting up a trap," Mocha voiced.

I shook my head. "If this was a trap, we would have been jumped by now."

"Wait, what's that?" Ryoko asked when she noticed movement in the alley.

Keeping to the shadows, I crept to the edge of the building to get a closer look. A man dressed in military attire set a slow pace down the alley. He cast glances over his shoulder every few moments, his pinkies twitching. *Cautious and nervous.* Made sense. If he really was serious about joining our cause, he'd be committing a pretty serious crime.

I motioned for everyone to spread out. This was our guy. Raikidan stayed next to me, no surprise there, but Ryoko surprised me by sticking with us as well. I would have figured she'd want to watch from another side.

The man walked into the only good light source down there, and I had to stop myself from gasping. I couldn't believe what I was seeing. Ryoko, Raikidan and I exchanged shocked expressions and then looked back down at Zo as he scanned the alley.

This couldn't be right. There had to be some sort of catch. Why would Zo, a high-ranking general, be here? Back when the rebellion formed, that was common, sure, but now? Now we were lucky to get anything higher than a foot soldier. Even a Tactician would be great every now and then.

Zo looked at his communicator to check the time. "Maybe I'm too late…"

Ryoko nudged me and I sucked in a tight breath. I wasn't going to find out any answers if protocol questions weren't asked. It was now or never.

Moving to the edge of the roof so he could see my shape but not my features, I chuckled. "Well, well, well. What do we have here?"

My voice echoed against the walls of the ally, prompting Zo to look around. As he did, the others moved closer to the edge so he was aware of how outnumbered he was if he was alone and tried to pull something.

When he still wasn't able to figure out which one of us spoke, I figured it'd be best to give him a hand. "In front of you."

He stopped looking around and peered up at me. "You're… a woman."

I chuckled. "Surprise."

He gulped. "My name is—"

"Zo." I chuckled again. "Yes, we know. We know a lot about you. But what we don't know is what a general like yourself is thinking, attempting to join the people who are rebelling against the one man that gave you your status?"

Zo hesitated, and I had a thought. "It wouldn't have to do with a particular shaman woman you're rather fond of, would it?"

Zo gulped, and the others laughed.

"No." I blinked when he answered. "It's not because of her."

I took great interest in this. "Oh really? Then tell me, why are you here?"

He licked his lips as he tried to word his reply, and I waited. "I… I don't know…"

"You don't know?" I laughed. "You really expect me to accept that answer?" Zo frowned but stayed quiet, and I grunted. "Well, I won't. This isn't something you do when you're bored and then leave when you've had your fill. This isn't a game! This is a real movement, with real goals with real lives at stake. We fight for a much different world than the one you live in. We fight for free choice, not forced subjugation. We refuse to see Zarda as some sort of god."

I shifted my weight. "I don't know why you're here, Zo, but I do know you are not ready for our cause. You do not have the conviction—the heart—to work alongside us. To go against the man that created you—to see the fellow soldiers you've fought alongside for years as enemies."

Zo looked down at the ground. "I see."

"You should leave," I advised. "You don't need to be caught."

He nodded, his gaze not lifting. It was as if he were still trying to process everything I said. When he started to walk away, the others withdrew from their perches, but stopped when Zo turned around again. "What can I do to prove myself?"

I chuckled. "What can you do? I'm afraid I can't tell you that, Zo. You must find the answer on your own." I slipped back into the shadows and spoke as I did, "If you manage to figure it all out, you know where to find us."

We all retreated to the backside of the building so Zo couldn't see us. I released a relieved breath when we heard him leave and removed my voice changer.

"That was impressive, Eira," Corliss complimented.

Rylan nodded in agreement. "You made the right call."

"Thanks," I replied. "I didn't want to send him away, but there wasn't anything there to tell us he could be trusted. I couldn't take that risk."

"It was the best choice," Seda agreed. "Zo didn't even know if he wanted to defect. He obviously didn't think this through."

"Do you think he'll contact us again?" Ryoko asked.

I shrugged. "It's anyone's guess. He needs to really think about it, though. It isn't something you can back out of after you've begun."

"I'm still surprised he even thought about joining us," Mocha said. "He's one of the last generals I'd expect to consider our movement as a positive thing."

I nodded with agreement, but Rylan shook his head. "I'm not. Think about it. Because of his infatuation with Eira, he's become more open-minded. It was only a matter of time before she got into his head."

"But I can't take all the credit," I said. "He needed to have his own doubts for anything I said to affect him. I've sensed his indecision every once in a while, so when I've had the chance, I've done my best to 'fan the flames' without revealing the truth about me. Still, I didn't think I had that great of an effect on him."

"She's right," Corliss agreed. "An idea is only as strong as its followers. If there is any doubt, there is a chance that opinions and sides will change."

"Well, let's hope he decides to join us," Ryoko said. "He may be a creep when it comes to women, but he's a good general, from what I hear. We could use someone like that on our side."

I agreed. Zo really could help us if we could convince him he was fighting for the wrong side. It seemed I had my newest task laid out for me.

26
CHAPTER

A light breeze rustled the leaves above me, speckles of sunlight splattering across the ground. I stared up at the canopy, my back against the rotting stump with nothing but the sounds of nature surrounding me. Even with the city mere feet away, the unusual nature of this spot held its noise at bay, making it a perfect place for me to come to and reflect. And reflect I did.

So much had happened lately, there was a lot to think about.

"If you want to talk to me about anything, I'm here."

"I need to figure out how to word myself so you can answer."

The voice growled. *"Yes, this block is frustrating."*

It wasn't just the past month's events running through my mind that had me asking for reflection. A dream I'd had drove me to seek time alone.

His strong ashy-musk scent and powerful presence filled my senses. My heart hammered in my chest. A gasp escaped my lips as his teeth grazed my neck, his hands sliding up my sides.

I hid my face in my hand. I needed to get that out of my head.

"Why fight what you want?"

"Because it's not right."

"You sure about that?"

Leaves rustled behind me, followed by the crunching of heavy footsteps. A familiar scent crossed my nose. *Raikidan.* I did my best to compose myself. "Hey, Raikidan."

"Eira, are you okay?"

I turned my gaze over my shoulder. "Yeah. I'm just reflecting."

He sat down next to me. "On what?"

I shrugged. "Everything. What's happened in this last year—hell, this last month. Who I was. How I've changed. Who I want to be." I shifted my sitting position. "How I need to get over certain obstacles to get to that point."

Raikidan arched an eyebrow, causing me to smile.

"I've learned a lot in these past months. I've always been afraid to be happy. Because when I am, something bad has always happened—but I've learned that I can't keep being afraid. I don't gain anything from it."

Raikidan gazed at me for a moment. "You've changed a lot."

My smile widened. "I know, and it's all thanks to you."

"Me?" His brow rose. "The other day you mentioned I'd gotten you to see something about emotions. But I don't remember doing anything."

"You got me to face my past—to face the trauma I've suffered all these years, instead of pushing it away and trying to ignore it as if it never existed. You understood me in ways others were unable to, allowing you to help me grow as a person and come to terms with many things. People say you should never change for another person, but what they don't realize is that there's nothing wrong with allowing others to help you become a better you."

I stared up at the sky. "My design was to be a first. The first soldier with no emotion. Jasmine refused to allow that to happen and tweaked my design, but not on paper. Contrary to what I've told others, told you, I came out of my tank with all my emotions intact. But I was still expected to be emotionless, or I'd be deemed a failure and put to death. I did what I could to fix Jasmine's actions. I tried to shove all my emotions away and pretend I didn't have them. I wanted to be able to do something right, except I couldn't. I buried most of them, but couldn't get rid of them all, and it left me all mangled inside."

I locked eyes with him, my voice dropping low. "Again, it's because of you I realized how wrong I was for doing that to myself. So, I've been trying to patch things back together. It's complicated, and downright confusing, but I'm getting there. It won't be perfect for some time, but I'm not going to run from it anymore. I can't do that to myself."

Raikidan brushed my bangs out of my eyes. "I'm glad I could encourage this change in you. I've watched you change from the person I met. You're becoming the real you. The one that would have existed had it not been for Zarda." His voice dropped to a whisper, the usual gravely tone deepening. "I like her a lot."

My brow shot up and he stammered over his words. "Th–that's n–not to say I didn't like the old you. Just th–that—"

I leaned over and lightly kissed his lips, his taste teasing me. "It's okay. I like this me much more, too. Thank you for helping me find her again."

"That's not why he was tripping over his words."

"Oh, shut up."

"You're the one who kissed him. Friends don't do that."

"I said shut up."

His lips twisted sideways. "I will continue to do whatever I can to help you become that person you wish to be." He reached out and cupped my cheek, caressing my skin with his thumb. "All I want is to see you happy."

My heart skipped, heat warming my face. "Why me?"

His lips spread into a half smile. "Because I care about you."

Is the space between us lessening? I couldn't tell for sure, my eyes couldn't break away, but it sure felt like we were drawing physically closer to each other. My eyes grew heavy and the space continued to lessen, until a twig snapped. Raikidan and I jumped to our feet and we both looked around.

Raikidan grabbed my hand and yanked me behind him. My brow furrowed and he stared in one direction, his body tense. I peered around him to find the familiar and unwanted sight of the revenant leading the Crimson Sanctuary. "Kir."

A sick, malicious grin spread across his ashen face. "So you remembered who I am finally."

From a sheath on my arm, I drew the special dagger Ryder crafted for me long ago. "No—had to ask the right people. Though after finding out, I'd rather not have wasted my time."

He scowled. "I will destroy you, Ancient Soul." *There's that name again.* "I will not allow your rebirth to continue."

My eyes widened. *What does he mean by that?*

The voice growled. *"He can't have you."*

Raikidan took a protective stance. "I will not let you touch her."

Kir sneered. "Your *champion* is just as moronic this time as before." He drew the sword strapped to his waist. "Makes my task easier. I will rend both your souls and send them to all halfling filth and their supporters as a message."

I slipped in front of Raikidan and held him back. "Rai, stay away from him." Raikidan went to protest, but I continued. "He's a revenant, remember? Revenants are dangerous, especially to those who are not skilled in handling them. Please trust me—I know how to deal with him."

Raikidan sighed, but didn't relax. "Fine, but if things get out of hand, I *will* step in."

I smiled and then squared off with Kir. His mouth twisted into an evil grin, and he rushed me with inhuman speed. I strengthened my resolve, and filled my body with spiritual energy as the shamans had taught me.

The day I let the shamans know about Kir, they had immediately set forth training on how to deal with him. All shamans would devote time to tracking him down until he was eradicated, but since I was a specific target of his, they wanted to be sure I could defend myself if the need came.

While revenants needed to be dealt with in a special way, I had no doubts Kir had extra tricks due to his revenant age. He wouldn't be easy to take down, but as a shaman myself, and a halfling, I couldn't allow him to continue his path.

My dagger morphed into a short sword when I came into range of Kir, and our weapons clashed. He took great interest in my modified weapon, but focused on attacking me. I dodged, evaded, and deflected blows as best as I could while looking for an opening. Each time I did, I reached for him with my free hand only to have him jump out of the way in time. *I need to get this paralyzing energy into him.*

"Don't give up. Predict his movements better."

"Easier said than done." While she was right, spirits were notoriously difficult to predict, and revenants were ten times worse.

My sword sliced across Kir's arm, my built-up spiritual energy shooting through the weapon and into him. Kir cried out and his form distorted. Then in a blink of an eye, he disappeared. I looked around. *Where the hell—*

"Eira, look out!" Raikidan shouted. He shoved me just as Kir came up behind me, his hand outstretched. Raikidan, now in my place, reeled back when Kir grabbed a hold of his arm.

Kir sneered. "Foolish boy."

No! I jumped to my feet and thrust my short sword at the revenant. It met its mark, his chest, and Kir screamed and writhed. I put myself between him and Raikidan when he backed away, but before I could continue my attack, the air to our left distorted into a portal and Arcadia rushed out.

Kir glowered and pointed at me. "This isn't the end, Isis. I will destroy you."

Isis? Who is that?

He ran to the center of the clearing, the air distorting around him and he vanished. Arcadia swore at her lateness while I focused on Raikidan. He held his arm, a blackish-purple handprint visible on the skin. My dragon cringed, his teeth clenched, and the mark grew, veining out first, and then consuming the healthy skin between veins.

"Let me see it," I said. Raikidan didn't protest. "I told you not to engage him. We need to get you to the shamans."

"No need." Arcadia approached. "I can remove the poison."

I stepped aside and the goddess held her hand over Raikidan's arm. Her eyes glowed blue-white, as did her outstretched hand. Raikidan cringed and I watched as the dark handprint pulled away from his skin in a gaseous form. The moment the poisonous marking finished leaving his body, the blackish-purple gas dispersed and Arcadia's eyes returned to their normal pale look.

Raikidan rubbed his arm. "What was that?"

"We call it R-poison," I said. "It's a fast-acting, painful poison that revenants inject into the living. Shamans are capable of fighting this poison with their use of spiritual energy, but an ordinary person has no way of fighting it. Without the help of a shaman, or a god like Arcadia in this case, they'll die within an hour." I looked to Arcadia. "Thank you. I'm sorry we delayed your pursuit."

She shook her head. "Don't apologize. Had he not left a trail of infected beings for shamans and myself to deal with, I would have been here sooner." She gazed around the clearing. "This place…"

"It's a thinness between the planes," I said.

She turned my way. "You knew?"

I shook my head. "While I've come here a lot to think, it wasn't until earlier today that I realized the reason for its odd nature."

Raikidan's eyes flicked between us. "What are you two talking about?"

Arcadia focused on him. "Creating the spiritual plane was no easy task for me. It took a long time to mirror the living plane and align the two without merging them. Unfortunately, due to the near-perfect mirror and the nature of the spiritual plane, it wasn't possible to keep both planes completely separate. There are areas, like this location, where the planes merge, making it easier for spirits and the living to pass between more freely."

I eyed her. "Wait, did you just tell us what the spiritual plane looks like to spirits?" She placed a finger up to her smirking lips and I laughed. "Your brother is rubbing off on you."

She shook her head. "The two of you should head home. Now that I know this place exists I will work on my vigilance of this area. I cannot allow this weakness be our downfall."

"Before we go, I have a question. Why did Kir call me 'Ancient Soul'? He's not the first to call me that. On top of that, he called me Isis." My eyes narrowed. "Everyone seems to think I'm someone important, but there's something missing. Are they mistaking me for her? Or is there something I don't know that no one wants to tell me?"

Arcadia stared at me, though her eyes remained soft. "I'm sorry, Eira, but like before, I am incapable of giving you the answer you seek."

Raikidan pulled me closer. I peered up at him to find his eyes narrow and dark. "What kind of god can't answer such simple questions? Especially important ones? A revenant is trying to kill her, calls her by names she doesn't understand, and yet others do? Who the hell do you think you are?"

I stared at him, my eyes wide. *Raikidan…*

"Good boy." I thought I caught a smile on the voice's words.

Arcadia smiled. "Your loyalty for her, even in this life, makes me happy." Raikidan and I exchanged glances, confused. "But sadly, there are unseen rules blocking my words. No god can tell you these answers."

No god?

"You will have to ask a mortal for them." She smiled. "Or look within yourself, as they also lie there." A portal appeared behind her and she stepped in. "Good luck."

She disappeared, leaving the two of us alone.

"Please tell me you're as confused as me," Raikidan said.

I nodded, though something stirred in my mind. Was Tel'les right about the reincarnation thing? Arcadia said something about "this life."

I turned to Raikidan. But that was directed to him as well. Was his soul older than we thought?

"I think it'd be best if we headed home," I said.

"Right."

I pushed my bedroom door open and Raikidan followed me in, today's events weighing heavy on my mind—especially the Kir situation. *So many unanswered questions.*

I went about doing laundry. Monotonous tasks tended to help me sort out my thoughts.

"Eira, are you all right?" Raikidan asked.

"Just have a lot on my mind."

He came up beside me. "Do you want to talk about it?

I shook my head. "Everything is too jumbled for me to make enough sense of it to talk about."

"Okay…" His gaze fell to my laundry basket. "Do you want help?"

My brow rose. "Since when do you know how to fold clothes?"

He gave a sheepish smile. "Since Ryoko made me learn so I wouldn't rely on you or her to do it anymore."

I looked down at the basket and then shrugged. "I guess you can help, if you really want to. Just don't make any comments about any of them. Mana has been wearing most of them."

"That explains why you have so much to fold."

I shrugged. "At least someone is getting use out of them. I wish Ryoko would just stop buying me clothes I won't wear. It's a waste of money."

Raikidan inspected a shirt he picked up. "You should wear some of these. They'd look good on you."

I examined the shirt in my hand and then folded it without replying.
"Don't be rude."
"I don't really know what I should say."
"Well, for one, you could thank him."
"That could potentially lead to certain unwanted conversations."
The voice growled with frustration.

The two of us folded clothes in silence, but Kir wouldn't leave my mind.

Raikidan stopped helping and turned toward me. "What happened with that revenant is bothering you, isn't it?"

I finished folding the shirt in my hands. "Yes. But it's more than just what he said today. Revenants are bad news. They have power no spirit should, and it's due to their strong will to continue on out of anger or grief. Such strong negative emotions twist their spirits until they cannot pass over without help."

I leaned on my dresser. "They use to be greater in numbers, several millennia before the War of End, but thanks to an elven woman of royal descent, those with spirit-touch abilities were organized and trained to deal with them. These were the first shamans. That was the shamans' original purpose. And that woman, Raina, became the first Ambassador. At least, that's what I've been told and have read in my recent research."

I shut my eyes. "Revenants are now just supposed to be monsters in stories told to children so they'll behave. They were supposed to have been eradicated, and our due diligence with lingering spirits is supposed to prevent beings like Kir from continuing to exist. But somehow we missed him—someone with a strong hatred of halflings. He's evaded us and now he's so strong, we might as well be taking on a god."

Raikidan cupped my cheek. "We'll get him. I promise."

My gaze lowered, and I sighed. I didn't know how to be positive about all this.

Raikidan let go. "Can I ask you something?" I gave him my attention. "It's about what you said to Arcadia. You said something about others mistaking you for someone else. What was that about?"

Oh boy. This would come up.
"Tell him the truth."
I plopped down on my bed. "I'm not clear on it myself. But ever

since my tank release, my mother told me I was someone special, that I had some unique gift or power that would be able to fix so many problems in the world. I never found this claimed power, and always figured she was just trying to make me believe in myself or feel better about my poorly handed situation."

I played with my fingers. "But then others started believing this, too. The shamans first, and now the dragons. Except they'd say things that don't make sense to me, and they get confused when I don't understand. I've come to realize they've all mistaken me for someone else."

"That's not true!"

"I don't know why they would, but it's the only reasonable explanation I have." I huffed and tucked a stray strand of hair behind my ear. "I don't even know what I did to make them think this way. All I know is that I don't have this profound, Lumaraeon-changing power they think I have, and it's going to crush so many hopes and dreams."

Raikidan sat down next to me. "I don't know about this Lumaraeon-changing power, but you are pretty special. Have you looked at what you've accomplished? Have you seen the kind of powerhouse you are?"

"Anyone can do what I've done if they try."

"That's the thing about having abilities that are so natural to us—we don't realize it's not that simple."

I met his gaze.

"Others could try as hard as they like, but not all of them could gather allies like you can. Not just anyone can have the control over fire like you. Not just anyone can tame a dragon like you have."

I punched him in the arm. "I've not tamed a dragon."

He rubbed his arm and then grabbed my hands, pulling me off the bed. One of his hands found my lower back and he held me close. "Not true."

He pulled me across the floor, his touch light and our movement floaty, but a bit choppy because of my bewilderment.

"Raikidan, what are you doing?" I asked.

He chuckled. "What does it look like? I'm dancing with you."

My brow rose. "Why?"

He grinned. "To make you feel better."

I laughed. "You're so weird. There isn't even any music playing."

"It's in my head."

"I feel silly."

"Then lighten up and have fun."

I blinked at his jest and then giggled. My laughter continued as we danced, and it became contagious, because soon Raikidan was laughing along with me.

When the supposed music in Raikidan's head seemed to end, he gracefully spun me around and backed up to sit on the windowsill. I expected him to let me go, but to my surprise, he pulled me with him until I was straddling his lap. He smiled at me.

I wrapped my arms around his neck and hugged him. "Thanks."

"See, you did tame a dragon."

I pulled away, but with Raikidan's hands on my lower back, I didn't go too far, resulting in my hands resting on his chest. Raikidan reached up and gently brushed a stray hair out of my face, and I smiled as I stared into his eyes. I couldn't help it. I loved the color, and the way the late evening sun filtering through the skylight reflected off them, I couldn't help but appreciate them even more.

My mind didn't send me any warning messages as my body leaned closer to him, and it didn't shout out at me when my eyes hooded, or even when Raikidan's grip on my back tightened. His hot breath teased my lips, but still I didn't pull away. His intoxicating scent numbed me to everything but him.

My lips parted and then pressed against his. One of his hands cupped my cheek, his strong fingers curling over the back of my neck, and his grip on my back tightened. Warmth swelled in my chest and my head swam as our lips synchronized. His fingers pressed into my spine, sending a jolt through me. A moan built in my throat. I liked this—craved it. I wanted more.

"Mana, wait," a hushed voice said.

Wait, this is wrong. I jerked away from Raikidan, realizing what I'd done. I put space between us, Raikidan staring at me with wide, confused eyes. "I—I'm sorry. I—I don't know what came over me. Just… forget that happened."

"Eira, wait—"

I snatched a folded towel and slammed the bathroom door behind me. I leaned against the door, my heart thundering in my chest and ears as I took gasping breaths. *What is wrong with me?* I knew better than to have done that. Nothing made any of my actions right. Pain clenched my chest. I grabbed it, struggling to cope with all the emotions hammering me.

"You're hurting yourself."

"I crossed another line I shouldn't have. I knew better. It wasn't right for me to do that. I deserve this pain."

"How long are you going to do this to yourself? When will you tell him?"

"Never. It's not right."

"But you want him."

"It doesn't matter what I want. He's not mine to have. He never will be…"

"He could be if you told him. He understands you. He wants you, too. That's why he didn't stop you."

The pain pulsed more. *"Please, stop… He belongs to someone else. I will not take away his happiness."*

"You would make him happy."

"Not like she could." I clamped my eyes shut. *"There's always… a better choice than me."*

"Stop it! Stop it right now. I will not sit here and listen to you degrade yourself. You've had plenty of young men vie for your attention. One of them includes a fine specimen of a dragon who sits outside this very door. You can try to deny the obvious signs all you want, but that doesn't change any facts. So, put on your big girls pants, face your fears, and take what you want! Zarda doesn't own you."

I stood there, my jaw slack and my eyes wide. I couldn't formulate a single response to that.

A hand rapped on the door, and then Mana's voice called out, "Eira?"

I took a quiet, controlled breath. "Yeah?"

"Are you okay?"

I tried to shake everything off. "Yeah, I'm fine."

"Okay. Would it be okay if I joined you?"

I chewed my lip and then decided it would help distract me. I headed for the bath. "Come on in."

The door opened and she slipped in, a smile on her face. I stripped down and sunk into the warm water, Mana joining me soon after. The two of us didn't speak. I was too lost in my chaotic mind. *I can't believe I did that…*

"Hey, Eira?" Mana said. "Are you sure you're okay? You look like you have something on your mind."

I smiled at her, attempting to reassure her and myself. "I'll be fine, don't worry. Just have to sort something out on my own."

She frowned. "Would you rather I left?"

My eyes widened. "No, of course not. Why would you think that?"

She avoided eye contact and shrugged. "I just don't want to be a bother."

"Mana, you're not a bother." *Really, you've been helpful with saving me from terrible situations. This time, you were just a bit too late.*

"Had she not shown up at all, you and your secret boyfriend would have had a fun night."

"Shut up about that. I'm not joking."

"Neither am I."

Mana lifted her gaze. "Then, can we hang out more?" My brow rose. She played with her fingers. "Well, Raikidan gets you all the time. And so do Ryoko and Elarinya. I want to spend time with you, too. I like you. You're really nice and you're friendly to me, and I feel like I should be able to hang around with you more. So, can I?"

I smiled. "Of course you can, Mana. But I'm not that much fun to be around. I'm pretty boring, really. I don't know why Shva'sika and Ryoko want to be around me so much, and Raikidan is around me because he's a lost puppy."

"A hunky puppy."

"Stop."

She giggled at my last add-in about Raikidan. "I don't care. I just want to be around you some more. It's been nice being around so many others. I miss it…"

I tilted my head. "You lived in a colony before being with Corliss, didn't you?"

She shook her head. "It wasn't big enough to be a colony. More like a clan. It was led by my father, and it consisted of my mother and a lot of their offspring."

I looked at the door when someone rapped on it. "Yes?"

Ryoko poked her head in. "Can Danika, Mocha, and I join you two?"

Mana nodded enthusiastically. "Of course, there's plenty of room!"

I smiled. "Sure. Mana and I were just talking about her family."

Shva'sika smiled. "That's sounds like a lovely topic."

"Well, we weren't talking about my family, really," Mana corrected. "Just how I used to live before becoming Corliss' mate."

"And how was that?" Ryoko asked as she slipped into the bath.

"I lived in a clan made up of my family and me." Mana said.

"And now you live with just Corliss? That's a bit of a change," Mocha said.

Mana nodded. "That's why I was telling Eira why I like being here with you guys so much. It reminds me a lot of what I had before."

"Have you and Corliss talked about having kids?" Ryoko asked. Mana frowned and looked down at the water, making Ryoko gasp. "I'm sorry! I didn't mean to upset you."

Mana shook her head. "It's okay. We dragons have low conception rates, so it's difficult for us to have offspring. It's not uncommon for mates to go several centuries before having their first clutch. Corliss and I want some… but it hasn't happened yet…"

"It will," I said. "When the time is right."

Ryoko nodded. "Yeah, she's right. I mean, would Corliss had come and helped us if you guys had kids?"

Mana shook her head. "No probably not."

"See, then maybe that's why it hasn't happened yet. Had you two had kids, he wouldn't have brought Raikidan back to us, and you two wouldn't have met us, either. And things would be going much differently now. I mean, Laz and I would probably be dead had they not come back when they had."

"Correction, I would have been dead," I said. "I would have made sure you left."

Ryoko rolled her eyes and Mana giggled. "Thanks. That makes me feel better about everything. I just have to be patient."

"It'll happen when you least expect it," Shva'sika added. "That's how I've seen it go with couples who try so hard to have their own children."

Mana nodded.

"Hey, Mana?" I asked.

"Yeah?"

"If you liked being around your family so much, why didn't you ask Corliss to stay with you guys instead of going off with him to his territory?"

Mana exhaled slowly. "That's because of my father. Unlike me, my father was rather mistrusting of the other races, and he didn't understand some of my siblings' and my curiosity about them. He thought our curiosity would get us into trouble, or even killed. So he was overbearing and made it hard for us to go out and have fun. As much as I liked being around my family, I didn't feel free, so I left to go out on my own."

My brow rose. "That's rather unusual for a female dragon to do."

She nodded. "I know. It's not common, and most of the time we don't stay on our own for long, since other dragons will insist we stay in their territory where it'd be safe, regardless of color difference."

"Except for half-colors," I muttered.

She nodded again. "Yeah, they're the exception, but there are dragons out there that don't care about mixed colored scales, so some dragons can find refuge—it's just harder."

"With you being on your own, is that how you and Corliss met?" Mocha asked.

Mana half-smiled. "Yes. When I left home, I traveled for some time, trying to find the right place for me. I ended up in Corliss' territory, but had only planned on resting for a moment or two. I smelled the territory marks of him, his brother, and Raikidan. I figured with so many males in one area, my presence could potentially cause some issues, and that was the last thing I wanted."

Mana splashed some water onto her arms. "That hope had been dashed when Corliss found me. The moment I met him, I felt some strong force between us. I wasn't sure what to make of it, but it scared me, making it easy for me to lie about my temporary presence. I told him I was just passing through on my way to visit family."

She sighed and shook her head. "My lie was short-lived. My father showed up, and tried to convince me to come home. I refused, and he resorted to an attempt at force, but Corliss wasn't going to allow that. He defended me, battling with my father. Both were formidable opponents, but eventually, Corliss overpowered my father and sent him away."

Mana scratched her head. "At that point, I couldn't make myself leave. He'd been wounded because of me, and had no regrets. It was only right I stay, for at least a little while. He gave me a nice cave to live in that was a little ways away from his, but not too close, so as to not make me uncomfortable. We got to know each other, and one thing led to another, and we became mates."

Ryoko hummed, a big goofy grin on her face. "Now that's a love story I'd like to see in a book."

The girls laughed at her and I rolled my eyes.

Mana pushed back her hair to rub water over her neck and shoulders, and I noticed a strange, round scar at the base of her neck. I thought to ask about it, but then decided against it in case it would trigger a possible bad memory.

Ryoko, who also noticed, wasn't so inclined to keep her mouth shut. "What's that from?"

Mana touched her scar. "This? Oh, that's my *mate mark*. All mated females have them. Our mates give them to us when we consummate our pairing."

I furrowed my brow in confusion. "Raikidan said males don't hurt females—at least, they're not supposed to."

Mana nodded. "Yeah, that's true, but this is the one exception. Along with another part of the mating process, the mate mark cements the bond between the mated dragons. It creates an unbreakable link for the pair. Though the process of creating it is rather painful, so males tend to add in an extra promise that it'll be the only time he'll ever hurt her. Some believe this promise deepens the bond, while others think the bond can't be deepened any further than it already is."

I nodded thoughtfully. "Interesting."

"How come your mark is shaped the way it is?" Mocha asked. "It's not really the shape you'd expect a mouth to make, even in a dragon form."

Mana smiled. "That's because the saliva of a green dragon is acidic. And even though Corliss has black dragon in him, he inherited more green dragon traits, such as the saliva."

Shva'sika looked at her with shock. "That sounds dangerous."

Ryoko nodded. "And kinda boring, since you can't kiss or anything."

Mana shrugged. "If we have the time to concentrate, we can actually remove the acidic properties for a time. It's not permanent, but the more skilled the green dragon, the longer that time is. But when it comes to mating, the mate mark changes a few things. With a mated pair of green dragons, their saliva's acidic levels become the same, making them immune since we can't harm ourselves with our own acid. And when it comes to a mixed colored pair, the non-green scaled dragon will become immune to his or her green-scaled mate. So when it comes to the mated pair, the acidic levels don't matter after the mate mark is made."

Mocha nodded. "That's rather interesting."

"My turn to ask a question!" Ryoko exclaimed. Shva'sika and I chuckled. "What's this other part of the mating process you mentioned? If it's not too uncomfortable for you to explain, that is."

Mana hesitated on her answer, and I understood why, so stepped in to help. "It's complicated."

Mana cocked her head. "You know about it?"

I chuckled. "Yeah."

"How?"

"I bullied it out of Raikidan."

She giggled. "How did you manage that?"

I shrugged. "He let a small bit of information about it slip, and I made him tell me."

Her giggling turned to laughter. "That's too funny! I can't believe you actually got him to tell you. He's the last dragon I'd expect to talk about it, even if he was bullied."

"Are you two going to tell us what you're talking about?" Ryoko demanded.

"Ryoko," Shva'sika scolded.

"What? I just don't think it's fair that Laz knows and we don't." She crossed her arms and pouted. "It's not fair she knows more about them when we're all supposed to be friends."

Mana glanced at her with a conflicted look, and I exhaled slowly. "We'll tell you, Ryoko, if you give me your word you won't laugh."

Mocha's brow twisted. "Why would we laugh?"

Mana gasped, her hands flying up to her mouth. "Eira, you didn't laugh when Raikidan told you, did you?"

I scratched the back of my head. "Yeah… I didn't mean to, though. It was just such a crazy idea, and the way he told me just made it sound like he was insane. I still feel bad about it."

"Is it really that crazy sounding?" Mocha asked.

Mana took a deep breath. "When they're ready to have a mate, the males develop a voice in their head that helps them locate and identify their destined mate."

Ryoko and Mocha blinked but Shva'sika nodded. "So dragons are the race that have that."

Mana looked at her quizzically. "You know about it?"

"A little," Shva'sika admitted. "My father talked about it once, but I never found out what race had it. I do know I always thought it was a gift any race would kill for."

"Well, if the perfect partner was basically handed to you and all you had to do was find them, who wouldn't want that?" Mocha asked. "Saves a lot of trial and error, and heartache."

"I always wondered why we dragons had the voice," Mana admitted. "It didn't really make any sense for us to be the only ones."

I grunted. "I doubt we'll find out, too. The gods aren't too keen on explaining certain things they do."

"But who's to say the gods did it?" Mocha said. "What if it was something the dragons developed on their own?"

"The idea is a bit farfetched, but I suppose that could be the reason."

"Mana, you don't know anything else that would help us unlock the secret, do you?" Ryoko asked.

Mana shook her head. "I'm afraid not. The mate marks and mate voice are ancient traditions. A lot of our ancient history was lost during a few wars, and knowledge of the origins of certain abilities we have was one of them."

Ryoko's lower lip puckered out into a pout. "Darn."

I splashed water toward her. "Cheer up. It's not a big deal. Especially for you."

"No kidding," Mocha agreed. "You got the man you wanted, so that's all in the past now for you."

Ryoko grunted. "Yeah, but it would have been nice to not have to wait so long. And Laz, we all know you would have loved it if Rylan hadn't chased after you for so long."

I chuckled. "Yeah, that's true."

I sunk under the water to wet my hair some more, and continued to chat with the others about whatever we felt like. It was nice, and I could see why Mana liked a clan-like setting. She was socially oriented, and was able to get along with anyone. It was a shame she couldn't have stayed with her family. I knew Corliss cared enough that he would have given up his territory to live with her had that been what she wanted. It made me hope the gods would bless them with a child, even if it was just one. They deserved that much.

And Raikidan… he also deserved that, as much as he seemed to think he didn't. *He deserves… a nice dragon…*

"He deserves you. And you him."

"No. He deserves someone better than me. Much, better than me."

CHAPTER 27

Fire swept past my face as I pivoted to dodge. The heat of the flame was impressive, but nothing I couldn't handle. The young shaman I faced threw another hot flame at me, and this time, I dispersed it. His face scrunched. He hated it when I did that.

The half-elf boy, barely thirteen years of age, tried a different tactic. He balled up his fire, compressing it with both hands. *Nope, sorry, kid.*

I rushed him, kicking his feet from under him. The kid lost his concentration and the flame fizzled out as he hit the floor. He groaned.

"Nice try, Es'tla, but that wasn't the right thing to do in that situation," I said.

"Yeah, I can see that."

I shook my head. He could use an attitude adjustment, too, at this rate.

I helped him up. "Do you know why it was a poor choice?"

He didn't look at me.

"Look at me when I speak to you." I kept my tone authoritative, but calm.

He didn't right away, but his eyes eventually snapped up to me. "You're going to tell me I suck at this."

My brow cocked. "Why would I tell you that?"

Es'tla looked away. "Cause my last teacher said I did."

My weight shifted to one side as I crossed my arms. I didn't know much about Es'tla. I'd called for a skill test for all shamans involved in the rebellion, to gauge what kind of fire power we were dealing with, personally taking on the task of testing the Rising Sun shamans. I wasn't as experienced as some of the older shamans, but I had the skill and mentoring knowledge to back me up.

This is how I met Es'tla. Del'karo brought him to me personally, piquing my interest. He didn't tell me much about the boy, just his name, age, and that he'd come from the North Tribe. He wasn't taking part in the rebellion, but Del'karo thought it'd be fine for me to use the time to gauge him regardless.

"Well, I don't know why your last teacher was such a moron, and that's not remotely close to what I was going to say."

Es'tla scrutinized me as if he were trying to find the lie in my words. "I'm listening."

Well, that was a good thing. I wasn't sure how parents dealt with preteens and teenagers. For the most part, Ryder skipped that, and I never went through it myself.

"You were a bit like this, too, when you first came out of your tank," the voice said. *"You just grew out of it quickly."*

"You have great control over your abilities. It's impressive for someone your age, as that control requires dedication and discipline."

His eyes fell away from me again, and I didn't like it. Not because of it was a lack of respect, but because I could tell this former teacher hadn't been good to him. Why else would he react negatively to dedication and discipline?

"The problem you ran into was proper judgment."

Es'tla lifted his gaze, this time curious. "What do you mean?"

"The last trick you tried to pull is an advanced technique. Someone like me, who has had years to temper my skills, could pull it off on the move in little time. But, someone of your skill level, it takes a great deal of concentration, as well as time, not something you had. With my close proximity, you should have forgone the idea, as it rendered you defenseless to my counter attack."

He took this advice in, his eyes flickering as he processed this new information. "So, you're not going to tell me how terrible I was?"

My brow furrowed. *What the hell kind of teacher did he have?*

"One not worth discussing."

She was right—and certainly not a shaman. No shaman would ever be that cruel.

I spit out a flame into my hand. The shamans loved seeing my fire-breathing ability. With their combined encouragement and Raikidan's continued interest, I was learning to be open with this again. It wasn't easy, but I managed. And I could tell this would help the boy.

He stared wide-eyed at the burning flame in my hand. I increased the heat until it burned white. Not an easy task for me, even when I was trying, showing my need for more training as well.

Sweat dripped down our skin from the prolonged intensity, the young boy staring at the brilliant flame.

"I want you to take it from me," I said.

His eyes widened. "Are you crazy?"

I grinned. "Only a little."

"Only a lot!" Telar called out.

I pointed at him, my eyes narrow. He grinned and went back to playing some odd game with a few of the young children who possessed early elemental abilities.

I focused on Es'tla again. "Now, try."

The boy hesitated. He stared long at the bright flame, and the longer he stalled, the harder it became to hold this flame.

"This isn't as easy as it looks, you know," I said through gritted teeth.

The kid's lips pressed into a line, and then he took a deep breath. Lifting his hand, he tried to tap into my flame's power. I sensed no change in my hold, but I knew he was trying based on the deep lines creasing his brow.

Then suddenly, the flame flickered. It wasn't a lot, but it was enough for me to notice why, and for Es'tla to pull back, his eyes wide.

I killed the flame, exhaling and enjoying the relief, and then smiled at him. "Very good."

His brow twisted. "Good? I couldn't take it from you."

"You weren't meant to." I placed my hand on his head. "All I expected was for you to try. I set a higher goal to gauge your skill, nothing more. And let me tell you, that was better than most your age could do."

He gazed up at me with bright blue eyes. "You mean it?"

I smiled. "Of course."

Es'tla wrapped his arms around me and buried his face in my chest. "Thank you…"

It took me a moment to register the unexpected reaction. When I did, I wrapped my arms around him. "You'll never feel useless with us, okay?"

He nodded.

After a few moments he pulled away and smiled at me, his face less closed off than before.

You did good.

I ruffled his copper hair. "Go on now. Your training is over."

He gave me one last hug and then ran over to Del'karo, who watched at the far end of the room. I went to sit down and relax for a moment, listening in.

"I want her to teach me more," Es'tla said. "Please?"

Del'karo chuckled. "We'll see what can be done. She's quite busy these days."

Es'tla sighed, his disappointment clear, but accepted the answer. I drank some water and watched him join Telar in entertaining the children.

Del'karo took in the sight and sat down next to me. "You did well with him."

"Wasn't too hard," I said. "I just had to get under the mess that his last teacher caused. Am I allowed to know?"

Del'karo nodded. "His father. As you may have guessed, he wasn't a good man. Es'tla's mother died in childbirth, and her husband blamed the boy. Didn't treat him well his entire life. His mother is the reason we found him. She begged for someone to find him, even just to put him in a better home."

I took a swig. "When was that?"

"About three months ago."

My brow furrowed. "Why did she wait so long?"

He shook his head. "We're not sure."

Did she also blame Es'tla for a while? I couldn't imagine a mother being so cruel, but there were all types out there.

"What do you think of his request?" Del'karo asked. "I know you heard it."

I grinned. "I wouldn't mind teaching him. Most would say it's about damn time I took on a student to train." I took another drink. "But you're right, I am too swamped right now to take on that responsibility."

My gaze shifted to him. "What about you? I know you have Vanya to care for, but if he wants me to train him, then an even better choice would be the man who trained me. You put up with all kinds of shit with my moody ass, and you have experience with teens, unlike me."

My elven mentor chuckled. "You could have fooled me. I've never seen a thirteen-year-old warm up to someone so quick."

"Ryder never hit that age. Not on a physical level, at least. He stayed ten for years, his mind struggling with identifying himself at such an age, and also comprehending such adult knowledge being thrown at him left and right." I shook my head. "And then one day he was seventeen, and then a few weeks later he was twenty-five. It took me a while to process. I knew watching your kid grow up was shockingly quick to most parents, but that was a bit extreme."

He snickered. "Yes, that would be quite the change, but a ten-year-old boy isn't all that different from a thirteen-year-old."

I snorted. "Puberty makes a huge difference. Ryder didn't go through that during his extended ten-years. Nothing changed about him physically or hormonally."

Del'karo went to say something, but was interrupted when we both flew apart and a strike of lightning zapped past us. Telar let out a strained exhale and put us back down.

My brow cocked, and Telar held up his hands as he shrugged. "I can stop a lot of elements. Lightning apparently isn't one. Who knew?"

Del'karo laughed while I shook my head. "Quite the character your friend is."

"That's one way to describe him."

My mentor's gaze shifted to Raikidan, where he sat braiding a little girl's hair. One of Xaneth's young watched the curious display. "I'm also impressed by Raikidan's ability to do hair. He doesn't come off as the type."

I laughed. "Oh, trust me, it's not by choice on his part. There's a girl at the orphanage we frequent—Panga—she insists he does her hair when we're there. No one else is allowed to do it. It forced him to learn, since nothing he said would deter her."

"But it is a cute sight, you have to admit."

She wasn't wrong. I enjoyed seeing the change in him. As much as he fought the instinct to ignore the children, he did well with them.

Del'karo's lips twisted to one side, his keen eyes darting to me. "He's showing far more fatherly qualities than I expected to find in him."

My eyes narrowed. "Don't."

"Do!"

His boisterous laugh startled me, and he wrapped his arm around me. "Don't be mad. I'm looking out for you like I would any of my children. But if he doesn't hold your attention, and your—"

We watched Telar lift up two children with his abilities and rotate them in the air. Their squealing giggles pulled their parents into the room to investigate.

"—unique friend, who is also good with kids doesn't either, then I'll have to keep looking out for you."

I shook my head. "Must you? I don't need someone. I do everything on my own just fine."

He pulled me tighter. "Need and want are quite different."

My brow cocked. Where was he going with this?

"You don't need someone to help you do chores, because you're able to do them on your own. But it's nice when they do. You don't need someone to dote on you, but it's certainly nice to be appreciated and loved."

My gaze wandered to Raikidan. He'd finished the girl's hair and now kept an eye on her as she played with Xaneth's child. He looked my way and smiled. It only lasted a moment before his attention was diverted by the two little ones again, as Xaneth's youngest stole the little girl's teddy bear. She started to cry, and Raikidan sprung into action, chasing the whelp down.

He returned a moment later, bear in one hand, whelp in the other. The little girl ceased crying immediately and hugged the bear tight. Raikidan turned his gaze to me again, the side of his mouth lifting upward. I smiled back, but only for a moment.

Del'karo was right. It was nice to be cared about for those reasons. But no matter how nice it was, it didn't make it right.

"If I could hit you, I would."

My mentor leaned over, gazing at me with a curious and confused eye. "I don't like that look. I've clearly missed something. What's wrong?"

I forced a smile and shook my head. "I'm fine. Don't worry."

He wasn't buying it. "I've been happily married for a *very* long time. You can't fool me with that line."

"Talk to him about it."

"I can't do that."

"Sure you can. He's always been there for you, like a replacement father—"

"Eira, look out!" Raikidan shouted.

The whistling of metal caught my ears. Before I could react, Del'karo and I flew across the room in opposite directions, hovering about three inches off the ground. The bench we sat on had been crushed, and metal met concrete. When I came to a stop, still hovering, I turned my head to find an armored man behind where Del'karo and I had previously sat, a bastard sword in his hands—which was now embedded in the concrete floor.

Who the hell—

"Eira, behind you!"

I cranked my neck back to find yet another man armored in a similar fashion behind me, his arms raised with a sword ready to swing down.

"Telar!" I shouted. "Move me!"

"What, why—what the hell? Where did he come from?"

There wasn't time. The man swung the sword down. I reached for my dagger on my arm and shifted it into a tower shield. Metal clashed, and my back slammed into the floor. I choked, the wind knocked out of me.

"Eira!" Telar and Raikidan both shouted.

The weight of the sword left me, and the sound of metal crashing into a far wall hit my ears. I gasped for breath, coughing and sputtering on the air my lungs struggled to take in. My shield reverted back into a dagger.

Raikidan rushed over to me and helped me into a sitting position. "Relax, Eira."

I did my best, and soon my breathing returned to normal. The clanking of armor caught my attention, and both armored men writhed on the ground. Telar had both his hands out, his face dark. Then, the suits of armor stilled and then winked out of existence.

My heart rate quickened.

"Sweet Thing, what's going on?" Telar asked, his head swiveling as he scanned the room.

I got to my feet, Raikidan standing as well. "They were spirits."

Several shamans began to gather, Telar still on edge. "Why did they attack you?"

"Good question…"

"Move!" Raikidan shoved me as another bastard sword grazed by me. I fell to the ground.

An ashen-skinned man stood behind us. He wore the same armor as the previous spirits, but his helmet was missing. Blue veins crawled against his skin, his eyes an unnatural red. A recognizable tattoo of a shield and blood drop covered his neck.

The voice hissed.

"Revenant!" I shouted.

Just then, more enemies appeared—some out of thin air, others through portals of some sort. The revenant looming above me bared his teeth as he lifted his sword, but his movements were slow. I recovered from my shock and rolled away, using the momentum to propel myself onto my feet. His sword carved into the ground.

That was close. This had to be the one who attacked me first.

"It is. The movements are the same."

Before I could think to defend myself, more people appeared out of thin air or odd-looking portals, men and women alike. All wore various attire, their features ranging. The only feature to tie them together was the same symbol on their neck.

I gauged the situation as shamans flooded into to the room and the rebels fell back. The enemies from the portals were living, that much was easy to differentiate. Beyond the ashen-skin characteristic of the revenants, the dim light of the room brought out their red eye attribute only seen in low- to no-light situations.

"Kir has been hard at work," the voice said.

"He's been too successful. Living supporters, I can understand. But more revenants?"

"Yes. It's troubling."

Chaos erupted. The Crimson Sanctuary clashed with the shamans; Telar forced back several enemies. Del'karo called for his focus on the revenants, due to his abilities proving to be oddly effective against them.

The armored man from before shifted, lifting his weapon up, and took a swing at me. I quickly rolled out of the way. I wasn't going to be able to focus on more than one of these guys with him around.

Raikidan moved to defend me, but I held up my hand. "You can't—you know this."

"Eira, I—"

"I know you want to help." My dagger pulsed as it took the shape of a falchion, my spiritual energy flowing around the weapon. "But you're not equipped to. Please don't do something rash like last time."

"Don't expect me to sit here and do nothing."

My eyes cut to him for a brief moment. "There are living Crimson Sanctuary members here. I need you to focus on them."

Raikidan hesitated, then nodded and charged the closest living enemy. Relieved, I focused my full attention on the revenant. He was already preparing another attack. I moved in, swinging my falchion. Metal met metal, and a wave of spiritual energy struck him.

The revenant howled and writhed, flailing wildly with his sword. I weaved around his attacks, trying to find an opening. Another revenant jumped into the frenzy, an elven man, his eyes intense. This man didn't carry heavy armor or a large weapon, instead favoring shortswords. He proved a quicker adversary, and I found myself turned on the defensive.

"Do you remember me?" The revenant's eyes bore into me. "Please tell me you do. I came back just for you, dear."

I refused to trade words with him. This wasn't the time. I slashed at him, making contact with his shoulder. He howled and doubled his efforts.

"You thought you banished us for good. But you didn't. Kir found us. He brought us back so we could finish what we started."

The voice inside my head hissed.

My eyes narrowed as I parried his swings. *That confirmed that.*

"You can't win, Raina. You might as well accept that."

My brow twisted as I dodged dual attacks from both him and the armored man. *Why did he call me by the first Ambassador's name?*

Two more revenants targeted me. *Shit.* I wasn't going to be able fight them all.

Telar grabbed two with his psychic abilities, pulling them away and inflicting all manner of pain to their souls, but three more took their place, my eyes darting about as I backed away. More revenants ignored their opponents and targeting me instead. The shamans, Telar, and other psychics that had joined the fray attacked the distracted revenants, but nothing they did stopped their advance.

"Kir's doing?" I asked the voice.

"Possible. More likely because our mouthy adversary called you Raina."

That was a better conclusion. If Raina had been the cause of their banishment, or whatever she'd done to remove them as a threat to the living, they'd focus their revenge on me—even if I wasn't her.

"You are the new Ambassador, though. That doesn't help your position."

Shit. Again, she was right. Raina was the first Ambassador. If she could get rid of them, so could I, in theory. It would be logical for them to deem me the greatest threat here.

Something female in form flashed passed me, forcing the revenants back in a fury of claw strikes. Long raven locks waved around the alluring female figure, her horns and tail hard to miss even in the confusion. *Rosa?*

Where did she come from? Did it matter? She was helping—*for some reason.*

Rosa proved a formidable fighter, her speed unmatched. Several living enemies turned their attention to her, seeing a demon as a bigger threat than even halflings and their supporters. A grin twisted on Rosa's crimson lips as she happily sliced into their flesh.

At that point, my talkative adversary from before slipped away from her and came at me. It proved far easier this time, with him as my only focus. I put everything I had into my attacks.

I quickly discovered that using a blade didn't help. The contact caused temporary pain, but it wasn't enough. I needed to take a riskier approach.

"Be careful."

Ducking low, I closed the gap and grabbed my opponent by the arm. He grabbed my arm in retaliation and pumped r-poison into my skin, his face lighting up with a sick excitement. He wasn't going to win, though. With my body filled with spiritual energy, the poison was nullified in seconds.

The realization quickly dawned on him, and he missed his opportunity to get away. I slammed him to the ground and pinned him there with my body, my hands clamped over his face. I wasn't sure if this was going to work, but I had to do something.

He grabbed my arms and attempted to push me off, forcing more r-poison against my spiritual shield, but the spiritual energy weakened him as it surged to defend me. My brow furrowed with concentration as I forced all the energy into my opponent.

He writhed and cried out, struggling more and more, until a wave of energy forced its way through him and burst his body apart. The same mysterious energy swirled around me. My head pulsed and pounded, my skin crawling with pain.

The voice gasped. *"Eira!"*

Images, voices, emotions flashed through my head. The pains of loss. The feelings of betrayal. The sight of loved ones walking away. It was so jumbled and jarring that I didn't know what was going on. What had I done?

A warm light flashed in the room. The revenants screamed. I swallowed hard, and looked up to find Arcadia in the room, her katanas drawn and glowing with powerful spiritual energy. In one swing, she'd dispersed almost all the revenants. The living Crimson Sanctuary members ran in retreat, leaving the same way they'd come. The remaining revenants also left, knowing they were now outmatched.

With them gone, Arcadia turned her focus on me. Words tumbled out of my mouth before I could think. "Arcadia, what did I do?"

Her somber expression bore into me, as if she were looking into my soul. "It's as you think."

Dread welled up inside me. "No… no, I didn't." I stared at my hands. "I… I didn't mean to…"

"Eira, you need to stay calm."

Raikidan placed a hand on my shoulder before focusing on Arcadia. "What are you two talking about? What did she do?"

"She rended his soul."

Telar stepped forward. "What do you mean by that?"

"I mean she destroyed it. His soul is no more. It has been erased from existence."

Gasps and murmurs filled the room. I continued to stare at my hands, praying they wouldn't shake as numbness fell over me. "I'm sorry…"

My words came out barely a whisper, and I wasn't sure if that was directed to her or to the now-gone soul.

Arcadia knelt in front of me and rested her hand on my head. "You don't need to apologize. I know you didn't mean to. But you also didn't do anything wrong."

I gazed up at her. "What do you mean? How can that not be wrong?"

"His soul was banished to a special place in the spiritual plane, along with thousands of other revenant souls. It was supposed to purify them of their twisted nature, so they could pass on to either hell or the afterlife. Many souls have passed through this process successfully, but there were many others that have not. They remained in this banished space, ever restless. This one had been in there for over ten thousand years. There was no way of saving his soul."

My eyes widened. Over ten thousand? How long ago did the first Ambassador live?

"A long time ago."

Her expression twisted into a reassuring smile. "I give you my word, this was for the best. Do not take any blame upon yourself."

I took a deep breath. "How did I do that?"

"That is the perplexing part." She stood. "Most mortals would not be able to. Those who have been able to in the past were severely wounded afterward due to the soul attacking theirs."

I took a deep breath and slowly let it out, trying to calm my still-twitching body. "I believe that did happen," My voice came out barely a whisper. "I think I saw bits of memories and felt various emotions that weren't mine."

She nodded. "Yes, that would be the moment I'm referring to. But you're unharmed, so to speak. I must look into this further."

Her eyes darted beyond me. "You have other tasks to handle."

I glanced back to see Rosa sitting on a chair, her legs crossed and eyes intent on the situation before her.

"You keep odd company, Ambassador," Arcadia said. "But I'd expect nothing less from you."

She then backed away, disappearing into a portal.

Raikidan helped me to my feet, and I faced the succubus. "Not to sound ungrateful for your help, but what are you doing here, Rosa?"

Her red lips curved into a smile and she rose to her feet. "Straight and to the point, as I expected you to be. And fun. I didn't expect you to lead such an exciting life. I'm so glad I chose today to be the day I cleared the life debt."

Interesting. I didn't think demons followed a code of honor such as that.

She walked past me, her hips swaying with confidence. "Now that I've done that, we're clear, and my beloved and I can go on our way once more."

My eyes darted to her. "You seem to have forgotten how to count. I am still owed one life debt."

Rosa halted, her lips pressing into a thin line. "I suppose there's no pulling that over you. Very well. One more life debt must be repaid."

The succubus' eyes glanced about at the audience we had. A woman hit one of the men next to her, his mouth agape as he gazed at Rosa. "Stop staring."

Rosa's lips turned up. "My, what a captive audience."

"I know it's been a long time since you've been human, but even you know it's because of your lack of clothing," I said.

Her grin slipped up the side of her face. "Yes, that's quite true. Though, clothing or no, this pretty face will be hard for many to resist."

We circled each other. Neither's posture aggressive, though neither trusting, either.

"I want you to seek out all members of the Crimson Sanctuary and assist with removing their threat. Living and undead," I said. "Do this, and I will clear the remaining life debt."

Shva'sika stared at me, horrified I would work with a demon. "Laz, what do you think you're doing?"

Telar motioned a hand, urging her to calm. "Have some faith in Eira."

I gave him a quick smile, appreciating his trust.

Rosa took interest in his presence and then shifted her eyes in Raikidan's direction. "You have interesting relationships. Were he not here, I would have been right, that he did lie to Zaedrix about being your beloved." She grinned. "Or you grew tired of him and traded for another. But here he is, still."

"Here I am," Raikidan said, his voice unwavering.

I glanced his way, to make sure that response wasn't due to hypnotism. *He looks fine…*

"And you'd best be careful around her." The protective warning in his tone made my pulse skip.

The succubus' lips pulled tight into a half smile. "Don't worry. You can be her favorite pet a while longer."

I bit my cheek. *He is so dead!* He had to go and make her think there was something between us like everyone else did.

"No, he's right to run with it," the voice said. *"It's best if you keep the lie up."*
"Why?"
"Because of how these demons work. Trust me."

I stared Rosa down. "You're getting off the subject. Unless you're rather me hold onto the life debt."

Her eyes narrowed. "I do this, then Zaedrix and I are clear. Our deal is finished."

"Your life debt will be clear, yes. But we still have an agreement."

"Once the life debt is paid, all agreements end."

She was right. I'd only made a verbal agreement with Zaedrix. Technically, even now, since no blood pact was involved, they didn't even have to abide by the life debt.

"Yes, they do," the voice said. *"Abax 39."*

"Abax 39," I repeated aloud before I could think to question the voice. Why hadn't I? I should know what something was before I called it to the table.

Rosa's eyes widened. "How do you know of the Abax?"

My lips remained closed. No way I'd tell her I was only repeating another's word. Whatever this Abax 39 was or did, it was going to be my ticket.

Rosa smiled all of a sudden. "I see. You're just as smart and resourceful as I imagined you'd be."

I did my best not to react, even though I was confused. What had my silence revealed?

"Per the terms of the Abax, I must disclose details to all who know of it." Her face scrunched in distaste for a moment. "The Abax forces us to obey the life debt agreement, even without a blood pact. And your knowledge of Abax 39 prevents us from concluding the agreement when the life debt is cleared. Zaedrix and I will remain bound to our agreement until your dying breath, even after the life debt is paid."

She regarded me. "However, I'd like to bargain an alteration to the agreement."

My brow rose. "I'm listening."

"Laz, what are you doing?" Shva'sika hissed. "You can't bargain with demons."

I ignored her. Technically, I could do as I pleased. But that wasn't why I was acting this way. This whole time, talking to this demon,

I sensed a strange amount of familiarity with the situation. Like I'd done this before with her a long time ago, beyond when I struck up the deal with Zaedrix. I needed to hear her out.

"You're doing the right thing."

The voice's knowledge in all of this was another reason. She wouldn't lead me astray, so this couldn't be all bad. *I hope.*

"We demons need to kill in order to survive," Rosa said. "That is the only way to obtain a soul. It's how we function. We can only sustain ourselves on animals for so long. It's what I agreed to when I sacrificed what little humanity I had."

We continued to circle each other. It wasn't a threatening maneuver. It felt right to do.

"I request altering the wording of our agreement to allow us to survive."

I grunted. "There is no need to alter the agreement. I said you were not allowed to kill innocents. That does not stop you from killing murderers, rapists, and others of the corrupted sort."

Shva'sika gasped. "Laz, you can't be serious."

Rosa smirked. "You fall under the definition of a murderer yourself, young Ambassador."

My expression remained neutral. What she claimed was truth.

She chuckled. "But, alas, the types of crimes you committed were not of darkness or corruption. Your soul is branded innocent."

My brow ticked up. She could see the level of corruption in one's soul?

Rosa surveyed the room. "You keep yourself in good company. There isn't one here that isn't labeled innocent, regardless of the crimes they've committed. Though that does not extend out of this room. I sense a great deal of dark souls working alongside you—some who reveled in their crimes before turning to the light."

A few individuals twitched, ready for any sort of fight she may cause.

Rosa grinned. "But they are off limits to me, for now. You broker alliances with them for the same reason you barter deals with two demons. A necessary evil to destroy a greater one. I quite enjoy this side of you."

She turned away from me, ending the dance of dominance, and headed down the hall. "Our agreement stands as is, then. Zaedrix and I shall not be allowed to kill any soul deemed innocent, though they are never the tastiest morsels anyway. And we shall find you this Crimson Sanctuary. Seeing to their dismantlement will be fun."

When she was out of sight, all eyes fell on me. Livid wouldn't begin to describe Shva'sika. "I can't believe you."

I made sure my expression remained neutral. "I don't make choices for the approval of others. You don't have to like what I've done. It won't change my actions, or my lack of regret."

Her eyes darkened. "I thought you were smarter than this."

Telar held up his hands. "Wait, hold on. How was this dumb? She didn't make any soul-sealing deals. And in the process, she came out on top, with two demons doing all her dirty work with this Crimson Sanctuary."

Del'karo came up to me and wrapped his arm around my shoulder. "The boy is right, Shva'sika. Besides, our girl here isn't one for sticking to rules. She makes her own up and enjoys breaking others."

I snorted.

"Quite the understatement, really."

He turned his gaze on me. "I'm more interested in something else. Your beloved?"

Irritation mixed with embarrassment flared up in me. I punched Raikidan in the arm. "That's his fault."

Raikidan made a wordless "ow" with his mouth as he grabbed his arm.

My eyes narrowed into slits. "He called me *his darling* as a stupid ruse when they attacked the village."

"It worked," Raikidan muttered, his eyes not meeting mine. "It's not my fault we ran into one of them again and she remembered."

Del'karo sighed. "Well, that's a shame. I thought you two were finally going to admit something here."

The room echoed with chuckles. I gave him an unamused look while trying to hide how I really felt about all this.

"You both just need to come clean. This won't go away until you do."

Del'karo patted my shoulder, a wicked grin on his lips. "All right, I'll stop heckling you for now. Let's get you somewhere comfortable to rest."

"Why? I'm not tired."

My mentor cocked his head. "Hon, you expended a great deal of spiritual energy. We all felt it. Don't try to push yourself."

I gave him a blank stare.

"You really have no idea what I'm talking about, do you?"

I shook my head and he sighed. "Figures. Well, regardless, you should rest a bit before going back to testing the others."

"Sure." I didn't feel like arguing. Even if I wasn't exhausted, it was good to rest after all we'd gone through.

Del'karo led me past Shva'sika, who still looked angry. It'd take her some time to calm down. I understood why she was mad, but she'd have to come to terms with my choice sooner or later.

28
CHAPTER

Dogs barked and people shouted, screamed, or made some sort of rude noises as Raikidan and I carried several bags through Quadrant One. A few on my shoulder slipped due to the smoothness of my cloak, and I grumbled as I fixed them.

"Are you sure you don't want me to help?" Raikidan asked. "It's no trouble."

"Go on. Let your ever-so-helpful dragon carry the load for you."

"No, you have more than me as it is," I said. "I'll just be glad to reduce what we're carrying."

"Do you not want to help?" Raikidan asked. "You agreed so quickly to do this, I thought you wanted to."

"Oh, I do, don't mistake that. As shamans or as rebels, my goal is to help people. It's just cumbersome carrying all these bags."

Raikidan adjusted a few on his shoulder. "I didn't think these void bags had a capacity."

"I had heard there was, but I'd never seen it reached myself."

Three shamans ran up to us, and we each handed them bags. They thanked us and then rushed off in three separate directions, handing out the contents to those who needed it. *It won't be enough.*

This part of the city was the worst. You were lucky to find a single person with a job that could feed themselves for a week, let alone clothe and house themselves, or worse yet, care for another needy mouth. Anyone with military background knew that if it weren't for the fact it'd be one more thing to reflect poorly on him, Zarda would have gotten rid of these people. But as it stands, not helping them worked fine in the citizens' eyes.

"It's disgusting, if you ask me."

I agreed. Most of these people needed just a little extra help and they'd be able to get on their feet.

A little girl with russet skin ran up to Raikidan and me, her big brown eyes pleading for help. Tattered clothes clung to her dirty body, and cuts and bruises covered her bare feet. Raikidan knelt and she whispered in his ear. I smiled as he interacted with her. He'd come a long way from the first time I'd introduced him to children.

"He'll make a great father one day."

"If that's what he wants."

The voice chuckled. *"I'm sure if you asked him for them, he'd jump on that."*

I did my best to not sigh out loud. *"Can you not?"*

"What? I think you two would make some cute little half-dragon babies."

I shut her out. I was getting tired of hearing this tune.

"If you'd just stop being stubborn, I wouldn't have to keep at it," she managed to get through. I did better with boxing her into my mind.

Raikidan reached into a bag and pulled out a pair of shoes. They looked a little big for her, and when she stepped into them, they were even bigger that I expected for someone her age. *I doubt she's had many proper meals.*

Raikidan rummaged through his bags looking for a pair her size, but wasn't having any luck. I went to set my bags down to look through them as well when a woman came out from the side of a building. Haggard wouldn't begin to describe her. *No… sickly is more like it.* Her russet skin was pale, and her eyes sunk into her head. She was barely able to stand by how she leaned against the building.

The little girl speaking with Raikidan smiled at the woman and called out to her. "Momma, they're going to give me shoes!"

A deep sense of dread washed over me as her mother tried to smile.

"Eira," the voice sounded as alarmed as I felt.

"I know."

Before I could consider approaching the woman, she collapsed. Quicker than I'd seen him react before, Raikidan launched himself toward her, barely managing to catch her. The girl shrieked and ran to her mother's side as Raikidan eased her to the ground.

I rushed over to check her condition as others around us looked on, murmuring. The woman took labored breaths and smiled at her daughter as the little girl fussed, but she didn't try to reassure her daughter. That worried me.

I whipped my head back and forth trying to find help. "I need a healer!"

A nearby shaman, who had been approaching to find out what was going on, nodded and ran off to find help. Raikidan bent closer to the woman when she tugged on his cloak and she whispered something into his ear.

Raikidan nodded and turned his attention to me. "She wants to say something to you."

I bent closer to the woman and she rasped into my ear, "Take care… of her. Get her… out of this… horrible place"—she coughed—"Please…"

I grabbed the woman's hand. "We're getting you help."

She shook her head, her lips curved in a smile that made my stomach drop. "I have been seen by… doctors and shamans. None could help me… over these two years."

Two years? That was a long time to fight without a cure for whatever she had.

"Promise me… she'll be safe."

I squeezed her hand. "You have my word."

She smiled and then turned her head to her daughter. Tears streaked down the little girl's face as her mother reached out and caressed her cheek. "Be good… Know that… I will always… watch over you… and that… I… love you…"

The last word came out as a half hiss as her breath left her. Her arm dropped and then she stilled.

"Momma?" The little girl shook her mother. No response. "Momma…"

"Poor thing…"

Raikidan placed his hand on her back and she sobbed into her mother's lifeless body. I looked up when several people approached in a rush, and frowned at Ken'ichi.

"We're too late, aren't we?" he said.

I nodded. He sighed, his shoulders slumping. Another shaman offered to retrieve a wagon, while others volunteered to wrap the body. Ken'ichi crouched next to the little girl to talk to her. As that all happened, I noticed how quiet the street had become. The onlookers watched the events with sorrow-filled eyes.

One woman, sitting on a front stoop, beckoned me over with a finger. I complied and sat down next to her.

"Her name was Lola," the woman rasped before taking a drag of a cigarette.

I did my best not to scrunch my nose over the foul-smelling substance. I couldn't understand how any nu-human could stand the smell long enough to get addicted. It was the same with my lack of understanding about Raynn's love for his cigars. "Can you tell me more about her?"

"I didn't know her well, but she isn't the only one with this condition." The woman took another drag. "Five years ago, Quadrant One found itself succumbing to a strange illness. Doctors and scientists had never seen anything like it before, and shamans weren't able to cure it with their abilities."

A long, drawn-out exhale left her lips. "The dead piled into the thousands, and the entire quadrant had been quarantined off to stop the spread. Three years ago, a vaccine was created, but no cure. Two years ago, a 'cure' came along."

The woman snorted and then had another drag. "It wasn't a real cure, by any means. It made it so that the condition could no longer spread, and slowed the rate in which it killed its victims—but that's all it did. Anyone infected was destined to die a slow and painful death. This is what happened to Lola's husband, and now her. Stella was lucky she wasn't infected, but now she's alone."

She hung her head. "Stella needs to be taken away from here. Far away, where she can grow up properly. All the children here do. They need something better. We can't even leave them at the orphanage. There'd be too many for the Matron to handle."

The woman lifted her gaze. "Will you help them? Zarda couldn't care less about us. But all of you seem to." She grabbed my hand. "Please."

"I promised Lola that Stella would be safe. I will not go against that promise. But I can't say what we can do to help the other children. Not yet, at least."

The woman nodded and sucked in another long drag. "As long as you try, that's all I ask. Hopefully those freedom fighters will liberate us soon. Then your help won't be needed. We'll be free to save these children ourselves."

"That would be a wondrous day." It didn't surprise me one bit she supported the rebellion. Most in this quadrant did. Zarda couldn't feed them lies since he didn't give them a reason to believe them.

I stood when the wagon arrived. "It was a pleasure speaking with you—"

"Anita."

"Anita." I nodded. "Thank you for telling me what you know. I won't forget your request."

"Thank you."

I approached the shamans as they loaded Lola's wrapped body into the covered wagon. Stella watched on, holding Raikidan's hand, her cheeks stained with tears. I stood next to Ken'ichi.

"What did you find out?" he asked.

"Her name is Lola, and she was afflicted with some sort of disease that plagued this quadrant for a few years. She lost her husband to it and had been suffering for two years herself."

He frowned. "I thought as much. I'd seen her ailment here before, but I don't know anything about it."

"I don't think the citizens do, either. Not from my talk with Anita. She didn't give it a name. Just told me when it sprang up, how long it took to combat it, and what type of 'cure' came about."

"What are we to do with Stella?"

"I promised Lola she'd go somewhere safe. I'd like for you to assist in getting her out of the city."

He nodded. "I can do that. I think sending her to the West Tribe will be best. I got her to talk about some of her interests, and I believe our tribe can give her what she needs to grow."

"I'd also like to have a meeting set up to find out what we can do about smuggling out more children."

Ken'ichi stared at me, his mouth agape. "Are you serious?"

I nodded. "It was a request from Anita. I don't know how feasible it is, but it's something I'd like us to look into. At some point I'd also like to move more than just children out."

"You really like to involve us in some shady things." He chuckled. "But it's not like we didn't sign up for it, either. Shady practices aren't beneath us if it means a better outcome for the people of Lumaraeon. It's not like we've had a squeaky-clean past."

"So, you'll pass along my message?"

He nodded. "Yes. And I'll personally see to it Stella is situated into a good home. I've got a couple ideas as it is."

"You?"

He jumped back. "No."

I snickered. "Gee, I didn't think being a parent scared you that much."

"It doesn't scare me." He relaxed as he stood next to me again. "I'm just not ready for that yet. I mean, I need to still work on winning over a woman's heart." He chuckled. "You could take her, though. I'm sure your son wouldn't mind having a little sister."

"I'm sure he wouldn't, but I'm going to pass. I'm not a good parent."

"Not true."

"I've met your son a few times now. I think you did well raising him. He turned out to be a good kid."

"Doesn't mean I didn't put him through hell that he didn't deserve."

He placed his hand on my shoulder. "Give yourself more credit. He does."

Ken'ichi patted me and then hopped up into the wagon, taking Stella from Raikidan as he lifted her up. I drew up next to Raikidan. Stella waved goodbye with her fingers as the wagon lurched forward. I waved back and put my best smile on for her. To my surprise, Raikidan waved to her as well. He also placed his hand on my lower back.

"I never thought I'd see the day a child would win you over," I said as the wagon moved out of sight.

"There was something about her," he said. "I can't put it into words."

I smiled and then collected our bags. "Well, if ever you want to be a parent, and she hasn't found a good match, I'm sure you'd make for a good candidate."

"I'm an unmated male." Raikidan shook his head and grabbed a few bags from me. "She should have human parents to raise her. They'd understand her needs better."

"I don't know." I started walking down the road. "Raising her may help bridge the gap between our species. I've learned quite a lot from you, Corliss, and Mana, but it was difficult. As a child, Stella would be able to adjust easier to that than I did."

"Maybe. But if I were crazy enough to take on that task as an unmated male, I'd want a human's help so I wouldn't mess her up."

"That's your cue."

"No it's not."

"You two would make great parents together."

"Stop."

Raikidan's focus shifted as we crossed the main road leading into the city. The front gates of the inner wall were mere feet from us. But that wasn't what caught his attention, and now mine. Two people stood at the gates, arguing with the soldiers guarding it. The pair carried backpacks and looked like they were attempting to leave.

I honed in my hearing to them, doing my best to block out the rest of the city.

"I have papers," the man trying to leave said. "My sister became ill, and we weren't able to travel until she was better. I have signed papers that show we can now leave."

"It doesn't matter," the general said, his voice eerily familiar. "You're past the allowed time. You're now a citizen of Dalatrend and do not have proper paperwork to pass."

"Bullshit!" the traveler shouted. "We're not citizens here. We'd never become citizens of such an awful city."

"Watch it," another soldier warned.

I'd heard enough. I wasn't going to allow them to do this to people. I changed my direction to head right for them.

"Eira, should we really get involved?" Raikidan murmured as he followed.

"No, but I'm going to anyway."

"Very well."

The soldiers noticed our approach. It was the general in charge who spoke to us first. "Ambassador Laz'shika."

My eyes narrowed. I definitely knew that voice. "Zo, is that you?"

His posture stiffened a bit. He'd caught my irritation. "Yes, ma'am."

"What is this I hear you're not allowing travelers to leave?"

"Travelers are allowed to leave. Citizens are not without proper permission."

"Oh, is that so?"

"We're not citizens." The traveler held up his paperwork. "I have the papers to prove why we were here longer than the standard visitation."

I turned to Zo. "Your city has visitation limits?"

"This has been our city's way for a long time," a soldier said. "It keeps our citizens safe—"

"Safe?" My voice rose an octave, and I was quite aware of the attention from citizens I was drawing. "You think taking people hostage for staying too long is making this city safe?"

"We're not taking anyone hostage," Zo tried to claim.

"Oh really? Then I'm imagining the trouble you're giving these two travelers? Their passage is not actually being barred?"

When he didn't have a comeback, I snorted. "I thought as much. Your leader is disgusting. Abducting people because he's power hungry. No wonder the citizens here are so miserable. They don't know what freedom is. And the fact you all so easily follow and defend such horrible behavior is unfathomable."

"Watch what you say, Ambassador," another soldier warned. "You teeter on a dangerous line."

"And if I don't?" I held myself higher. "You wouldn't have the power to stop me. None of you could stop a shaman. That is why there is a peace treaty. Not because we're weaker than Zarda and the force he has, but because he fears us and what we can do. We don't like war, so we agreed to peace with him, but that doesn't mean we won't fight back when needed. So, I'd recommend you be careful what you say to the Ambassador of the Shamans."

The soldier backed down and flicked concerned eyes to his comrades, unsure how to handle me now. Zo peered around as the crowd of civilians drew closer to the confrontation.

"You're free to pass," Zo said after another moment of looking about. "We're sorry for causing you trouble."

The traveling man snorted and stored his papers away. "Half-assed apologies won't save you face."

The woman with him turned to me and spoke, her voice raspy. "Thank you for your help."

I lifted my hand to my mouth and muttered an incantation before breathing out a small flame. Taking control of it, I formed the flame into the shape of a bird with a long flowing tail and had it fly over to them. The flaming bird circled them a few times before finding purchase on the woman's shoulder. Her eyes lit up and she touched it, finding it didn't harm her.

"This flame will keep you both safe for several miles," I said, smiling. "And if you're heading west, the West Shaman Tribe welcomes all travelers."

The traveling man placed his hand on his sister's back. "Thank you. We appreciate what you've done, and your invitation."

The two left, not without shooting nasty looks at the soldiers as they passed. Zo turned his head toward me, but I spun on my heels and headed into Quadrant One. I had people to help, unlike them.

Raikidan lagged behind, probably to be standoffish with Zo like usual, and then rejoined me. "That was… an interesting way to handle that."

I chuckled. "Yes, but I believe it worked well."

"What exactly were you trying to do? Besides nearly get us to start a visible war between Zarda and the shamans?"

"That wasn't going to happen. The soldiers don't have the guts to test that line. They did, though, need to see their actions have consequences. My accusations drew out the harbored negative feelings of the citizens of this quadrant. And it showed the shamans are not pleased, either. Their actions also further angered outsiders, as you can bet they will report this to their city, and that isn't good for Zarda."

"Do you enjoy causing trouble?" I could see the smirk on his face, so I knew he was teasing me.

I chuckled. "Sometimes."

"All the time."

"Well, as crazy as the idea was, I think you did the right thing," Raikidan said.

I smiled. "Thank you."

"I could see the effect it had on Zo, even with that helmet on. His posture said everything." Raikidan placed a hand on my lower back. "You're going to win him over sooner than you think."

"You don't sound happy."

He chuckled. "Means I'd have to deal with him more. And you know how I feel about him, especially around you."

"See, see!"

"Well, if he's on our side, I don't have to keep pretending to be sort of interested in him."

Raikidan thought about this, but before he could say anything, a woman ran up to us, frantic. "Please, can you help me? My daughter is sick. She needs help."

I held up my hands and did my best to calm her. "Don't worry. We'll take a look at her and help where we can. Lead the way."

29
CHAPTER

I glanced over at Mana and Genesis as they helped me care for my plants in the greenhouse. Mana, unsurprisingly, was doing well. Raikidan had told me green dragons had an affinity with plants, and seeing how well Mana did with mine, I could believe it.

Genesis, on the other hand, was the one who surprised me. She, too, had quite the green thumb on her, especially when it came to my more delicate flowers.

Genesis giggled. "Mana, what are you doing? It sounds like you're talking to the plant."

Mana smiled. "I am."

Genesis blinked. "Why?"

"To help it grow, of course." Mana continued to smile as if she wasn't doing anything strange in the least.

Curious, I walked over to her and looked at the plant. "Raikidan told me green dragons have an ability to help plants grow. Are you capable of doing that by talking to it?"

Mana nodded. "We can control plants like human and elf elementalists do, but the plants die afterward. We're not fond of that result, so we rarely use that ability. In its place we use an ancient dragon language to speak to them and help them grow."

My brow twisted. "Ancient dragon language?"

"It's the language our current one evolved from. It's far more primal and affects the world around us depending on how it's used. The green dragons and the violet dragons are the only ones that have any forms of knowledge left of our ancient tongue, and it's not exactly extensive."

"Violet dragons?" Genesis said. "Never heard of those."

"They're now extinct," I said. "And they were the ones with the knowledge of magic."

Genesis brought a dirty finger up to her chin. "So that's what happened to magic…"

"Mana?" I asked. "What the green dragons know and what the violet dragons knew when they were around, was it only related to your abilities?"

Mana nodded. "Green dragons only know enough of the ancient language to help with plant growth and the violet dragons only knew enough about magic."

"Could you talk to this plant some more?" I requested. "I'd like to see if I can understand what you're saying."

Mana smiled. "Sure. It's nothing like our current version of the language, just keep that in mind."

I nodded and listened as she whispered to the plant. The words rolling off her tongue were primal, but felt exceptionally familiar. I continued to listen until she was done.

"How long does it take for a plant to grow?" Genesis asked.

"It depends on the plant," Mana said. "Sometimes it can take a few days, and with others, it can affect them immediately. This plant is a bit stubborn, so I'm thinking it won't show signs for a few hours at least. Eira, something the matter?"

I was rubbing my chin and only vaguely aware of their conversation as I thought about their language. "I'm just thinking. There's something familiar about that language."

"You have the answer."

"Thanks, Captain Obvious."

"Like familiar how?" Genesis asked.

I thought some more, and then it came to me. "It reminds me a lot of Old Tongue."

"Really? That's strange."

I nodded. "It's as if the language we humans speak now and the one the dragons speak were once the same, but that would mean that Old Tongue isn't the oldest language out there."

"And that dragons and humans used to be close." Genesis shrugged. "Or in theory, at least."

I looked at Mana. "What do you have to say about that idea?"

Mana chewed on her lip for a second. "Well, to be honest, it might not be far off. There's a theory among our kind that states dragons used to be human."

My brow lifted, my surprise evident. "That's an interesting theory."

She nodded. "And I honestly don't think it's too far off. Of all the shapes we can shift into, humans in particular are the easiest for us. Even nu-human isn't hard for us to learn."

Genesis turned her attention toward the house. "Seda needs me for something. I'll be back."

"Sure," Mana and I replied.

The two of us looked at each other and then giggled. It was nice spending this time with her. We were quite different, but had enough in common to be able to spend time together comfortably.

The door to the house shut and the two of us went back to work, except something nagged me about the languages.

"It's okay to ask her. She won't judge you."

"I know. Of all the individuals I know, she's in the top five when it comes to acceptance."

"I see the question forming in your head. Ask her."

If the voice was encouraging this, I had to. It might help me with some things. "Hey, Mana?"

She stopped tending to a hibiscus. "Hmm?"

"I have a question. It might be a strange one, but you mentioned the theory your kind has—it has me thinking about something Raikidan and I had talked about in passing once."

"Okay, what's on your mind?"

"You said many dragons theorize you were once human, or even possibly vice-versa. Raikidan told me of a legend about a human-dragon hybrid, and a dragon I know claimed to have known one herself. Does this origin theory stem from this potential hybrid capability?"

Mana nodded so enthusiastically I thought for a moment her head might pop off. "Yes! I'm so glad you know about that, because I've wanted to talk to someone else about it for so long. There's only so many times Corliss and I can talk about it. I need someone else to discuss this with."

I blinked. Apparently she really liked the idea of this child, or at least talking about it. "I don't know much about it, honestly, but I'm wondering—if the evolution theory is correct, then maybe the child would be a missing link between the two?"

Mana rocked her head side to side. "I guess that could be it, but Corliss and I think it'd be more like a sign our bodies are still compatible."

"Like our genes are close enough to still mix, but different enough to create a new species or race?"

She nodded. "Exactly!"

"Hmm…" I thought about it. "That actually makes a lot more sense than what I said. Since my aunt was a geneticist, I have a decent grasp on how genetics work and how they're passed to offspring. If dragons and humans had enough compatible DNA, they could mix successfully just like humans, elves, dwarves, grekeleon, and wogron can."

"But what would happen to that said child if it bred with a human or with a dragon?" Mana asked curiously. "Would it make another type of species?"

I scratched my head. "Well, when you put it that way, I guess it wouldn't be a new species, but more like a subspecies… or maybe it wouldn't even be that. I'm not fully sure. I don't know enough about that stuff to know how that works."

"Hmm, that sucks. Oh well. I guess I'll have to wait to find someone else to talk to about that."

I chewed my lips. "Mana, out of curiosity, why are you so into this theory?"

"Well… because of my grandmother, honestly. She was obsessed with the idea that humans and dragons were related, and it stemmed from her mentor."

"Mentor?"

She nodded. "Yeah, we take on mentors to learn the ancient dragon language when we don't have family or friends to teach us. My grandmother lost her family early in her life, so she wandered around until her mentor took her in and taught her a lot. He was one of the oldest dragons of the time, and he had a lot of knowledge of the world. It's said he was around when the War of End happened, and he himself claimed to have actually met four human-dragon hybrids."

"Four?" I wasn't sure I could believe that.

"Yeah. While the legend only talks about one child ever coming to be, he claimed to have met four, and said there had been a least fourteen born in Lumaraeon's history."

"That's… interesting…"

"I wish you could talk to him about it. I think that with the knowledge you both possess, you would have been able to do something really good with this theory. He died a few decades ago when he lost my grandmother. Her loss broke his heart. He couldn't bear to live without her."

My brow rose. "I think I'm missing something. Are you saying beyond acting as her mentor, he loved her?"

Mana smacked her forehead. "Right, yes, that's what I'm saying. During the mentorship, they became mates."

My lips pressed together. "I'm confused. Wouldn't you mentor with someone who is older than you?"

She nodded. "She did. Age is handled far different with us dragons. As long as dragons are of mating age, coupling with large age gaps are a non-issue."

I rubbed my chin. "Interesting."

She smiled a bittersweet smile. "I miss him as much as I miss my grandmother. I liked hearing all his stories and theories."

I looked at her sympathetically and let her keep to herself for a few moments before asking her another question. "So, you really don't hate the idea of a human-dragon hybrid, do you?"

Mana shook her head. "I like the idea, and Corliss is of the same opinion. We don't care if someone is a halfling or not. We see everyone the same way. If they're good, then that's great and I want to be around them. If they're bad, I want to avoid them. Blood shouldn't determine if someone is good or bad. Just how they act."

I felt something shift in me. Like the bond I was building with Mana had just strengthened tremendously.

"See. You can trust her."

I smiled. "Thanks."

She tilted her head. "For what?"

"For being honest and accepting us."

Mana blinked and went to speak, but Ryoko burst through the door leading to the house, and she looked frantic. Interested in what was up, I headed for the entrance of the greenhouse but she beat me there.

"Ryoko, what's—"

"We need to go now!" she exclaimed. "A bunch of people defected from the military just now, and it's made a mess of a scene. Intel also says some of your brothers are a part of this group!"

My heart stopped. That couldn't be right. They wouldn't do something so reckless.

Ryoko quieted her voice. "And a scout said he thought he caught a glimpse of Ryder in this group, too."

My blood ran cold. "N–no. That can't be right."

Ryoko shook her head. "I don't know if it is, but we won't find out until we get to the battle."

"Battle?"

"Yeah, like I said, they made a mess."

"You need to go and save him."

I nodded and rushed inside the house to get ready. Now wasn't the time to freak out about who defected and who didn't. I needed to focus so I could get them out of this situation.

I pulled the trigger on my carbine until the magazine emptied, and then hid behind debris from a fallen building to reload. Saying that the defecting soldiers had caused a problem was an understatement. We had been fighting for at least an hour, and neither side was giving an inch. There were still a few defecting soldiers who weren't in a safe location, so we weren't willing to fall back, and the military, not surprisingly, wasn't willing to let us win in any way.

"Laz, fall back," Seda messaged. *"We got the last of them underground."*

Relief washed over me. *"Thanks, Seda."*

I made hand motions for people to fall back, but the military unleashed a wave of rockets our way. I ducked behind a pile of rubble and prayed. The moment the rocket fire ceased, we rebels retaliated with our own fire and took the moment to break away.

I slipped into a side alley and attacked advancing soldiers, when I came out the other side. A round of rockets came from behind me, and I glanced back to see Mocha giving me a hand, with Raikidan keeping her safe when she needed to reload. He also watched for rogue soldiers in an attempt to keep me alive as well. Unfortunately, we were limited on man- and firepower, while the military seemed to have an endless supply of both.

More soldiers filed in, making it feel as though the entire army had been mobilized. *It's as if Zarda is particularly desperate to keep these defectors from getting away.* Or he was taking the opportunity to take as many of us out as possible, to lessen the chance of us succeeding with our end goal.

Fire blasted out of a side alley, and soon after, Raynn waked out with a pulled grenade. He tossed it toward the advancing military and made his way over to my left flank.

"Raynn," I greeted as I fired my assault.

"Keep your eyes open, Fire Bug," he advised. "They were pulling some sketchy maneuvers a few streets over.

Did he just— I couldn't believe he just called me Fire Bug. He hadn't done that in forever. Not only that, he just gave me a warning. Was him being stripped of his rank and exiled from his team the reason? Had it taught him something he forgot?

I nodded. "I'll keep that in mind."

"We should continue to fall back."

I looked at him funny. "Who are you and what have you done with Raynn?"

He chuckled as we made a slow retreat. "Getting me into trouble was the best thing you could have done for me. I owe you."

"You owe me nothing. It was the least I could do after—"

"Get down!"

A flash from my past came to me all at once.

"Eira, look out!"

I didn't have time to react. Raynn pushed me just as a soldier rushed out of an alley and shot at us. My blood froze when Raynn screamed in pain and fell to the ground.

"Tannek, no!"

"Raynn!"

I aimed my finger gun at the soldier, and used the last bullet it contained to take him out before focusing on Raynn. He clutched his chest, blood pooling everywhere.

"Raynn?"

"Raynn!" Mocha screeched. She threw down her rocket launcher and rushed over to us.

Raynn chuckled. "I'm good."

I knelt next to him. "Don't lie to me."

He chuckled some more and then coughed. "All right, I'm pretty sure he got a vital organ…"

"Raynn…" My hands shook a little, but I took a deep breath to control myself.

Just then a psychic swooped down and created a barrier for us.

My eyes widened. "Telar?"

"Get him out of here, Sweet Thing!" Telar ordered. "I'll help keep these guys at bay."

I nodded and grabbed Raynn's large arm and hauled him up as best as I could, ignoring his pain-filled cry. "Mocha, give me a hand. We need to get him out of here."

She nodded and we worked together to fall back before having to hide in an alley due to Telar being overwhelmed by enemy fire. We laid Raynn flat on the ground while Raikidan and Telar kept the army out. Mocha rested Raynn's head on her legs and ran her fingers through his hair.

Ryoko and Rylan appeared in the alley just then, as well as Genesis, who had insisted on joining us in the field this time.

Genesis gasped. "Raynn…"

"We need to get him out of here," Mocha insisted. "That way we can get him fixed up."

Raynn shook his head. "Too… late…"

"No, don't say that," Mocha begged.

"Too many soldiers…" he mumbled. "Too injured."

"No!" Tears welled up in her eyes. "I won't accept that answer."

"But there are too many out there," Telar said. "The only reason we haven't been stormed is because I'm shielding us, and I can't keep this up for much longer."

Mocha shook her head slowly. "No…"

I knelt next to them. "Why'd you do it, Raynn?"

He chuckled. "Cause you did it… for me once, remember?"

I touched my right shoulder. "Yeah, I remember that."

He smirked. "Took a bullet right in the shoulder… and kept on fighting like… nothing happened." He frowned. "I'm sorry."

"For what?"

"The way things turn out." He coughed. "For turning my back… on you… when you had never done it to me."

"Why did it end up like this, Raynn? What changed?"

"Remember when you warned me about Jero?" he asked. I nodded. "He's what happened."

"You were the one caught up in that mess?"

"Yeah… I forgot you were gone on your own assignment… when I barely managed to drag my half-dead ass back and bring everything to light. And instead of taking my anger out… on Jero only, I did the one thing I shouldn't have. I became him."

"Why?"

"Because… I was angry. I was angry no one was there for me when I needed it most. I was angry no one believed my story. I was so angry… I stopped caring about everyone else, since it seemed like they didn't care about me. I was so angry… I forgot what used to be important…"

I watched as he struggled to keep his eyes open.

"Tannek? Tannek, no…"

"I'm… I'm sorry…" he murmured.

"Don't," I said. "Don't say that."

"I can, though. Because it's my fault our—"

"It's my fault, too." I looked down at the ground. "I should have tried to fix everything from the start, instead of letting it get to this point."

He smiled. "You're a good kid… Stay that way. I'm sorry things ended this way…"

"Raynn…"

He did his best to look at Mocha. "I'm sorry to you, too, Mocha. I should have treated you better…"

Mocha shook her head. "Raynn, no…"

Raynn's eyes closed and we listened as he took his final breath.

"No, Raynn, don't die on me," Mocha sobbed.

"Tannek!"

"Raynn!" she screamed.

The voice remained quiet, as she had throughout this fight to allow me to concentrate, but I felt a shift in her in my mind. It was as if she'd come closer to me, making some sort of attempt to embrace me.

"Oh, no… Don't tell me I'm too late to help." I looked up at the sound of Shva'sika's voice to see her and Seda running toward us.

"What are you two doing here?" I asked.

"I saw what was going to happen to Raynn, and I tried to get us here as fast as possible to prevent it," Seda explained. "It looks like I didn't react fast enough…"

Shva'sika knelt next to Raynn and attempted to heal him. Within seconds, his wounds healed, but he didn't stir. Shva'sika still tried to heal him in hopes it would bring him back, and Mocha tried in her own way to get him to come back, but their efforts were futile. He was lost to us.

Shva'sika sighed and cased her attempt. She knew it was over, and Mocha sobbed as she held onto Raynn.

"Do something," she begged. "Anything!"

Shva'sika placed her hand on Mocha's shoulder. "There's nothing else we can do. I'm sorry."

"There has to be!" she shouted. "There has to be…"

"Danika, since you're a shaman, can you, I don't know, bring his soul back?" Ryoko asked.

Shva'sika shook her head. "No. It's forbidden for us to do that. If we did, we'd be immediately judged by the gods for corruption."

Mocha sobbed louder and I clenched my fists. It shouldn't have been this way. It shouldn't have ended like this. Raynn's death wouldn't be in vain.

"Show them what it means to cross you," the voice said, rage laced within each word.

I stalked toward the main street. "Genesis, come with me."

"Um, why?" she asked. "Shouldn't we be trying to get out of here?"

"We will, once we show the military the mistake they made."

"Eira, you don't mean you want me to"—she gasped when I nodded—"Are you sure? You've always been vocal about your dislike for my necromantic ability."

I nodded again. "Just this once, I'll allow it. I want them to understand who they're up against. Who they *pissed off.* Shva'sika, I need you to do your best to make sure no soul is attached to Raynn's body."

"I'll do what I can," Shva'sika promised.

"Why can't we use her ability to bring Raynn back?" Mocha asked.

"Because I can't choose which soul attaches to which body," Genesis explained. "And after I release my necromantic hold, the soul leaves the body. It wouldn't be a permanent solution."

Her gaze fell.

Shva'sika looked to Seda. "Seda, I need you to create a barrier around us to help—a psychic field to deter spirits."

Seda nodded. "All right. Telar, you keep Eira and Genesis safe."

He nodded, his usual cocky demeanor gone. "With my life."

"Eira, I'll be cloaking both you and Genesis in a fake disguise," Seda said. "That way you can do as you please without consequence."

"I appreciate that. When the coast is clear, everyone is to get underground," I instructed. "Raynn is to be brought with you so we can give him a proper burial later."

"I'll do that," Ryoko offered.

I nodded and headed out of the alley. The military, unaware of the cloaking shield Telar had up for us, were taken by surprise when Genesis and I appeared, but then relaxed when they realized we were the only ones who were appearing, unaware of the force the two of us were about to unleash on them.

Without hesitating, I breathed a large flame at them, starting up my assault. I breathed another as soon as I ran out of air for the first flame, forcing the military back. Thanks to Telar, their bullets weren't able to touch me when they retaliated and this scared them. When the dead bodies strewn about the street stirred, I knew I had given Genesis enough time and I picked up my attacks.

The dead rose up and advance toward the military, completely unnerving them. Not only could they not kill these risen bodies, but many of them were comrades they had just fought alongside.

"Eira, I'm not going to be able to hold this up much longer," Genesis said. "I don't have the practice to go for long, and I'm trying to help as many streets as possible, making that time shorter."

I nodded and increased my attack. Building up a fire cyclone, I unleashed it on the enemy, forcing their retreat. They knew they couldn't win, but I wasn't going to let them go so easily. Building up more fire, I combined all the fire I could into one giant flame and shot it skyward.

"Telar, I need a map of the street," I thought, knowing he'd be tapping into my mental thoughts for this situation.

"Of course."

An aerial view of the streets appeared in my head, and I forced my fire higher into the sky. As I did, it took the shape of a large bird. When I determined it was high enough, I split the fiery bird apart and rained fire down on our enemy. The military was sure to flee on all streets at this point, but not without losses—between Genesis' and my combined assault, as well as the assault the rest of the rebels threw at them.

"We're getting out of here now," Seda messaged. *"All those who defected from the military are now in the Underground, and the military is retreating. You should get to safety."*

"Gen, Telar, we're falling back," I ordered.

They nodded and we rushed down the street. Darting into a side street, Telar lifted a manhole cover via telekinesis, and then the two of us, getting us all down the tunnel swiftly and safely. Once our feet were planted on the ground, we headed for the Underground.

Telar forced the doors open to the training room when we arrived, and I looked around. The room was nearly empty, but that wasn't a surprise. The Council had sent out all able-bodied rebels to help get this situation under control.

Aurora jumped down from her computer station when she noticed us and ran over. "They have everyone in a lounge room. I'll show you which one."

"How many in total were there?" I asked.

"Ten."

I narrowed my eyes. "That's a lot. Do we know why they chose to defect?"

She shook her head. "They refused to talk until you got down here."

"Why?"

She didn't reply. Instead, we took a corner in the hall and ran down another corridor. Halfway down, Seda waited for us. She joined up with our little group, but no one spoke, and we ran into the lounge at the end of the corridor.

"This is why," Aurora said.

My blood froze at the sight of Ryder and some of my brothers sitting on some ottomans.

Ryder, hearing our arrival, lifted his head, but he didn't smile like he typically would have. "Hey, Mom."

"What the hell is going on here?" I didn't mean to sound so angry but the truth was, I was livid. They should have known better than to defect like this. Ryder especially.

"We have a good explanation, Sis," Rhaec insisted.

"You'd better. I lost a good man today because of all of you."

Ryder sighed. "They were going to implant tracking devices into us."

My brow furrowed. "Come again?"

He patted the seat next to him, and I went over to sit down. "They've developed a new tracking device that would make the clunky external ones obsolete. They selected a handful of soldiers to test the effectiveness, and we're that group. We'd have no choice in the matter, so we couldn't stay. And I don't know about you, but I didn't want one of those things implanted in me. Sorry we caused you trouble, but we just couldn't stay."

I shook my head. "Don't be. I was irritated because of what I just went through. I can't blame you guys. I don't want those trackers in anyone, and it makes me worry that Zarda will start forcing it on the civilian population. It's only a matter of time."

I scanned the group. "I'm noticing not all of those here are related to me. I don't even know some of you. Any cues to the reason for selection?"

Ryder shook his head. "I figured I was chosen because I knew you. Even though a Hunter came in with a body that looked like you, and convinced everyone she was the real deal, including the geneticists that tested the body, Zarda has remained suspicious of your claimed civilian status. But when Trigon, Bone, Yára and a few others weren't picked, I wasn't sure what to make of the selection."

"I believe Zarda is targeting you, Commander," a former soldier I didn't know said. "But he's trying to hide it by throwing us into the pool, while also leaving out some other obvious choices."

"You seem pretty sure."

He snorted. "He's obsessed with you. It's why that ruse of yours didn't work on him. As good as it was, Zarda is a nutcase. Hell, he made Yára, for Satria's sake. And when she didn't come out looking like you, he forced her to change."

My brow furrowed. "What are you talking about?"

"He's talking about this." Ryder reached into his pocket and pulled out a folded piece of paper. "Yára wanted you to know. And since I was running, she asked me to pass the message along."

I took the paper and opened it, and nearly dropped it in shock. Now I knew why Yára's hair appeared more blue than mine. There wasn't a strand of violet hair on her head in this picture. Her hair was the same blue shade as Shva'sika, and it also wasn't as straight as my hair, or my mother's for that matter. It curled a bit, and was pulled back into a loose bun, creating a wild, untamable look.

"He makes her dye her hair?" I couldn't believe this.

"Told you he was insane," the soldier murmured.

Ryder chewed on his lower lip. "There's something else you need to know, and it's not about Yára. It's about me."

Panic flashed through me. "What's wrong?"

"I'm not really sure if anything is wrong, per se, but it is something I can't ignore now."

He tugged on his right hand glove, and my panic rose. Ryder didn't wear gloves. Ever since he was a boy, he couldn't stand them. Told me they were too restrictive or something like that.

He pulled a glove off, and I blinked. His hand seemed normal to me. I reached over to touch it, but he jerked his hand away. "Don't."

"Ryder, what's wrong?" I asked. "You're acting funny about this. You hand looks fine."

"It may appear that way, but it's not. Elgren, where did you put that piece of metal I picked up?"

One of my brothers I vaguely recognized reached behind him and picked up a small sheet of metal. He handed it over. Ryder took it with his gloved hand, and then grabbed the side of the metal sheet with his ungloved one. Instantly his hand paled, and the part of the metal he touched froze up.

My eyes widened. "Ryder…"

"That's not all."

Handing me the piece of metal to hold for him, he put the glove back on his hand and took off the one on his left hand. He took the metal sheet back with his gloved right hand, and then touched it with his ungloved hand. Like before, his hand reacted, but instead of paling, it reddened as if it were warm, and the metal it touch heated up.

"This is why I didn't want you touching my hands," Ryder explained. "I can't control it right now, and the gloves are the only thing that protects anyone."

I stayed quiet, my head buzzing too much to speak. Given his hair color and who his father was, I assumed one day Ryder may exhibit ice abilities. But I never expected this.

"Mom, are you okay?" Ryder asked as he put his glove back on.

I nodded slowly. "Yeah. I'm just trying to process this. How long has this been going on?"

"The lack of control has been going on for about a week."

"No, how long have you had this ability? You've never told me about this before."

"A while…"

His elusive reply didn't sit well with me. "Ryder."

He sighed. "Since just before I made your special dagger."

I tilted my head. "Why didn't you tell me?"

He shrugged and avoided eye contact. "I didn't know how to tell you. I thought it was weird and I had some control over it, so I just kept it to myself."

I nodded, understanding that position. I knew all too well what it was like to feel weird about an ability that came to you naturally. "Right. I shouldn't be fussing about that anyway. What is a concern is the fact you could control it to start with, and now you're having difficulties. That's a bit backwards."

Ryder chuckled. "I guess that means I really am your son."

I shook my head, a small smile spreading across my face. "We're going to have to bring you to the shamans. I don't know anything about this ability you have. If anyone does, it'd be them or the scholars."

"Meaning I'm going to have to leave, aren't I?"

"I don't know. It all depends on whether they can help or not."

"I'm not leaving."

"It won't be negotiable if that is the best choice."

"I'm not leaving. That is my choice."

"Ryder, don't argue with me."

"I'm not leaving."

"Ryder!"

"I'm not a child, Mother!" I almost flinched from the force in his voice. "I'm an adult, and I make my own decisions. I'm not leaving." His voice quieted. "Not without you, at least."

I let out an exasperated breath and tapped the picture of Yára on my knee as I went to thinking. Everything was just so messed up right now. As I did, I notice Rhaec was acting really funny—anxious, even. "Rhaec, what's wrong?"

He shook his head. "Don't worry about it, Sis."

"Rhaec."

He huffed. "Just worried. Two friends helped us get out, but they lagged behind to buy us some time. They figured because they're psychics they'd be able to it better than anyone else. They told us they'd be fine, but I'm still worried..."

"What are their names?" I asked.

"Saléna and Nyra."

This caught Seda's attention. "Come again?"

"Their names are Saléna and Nyra."

"Those are my sisters!" she roared. "You dragged them into this mess?"

Rhaec glowered at her. "We didn't drag them into anything! They chose to help us, as much as I protested."

A soft chuckle came down the corridor leading to the room we were in. "Take it easy, Sis. We're fine."

Seda turned just as Saléna and another blonde-haired woman I presumed was Nyra walked into the room. Seda's shoulders sagged, relief registering on her face. "You're safe."

Saléna grinned. "Of course. We knew what we were doing."

"We had to fake our deaths. That's why it took so long," Nyra said. "So everyone can calm down. Especially you, Rhaec. You worry too much."

Rhaec, overcome with emotion, rushed over to the two psychics and pulled them in for a giant bear hug. It was a bit obvious he was fond of them, though I couldn't blame him. They were pretty, and if they were anything like Seda, probably enjoyable to be around.

Nyra turned her face toward me. *"Your brother is a lot like you. Always worries too much about those he cares about, even when it's not necessary."*

I chuckled. *"Can you blame him for worrying?"*

She looked at Rhaec with a smile as he put her and Saléna back down on the ground. *"No, not really."*

I smiled. I sensed a great deal of fondness coming from her toward him. I was glad my brother had a friend, and I hoped she would be able to help him achieve the normal life we all deserved.

My ears perked when I heard several pairs of footsteps coming down the corridor leading to this room. It wasn't long before Ryoko, Rylan, and Raikidan entered the room.

"How are things?" I asked, knowing they'd understand what I was referring to.

Ryoko let out a sorrowful grunt. "Mocha is still crying. Doppelganger and Chameleon are with her, but nothing is going to ease her grief right now. Danika had a private conversation with his spirit. He wants to be buried instead of burned, so she made arrangements for some shamans to come down and preserve his body until we can get that accomplished."

I nodded.

Someone approached from behind. Everyone around me was calm, so my brain found no need to go on alert, but my body seemed to think differently. In the end it had made the better choice because whoever this new person was had slapped me in the rear, and I was not okay with that. I spun around and slammed my fist into the man.

"Mom, if I can ask, who did you lose?" Ryder asked.

He fell back and rubbed his face. "Ow. You didn't need to do that."

My mother laughed at him. "I told you to watch yourself. Someone was going to put you in your place one of these days."

Rylan grunted. "He's lucky Eira is in a good mood."

The man climbed to his feet. "So you're Eira, Amara's mute daughter?"

My lip curled and he held up his hands defensively. "Easy, that wasn't meant to be an insult. I don't care if you can't speak." He held out his hand for a handshake. "Name's Raynn."

My gaze lowered and I was quiet for a moment. "Raynn…"

"Mom…" He leaned over and I wrapped my arms around him and rested my head on his. "I'm sorry. I know you two were friends once."

I eyed this Raynn character. He was a handsome man for an older person; I'd give him that. He probably got away with his rude antics a lot because of them, but I wasn't going to be one of those. I spit on his hand and stormed off.

"Great, we have another Amara," Raynn said, his tone amused.

My mother snickered. "Oh trust me, she'll be worse. She's got one hell of a fiery personality."

"Well, then she should be interesting to get to know."

Amara snickered. "Good luck getting on her good side now."

My grip on Ryder tightened and my gaze focused on the ground. "We still were. It just took today to realize it…"

Rhaec left Saléna and Nyra and sat down next to me. He rested his arm over my shoulders and laid his head on me. My other brothers also came over to me and sat as close as they could. I was glad for their comfort—it made the loss a little easier. But only a little.

Telar entered the room, but didn't say anything. I could tell he wanted to have a word with me, but was thankful for his patient respect. After a few minutes had passed, I excused myself, allowing Seda and the others to work with my family and the other former soldiers to get them situated.

I followed Telar down the hall until we came to a more secluded location. "So, what's up?"

"I wanted to apologize for arriving so late," he said, his head turned, indicating he couldn't look me in the eye. "I tried to get to you in time; to avoid you having to go through that situation a—"

I place a hand on his arm. "It's okay. It's not your fault. You aren't responsible for either death."

"But had I reacted sooner, both situations would have turned out different."

"Maybe—maybe not. Fate is funny like that."

He sighed. "I wish you'd see life better than that."

I shrugged. "I've become desensitized to a lot of things. Death, hope, all of it. Raynn's death hurts, but not as bad as it should, and I hate that. Each time I've held onto hope, it's been crushed to the point I don't have much left."

He grimaced. "Well, here's some you can hold onto. Those shamans you hooked me up with, they were the best direction I've been sent. I doubted someone could help my sister at this point, but you proved me wrong. We think a cure for her is around the corner."

I smiled wide, the hope he mentioned swelling in my chest. "That's wonderful to hear. I guess that means—"

He nodded. "I was going to your place today to let you know I was leaving the city when all of this went down. I want you to know how grateful I am for the help you gave. May not mean much to most, but Avila is everything I have. I need her."

"I know how much it means to you, Telar." I smiled. "I really do."

He pulled a folded piece of paper out of his pocket and handed it to me. "No, I don't think you do."

My brow creased and I took the paper. Unfolding it, I found a letter, written in the symbolic code I created due to my abysmal common reading skills.

> *Brother,*
>
> *I'm glad you made it to Dalatrend safely, though your comment about finding Commander Eira has me concerned. Don't go putting the moves on her, you hear? It failed in the past, and from what I've seen of your and her futures, it won't work now. She's not the right one for you. You both have someone else that is better suited for your personalities.*
>
> *Please don't be stupid. And tell her I say hi and thank you.*
>
> *I love you,*
> *Avila*

The letter surprised me, though not because of what it revealed. With the way Telar has treated me, both past and present, I had already come to the conclusion he may have had, at the very least, passing feelings for me. Why, I couldn't understand, since we were so different.

What surprised me was the fact that he so willingly gave this to me to read. I looked at him. "You never told me she says hello or thank you."

He rubbed the back of his neck. "Yeah, I kept forgetting."

I shook my head. "Why did you show me this?"

Telar shrugged. "I kinda assumed you already knew, so I might as well put it out in the open. I came back to help Avila, but also to see if maybe things had changed enough where I might get a chance. I know now, we'd be good, but not perfect, and it wouldn't last like I'd want."

"Maybe if life had been different, I'd have been able to give you a different answer," I said.

He nodded. "It's possible. And maybe in another life it'll be different, but this is our reality, and there's definitely someone better for you and he's right under your nose."

"*See!*" the voice shouted at an awful volume.

I huffed. "Please don't bring Raikidan into this. It's not like that…"

Telar leaned closer and planted a firm kiss on my forehead. "I wouldn't say that. Not from what I've gotten glimpses of. He's a good choice."

He pulled away and headed toward the virtual training room. "I'll catch ya later, Sweet Thing, when my sister gets sick of me and kicks me out again."

I chuckled and shook my head. *That man is something else.* I hoped for the best for not just Avila, but also him. I hoped he'd find that right woman who could handle someone like him. He deserved that much. Even if he was wrong about Raikidan and me. *It's just not meant to be…*

"*Not true,*" the voice's tone was more sing-songy this time. She was acting weird again.

I jumped when a masculine hand touched my arm and Raikidan held up his hands. "Sorry. I didn't mean to startle you. And don't say you didn't hear me, because I kicked a bucket."

I closed my mouth and huffed air out of my nose. I needed to pay more attention to my surroundings.

His eyes softened. "How are you feeling, really? No lying to me."

My shoulders slumped. "Like a building fell on me, when it should feel so much worse."

Raikidan reached out and cupped my cheeks with both hands, framing my face. I rested my hands on his arms, but didn't push him away as he looked deep into my eyes, those brilliant sapphires snaring me. He leaned closer and my heart thumped in my chest.

I went to say something, but he rested his forehead on mine and spoke, "No matter what I say, it won't take your pain away, but I am here for you. Lean on me as much as you need when you can't hold yourself up."

He let go of my face and wrapped his arms around me. "I will always be here for you."

"Thank you…" was all I could say. I appreciated his words, especially in a time like this. *He'll pay for this, Raynn. Zarda will pay for what he's done. I swear on that.*

I spun the daggers in my hand before straightening. Another target dummy laid on the ground from yet another perfect assassination demonstration.

"That's all for the demonstration," I told my two students. "Practice what I taught you. You'll be tested tomorrow on it, as well as the techniques I taught you these past few days."

"Yes, ma'am," they replied in unison before doing as instructed.

I watched them, refusing to offer help unless they absolutely needed it. I knew they were capable of perfecting this technique, and if I babied them, they'd never see their potential.

"Geez, Fire Bug, you don't go easy on anyone, do you?"

I turned to see Raynn approaching. "You can't complete an assignment if you're soft. A target is a target regardless of their background."

He shook his head. "You're something else, Kid. Not out of your tank twelve years yet, and here you are talking as if you've been doing this for half a century."

"I'm nothing special," I replied.

"Nothing special?" He laughed. "You're the youngest soldier to get the title of captain, and that was when you were at eight years released. And now you have not one, but two students of your own. No one has been given a trainee before they've been out of their tank for fifteen years."

I rolled my eyes and he nudged me, making me chuckle a little. "There. There's that smile I was looking for."

I frowned. "I'm not supposed to smile."

Raynn sighed. "I don't get what Zarda is aiming for with you. I really don't. First he just wants you to be an emotionless soldier. Then he starts looking at you like he does Amara. Now he's still expecting you to be emotionless while still giving you those looks?"

I shrugged. "What's there to get? He doesn't know what he wants. I just do what I'm told."

He chuckled. "For now."

I looked at him strangely. "What's that supposed to mean?"

"Just means that one of these days you're going to want to make your own choices. Everyone wants that eventually, and that's when we are marked as failures."

"I don't fail."

Raynn rubbed my head. "Of course you don't."

I swatted him away, and he laughed, though it didn't last long when someone called for him. I turned to see who it was and nearly snarled. The dark-skinned, dark-haired, dark-eyed man was none other than Jero, and I couldn't stand him. Raynn waved him off quickly and Jero nodded before leaving.

"What was that all about?" I asked.

"That was my call to head out," Raynn said with a sigh. "You be good, Fire Bug. I'll see you when I get back."

I grabbed him by the wrist when he tried to leave. "Raynn, you're not going on an assignment with Jero, are you?"

He nodded. "Yeah. Me and a few others. Why, what's wrong?"

I took a deep breath. "Jero is known for leaving comrades behind to save his own skin and passing it off as an accident. Promise me you'll be careful."

Raynn nodded slowly. "Yeah, I'll keep my eyes on extra alert. But if I, uh, for some reason don't come back and he does——"

I grinned. "I'll make him beg as I tear him limb from limb."

Raynn laughed. "That's the Eira I know. I'll see you when I get back, and I promise I'll be careful."

I smiled. "You'd better."

"And I don't care what Zarda says. Smile more. You have a good smile."

"I'll see what I can do."

"See ya, Kid."

"Bye, Raynn."

CHAPTER 30

I finished drying the plate in my hands and put it away in the cupboard with a quiet sigh. After everything had calmed down last night, I managed to get Ryder to the shamans, who immediately took him in. None of them knew anything about his ability, but they were determined to help in any way they could.

Ryder, on the other hand, wasn't thrilled about having to stay with them. He insisted he should be underground with everyone else, and that his control issue wasn't a main priority. I wasn't having it. I understood where he came from, but I also knew it was a big problem. Too many accidents could happen if he wasn't in control of his abilities, and I wasn't going to risk that.

"He gets his stubbornness from you."

"Don't I know it."

I hung my drying rag on a hook for later use and headed for my room to grab my Library access book in hopes of finding information in there. I didn't take more than three steps into my room before everyone in the house heard something strange at the front door. Before we knew it, the front door flung open and a group of people thundered up the stairs and into the living room.

Surprised to see so many soldiers in our house so suddenly, everyone was caught off-guard and unable to react, except Rylan, Raikidan, and

Corliss, who had been downstairs. Hearing them barge in, they were quick to rush upstairs to see what was going on.

Ryoko, finally recovering from the intrusion, stood from her spot on the couch and placed her hands on her hips. "What the hell is the meaning of this?"

"We're here for an emergency inspection," the general leading the squad informed us.

I crossed my arms. "If this was an inspection, you would have knocked on the door and waited to be let in like civilized people."

"Making this a raid," Rylan said. "What reason do you have to raid our house this time?"

The general ignored him and set his attention on me. "You're Eira, correct?"

I nodded. "Yes."

"Then you'll have to come with me."

"Why?"

"For questioning."

I raised an eyebrow. "What for? I haven't done anything wrong."

"I'm afraid I can't tell you."

I sensed the voice's presence close in my mind. Her irritation matched mine, but she remained silent, for now.

I crossed my arms. "Then I'm not going anywhere."

"Ma'am, this isn't negotiable."

"Then you'd best tell me why you need to question me or you're all getting thrown out of here."

The general sighed, clearly annoyed. "You're acquainted with a man named Ryder, correct?"

"Yes. He's a friend of mine."

"And a man named Rhaec, yes?"

"I know him because I was helping Zo with an issue that involved him, but he isn't a friend."

"Well they are the reason you need to come with us for questioning," the general explained. "Both were accused of treason last night and promptly disappeared."

"And you think I either had something to do with it or know where they are, right?"

"We don't know. That's why we need to speak with you."

"Well, I wasn't involved, and I don't know where he is," I said. "Now you have your answer, and you can all leave."

The general exhaled slowly. "Ma'am, please cooperate with me."

"Or what, you'll take me in by force?" I held my head high. "Like you could. You're aware of who I am. You only asked my name out of formality. This means, you take me in, there's going to be trouble."

"We just want to ask you a few questions."

"And I'm actually a rabbit."

"Ma'am, you're testing my patience."

"Not that you have much to begin with." I rested my hands on my hips as his upper lips curled back. "I'm not going anywhere. Ryder may have been my friend, but he was a soldier and I'm a shaman. We don't discuss everything with each other. If he did something that would be considered treason, that'd be on him and I'd know nothing about it. Now leave our home before I get ugly."

The general's face relaxed and surprise flashed through his eyes. "Our home? You live here?"

"Yes. Zane is an old family friend. He offered to allow Rai and me to stay here, and since there were no rules about shamans living with civilians, I didn't see a problem with it. Is there a problem, General?"

"You have quite the attitude."

"You have no idea." My attention was pulled away when I heard someone rushing down the hall. I tilted my head slightly when Seda ran into the room. She wasn't disguising herself, so it was bound to be important. "What's wrong, Crystal?"

"You need to leave now," she said. "These raids are targeting the shamans, too."

The voice snarled and my anger boiled. My attention snapped back to the general. "She had better be ill-informed."

"No, ma'am, she's not." The general was either brave, or stupid for admitting that. "Due to the circumstances, no neutral party is given an exception. There is no negotiating this."

My fists clenched. "Get out."

"Excuse me?"

The heat in my body rose. "I said get out, the lot of you."

The general held his ground. "We have our orders. And all those present in this city are to abide by the rules."

"Sir," a soldier whispered to him. "It might be wise to listen to her. She's rather angry, and if you hadn't noticed, the temperature in the room is rising at the same rate as her anger. If we don't leave, she might just cook us alive."

"That'd be impossible," the general argued. "No one can do that."

Shva'sika rose to her feet, also having had enough of this nonsense. She let a few electrical sparks crackle between her fingertips. "You underestimate the Ambassador's power. Now leave before this situation gets violent."

The general went to argue, but Raikidan and Rylan weren't going to have it. They forced the military squad back and down the entryway stairs. I ran into my room before making sure they managed to get the soldiers out of the house. I needed to dress quickly and help the shamans as best as I could.

"Take a deep breath."

"I can't. I need to get there now."

"You can't help them if you're all out of sorts. At least take a second to breathe and calm your mind."

Raikidan appeared in my room just as I threw my cloak around my shoulders. He was already dressed appropriately, so I assumed he either had gone to change, or was wearing the cloth armor, which was more likely the case.

I didn't speak to him as I headed for the front door but I did stop when Shva'sika's bedroom door flew open. I watched as she struggled to clasp her cloak around her neck in her rush. "I'm coming with you."

I nodded. "I wouldn't have it any other way."

"Eira, be quick," Seda said. "Most of the shamans are handling the attempted raids well, but I got a quick glance at a squad heading for the home harboring Ryder, and I'm worried."

I nodded. "I'll head there first. I don't need the shamans getting into any possible trouble because of me, and I don't know how well these encounters are going to go."

Before anyone could say anything else, I headed down the stairs and rushed out of the house.

My heart pounded as we rounded the last corner on our route. Our hurrying had warranted some attention from squads of soldiers following their orders for the raids, but luckily we hadn't been stopped.

My anger rose as the house came into view and there was a squad of soldiers standing outside. It appeared that some were already inside, since the front door was wide open.

When we arrived, soldiers tried to prevent us from entering the building, but I wasn't having it. Forcing my way in, I managed to get into the living room just as a shaman grabbed an aggressive soldier by the arm and began freezing the soldier's arm.

"I told you not to touch her!" the shaman yelled.

I nearly sighed at Ryder's recklessness. He may have had a cloak on to help disguise him, but by using his abilities, he risked exposing himself and getting everyone into trouble.

"Reckless, like you…" The voice chuckled. *"And Raikidan."*

I ignored her. "What the hell is going on here?"

Ryder released the soldier. "Ambassador…"

"Ambassador, these soldiers are trying to force us to remove our cloaks!" a woman shrieked.

I looked at Ryder. "Is that why you grabbed him?"

He nodded. "Yes. This one here was being aggressive toward one of the women. I wasn't just going to let that happen."

"I understand. All soldiers are to leave this house now."

"Ma'am, we have—"

I lit a fire in my hands quickly and made sure the fires were large and hot. "Now! I will speak with you outside."

Most of the soldiers left. A few remained for a moment out of defiance, but their rebellion didn't last long. Raikidan and I followed, but Shva'sika stayed inside.

I didn't give the soldiers any time when I stepped out of the house. "Where is your commanding officer?"

Several soldiers stepped away and a curvaceous, blonde-haired woman with light makeup dusted over her face in a black uniform stepped forward. While obviously beautiful, it was her demeanor that awarded her the rank she held. As she walked, she exuded confidence, and I could sense her attempt to intimidate me even before having to converse with me.

"I don't like her."

"You have a lot of nerve interfering with us," the general sneered.

I held my head high. "Zarda has a lot of gall to attack us in such a way."

"You're not under attack. This is a mandatory raid that no one is exempt from."

I grunted. "I'd find that believable if you weren't also making an attempt to force us to go against our customs and reveal our identities."

"We have several fugitives on the loose. We can't take any chances of them infiltrating any systems. That includes pretending to be one of you right under your noses."

"Like I'd believe that rubbish. I'm sure you're rather aware of the agreement we have, and the consequences if that agreement is broken, regardless of the reason behind it. Or do I have to march into Zarda's throne room myself and remind him?"

"Is that a threat?"

I smirked. "It's a warning. If you do not cease these illogical activities at once, I'll be sure to storm into that eyesore of a fortress you call home and show Zarda exactly who he's dealing with. And trust me, you don't want me doing that. It won't be a pretty sight."

The general exhaled, her breath tight, showing how little power she had to fight against me.

"Now, I suggest you get on those communicators of yours and let the others soldiers know the searching of shaman homes will cease."

The general growled, but did as asked. Once she made the order, and argued with a few other officers over the decision, I watched them leave and go about searching civilian homes.

"Good riddance."

When I was sure they weren't coming back, I entered the house again. I exhaled and pulled my hood down when Raikidan shut the door behind us and we made it into the living room.

I looked around before speaking. "Is everyone okay?"

Shva'sika smiled at me. "Everyone is fine. Question is, are you okay?"

I blinked. "Yeah, why wouldn't I be?"

"Your fire ability."

"Yeah, what about it?" She was acting like there was something wrong with my ability.

"Mom, you heated this whole room up when you were angry," Ryder told me.

"I only did that at our house," I said.

Shva'sika shook her head. "No. You did it here as well."

"She was heating the air outside too," Raikidan said. "But she was too focused on the general to notice the other soldiers messing with their uniforms."

I gave the three of them funny looks.

"They're telling the truth."

"You sensed it, too?"

"I'm here with you. Of course I did."

"You didn't notice it at all?" Ryder asked.

I shook my head. "No."

"When the heat rose at the house, were you aware you were doing it?" Shva'sika asked.

I shook my head again. "No. I only knew because someone said something."

She nodded, her brow knitting with thought. "Your abilities are growing again."

I pushed the thought aside. "Makes sense with everything going on, but I'm not concerned with that right now. I don't think the rest of you should be, either."

"It's because you need to keep your abilities in check," Shva'sika scolded. "If you're able to raise the temperature around you without even realizing it, Laz, terrible things could happen. And who knows what else you'd be capable of because of this. You need to focus on training for once.

I threw up my hands. "On top of everything else that I'm expected to do, right? I have enough on my plate as it is right now. So if you think you can do something better than me, please, be my guest and do it."

Shva'sika placed her hand on her hips. "Stop putting words in my mouth."

"She's not," Ryder said. "She's making a point. You really do expect too much from her, and there's only so much one person can do. She's only human."

"I only give her what I'm sure she's capable of handling," Shva'sika argued.

"And how do you know for sure what she's capable of handling?" Ryder challenged. "You're not her."

Shva'sika frowned and I had to refrain from sighing. I wished the two would just drop it. This really wasn't the time.

"I side with you. You've got enough on your plate. Someone else should step up and help."

"Wow, we agree on something?"

"We agree on many things. Just not one topic in particular."

"I think we should be heading home now," Raikidan said, attempting to diffuse the situation. "We've settled the issue we came here to handle, and Eira is fully capable of handling herself and her advancing abilities. She'll work on it on her own as time permits."

He looked at me. "Right?"

I nodded and he nodded back. "See? Now let's go."

Shva'sika sighed and gave in. I smiled my thanks to him for the backup and then gave Ryder a goodbye hug.

"When will you be back?" he asked.

"When things calm down."

"Promise?"

"Of course."

He smiled. "All right. I'll be waiting."

"He's such a good boy."

I said my goodbyes and the three of us headed back home, making sure to keep an eye out for soldiers who weren't listening to my threat, which was definitely not empty. With this blatant attack on the shamans, I could have used this as an opportunity to end this rebellion. Thinking about it, I should have. I should have demanded an audience with Zarda and just taken him out. Now it was too late and we'd have to wait.

"I'm not convinced that would have been the safest route to go. It's no better than you going rogue."

She had a point.

"You'll get a good opportunity soon. Just be patient."

Again, I couldn't argue her. I just had to bide my time—that was something I was good at.

31
CHAPTER

Keeping an eye out for any trouble, I cleaned a glass behind the bar. Today was slow, but when the military did raids it always threw off businesses. Most people either didn't want to go out because of their mood, or they figured businesses would be down for a while.

My decent mood soured when I spotted Zo entering the club and heading straight for me.

"What do you want?" I asked when he arrived at the bar. I was in no mood to be civil with him.

"You should reconsider your approach. We need him to join the cause."

Zo held up his hands. "Hey, take it easy, I'm not here to start trouble."

"That's all you do these days."

"Eira, I'm sorry you're upset about what was going on, but we—"

"Were given orders?"

"Yes."

"And that makes what you did okay?" I nearly spat on him. "Do you think I'd be okay with hearing such a pathetic reason?"

"Eira, you don't understand."

"Oh, I understand." I slammed a glass on the bar. It cracked from the force.

"Eira, watch your temper."

I ignored her. "I understand that you're all nothing but lowlife scum who prey on those you think are weaker than you. You blindly follow orders instead of thinking for yourself. This is why the shamans and soldiers are never getting along! That is why peace feels so unattainable. You're all nothing but pathetic pieces of shit out to terrorize innocent people!"

Zo stared at me, in utter shock at my accusations. "E–Eira—"

I threw the glass I had into the rack behind me and everything shattered, drawing attention from most everyone in the club, including Raikidan, Rylan, and Azriel. "Don't you even start with your lame excuses. I don't want to hear it! You've pissed me off for the last time, Zo. You try to make the rebels look like the bad guys, when you've done nothing but make this city a miserable jail cell. That is why they fight against you. You don't know what it means to make your own choice, unclouded by lies and deceit. You don't realize you're no better than the soldiers who killed my family."

Patrons whispered amongst themselves, and the air around us warmed as my anger boiled. My control over fire and heat really was growing at an abnormal rate. It was… odd.

"Now get the hell out of this club! I don't want to see your damned face again." I turned away to clean up the mess I made. "And that means outside the club, either."

"But, Eira—"

I spun around and tossed a glass at him. "I said get out!"

Just then, Rylan and Raikidan rushed over and grabbed Zo.

"I think it'd be best to listen, if you want to live," Rylan warned. "She's not playing around."

Zo shook them loose, not that they had a tight grip on him. "Yeah, I can see that. I'll leave peacefully on my own, don't worry."

I grunted and headed for the back room. Azriel and Raikidan followed while Rylan made sure Zo left.

"Eira, are you okay?" Azriel asked.

I took a deep breath and then exhaled slowly before chuckling. "Do you think that was convincing enough?"

"Wait, seriously?"

Azriel blinked with bewilderment. "You did that on purpose?"

I grinned. "Course I did. He needs a push."

"You brat!"

Raikidan shook his head. "You really think that display will convince him?"

"She convinced me!"

I shrugged. "I don't know, but he needed to see what problems his actions caused. I'd already been pushing it lately, so the raid was the most logical tipping point. Now he can't deny how his actions change people's perception of him."

Azriel scratched his head. "But did you really have to break so much glassware and product to get him to understand?"

"He's right."

I ducked my head. "Uh, yeah… about that. That was an accident. I meant to only break one glass. But remembering what they did… got my blood boiling. I'll pay for the replacements."

He shook his head. "Don't worry about it. Rylan gave me a rundown about what happened earlier—he figured you'd be a little on edge. I can't blame you for being angry. If anyone should pay for the replacements, it should be the military, but we both know that won't happen. It's not like I don't budget for these kinds of problems anyway. Kinda have to, with you running this place with me."

I crossed my arms and rolled my eyes. "Ha ha."

He held out his hand suddenly. "Hand me your name tag. I'm going to send you home for the night. Raikidan and Rylan, too."

I cocked my head. "Why?"

"Because I was just contacted by Seda. Your team is needed for something."

"Do you know for what?"

He shook his head. "She didn't say. I can only guess you'll find out when you get home."

I nodded. "All right. Sorry again about the mess I made."

He rolled his eyes and shooed me away so I'd go do whatever it was that the Council needed done.

I adjusted my voice-changing device and then tapped my fingers on my knee. The Council informed us a possible recruit who had been sent away the first time was going to attempt to join us again. But the Seers looking into it weren't able to pinpoint who or when. This forced us to sit here for three and a half hours. No sign of anyone showing up.

Ryoko removed her voice changer and kept her voice low. "This is pointless. No one is coming. Let's just leave."

"He is coming," Seda insisted telepathically. *"I don't know when, but I did see a glimpse of him talking with us."*

Ryoko huffed. "He'd better show up. I feel like my change is going to start early this month."

Blaze moved from his spot from his lookout point and came over to us. "Someone is coming. They're alone."

"Let's hope it's our guy," Ryoko muttered before putting her changer back on.

I nodded, then planted myself in my agreed-on spot. Within minutes, someone came around the corner and walked into the alley. He was in uniform, and it took me a moment to realize who it was.

"Color me impressed," the voice said.

I chuckled. "Well, well, well, look at what we have here. We heard about the 'conversation' with that woman you're so fond of, but we didn't think you'd be swayed so easily, Zo."

He looked up at me wide-eyed. "You know about that?"

I chuckled. "Wasn't much of a conversation from what I heard. Just her doing a lot of yelling and breaking of glassware."

"You've been spying on me, then."

"Of course. We keep tabs on all prospective recruits. Especially when they hold positions like yours."

"So, you know what I'm going to say to you."

"Only because you came back. But I want you to say it."

Zo took a deep breath. "I want to join the cause."

I smirked. He used just the right words. "Are you sure? You're willing to go against the one who created you?"

"I am a man, not a tool—"

The voice snickered.

"—I want to be someone these people don't have to fear."

"Not just the people of this city, Zo. All the people of Lumaraeon, regardless of race. We fight for them."

"Then I fight for Lumaraeon."

"And in that fight, you're willing to turn your back on those you have fought alongside all these years? The ones you call comrades?"

"No, I am not turning my back on them. I am saving them. And I will unify them with the new ones I make."

Right answer, Zo, right answer. "I believe your intentions are pure. You will join us."

Zo smiled, but it went away when I spoke again. "But you will need to prove yourself. You won't have direct contact with any of us for some time. The Council will deliver orders to you that you will need to carry out. Once you gain our trust, then you will be allowed to interact with us more like a true comrade."

"Who is the Council?" Zo asked.

"You will find out in time. For now, I cannot tell you because we cannot fully trust you."

Zo nodded. "I understand. I won't fail you."

"Let's hope not. Now go, before anyone gets suspicious."

Zo nodded and spun on his heels. We watched him leave before shrinking into the shadows.

"Well this is going to be interesting," Mocha said as she took off her voice changer.

Argus nodded. "I hope we're not making a mistake."

"I don't think we are," Rylan said. "I was there when Laz chewed him out. She really knows how to get someone to do what she wants."

"Well she had it easy because Zo's so infatuated with her," Mocha said.

"Even if he wasn't, she'd still manage," Raikidan said. "I'm here, after all."

I held up my hands. "It's just one of the perks of being me."

Raikidan grunted and I smacked him in the arm, making the others laugh.

"Let's head home," Rylan said. "We have one new recruit. May not be much, but it's something, and I think it's worth celebrating over."

Ryoko gasped. "Can we have an ice cream party?"

Mocha's eyes lit up at the idea, and Rylan was overwhelmed by their pleading eyes.

Rylan groaned. "You women don't play fair."

I snickered. "You're just weak. But I think Ryoko has a good idea. Ice cream sounds real nice."

Ryoko squealed and took off. "So picking out the flavors!"

"Not alone you're not!" Mocha shouted as she ran after her.

The rest of us laughed and were soon to follow.

A *ting* echoed through my room when my spoon clanged against the ceramic bowl in my attempt to scrape out some peanut butter with my ice cream. I hummed the dragon lullaby and kicked my feet hanging over my bed. This ice cream idea was the best. The dragons' reaction to the whole Sunday buffet special had been amusing. Mana jumped right in on the concept, while Corliss and Raikidan took it in best they could.

I looked up when someone entered my room. *Speak of the devil.* "Hey, Rai."

He shook his head as he chuckled. "Another bowl of that stuff? That's what, your fifth?"

I ducked my head. "Seventh."

Raikidan shook his head again. "Why can't you eat like this with *real* food?"

I took another bite of ice cream. "Cause I have a sweet tooth the size of Lumaraeon, and no one can stop me."

He sat down next to me and reached for the bowl. "I can if I take it from you."

I pulled it out of his reach and snapped my teeth. "Don't you dare."

Raikidan jerked back, confusing me. "Uh, Rai?"

"Sorry. That was similar to a dragon's warning response for having their possession taken."

I frowned. "I'm sorry. I didn't—"

He shook his head. "There's no need to be. It was a gut reaction I had—instinct driven. I know you were joking. Though, I have to say, you've improved on your possessive behavior with food."

I looked down at my bowl. "Ryoko and I are working on that together. She's been getting snippy lately with her own food, a possible side effect from the wogron transitions she's experiencing. It's been the perfect way for us to fix our issues."

He patted my shoulder. "I'm glad."

I held my bowl out of reach again. "No, you can't take it."

He snickered. "Fine. But as compensation, I'd like for you to keep singing."

I pursed my lips. "You don't get tired of me singing that?"

Raikidan leaned back. "Not in the slightest. I like hearing you sing." He chuckled. "I might have to steal you away after all this, so you can sing for me all the time."

I smacked him in the abs, a smile curving up half my face. "We talked about this before. You're not allowed to steal maidens for their voice."

He rubbed the area I hit, a slight pout on his lips. "You're no fun. I'd feed you. And take you for walks. And be sure to tell you how pretty you are all the time."

I found myself on my back, rolling with laughter. Raikidan watched me, amused.

Ryoko poked her head into the room. "Is all that sugar finally getting to her?"

"I think so," Raikidan said, not looking away from me.

I pointed at him as I tried to calm myself. "His fault."

Raikidan held up his hands. "I don't know what you're talking about. You're the one who fell over laughing for no reason."

I smacked him again and ate more of my ice cream. "Liar."

"Man, you're violent today."

Ryoko snickered. "I'll leave you two to your squabbling."

She closed the door behind her.

Raikidan smiled. "Now that your fit is over, will you sing?"

"Can you teach me another song?" I asked. "Just to vary it up."

He frowned. "We… don't have many others. We have ones that are sung in remembrance, for loss, and one we sing to a mate. That one isn't sad, so I guess I could teach you that one."

I wasn't sure about that idea.

"It's a sign. Let him teach it to you."

"No, that's okay. I'll just sing this one I know."

"No, that's not what I told you to do."

I ignored her and took another bite of my frozen treat before preparing to sing some more.

Raikidan stopped me the moment the first note escaped. "Wait. I'll teach you the song."

My brow rose. "I said it was okay. I don't want to put you in a weird position teaching me something so…"

"Intimate?" He nodded, though his eyes couldn't meet mine. "It's not as intense as you may think."

"Uh huh. That's why you can't look at me?"

Raikidan's eyes snapped to me. "Yes I can. I was just thinking."

"Lying shit."

"My thoughts exactly." I shook my head. "It's fine, Rai. I know this song, and you like it, so I'll sing it."

He climbed farther onto the bed and lay back on my pillows. "I'm teaching you, so listen carefully."

My brow twisted. "Why?"

"Because you may need it one day."

I snorted. "Yeah, right."

He looked at me, confused.

"It's a dragon's song. Only a dragon could truly appreciate it sung to them, and it's not like I'd run into one that would try to claim I'm their destined mate." I shook my head. "Besides, I'd be lucky if a human could stand what a broken mess I am."

"That's not true."

Raikidan frowned and brushed my bangs away from my eyes. "Don't say that. It's not true."

My gaze went elsewhere and I ate another spoonful of my melting treat.

Raikidan slipped his arm around me and pulled me closer to him. "None of that. I'm going to teach you a nice song and you're going to be happy, got it?"

My brow lifted and I refused to take the spoon out of my mouth. It didn't matter, though. Without considering I'd have some sort of response for him, Raikidan hummed a tune I'd never heard before. I listened as it developed and found myself no longer interested in my snack.

The tune interested me—soft, but still equally powerful and compelling. I relaxed into him as he continued and I tried to find the pattern in the tune. I lost myself in the song as it continued on and on. *He has to be looping it at this point.* It only made sense. No way could this song be this long.

That also told me this song was designed specifically to not end. *Much like their pairing.* Made sense. What didn't make sense was Raikidan's continuing of the song and not actually teaching me. *Maybe he's expecting me to pick it up in some way.* That I could believe.

So I did.

I listened more intently this time, finding the patterns and inflections better, until I decided to try it myself, but at an octave I was comfortable with.

I didn't do too badly at first, but a few seconds in, I messed up. I cringed and Raikidan's singing stopped. "Sorry. Didn't mean to mess you up."

He chuckled. "No need to apologize." He brushed my hair to the side again. "I'm just glad you listened to what I'd done. It's not easy to teach the song unless you've heard it enough to give it a try on your own."

"I'd like to try again. I like this song."

Raikidan nodded and then continued where we'd left off.

32
CHAPTER

The crate lid creaked as I pried it off. Peering inside, I smiled and snatched up all the ammunition I could without caring about the type. Anything was better than our current supply. The fact we even managed to slip into a warehouse with ammunition was a feat.

The rebellion had been running low for some time, but due to high security, either no one was able to get into a targeted warehouse, or warehouses believed to house ammunition were either completely empty or had empty crates. This find was exactly what we needed.

"How's your search going?"

I turned to see Raikidan walking toward me. "Great. I can see yours isn't, since you're not helping."

"I heard some commotion outside, so I thought it was best to move about and keep an eye out instead of searching," he said.

"And what did you do with your backpack?"

"Gave it to Mocha," he said as he continued to advance. "She came across a good find, so I figured she'd need it."

"Well, you should think about helping grab ammo instead of being a lookout. The faster we collect this stuff, the faster we get out and don't need to worry about any soldiers guarding this place."

He sighed. "Then I'll help you."

I nodded. "Fine with me."

I moved to another crate and opened it up, only to find it empty. A strained breath left my nose and I moved to another. This crate did have useful contents and was different from my first find, making it even better.

Raikidan helped me, but it wasn't long before he started acting funny. I noticed he stood closer to me than needed, and he seemed to be paying more attention to what I was doing than what he should be doing.

"Is there something wrong?" I finally asked him when I was sure he had moved even closer to me.

"No, why?"

"Because you seem to be forgetting about my personal space rule."

He took a visible step closer. "I am?"

"He's acting strange, even for him."

"Don't start with that. We have a job to do. I don't have the time or patience for your games."

He placed a hand on my hip and invaded my personal space. His strong scent hit me, but something was… off about it. "What game?"

I push him back. "You know not to do that."

He grinned. "Do what?"

"Eira, who are you talking to over here?"

I blinked in confusion when I heard Raikidan's voice come from somewhere in the warehouse behind me. My confusion grew when he came around a stack of crates. I stepped away from the Raikidan next to me and looked at them both. This situation was all too familiar.

"What's going on here?" the new Raikidan demanded to know.

The Raikidan near me chuckled. "Looks like I was too slow and got caught. Oh well."

The Raikidan near me reached out and aimed to grab me by the throat, but I ducked and moved farther out of reach. The Raikidan that was seemingly on my side rammed the other Raikidan into the crate I had been searching prior to this incident.

The commotion caught Ryoko's and Mocha's attention and they ran over to investigate.

"What's going on?" Mocha asked.

"Why are there two people who look like Raikidan?" Ryoko asked.

"I don't know!" I said.

"This is like the situation with Rana," Ryoko said. "You don't think she—"

I shook my head. "No. I burned her body after she asked me to. Even if I hadn't, she wouldn't be doing this. We ended on good terms."

One Raikidan shoved the other into a crate and then pointed at me. "Don't you talk about her like that! You have no right."

I stared at him. How did this guy know Rana? The man, angry with my lack of immediate defense, shifted to his natural look and my breath caught. "Sabel."

He was a tall, slightly muscular man with alabaster skin, crystal blue eyes and silver hair. Sabel clenched his fists as he stalked over to me. Ryoko attempted to put herself in front of me, but I motioned for her to stand down. This was between him and me.

"So, why don't you tell me what problem you have with me, Sabel," I said. "Just let me have it and we'll see if it's justified or misguided."

"Everything!" he seethed. "The way we were treated. My poorly chosen assignments. My loss of friends. Rana was the last friend I had, and you took her away like all the others!"

"You're talking about the executions."

"Of course I am. You played favorites, like all the ranking officers. Whoever didn't suck up to you was given the boot."

I sighed and shook my head. "You're misguided by anger."

"Don't! Don't even start acting all high and mighty on me."

"Do you really think I enjoyed making those choices? Do you really think I was that twisted?" I crossed my arms. "Well I'm not. I didn't pick favorites. I didn't pick at random. I lost sleep over those choices that Zarda took sick pleasure in forcing me to make! I knew those soldiers I chose had friends. I knew they had family. But that didn't matter."

I took a controlled breath. "I had to make a choice or Zarda would have, and his choice would have been worse. He would have selected them all for his sick pleasure! I picked who would benefit the military the greatest, not who I liked more, and chose humane deaths when possible. I didn't want that curse, but I had no choice but to accept it."

Sabel's eyes tightened. "And Rana? Why her?"

"Rana had a personal vendetta against me. She attacked me and she attacked my comrades. She died because I protected them and myself.

I didn't want to do that, Sabel, but she forced my hand. And in death, she asked me to burn her body so she couldn't come back, because she understood she was wrong. And she believed she had no place in this world because of some of her more unfortunate abilities."

"You're lying!"

"No I'm not, Sabel. And I can prove it."

I pulled out a spiritual crystal from a pouch attached to my belt loop and forced spiritual energy into it. Within seconds, a small spiritual field formed around the crystal and I made an attempt to find Rana. I didn't have to look far.

"I'm here, Eira," Rana whispered. "He may not believe this, but we must try."

I forced more spiritual energy into the crystal, and when there was enough to create a large spiritual field, Rana's translucent form appeared in front of me.

"R–Rana?" Sabel stuttered out. "No. This is some sort of trick."

"This isn't a trick, Sabel," Rana said. "This is me. Just without my body. Everything Eira just told you is the truth. What I did and what I forced her to do is the truth. I told her to burn my body so I couldn't come back."

"No. No, Rana wouldn't say that," Sabel said. "She wouldn't have wanted to die."

"I didn't have a chance at a real life, Sabel. Nothing was going to change that."

"But…" He looked distraught. "We were working on an antidote together. We were working on a way… Why would you do that to me?"

Rana's eyes were filled with sympathy and a bit of regret. "I know you cared, Sabel, but we both know the antidote wasn't working like we needed it to. It's better this way."

"No it's not! No it's not… How could you say that? How could you give up on me like that?" He shook his head. "Rana wouldn't have given up on me. You're not Rana!"

"Sabel, please," Rana begged. "It's best this way. I wasn't good for you…"

"No… that's a lie…"

"Sabel," I said before tossing the spiritual crystal to him.

Sabel caught the crystal out of reflex, but almost dropped it the moment it made contact with his hand. I knew, by the way he jerked, he had felt the artificial heartbeat the crystal gave off.

Sabel stared at the crystal as he felt the artificial pulse. "It's…"

"An artificial heart," Rana said. "I'm really here, Sabel, but only temporarily. I'm here only to get you to open your eyes."

Sabel stared at the crystal for some time. I could understand his struggle, even with the evidence. Like Rana, he convinced himself he had the true answers. I just hoped violence wasn't going to be needed with him as well.

His eyes lifted to meet mine. "I'm sorry for my accusations. And for attacking you."

I relaxed, as did everyone else, and nodded. "It's fine." I glanced at Rana. "I'm glad this outcome was better."

"I guess this means I have no real reason to stay loyal to Zarda anymore," Sabel murmured.

"You can join us," Ryoko offered.

Sabel nodded. "I think that would be—" He froze and the spiritual crystal slipped from his hands.

"Eira, something is wrong."

I stepped forward. "Sabel?"

Ryoko and Mocha looked at each other with worried expressions, and Raikidan took a defensive stance.

"No… don't…" Sabel said as he held his head. "Please… no!"

I gasped. "By the goddess!"

"What? What's going on?" Mocha asked.

Before I could say anything, Sabel came at me, his movements jerky and slow, making it easy for me to dodge him.

"Sabel, fight it!" I ordered. "Get him out of your head."

Ryoko gasped. "A psychic is controlling him!"

"Sabel, fight it." I said again as his body continued to go after me. "You need to force him out. Take control."

"C–can't stop… C–can't get him o–out…"

Rana moved in front of me, but before she could say anything to Sabel, his body attempted to attack her as if it believed she was actually there.

"You need to disable him."

I punched Sabel in the face. It didn't do much, so I tried again. Same result.

"That's not working. The psychic is suppressing his pain."

"I'm well aware of that now."

"K—kill… me…" Sabel managed to beg as he took another swing at me.

I shook my head. "No, Sabel, I won't do that."

"P—please," he begged. "Please s—stop this."

"Sabel…"

"I w—won't blame you. D—do what you have to…"

Rana set sad eyes on me. "You have to. It's the only way."

I hesitated. It wasn't right to have to do this. It wasn't fair to him.

"The psychic will kill him if you don't. You know this. End his suffering."

Taking a steady breath, I drew my dagger and maneuvered around Sabel's poor defenses. I plunged the dagger into his heart and then pulled it free so I could slip behind him and thrust it into his back. Sabel screamed out in pain, and I cursed the psychic for letting go of his control right at that moment. The sick, twisted prick would pay for it if I ever found out who it was.

I caught Sabel as he fell, and rolled him over to lay him on his back. "I'm sorry, Sabel…"

He coughed up blood. "D—don't be… This is my… fault. T—they knew… I was going after you…"

He coughed up more blood and his voice became weaker. "I should have known… they would monitor me…"

"Sabel…"

"I'm the one… who is sorry. I shouldn't have… accused you of all those things. You proved to me, with your hesitation… to kill me… that you were telling me the truth…"

"Sabel, I"—I listened as his breathing ceased—"Sabel?"

"He's dead," Rana said. "I see him crossing over."

My head lowered in silent prayer. "Take care of him."

"You know I will. When he's ready, we'll let you know how to handle his remains."

I nodded. She faded away and I exhaled a slow breath before closing Sabel's eyes and then hauling him over my shoulders.

"I'll take him," Raikidan offered.

"No, I'm fine," I replied. "I do need someone to grab my spiritual crystal, though. We need to get out of here before soldiers start swarming the place."

He nodded and retrieved my bag of acquired ammunition and then snatched up the spiritual crystal.

"Are you going to be okay?" Ryoko asked as we left.

"I'll be fine," I said. "I just want to get out of here."

"Okay…"

I pulled myself out of the bath and wrapped a towel around my body before heading into my room. We had left Sabel's body with the Council to be buried later. I also had to deal with a lengthy lecture on how I shouldn't have left the location without collecting more ammunition. Apparently what we'd gathered wasn't good enough and the fact we'd been discovered wasn't an appropriate reason to leave so soon. *Well, for a few of them at least.* There had been a number of Council members who didn't agree with the reprimand and made it known.

I didn't care. They could reprimand me all they wanted, I wouldn't have risked everyone's lives for the sake of ammunition. We'd just have to keep rationing.

I pulled out some clothes to wear to bed and I untied my towel. Mid-motion while discarding it, the fire escape creaked and Raikidan appeared in the window. Raikidan froze when I gasped and attempted to cover myself with my towel.

"Raikidan, get out!"

He stayed where it was, staring at me. My heart hammered in my chest as heat spread through me.

"I said get out!"

Raikidan shook his head and turned around, but he glanced over his shoulder. His sapphire eyes glowed a brilliant hue.

"Why are you looking back in here? I told you to get out!"

He grinned and left. "I just like what I see."

He what? I licked my lips in my shocked state and tried to think straight, but my body didn't want to listen.

As I took some steady breaths, I looked over at my reflection in the mirror on the wall and swallowed hard. My attempt to cover myself hadn't gone so well. The towel hung in front of me, covering some of my more vital areas, but my waistline and hips showed a lot of skin still, and my arms had done a better job covering my breasts than the towel, though even that coverage was minimal.

Heat rose in my face. *He said he liked—*

The voice chuckled. *"See."*

I shook the thoughts from my head. *No, he was just messing with me.*

The voice let out an exasperated sigh. *"Stop trying to deny what's right in front of you. He liked what he saw. He would have preferred the towel not be in the way of his viewing pleasure, but you're too prudish to allow for that."*

I went about dressing for bed. *"It's not like that."*

"I wish you'd stop being so ridiculous about this. All signs point to this being right for you. Jump on it." She chuckled. *"Well, him."*

I sat down on the bed. *"Why are you so insistent on this? You told me you want me to be happy, but you've never explained your stance on this topic."*

"I'm sorry, Eira, but I can't explain it to you."

Of course she couldn't.

"Dear, I know you get annoyed with me, but I wish you'd listen to what I'm saying. What others say. Raikidan took the time to get to know you, the real *you, even when you did what you could to push him away. He taught you about himself and his kind at lengths he hasn't gone for others. He's taken you out on a date. He showers you with gifts and affection. A lot of affection. And just now, he didn't shy away from telling you what was on his mind."*

I played with my fingers, my eyes finding interest in the floor, as if trying to avoid her nonexistent gaze. *"It's not me he should vie for. There's someone out there that's his perfect match."*

"There can be more than one that meets that criteria. You know that first hand."

Tannek's face flashed in my mind, then Telar, and then, to my surprise, Ken'ichi. Though, as I thought about it, it wasn't really that much of a surprise. Early into getting to know him, I denied his interest in me when Raikidan made mention of it. I couldn't deny, now, that had I not been so adamant about pushing others away, and holding onto the past, something may have happened between Ken'ichi and me. *Same with Telar.* Though, like he'd said, it probably wouldn't have worked out in the long run.

I shook my head. *"Doesn't matter. Gods chose her."*

"The gods wouldn't be able to tell the difference between 'there' and 'they're' if it weren't for the creation of grammar tyrants."

I snorted through my nose, then giggled uncontrollably, nearly falling on the floor.

"Your laughter makes me happy. You've come a long way."

"So have you."

"It's because of him."

"I wish you could tell me what that meant. You've said it before, and yet I'm no closer to understanding." I shook my head. *"And don't tell me the answer lies within. I'm so tired of hearing that. You can't find answers if you don't know what you're looking for."*

"You've made it so close to the answer already. Stay the course and you'll figure everything out."

"So, don't tell Raikidan how I feel."

"No, tell him. He's an important key."

I straightened. She was able to reveal something right there. How, I wasn't sure, but I wasn't going to take it for granted.

He's a key… A key… I jumped to my feet. *"The voice I heard, when Raikidan and I were exploring that manifested building in my mind, was that you?"*

Silence.

I paced. That was an answer, of sorts. It was a yes or no. It had to be. Every question in the past that met the same silent treatment due to this strange block had been close to the truth. *So it's a yes?*

I rummaged through my stuff for a pencil and paper, finding a sketchbook I used for my jewelry every now and then. *Good enough.* I plopped down on my bed and sketched out the door I'd seen, losing myself in remembering what details I could.

Each contact with the paper—every line—each shape created, my thoughts drowned in the image burned into my mind. Just about when the image was finished, the sketchbook left my hands. My eyes widened and panic flooded into my chest. I snapped my head to Raikidan, who now sat next to me on the bed.

I snatched the pad back. "I'm not done."

"Eira, what has gotten into you?" he asked.

"Ideas…" I continued to sketch.

"Uh, how about more of an explanation?"

"It's all connected somehow." I stopped sketching. "But how?"

Raikidan watched me for a moment as I thought, and then took the sketchbook again. I didn't take it back—my mind now moved on to thinking. I stood and paced.

"The images on that door mean something. You mean something. That voice I heard… it all means something. Something… important."

"You're not making any sense."

"I know." I couldn't explain it to him. Not without telling him more about the voice, and I couldn't do that right now. *He'd think I'm crazy.* "The answer is on the tip of my tongue…"

Raikidan's eyes flicked down to my sketchbook. He flipped it around so I could see it. "Did you even look at what you drew?"

It probably looked like a scribbled mess, but I humored him. To my amazement, it was far from that. A crisp, detailed depiction of the stone imagery on the door met my gaze.

"I've never seen you draw something so nice," he said. "Not to be insulting or anything."

I took the sketchbook from him and stared. So much detail on the page. "No offense taken. I've never drawn this well before."

How did I manage it? Was it related to all this? Or was it because the building existed in my mind I was able to create it on paper better?

I handed the sketchbook to Raikidan and paced, the image now weighing on my mind as well. Why couldn't I get the words to come off my tongue? It was right there!

Raikidan sighed and grabbed my hand, forcing me to stop. "You need to calm down. You're going to burn a hole into the floor."

I held his gaze and then slipped from his grasp to pace some more. "My mind is going a million miles a minute. I need to move as I sort this out."

"It's not helping." He grabbed both of my wrists this time, his warmth seeping into my skin. "You're just working yourself up. Take a deep breath and sort out your thoughts."

We stared at each other, my mind not cooperating in the least. I tried to pull out of his grasp again, but he held on tighter. Raikidan frowned and yanked me toward him. I stumbled but had enough of my wits about me to stay upright and not fall on him. Even holding his gaze, I still felt the pull to pace and think.

Raikidan's eyes narrowed. "Okay, that's it."

He let me go, but then wrapped his arms around my lower body and lifted me up, only to throw me on the bed right after. I let out an *oof* as I bounced on the soft, springy surface. Raikidan climbed onto the bed and laid his head down on my chest.

"There, now you have to calm down."

I stared at the ceiling, bewildered, and then tried to get up. He wasn't having it. He wrapped an arm around my waist, pinning me there on the bed. "No."

I let out a deep exhale. "Rai."

"You need to calm yourself."

I lifted my hand and held two fingers close to each other. "The answer is right there. I'm so close."

"I know. But you're getting yourself so worked up you can't actually think. You only think you're thinking."

My arm dropped and I looked down at him. He gazed up at me. Was he right? *Duh, Eira.* Of course he was.

I took a deep breath as I closed my eyes. I needed to relax. After a few more breaths, my head cleared a bit. It wasn't enough to get it to stop freaking out, but it was better.

"Can you now explain to me, in an organized fashion, what's got you all worked up?" Raikidan asked.

"I had a thought about that temple. And then so many ideas came flying into my head. They were all connected somehow, but I don't know how. The answer for everything is right there. It's frustrating to know I have the answer, but I don't."

Raikidan reached up and intertwined his fingers with mine. "It's okay. You'll figure it out when you're meant to."

My hazed flicked to our hands, noting how much I liked they way they fit together. "I feel like I was supposed to a long time ago."

"Don't fret about it." He half-smiled at me. "I know you'll figure it out soon. I'll help, like I promised. From what you said in all your gibberish, I'm connected to this somehow, anyway."

I pressed my lips together as I thought. "You're a big key."

His brow rose. "I assumed I had something do with it, that much I told you when I first found out about this temple in your mind. But if you're saying I'm a big key, I'm curious to know what has you thinking that."

"You changed the course of everything. You made me aware of what that place was. You got me to that temple. Those dragons carved in stone? They mean something. The way you got me there, it means something."

Raikidan sat up, letting me go as he did, and retrieved my sketchbook.

This allowed me to sit as well, but unlike before, I didn't have the urge to stand and pace. He scooted next to me and we examined the drawing I'd made. I couldn't help but trace some of the lines of the woman on the far right. She shared many similarities to Tla'lli and the other South Tribe shamans.

"Maybe if you bring it to life, it can help," Raikidan said.

My brow rose. "What do you mean?"

He pressed his lips together for a moment. "We never talked about it after it happened, but that memory magic ability you used…"

I shook my head. "I don't know what that was, Rai. I really don't. I'd never done anything like that before. Something inside me said to breathe on the painting, so I did."

It wasn't a total lie. I wasn't sure what that voice was that told me to do it. But my wording kept me from sounding insane. "For all I know, it was all a trick by some psychic, and you had the intelligence to capitalize on it and make up a story."

Raikidan shook his head. "No. I told the truth that time. It was memory magic. I've seen it once before, at the town my mother and I used to frequent in the past. A traveler used it to make some coin."

His nose scrunched. "And seduce some of the more impression-able females."

I did my best not to laugh at his reaction, but a chuckle escaped my lips.

Raikidan shook his head to rid himself of the thoughts. "I don't think I'm going to ever understand that side of you humans."

I patted his arm. "It's okay. There's going to be a lot of things that we do so differently we will struggle to understand." I grinned. "But this particular situation, you'd understand better if you had a mate. That feeling is what some humans seek out, in a temporary sense."

He shook his head again. "Anyway, that's not what I was aiming to talk about."

I chuckled but let him get us back on track.

"It was a real thing you did."

"But how?" I said. "I don't know how I did that."

Raikidan stared at the drawing. "Maybe the same way you made this."

I cocked my head, failing to understand.

"Remember how those shamans had that theory you've been rein-carnated?"

My eyes widened. "You think that ability might prove it?"

He nodded. "It's possible you managed to tap into an ancestral memory of sorts. If you knew magic, even just memory magic, in a former life, then it's quite possible."

I took the sketchbook from him and traced another image of a woman, this one an elven woman with a flowing dress. Did I tap into some ancestral memory in my mood and make this, too? "What if… these are those lives?"

Raikidan touched each depicted person. "That'd be sixteen." He cocked his head and tapped two women drawn next to each other, almost touching. "Fifteen maybe? I'm not sure, but these look a lot like twins."

I frowned. "Sixteen or fifteen, makes the idea a bit of stretch regardless."

"I don't know." He counted them again, as if trying to piece something together. "That might be what it takes to get as strong as you."

I tapped a dragon. "But what about these? Why dragons?"

"Well, we both know that our meeting was no accident—that it was destiny. Maybe it was, and not a big elaborate joke the gods are playing on us. Maybe in the past you tamed dragons, too."

I punched him in the arm. "I didn't tame you."

He looked me in the eye. "Yeah? Then what would you call this?"

I held his gaze. "Befriending."

He reached up and brushed my bangs away from my eyes, resting his hand comfortably on my cheek. A smile slid up half his face. "I'll take that answer."

The longer we stared at each other, the more those feelings I'd been trying to bury threatened to surface. The thought brought warmth to my face and I couldn't allow him to see. I ripped my gaze away and stared at the drawing.

The voice sighed. *"You were doing so well."*

"If you *befriended* a dragon in the past," Raikidan said, "more than once, especially, that might also explain how you've excelled learning our language."

My brow rose. "Excelled? I don't excel at that."

He gave me a pointed look. "Compared to other humans, yes, you do. In just a few months, you've learned more words and sentence structure than the average human could in a year."

I chewed my bottom lip. Was I really that good? I was so certain I sucked. In either case I sounded stupid when trying to speak it, regardless if he thought otherwise.

Raikidan brushed my hair aside again. "I'm losing you to your thoughts again."

I snickered. "Don't worry, I'm not going to start pacing. Just trying to piece this all together. I'm not quite sure we have this right."

"Why don't you sleep on it, then? It'll let you clear your head so you can think better on it later."

I nodded. Sound idea. And if I was lucky, I'd end up at the temple again to investigate it more.

Raikidan slipped off the bed and placed my sketchbook on the dresser with my pencil as I situated myself for sleep. A pitiful squeak escaped me when he jumped back onto the bed and snuggled up to me. My body curved comfortably against his hard form, his tantalizing scent teasing me. A comfortable warmth washed over me.

I wanted to question him, but the words lodged in my throat. I knew I should. I should keep fighting this desire because it was wrong to indulge, but I didn't have the strength right now. I wanted this contact.

Raikidan glanced down at me. "Not going to chastise me?"

I snuggled in deeper. "No."

Raikidan smiled and then rested his chin on my head. He made me feel safe—wanted. Even for just a moment. It was nice.

"Keep this path up, and you're going to find the answers."

I decided to bite the bullet. *"Rashta?"*

No response. *Dammit.* It was worth a shot. A long one to be sure, given she hadn't responded to the other times I'd inquired, but my talk with Raikidan had been strange enough it couldn't have hurt to try. Soon, though, I'd figure this out, including her. I wasn't going to give up.

Raikidan pulled me in even closer, and his unusual dragon "purr" reverberated through his chest, soothing me into a restful trance.

"The answers will come to you in due time, dear. Just you wait."

I threw on a light jacket and stepped outside the club into the alley. I needed some fresh air. Sitting down on some plastic crates, I let my mind wander. I didn't want to think about club responsibilities, and I didn't want to think about the rebellion. I wanted the latter to be done with.

Spring was upon us, and the Council had agreed to end Zarda's reign by spring, but nothing had changed. The assignments were the same and came at the same rate. If I knew how to get in and do the job myself, I would have done it a long time ago—but unfortunately I wasn't that skilled… or smart.

"Don't say that, you are smart. Killing him is more complicated than a simple assassination."

I peered over to the front of the alley when someone stumbled in. I figured it was a drunk, from either this club or one of the ones down the street and normally I wouldn't care, but since I'd been jumped in an alley before, I didn't want to take any chances.

I was surprised to see it was Zo. Last I knew, from the information I had dug up on him over the past year, he never drank enough to be wasted. But here he was, struggling to stand. Had this been going on a few weeks ago, I would have let him stumble, but now that he was part of the rebellion, it was my responsibility to make sure he was going to be okay.

I took several steps closer to him. "Zo, you okay?"

Zo muttered incoherently and fell over. My pace quickened and I knelt to help him up, but he pushed me away. "Don't touch me."

"Zo, take it easy." I kept my voice soft. "I'm just here to help."

"Leave me alone!"

I grabbed him by the arm and tried to pull him up. "Don't be like that. Let me help you."

He didn't protest this time, but he also didn't try to help me in getting him up. He was heavy, but nothing I couldn't handle.

"You're pretty," he slurred.

"Um, thanks." I turned toward the road. "Let's get on the main street so I can call you a taxi."

He chuckled. "You'll come with me, right?"

"I'll bring you to the cab."

"No, you'll come home with me."

"No, Zo, I'm not going home with you. I'm getting you a cab and then going back to work."

He stopped walking and grabbed onto me. "Why? Eira, I l—"

"Zo, stop. You're drunk. You need to go back to the barracks and sleep this off. There's no negotiating this."

Zo gave up standing, yanking me down. "What did I do wrong? Why do you hate me?"

I sighed. "Zo, I don't hate you. You drank too much and I'm trying to get you home. That's all that's going on here."

He shook his head. "No, that's not what this is about! You can't stand me. I'm just a jackass to you, and you're just too nice to tell me to get lost."

Great. He's an emotional drunk. Explained why he didn't drink in excess. I exhaled slowly. "Zo, I don't hate you. Please, believe me."

The side door to the club opened and Raikidan came out. "Eira? Your break ended ten minutes ago. Everything okay?"

When he noticed me with Zo, alarm registered on his face. "What's going on?"

"What do you want?" Zo didn't refrain from being rude. "No one wants you around, you prick."

Raikidan's eyes shifted to me, brow cocked, and I shook my head. "Don't listen to him. He's drunk. I could use your hand getting him to the street, though. He needs a cab."

Raikidan nodded and came over to assist, but Zo wasn't having it. "Don't touch me!"

Raikidan sighed in aggravation and I felt a little bad. This was something he dealt with a lot since being forced into this job.

"Zo, stop. He's just trying to help," I said.

"He's the reason for all of this, isn't he? He's why you won't give me the light of day anymore." Zo tried to push away from us. "You showed your interest when it was convenient, then went back to him when you were bored. You're a slut like all the other—"

Raikidan punched Zo in the face. "Don't you dare call her that!"

"Rai!" I shrieked. "He's drunk."

"I don't care. Nobody, drunk or sober, calls you that. And now he'll have a nice reminder why he won't ever again."

I huffed and went to help Zo again. He pushed away my offered hands and stumbled to his feet only to fall into someone else. "Whoa, easy there."

I blinked. "Corliss?"

Corliss smiled. "Hey."

"Who are you?" Zo asked.

"Just a concerned citizen. Let's get you to a cab," Corliss said.

Zo nodded, allowing Corliss to escort him away. "Yeah… that sounds like a good idea."

I relief washed over me. When Corliss returned, he was alone and smiling. "Got a little worried when Raikidan didn't come back after going to search for you. Glad I came out. Looked like he wasn't going to listen to either of you."

I crossed my arms. "Drunks do stupid things."

"Speaking of stupid"—he held out his hand that was clenched and opened it—"I'm going to ask you a possible stupid question. Can you possibly tell me why I found this tucked inside his uniform?"

"Is that flesh?" Raikidan asked.

My body locked up when the scent of the tissue wafted into my nose.

The soldier behind me pushed me down the poorly lit hallway. I didn't know what I did or where I was going, but I had a feeling this wasn't going to end well.

It wasn't just any flesh. Now I knew why Zo had been drunk. Corliss held the piece of fleshy tissue closer to me, and I stepped back with wide eyes.

"Eira, what's wrong?" Raikidan asked, worry clear in his voice.

I shook my head and stepped back again.

We came to a metal door, and an awful smell drifted into my nose. I recoiled, my instincts screaming at me to run, but the soldier behind me pushed me forward, forcing me to the the door at the end of the hall.

"T—that's human flesh," I managed.

"You've dealt with dead humans before," Corliss said. "Why is the flesh—"

"Corliss, stop." Raikidan turned his attention back to me. "Eira, what's wrong?"

I swallowed but couldn't find the words to tell them.

The door creaked open, and before I had a chance to look around, the soldier pushed me through. I fell about four feet down, into a pool filled with a warm liquid. I scrambled upright and tried to push myself up the slimy wall, when I felt an unmistakable mass of human bodies underneath me. The door closed and I snapped my head in multiple directions, frantic for a way out. I was met with four walls, a nearly burnt-out light, blood, dead bodies, parts, and bits of flesh.

"Eira!" Raikidan yelled. I jumped and he shot me an apologetic look. "Sorry, but I needed you to come back to us."

"I—it's fine," I stammered as I tried to get a hold of myself.

"What's wrong?" Raikidan asked. "Why is this bit of flesh upsetting you?"

I licked my lips. "That piece of flesh was on Zo because he did something wrong."

Corliss's brow knitted. "What do you mean?"

I took a deep breath. "There's a room, deep in the fortress underground. It's where Zarda performs one of his most horrifying tortures."

I licked my lips again. "And it's where all the experiments that didn't make it through the growing process go."

The dragons stared with horrified eyes. "Eira?"

"It's called the *Blood Room*. Since the experiments were failures, Zarda didn't believe they deserved to be buried or disposed of properly. Instead, he had them dumped into this room, along with blood from tests that were no longer needed, and body parts and flesh removed from living experiments for various reasons. And when Zarda felt the need to teach one of us a lesson, he'd throw us in there for a few hours."

I took a shaky breath. "Typically, one time is enough to prevent you from doing anything wrong again. Zo must have done something Zarda deemed wrong and threw him in there. I can only guess he didn't listen to an order. That's the most common reason an experiment is punished in such a way."

Corliss tossed the flesh and wiped his hand on his pants. "Sorry I brought it up."

I nodded. "It's fine."

"Eira, have you ever been to this room?" Raikidan asked.

I took a quick breath and turned on my heels. "I need to get back to work. I'm really late."

"Eira, stop."

I halted and sighed. "It was during my earlier years when I was more reckless. I didn't perform a task as asked, so Zarda threw me in there. It was almost two decades before I disobeyed again."

I chewed on my lip. "I… I wouldn't even wish that torture on Zarda. That's how horrible that place is…"

"Eira…"

I took a quick breath to collect myself and headed for the door again. "Now I have to go back to work."

Raikidan grabbed me by the arm. "You're going home."

"What, why?"

"You're not in any condition to go back to work."

"Rai, I'm fine."

He turned me around and forced me to walk toward Corliss. "No, you're not. We caused you to remember something traumatic. You shouldn't go back to working after that. Corliss, I need you to take her home."

"Sure," Corliss agreed. "Mana is with Ryoko, so I know she's safe, but I'd like for you to keep an eye on her for me while I'm gone."

"Yeah, I can do that."

"Thanks."

"Guys, I'm fine, really," I insisted.

"I have a car parked down the street," Corliss said, ignoring my plea.

I huffed. "Fine. I'll go home." I pointed at Raikidan. "But I expect you to be able to make the same amount tonight as if the two of us did the work."

Raikidan held up his hands. "That's not possible!"

I shrugged and followed Corliss out of the alley. "Not my problem. You're the one sending me home. Have fun."

Corliss snickered and pulled his keys out of his pocket.

I stared up at the water above me in the bath. Raikidan had made the right call in the end. Not long after I'd gotten home, I had another episode. Seda helped me through it, as did the voice. After it passed, I had chosen to come in here to work on my spiritual plane walking. More specifically, I worked on a technique to make myself aware of what was going on around me while being able to focus on spiritual plane matters. It wasn't going well. I was still on the physical plane, holding my breath, with few moments of only partially passing over to the spiritual plane.

I knew it would take time, but I wanted this technique to work. The only thing it seemed to do was help me learn to hold my breath longer, and that wasn't what I wanted. I wanted to be able to protect myself no matter the situation. I couldn't rely on Raikidan to do it in the future. He may have taken an oath to be my permanent Guard, but he had a life to get back to. I couldn't take him away from that for my sake. It wasn't right.

I sat up and took a deep breath of fresh air when a dark shadow flashed through my vision. The bath appeared fine, so I wondered if it was something on the spiritual plane. Curious, I decided to submerge myself again and head over to the spiritual plane to check it out.

I looked around when I crossed over. It was dark and dreary, and it felt like I wasn't alone, but as I scanned my surroundings I saw nothing. I had to have imagined the—

"Be wary," a voice hissed.

My head swiveled back and forth. The voice was rough, male, and sounded familiar somehow.

"Be wary," the voice warned again. "The path you walk is paved with treachery."

I grunted. "Yeah, I know. I plan to kill the man that rules this city and the surrounding area. That's considered treachery."

"Not that treachery. Another form, from someone you place trust in."

"What?"

"Be wary."

"Be wary of who?"

The voice didn't answer. I waited a few moments, but when it didn't answer, I knew it was gone. That's how spirits worked. And typical of spirits, their message wasn't always clear. I had no idea who he was warning me about.

A part of me wondered if it was related to the warning about my fate that I already knew and was trying to avoid, but I couldn't be convinced just yet because there wasn't enough to go on. Whatever it meant, I couldn't think about it on this plane.

Closing my eyes, I slipped back to the living world, and when I opened them again, I was met with a blurry vision of Raikidan standing over me. He offered his hand to me and I took it without question. I took a deep breath of air when I broke the surface of the water.

"Do I want to know what you were doing?" Raikidan asked. "Because for a moment I thought you were drowning."

I chuckled as I relaxed in the bath, thankful I'd put a bathing suit on before doing this. "I was working on a technique, and I thought submerging in water would help."

"Did it?"

I shrugged. "It's a work in progress. I didn't expect you to be back so soon."

Raikidan smiled. "Azriel let me out early so I could come check on you."

I smiled back. "Well I'm fine, thanks."

"You sure?"

I nodded. "Yeah. I've had enough time to be alone and calm down."

He chuckled and shook his head. "Being alone in water to relax after what you remembered is the last thing I'd expect to hear come from your mouth."

I relaxed more. "Yeah, well, I'm weird like that."

"You sure are. But if you really think you're okay, then I'll leave you alone."

I nodded in response, a smile on my lips, and he accepted my assurance. He turned to leave, but as he took a step, he slipped.

"Raikidan!" I gasped when he fell into the bath water. I scrambled over to him and helped get his head above the surface to gasp for air. "Are you okay?"

He nodded. "Yeah."

"You didn't hit your head at all, right?"

I fussed, checking him all over and he started laughing. "Eira, I'm fine. Really."

When I realized he was okay like he claimed, I relaxed. "Sorry. I'm acting like a worried mom."

Raikidan calmed himself and then reached up and brushed my wet hair aside. "Not a worried mom."

He leaned in closer. My heart rate quickened and my body froze. What was he doing? Why couldn't I move?

Raikidan pressed a firm kiss on my forehead, drawing out a warm flush on my face.

The voice hummed. *"Oh, that's a nice one."*

"I appreciate your concern," he spoke against my skin.

When he pulled away, I smiled as I looked him in the eyes. "Someone has to look out for you."

He let me go, allowing me to put some needed space between us. "I guess I should go change out of these wet clothes. Since you insist I wear something."

I shook my head. "Once you go back to your normal life, you can strut around in the nude all you want."

Raikidan chuckled and climbed out of the bath, more careful this time, his wet clothes clinging to his muscular form. He proceeded to pull his shirt over his head, corded muscle stretching and flexing with the effort. Water dripped down his chiseled chest. I leaned back, taking in the impressive sight.

Raikidan glanced my way as he wrung the shirt out. "What?"

I shrugged and looked away. "Just like what I see is all."

He stood there, watching me for a moment, before chuckling and leaving. When the door closed, I sunk deep into the water, my face hot. *What the hell is wrong with me?* Why had I said that to him?

The voice chuckled. *"You can only run so long."*

I feared she was right. *I'm in so much trouble.*

CHAPTER 34

I pulled into my parking space in the garage and cut the engine to my motorcycle before compacting my helmet with a sigh. I was exhausted and it was only just past midday. Ryoko and Raikidan pulled their motorcycles into spots near me while Rylan parked the truck a little ways away.

"Anyone else beat?" Mocha asked as she jumped out of the truck and deactivated her cloaking watch.

I swung my leg over my motorcycle. "I am."

"The Council is insane, thinking today was a great day to do surveillance assignments," Ryoko muttered.

I stretched. "Problem is, a day like today is the best day to do them."

Rylan nodded as he walked over to us. "She's right. With so many people out and about, it's the perfect time to see something worth knowing."

"Why is it so crazy out today?" Mana asked as Corliss helped her out of the truck. She had insisted on seeing what a surveillance assignment was like, and of course that meant Corliss had to come with us as well, not that we minded. Surveillance assignments benefitted from having more eyes on the job.

"It's the spring equinox," Ryoko said as we all made our way toward the basement stairs. "It's kinda a big thing for us humans."

"But I thought the equinox was weeks ago," Mana said. "I felt it in my body."

Mocha shook her head. "No. That was seasonal change. Most are affected by the arrival of spring, but the equinox doesn't happen until after that."

"Oh…"

When a familiar smell drifted into my nose, I came to an abrupt halt on the stairs; Ryoko nearly walked into me. "Laz, what's wrong?"

"Nothing's wrong," I murmured as I sniffed the air. "Just… different."

"Guess who."

I bolted up the stairs when realization dawned on me. The moment I burst through the door, a hearty, familiar laugh echoed through the living room and hallway. "Told ye she'd run up here."

My eyes lit up. "Daren!"

The familiar stout, pot-bellied human man with bronze skin came out of the kitchen. "Good to see ye, lass."

I smiled and ran over to him to give him a hug. "It's good to see you, too."

He smiled before turning me around. "Brace yerself."

I barely had time to listen before Valene ran into me. I laughed as I struggled to keep myself upright. "I should have known you were here, too."

"Hug her extra tight for me."

"Of course!" Her smile reached her ears. "I wouldn't dream of missing a chance to see you, especially if it's a day like today."

I chuckled. "You want to go to the carnival, don't you?"

She nodded, practically bouncing in my arms. "The traveling merchants come here every year at this time, because Dalatrend puts on the largest festivities in all of Lumaraeon! When I was little, they'd tell me all about it, but mom couldn't take me because we're human instead of nu-human. And I thought, because I was with you guys, we might be able to figure out a way to allow me to go this time."

"I think we can figure something out for you." Daren's cooking teased my nose again. "What are you making, Daren? It smells amazing."

He chuckled and scooped a ladle into the giant pot on the stove. "Yer favorite."

My eyes lit up. "This day just got even better!"

He dropped the food into a bowl and scooped up another ladleful with a smile and then held it out to me. I took it eagerly and dug into the stew. A delighted moan rumbled through my neck and I leaned against the kitchen wall as I savored the delicious tastes dancing along my tongue for a moment before gobbling up the rest of the stew and asking for more.

"She really likes that stuff," Mocha observed. "What is it?"

"Daren's famous beef stew," Valene said. "It has five types of meats."

"What kinds of meat are in it?" Rylan asked.

"This ol' stew recipe has elk, bear, venison, rabbit, and mountain goat, lad." Daren winked. "But it's the spices that make it all work."

"So good," I said through a mouthful of food.

Ryoko raised her hand. "I want some. That just made my mouth water."

"You mean the smell alone hasn't?" Blaze asked from where he sat on the couch. "Because I've had to sit here drooling for over thirty minutes."

Ryoko leaned on the bar and held out her hands. "Please?"

Daren nodded enthusiastically with a smile and gave her a serving.

Ryoko's eyes lit up when the food touched her lips. She squealed with glee and she half rolled on the bar. "This is amazing!"

Blaze got to his feet. "That's it, I want some."

Daren chuckled. "There's enough for all of ye to have. But get it quick, 'cause Eira here will eat it up on ye in a few moments if ye don't."

Mocha shook her head. "She couldn't eat all of that."

"Wanna bet?" Rylan challenged. "Between her and Ryoko, they could probably finish off five of those pots."

"That's insane…"

Ryoko shook her head. "No. I could finish five pots of this alone. It's that good."

Rylan shrugged. "Guess I'm going to have to try this amazing stew."

Daren chuckled and scooped stew into several bowls.

"This is good," Rylan complimented as he ate.

"It's okay." Everyone gave Mana funny looks when she spoke. "I think Eira makes a better stew."

Ryoko blinked. "Wait, what?"

"I have to agree with Mana," Corliss said. "This is good, but the stew Eira makes does taste better."

Raikidan nodded in agreement as he ate.

Everyone looked at me and I shrugged as I went over to the pot of stew and helped myself to some more. "Don't ask me. I think the three of them are insane. We all know I'm lucky to make a decent tasting grilled cheese or pancake."

Ryoko shook her head. "You guys are crazy."

"So, Mana, we still owe you an explanation, don't we?" I said through a mouthful of food.

Mana nodded. "Yes."

I licked my lips after swallowing. "Well, the spring equinox is pretty important to us. It's a sign the seasons have started over. It represents the renewal of life as it continues to cycle. We humans make a big deal about it and celebrate. Dalatrend puts on a big carnival all day, and at night it turns into a lantern festival."

"What's a carnival?" Mana asked.

"It's a collective of amusement rides, a variety of food and merchandise vendors, games of chance and skill, and sometimes thrill and animal acts under a large tent, though the thrill and animal acts are usually only seen in circuses. But every now and then, the festival has one."

Her face lit up. "Oh, that sounds like a lot of fun. I wanna go!"

Corliss chuckled. "We can go, don't worry."

"It'd be good for all of you to enjoy yourselves for once."

"But first we have to get Valene situated to be seen in public without being harassed," I said.

"What about Daren?" Ryoko asked

Daren shook his head. "I won't be goin' with ye. Don't like crowds. Ye all have fun though."

Ryoko nodded and I placed my empty bowl in the sink before leaving the kitchen, but didn't have to go far because Argus was already coming down the hall with two cloaking devices.

"Smart choice."

"Already ahead of you," he said. "I wanted to make sure we didn't have any malfunctions, so I went to make some overdue adjustments."

He held up a necklace and a watch. "I worked on one for you, too, Mocha, just in case. You two can fight over who gets what."

Mocha smiled. "Thanks. I'll take the new watch, unless Valene does."

Valene shook her head. "No, I like the look of the necklace. I'll use that."

"Are you sure we shouldn't just use prosthetics for Valene?" Ryoko asked. "She only needs nu-human ears. A cloaking device seems a bit overkill."

"The prosthetics are more temperamental than the cloaking device, you know that," I said. "It's easy for them to fall out of place, or off completely, even when properly fastened."

She placed a finger on her lips. "Yeah, you have a point."

"So, how do I use this?" Valene asked as she examined the necklace when Argus handed it over to her. He enthusiastically gave her the run-down for the device.

While he did, I slipped into my room to retrieve some of my personal stash so we'd be able to do more than the rides. My ears picked up "almost like magic" from Argus and I chuckled.

When I returned, Valene wore the pendant, and her ears had transformed into a nu-human's. It looked strange on her.

I clapped my hands together. "Ready?"

Valene's eyes lit up and she grabbed one of my hands, yanking me for the door.

"You guys catch up when you're ready," I called over my shoulder.

"Lass," Daren called out. "Money?"

"I got it, don't worry," I said.

"Yeah, she's being a good adoptive mom."

He shrugged. "If ye say so."

Valene wouldn't allow me to stall any more, and dragged me out of the house.

Getting to the carnival was difficult with the people on the streets. Even streets that had been closed off to vehicle traffic were a nightmare, but the moment we arrived at the carnival and Valene's eyes lit up, I knew it was all worth it.

"What's that over there?" Valene asked as she pointed to a small food stall after we had gotten off a spinning ride she insisted on going on three times.

"Cotton candy," I said.

Her eyes showed her interest. "I've never had cotton candy before."

Ryoko and I exchanged a grin and ushered her over to the vender. I bought a stick and held it out to Valene. She eyed the pink and blue fluff, unsure what to make of it, and Mana stared at the treat longingly.

"You can have some too, Mana," I said.

Mana smiled and picked off a wad. "It's sticky!"

I laughed. "It's just spun sugar."

Mana looked at Valene. "We'll eat some together?"

Valene nodded and grabbed a wad of the sticky sweet. The two popped the treat into their mouths and their eyes went wide. "It disappeared!"

Ryoko and I laughed. The voice also chuckled.

Mana grabbed a larger chunk from the stick. Valene took more, too. "Save some for me."

I smiled at the two and bought another stick and offered it to Corliss and Raikidan. "Wanna try?"

The two dragons hesitated.

"Hey, if they won't, I will," someone said as they came up behind me and snagged a wad.

I turned around and my eyes widened when I saw Ryder. "Ryder…"

He smiled. "Hey."

"W—what are you—"

"Hey, I want to try some," someone else said.

"Me too," someone said.

I watched as both my brothers Trigon and Rhaec came up on the other side of me and grabbed a handful of candy. "What the hell are you three doing here? Do you not realize how dangerous it is for you to be here?"

"Hey, relax, Sis, it's cool," Trigon tried to assure. "Council gave the okay. They said there'd be so many people out there'd be a low likelihood of being caught."

"Morons."

I stared at them. "Are you insane? That doesn't make it safe! Being seen with us would make it—"

"Mom, relax. Everything is going—" I glared him down and he let out a terse exhale. "We already have a plan worked up if anything looks like it might get hairy. Please calm down."

"Where are Elgren and my other brothers?" I asked.

"They, uh, thought it wouldn't be safe," Rhaec admitted.

I threw my free hand up in the air and then offered the cotton candy to Corliss and Raikidan in an attempt to move on. "Do you guys want any of this?"

Corliss went to say something, but someone came up and took the treat from me. "Thanks."

"Ebon!" I complained as he chowed down on the sugar before handing it to Nyoki. Corliss had called them earlier, and they had met us at the entrance to the carnival when we first arrived, but disappeared soon after. This was the first we'd seen them since, and we'd been here for about an hour.

"What? You offered," he said.

I blinked when I was handed a stick of cotton candy, and I looked at Raikidan in confusion.

"Do you want it or not?" he asked.

I took the cotton candy from him and ate a small wad. Raikidan then grabbed some for himself, and before I knew it, he took it back to eat himself. I shook my head, but didn't bother asking for it back or buying another one. I wasn't the biggest fan of cotton candy, so it wasn't a real loss. *Now if it was funnel cake, it would be an entirely different story.*

"What's that?" Valene asked, pointing to a strange-looking building.

"A funhouse," Ryder said.

"What's a funhouse?" Trigon asked.

I grinned. "Go find out."

Valene ran for the funny-looking building. Trigon and Rhaec exchanged glances and shrugged before following her, Mana accompanying them. I trailed behind at a much slower pace, to allow them time to figure out the attraction before going in.

"You want to give it a shot?" I asked as I reached them.

"I don't know what it is," Rhaec said.

"There are two entrances and one exit. We'll race to see who gets to the end first."

"But we don't even know what this is!" Trigon said.

I headed for one of the entrances. "What, chicken?"

Trigon's eyes narrowed. "Don't call me chicken."

I pulled my arms in and flapped them, and Valene joined in my teasing by making clucking noises.

"Fine, you're on!" Trigon took off for the other entrance of the glass house.

"Stupid," Rhaec muttered as he followed our brother.

Ryder shook his head, smirking as he glanced my way, and then went to join the other two. I was glad he wasn't ruining my fun.

This is going to be entertaining.

"I don't understand what Eira is doing," Nyoki said as I flashed my wristband to the carnie working the right entrance of the ride. "Everyone can see this funhouse has a glass maze."

Rylan chuckled. "Trigon and Rhaec are new to these."

"But if they don't know they'll"—Nyoki gasped—"that's so mean! Why would she do that?"

Ryoko giggled. "Because they're her brothers. Why wouldn't she pull a prank like that on them?"

"Oh. I didn't realize they were related. That makes a lot of sense now."

"Eira, is this really a maze?" Valene whispered.

"Yep," I said. "Well, the first part at least. There may be another later in this house, but I'm not sure."

"But why didn't you tell the others?"

I grinned as I walked into the entrance of the maze. The panes were made of thick plastic, like glass house rides had, but they were kept exceptionally clean. "Stand here and watch."

Confusion crossed her face before she nodded. We waited for Ryder and my two brothers to appear on the other side of the maze.

Trigon shrugged and walked toward us. "I don't know what the big—"

Valene and I burst out laughing when he walked right into a pane, and even Ryder and Rhaec joined in. When I glanced over to the others outside the ride, they, too, were enjoying his misfortune.

Trigon rubbed his face. "Ow… What the hell? What is this?"

"A maze," I said as I maneuvered into it.

"Seriously? Why didn't you tell me?"

I chuckled. "Because it was more fun not to."

"I'm going to beat you!"

Valene giggled. "You gotta get through this first."

"I could just go back," he muttered.

"I wouldn't let you live it down, you big chicken," Rhaec teased as he entered the maze.

"I'm not chicken!" Trigon roared. "And I'll prove it to you."

"He's so adorable when he's mad."

I chuckled and turned to the right when I came to an open area, but Valene didn't follow. "I think we should go this way."

I shrugged. "You can go that way if you want. I'm going to try this one."

"Okay. Good luck."

We parted, and it wasn't long before I took another turn and ran into a dead end. I grunted and tried another possible route, but it, too, was a dead end. *Looks like my way was wrong.* I backtracked until found myself on the path Valene chose.

I took a few more wrong turns and even ran into Ryder on the way, but we chose to go separate ways soon after. Trigon and I almost collided. Lucky for me, a pane kept us apart, though he wasn't as happy about it.

I fell to the floor when Rhaec ran into me. "Ow…"

"Sorry, Sis." He helped me up. "I wasn't paying attention."

I chuckled. "It's fine. I guess the way you came from was a dead end?"

"Yeah, yours?"

I nodded and then looked toward the corridor I headed for. "I'm about to check this one, if you want to follow."

He went to respond when someone knocked on the plastic panes. Our eyes fell on Valene, who was now out of the maze part. She grinned ear-to-ear and waved.

Rhaec groaned. "She beat us there."

"It's okay. As long as Trigon doesn't get there first we're safe," I said.

"You mean, you're safe."

I pointed at him. "Yeah, that."

"Thanks for not sending us back underground, Sis," Rhaec said when we ran into a dead end. "I like being allowed to spend time with you. The others wanted to as well, but were too afraid of being caught."

I chose a new path for us to try. "You should have been, too."

"You're worth being caught over."

"You don't know me."

"You're family, what else is there to know?"

I shook my head. Valene knocked on the plastic pane to get our attention and pointed at the floor. My brow twisted, but when she continued to point, I looked at my feet.

I laughed when I saw the little vine crawling over to me. "Guess we have a way out."

"Isn't that cheating?" Rhaec asked.

I grinned. "Not if no one knows."

He chuckled. "You're so bad."

"I don't see you complaining."

"Hey, if it gets me a leg up on Trigon for once, I'll take it."

"You act like that's rare."

"Yeah, well, that's because it is. He's better at most things."

"He's not better at getting a pretty girl to notice him."

His face reddened. "I–I don't know what you're talking about."

"Aw, he's embarrassed."

I snickered. "I'm much older than you, Brother. You can't fool me. Between how you acted when you found out Nyra was safe, and your embarrassment now, you can't tell me you don't like her even a little."

"All right, fine. So what if I do? Doesn't mean anything. It's not like she sees something in me. It's a phase that'll pass."

"I don't know about that. She seemed pretty fond of you when I talked to her."

"Really?" He sounded hopeful.

I shrugged. "That's just what I got."

His eyes cut away. "Well, I hope not."

This change confused me. "Why not?"

"It wouldn't be right for me to involve her with us… We're just not stable enough still."

I frowned. "Has today been hard for you?"

He nodded. "I struggle the most out of us, and I know I'm doing a lot better than before, but I still have a ways to go."

"Well, if it's any consolation, I'm proud of you." I said. He turned his gaze to me and I smiled. "I mean it."

He smiled back. "Thanks."

"And don't give up on a personal life. You'll get there. It just takes time. Trust me."

"'Bout time you two came out, slowpokes," Valene teased, interrupting Rhaec's next reply.

I rolled my eyes. "What? Too afraid to go on by yourself?"

She bit her lip. "No. Of course not."

I chuckled. "Right. Let's get going before Trigon figures out our little trick and catches up."

"He can't. I retracted the vine back into seed form. They're on their own."

Rhaec gaze at her, amazed. "You can do that?"

Valene nodded as if his surprise wasn't an uncharacteristic reaction. "Yeah. I'm a plant-based earth shaman. It's way easy to do."

An interested and slightly awed expression crossed Rhaec's face, but he didn't inquire further.

I led them into into the next part of the funhouse, finding it a small hallway with a floor that moved. Valene and Rhaec found this room far more fun. I was amazed Rhaec was even able to get through this hall with such little effort. He was a big guy.

When we managed to get to the end of the hall, we took the corner and climbed up steep moving stairs before having to go through another hall, but this time mirrors covered the walls and ceiling, and the hall itself felt tilted.

"This is disorienting," Valene said.

"I can carry you if you'd like," Rhaec offered.

"No, that's fine. I'm pretty sure I can make it to the end of the hall. Thanks for the offer, though."

Rhaec shrugged. "All right. Whoa…" We stopped walking. The hall ended, but it merged with a room of mirrors. "This is different."

"This is why it's called a funhouse," I said as I walked into the room. "The good ones have mirror rooms."

Valene giggled as she jumped between two mirrors that distorted her body. "These are fun."

Her giggling continued when she noticed the distortion of the mirror behind me. "That one makes you look buffer than Rhaec."

I flexed. "You think?"

"No way." He came over and flexed behind me. The mirror had the reverse effect on him and he slimmed down. We all erupted in laughter.

The voice also laughed. *You three are killing me.*

Once we calmed down, we continued on.

"This room has too many turns. Something is odd about this room. Don't think…" I looked around when I realized I was now alone. "Guys?"

"Great."

"Eira, Rhaec?" Valene called. "Where'd you both go?"

"I was just walking," I replied. "Then you guys were gone."

"Same here," Rhaec called out. "You don't think this is a maze, too, do you?"

I sighed and stopped. "I know it is. I just came to a three-way intersection. These mirrors were so distracting I couldn't see the extra walls."

Valene huffed. "Great. Guess I'll see you guys on the other side."

"Once you get out of this maze, just continue on. It'll save time," I said.

"Okay," Valene and Rhaec replied.

I chose to go right and followed the path until I came to another choice. I repeated these choices until I ran into a dead end and had to backtrack and repeat the whole process again.

"Eira? Eira, are you in here?" Trigon's voice ran through the reflecting corridors. When I didn't answer, he growled. "Eira, if you're in here, you'd better answer!"

"Stay quiet, it's more fun."

"Planned on it."

"Trigon, calm down," Ryder coaxed. "If you pick a fight with her, she's going to kick your ass."

"I don't care."

"So she pulled a prank on you, big deal," a familiar voice teased. "She could have done worse, trust me."

"Azriel, is that you?" I called out.

Azriel chuckled. "Yep, it's me. I figured I'd come help these two since they seemed a bit lost."

"When did you get here?"

"I'm going to say about five minutes ago."

"Okay." I turned a corner.

"Hey!" Trigon called out. "You purposely ignored me."

I chuckled. "Of course I did. I figured you'd start storming through this maze like a maniac."

"Another maze?" he whined. "I hate this place!"

"But this maze is better!" Valene shouted in protest. "The crazy mirrors make it fun."

I heard Trigon sigh. "I just want to get out of here…"

"I'll make it up to you," I promised him.

"Yeah, right."

"She will," Ryder assured. "Trust me."

"She's always good with her word, boys, don't worry."

I took another corner and exhaled an annoyed breath when I came face to face with another dead end. This really wasn't much fun anymore.

"You're not a maze lover."

I continued to stumble around blindly until I came to a corridor that appeared a bit brighter than the others. I took a quick sniff and caught a whiff of Valene's scent. I figured the chances of this being the exit were high, so I didn't see a reason not to try it.

The corridor lightened as I made my way through, and when I took the corner at the end, I was met with a view of the outside and a striped spinning tube. I unsteadily walked through the spinning tube exit, and Valene greeted me with a smile. I smiled back and glanced over my shoulder to see if the others were close behind, but no one showed up.

I looked over to our group and noted the head count was a little different. Blaze, Rylan, Corliss, and Raikidan were gone, and Genesis and Seda had shown up. Argus had let us know they'd meet up with us once their Council meeting ended. Genesis' choice to join us surprised the majority of us. Even though she was trying to reintegrate into the world now that she had her adult body, she didn't enjoy being out around people.

"It's been a long time since she's gone to a carnival," the voice said. *"I'm sure she wants to experience that again, and with friends, that makes it more fun."*

"That's a good point."

"What happened to our group?" I asked as Valene and I walked over.

Ryoko pointed at the funhouse, where two of the four were trying to navigate the first maze. "Blaze decided to make a comment about how long it was taking you guys to get through the funhouse, so Rylan challenged him to go through it faster."

"And Corliss and Raikidan somehow got dragged into it," Mana added. "They figured the maze out quickly, though. You just missed them going into the next part."

I chuckled. "That would figure. I'll be right back while we wait for them all. I owe Rhaec and Trigon some food."

"I'll help," Valene offered.

"Me too," Mana said. "Corliss was getting a little hungry."

I nodded and the three of us headed over to a food stand to pick out something to eat. We came back with several small boxes filled with food just as Ryder, Rhaec, Trigon, Rylan, and Azriel came out of the funhouse.

"Where are Corliss, Raikidan, and Blaze?" I asked.

"Raikidan and Corliss ended up backtracking to the glass maze by accident before getting lost in the mirror maze, and Blaze is just lost in the mirror maze," Seda said. "They might need some rescuing."

I shook my head. "Great."

I held up two boxes of food. "Rhaec, Trigon, here you go."

"All right, food!" Trigon cheered before taking his box and attempting to steal Rhaec's.

"That's mine!" Rhaec pushed our brother's hand away from his food.

Valene held out a box for Ryder. "We picked up some for you, too, for being a good sport."

Ryder chuckled and gratefully took the meal.

"I think someone is going to have to go on a rescue mission," Ryoko said. "I don't think any of us like the idea of waiting all night for them to figure out the maze themselves."

"I'll do it," I offered. "It was my fault this all happened, so I might as well."

"I'll go with you," Mana offered.

Ryoko held out her hand. "I'll hold your food until you get back."

"And I'll guide you," Seda said. "We don't need you two getting lost as well."

Mana and I smiled our thanks before heading into the funhouse. Seda projected an image of the correct path to take into my head and I set a quick pace through the glass maze.

"Sorry if you wanted to enjoy this," I said to Mana as I led her up the moving staircase.

She shook her head. "I wasn't interested in this ride, so I don't mind."

I nodded and led her down the mirrored hallway. When we came to the mirror maze, I waited for her when she decided to play in front of a few and then continued on until we came to a fork.

"Corliss is down the left corridor, and Raikidan is down the right," Seda messaged.

"I'll go get Corliss," Mana said. "It'll surprise him."

I nodded and headed down the corridor leading to Raikidan. After a few turns, I found him at a dead end grumbling to himself.

"Lost?" I giggled out.

Raikidan whipped around. "I called for you and you didn't answer, so I thought you left."

I nodded. "I did, but then came back to rescue you."

He frowned. "Great."

I grabbed his hand and pulled him back the way I'd come. "C'mon. The sooner we leave, the sooner we can do something a bit more fun."

Raikidan grunted and I frowned. "You're not having fun, are you?"

"Hard to with things like this."

My shoulder slumped. "I'm sorry… You can head home if you want once we get out of here."

"I don't want to go home."

"But if you're not having fun, there's no point in staying."

"I am having fun. Just not with this ride."

"This is the only ride you've tried, and you're not having fun with it. How can you be having fun?"

"I just am."

I glanced at him doubtfully but continued to lead him.

'Mana and Corliss have Blaze with them, so you can head straight for the exit,' Seda said as she swapped the map in my head.

"Thanks."

"Is Seda giving you directions?" Raikidan asked when we walked through another flawless corridor.

"I'd be getting us lost instead of saving you if she wasn't."

He grinned. "So, if you're saving me, you'd be your human story equivalent of a knight in shining armor?"

I laughed. "Not really."

"Why not? Just because you're female doesn't mean you can't be similar."

"A knight in shining armor saves the woman and gives her a happily-ever-after. I'm just getting you out of a funhouse."

"Yeah, well, I'll be pretty happy when we get out of here."

I chuckled. I couldn't argue that logic.

I let him walk on his own when we came to the exit hallway. I nearly fell when I tried to run through the spinning exit, but managed to save myself the embarrassment and the two of us joined up with the others.

"Finally!" Ryoko cheered. "Now we can go do something."

Valene pointed to a spinning ride. "Let's go on that ride!"

"I don't think that's a good idea," I said.

Valene blinked. "Why not?"

"Because you just ate, and unless you want to puke it all back up, it's really not a good idea to go on it yet," Ryoko said.

"Well, then what can we do?" Valene asked. "Almost all the cool-looking rides have some sort of movement."

"We could go play some games," Blaze said. "Those are better than that stupid funhouse."

Genesis raised a hand. "I'm in favor of playing some games. I'm not much of an amusement ride person."

Argus raised his hand. "I'd like to grab something to eat first."

We agreed to buying food first then played games. As the others ordered their food, I looked around keeping an eye out for games to try.

"That's not why you're doing it."

"Keeps me preoccupied."

Trigon approached me. "Sis, can we have some money? We're still hungry."

I shook my head. "I don't have any left."

His brow furrowed. "You're out of money?"

"Carnival food is expensive. I bought food for you, Rhaec, Ryder, and Valene."

"And don't forget all the cotton candy you bought," Valene said.

"You didn't mention yourself eating," Rhaec said.

"That's because I only got a little bit of the cotton candy." I shrugged. "It's fine. I don't eat much."

My brothers exchanged glances, regretting eating all the food I'd given them.

"Here," Raikidan said as he came up next to me. In his hand he had a corndog. "Don't tell me no, either."

"Good boy."

My brow furrowed and I accepted the offer. "Uh, thanks?"

"I know when you're not eating." He held up a plate with a funnel cake topped with ice cream, chocolate syrup, and some candy pieces. "And once you're finished with that, you can have this."

My eyes went wide and I grabbed for it. "Gimme."

Raikidan chuckled as he held it out of my reach. "You get this last."

I tried to jump for it. "Gimme!"

The others laughed as they watched. Even the voice was amused.

Raikidan tried to keep himself composed. "Eat your… corn dog first."

I pouted and bit into the batter-covered hotdog. Raikidan also ate one, and he appeared to like it, based on how quickly he finished it. He allowed me to eat my funnel cake just as Blaze and Argus picked a game of ring-toss to play. While they did that, Ryoko and Mana went over to a goldfish catching game. Our groups slowly dispersed to the games nearby until Raikidan, Valene, and I were left. She stared longingly at all the games to try.

I dug into my coin pouch and pulled out a smaller one, handing it to her. "Here. I set this money aside just for you to play games."

She gasped. "You don't have to do that."

I made her take it and nudged her. "Go have fun."

A wide smile spread across her face and she ran off to the goldfish station to find out what it was all about. I ate my snack, noticing Raikidan staring longingly at it.

"I'd offer you some, but we know how bad that's turned out in the past," I said.

Corliss snickered nearby, catching Ebon's attention. "Sounds like a good story."

"Don't you dare tell him," I warned Corliss.

Corliss ignored me and whispered to Ebon. Nyoki listened in, giggling as the story played out in some fashion. I snarled and ate more of my cake.

Raikidan bent closer to me. "It won't turn out like that."

My eyes narrowed. "That's what you said last time."

The three dragons laughed and I shot them a dirty look.

"I promise this time will be different."

I studied him and then broke off a piece of the funnel cake and scooped it into the ice cream. "If you start acting weird, I'm locking you in a closet."

Nyoki held herself up on a game station as she lost it. Everyone's heads turned her way, not understand what was wrong with her, and both Corliss and Ebon laughed at her reaction.

Raikidan ignored the other dragons and took the offered treat. He broke off more almost immediately. I shook my head, and together we finished off the funnel cake in no time.

"Hey, Eira," Blaze called out. "Come over here, would ya?"

I wandered over, licking some chocolate off my fingers as went. Raikidan disposed of the plate and then followed. "What's up?"

He scratched his head as he stared at the hundreds of bottles before him. "We can't seem to get a single ring on these bottles. It feels… rigged. Wasn't sure if you could give it a try, since you're good at throwing games."

He wasn't wrong. My time in the military made me good with games requiring good hand-eye coordination and throwing. "I don't have mon—"

Raikidan held up a few coins. "This should be enough, right?"

I pursed my lips. "I don't want you to pay for my games."

He made me take the money. "You can pay me back."

Nyoki snickered and spoke mostly to herself, but I suspected the other dragons could hear her. "That's a lie."

Raikidan shot her a dark look. I sighed. She was right. I knew him well enough he wouldn't take repayment for the food or the game. And he wasn't going to take no for an answer right now.

I examined at the prizes and spotted a keychain I liked. "How many wins do I need for a prize like that?"

The carnie looked where I pointed. "Those small prizes are three rings."

I inspected the sign detailing costs to play, finding it was made easy for everyone, including those who couldn't read, by using pictures along with the words. *I know it's probably meant for kids, but it certainly helps me.*

"You've been doing well on your own these last few weeks."

I hadn't told anyone, but I'd been trying to learn again. It was after I'd read the elvish sign of Éan Ag Eitilt at the mall. I realized that if Shva'sika and Xye could manage to get me to understand that script, then maybe I could finally learn the letters that made up common. It wasn't going well.

I didn't understand why, either. Why was it so hard for me to learn this?

"If you ask Raikidan, I'm sure he'd be able to help you understand common better."

"Why would I ask something so embarrassing?"

"Because it's not. And we both know he would understand why you'd come to him for lessons and not someone else."

I sifted through the bit of money Raikidan gave me and handed the needed amount to the carnie. "I'll pay for five tosses."

He nodded and handed over the rings. I got a good feel for their weight and then tossed the first ring, not putting any strategy into the throw. I bought the extra two rings to get a good feel for them.

The ring bounced off a few bottles with a *ting ting ting* before disappearing beneath. Blaze's brow rose, but was smart enough to stay quiet.

I didn't like how that ring flew. The weight didn't feel right about it. I allowed the next ring to dangle from my finger as I figured it out. This one had a different weight than the first.

"They make them all with imperfections."

"Seems that way."

This would make it difficult, but not impossible. I place strategy behind this next toss, and I almost made it onto a bottle neck. *I think I figured it out.*

"Are you sure?"

"Yep."

I weight-checked the rings and then tossed them in quick succession, all three making their mark. Blaze ran his fingers through his hair, exhaling slowly, and the carnie couldn't hide his astonishment.

Argus chuckled. "That's Eira for you."

"Trust me, I just made it look easy," I said. "That took a lot of calculating."

"More than I was able to put out, so good on you."

The carnie nodded. "Yes, very good indeed. You've won a small prize."

I pointed to the keychain and he handed it over. The three men next to me peered over my shoulder.

"Is that supposed to be Phyre?" Argus asked.

I smirked. "Yep."

The rubber depicted a cartoon image of Phyre. His head was much larger than his body, and his eyes filled most of his head. He looked like the spikey-haired troublemaker I was learning he was.

"I think it's a great depiction of me," came a familiar smooth and commanding voice.

"He would show up here."

The boys jumped back and I smiled at Phyre, holding it up to him. "I think it's it's cute."

He chuckled. "Quite."

Phyre then surveyed the game, allowing me to notice the stunned carnie. "I'd like to play, if you don't mind."

The carnie tried to speak, but no words came out. *Poor guy.*

I nudge Phyre. "You have to pay."

"Oh! Right, right." His voice lowered. "Can I have some money? Mom didn't give me my allowance this month."

I couldn't stop the boisterous laugh. He was something else. My friends also found it amusing. People we didn't know either stared or whispered, in their excitement to see a god. It was one interesting thing about gods. They had an aura that no one could mistake, making it impossible for just anyone to walk around as an imposter.

I used the money Raikidan had "loaned" me, and handed it to Phyre. He tried to give it to the carnie, but the man stuttered out a refusal. "N—no, no need."

"I insist."

The carnie's hands shook as he accepted the coins and handed over the five rings, his eyes unable to meet Phyre's gaze. Phyre appeared amused by the man's behavior and went about tossing his rings. He missed the first and third throws, but managed to land all the others. Pleased with himself, Phyre gazed at the carnie expectantly.

"Well done, sir." The man pointed to the prizes. "That would award you a choice from these rows here."

Phyre went to point to something but then stopped, his body going rigid. "Oh no. She found me."

He shifted panic sticken eyes to me. "If my sister asks, you didn't see me."

Before anyone could react, he ran off, but then called back over his shoulder. "You can have my prize!"

He disappeared in a puff of dark smoke, and not long after, a portal opened in the opposite direction he'd gone. This one I recognized.

Arcadia appeared, her usual sullen expression twisted with rage. "Where is he?"

Everyone pointed in the direction Phyre ran and I spoke for them. "He played a game, then booked it when he realized you were coming."

She nodded, then sprinted in the direction that had been pointed out, her wooden shoes clomping on the ground. Maiyun padded after her, ever faithful, the two disappearing into a portal.

The voice sighed. *"Those two are something else."*

"That… was weird," Argus said.

"That is becoming our normal," I said.

The carnie's shaken voice interrupted us. "Uh, miss?"

I looked at him.

"Are you, uh, a priestess?"

Raikidan chuckled. "If she is, she's terrible at her job."

Blaze snickered and I smacked them both.

"It's just, you seem so used to conversing with those two. I've heard only priests and priestesses have regular contact with the gods. If you're not a priestess, then you must be someone special."

"Oh, she's special, all right."

I noticed the extra attention on me with all the strangers around now interested in the woman who interacted with the gods so freely. I gave a weak smile. "It's… complicated."

He gave a slow nod and then pointed to the prizes. "Well, he did say you can have his prize, so feel free to pick."

I took in the selection and chose another keychain. When the carnie handed it to me, I offered it to Raikidan.

Raikidan's brow rose. "Why are you giving it to me?"

"Because you gave me the money, and I think you'll like this keychain."

He accepted the gift and examined it.

"Who is it of?" Corliss asked.

Raikidan held it up, revealing the depicted god was none other than Raisu.

Ebon nodded. "It is fitting. That's a nice gift, Eira."

Raikidan gave me a dubious look. "What am I supposed to do with it?"

I shrugged. "Use it for your keys, so you stop losing them."

The others around me laughed. Raikidan didn't like carrying around keys, as he had a habit of misplacing them all the time.

I went about hooking my new keychain onto a beltloop, and Raikidan copied me. I wasn't sure if he actually appreciated the "gift," but at least he wasn't refusing it in front of everyone. If he gave it back later, I'd keep it. I thought they were adorable.

Ryoko, Valene, and Mana approached. They carried bags with goldfish, and a few other prizes they'd won from other games.

Valene held up her bag to me. "Look, I won cute little pets."

Mana held up hers, containing a lot of fish, though not as many as Valene. "Me too."

I chuckled. "Well, I guess we need to invest in a fish tank for your room."

"We have one," Ryoko said. "It's stored downstairs from when Argus' snake was smaller."

That worked out well.

Valene's attention waned and she sought out the games. "Oh, what's that?"

I peered in the direction she pointed. "It's a type of racing game. You shoot water at a tiny target and try to be the first to fill the tube. Winner gets a prize."

"That sounds like fun!" She dashed off toward the game.

Argus chuckled. "I'm enjoying her enthusiasm."

"It's refreshing," Azriel agreed.

I ran to catch up with Valene. She already sat at one of the stations when I caught up. Raikidan handed me some more money, not allowing me to protest, and I paid the carnie. Ryoko took a seat next to us and Azriel sat next to Valene.

Valene huffed playfully. "If this is a shooting game, then I'm going to definitely lose."

I chuckled. "It's okay, you can lose with Azriel. He's a bad shot."

"I am not," he said.

"Worse than us," Ryoko replied.

Azriel grumbled and turned his gaze to Valene. "Don't worry. Losing to them isn't that bad. I should know."

Rylan sat down next to Azriel, and Azriel chuckled. "Now, losing to Rylan is a different story."

"That's just quick-draw games," Ryoko said. "He's easy to beat with these games."

"I'm just as good as you," Rylan argued.

"Why don't you put your money where your mouth is?" Ryoko challenged.

"You're on."

Valene giggled. "This is going to be fun."

My eyes flicked to the carnie running the game, who grinned and pressed a large red button. The button activated a timer and this sent Valene into a panic. "Wait, how do I play this game?"

"Aim the gun at the small target in front of you and press both buttons," the carnie said.

Her face twisted. "That's it?"

"That's it. The guns are fixed with little rotary movement. Keeps the game simple for adults and children."

She exhaled. "Okay."

The timer hit zero and a buzzer rang. The five of us pressed the buttons on our guns and raced to get our meters to the top. Valene and I doubled over in laughter when she did terribly at keeping her aim straight. Poor focus ended up screwing me up, which made us laugh even more. Azriel began laughing with us, and Ryoko and Rylan joined in our contagious laughter, but they did better at keeping focus.

The winning buzzer rang when Ryoko's meter reached the top just before Rylan's, and she squealed with joy. The carnie chuckled and pointed to the row of prizes she could select from. She picked a purple and blue monkey and hugged it tightly when the carnie handed it to her.

Valene sighed and played with the gun. "I don't get this thing."

"It's actually not as hard as it seems," Blaze said, slipping behind her. He placed his hands on hers and moved the gun. "I'll show you."

"O–okay," Valene stammered.

Annoyance pulled deep in side me. I left my seat. "Seda, Argus, take my spot."

"Why?" Argus asked.

"Oh, oh, teams game!" Ryoko cheered. "Great idea! But wait, why did you get up, Laz?"

"I'm going to go walk around," I said. "I'll be right back."

"But someone can be your partner."

I shook my head and headed off. "I'm good. You guys have fun. I'll be back."

I didn't know where I was going, but I didn't care. I needed to wander around.

35
CHAPTER

As I wandered, the sound of someone following caught my attention. I glimpsed over my shoulder to find Raikidan. I shouldn't have expected anything less.

"He is your faithful lost puppy."

"You didn't have to follow me," I said when he caught up.

He shrugged. "Better than watching the others play a game. And I'm more concerned about you."

"Uh, why?"

"I saw how you reacted. You're walking because of what Blaze did."

I continued on. "I figured it was best if I didn't grab him by the throat."

"Why?"

"Because Valene is an adult and she doesn't need me to protect her. If I stuck around, I would have caused a scene."

Raikidan smiled. "You sure you're not her real mother?"

I laughed. "I guess I do sound like an overprotective parent."

He took in the events around us. "So do you have a particular destination in mind?"

I shrugged. "Just walking, really."

"Step right up, folks, and try your skill!" a carnie working a game station shouted.

"What's that game?" Raikidan asked.

My eyes narrowed. "Only the most rigged game here. You throw a ball at a stack of ceramic bottles and try to knock them off their platform in one throw. You get three chances to try, and if even one bottle remains after a throw, they get stacked back up."

"Doesn't sound that hard, or rigged."

"Trust me, it is."

His brow rose. "Personal experience?"

"When I was in the military, I was assigned to monitor this event quite often, but stayed out of any interactions until Azriel convinced me one year to give that stupid game a try. I almost won three times, but each time there was this one bottle that fell over and rolled toward the edge. The damn bottle teetered but never fell off!"

Raikidan took a decisive breath and headed over to the game.

"Rai, what are you doing? I told you it's a rigged game."

He grinned at me. "I'm going to give it a shot."

I shook my head and followed. The carnie smirked when Raikidan approached, and then explained the rules of the game and what level of prizes could be won depending on how he beat the game.

Raikidan took in the alignment of the bottles and felt out the balls he paid for. I was rather surprised how much calculating he put into this. I had honestly thought he'd throw caution to the wind as if he hadn't believed my warning about the game.

I giggled when Raikidan missed with his first throw, and then again when he missed with his second throw. Raikidan shot me a warning look, but I continued to laugh at him. He tossed the last ball and this time it hit the mark but only two of the three bottles fell off the platform. The last bottle rolled to the edge and teetered, just like it had for me all those years ago.

Raikidan huffed and I chuckled. "Told you so."

He reached for more money. "I'm going to give it another shot."

I stopped him. "Don't. It's not worth it. We can play a different game that's more fun."

"No, I want to play this one."

"But why?"

"Because I do."

"He's going to be stubborn, so let him be."

I sighed and let him try again. As the carnie handed Raikidan the three balls, I noticed a trio of soldiers walking toward us. I spotted Zo amongst them.

"You're really giving this rigged game a shot?" Zo asked as he approached.

Raikidan shrugged. "I figured it didn't hurt to give it a try. I'm supposed to be here having fun, after all."

"Fair enough. Good luck."

Zo's behavior caught me off guard. He wasn't acting normal at all. Or, what I'd consider normal.

Zo glanced my way. "You haven't seen Yára, have you?"

My brow furrowed. "No. Should I have?"

"Well, she was hoping to see you here because she wanted to give you something. Then we lost her and Bone in a crowd. I hoped you and her might have crossed paths." Zo pointed to the psychic with him. "Agren here tried to search for them, but there are too many people around."

I shook my head. "Sorry, I haven't. I wonder what she wants with me."

"I wish I knew. She wouldn't tell anyone."

"Well, I'll keep an eye out for her, at least." I turned my head when Raikidan threw his first ball and missed. I laughed at him again. "You suck at this."

He handed me one of the balls. "Then you try."

I took the round object and pushed him aside. I tossed the ball in the air a few times as I scrutinized the set up of the ceramic bottles. I remembered how angry this game had made me in the past and then threw. The ball sailed through the air and slammed into the ceramic bottles with such force it made the others around me jump.

I huffed when one bottle was left teetering on the edge of the platform. "Every time."

"How many times have you tried this game?" Zo asked.

"Just once. Each throw resulted in the same ending as just now."

"Makes sense why you threw with such force," Agren said.

I stepped aside so Raikidan could try again, but his result was no better than mine.

"So, we done yet?" I asked him, though not looking at him.

He pulled out a coin. "One more throw. Just one."

I shook my head but didn't stop him. The carnie stacked up the bottles again and handed Raikidan the one ball he paid for. Raikidan tossed the ball into the air for what seemed like forever before he was ready to give this game his last shot. Raikidan chucked the ball with everything he had, and the bottles went flying.

I stared at the empty pedestal, jaw slack. "You did it… You actually did it…"

The carnie laughed. "Well I'll be. That was mighty impressive."

"No kidding," Zo murmured.

The carnie gestured to the prizes hanging above us. "You're the first to win the one-shot challenge since I've been doing this. Pick any prize you want."

Raikidan studied the selection and pointed to one that I couldn't make out. The carnie reached up and pulled down a white stuffed animal.

The man handed Raikidan his prize, and he transferred it over to me. "Here you go."

I blinked. "What?"

"It's yours. Take it."

I smiled and took the prize. "Thanks."

The prize was a stuffed unicorn, a creature that resembled a white horse with a horn on the forehead that had gone extinct at least five millennia ago. The unicorn's mane was white and purple and its eyes were rainbow-colored, a typical fantastical trait of the creature. I started laughing when I took a good look at the eyes.

Raikidan nearly panicked. "What?"

I turned the unicorn around. "Look at its eyes!"

Raikidan jerked back when he saw the cross-eyed nature. "That's freaky. Do you want a different one?"

I shook my head and smiled. "No. I like it this way." I headed off in a random direction. "Reminds me of you."

"Hey, what's that supposed to mean?" He ran to catch up.

"It's just as derpy as you."

He wrapped a strong arm around my neck and pulled me into a headlock. "I'm not… derpy."

I tried to pull out of his hold. "You don't even know what it means!"

"I don't need to, to know it was an insult. Now apologize."

I struggled. "Never!"

"I'll mess up your hair."

"He did not threaten that."

"Don't you dare."

"Then apologize."

"No!"

Raikidan's presence disappeared suddenly, and it was replaced by someone else. I squeaked when this new person crouched down and hoisted me onto their shoulder. I peered down at the man with bewilderment. He gazed up at me, a large smile on his face. He was a well-built man with sandy blond hair, tanned skin, and green eyes. Something about him felt familiar, but I was sure I had never met him before.

There were two other men with Raikidan. The slimmer of the two had black hair, green eyes, and alabaster skin, and the burlier man who had Raikidan in a headlock had dark hair, eyes, and skin. The three of them wore black watches and the realization of who they were hit me like a train.

"Ah, smart boys."

"So is this why you three weren't worried?" I asked.

"Yep," my brother replied. "We had the watches in our pockets the whole time and knew to activate them when we noticed soldiers in the vicinity. We told you not to worry about it."

I chuckled. "So am I sitting on Rhaec? I'm still getting used to your voices."

He nodded. "Trigon has been dying to get Raikidan into a headlock. Don't ask me why, 'cause I don't know."

"And Ryder is watching… because?"

"He wanted to give your friend shit about something. Not sure what, but I can only guess it's because he hangs around you all the time."

"It's because he cares."

"Men are weird."

Rhaec looked at my stuffed unicorn. "Can I see the prize he won for you?"

"He didn't win it for me. He just gave it to me after he won the game he stubbornly wanted to play."

"Yeah, uh huh."

"Yeah, sure, we'll go with that." He took the stuffed prize and cocked his head. "What's with the eyes?"

I laughed. "Aren't they funny? I told Raikidan they were derpy and they reminded me of him."

"Is that why he had you in that headlock?"

My scrunched. "And threatened to mess up my hair."

Rhaec gave the unicorn back to me. "Now I'm glad Trigon grabbed him."

I scanned the area and gasped when I spotted a pen filled with horses. "Let's go over there! Now."

"What? Wait, why?"

I didn't answer. I just jumped off his shoulder and ran over to the corralled horses. I slowed my pace when I came close so I wouldn't startle them, and leaned on the wooden fence that penned them in and watched them graze. They were beautiful.

One horse, a Gypsy Vanner stallion with the traditional paintcoat pattern, picked up its head and watched at me for a moment before strolling over. The Vanner came right up to the fence and remained calm as I reached out and scratched his nose.

"He's beautiful."

I smiled as I pet the gentle creature, a peaceful calmness flowing through me. It wasn't a foreign feeling. Certain animals did this to me. Horses happened to be one of them. I liked horses a great deal because of this.

"His name is Legacy," someone told me.

I turned my head to see a young brown haired, blue-eyed cowboy walking over to me. I recognized him. He was one of the shamans that had arrived late to my ceremony party, whom I had sent Iana over to hang out with.

"Shamans aren't supposed to work these events in a direct way such as this," I said.

The man chuckled. "Well, I'm not a shaman. Just an elementalist. The shamans taught me how to control my abilities and they let me attend their parties."

"Fair enough."

He held out his hand. "Name's Alistair."

I accepted the gesture. "Eira."

Alistair grinned. "I know."

"I know, you know. I remember you. You were carrying that lamb when you showed up at the party."

"Yeah, she was my abandoned lamb from this year's breeding. I couldn't leave her home."

I shrugged. "Didn't bother me. The kids liked her."

"And you seem to like Legacy."

"I like horses."

Alistair leaned on the fence. "You sure that's it?"

"He came to me. I'm just petting him."

His brow furrowed. "You didn't call him at all?"

"No."

Alistair scratched Legacy's neck. "Interesting."

"She has that effect on horses." I looked back to see Ryder leading Raikidan and my brothers over. "It's always been that way."

"So, you must know a lot about them," Alistair guessed.

"A bit," I said. "Legacy here is a Gypsy Vanner and has the traditional piebald coat pattern called tobiano. You have a Friesian mare over there, and next to her an Appaloosa mare with a blue roan blanket-spotted coat. You have another Gypsy Vanner, this time a mare, with the highly desired silver tobiano snowflake dapple pattern, a few paints with various coat pattern types, an Arabian, a few more Appaloosas with coat patterns I don't know the name of, and in the back, fenced off from the rest of your herd, you have a black and a white Percheron. The rest of the horses, I'm not sure, since I have a feeling the majority are cross breeds."

Alistair nodded. "Impressive."

Trigon whistled. "I'll say."

I shrugged and pet Legacy some more. "Not really."

Alistair whistled a quick tune and a Paint mare picked up her head, turning it our way Alistair whistled again and she trotted over. A little colt was quick to follow her. Alistair gave the mare a quick scratch on the nose before letting me reach out to pet her. The mare responded positively, and before I knew it, she'd pushed Legacy to the side.

The tiny colt that came over with the mare lifted his head to get pet, but he was so small, his nose barely reached the top of the fence. I giggled and knelt so I could reach him through the fence bars. The colt was definitely the progeny of the mare with his painted coat, but based on the spots on his rump, I guessed the sire was of a different breed. *Probably Appaloosa, or a cross breed with Appaloosa genes.*

"He's young. Any particular reason you brought him here?" I asked.

"Stargazer may be young, but he's not weak. He can keep up just fine with the herd, and has the right instinct to stay close to his dam while the herd is moving."

"Why are there horses here anyway?" Trigon asked.

Alistair tossed his thumb to where a group of men lead around some horses with children on their backs. "Horse rides. Brings in good money because of the kids, and no one here in this city gets out much."

Trigon nodded.

I looked over at the two Percherons fenced off from the rest of the herd. "How come those two are separated from the rest?"

"Nightshadow and Moongrace aren't from this herd, so it's best to keep them separated, or Legacy and Nightshadow might go at it. And Nightshadow and Moongrace pull the wagon, so we make sure there's little chance they're accidentally picked for rides. This ensures they get the rest they need before having to be harnessed up again to head back to the ranch."

I nodded. "Understandable."

Alistair cranked his neck over his shoulder when someone called for him over at the horse rides area. He excused himself and ran over to find out what was up.

"So, what are we going to do now?" Rhaec asked.

I didn't answer. Instead, I gave Rhaec my stuffed unicorn and slipped inside the horse pen to make my way over to the two Percherons.

"Eira, don't go in there!" Ryder hissed.

I ignored him and continued on, careful not to spook the other horses in the pen. Stargazer trotted alongside me until his mother made a low nicker and he trotted back over to her.

I leaned on the fence and watched the two draft horses graze on the short grass around them. The black male Percheron I assumed was Nightshadow lifted his head and put his attention on me. I didn't call him over. I wanted to see what he'd do about me standing here.

I did, however, nearly jump out of my skin when something warm bumped my shoulder. I turned around to find Legacy standing behind me. He nickered and nudged me again.

I laughed and patted him. "I don't have any treats for you."

Legacy exhaled and enjoyed his attention, which ended soon after when hot breath hit my neck. I turned around and was faced with Nightshadow staring down at me. His presence was incredible.

I reached out and held up the back of my hand for him to take in my scent. Nightshadow breathed normally with my hand in front of him, and when he didn't react after a few moments, I reached out and rested my hand on his soft nose. He exhaled and then leaned into my touch. I took that as a sign of approval and rubbed his muzzle. He nickered, making me smile, and then I laughed when Legacy nudged me again for attention, so I scratched his cheek.

"What wonderful creatures."

Alistair approached, and I gave him a sheepish smile. "Go ahead, scold me for entering the pen without permission."

"Normally I would, but for you I'll make an exception—only because this behavior with the horses is unusual."

Before I could question him, a sharp whistle pierced the air. We turned to find Trigon waving and then pointing to two people. They were Yára and Bone.

A wide smile spread across my face and I waved them in. Bone shook his head. Yára, on the other hand, slipped through the fence.

I put on a fake pout when she joined Alistair and me. "So I only get to see you?"

Yára smiled. "Bone said he didn't want to risk bringing any unneeded attention to you with Rhaec and Trigon nearby. Though, if you want my honest opinion, it's cause he wants to catch up with them. He's been a little lost with them gone."

I understood. "I wouldn't doubt you're right. I'll have time to catch up with him later. He always seems to find me."

Yára giggled. "That's true."

"You know, Zo is looking for you," I said.

She nodded. "I figured. He's supposed to be keeping an eye on me. If it weren't for that crowd that separated us, he'd still be doing a good job of it."

"So, he's your glorified babysitter?"

Her face scrunched. "Yeah. Zarda doesn't trust me to not run off."

"He did the same with me and he's going to be extra cautious with you. That's my fault. I'm sorry."

She shook her head. "Don't be. You did what you had to. And you weren't expecting him to make us."

"True."

"So, you two are related," Alistair mused. "I worried I was overthinking the near-identical nature of you two."

I nodded and gestured to him. "Yára, this is Alistair. He's an elementalist that works with the shamans. He's also running this horse ride business. Alistair, this is my sister Yára."

Alistair held out his hand. "Pleasure."

Yára shook his hand and smiled at him. She then jumped out of her skin when Legacy her nudged her shoulder with his nose.

Alistair chuckled. "He really likes you both. I've never seen him come up to anyone seeking out attention like this. Not even with me, and I've raised him since birth."

Yára held her hands close to her body, her eyes flicking from the horse to me.

"He's not going to hurt you," I said.

"I kinda figured that. I'm just not sure what I'm supposed to do. I've never been around a horse before."

"All you have to do is reach out and touch his nose."

Yára nodded and reached out to Legacy. He nickered at her touch and Yára smiled. "He's nice."

Alistair pointed to a saddle that rested on the fence. "I can tack him up for you."

She shook her head. "Thanks for the offer, but I have to go back to work and find my commanding officer. I actually came to give you something, Eira."

I tilted my head. "Something for me?"

She nodded. "You were planning on going to the lantern festival tonight, right?"

"Well, yeah."

She grinned and dug through a pouch attached to her belt and pulled out a folded envelope.

I took the envelope and opened it, peering inside. "Tickets?"

She held her hands behind her back. "They're lakeside passes."

My eyes widened. Lakeside passes for this event weren't easy to come by, and were highly sought after. "Really?"

"Yeah. The one good thing about Zarda's interest in me, I get what I want. I told him I wanted to see the festival, but wanted to bring a couple of civilian friends I've made in my trips outside the fortress. I had clearance to bring as many friends as I wanted right then and there."

I smiled. "Thanks, Yára. I appreciate it. Just be careful when asking for things."

"Yeah, I know." She stuck out her tongue in disgust. "I try not to do it whenever possible, since I never know if he's going to demand something in return. But I was willing to take a chance this time. I should get going, though. I don't want Zo getting into trouble because of me."

I nodded. "Okay, I'll see you at the lake, then."

She gave Legacy a quick pat goodbye before heading back to the others and leaving with Bone. Bone gave me a quick wave and I waved back.

I turned my gaze on Alistair. "I should go as well, and not keep you from making any more money. Thanks for allowing me in here."

"I'll admit, allowing you in was to sate my own curiosity."

My brow twisted. "Care to explain?"

"They say the Ambassador has special gifts. These gifts aren't always big, and don't come off as such. Seeing how you and the horses inter-acted with each other, I'm certain that's the case."

"He's not wrong."

I rolled my eyes and he laughed. "Of course, that doesn't mean you have to believe me. And I could be wrong. Who knows."

He reached for his back pocket and pulled out a large folded piece of paper. "But, as a small token of thanks, maybe we can help each other out. My ranch is large, and I'm always looking for new hands. If know anyone who would be interested in working for me, send them my way?"

I unfolded the paper to find a map with the location of his ranch starred on the West side of the Larkian Mountain rage that separated the western plains from the eastern forests and basically split Lumaraeon in half as it intersected the North Hyberia Mountains. "I'll see what I can do for you."

I gave Nightshadow a quick pat on the flank and then rubbed Legacy's muzzle before heading over to everyone else. There were still a few hours before the lantern festival, and I wanted to rejoin the others and have more fun before then.

I held the box containing my lantern close as we pushed our way through the crowd in the park. We'd gotten so wrapped up in having fun at the carnival, we'd all lost track of time and forgotten about the lantern festival. That was, until one of the carnies let us know the carnival was closing down so they could attend the festival themselves. Then a bunch of us ran back to the house to grab our lanterns.

Now we were here, but it was almost time for the event to start. Lanterns were already hung and lit in the trees, as well as lining pathways and set down in shapes on the grass around people.

We finally managed to get to the blocked-off area and showed the soldiers our passes. They let us in without incident and we searched around for a good spot.

"Eira, over here!" someone called.

I looked about and found Bone and Yára standing on a wooden dock waving to us. I waved back and led everyone over to them. The soldiers nearby gave us suspicious glances, but we ignored them.

"I'm so glad you could make it!" Yára beamed. "I was afraid you weren't coming."

"I told you we'd be here," I said. "Have some faith in me."

"But we almost didn't make it," Blaze muttered.

I punched him in the arm and he rubbed it, his eyes dark.

Bone chuckled and pointed to the lanterns by his feet. "Do you all have lanterns, or are you going to need some?"

We held ours up and he nodded. "Okay, good. We have lighters, too, if you need any."

"Thanks for the offer." I crouched down and unpacked the water lantern I had in my box. The prices for lanterns this year were outrageous, so I had only been able to purchase two sky ones. With Valene's arrival I gave her one, and before I knew about Yára's surprise, Seda had taken our extra lanterns back to the shop and swapped them for water lanterns.

Valene knelt next to me on my left and unpacked her lantern. Ryder flanked me on my right, and Trigon and Rhaec crouched down behind us to unpack the lanterns they had. Seda handed me a hanging lantern; a gift from Arcadia that'd been left on my bed. I secured it to a post on the dock.

Bone and Yára sat next to Valene and set their lanterns in their laps.

"So when do we start?" Valene asked when her lantern was ready.

I pointed out to the middle of the lake. "There's a raft out there that'll light lanterns. When they release them, we light ours and let them go. Then we watch."

"Well they better start soon!"

"Someone needs to learn how to be patient," Trigon teased.

Her eyes narrowed at him. "Shut up."

The group of us laughed, but it was cut short when someone lit up a lantern on the lake. Valene squealed but I hushed her. It was important this moment remained tranquil.

More lanterns lit up on the raft, and then were let go one at a time. Some were sky lanterns while others were water. All around us, lanterns lit up in response. I lit the tiny candle inside my lantern, then helped Valene light the round wick on her sky lantern. Bone pulled out a lighter and lit his lantern as well as Yára's before handing it off to the others who didn't have a lighter themselves.

I set my lantern down into the water and pushed it away while Valene lifted hers up and let it go after watching some other people with their sky lanterns. I watched as everyone around us let go of their chosen lantern, surrounding us in orange lights. A peaceful sensation fell over me. I smiled.

"This is so amazing," Valene breathed. "Thank you for bringing me to this. It was worth the wait."

I wrapped my arm around her. "Any time."

My arm didn't stay around her long when something caught her eye and she moved away. Raikidan swooped in and took her place—two lanterns in his hand. I peered at them and noticed they were different from the ones the rest of us used.

They appeared to be from another region. I opened my mouth to ask about them, but Ryoko beat me to it. "Whoa, those are some cool-looking lanterns. Where did you get them?"

Rylan nodded. "I'd like to know as well."

"Ebon came by last week and dropped them off for me," Raikidan said. "He had been out in the area we'd grown up in and purchased some."

"Is that why they look so different than ours?" Ryoko asked.

Raikidan nodded. "Depending on the region, the lanterns will look a bit different. While we lived on the east side of the Larkian Mountain range, there was cultural crossover due to our close proximity to the west side. They use lanterns like this."

"That's cool," Valene said.

"The shamans, druids, and gypsies also have their own lanterns," Shva'sika added. "Right, Laz?"

I nodded. "If you look at some of the lanterns floating around, you'll spot a few here. There are also certain races that have their own styles, and even families with long lineages have family lanterns. Different lanterns are a lot more common than people realize."

"*You knew about this festival?*" Mana whispered to Raikidan in Draconic. It surprised me momentarily how well I was able to pick up the sentence. I didn't think I was that good at their language yet.

"*Yes.*" His reply came out curt, showing it wasn't open for discussion. I figured it had to be because of his mother. I wouldn't doubt he attended these festivals with her before her death.

"I have more, if any of you want to light one up and let it go," someone announced behind us.

We turned around to see Ebon and Nyoki approaching.

My eyebrow rose. "How'd you get in here?"

Ebon flashed a devilish smirk. "I have my ways."

"*With that face, he sweet-talked his way in.*"

I didn't doubt it for a second. I'd seen Ebon persuade the most unsure customer into buying more than they should.

"Well, I don't care how they got here, I just want one of these cool lanterns!" Ryoko exclaimed.

Ebon chuckled and handed one to her. As he distributed them, Raikidan nudged me to get my attention.

I cocked an eyebrow when he held up a paintbrush. "What's that for?"

"It's a tradition to write a word on the lanterns in black ink," he said. "Then you trade it with someone else and let them go."

"What do you write?"

"Something to wish for on yourself. Tradition states your wish floats to the skies toward the celestial plane, and the higher it goes, the more likely it'll be granted."

Sounded quite selfish—and flawed. "But if someone else lets it go, wouldn't that mean the word is actually for them and not yourself?"

Raikidan blinked and then thought about this. "Well… I guess you'd be right."

I took the paintbrush from him. "All right, then I'll write something to wish for you."

I thought about what to write and then dipped the paintbrush into the ink vial Raikidan had set down between us. Choosing the lantern I wanted, I painted the word in Draconic. *It's fitting for this occasion.*

"This is a good choice."

"What are you writing?" Raikidan asked.

"It's a secret."

"You know I'll see it in the end."

"It's a secret until then."

He chuckled and shook his head. "Fine, then my word is a secret."

"You've probably written it in your tongue and used a word I don't know, so I wouldn't know it anyway."

Raikidan laughed. "Smartass."

I grinned and then finished off my word. I scrutinized my work to make sure it was as close to perfect as possible. *Regguvyll.*

The two of us swapped lanterns when he'd finished his word. He didn't look at what I wrote, though. I watched him purposely face it away. Even though I suspected I couldn't read the word he wrote, I did the same. He'd tell me in the end anyway.

Raikidan held up the lantern. "Ready?"

I held up my lantern. We both lit them and then tossed them into the sky.

We gazed up at the lanterns as they floated away. Raikidan then spoke, "So, what did you write on the lantern?"

"*Regguvyll.*" I let him take in the word for a minute before smiling wide at him. "*Happiness.* Because you deserve it."

A half-smile spread across his handsome face. "Thank you."

I struggled to not get sucked into those eyes of his. "What did you write for me?"

"The same thing."

I stared at him, surprised, and then smiled as a warm sensation fell over me. "Thanks."

We gazed at each other for several moments, everything around us but the light of the lanterns disappearing. The dappled lights reflected off his strong features, his eyes drawing me in as they usually did. If everything stopped, I'd be okay with it. I could take in this view forever. This was all that I—

"See something you like, Laz?" Ryoko's words cut in behind me, pulling me out of my trance.

The voice growled. *"She had to ruin the moment!"*

While I was a bit glad she saved me from my stupidity, I knew what she was after. A blue lantern floating about caught my eye. It was time to mess with her.

I pointed leisurely in Raikidan's general direction. "Just a mesmerizing blue lantern."

She was so close, I could feel her grinning. "And you, Rai?"

He made the same gesture in my direction. "A lantern with a spectacular shade of green."

Her excitable energy was palpable. "Oh, really?"

The blue lantern floated closer, my finger following, until the two lanterns crossed paths. The two of us spoke at once. "Yep."

Ryoko's energy died. The others around us roared with laughter and I glanced back in her direction, a grin on my lips. "What, did you think we were using metaphors or something?"

Her face scrunched and she stomped away. Raikidan and I chuckled some more and bumped knuckles. That had worked out better than I could have hoped. The green lantern was a surprise, quite convenient really, but I didn't care.

We went back to watching the lanterns. It was such a peaceful night… a fun night. It had been nice to forget about all our troubles and let ourselves be normal people.

Raikidan's presence grew as he scooted a bit closer to me. I was okay with this. I was okay with all of this.

CHAPTER 36

An East Tribe woman put forth some concerns around trade with other tribes. A North Tribe man also voiced a similar concern, and other members in the meeting offered up potential solutions. I sat there, patient as ever, taking in what I could. I didn't know anything about the brought-up topics, which was why Shva'sika suggested I sit in for this meeting.

While everyone knew my main priority would be the rebellion right now, I was expected to fill my role come its end. This meant I needed to learn how the tribes interacted with each other. With how much I needed to absorb, I wasn't sure how I'd fare when this became a full-time gig. I also wasn't sure if I wanted to do this. Could they force me to continue if I couldn't get it right? Could I pass the buck to someone else?

"You're going to do fine."

"Possibly, but will I enjoy doing this?"

"I'm not sure I understand."

"This job is a life-long commitment I didn't jump up and volunteer for. I had military responsibilities for half my life, and I hated it. I'm also not a people person. I don't think I can do this for a lifetime."

"Give it a shot at the very least. If you don't like it, then you can rescind the title, but you have to try it first."

I jumped when someone landed on the ground near me and then rushed to aid Raikidan as he rolled on his side, groaning in pain. "Rai, are you okay?"

"Ry…o…ko," he managed.

My brow twisted and I turned in the direction he'd flown from. Ryoko, a dark look in her eye, snorted indignantly and turned her back, focusing on the Fractured Crystal shamans around her.

When the shamans heard I would be in on the meeting, they requested I bring Ryoko along. Peacekeeper Ryoko wanted them to train her, as the seal Zarda placed on her elemental connection was now broken.

"You refused to fight her, didn't you?" I said as I helped Raikidan sit up.

Raikidan took a deep breath. "Yeah. She didn't take too kindly to it this time."

I shook my head. "I wish you'd listen to me about sparring with her, but you're almost as stubborn as me."

He grumbled and got back on his feet. After allowing a Cleansing Spirit shaman to give him a once-over, he went back to working with the earth shamans and Ryoko.

My meeting continued, the shamans asking for my input now and then. I did my best with suggestions, though most weren't well-received. The voice tried to encourage me, but I wasn't feeling great about my position here.

My salvation came in the form of Shva'sika. She sashayed up to me and whispered in my ear. "Seda needs your assistance with her charges."

Seda was another reason we were here. Some time back when Tla'lli asked for her assistance, it turned out to be a major situation, and Seda wanted to check up on the progress.

I turned my attention to the shamans before me. "I'm needed for something. Please excuse me."

They understood and allowed me to leave.

"Seda doesn't actually need you," Shva'sika said. "She said you could use a break."

"Thank you."

"You were doing well at being polite."

I sighed. "At least I was good at something."

"Don't beat yourself up. It'll become easier in time."

We'll see.

She led me to another room in the underground, where Seda sat with two children—a young boy with short sandy blond hair and a cloth wrapped around his eyes, and a young girl with long sandy blonde hair who looked to be the same age as the boy. She too had a cloth wrapped around her eyes.

The situation Seda assisted with was these two—psychic shamans. The twins didn't manifest their psychic nature until later in their development than what was considered normal, and the strength of that power exceeded what most children their age should have. When I sat in for their first assessment with Seda, they also showed off their elemental abilities, water and fire both. Such rare children, making them major targets for the military. It made sense the shamans sought our help to conceal them.

The girl turned her head up when I approached and broke out in a wide smile. "Hi, Eira!"

I smiled back. "Hey, Nisa. You and Kelen look good."

Kelen gave me a wide, toothy grin. "We're great! And Seda told us she can tell we've been practicing on controlling our power. She says more than half of what she felt when we last met has disappeared!"

Seda turned he head toward me. "Apparently Telar took over their training for a while before he left. It's a good thing, too. Their power has grown even more."

"That's not an intelligent choice for a teacher in the least."

I snorted and sat down next to Nisa. "Good thing? Like I trust him not to turn these two into little trouble makers."

Seda laughed. "Oh, I already know he's taught them a thing or two." Her head turned toward Kelen. "I caught *someone* trying to play a prank on a Council member."

Kelen ducked his head. "They're all so stuffy. I wanted them to laugh for once."

"All right, maybe it was a smart choice."

I snickered. "I can't disagree with him there."

Seda shook her head and went back to teaching. I took the time to analyze the twins. Kelen held himself high like before, but Nisa still showed a lot of timid behaviors. She talked more today, showing her growth, but I suspected she'd fall under the Seer order at this rate, while her brother would be a Battle Psychic. *Though, once we win this war, who knows if those names will be needed anymore.* I honestly wasn't even sure if they'd come about because of the military training segregation, or if they existed long before then.

Seda concluded her lesson, and turned her attention to me. "Would you like to do your own evaluation?"

I nodded. "How is your shaman training going?"

"We can't touch the spirit plane yet, not even a little," Kelen mumbled.

"But we can hear spirits talking to us," Nisa said.

I nodded. "That's good progress. Spiritual plane walking is difficult, so don't be too hard on yourselves. Communicating with spirits is much more important in this stage of your training." I glanced between them. "How is your elemental control doing? I know it's been tough trying to grasp both elements at the same time."

"We're having trouble, but water is easier for us right now," Nisa said. Her lower lip trembled and she her head tipped down, drawing my eye to her arms covered in bandages. "Kelen is better than me, though, when it comes to fire. I'm no good."

There it was. She wasn't solely timid. A lack of confidence gripped her tight and we couldn't have that. "Hey, don't say that. I bet you're plenty good."

She shook her head. "No, I'm no good at these things."

I exhaled a small flame into my hand. She watched as I formed it into the shape of a tiny bird. "I want you to take it from me and control it."

"But I don't know how to do that yet."

"Yes, you do. You just don't know it yet."

"Laz, is that wise?" Seda messaged. *"Your fire is strong."*

"She'll be fine. I've lowered the power significantly, but I've gotten pretty good at guessing a person's elemental potential. I know Nisa can do this. She just needs confidence."

I placed my focus back on Nisa, who stared at the bird. Even without seeing her eyes, it was easy to tell she struggled with getting herself to even try.

Finally she reached out and attempted to take the bird from me, but nothing happened. She continued to try several times until her shoulders slumped and she gave up.

"Let me show you, Nisa," Kelen said as he reached for the fiery bird.

I grabbed his wrist. "No."

"But I was just gonna—"

"No," I repeated. "This is your sister's task, and you will respect her and let her do this, understood?"

He nodded with a frown and sat back down. When I focused on Nisa again, he whispered to Seda, "She's mean."

Seda chuckled. "No, she's making a point."

"I just wanted to show Nisa how to do it…"

"This test isn't for you, and by trying to take it from your sister, you're disrespecting her and Laz. Let your sister figure it out. She needs to find her confidence on her own."

"Okay…"

"Keep trying, Nisa," I encouraged.

She shook her head. "I can't do it."

"Yes, you can. I believe in you."

"I believe in you too, little one," the voice said. *"You can do this."*

Nisa watched the fiery bird. It flapped its wings, as if taunting her. She reached out and made another attempt. This time I could feel the power of my fire drawing away from me and watched as she eventually managed to fly the bird over to her.

"Very good, little one. Very good."

Nisa's eyes sparkled. "I did it!"

I smiled. "See? Just like I said you could."

"Thanks, Eira!" Her smile reached her ears and I smiled back. She had a tough road ahead of her, but as long as she didn't get discouraged and her brother didn't continue to show her up, I knew she'd be able to conquer all the obstacles.

The five of us jogged up the steps to the living room. After I'd assisted Seda with the twins, I'd been called back to my meeting. It went smoother that time, including when I gave input, prompted or not. I didn't feel great about my position as Ambassador still, but at least I wasn't a total failure.

"Because you're not."

The moment we stepped into the living room, Crystal came scampering over to us and rubbed against my leg. I bent over to pet her.

She then ran over to her favorite dragon and begged for attention. Raikidan picked her up and scratched her into a purring fit.

"How'd everything go?" Rylan asked.

He hadn't come with us, much to Ryoko's and my disappointment. He chose to work on his music instead of his ice abilities, but I couldn't really blame him. Music was his passion, and I knew he was working on a secret song just for Ryoko.

"Great!" Ryoko beamed. "Laz played boring old leader with responsibilities, so I can't say much for her, but I had a great time. I learned a lot. Wanna see something cool?"

Rylan chuckled. "I don't think it's a good idea for you to do any earth-moving abilities in this house."

"I'm not talking about the earth abilities. I'm talking about my shell ability."

Rylan blinked. "Come again?"

Ryoko took a deep breath and then hardened her skin, but this time, instead of hardening into a pattern like it normally did, her skin morphed and hardened into large plates that protruded from her body. "Ta-da!"

"That's impressive," Argus said.

What she didn't tell them was this happened by mistake during her training. She'd gone to block an attack and accidentally activated her skin-hardening ability, with a smaller twist. It then became the new focus of her training.

Rylan's eyes raked over her body. "You're not freaking out about how you look."

Ryoko put her hands on her hips. "Is that a problem?"

He smiled. "No, of course not. I'm happy you're not. It's just a bit surprising, to be honest."

"She didn't even freak out when it first happened," I said.

"That's because I'm done being like that," Ryoko said. "I decided that some time ago."

So, when you and Rylan got together. I bit my tongue, figuring it was best.

"So, I was thinking, in celebration of this new discovery, we should go to the club!" Ryoko announced. "What do you think?"

Rylan nodded. "Sure."

I shrugged. "I guess."

Raikidan also shrugged.

"You two aren't any fun," Ryoko said.

"We aren't objecting to going," I said.

"No, but you're not happy to go."

"Well, if I didn't want to go, I would have told you I was going to pass."

"Raikidan and Rylan are going to need to pass for now," Genesis announced as she walked into the room. "I have an assignment for them. Seda, I need to go over a few things with you as well."

"Can't it be given to another team?" Ryoko whined.

"You can go to the club after they finish," Genesis said. "It shouldn't take them long if they do it right."

Ryoko huffed. "Fine."

Genesis waved the boys over. "Come with me so I can explain what you have to do."

Rylan and Raikidan nodded and followed her back to her room. Seda prepared something quick to eat and then also went to the same room.

Ryoko huffed again. "So what now?"

I stretched. "I was thinking of giving Zo a heart attack."

She cocked her head. "Huh?"

I shrugged. "I'm thinking keeping him in the dark about my real identity has been going on long enough, and I should talk to him at the Underground."

Her eyes lit up. "I'm *so* going to be there when you do! I wanna see his face."

I chuckled. "All right, let me go change. If you could contact the Council for me so they can get him there to save time, that'd be great."

"Of course!"

She ran off to do her task while I headed into my room. Shva'sika followed.

"Are you sure about this?" she asked.

I shrugged. "It could cause a total disaster, but I'm going to have to tell him eventually, and a few days ago the Council told me they wanted him to be assigned to our team eventually. If that's going to happen, I have to take a chance with him knowing at some point."

"But is it too early?" she asked. "I mean, he's still under evaluation."

"I know, but we need to end this rebellion. We were determined to have this over with when spring hit. It's spring, and there are no signs of it ending. Not with any help of the Council, that is, so I need to push things along myself."

Shva'sika nodded. "All right. I'll let you do this. I just don't want to see the military storming this house later, claiming us to be traitors."

I laughed and went about getting dressed. *"Do you have any input?"*

"Not this time. I trust your judgment."

When I finished, I met Ryoko in the living room.

"They're getting him now," she said. "He should be there by the time we arrive."

I nodded and the two of us set a quick pace to the Underground, Ryoko opening the heavy doors on her own when we arrived. We headed down the hall leading to the interrogation rooms, where Council member Adina met us.

"He's inside waiting," she said. "Are you sure about this?"

I nodded. "Now is as good as ever."

"Very well. Have at it." She turned around and walked into the viewing room.

Ryoko gave me a thumbs up and followed. I took a deep breath and then entered the room Zo waited in. He stood in the room, his back to me, but the moment the door closed, he turned around. The look on his face was priceless.

"Worth it."

"You have got to be kidding me."

I chuckled. "Surprise."

He went to speak, but then scratched his head and tried to figure out something to say. "I feel like a complete idiot."

"Because you are."

"Trust me, a lot of people thought you were. Including me."

He chuckled. "Gee, thanks." He shook his head and then sat down on the only chair in the room. "I need a minute."

"Sure."

I waited until he was ready to talk. "Okay, let's start from the beginning. And by beginning, when we first met and why you didn't use a better cover name."

I nodded. "I had spent some time outside of the city and had just returned the day you stopped by. I hadn't thought I'd need a cover name and story so soon, so when you asked for my name, I had made some less-than-stellar choices that everyone had to work around."

He nodded. "And since I'd never met you before, I didn't see any issues at the time."

"Question is, why didn't you start to, later, when everyone was insisting I was lying?"

He rubbed the back of his neck. "Because I wanted them to be wrong since, I was interested in you. And then that trick you did during the night of that party to have someone else look like you to throw everyone off, I took advantage of that to believe I was right, along with other tactics you threw out to get us off your back. Especially that last one. How did you make such a convincing body?"

"A lot of resources." I shook my head. "So, how stupid do you feel?"

He sucked hair through his teeth. "Well, we're on the same side now so I shouldn't, but I feel stupid that I let my feelings cloud my judgment."

I nodded. "If it's any consolation, I never wanted to lead you on like that."

"I'm guessing you were told to?"

"Yeah. It was thought I might be able to get some information out of you, even though I didn't have that kind of training."

"Training?"

"Extraction by use of seduction. I'm not the first person you should turn to for that."

Zo chuckled. "You should give yourself more credit. Had your friend not gotten in the way all the time, you might have been able to get quite a bit out of me."

"He got in the way because I wanted him to. I wanted nothing to do with that plan. I wanted you to stay away from me."

He scratched his head and chuckled. "Yeah, I was getting that impression after a while."

"Took you long enough. You're really dense."

"Yeah, I get told that a lot."

"And you need to work on your dating skills. You're terrible."

He placed his hand on his chest. "Ow. I have feelings, you know. You don't have to be so mean about it."

I crossed my arms. "I'm being nice about that."

"Seriously? You thought I was that bad?"

"Yes, you were. Her handsome dragon has better skills than you."

"I had never been on a date before you came along, and I knew they weren't supposed to go like that. There was only one decent one, and it was good until you forced me to kiss you."

Zo held up his hands. "Wait, back up. You'd never been on a date before me?"

"Nope."

"But, your friend."

"He and I are just friends. Anything that appears more is all an act."

"Stop lying."

"We're just friends!"

"But he acts like he hates me."

I chuckled. "Oh, he does. Don't mistake that. But we're not together."

"You should be…"

"So that story about you, that you are supposed to be his wife, is also a lie."

"Duh." I shook my head. "My whole immigrant story is a lie. But that wife part, he made up on his own, and it's definitely a lie."

"Wouldn't have to be if you'd stop being stubborn."

"You didn't know about it?"

"I didn't know until after he told you. He had planned on discussing it with me first, but it just came out when you two were brawling it out outside the club."

Zo nodded. "All right. And you being a shaman?"

"That's true. And I'm also their Ambassador, though I do believe someone else should have been given that role."

"But that goes against the agreement they signed," Zo said.

I rocked my head back and forth. "Depends on how you look at it. Them training me in the ways of a shaman and naming me Ambassador doesn't go against the agreement. Based on the laws of the shaman society, anyone can be chosen, regardless of background. So, even a fugitive like me can be taken in, and all my past transgressions are null and void as long as I embrace the shaman way. This keeps the pact clear of infringement, as it's stated quite clearly."

I smirked. "Them allowing me to be a rebel still, and some even helping me with that, now that would be a breach of the pact. But no one said they were happy to abide by it."

Zo chuckled. "I see."

Someone knocked on the door to our room, and I cracked it open so he couldn't see who was on the other side, just in case. I was surprised to see Ryoko. "What's wrong?"

"We need to go," she said. "It's urgent."

"All right, I'll finish up here." I shut the door and faced Zo. "I'm needed, so I have to cut this short."

Zo nodded. "That's fine. I need time to process all this as it is. But before you go, I just want to apologize for what happened at the club a few nights ago. I—"

I held up my hand. "No need. You were drunk."

"But I said horrible things to you."

"Zo, I said it's okay. Just tell me this. Were you drunk because you were in the Blood Room?" Zo froze and I nodded. "I thought as much."

I opened the door to leave, but Zo stopped me. "How do you know about that place?"

"Everyone knows about it."

"How'd you know I was there?"

"Because we found some flesh on your suit." My gaze faltered. "And you're not the only one who's gone there."

I closed the door behind me and faced Ryoko. "What's going on?"

She moved down the hall. "Raikidan and Rylan were caught!"

"Oh no…"

My eyes widened. "Tell me you're joking."

She shook her head and my pace picked up to a run. "I wish I was. They were lucky enough to escape capture, but they're being pursued. Seda said if we can get to them and split up, then we might be able to throw the military off long enough to get away."

I nodded. "It's the only shot we got."

I waited in the shadows of a dark alley; Ryoko crouched on the other side of the street. Seda was having Raikidan and Rylan run our way so the two of us could split them up, but we didn't know when they'd be here. All we were told was *soon.*

The voice's presence bubbled in my mind. She didn't speak, but her constant "aura" helped me stay calm. I appreciated it, even if the sensation was strange. All these years she'd haunted me. I never thought I'd ever come to enjoy her company, as annoying as it could be at times.

"I heard that."

Ryoko waved at me when her ears picked something up. I listened and caught the sound of two pairs of feet running our way. It had to be the guys. I peeked around the corner and was able to confirm my suspicion. I signaled for Ryoko to get ready. When the guys came into arm's reach, we grabbed them.

Surprised, Raikidan went to strike me, but managed to stop himself when he realized it was me. "Don't do that!"

"You knew we were going to meet up with you," I hissed as I pulled him down the alley.

"I didn't know you were going to jump me."

"I didn't jump you."

"Yeah, sure you didn't."

"Not in the way he would have liked, at least."

"I could leave you to deal with your own mess," I said to him, ignoring her.

He scowled. "It's not my fault we were spotted."

"And? I still had to come and save your ass."

"Well, miss hero, what's the plan, to whisk me to the safety of your castle?"

I chuckled. "Right now, it's to run and put as much distance between us and them as we can."

"Not much of a plan."

"If you have a better one, I'd love to hear it."

"We could hide in one of these alleys. It's dark out so we could remain in the shadows pretty easily."

"Except they're going to scour every inch of this place."

Raikidan clamped his mouth shut, clearly unable to provide any more alternatives. We ran through several more alleys before having to backtrack due to a patrol we nearly ran into.

As we ran, I noticed something was up with Raikidan. "You okay?"

"I'm a little tired."

"Why?"

"I made an attempt to shift Rylan and myself into something small so we could hide, but was interrupted, wasting a lot of my energy."

I nodded. "Let's hope we don't need that ability, then."

"Yeah, let's hope."

"*Laz,*" Seda messaged. "*The military gave up chase on Ryoko and Rylan and have now turned their sole focus on you two.*"

"*Are they safe?*"

"*Yes. They've taken refuge at Zane's shop.*"

"*Good. I'll figure something out on my end.*"

"*You're almost outside the restricted area. I know you can make it.*"

Raikidan seemed to notice my mental conversation with Seda. "Everything okay?"

"Military is on our ass. They gave up the chase with Ryoko and Rylan," I said.

"Perfect."

We kept running and Seda gave me periodic updates on the military. Unfortunately, we weren't doing well enough with losing them.

I bit my lip as I took a chance with a small alley. "This way." We rushed into the side street, only to find it was a dead end. "Shit."

"*You're out of time, they're almost on top of you. You need to think of something.*"

"*Can't we get Chameleon out here to help?*"

"*No. He's still tied up with his assignment.*"

Shit…

"Let's try another one," Raikidan suggested.

"No, we're out of time. You still don't have the energy to shift, right?"

"Yeah, sorry."

I tried to think quickly. I could scale the wall, but I was sure Raikidan couldn't. "You're wearing the armor cloth, right?"

"Of course, why?"

"Change to your Guard clothes," I instructed as I willed my cloth to swap to my shaman clothes.

He did as asked. "Okay, now what?"

I pulled out a map device and located our position. We were just outside the restricted area. It'd save us, but barely. We couldn't be standing in an alley doing nothing, though. I bit my lip and put the map away. *It has to be done.*

"*I'll retreat now,*" the voice said. "*Have fun!*"

"Are you going to tell me what you have planned?" Raikidan asked.

I gazed up at him, slipped my hand into the hood of his cloak to tangle my fingers into his hair, and pulled him closer until our lips met. Raikidan froze, shocked by my choice of action, ultimately cutting this kiss short.

"Rai… you need to kiss me back," I murmured, my lips hovering over his.

"You sure about this?" His hot breath sent a shiver down my spine.

"It's the only alibi I have to work with."

Raikidan placed his hands on my hips and pushed me against the wall. He leaned closer and captured my lips with his. My pulse quickened as our lips synchronized, and I pressed against his sculpted chest when I slipped my tongue into his mouth. Raikidan inhaled deeply, but met my action, hungry and demanding, and tightened his grip.

The world around us melted away and one of Raikidan's hands migrated from my hip and grabbed one of my hands, lacing his fingers with mine and pinning it above my head. My body filled with warmth, intensifying the kiss, and the longer the sensation stayed, the more my brain tried to make me believe this was right—this was how it was supposed to be between us. But I knew better than to believe it.

Our lips parted, but that wasn't the end of it. Raikidan's lips grazed the side of my face and trailed down to my neck. The warm sensation in my body intensified and nearly took my breath away. I felt weak—vulnerable. It was an irritating feeling, but I didn't have the strength to fight it.

A strange noise escaped Raikidan's throat that startled me. It was such a rough sound that it almost seemed like some sort of possessive growl. In my startled state, I was brought back to reality and realized what Raikidan was doing with his teeth.

I pushed him away. "You're going to leave a mark."

"You want this to be convincing, right?" he said, his voice taking a huskier tone.

Before I could reply, he crashed his lips into mine. My heart hammered in my chest.

Someone came into the alley and shone a light on us, cutting everything short. I turned my face away, and Raikidan held up his hand to shield his eyes while trying to figure out who was here.

"Don't move," someone ordered.

My hand went on to the side of my neck as I pretended to be embarrassed and a bit nervous. The patch of skin I touched felt rough instead of smooth. *Great, not this again.*

"Get that light out of my face!" Raikidan barked, pulling away from me a little."

"I said don't move!" the soldier shouted again.

"The hell I won't. What right do you have?"

"Put the gun down, Corporal," someone familiar said.

I groaned internally when I realized it was Zo. *Just my luck.*

The soldier obeyed and the light moved from our eyes, allowing us to see Zo and several other soldiers standing in the alley.

Zo approached. "Care to explain yourselves?"

Raikidan went to say something but I beat him to it. "Minding our own business. Didn't realize that was a crime."

Zo's head twisted a bit, not expecting the hostility. "It's not. But you're near a restricted military area—"

"Also not a crime."

He exhaled. "No, but we're in pursuit of two suspicious individuals—"

"So you're going to cause trouble for every pair of people you come across until you find the right pair?" Raikidan said.

Zo sucked in a tight breath. "Corporal, Bone and I will continue to deal with the Ambassador and her Guard. You take the rest to continue the search."

The officer saluted. "Yes, sir."

When Bone joined Zo, and the other soldiers headed out, Zo waved us over. "Did you have to make this that difficult?"

I chuckled. "I had to keep up appearances. We all know I won't take just any answer for a hostile situation."

"Fair. I'm rather impressed with how fast you got here. I received the call while I was still in that room. Took me forever to get out and help."

"What story did you come up with?"

"That I was checking out some suspicious activity in the sewers."

I nodded. "Good."

"I've obviously missed something," Raikidan said.

Zo chuckled. "While you were getting yourself caught, Eira and I had a good heart-to-heart about telling the truth. I wouldn't expect you to know that, unless that's what the two of you were talking about back in that alley."

"Shut up, Zo," I warned while trying to hide my embarrassment.

He held up his hands. "Hey, whatever you chose for a cover is your business."

I noticed my brother glaring at Raikidan. "Bone, stop."

Bone pointed at Raikidan. "We had an agreement."

"I'm still honoring it," Raikidan said. Bone snorted. "I'm serious."

Bone still didn't like Raikidan's answer, but I was more interested in this *agreement*. "What are you two talking about?"

"Don't worry about it," Raikidan said.

"If it's about me, you'd better start talking," I threatened.

"Really, it's nothing to worry about," Bone said.

I ground my teeth together and grabbed them both by the ear and twisted. "Tell me what you're talking about, or you're both dead. How does that sound?"

"Please stop, Sis, that hurts," Bone begged. "It's between him and me, nothing major, and nothing more."

"Yeah, no kidding," Raikidan muttered.

Zo chuckled. "So you really are the one they're cloned from."

"Yeah we are," Bone responded for me.

"And she's the more violent one of the bunch," Raikidan said. I twisted his ear more and he winced. "See?"

"Sis, I have something for you," Bone said.

I blinked. "What?"

He pulled a small, rectangular metal object from his pocket and I let them both go so I could take it.

I inspected the item. "What is it?"

"Something important."

I grunted and put the item into a pouch. "This doesn't take either of you off the hook."

He blew out a breath. "Please just trust me when I say it's not important."

"If I find out it is and I don't like it, you're both dead."

Zo chuckled but refrained from making any comments. Probably for the best, or he'd end up on the list, too.

The four of us walked in silence the rest of the way to the house, following protocol according to Zo. I was aware of how close Raikidan walked to me this time. He typically stuck close by, but this time felt a bit different.

When we arrived at the house, I gave Zo and Bone my thanks and headed inside with Raikidan in tow.

"Was it wise to tell Zo the truth?" Raikidan asked when he closed the door.

I shrugged. "I don't know. But we'll find out in time."

"All right, I'll trust your judgment."

"Glad to see you back in once piece," Seda said when we entered the living room. "You wouldn't happen to have something for me from Bone, would you?"

I pulled out the object he handed me. "I'm guess this is it. It's all he handed me."

She nodded and used her power to levitate it over to her. "You should get some rest. I've been seeing glimpses of tomorrow and it looks like an interesting day."

I nodded my thanks and headed for my room, Raikidan still strangely close behind. My clothes changed at will when I walked over to my bed and flopped down on it. I then took my hairclip out of my hair and placed it on my nightstand before rolling onto my back to stare up at the ceiling. I wondered what kind of day Seda was seeing. Hopefully it was a good one.

"Hmm, I think it's going to be a good one after earlier."

"Don't bring that up."

Raikidan lay down on the bed next to me and relaxed. "You don't mind, do you?"

I shrugged and rolled onto my side to face him. "I guess not."

He rolled over. "So, this isn't weird?"

I pursed my lips. "Why would this be weird?"

He shrugged. "I don't know."

Raikidan reached over and tucked a stray hair behind my ear. The warm sensation from earlier flared up again. *Not good.*

No matter how many times I continued to tell myself to keep myself in check, it was proving easier said than done. I knew better. I knew it couldn't work—how much of a mistake it would be to try to pursue these feelings. But even still, it was becoming hard to not wish things were less complicated.

I slid off the bed and headed for my dresser.

"What are you doing?" Raikidan asked.

"Looking for something." I dug through drawer after drawer. I couldn't remember which one I put it in. It had been such a long time since I'd laid eyes on it. When I wasn't coming up with anything in my search, I was beginning to think it wasn't here after all. "Ah, there you are."

The object was long and wrapped in black silk. I took it out of the drawer and headed back over to the bed. Sitting down, I handed the item to Raikidan.

"What's this?" he asked.

I relaxed on the bed. "Unwrap it to find out."

Raikidan eyed me before removing the silk. His eyes widened upon revealing the glass-bladed dagger with a gem-encrusted hilt. Raikidan rotated it in his hands. "This is amazing. Where did you get this?"

"It's given to all officers when they are promoted to commander," I said. "It's supposed to be worn for show, but I put it away since the gems and size made it a problem for me. Now I want you to have it."

"Eira, I told you I didn't want payment for helping you."

"I never said it was payment for anything."

"Then why give it to me?"

I shrugged. "I have no use for it. It's not made to be used, and I won't display it after this is all over because I don't want that reminder. It'll always sit in my dresser if I keep it. I figured you'd have better use for it. Even if that use is to sit in your hoard, at least you'd look at it from time to time, unlike me."

"Eira, I... I don't know what to say."

I smiled at him. At least he liked it. My cheeks flushed and that stupid feeling buzzed inside me when Raikidan's lips touched mine. His taste teased me, reminding me of what we'd done earlier.

"Hmm, he's so good at that!"

"Thank you," he murmured as he pulled away.

"Y–you're welcome…"

He smiled and I found myself smiling back before laying my head down on my pillow.

Raikidan rested his hand on my head. "Dream well."

I closed my eyes. "I'll try."

37 CHAPTER

My head felt heavy as I woke. My eyes didn't want to open, but when I managed to crack them, I noticed it was still dark. *Great, another one of these nights.*

I wiggled around to get comfortable so I could go back to sleep, only to notice something heavy on me. I opened my eyes more to find an arm draped over me and I had to refrain from panicking. Instead, I rolled over to find Raikidan in his nu-human form. I jerked back, surprised, and then became confused when I realized he was fast asleep. *Since when could he sleep like this?*

"Interesting, isn't it?" a familiar voice said.

I sat up to find Corliss sitting on the windowsill. "How long have you been there?"

"Long enough."

"You know that's really creepy, right?"

He shrugged. "Doesn't matter. What does is what's going on between the two of you."

I looked away. "Nothing is going on."

"Stop denying it."

"Oh really? Then can you tell me how Raikidan is capable of sleeping in that form?"

I shrugged. "It's news to me, too."

"I think you do know. You just don't want to admit the reason."

My eyes snapped to him. "Then why don't you enlighten me? What am I not willing to admit?"

"How much you two actually care about each other."

I frowned. "Why won't everyone just drop this?"

"Because you won't stop running away."

"I'm not running from anything!" I glanced at Raikidan when he stirred from my outburst. When he didn't wake, I glared at Corliss. "There's nothing between us. Just ask Raikidan."

Before Corliss could say anything, Raikidan stirred again and this time his eyes cracked open. He glanced up at me with a groggy smile and reached out to touch my face. "Come back to bed, beautiful."

My heart stopped and my mind went blank. *Why did he just call me that?* Before I had the chance to recover, his hand fell and he was asleep again.

Corliss chuckled. "I think you just got your answer."

"He wasn't exactly conscious enough to be aware of what he was saying."

"He targeted you specifically."

"He could have been dreaming of someone and in his half-awake state confused me for her."

His eyebrow rose. "You really believe that?"

"Yeah, I really do."

"And there's no way he was dreaming about you."

"No."

Corliss watched me. "You want him to be."

I had to look away from him. "No, I don't."

"Yes you do, because you want him."

"Even if I did, he's not mine to have." I lay back down and curled up, facing away from Raikidan. "Now go away."

"If you woke up tomorrow and he was awake and still right there, would you believe me?"

"He won't be."

"We'll see about that."

38
CHAPTER

I sighed and ran my fingers through my hair for the millionth time. Like I expected, I had woken up alone. I knew this would be the case, so I couldn't understand why I was so worked up about it. I pushed these feelings away so I wouldn't end up in situations like this. It wasn't right to think that way about him… *So why can't I get myself to listen?*

"Because the two of you are meant to be."

Someone knocked on the door. I ran my fingers through my hair to make sure it wasn't obvious I was a stressed-out mess and made it look like I was just hanging out in my room. "Come in."

Ryoko strolled in and looked at me. "What are you doing in here?"

"Thinking."

She sat down on the bed. "About what?"

I shrugged. "Nothing important."

"You sure?"

My brow twisted. "Yeah, why?"

Ryoko flipped my hair over the back of my shoulder and poked at a tender area on my neck. "Because of that! You have a hickey. Spill the beans, missy!"

"I have a what?" I shrieked. I grabbed my neck and found the sensitive area where Raikidan had targeted my neck last night.

Ryoko nudged me. "C'mon, tell me."

"It wasn't supposed to happen like that… it was just supposed to throw them off…"

Ryoko's eyes softened. "Laz, tell me what happened last night."

I hung my hands over my knees. "The military caught up with us and I had to think of something quickly that would make them less likely to question our reason for being so close to a restricted area. Only one thing came to mind. I…"

The words died on my lips. My shoulders slumped, the weight of what happened growing heavier.

Ryoko nudged me. "Told you so. You like him. And don't even try to lie about it. You made out with Raikidan as an attempt to throw off the military. You would have rather been caught without an alibi with anyone else."

"It's not like that."

She gave me a stern look. "He left a mark on your neck and you're freaking out over it, so it wasn't part of the plan. He got carried away. Meaning it's not one-sided."

"He's promised to someone else…" The words came out barely a whisper.

Ryoko blinked. "What?"

My lips pressed together, the reality of those words harder on me than anything I wished them to be. "It's exactly as I said. He's promised to someone else. So it doesn't matter how I feel."

"Are you sure it's not—"

I nodded. "Yeah, I'm sure."

"How long have you known?"

"Since the beginning. That's why it never mattered what anyone said. He's not mine to have so I've done what I can… to ignore how I feel."

"You admitted it to me."

I shrugged. "No point in lying. It is what it is, but it doesn't matter. Doesn't change anything."

"I don't think you have the whole story."

Brow cocked, my gaze rose to meet hers.

"Remember that date you two went on, and how I told you I helped him plan?" I nodded, though I didn't understand where this was going. "I didn't prompt him. He asked me to help him come up with the plan. And I made it clear I was setting it up as a date. He didn't flinch or hesitate." She slid off the bed. "So, you should tell him."

I stared at her, unable to process what she said.

The voice chuckled. *"Told you so."*

Ryoko winked and left me to think. That was the last thing I wanted to do. If I thought, I'd do something stupid.

"Telling him how you feel isn't doing something stupid."

I headed for the fire escape. Climbing up to the roof, I went to my greenhouse, walking past all the flowers and my messenger hawk. I passed the fountain and over to a desk I had set up in the back by a few small potted fruit trees.

Pulling out a key hidden under the dresser, I unlocked the only drawer that stored anything and pulled out a journal and pen. I sat down and flipped through the used pages until I came to the empty ones. I wrote out the date.

2035 Xerix 5

This paused my thoughts. *Same month as when Raikidan and I met.* I didn't know the exact day, but it was somewhere around this time. *Was it today exactly?* That'd be way too coincidental. But life was funny like that. Regardless of that accuracy, I couldn't believe we'd known each other for a year at this point. That day felt so long ago.

I tapped my pen on the paper and then began to write. I wrote about my feelings and what I thought. I wrote about what had happened in the past few days. I jotted down whatever came to mind, unhindered by fear.

Seda had insisted I try this. She thought it would help me since I struggled with talking to others. She was right.

I exhaled through my lips when I finished. The sun was going down now and I fought with myself over this decision, but it was what I had chosen. I couldn't tell Raikidan how I felt. I knew that wasn't right. Even if he'd planned the date like Ryoko claimed, stealing him away from that happiness he deserved… it wasn't right.

And I couldn't tell him the truth about me. A few may accept my existence, but that was because they thought I was someone else. Raikidan was better off not knowing either truth.

"You're making a big mistake."

I locked away my journal and pen, fed my messenger hawk, and left my greenhouse. With nothing left to do on this problem, I chose to put my clothes away and clear my mind. I'd forget last night and eventually things would straighten out.

The rebellion was going to come to an end soon, and Raikidan would be free to go back to his life. I could put some distance between us for a bit and these stupid feelings would go away, and our friendship would remain intact.

"I wish you'd listen to reason."

"Mind your own—"

"This is my business. I'm attached to you, remember?"

"I make the choices for my life. Not you. I don't care if you agree with them or not. That's not your decision to make!"

She sighed and stayed quiet.

I closed my bedroom door behind me and jumped out of my skin when Raikidan landed on the fire escape. "Don't do that!"

He looked at me apologetically. "Sorry."

"What have you been up to today?" I asked as I headed for my dresser.

"Another surveillance mission."

"Surveillance?" I looked at him askew, but before I could continue, I noticed he was hiding his hand behind his back. "What do you have there?"

He grinned. "Something for you."

I tilted my head. "Me?"

"Yeah, come here and I'll give it to you."

Curious, I abandoned my clothes. When I was in front of him, he smiled and then revealed what he was hiding. My eyes grew wide at the sight of the bonsai tree.

"Is this really for me?" I asked as he handed it to me.

"No, it's for Ryoko and I just wanted to see what you thought of it."

I blinked and he grinned. I laughed, the warm feeling from last night returning. It worried me. I knew better, and yet that other side of me didn't want to listen. *It doesn't learn...* I needed to put distance between us.

"Well, thank you." I headed for my dresser again. "I'll put in my greenhouse in a bit. I want to get these clothes folded and put away before I forget again."

"Sure." His reply sounded a bit odd to me, but I brushed it off and set my mind on my chores. The room was quiet for some time, until Raikidan spoke again. "Eira, can I ask you something?"

I continued to fold. "Yeah, sure."

"Are you positive you want to help me find my destined mate?"

I paused for a moment before continuing with my task. "Of course I am. Why are you questioning this again?"

He ignored my inquiry and entered the room further. "What if I told you I was choosing someone else?"

I stopped folding and turned to look at him. "Why in Lumaraeon would you do that?"

My breath caught in my throat and I dropped the shirt in my hands when Raikidan closed the distance between us. He rested his hand on the dresser, boxing me in. Our gazes locked. "Because you're a better choice."

I froze and my mind went blank. He wanted me? Why? What made me a better pick? It didn't matter. It wasn't right.

My eyes flicked away, fearful I wouldn't be able to say the right thing if I continued to hold eye contact. "R–Raikidan, y–you can't do that. You're better off with her—whoever she is—than—"

"Look at me and say that, then. Look at me and tell me you don't feel the same and I would have been better off keeping my mouth shut."

I hesitated. Could I do that? I had to do it. It was for the best. I lifted my gaze, but the moment our eyes met, my resolve disappeared. I couldn't lie. I couldn't remind myself of the past and the pain that had come with those choices. I couldn't hide from the truth.

"It's okay to want to be happy, Eira," Seda messaged telepathically. *"It's okay to let go and try again."*

"I don't want to be hurt again."

"Would that pain be any different than the pain of ignoring your feelings and making yourself more miserable?"

As usual, she was right. Pain was pain, regardless of who inflicted it on me.

Raikidan remained still as he waited for my answer. I reached up and grabbed his face with both of my hands, lifting myself up on my toes.

"You are mine," I murmured in Draconic before claiming his lips with mine.

Raikidan's hand left the dresser and flew to my back, pulling me closer to him. His lips became more demanding—needy—and the warmth of his mouth sent a current rushing through my body, making my head swim.

Raikidan's hands slid down my back until they touched my ass. He lifted me up onto the dresser and I held onto him instinctively with my legs. Once seated, I was able to relax a little, giving me the opportunity to drag my fingers down his neck, over the bone and sinew choker I had made him, and across his chest. His pectoral muscles rippled with my touch. A possessive growl rumbled in his chest and he pulled me closer, though we didn't stay that way for long. His shirt was in the way and I needed to rectify that.

Our lips parted when I slid his shirt up. I was in no hurry to rush any of this along, but Raikidan was another story. He whipped his shirt over his head and tossed it, grinning as I appraised the sight before me. I had always liked the choker on him, but seeing him wear it on his half-naked form gave me a greater appreciation for the piece of jewelry.

My teeth caught my lower lip, my cheek flushed and hot.

Raikidan leaned closer and grabbed my chin with his finger and thumb to make me look at him. "Let me help you with that."

My heart thumped in my chest, but before Raikidan's lips touched mine again, the fire escape creaked.

"Eira?" It was Mana. "Eira, are you in here?"

Raikidan braced himself on either side of me and let out a heavy exhale. I noted his tight shoulders. Mana poked her head in through the window, but before she could say anything, Raikidan cut her off. "Get lost, Mana."

She blinked and I gave him a look. I could understand he was irritated, but he didn't need to be so rude.

Mana pouted. "No need to be mean."

He glanced back at her. "I said—"

I placed a hand over his mouth and gave Mana a sympathetic gaze. "Mana, we're in the middle of sorting out something important. Do you mind coming back later?"

Raikidan removed my hand. "Much later."

Mana's nose twitched as if a scent I couldn't detect crossed her path, and then she giggled. "Sure thing. I'll come back in a couple days. Have fun."

She slipped outside and my cheeks flushed. *Days?* I shook that thought out of my head. She was just messing with me. *Right?*

I turned my focus to Raikidan. "So, tell me, why did you bite her head off?"

He let out a strained breath. "Because I got fed up with her showing up and ruining everything for me every time I tried to bring this up with you. She's been nothing but a pain in my ass, and Corliss won't keep her on her leash."

I snickered. "Sounds like I need to put you on a leash and teach you few things."

His tongue dragged long his lower lip. The look he gave me as he leaned closer brought my brain to screeching halt. "If training me would please you, then by all means."

I swallowed hard and my heart thundered in my chest again. I looped my finger into the choker. "What a tempting offer."

"One week," he murmured, his lips hovering over mine.

I pulled back, my brain on the verge of a malfunction. "Huh?"

"Dragon mating rites give me one year uninterrupted with you. But with everything going on, we can't do that. So all I ask is one week, just the two of us."

"Rai, we have a rebellion to win. We can't—"

"One week, please," he begged. "It can be done my way or your way. I just want one week with you."

My pulse quickened. While I wasn't sure we could have a week to ourselves with everything going on, that wasn't what my mind clung to at present. It was how he was handling our relationship. I had the choice of pace.

I knew how quickly dragons came together after accepting each other. Humans would take more time, usually, and while I would normally opt for the human way, I wanted him and didn't want to chance him changing his mind so quickly about wanting to be with me. It didn't mean he couldn't later, even if a dragon claimed it not possible, but I would indulge in what I could, even if it were for a short time.

"He's yours," the voice said. *"Claim him. Then no one can take him. He's proven himself worthy of this claim."*

She then receded into the back of my mind.

I smirked and held his gaze, not knowing if the face I was making was appealing or not. "Who said the two choices were different?"

Raikidan's hands flew up and grasped my face, pulling me in for a hard, rough kiss that turned my mind to mush. One of his hands let go, and my hair spilled over my shoulders when he removed my hairclip and placed it on the dresser. With the same hand, he caressed my skin, setting it ablaze.

I held onto him tightly when he lifted me up and carried me. As needy as this kiss was, Raikidan showed restraint as he laid me on the bed and knelt over me.

Our kiss broke when the bedroom door opened suddenly and Ryoko strolled in. The three of us stared at each other. Ryoko grinned, and I was aware of the flustered flush on my cheeks from being caught in this position.

"Do you mind?" Raikidan asked. "We're a bit busy."

Ryoko chuckled. "I can see that."

I frowned. She would act like this. Using what strength I had, I flipped Raikidan over onto his back and straddled him. I stared Ryoko down. "Get out."

She snickered and raked her fingers in the air like claws. "Down, kitty, I'm going." She started to close the door behind her and winked. "You two just be safe now."

The door shut, and I stared at it for a few long moments before looking down at Raikidan, his signature grin spread across his lips. He lounged under me with one of his arms tucked under his head. A strong air of confidence surrounded him. *He likes something about this.*

"What are you smiling about?" I asked.

His grin grew deeper. "I'm starting to like this position."

I leaned in closer to him, not taking my hands off his sculpted chest. "Oh really?"

"Yes, but"—he seized my hands and before I knew it, he'd flipped me onto my back. He hovered over me with my hands pinned to the bed on either side of my head—"I still prefer this one."

I did my best not to panic. I didn't like this position. I didn't like feeling so trapped.

Raikidan leaned in and his lips brushed the side of my face. "I'm not going to hurt you, Eira."

"It's not you," I murmured. "It's this particular position. I don't like feeling so—"

I gasped when he began leaving a trail of warm kisses down my neck.

"It's okay to feel vulnerable," he murmured. "I'll protect you, even if you don't want me to." His teeth nipped at the tender spot on my neck he had left the previous night. "I will have to mark you. It will—"

"I know all about the mate mark. I know it'll be painful."

Raikidan's lips traveled over to my collar bone. "I promise, it'll be the only time I ever hurt you."

He kissed my collar bone and he slowly slid his hands down my arm. A tingling sensation pricked my fingers and toes. "But first, I'll claim even inch of you. I'm going to show you what it means to be loved by a dragon."

"Physical attraction, I see." My words came out breathy. "Primal want, I can agree with. But I'm too jaded for love."

He continued to kiss me, sending bursts of tingling sensations through my body. "I'll prove to you it exists. I'll love you right and never betray you. A challenge I accept with every fiber of my being."

I found myself unable to respond as his kisses became more fervent, until his lips found mine once again. I laced my fingers into his hair and his hands slid down the sides of my body. They found the hemming of my tank top and slowly pushed it up.

Our kiss broke when his hands reached just under my breasts. My bottom lip quivered and my body tightened.

"It's okay, Eira," he murmured. "I won't do anything you don't want me to." He lightly kissed my lips. "If you want me to stop, no matter when, I will listen. I only wish to please you."

"I'm fine," I managed. "The slow pace is allowing me to think too much about this."

I took a deep breath to calm myself and then ripped my shirt over my head and tossed it. "That should help."

Raikidan huffed, his eyes keeping contact with mine and never wandering. "I wanted to do that."

My heart fluttered, surprising me. With my reaction moments ago, that comment should have made me uncomfortable. Lying beneath him without a shirt on should make me uncomfortable on its own, but right now I felt just fine.

It had to be because his gaze wasn't wandering. I felt safe… wanted… with his attention focused on me, as if he knew exactly what would please me.

I reached behind my back and unclasped my bra—my supple breasts spilling out of the undergarment. Raikidan's eyes glowed with lust as I dropped the bra on the floor, and his gaze finally raked over me with appreciation. He spoke again, the gravely edge to his voice intensifying with the deepening of his usual tone, "I take back my complaint."

My cheeks flushed hotter and I found myself unable to look at him—my arms threatening to wrap around my chest to hide me. Raikidan grabbed my face with a firm, yet gentle hand, and made me look at him before aggressively claiming my lips with his. Our tongues wrestled with each other, an intense hunger building up in me with each passing second.

Raikidan's free hand found my waist and slowly glided up my skin, specifically targeting the large scars I had, sending tingling sensations through my torso. Our kiss broke when his hand reached the base of one of my breasts. My fingers and toes tingled. My teeth caught my bottom lip. Raikidan held my gaze before flashing me his signature cocky grin and leaning over to reverently trail kisses down my neck, his hand sliding over my swollen breast.

A quiet gasp escaped my mouth that repeated when his other hand released my face and claimed my free breast. My heart hammered against my ribcage, and my fingers laced into his hair when his fingers rubbed my sensitive peaks as he continued to kiss and nip across the skin of my chest.

Desire flared through my core; a moan escaped my throat when Raikidan's lips claimed one of my aching buds. His tongue flicked and circled my taut nipple, intensifying the need building inside me.

Through hooded eyes, I looked down at him just as he gazed up at me. A grin spread over his face, stoking the flames burning inside me and sending startling desire throbbing between my thighs. Raikidan's hand let go of my breast and slid down my stomach to my hips, but only remained there for a moment. Slowly, his hand migrated across the band of my pants until they reached the button. I tensed and my lip quivered again. I mentally cursed. I didn't want to act this way. I didn't want to be afraid of any of this.

Raikidan pulled away with what I could have sworn was a sigh, and pinned both my arms above my head. He rested his forehead on mine. "Don't make yourself do this. You're not ready."

I narrowed my eyes as irritation flared in me. Zarda had taken a lot away from me. But before him, there were pleasant memories—some I shared with Tannek that reminded me how good it was to lose yourself with someone else. *Zarda has no hold on me any more!*

I yanked my arms free and grabbed onto the band of his pants, pulling him a little closer. "Don't tell me what I'm ready for."

In one swift motion, I unbuttoned and unzipped his pants. Raikidan stared wide-eyed in shock when I reached into his pants and grabbed his throbbing manhood. The shock slowly melted to desire, and his grip on the sheets on each side of my head tightened as I continued to hold onto him, occasionally changing the pressure of my grip. "Eira…"

A wicked grin spread across my lips as I held his gaze. "*My* dragon is about to find out what I mean when I said we humans do this for *fun*."

Releasing him, I took hold of the band of his boxers and pants, and pulled them both down with ease, his erect member released from its material confines. My cheeks flushed hotter at the thought of breaking our locked gaze to peek. As if he could see the thought, his eyes glowed with lust, the captivating color of his eyes deepening, and he pulled away and off the bed to finish the job I started. I sat up and allowed myself to take in every viewable inch of him, slowly, as if I had all the time in Lumaraeon. Heated desire spread through my body.

Our gazes locked again and I beckoned him with a finger. "Come here."

As if unable to ignore my request, he climbed back on the bed and captured my lips with his. I dragged my fingers down his chest, but when I reached his navel, I found myself on my back again and Raikidan fussing with the button of my pants. His possessive claim on my mouth didn't let up until he conquered the button and zipper and yanked my pants off, tossing them carelessly.

His eyes glowed as his fingers touched my underwear. "Silk. How did you know I loved it?"

I grinned. "I'm good like that."

He slid his thumbs up my inner thighs and slipped them into the band of my underwear. My breath caught momentarily with anticipation as warm desire throbbed between my thighs. He nipped my lip, and then my neck. "And now *my* human is about to find out what I mean when I say we dragons will do anything to please our mates."

Raikidan slipped a finger between my thighs and a gasp escaped my lips as pleasure surged through me. "Rai…"

He grinned against my neck and continued his rhythmic motion.

"Rai…" I moaned. "Rai…"

Pleasure pulsed in my core, spreading outward across my entire body and my hips bucked. Any words beyond his name came out, between moans, as incoherent gibberish. Raikidan slipped another finger into my burning desire, pushing me over the edge. My back arched, and I cried out as ecstasy flooded over me.

Raikidan pulled his hands away as my breath came in short, heavy bursts. I gasped when he nipped the sensitive skin on my neck and he chuckled. "Did that please you?"

"Yes." I took a breath. "Gods, yes."

He kissed me on the lips. "Good. There's more where that came from."

I grinned as I placed my hands on his chest. "I hope so. But until I'm ready for more"—I pressed hard on his chest and flipped him over until I straddled him, Raikidan grabbed my hips instinctively—"it's your turn."

Raikidan merely stared at the sight I presented him. With a grin, I began grinding my hips into him and his grip tightened. "Eira…"

I ground my hips into him some more. "Eira, if you want something, ask."

I slipped lower and dragged my fingers down his chest. "I'm not asking."

He sucked in a deep breath when my touch passed his navel. "Then tell me, what are you doing?"

I briefly bit my lip, before continuing my path. "Doing."

His breath caught when my hand took hold of his erect member and slowly stroked him. His eyes closed and he sighed with pleasure as I continued. "Eira…"

I smirked and bent closer. Raikidan opened his eyes and looked at me, but before he could say anything, he moaned as I slowly eased my lips over his throbbing manhood.

He moaned as I sucked and slid his shaft in and out of my mouth rhythmically. "Eira…"

The sound of him moaning my name surged a new hunger—need—inside me. My rhythm picked up speed. Raikidan's hands tangled into my hair as he groaned and rocked his hips, his hard member continuing to swell. Then suddenly, he sat up and forced my head away. After taking a few controlled breaths, he seated me on his lap and claimed my lips, his hand firmly curled around the back of my neck, and the other crushing me against his hard body. I threaded my fingers into his hair, meeting his need, and ground my hips into him. Raikidan growled with a possessive, hungry want.

One of his hands slid down my back and hooked into the band of my underwear, pulling it down. When he got to the point where I needed to reposition for it to go any further, he did just that. The two of us rolled until I was under him, and he slipped the silk undergarment off my body and deposited it on the floor. Raikidan caressed my bare skin wherever he could reach, his hands always coming back to my thighs, burning with need and anticipation.

I broke our kiss and spoke breathlessly, "What are you waiting for?"

He grinned. "That invitation."

With firm hands, he lifted my hips toward him. My back arched and my breath came as one long inhale as he filled me. Raikidan's breathing hitched as the new sensation rocked him to the core. He placed his hands on either side of my head as he held himself over me, but remained unmoving. I grinned and thrust toward him once.

His breath hitched. "Eira, wait."

"No," I said, thrusting again.

He lowered himself and nipped my neck. "If this ends quicker than we want because you're impatient, don't blame me."

"I thought you wanted to please me?"

Raikidan thrust deep inside me, rocketing pleasure through me. My arms wrapped around him as a moan escaped my throat, and his momentum increased. I met his thrusts, pushing him farther inside, increasing the pleasure for us both.

His breath came hotter on my lips than normal—the taste of his flame heavy in each breath. I kissed him with need, and he jerked his head back when my advance pulled him away from his concentration of keeping his fire at bay, but I was persistent. His fire teased my lips and I began consuming it, almost as if instinct drove me. As this exchange continued, my own fire stirred up in my chest, and before I knew it, Raikidan's flame died and he took mine from me.

I gasped and my nails dug into his back when Raikidan ended our kiss abruptly and nipped at my neck. He continued until his teeth found the area where he had marked me last night. I winced, but didn't fight it. I had to endure and focused more on the pleasure pulsing through me.

Raikidan's left hand reached out and grabbed a fistful of damp hair, exposing my neck more, while his other hand slid down my side until he slipped it between my legs and increased the pleasure. I cried out, my nails digging into his skin more, and I barely noticed the change in the shape of Raikidan's teeth as I hit my second climactic release. Raikidan abandoned himself to the pleasure building inside him, and his breath staggered as his body convulsed and his teeth clamped down on the flesh of my skin, sinking in deep. I cringed, but managed to relax as the heat of his flame caressed my skin on the wounded area.

"*You are mine*," he murmured in Draconic when he unlatched his jaw. "*Always mine. Forever.*" He nuzzled the side of my face as his breath came out in staggered gasps. "I'm sorry I hurt you. I'm sorry…"

He continued to murmur the apology until I placed a finger on his lips. "It's okay."

"No, it's not." He buried his face into my neck. "No, it's not."

Rolling my eyes, I pushed him off me so he'd be lying on his back and curled up to him. The heat and strength of his body against mine, elicited a need to be forever close to him. "Yes, it is, because everything leading up to that made it worth it."

"I'm glad you're pleased." Raikidan wrapped his arms around me and squeezed. "And I promise I won't hurt you again." He inhaled deeply, taking in the scent of my hair. "I love you."

I bit my lower lip. I knew I should say it back, even if I didn't believe the words, but they died on my tongue. Pain twisted in my chest.

That's what you're supposed to do, right? Even if you didn't mean it because it made them happy?

Raikidan kissed my head and rubbed my back. "You don't have to say it back, or believe me. I just want you to know that's how I feel. I'll tell you every day—every hour, every minute if I have to, until you do believe me."

I rubbed my thumb on his chest. "Maybe you'll be able to convince me otherwise, but for now, they're just words. I'm sorry."

He continued to rub my back. "Don't be. Means I have to work extra hard to prove myself."

I chuckled. "Well, if your performance just now is any indication how well you'll prove yourself, I think I'm in trouble. For a dragon that claims to know nothing about human copulation, you performed *very* well."

"I don't know how to explain it, really. I just knew what to do, as if I'd done this with you before, but I know I haven't." Raikidan inhaled deeply again. "Though I wish I had. That was a lot better than I imagined it would be."

I smiled despite myself and continued to rub my thumb on his chest. That is, until I noticed something on the back of my hand. Turning it to get a better view, my heart raced and my eyes widened at the sight of the patch of scale-like skin. My hand flew up to my neck, only for me to find that it, too, had changed in areas. I pulled away from Raikidan, sat up and frantically looked myself over. To my horror, my sides, legs, arms, even my thighs were covered in the leathery scaled skin, though the ones on my thighs were much larger than the ones covering the rest of my body.

Raikidan placed a hand on my shoulder. "Easy, Eira. It's okay. Calm down."

I found myself unable to listen. The change had never happened like this. A few scale-like patches and my hand shifting shape were the only involuntary changes that had ever happened in the past. Anything more were deliberately initiated. This wasn't supposed to happen to me. I was supposed to look normal—to look—

Raikidan forced my focus to him. "Eira, stop. There's nothing wrong here."

"Yes there is. This isn't supposed to happen. I'm not supposed to look—"

Raikidan's lips crashed into mine, the intensity stealing my breath away. "You're beautiful. Doesn't matter how you look, or what types of metamorphosis you go through. You'll always be beautiful to me."

Again words escaped me. Was there truth in those words? Or were they said just to make me happy?

Raikidan moved, positioning himself over me while I still remained facing the bed. He nipped my shoulders. "No matter what you look like, you're still Eira. And I will prove it to you."

I gasped when he bit the base of my shoulder blade and continued to pinch my skin with his teeth as he migrated down. Either he'd prove it, or distract me long enough for me to not care for a while. Both outcomes worked for me.

39
CHAPTER

A deep breath of air filled my lungs as I stirred. My eyes fluttered open and I rubbed them, only to realize the sun had yet to rise. *Great.* The sound of Raikidan sleeping soundly next to me had me rolling over, the sheet he'd pulled over me moving with me.

Raikidan slept on his stomach, his arms tucked under his pillows. Tilting my head, I reached out and played with his hair. Him sleeping in his nu-human form was still a perplexing sight. I had asked him about it before we went to sleep, but he didn't know much about it either. What he did know was the past two nights hadn't been the first.

Back during the summer, when he had first agreed to work closely with me on my personal space issue, we had both fallen asleep on the couch. Apparently Ryoko had taken the liberty of photographing us. But, beyond that, he wasn't sure how he was capable of it.

I looked at my hand and noted its normal state. Touching my neck and cheek, I confirmed that was back to normal as well, and then gave the rest of my body a once-over. For the most part, my skin was back to normal. The only signs left were faint and on my hips, the one spot that had changed the most. A light pattern of scale remained, but at its peak, the skin began to protrude into long and wide shapes that resembled plating.

Raikidan had done a good job proving he didn't mind. Better than good, really. I could have sworn that with each physical change, he got more excited.

"Duh, stupid. He's a dragon."

She had a point. *Should have thought of that.* Him being a dragon, it'd be natural for my scales to appeal to him. If it weren't for the other physiological changes my body went through, I was sure I'd be able to accept the metamorphosis better, but that wasn't the case, and eventually my body reminded me of that.

I stretched my shoulders expecting pain or stiffness, but found none. I finally convinced Raikidan to let me rest when my back began to hurt, although it was not from our *activity*, like I let him believe. I couldn't believe that in the few hours we spent together, my body had tried to transform *that* much.

"You really need to tell him the truth."

"I know. I just… don't know how."

"You just say the words: 'Raikidan, I need to tell you the truth about my origins.' And then just say it!"

She made it sound so easy. But I'd fought that truth for so long, the words lodged in my throat now. Discomfort crawled under my skin at the thought of telling anyone, even Raikidan, like some defense mechanism.

I glanced at Raikidan again, watching him sleep. His words about picking me over his destined mate tugged at the back of my mind. The idea that he thought I was a better choice elated me, but at the same time, I couldn't shake the nagging doubt that this wouldn't last.

"Don't go there."

What if we crossed paths with her and he realized he'd made a mistake?

"Stop it."

What if she was that much better and he wanted to leave? How would I cope?

"I said enough! You're ruining a perfectly good moment by giving in to your insecurities. If you cross paths with her, you kill her and then bury the body, keeping him all to yourself."

I almost choked. *"I'm not psychotic!"*

"Then what would you do?"

I chewed my lower lip. *"I'd let him go. It'd hurt, but why try to convince someone to be with you if they don't want you anymore?"*

The voice growled. *"I really wish I could smack you right now."*

"I'm just being practical for my situation."

"No, you're being stupid."

My brow furrowed when I realized there was someone else breathing in the room, cutting my argument short. I remained still as I listened in attempt to locate the source. *The window.* Hugging the sheet, I sat up to find Corliss sitting on the sill with his back facing the room.

"Do I want to know why you're here?" I asked.

"Tradition," he said without turning to look at me. "Mating rights gives the dragons involved peace of mind for one year. No dragon will try to push the territory boundaries, and if the male dragon has a friend nearby, that friend will keep watch the first three nights. That's what I'm doing."

"Why, when Raikidan didn't do it for you?"

He partially turned. "How do you know that?"

"I know a lot about the tension between the two of you. Raikidan told me some, and how he felt, but that was after I had been shown what happened."

"Should I ask what you mean by shown?"

I chuckled. "Being a shaman means I've seen things even if I didn't ask or want to be shown."

Corliss gave a curt nod. "I understood why Raikidan was upset. I wasn't open with what was happening between Mana and me. I only told him I was keeping her safe since she didn't have a home. I worried he'd start to think she'd drive a wedge between us if he knew she was my destined mate and I was just biding my time."

He exhaled through his lips. "I now know how stupid that notion was. He would have taken it all better had I been honest. But because I wasn't, he felt betrayed. I honor this tradition even when he didn't do it for me, because I value our kinship, as broken as it is still."

"It'll mend. Just takes time."

He smiled. "Yes, now that he's got you I think that will be easier. Too immature to say I told you so?"

"Told me so what?"

He turned and gave me a pointed look. "That you were his destined mate."

I shook my head. "No, I'm not. He chose me over her."

Corliss' brow furrowed. "What?"

"It's as I said. He's promised to someone else but chose me."

His head turned toward the outside a little, his eyes indicating that he was thinking. "I was certain it was you." He shook his head. "No matter. He wanted you more. That's the end of it. Screw what the gods said. He's chosen his path for happiness."

"Unless we run into her."

"Arg! Corliss, help me get this woman to understand!"

Corliss' eyes narrowed. "Oh, don't you start thinking he'll leave. We've all made it clear how dragons work." His mouth bent to one side. "Like it or not, you're stuck with him, Eira. It's a lifetime commitment."

"Lifetime." My gaze faltered and I grunted. "We'll see."

"Eira, don't let one wrong corrupt that. I mean it when I say it's permanent."

An image of my mother flashed through my mind. One of her standing alone, staring out at the sky. Wondering when promises would be kept.

"Eira..."

"Good night, Corliss." I lay back down and closed my eyes, slowing my breathing. Sleep didn't come, but I continued the act to keep Corliss quiet.

Raikidan stirred. He sucked in a deep breath and then reached out and grazed my shoulder with the back of his fingers. His touch retracted and he bolted upright when he noticed Corliss' presence. "What are you doing here?"

"Standing watch," Corliss said.

"I didn't ask you to."

"I know, but I still want to."

Silence filled the air until Raikidan spoke. "Why, when I didn't for you?"

"Because I understand why you've been upset with me and can't blame you since it's my fault it got to that point. I should have been more up front with you, even if I wasn't sure how things would go. You deserved that much."

"So you want my forgiveness?"

"Only if you want to give it."

"Will you give me some for overreacting?"

Corliss was quiet for a few seconds, as if shocked by Raikidan's words. "I don't think I've ever heard you admit something like that. Eira has really had an effect on you."

"Shut up. You going to accept it or not?"

"You told me to shut up." Raikidan snorted and Corliss chuckled. "Yes, I forgive you. We'll work on making things better now."

"Deal. Now go sleep."

"Before I do, I want to talk to you about Eira."

"What about her?" He almost sounded alarmed.

"She woke up earlier and said something that doesn't make sense. Give me an honest answer. Is she your destined mate?"

Raikidan was quiet for a moment and I listened. "I don't know."

"Oh, in Zion's name—what kind of lame-ass answer is that?"

"What do you want me to tell you?" Raikidan growled. "Her name doesn't match, but everything else does. I can't explain it. So I chose her. I want her, Corliss, and that's all that matters."

"Did you explain to her how this is a lifetime commitment? And I don't mean just say it is."

Raikidan was quiet for a moment. "No. I didn't think it was needed. Why are you asking?"

I could swear I heard Corliss smack his face into his hands. "Why are you such an idiot? No wonder she thinks you may leave her."

"W–what?"

"It's exactly what I said. Because she knows you *picked* her over your destined mate, she's convinced there's a possibility you'll run into this other female one day—and you'll realize you made some sort of mistake. I don't know what's more painful, hearing her say the words, or how accepting she was of it."

The bed shifted. "I wasn't going to lie and say she was my destined mate. That'd be the worst thing I could do."

"You need to tell her everything, cousin. What the mate bond is. What choosing her means. Hell, even telling her the name."

A low growl came from Raikidan. "I will not."

It took a moment for Corliss to respond. I didn't blame him. That response surprised me too. "You *need* to, Raikidan."

"The name doesn't matter."

"Yes, it does."

"I want Eira. The name doesn't matter."

His refusal to answer more than irritated me. Why was it such a big deal to say the name?

"Eira, don't overreact."

I opened my eyes and rolled over. "What's her name, Raikidan?"

Raikidan stared at me. "You're not asleep…"

"I never went back to sleep like Corliss thought."

Corliss sucked in a tight breath. "I'll leave you two to talk."

The fire escape creaked and I spoke to Raikidan again. "What is her name?"

He hesitated. "Her name doesn't matter."

I sat up. "It does to me."

Raikidan's eyes softened, but he didn't speak. I sighed and pulled the covers off to hop out of bed. "So you do want her. Good to know."

"Wow. Way to jump to conclusions."

Raikidan stopped me. "I never said that. That's not how it is."

I gave him a sidelong glance. "And how is it supposed to be, then? Why not tell me, other than to keep me in the dark if she ever does show up?"

He looked taken aback and offended by the accusation. "This is my burden to bear, Eira, not yours. It's one I accepted for choosing you. I chose you because I want you. I claimed you because that's all I want. She will never matter. It will only ever be you until I die."

I scooted to the edge of the bed and he looped his arm around me. "You have secrets, too."

I grunted. "I do. And I know where this is going. You want to barter my secrets for yours."

His grip loosened a bit. "You make this sound devious. I was going to say compromise. Lay everything out so there aren't any more secrets. For instance, you lied about being grekeleon."

Tightness formed in my shoulders.

"You can't tell me I'm wrong. The change you underwent last night isn't one of a grekeleon, or even a half-grekeleon. They have flat scaled skin like snakes, not plated scales."

"I want to tell you. I thought about it earlier, and the discomfort made me realize I still need to work on that. But now I'm not so sure I want to."

"Wow, childish much?"

"I don't understand why you're acting like this."

"Then you've really not been paying attention to how these secrets affect me." I pulled myself free climbed off the bed. "I doubt the thought of speaking this destined mate's name aloud will cause you so much pain you want to vomit."

"Eira, where are you going?" Raikidan asked as I headed into my closet. "Come back and talk this out with me."

"I'm going for a walk. I need to calm down." I threw on some clothes and fixed up my hair to look decent. As I headed for the door, I caught a glimpse of Corliss standing out on the fire escape, but he didn't come in.

"Eira, please don't walk away from me. We can work this out now."

"Raikidan," Corliss said. "Know when to pick your battles."

Raikidan growled. "Do not get involved."

"Heed my counsel, cousin. Do not stop her."

I left my room only to find Seda slipping on a jacket, the TV on, and our half-wogron friend half watching it. From the looks of it, she was having a small telepathic conversation with Seda. Ryoko looked at me with a grin. "Hey there, screamer."

Her expression dropped immediately when she noticed my state. "What's wrong?"

"I'm going for a walk to clear my head."

"You're welcome to join me," Seda said. "I also need a walk to clear my head. I won't pry unless you want to talk about it."

Ryoko's eyes flicked between us before focusing on Seda. "Wait, you just said you were going for a walk and it wasn't a big deal. Trouble in paradise is far from not a big deal. Let me get dressed and I'll join you. Maybe I can help."

I held up my hands. "Don't worry about it, Ryoko. I can't speak for Seda, but I just need to clear my head."

Seda nodded. "Same."

Ryoko turned off the TV. "No, you both need some good old fashion girl time to vent and figure things out. Give me two shakes and I'll be ready. We can walk to Café Lanada a few blocks down. They're one of the few cafés open at this hour."

I pursed my lips and nodded. There was no changing our friend's mind. While we waited, Mana poked her head out of hers and Corliss' room.

"You looking for Corliss?" I asked.

She nodded. "He said he'd be back at sunup but since you're out here, I assumed he'd be back already."

I jerked my head toward my room. "He's in there with Raikidan. You're welcome to go in."

She tilted her head and listened for a moment, picking up the Draconic words spoken beyond the door. "No, I think it's best I not. Can I come with you?"

Seda smiled. "I don't see why not."

Mana's eye lit up and she pulled herself into her room to change into some new clothes. When everyone was ready, the four of us headed out into the night down the street. No one spoke. Mana was too caught up in gazing around; Seda and I each lost in our own thoughts; and Ryoko studying us.

I kept running my situation through my head. I went back and forth between him just not being fair and me realizing how much I was overreacting. I knew I was. I knew his request for no secrets was a fair one. And at the same time, I couldn't get over his adamance for keeping this name a secret. Why keep me in the dark? We were supposed to be partners, right?

"You are," the voice said. *"And that's why he wants all secrets gone."*

"Right—so he can use them for leverage."

"No. Stop. Take a deep breath and don't twist my words."

I did as she said and the tenseness in my body lessened, though it came right back as my mind jumped back into the same loop. Why couldn't I know? Why couldn't I at least know when she showed up and threatened what we were building together?

The voice sighed. *"Stop right there. He isn't going to pick her. He's not keeping this from you because he wants to pull a fast one over you."*

I pinched my nose and took another deep breath. This time, it didn't help, and the voice exhaled hard again. This cycle was hard for me to break. And even she wasn't sure how to stop it at this rate. Unfortunately, I couldn't seem to let it go. Right now that just wasn't an option.

The four of us arrived at Café Lanada and placed an order with the barista before finding a table in a far corner. I really didn't want to talk about my relationship issues, but the way Ryoko stared at Seda and me expectantly, I knew there was no getting out of it.

To my surprise, I wasn't her first target. "Let's start off with talking about your issue, Seda. It takes a lot to get you worked up, so what's got your goat?"

Seda chuckled. "You and your expressions today. It's nothing really to worry about. Argus is spending his nights inventing and not coming to bed when he promises to. I'm just overreacting."

I regarded her for a moment. "You're not the type to overreact."

Ryoko pointed at Seda, "Yeah—details, missy!"

Just then, the barista called out our number, and Seda used it as an excuse to leave the table. Ryoko and I exchanged worried glances. Seda had always been that person you could confide anything in and she'd help in any way possible. She also knew that it would be reciprocated if she needed help. So if she didn't want to talk about her problem, something was up.

Seda returned with a tray and used her psychic abilities to hand out the drinks and snacks. She sat down. With her hands wrapped around her café latte mug, she spoke in a low tone, "He's a smart man and loves his inventions. I accept that with gusto. With him working hard at the shop and me dealing with the Council and trying to balance my mandatory meditation, nights are the only time we have together right now."

She took a sip of her hot drink. "So for him to spend so much time in his workshop to the point he's falling asleep in there or not going to bed until I'm rising for a new day, I… feel alone. I've tried to talk it out with him, but nothing changes. I'm just not sure what to do anymore besides move my things back to my old room with Genesis, or even set up my own room."

Ryoko's ears drooped. "Fudgesticks, that's not good."

I couldn't help but chuckle. "And now we have euphemisms from her. What will she think of next?"

Ryoko glowered at me, but Seda laughed. "Thank you, I needed that."

"Have you tried to involve yourself in the work he does?" Mana asked.

Seda sipped her drink and nodded. "When I can and I'm not exhausted from my long day. I'm also nowhere near as smart at that man—"

"Don't sell yourself short!" Ryoko said. The ironic wording got me to snort just before drinking my hot cocoa. She narrowed her eyes at me before focusing on Seda. "You are really smart."

Seda smiled. "I'm not disagreeing with you. I'm just not Argus smart. I read his notes or listen to him speak passionately about his projects and it goes right over my head."

"To be fair, the rest of us are in that same boat," I said.

"Yes, well, it makes it hard to get into what he does, or prove that I do like hearing him project his enthusiasm."

My brow rose. "He questions that?"

She nodded, a frown on her lips. "Argus thinks he's bothering me and I can't convince him otherwise."

I set my mug down on the table. "How do your conversations go with him when you bring up your concerns?"

She chewed her bottom lip. "Either he promises to do better or tries to explain why a part of the project took longer than he expected. The latter I can understand, but neither answer fixes the issue."

I frowned. Psychics may wear a face covering, obscuring a good portion of their expressions, but that didn't hide the other body language. She felt neglected. *I know how that feels…*

"He's not neglecting you. And you know that."

Ryoko pursed her lips. "Then maybe putting some space between you would be good for you. I mean, it's not ideal, but it could give you both time to think about all of this without pressure from each other."

Seda's lips twisted, showing the turmoil of emotions raging inside her. "I had just hoped it wouldn't come to that…"

"Sometimes time apart is how we figure out what's best for us," Ryoko said. She then looked at me, allowing Seda to think. "Now, about your issue."

My gaze fell to my cup. "There's no need for us to talk about it. I'm just overreacting and need to sort out my head."

Ryoko tilted her head down and narrowed her eyes, but it was Mana who spoke. "I've seen a lot of inter-species relationships and they are by far the most complex due to the differences of culture and communication. Even a coupling as common as elves and humans isn't straightforward."

Ryoko snorted. "No relationship is straightforward."

All of us couldn't help but laugh.

I calmed down and sucked in a breath through my teeth. "All right, I'll tell you what's up. Remember when we had that chat in the bath about dragons having that voice gift?"

They nodded, though Mana's brow creased with a bit of concern.

"Well, Raikidan has one, but it's not me."

The three of them stayed quiet—Ryoko surprised, Mana confused, and Seda... impossible to read.

"I knew he was choosing me over her, but... Raikidan won't tell me her name. He's insisting I don't need to know, but it feels like he's keeping it from me for a big reason. I won't even know if she shows up and will be blindsided when he realizes she's better."

Mana opened her mouth to speak but I continued, unable to stop myself from spewing out my inner turmoil.

"On top of that, he wants to know all my secrets—like my halfling origin. Heck, I haven't even told him my given first name—the one I never use for personal reasons." The others remained silent as I took a deep breath. My voice lowered. "Part of me wants to tell him, but I have so many issues talking about it with others. He even knows this, and yet chooses to ignore it."

My hands clutched around my mug. "It's feeling like I walked into one giant lie... again." I shook my head.

Everyone gazed at me with sympathy. Ryoko reached out and grabbed my hand.

I took another deep breath and exhaled slowly. "I know I'm over-reacting. I know Raikidan has no malicious intent behind it and just wants there to be no secrets. I know there's got to be a better reason why he's not telling me this name—at least beyond 'it's my burden to bear' heroic bullshit."

Ryoko giggled a bit when I altered my voice to mimic his words, but quieted quickly. I didn't have anything else to say, staring into my half-consumed mug. I was to blame in this. I was acting like a spoiled child.

"No, don't do that! Don't start throwing blame on yourself. Yes, you're over-reacting, but that doesn't mean you can start playing blame games like this."

Mana's eyes softened. "Eira, I think you're missing something important here."

My brow ticked up. "What do you mean?"

"You said you felt like he was lying so that if he wanted to leave later, he could. But that's not possible for us. We dragons mean it when we mate for life. The very thought of breaking that commitment gives us physical pain. It's an effect of the bond we've been bestowed. Yes, he picked you instead of the mate the gods chose for him, but that doesn't matter anymore. Halfling, human, it doesn't matter to us dragons. You're not dragon. He was okay with this fact when he chose you, and there's no going back for him on that choice. And because he picked you, not knowing your non-human side, if he were to find out later, his stance won't ever change."

She tapped her lips with her fingers. "What I don't quite get is this 'it's my burden to bear' bit you quoted from him." She paused and then her eyes widened. "Wait, I do. Oh, no. His parents didn't tell him."

The rest of us looked at each other, confused. I spoke. "Tell him what?"

She shook her head. "When our mate bond is made, the voice goes away. Slowly, but it does leave."

My eyebrow rose. "How long does it take?"

"About a year. Hence the reason for… oh, what's the word you humans call it… our way is an extended form of it."

Ryoko snickered. "Honeymoon." She then threw her hands up in the air with excitement. "Meaning Eira's hitched!"

My cheeks burned hot and I hid my face in my hand as the other two laughed.

"Oh wait, that sucks. I wanted to plan the wedding."

I tilted my head and narrowed an eye at her. "No weddings."

She threw her hands out. "But it'd be great! There'd be a beautiful ceremony. And lots of flowers. And amazing food, especially the cake. You'd look so gorgeous in a wedding dress."

Seda's lips spread into a grin. "She'd wear her shaman attire, actually."

Ryoko gasped. "You saw it? Even after all this?"

"It's a possible event in some timelines."

Ryoko squealed.

Mana cleared her throat and continued. "Like I was saying before we were sidetracked, this isn't an issue. Destined or chosen, the bond still exists between you two, and the voice will go away."

"You're confident?" I said.

She nodded. "I know a male who did this with another dragon. He found someone he liked far better than the voice. His voice was mean and nasty, and not what he wanted. His mate is exactly what he hoped for and they're happy. Their bond is as strong as any mated pair and the voice left at the same rate as any other mated male."

My eyes lowered to my cooling mug. "So, I really am overreacting."

She tossed her head back and forth. "Yes and no. He could have handled this a lot better, even with him not knowing about the fading voice bit. He's a handsome male, but he's not the brightest."

Ryoko snickered. "It's a perk of being him."

I laughed despite myself. She wasn't wrong.

Mana glanced at Seda. "There's one last thing about this situation that I hope you may be able to confirm. I also suspect Raikidan has similar concerns as Eira on the possibility of abandonment. I don't know if humans are bound to the same sensations with the mate bond as we dragons. He may be afraid that if Eira knows this female's name, she'll force him to go after her if they ever meet or she catches wind of her presence at some point."

Seda nodded. "While I've attempted to not glimpse his mind, trying to allow the two some privacy, I've seen enough. Raikidan is about as tactful and communicatively inclined as a steel door—"

"So, a female version of Laz," Ryoko snarked.

The four of us laughed. I couldn't say she was wrong on that claim.

Seda calmed herself. "Yes. Makes them perfect for each other."

Her face softened and her lips spread into a friendly smile. "Raikidan's feelings for you, Laz, are genuine. All he cares about is your happiness, and he knows this voice upsets you. Its existence brings on a great deal of anxiety for him. He wishes every time it speaks, it was you instead. He doesn't want to cause you any grief, but he's also afraid if you know, you'll try to pull away for her to take your place. He doesn't want that."

I rested my cheek on the palm of my hand and stirred my lukewarm cocoa, thinking over her words.

Ryoko bounced a little in her seat. "Say it. Say it!"

"He loves you."

Ryoko squealed with delight. I continued to stir my liquid chocolate, my lips turned down into a frown. The talk had started to make me feel better until that.

Noticing my lack of joy, Ryoko's ears drooped again. "Laz…"

Mana frowned. "I don't understand this reaction."

"It's complicated," I muttered.

She let out a terse sigh. "Well, we can't help you unless you have the backbone to tell us."

I stopped stirring and stared at her; Seda and Ryoko also looked at her with surprise.

Mana's shoulders slouched and her gaze fell to the table. "Sorry. I shouldn't have been so rude."

I smirked. "Don't be sorry. Such a response from you is refreshing."

I then took a deep breath. "The phrase carries a lot of anger with me. It stems from my father, who is the reason I'm a halfling. He made a lot of false promises that ultimately killed my mother. Prior to her death, I tried to give someone a chance to prove to me such a phrase isn't empty, but it's also the reason he's dead."

I stared at my mug. "I have come to associate the phrase with pain and failure. It's why, up until recently, I had a habit of blaming my halfling side for my problems and men for being liars. It wasn't right. There are always a few bad apples in a bunch, so I've been trying to curb that opinion, but that change doesn't happen overnight."

Her brow creased and her eyes softened. I thought I could also see moisture welling up in her eyes. "That's awful! And completely unfair to you."

I gave her a half smile. "Life can't be fair to everyone."

She shook her head. "I don't care! You deserve to be happy. All of you do."

My half-smile spread into a full one. Her passion was endearing.

Mana reached out and grabbed my hand. "And you. You need to tell Raikidan. I know you said it was hard, but he will accept what you tell him. I know it."

She was right. I really did need to tell him. I just needed to figure out how without hurting myself.

"Don't allow fear get in your way," the voice said.

Seda turned her face to me. "What was that?"

Ryoko cocked her brow. "What was what?"

Oh shit.

Seda bit her lips. "I didn't mean to say that out loud. Sorry."

Ryoko's eyes flicked between the two of us. "Yeah, well you did, so spill the beans."

I kept my lips closed. This was not something I wanted to talk to them about. Seda had never asked about the voice before, so I suspected she didn't know about its presence, and I preferred to keep it that way. I didn't want everyone thinking I was crazy.

"It's okay, you can tell them."

"How can I when I don't even know what you are?"

"The thing is… you do know."

"What?"

Ryoko waved her hand. "Hello? Anyone going to clue us in?"

Mana turned to her. "I don't know about you, Ryoko, but I'm noticing a lot of hesitation. It may not be good for you to keep asking."

"We're friends here." Ryoko crossed her arms. "And we should be able to talk to each other about things."

I worked my jaw. "All right, but you need to promise you won't laugh or call me names."

Ryoko pulled back and her eyes widened, offended by the call-out, but then grew serious and nodded.

I took a deep, hesitant breath. "What Seda is asking about is a voice that speaks to me."

My three friends stared at me.

"I don't know what it is, but it's there… chatting my ears off."

"I do not!"

Seda tilted her head. "How long have you know about this voice?"

"Most of my life," I admitted. "My first experience with it was when Zarda forced me into that gladiatorial massacre. She had my back, and while her approach to some situations have been… less than stellar, she's proven to be on my side."

"That was in the past. I behave far better now."

"Except for your comment when I woke up."

"That was supposed to be a joke. Though… it's still a viable option."

Seda regarded me for a moment. "You said she, as if it's a separate entity from you."

I nodded. "I've determined as much in the past few months, which is as long as she's been so much more active. Before then, she would only pop in occasionally."

Seda rested her elbows on the table and leaned forward. "This is my first time hearing it, and while you're good at keeping your thoughts hidden, you're not perfect or impervious to the psychic ability. This means I should have been able to hear every now and then. If it's a separate entity from your mind, this has to be strong to keep itself hidden."

She held out her hand. "Do you mind if I probe?"

While I didn't like psychic probes, this might prove useful to unlocking answers. I nodded to show my consent.

Seda reached across the table and touched my temple with her fingers.

"Hello, Seda," the voice greeted. *"It's a pleasure to finally be able to communicate with you now that this—"*

Seda's lips tightened into a line and I knew she was about as confused as me about the sudden stop.

"Can you still not tell me the reason?" I asked it.

"No." The voice growled. *"I thought I was close to a breakthrough. This is so frustrating!"*

Seda snickered. "She sounds like Ryoko."

"She acts like her sometimes, too. The two would get along swimmingly."

Ryoko gasped. "I want to talk to her then!"

Seda and I snickered, and the voice did, too.

"Well it's a pleasure to communicate with you as well," Seda said to the voice. *"Based on how Laz responded to your conversation interruption, I guess there are things you cannot—"*

Before she could finish, out of nowhere, several female voices spoke at once—all trying to say hello or fighting over who should be have the next turn to speak. Seda pulled away and held her head, though she wasn't the only one.

I held onto my head as it pulsed with pain. "What the hell was that?"

"I think I counted fifteen voices just then." She moaned in a bit of pain. "That doesn't include the one we were trying to communicate with."

Fifteen? Why did that number feel significant? I cringed as my head throbbed. *If only my head didn't hurt so bad.* I'd be able to bring up the answer so easily.

An image of the temple door flashed through my mind. *Wait. Fifteen women...*

Ryoko giggled. "See, Laz, you do have a multiple personality disorder."

Seda reached over and flicked Ryoko in the forehead. "Don't make light of a mental disorder like that."

Ryoko rubbed her forehead and grumbled. "Well how else are you supposed to interpret hearing a total of sixteen voices in her head?"

Seda took a calm breath. "What Eira is experiencing is far different. Dissociative identity disorder, the proper way of calling it, is a mental disorder characterized by at least two distinct and relatively enduring identities or dissociated personality states that alternately show in a person's behavior, accompanied by memory impairment for important information not explained by ordinary forgetfulness."

She clasped her hands together. "Eira shares none of these characteristics. Each voice had a distinct vocal pitch and personality characteristic that does not come with an identity Laz projects."

Ryoko and I glanced at each other. I grinned. "Well then, *Doctor*, how would you explain all this?"

Seda's face reddened and she ducked her head. "Sorry about that. The ability to see into minds has given me a slight obsession. In my free time, I do a lot of reading on different studies published about the psyche."

Ryoko smiled. "Have you thought about becoming a psychologist?"

Seda took pause for a moment. "Well, no, but now that you mentioned it…"

I sipped my cooled-off drink. "I think you should. Between your personality and your ability, you'd be good at it."

Ryoko held up a finger. "Don't forget her intelligence."

Seda chuckled. "Well, I'll think about it more. Laz, would you mind if we did more sessions like what we had? To learn more about the situation."

"I'd be happy to work with you on this." If anyone could help me with these mind games, it was her. I was so close now, I knew it. That last situation was something I needed. Once Raikidan and I patched things up and worked on this issue, then maybe we could examine the temple again.

Ryoko giggled. "After the honeymoon."

My face reddened, but before I could spit out a retort, I noticed how quiet Mana had been. The others realized this, too, and looked at her. Mana, brow twisted with thought, jumped when she noticed the attention.

"You okay?" I asked.

"Yeah, just thinking." Her gaze went to Ryoko. "Do you have any issues you want help with?"

Ryoko's brow furrowed while I regarded Mana. *What's up with her?*

"Um, no, Rylan and I are fine as far as I know. Sure, we've had our share of disgruntled communication, but we got through it."

Mana cocked her head. "Then how come you were watching TV in the middle of the night?"

Ryoko smiled sheepishly. "I've been having trouble sleeping. I try to curb it by reading until I'm tired enough to sleep, and if that doesn't work, I watch TV."

I leaned on the table, lacing my fingers together. "Does Rylan know about this?"

She nodded. "Yeah, but he doesn't know how to help… except offer sex, as if it'll fix anything."

We roared with laughter, gaining glaring looks from the few employees and other customers in the building.

I shook my head. "Such a typical male response."

"To be fair, it's not a wrong assumption," Seda said. "It does fix a lot, just not as much as many would like."

I smirked, my eyes narrowing with mischievous intent as I glanced her way. "Maybe that's the trick you're missing with Argus."

Seda looked at me, lips tight, and then laughed. "Maybe you're right."

Ryoko rolled her eyes. "Like that would work for him. If he's anything like Rylan, when he's focused on something, there's no distracting him, even with something far more fun."

Seda wagged her finger at Ryoko. "You underestimate my power. As a psychic, I can play with all the little pleasure centers in his brain. He can resist, but not even he's capable of ignoring it in the long run. And, if I was a horrible girlfriend, which I'm not, I could turn it all off so he can't enjoying his time creating."

Ryoko's eyes crinkled as she laughed. "That's evil and amazing all at once."

She then turned to Mana. "How about you? Do you have an issues you want help with?"

Mana shrugged. "Corliss and I don't have these types of issues. Communication issues are a problem every now and then, but that's normal for anyone."

She blew out a breath. "Well, I guess there's one thing. There's him treating me like I'm helpless and in need of coddling. That's always been an issue for us."

The three of us exchanged glances. We all had seen this going on, and we all knew the solution. Ryoko decided to be the one to bring it up. "You need to stop being so passive-aggressive about it."

Mana tilted her head as Ryoko continued. "We all see this between you two. Sure, he could chill out more on his own, but you have to stand up for yourself. You're always beating around the bush, making comparisons to the situation, or feeding into the behavior by not being straightforward." She set her hands down on the table. "If you want something, say so. If you don't want something, do the same. Lay down some ground rules. He can be protective, just not smothering."

Mana's brow furrowed with concern. "I… just don't want to upset him. He's good to me, just a little…"

"Pedantic," I said, before chuckling. "You're overthinking this. You don't have to be aggressive, just stand your ground and be assertive. Show him you can hold your own, but want him there to help because you want him to." A sly grin spread across my lips. "Human or dragon, assertiveness will get you far."

She cocked her head. "Huh?"

Her innocence amused me. "It's okay to be a submissive type; Corliss definitely likes that. But even a male like him will find appeal in assertive tendencies now and then."

Mana's brow furrowed in thought. "That's going to be hard for me. My sister was the assertive one. She didn't put up with our father's antics and left home first."

Seda fanned out her fingers on the table. "But you still left. Even if your sister did it first, you were still capable of the same action. And there's no shame in that."

Mana nodded. "Okay, I'll try. I don't know how, but I will."

Seda smiled. "I'll help you when I can, how's that?"

Mana smiled wide and nodded again.

With everyone relatively satisfied with each talk and the advice they were given, we decided it was time to head home.

As we headed down the sidewalk, my mind wandered back to my issue. How was I going to go about this? I wasn't sure I could stomach the truth right now, as much as I wanted to.

And of course, I couldn't shake that nagging feeling this female dragon would be a better partner for him. But I was also a selfish person. I had claim to him. If she came around, she couldn't have him, no matter how much she tried.

"Dead body is always an option."

"Stop."

"Laz," Seda messaged. *"I'd like to inquire about something. It wasn't for the others to hear, so I wanted to wait until now."*

"Okay, what's up?"

"Does some of your issue stem from the prophecy I told you? You've used it to guide many of your actions, and honestly, go about your life in the wrong way, if I may be so bold."

Was it? I hadn't thought of it as of late. *"I don't think so. It hasn't been on my mind lately. Though now that I think about it—"*

"Don't think about it."

"Huh?"

She sighed. *"I shouldn't have told you about it. I'd done so to gain your trust back then, but I hadn't looked into its meaning before revealing it. Nor had I explained how prophecies work, many of them never coming true."*

"I asked you this before and you said you couldn't answer, but I'm going to ask again just in case because maybe I'm dumb, or even overthinking its complexity. What does 'your heart will betray you' even mean?"

She chuckled. *"What you think it does, but expanded. It means you will sacrifice everything, even your life, for any attachment you have. Not just one person, like you once always thought, but for all those you care about."*

I took this in. *"So it really wasn't anything new. It followed what I told others when it came to those I cared about."*

"Yes."

"And it's not guaranteed to come true?" My mind went to Raisu. He'd mentioned fate was ever-changing. Or something like that.

"That's right. Depending on choices we make, the prophecy can be null."

"It's okay to trust him," the voice said. *"Let go of your fears. They're part of what is hurting you the most."*

"What she said."

I chewed on my lip as I thought this over. I'd always held back because of this prophecy. I didn't want to end up like my mother. It made a lot of sense, if this fear caused the physical pain I experienced. Not many wanted a halfling. And even less would want a damaged one like me.

"Stop," the voice said.

But Raikidan chose me even knowing this. And I couldn't expect he'd do the same as my father. To blame an entire race or gender because of one or two individuals was wrong of me, I knew that. *So for me to expect the worst from him over this voice isn't right either.*

"Finally!" the voice shouted. *"I thought you'd never come to your senses."*

"Shut up."

"Yes, I can see why you think Ryoko and she would get along," Seda said. *"I can't wait to meet her."*

Seda and I looked at each other before I spoke to the voice. *"What?"*

My question, unsurprisingly, was met with silence.

"I shouldn't tell you this, but I don't care," Seda said. *"While we were at the café, I searched into your future timeline, beyond the wedding bit."*

I snorted but let her continue.

"It's a branching mess, like most, but one thing that most of them had was you happy with someone."

"Someone?"

She chuckled. *"That someone being Raikidan. I've never seen you as happy as you are in these threads of time. Just keep that in mind as you figure things out."*

The rest of the walk home was uneventful. My mind went to the thoughts of telling Raikidan the truth. Fear and pain welled up each time I thought about going ahead with it, and it made things difficult.

"Try to remember, dear, there's nothing wrong with what you are," the voice said. *"You're so important. You know this. Your mother told you much. But there is also so much more you don't know. I wish I could tell you more. You deserve to know. You need to know."*

We made it to the house several steps before I could inquire with her. Single file, the four of us entered the building to find the living room occupied by several unexpected bodies. Rylan lounged on the couch, and Argus and Corliss stood nearby. All three watched Raikidan pace a hole in the floor.

The others acknowledged our presence, looking our way, but it took

Raikidan a few moments longer to notice. He stopped and made eye contact with me, but before anything more could be done or said, Argus grabbed Seda by the hand and dragged her down the hall. His posture wasn't aggressive, so no one found reason to think she'd need help. Seda openly questioned Argus about his behavior, but he insisted they'd talk in private.

Rylan looked to us when the two disappeared from sight. "Well, that was rude of him. Welcome home, ladies. Hope your walk was pleasant."

Ryoko smiled at him. "It was. Why are you up?"

"I came to check on you and found out from Corliss you went out for a bit. I then decided to watch Raikidan pace a hole into the floor while I waited for you to return."

"You could have gone back to bed."

He shrugged and got up from his spot, his hand out to her as he moved around the couch. "Didn't want to. Now I do."

Before she could accept his invitation, Mana skipped over to Corliss and grabbed his hand. "You're coming to bed, too."

"Oh, okay." He followed her down the hall without a fuss.

Ryoko and I glanced at each other with big grins. We both saw the look in his eye. Mana pulled off cute and assertive well, and Corliss couldn't resist the charm. Rylan appeared confused by our exchange, but brushed it off and invited Ryoko to head to bed with him. She eagerly complied. This left Raikidan and me.

He hadn't taken his eyes off me for a moment. I shrugged off my jacket and headed for my room. Raikidan closed the distance and wrapped his arms around my waist, pressing his face into my hair and inhaling deeply. "You came back."

I snickered as he continued to take in my scent. "Well, yeah. I just went for a walk to clear my head."

"I know, but…" He squeezed me and then hauled me into his arms, carrying me the rest of the way and laying me down on the bed. He lay down next to me and held me close. "You were so angry you weren't yelling. I thought I drove you away because I was being stubborn. I'm—"

"I'm sorry," I said.

He pulled away just enough to look down at me. "What?"

"I'm sorry," I repeated. "I overreacted—"

"You reacted just as you should have. I shouldn't have tried to keep this from you. I should have realized you'd see it the way you did because I didn't explain all the details." He rested his forehead on mine. "I made an assumption and paid a price for it."

"That still doesn't excuse my behavior. And you were right. I have my own secrets that aren't out on the table. They should be, and I want them to be, but I'm fighting with it. And because I'm struggling, I can't expect you to let go of everything, either." I pulled away. "I don't want to know her name."

His brow furrowed. "I don't understand."

"Uh, me either!"

I took a deep breath. "Let me amend that. I don't want to know her name right now. I don't want to know until I'm able to tell you my secrets, too. It'd be unfair of me to demand anything from you if I don't give anything in return."

The back of Raikidan's hand stroked my cheek. "How long do you think that'll take?"

"One week. That's all I'm giving myself."

He leaned in close. "And what if I come up with another guess?"

I poked him in the nose. "No left-field guessing. You need to be absolutely sure."

"But I can try to figure it out."

"We can make it a fun little race."

Raikidan rested his forehead on mine again, his hot breath hitting my lips. "And what does the winner get?"

"Whatever they want." I grinned. "Deal?"

"Anything?"

"Within reason."

His lips brushed mine. "I like the sound of that." He kissed me lightly. "I promise you, Eira, I'm not going anywhere. You won't lose me like you lost Tannek."

My eyes widened. "How do you know about him?"

"I heard enough things here and there, where I decided to talk to Azriel. He told me a lot about what happened between the two of you. And how he died."

My gaze lowered. "I don't want to talk about that…"

"I understand. Losing someone you love is the worst pain imaginable, and you've lost so much in the worst ways. You've coped as best as you could alone, but you don't have to anymore." He rested his head against mine again. "I'm here. I'll prove it to you every day if I have to. I didn't have to choose you. I could have chosen her, but I didn't. I want you more."

He grinned. "Down to every last overreacting freak-out. The gods can't possibly know me if they think anyone but you is best for me."

I laced my fingers with his. "You mean it?"

Raikidan tightened his grip and leaned in to nip my neck—my pulse quickened. "We're bonded. Even if you can't feel the power of it, I do. It strengthens every moment I'm with you."

I gazed up at him. "What does it feel like?"

His brow creased. "Hmm… it feels like a buzzing or humming of energy between us."

I frowned. "I don't feel that."

His hand slid over my shoulder and down my side to the hem of my shirt. "Maybe these clothes are just in the way."

I chuckled. "You don't waste any time, do you?"

"Now that we've cleared things up, I don't want to waste any more of this week I have of you to myself. And who knows, maybe you will feel the bond if we keep trying."

I grinned against his lips and then pushed him on his back, using the momentum to straddle him. Raikidan relaxed under me, placing one hand under his head and the other on my hip. He really enjoyed this. It gave me an idea.

I leaned forward, gliding my hands against his muscular chest. "Wait here, I'll be right back."

He tried to stop me, but I managed to slip away and into my closet. "Eira, come back. I can help with those clothes."

"It's a surprise. You can wait two minutes. It won't kill you."

He huffed, but I didn't hear him climb off the bed, so at least he was complying.

"Do you think you can handle that one-week timeline you gave yourself?" the voice asked.

"I'm going to have to. There's no negotiating these terms. Our relationship is going to crumble if I don't, and I don't want that."

"And you're not going to act all weird on him for keeping the name quiet? Though if you ask me, I'm still not convinced it's not you."

"You've said that before once. Why do you think that?"

"I'm not able to put it into direct words. But you meeting him was destiny. You falling in love with him is no mistake. You being halfling, I believe, is the missing link between this."

"You think my halfling name is what he hears?"

"I do, Laz. Why else would he tell Corliss everything but the name matches up?"

"We could be similar individuals."

"I'm not convinced."

"You know, I'm surprised you're wearing pants," I called out to Raikidan as I sifted through a small collection of nightclothes on hangers.

"Except, I'm not."

I laughed. Of course he'd drop them that quickly. "I meant before."

"Yeah, well, Corliss made me, if I was going to leave the room."

"At least one of you has some decency," I muttered under my breath.

"What was that?"

"Nothing!"

He grunted and I chuckled. My searching ceased when I came to the red and black lace babydoll set Raikidan had picked out for me several months ago. *There you are.*

I peeled my clothes off and took the nightgown off the hanger, slipping it over my head. I pulled on the matching panties and then looked myself over in a mirror. My cheeks tinted several shades at the sight of myself. The babydoll, while made to be loose-fitting, still fit every curve of my frame, accentuating them just right. *He's got good taste, I'll give him that.*

"Hey, you done yet?" Raikidan called out. "I know you want this to be a surprise, but I'm about ready to come in there and grab you so I can throw you back onto this bed."

I shook my head. "You need to learn how to be patient."

His eyes bugged out when I emerged from the closet and leaned against the doorframe, one arm held above my head and my other hand resting on the curve of my hip.

"You like? You picked it out."

Raikidan swallowed hard and struggled to speak.

I grinned. "I'll take that as a yes."

Slowly and with a clear purpose, I pushed away from the frame and sashayed my way over to him, aware of how widely I swayed my hips and how the nightgown clung to my moving form. Raikidan's appreciative gaze took in every inch of me, but he wasn't the only one. I noticed how his muscles tensed and his shoulders pulled back, broadening his frame. The lust in his eyes deepened with each step I took, and his erect member didn't escape my eye, either. *Perfect.*

I liked how confident I felt because of him. I liked being genuinely appreciated, both physically and mentally, and not reeling back from any of it.

I smirked as slipped onto his lap, fanning my fingers over his muscular chest, his hands instinctively cupping my rear. "Regretting being impatient?"

He struggled to form a sentence as my fingers glided across his bare chest. "Maybe a little. Now I'm not sure if I want this to stay on or to rip it off of you."

I leaned closer, my lips hovering over his. "If you rip it, I can't wear it again."

A half-smile slipped up the side of his face. "Would you need it again?"

"After our one week is up, I would." I pushed him onto his back, placing my hands on his chest so it'd be harder for him to sit up. "And really, it's fun to spice it up a bit, don't you think?"

Raikidan rested his hands on my thighs, his eyes showing how interested he was to see this all play out. I grinned and ground my hips into him, his hardness pressing against my barely protected hot spot. He tried to sit up, but I kept him down, eliciting a low, frustrated hiss from him.

"I'm going to show you a new type of fun. Make sure you tell me how much you enjoy it."

CHAPTER 40

ocha peered around the wall the two of us hid behind. Doppelganger and Chameleon were supposed to meet up with us, but they were late, very late. *They're lucky I can't dish out a punishment on them.*

A presence slowly appeared behind me, and I whirled around to find someone sticking halfway out of the wall. Before I could register it to be Chameleon, I threw out a fist and hit him in the face. I immediately retracted my hand as he groaned in pain. Doppelganger laughed at him as he strolled around the corner. "Told you not to do that."

"Yeah, I didn't think she'd flat-out hit me," Chameleon complained.

"Well, you should have," I hissed. "Every time you've done it to me in the past, I've hit you."

Back in the early times of our military days, he had tried those pranks. That was all before Raynn went off the deep end, bringing them all with him.

He chuckled and fully came out of the wall. "Well, I thought your reaction would be different this time, since you're proving how quickly you've actually changed in the last few years."

My brow rose. "Huh?"

Doppelganger chuckled. "Don't go playing dumb. We know you've been knocking boots with the rookie."

My face flushed several shades. "H–how did you find out about that?"

Mocha chuckled and hung her arms over me. "Ryoko has been quite the blabbermouth about it."

I rested my face in my hand. "Perfect."

Doppelganger smirked. "Well, to be fair, a lot of us had bets going on how long it would take to finally happen."

I looked at him incredulously. "Seriously? You guys need to get a hobby."

Someone chuckled. "Picking on you is risky, but a fun hobby."

We looked around, ready for a fight, but saw no one. *Where are you?* A damp, musky smell crossed my nose and I continued to look around. *I know that scent.* Just then, a mist filtered in behind me and two men materialized. *Greeve and Helkin.*

Greeve smirked. "I've made quite a bit of money off you myself. It's fun."

I snorted. "I'm glad I can be a source of amusement."

Helkin patted me on the shoulder. "You love it."

"Yeah, yeah. I guess you're giving us a hand with this?"

He nodded. "Little birdy told us you may want some help with this."

Greeve's eyes twinkled with mischief. "He means his little birdy."

Helkin smacked Greeve in the arm. "Do not."

I snickered, seeing the redness in his cheeks. "Just tell Sendara I said thank you."

I moved away and glanced back at him. "Of course, I expect you to give her a kiss on the cheek for me. She liked it when I gave her little things like those."

Helkin's face turned several shades of red. "Y–yeah, sure."

The group of us chuckled. It wasn't a secret to most that Helkin had a thing for her, but Sendara was quite picky in the men she showed interest in. So he had always kept it to himself, instead of creating any potential issues for the team. Of course, what he didn't know was that Sendara and I had agreed that if I found a good pick for her, that thank-you kiss would be a calling card that they came with my approval. *You're welcome, Helkin.*

Doppelganger rubbed his hands together. "All right, so we have two extras for this."

"Three," Chameleon corrected. "I bumped into someone who had a skill similar to mine. He's off scoping the place out."

"That would be Shyden," Greeve said.

My brow rose at Chameleon. "You knew?"

He shrugged. "Just that guy. I didn't get a chance to say anything because these two clowns showed up."

Greeve and Helkin glowered at him and I chuckled. "Well, regardless, it works out. This means we can get in with two groups."

"What are we doing here?" Greeve asked. "Sendara didn't have any information on the assignment you were doing."

"Several of our operatives were captured last night and moved between facilities," I explained. "Two of them are here. We were going to split up into pairs to extract them, but with you, Helkin, and Shyden, this extraction should go smoother."

"The extra hands may help with setting up a diversion, actually," Doppelganger said. "If we use one group to distract the compound, then we can focus our efforts on the extraction with little resistance."

"Sounds like a solid idea," Greeve said. "Question is, how are we going to distract?"

"Easiest way is to disable some of their systems. That'll send them in a panic," Chameleon said. "My abilities would be good for this. I can get into their security system in a way that they won't suspect foul play."

"Shyden would also be good for that," I said. "As well as you, Helkin."

"Well, if three people are good for the distraction, why don't we have three groups?" Mocha suggested. "Two groups get the targets, and the third does the distraction."

I nodded. "I like the idea."

"Wait, that'd bring the two groups back down to two per extraction group," Doppelganger said. "Doesn't that defeat the purpose?"

"No, I think it just brings the extraction teams to their original size, with a little extra help from the distraction group," Chameleon said.

"He's right. It doesn't matter how many each team has, as long as we get the job done," I said.

"So, which group is getting Eira?" Helkin asked.

"Both can, actually," Doppelganger said.

I tilted my head. "What?"

"I've been practicing a technique that can allow me to create copies of others for a period of time," he said. "I can create up to three copies of them, though the more I make, the less time before they go away."

"What does it look like when that time ends?" Greeve asked.

"Depends. If you're close enough, they'll absorb back into your body. If you're not close enough, they rapidly decompose on the spot. It's not a pretty sight."

I grimaced. "I'll take your word for it."

While momentarily grossed out, I did wonder how his ability affected his spirit. This wasn't the time to look into it, so I stored it away for later consideration.

"But that makes one team uneven again," Mocha said. "Should we just stick to two per extraction team?"

"Copies have special abilities, remember?" Doppelganger said. "It'll make keeping tabs on both groups easy so we don't have to use the communicators as much. Plus, the team with me would have extra use of my ability for extra bodies."

"Well, it's nice to have some meat shields if things go wrong," Greeve said.

"Uh, that's not exactly what it's meant to do," Mocha corrected.

"Yeah. I don't need to feel all that pain, thanks," Doppelganger said.

Greeve's brow furrowed. "Wait, what?"

"My ability comes with a heavy side effect. Since the copies aren't projections, they have nerves and all that fun body stuff that makes them real. What they feel comes back to me when they cease to exist. Too many wounded or dead ones could seriously harm me—or worse."

Greeve frowned. "Well, damn."

"How does that work with virtual simulation?" I asked.

"Luckily, that's where I don't have to worry about it. The system isn't able to simulate a full connection, so pain isn't something I have to worry about coming back to me."

"That's a relief." Just then, his shadow warped and a figure rose up out of it. I smiled at the one-eyed newcomer. "Hey, Shyden."

He nodded. "No time for pleasantries. I've altered some of the communication methods to help clear out some of the guards. We only have a little bit of time."

"Thanks for the heads up. FYI, you'll be part of a group that continues doing that. Helkin, you can fill him in." I looked to Doppelganger. "Let's get your little idea rolling, then."

Doppelganger nodded and placed both his hands on the sides of my face, being sure to press his thumbs on my forehead. "Close your eyes and relax. You may hear some weird sounds and feel some tingling sensations. It's normal. Even happens to me still."

"I've had forced shapeshifting placed on me. I can handle some discomfort."

"Very well."

He took a deep breath as I closed my eyes. Immediately, the warnings he gave me came to fruition. My back, arms, and legs all crawled with various sensations. It was easy to ignore all that. My mind, on the other hand, that was something I had a harder time dealing with.

Audible voices rang through my head. Some I knew from my own memories; others, I didn't. Even names I was sure I'd never heard before. *Verrak. Atria.* Those two names repeated in my head several times. Then, nothing.

Doppelganger's hands left my person and my eyes fluttered open, assuming the process had completed. The shocked look on his face perplexed me. "What?"

He made a motion for me to turn around. Brow arched, I turned and then jumped back when I came face to face with an olive-tan skinned human woman. Her sapphire eyes twinkled with amusement and her slightly wavy black-to-red ombre hair blew in the wind. She wore a completely different outfit from me, made of leather pants, bracers, and knee-high boots, and a tight cloth shirt, though it fit our assignment need with all the daggers she had tucked away in belts. She stood at my height and was gifted with a curvaceous figure. *Lucky her.* It wasn't that my athletic figure was bad, I had just always wanted one more like hers.

The mystery woman waved her fingers as me. "I'm ready to work."

I looked at Doppelganger and he shook his head. "Don't look at me. That's never happened before."

"Sure it hasn't," Chameleon teased. "Don't lie. You wanted to use Eira so you could create the woman of your dreams."

Doppelganger's face tinted a shade of red. "She isn't, and this isn't my doing."

The odd copy of me crossed her arms as she looked him up and down. "Don't worry. You're not too high up on my list either, sweetheart."

Greeve and the rest of us laughed. "Well, it sure does sound like our Eira."

"But why doesn't it look like her?" Doppelganger mumbled to himself, completely ignoring our teasing laughter.

I slapped him in the arm. "It doesn't matter. She's perfect for this assignment, as long as you teach me how this works."

He nodded. "Copies move and think independently from the original, but can be controlled if you take the time to concentrate on them. You can also see through them in the same manner. This allows you to be aware of all of the details of your copy's environment, right down to smells and sounds."

"That's handy," I said. "Let's give this a shot."

I took a deep, concentrated breath and closed my eyes, focusing on my copy's presence. I thought it'd take me a bit to get used to the technique, but I was surprised by how quickly I found myself able to lock onto her essence. A disorienting sensation fell over me as I tried to look through her eyes, and my own eyes snapped open when I felt myself falling over.

Doppelganger caught me. "Whoa, easy. You okay?"

"Yeah, that was weird," I said.

"What happened?"

"I just tried to do what you told me and look through her eyes. I got disoriented and almost fell over."

"That's unusual," he said. "No one else has had that issue."

"Maybe it's a side effect due to the strange copy produced," Mocha suggested. "Could be a bad connection."

"Will that cause an issue?" I asked.

Doppelganger shook his head. "Nah, it'll be fine. You will just have a hard time checking in on the other group."

I nodded. "I can deal with that. How long will she last?"

"About an hour, less if things don't go well and I'm put under too much stress."

"Very well, let's get moving, then. You'll come with me. Mocha, Greeve, and my copy will be part of the second extraction team. Chameleon, Helkin, and Shyden, we're counting on you two to keep the guard distracted long enough to get these two out of here."

"Understood," they said in unison.

I nodded. "Let's move out."

We split off into our groups, Doppelganger close on my heels. We slipped through security, the men too preoccupied with their communication issues, and made it to the target building in record time. I fiddled with a locked door until it *clicked* and we slipped in.

Dimmed lights illuminated the hallway as we crept through. The two of us were extra cautious when we came to any door along the way, and even resorted to hiding in one when a patrol caught our ears. Doppelganger took point at the door, and waved me to follow him when the guards had passed. We turned several corners and took a flight of stairs before running into another obstacle.

A soldier stood in the new hall, on guard in one spot. We needed to move him or we'd never make it to our target. An idea came to me. I motioned for Doppelganger to stand on the other side the hall opening and then spoke directions with my hands. He nodded his understanding.

I rapped on the wall, catching the attention of the guard. He mumbled to himself, but shrugged off the sound and kept his post. I knocked again and this time he took a few steps our way, his gun at the ready. Doppelganger and I remained still until he came in range. I moved back to catch the soldier's attention, and Doppelganger quickly disarmed him and then knocked him out.

I bumped arms with him for a job well done, and then searched the soldier while Doppelganger found a suitable location to hide him. I found nothing of interest on him until I located a small hidden pocket on his vest.

Doppelganger returned just then, and I held up the keycard. "This will come in handy. Argus handed me a code reader, so I'll know what type of access it gives."

"Your group is full of helpful surprises." Doppelganger then shoved the soldier in a closet down the hall.

While he did that, I took out the reader and scanned the card. The screen flashed with the number two. *Second-level security clearance, not too bad.*

I rejoined Doppelganger when I tucked the scanner away, to find him peering into a room near where the soldier had been standing. Tied to a chair sat a man with a strange contraption on his head. His head slumped toward his chest, but I could see the eye coverings. *A psychic?* He wasn't our target, but I was curious.

Clicking my video feed button, I recorded a few seconds of the man and sent it to Argus. "See if Seda knows him."

He spoke with her, and I heard her gasp and knew what to do before he came back. "Definitely get him."

I swiped the keycard across a black scanner. I held my breath when nothing happened, worried it'd set off an alarm. I sighed with relief when the door unlocked and slid open. Doppelganger and I slipped into the room and the man lifted his head. "Who's there?"

"We're here to get you out," I said as I fussed with his bindings, noting how banged-up he looked.

He chuckled. "You're not here for me."

"Originally, no, but we're not going to leave you behind, either. Is your sibling here, too?"

He nodded as best he could. "She's down the hall… I think. This device blocks my telepathy enough where it's hard to get a lock on her."

"I'll get him, you go find her," Doppelganger said.

I nodded and rushed out the door and down the hall, looking into every room I came across, only to find them empty. I started to worry about the psychic when I came to a corner with some voices coming from the other side. I stalled, thinking they were coming this way, but as I listened they remained in the same place.

Creeping up, I peered around the corner. A male and female soldier stood on guard, casually chatting. *I can't take them both out without risking an alert.* Reaching into a pouch, I pulled out a finger gun and two micro tranquilizing darts. Most darts I used were larger than this, but thanks to all the work the teams put into collecting technology information, we were able to come up with more discreet darts.

Loading one dart after I'd pulled the glove over my hand, I took aim at the woman's neck and fired. She flinched and grunted a complaint. I took the time to load the next dart as her male counterpart showed concern. He walked over to her and I waited for her to finish insisting she'd be fine. Once he accepted her words, he took up his position again and then I shot him as well. He twitched and smacked his neck as if a mosquito had bit him, but that was it. *Hopefully that's enough for him.* He was a big guy, so there was a chance he'd need more of the serum.

I stored the gun as I waited, ready for surprises. It wouldn't take long for the serum to take effect on the woman, as long as it got into her bloodstream, but her male counterpart could take a few minutes, and that could get messy if I wasn't ready.

Half a minute passed and the woman started to sway. She caught herself and shook her head. Her male companion made his concern known, but she continued to be stubborn. *I like her.* Too bad we were on opposite sides of this war at the moment. The female soldier swayed and then fell. He tried to get her, but his movements were sluggish. *Ah, so it did work on him, good.* The woman attempted to get up, but failed and ultimately fell asleep.

The male soldier tried to speak to her, but the words came out muffled and soon he, too, collapsed in a heap. I walked over to them and rifled through their pockets to find the female soldier also had an access card. After scanning, I found it to be the same as the first one I'd stolen, giving me hope. I then peered into the room they guarded to find a woman in a similar state as the psychic in the other room. *Found her.* Swiping the card, the lock registered and the door slid open.

Before I could get inside, she whispered out to me. "Is my brother okay?"

I went about untying her. "He's about as worse for wear as you."

She deflated. "I'd have hoped they'd go easier on him since it was my fault we're in this predicament."

"It's not your fault," came a male voice.

I turned my gaze over my shoulder to see Doppelganger with two of his clones, one of which carried the male psychic on his back.

Her brother spoke again. "We're both in this together. Zarda doesn't matter to us anymore."

His sister frowned and I flicked her in the nose. "Be grateful you get a second chance."

She nodded. "I suppose you're right. Thank you."

I slipped her arm over my shoulder and helped her stand. She struggled, but managed. Doppelganger held out an arm. "I'll carry her. I'm stronger."

I nodded my thanks and then scrutinized the three versions of him. "Which is the real one?" All three raised a hand and I huffed. "Real funny."

The male psychic chuckled. "This one carrying me is the least stupid of the trio, if that helps."

The three Doppelgangers glowered at him and I chuckled. "Actually, I'm looking for the exact opposite."

He pointed to the one who didn't have a person attached to them. "That one, then."

The lone Doppelganger held out his hands. "Hey!"

I smacked him in the shoulder. "Let's get moving. We still have someone to find."

"Can you connect to the others and find out how they're doing?" Doppelganger asked. "Would be wise with how much time has passed. The copy I made of you will disappear soon."

"Good idea." I leaned against a wall. Closing my eyes, I sensed out my copy. She was running, and I could sense others near her. I continued to connect, ignoring the disorienting feeling that flooded over me, until my vision came to me—though I could tell it wasn't my body. My copy came to a stop in a hall and glimpsed around a corner. Noting the coast clear, she waved the others to follow her. Greeve had a man slumped over his shoulder, and Mocha helped a young man, maybe in his late teens. *That's strange. Why such a young kid?*

"*Hello, Eira,*" my copy said, startling me. "*Your friends are fine, don't worry. I won't allow any harm to come to them. I like them as much as you do.*"

Something wasn't right about this copy. "*Who are you?*"

She chuckled. "*You already know.*"

Disorientation came over me and I was thrown out of her body. I shook my head. Doppelganger bent over to get a better look at me, concern creasing his brow. "Are you all right?"

"Yeah, but... there's something off about that copy you made of me. It doesn't talk to me like I would."

Doppelganger tilted his head. "It talked to you?"

"Uh, yeah, is it not supposed to?"

"No. It can talk to others, but not telepathically to the original."

"*Do you know anything about this?*" I asked the voice. I was met with silence. "*Hello? Important question that affects my safety.*"

Yet more silence. Something was off. She hadn't spoken at all since I'd received this assignment.

I took a deep breath. "Well, this one is definitely an abnormality. I hope it won't cause the others any issues."

"For some reason, I'm confident it won't."

"They do have one of the targets, and an extra as well," I said. "A teen boy."

The female psychic sighed. "I'm glad to hear that. He got caught up in my mess."

I nodded. "Well, at least we could help. Means you can have your pity party together. Now let's move."

The male psychic chuckled. "I like her."

"All right, up we go," Doppelganger said to the female psychic.

"Watch where you put those hands of yours," her brother warned. "Or you'll lose them."

"Look, I make be a jokester, but I'm not some creep who goes around copping a feel without expressed permission," Doppelganger said.

I rolled my eyes and grabbed the two soldiers I'd knocked out and dragged them down the hall until we came to a locker room. Doppelganger went about locking the two up together, though I had to warn him about playing too many games with the pair as he tried to position them in a rather compromising way. Not that being caught in a locker together wasn't compromising in itself.

I nodded to him when he completed the task and we continued on, careful of our injured rescues. We came across no other guards, and it smelled of suspicion.

"Your communicator is blinking," Doppelganger said.

I attached it to my head and answered the call. "Yes?"

"You have ten minutes to get in and out," Shyden's voice came over. "We've caused a bit of a stir over here that you'll be proud of. All hands on deck for them."

"No alarms?"

"All disabled."

I chuckled. "Explains the empty building. Good work. Keep them busy as long as you can."

"Of course."

The line cut and I motioned for Doppelganger to continue with me. The "two" of us rounded many more corners, so many I called in for a location update on the target to be sure we were going the right direction. The answer wasn't exact, but showed she was here, just deep within the building.

"You think I should check on the others?" I asked Doppelganger.

"Normally, I'd say your copy is gone, but…"

His trail off perplexed me. "But?"

"Well, it's complicated. When I make copies, there's a small energy change in my body and when a copy disappears, that energy returns. When I do the force copy on someone else, that energy depletes at a higher rate. When I made your copy, it didn't deplete at the same rate as the others I practiced with. And now, even though we're at the point that copy should be gone, I haven't felt any different."

"I also don't feel different," I said. "And you did say once it went away, I'd know."

He nodded. "Let me know if that changes."

We continued on until finally coming to a large, open room. In it, two more guards and one enclosed room. *That has to be where they're keeping her.* I motioned for Doppelganger to back up, and I loaded my finger gun with tranquilizers. Staying hidden and taking aim, I fired at one guard and reloaded as quickly as possible.

The second guard took notice of his counterpart's pain complaint and, unlike the past pair, became suspicious. With their communication system down, they wouldn't know as much as the rest of the compound, so he just had to be smart… or paranoid. His posture alert, he checked his comrade, who complained of pain in his neck. The man checked him out and found the dart, but I didn't panic when he readied his gun and looked about. Instead, I took aim and waited for him to give me an open shot. When it came, I pulled the trigger.

With the two on high alert, they heard the *pop* of my gun. The weapon used pressurized air to push the darts, meaning it was not silent to those aware of my presence. The soldiers readied their guns. The second soldier to be hit by my darts advanced.

I motioned for Doppelganger to move back some so I could position myself just right. The first target dropped, and his comrade spun around. He rushed to his friend's side and then radioed in for help, only to find the line dead. He continued to try, each time slurring his words.

He swore and aimed his gun my way. Stumbling, he fought the tranquilizer, but wasn't any good at defending himself. The barrel of the gun passed the corner threshold and I made my move. Grabbing hold of the barrel, I yanked the weapon closer and jabbed the soldier in the throat with my elbow. In his weakened state, he dropped the gun. I followed up by sweeping my leg behind his and grabbing him by the head, slamming it against the wall. He collapsed and didn't get back up.

"Remind me not to pick a fight with you," Doppelganger said.

I chuckled. "As long as you're not drugged up, you'll do okay."

He grinned. "Who said I wouldn't be?"

I rolled my eyes and went to the door. Peering in, I found a woman lying on the floor, her condition worse than the two psychics. Without thinking, I swiped the access card for the lock and the light flashed red. It continued to flash and I mentally swore. I didn't know the state of the alarm systems, and an alarm wasn't blaring, but more than ten minutes had passed.

Thinking quickly, I searched the body of the guard closest to me, but found nothing. Doppelganger searched the other man and called out to me. I looked up in time to catch an access card. Scanning it, I found it to be a level-three access. *Of course.*

Swiping the card over the lock, the light flashed green and the door slid open. Without hesitation, I rushed into the room to the target's side. I checked her pulse to find it weak. *No time to stall.* Slinging her arm around my shoulder, I hauled her onto my back as best I could. Doppelganger tried to take her from me, but I refused. "We don't have time. I'll manage. You take point."

He nodded and we rushed out of the room, only to find we weren't alone. My instincts to fight flared, but I relaxed when I realized it was Helkin and Shyden.

Helkin smirked. "Need help out?"

Doppelganger and I looked at each other and then back to them. "Yes."

Shyden held his arm out to me. "You and the woman can come with me. If your friend gets rid of one of these copies, I can manage a third person, but I'll need to make more stops."

"Will it be safe for these three?" I asked. "They're pretty banged up."

"Unlike your other friend, our abilities won't put stress on them," Helkin said. "It'll be safe."

I nodded. "Well that would have been nice to know before we did all this."

"You wouldn't have found the two extra captives, had we gone that route."

"True. Let's get moving, then."

Doppelganger set down the male psychic, and handed the female one to Shyden, before reabsorbing his copies. The process went quicker than I thought it would, but it was no less disturbing. Once done, he lifted the male psychic onto his back again.

"Hope you ladies are ready," Shyden said.

Helkin moved so a shadow cast onto my mentor's feet, and it then distorted and lashed out for the shadows of those Shyden was about to carry off. I took a calming breath as the four of us sank into the floor. It had been some time since he'd use this technique on me. Darkness swallowed us, and then nothing.

Unlike Chameleon's ability, you didn't feel anything while moving around. The emptiness clawed at the psyche. The only reassurance I had was Shyden's firm grip on me.

Shyden popped us up outside next to a building, and I took a deep breath. I looked around and noted we were still in the compound, and soldiers scrambled around on full alert. A few turned our way, but Shyden had us covered and we were back in the shadows. How he knew where to go was beyond me. I didn't quite understand his, Helkin's, and Chameleon's abilities, but they were unique, to say the least.

The four of us slipped out of the shadows two more times before we found ourselves in the sewers. Shyden released me, pulling the psychic woman more onto his back in order to support her better. Once he was good, we set a quick pace to the Underground.

We reached the door, and I hadn't gotten a chance to think about how we'd open it yet when Shyden placed a hand on my shoulder, and we were pulled through a shadow to the other side. Several people were waiting for us, three of whom were Seda, Council member Akama, and Corliss, and gave us a hand with our rescued captive. What Corliss was doing here, I hadn't the faintest.

Seda and Akama immediately went to tending to the psychic woman. I watched as the two used their abilities to pry off the device from the psychic woman's head.

She blew out a relieved breath. "Thank you."

"It's concerning they were still able to make these devices," Seda said.

"I was sure we'd sent in enough teams to dispose of any schematics and prototypes.

"We'll have time to debrief you later on the position you're in, but right now you need to recover," Akama said to the injured woman, surprising me. Usually the Council was a bit stricter.

"It's because we've been keeping tabs on the pair," Seda messaged to me. *"We lost all contact with them a week ago. We assumed the worst."*

"Fair. Is her brother here?"

"Yes, he's resting, though not willingly, as he's concerned for his sister."

"Well, he can stop being a worrywart."

She chuckled and motioned for me to follow. *"You're going to want to help out with another situation."*

My brow furrowed, but I followed, Shyden inviting himself and no one protesting. Seda led us over to a small group of people, one of whom was Doppelganger. I then noticed Mocha and the others from our assignment.

"Good, you're here," Doppelganger said. "You were right, something is weird about that copy."

My brow arched. "Huh?"

He stepped away, revealing the "copy" he made of me sitting down on a bench. She jumped to her feet when she spotted me. "Finally! I thought I was going to die of boredom waiting for you. You're so slow."

I snapped my attention to Doppelganger. "What the hell is going on?"

He held up his hands. "I don't know. I really don't."

The copy sauntered over to me. "Well, I have to go back now." She moved behind me and gave me a quick hug. "Thanks for letting me out. Let's do it again soon."

Then the most uncomfortable, skin-crawling sensation washed over me as she was reabsorbed into my body. I struggled to stand, but Corliss reacted quickly and caught me before even Shyden could.

"Are you okay?" he asked.

My skin crawled and my stomach flipped. "I think I'm going to be sick…"

Someone grabbed a bucket and threw it to me just as I lost the meal I'd consumed before the assignment. My legs buckled underneath me, and Corliss held onto me tighter so I wouldn't fall.

"Eira, I'm really sorry," Doppelganger said.

"Never again," I said before retching into the bucket again.

"I don't know why this was so different," he said. "This has never happened before."

Corliss nudged me. "Maybe your multiple personality disorder caused the issue."

I laughed and hit him. "I don't have a personality disorder. I don't care what Ryoko says."

"No, she's just hormonal all the time, like all women," Shyden said.

I glared at him. "Watch it."

He smirked and tossed me a bottle of water. Once I'd gotten cleaned up, I stood and pointed at Doppelganger. "That was handy, but seriously, never again."

He nodded. "No worries there."

"We should get you home," Corliss said.

"I need to debrief with the council first," I said.

Seda shook her head. "No need. You did your job and then some. The Council will be busy with the rescues and dealing with these devices used on them, so head on home. If they need further detail from you, they'll make it known."

I nodded. "Very well. Don't stay out too late, now."

She smiled and then left for the Council chambers. Shyden came up behind Corliss and me and placed a hand on each of our shoulders. "How about I give you two a lift?"

Before either of us could agree to the offer, our shadows distorted and darkness swallowed us. Corliss panicked and grabbed my arm. I rested my hand on his to reassure him, and waited for our ride to be over.

Minutes passed before the shadows slipped away, and we were left standing in my bedroom with Raikidan standing in the door way, mid-bite into a burger.

"That's sexy," I said.

"You're back," he said, his mouth full of food.

"He's stress eating," Corliss said. "It's why I suggested getting you home so quickly. I didn't want him eating us out of house and home."

Raikidan swallowed his food. "I am not stress eating." He then noticed Shyden and glowered. "Who is he?"

Shyden chuckled. "Too old for her, don't worry." He then ruffled my hair. "I'll catch you later, Sweetheart. And don't worry. Your cat-like friend had other arrangements to return home."

He then disappeared into my shadow on the floor. Raikidan's unhappy look didn't disappear and Corliss excused himself, taking the fire-escape route.

I shook my head and headed for my dresser. "I smell like sweat, vomit, and a sewer, so I'm going to take a nice long bath."

"Why do you smell like vomit?" Raikidan asked, his voice strained with mild panic.

"Bad reaction to something. I'm better now."

Raikidan ran over to me and fussed. "Are you sure?"

I laughed and put some distance between us. "Yes, I'm sure." I removed my shirt as I headed for the bath and glanced back at him. "Finish eating and you can join me."

He put his half-eaten burger down and smirked, his eyes glowing. "I'm done."

My pants were next, and I slipped into the bathing room, Raikidan's heavy footsteps hot on my heels.

CHAPTER 41

My eyes scanned the dark forest for any movement as I sat on a weak tree limb. I would have preferred something better, but the trees here could hardly be considered healthy, and this was the best tree I could scout out in my limited time.

There was something out there; I could sense it. This whole assignment felt off, and the moment we had entered this half-dead forest, I couldn't help but feel... watched. My scanning stopped when I heard rustling behind me. As I listened, I identified them as human. It wasn't time for me to head back to camp, so I was convinced it wasn't a comrade coming to relieve me of my post.

I slipped out of the tree and pressed myself against the trunk with a drawn dagger held close to my chest. The snapping of a twig just on the other side of the tree sent my instincts into overdrive and I lunged for my target. I pushed the man against the tree and held my dagger to his throat, but stopped my attack when I recognized the brown-haired, brown-eyed man. "Tannek?"

He chuckled. "I'm willing to try a few things, Chickadee, but this isn't one of them, sorry."

I scowled and pushed away from him roughly. "What are you doing here? You should be back at camp."

"I came to see you," he said.

I snorted and walked off to scout. "Go back to camp."

He grabbed my wrist. "Please stop being mad at me, Eira."

"I'm not mad," I said. "You're discharged in three days. You can go make normal friends and have a normal job. You can have a normal life and find a normal girl to spend time with. I'm just making it so I can handle that."

I ripped my hand free. "Now go back to camp."

He grabbed me again. "No. I'm not letting you think things are going to change because I'm forced to leave service. I don't have a choice, Eira. I had to sign the paperwork, but that doesn't change how I feel about you. You can't be replaced."

He pulled me closer and stroked my cheek. "You're my girl, and there's no replacement for you. You are my normal, and I like that. I don't know how we'll make this work, and I don't care if Zarda is under the delusion you belong to him. We both know he's wrong, and I'll defy him and sneak into the fortress to see you if I have to. I won't let him get between us."

My gaze lowered. He made it sound so easy.

Tannek lifted my chin so I'd look at him. "I love you, and nothing is going to change that."

He kissed me lightly on the lips and I couldn't stop myself from kissing him back. I didn't believe for a moment things would stay the same. He'd get a taste of his freedom and eventually I'd be nothing more than a memory. But no matter how much I wanted to stay away from him, I couldn't.

I pulled away and pushed him. "Now go back to camp."

Tannek shook his head. "I want to spend time with you. I don't get alone time with you like I want."

I sighed. "Tannek, this is an assignment. I need to do my job."

Tannek frowned. "I can't even have a few minutes?"

"If Zarda finds out we're sneaking around, especially on an assignment, you're dead and I don't want that."

Tannek blew out a breath through his lips. "All right, fine. Your logic wins."

My fingers brushed his cheek. "I do it because I care, not because I want you to go away. I'd prefer you to be around, but you're not quiet enough, and you'd be a distraction."

He grinned and planted a light kiss on my forehead. "Well, if you need a distraction, you know where to find me."

I watched him head off toward camp before turning to resume my watch. I nearly jumped out of my skin at the sight of the dark-haired Battle Psychic standing behind me. "Telar—"

He held up his hands. "Easy. The whole platoon knows about you two. We keep our mouths shut because we know why you two have to sneak around, and that's not fair."

I snorted. "Right. What do you want?"

"I've come to relieve you of sentry duty," he said. "Larsen is already scouting the east side of the camp for you, and I'm going to take this area."

My eyebrow rose. "You?"

He chuckled. "I can do quite a few things you assassins can, and that includes sneaking up on one of you and taking care of sentry duty."

"Right." I turned and headed for camp.

"Oh, and one bit of advice, Eira."

I stopped to listen to what he had to say.

"Instead of covering up your embarrassment with anger, try letting the embarrassment out. You'll look adorable—and get what you want more often."

I grunted and continued on. As I came into the clearing, everything appeared normal. Comrades spoke amongst each other, ate, and some were even "resting" their eyes. Tannek was already doing his rounds to make sure everyone was in the proper fighting condition. I headed over to Ryoko and Rylan by the fire.

Rylan greeted me with a smile, and Ryoko handed me a plate of food.

"Quiet out there, I can assume?" she asked.

I took the food and sat down. "Only the sound of crickets trying to serenade me."

She giggled. "How romantic. You going to ditch Tannek for them?"

I shoved food into my mouth. "I don't know what you're talking about."

She sighed, her aggravation hard to miss. "Don't be like this, Laz. Everyone knows. No one is going to tell Zarda. Just be honest with us."

I remained quiet and ate. It didn't matter if others thought they knew. The reality was no one could officially know. Zarda was too much of a threat for Tannek and me to be open about our relationship. It was why I hoped, more than anything, he'd forget about me when he left service. He was too good of a guy to have to deal with this. He deserved to be happy...

I stopped eating and looked around when a chill ran down my spine.

Ryoko turned her head. "What's up?"

"Not sure." I continued to scan the campsite.

"Ambush!" someone screamed in warning from the woods.

But the warning came too late. Before anyone could react, gunfire light up the night and the campsite was overrun. We all reacted as quickly as possible and defended ourselves.

Bodies quickly fell to my blades as I cut down the enemies. Who they were and where they came from were not of any concern to me at the time. Their elimination was the only important thing.

"Eira, look out!"

Something heavy crashed into me before I could process the warning, and I heard a gun go off. I hit the ground hard, but immediately pushed myself up and spun around. To my horror, Tannek fell to the ground next to me. "Tannek, no!"

I rushed to his side. Blood pooled out of several bullet wounds. He shook and gasped for air.

"What the hell were you thinking?" I shouted.

"I—I wanted to protect you," he said with an out-of-place smile.

"I'm wearing armor! You're not." I knew I was being too harsh on him, but I was upset. "I don't know how to fix this…"

He reached for my face. "Eira… I—"

Before he could touch me, his hand fell and his eyes dulled. My heart stopped. "Tannek?"

I shook him, but he remained motionless. "Tannek, no… Tannek!"

Numbness fell over me and the battle around me faded away. He couldn't be dead. He was supposed to be let go in a few days. He was supposed to be stubborn and figure out a way to see me even when I would protest and tell him to move on. He couldn't die. He couldn't… leave me…

My eyes snapped open and I flew up into a sitting position—my breathing heavy and sweat pouring off my skin. My hands trembled and my heart raced. *Tannek…*

"Eira?" Raikidan asked groggily. He bolted upright and touched my shoulder. "Eira, talk to me."

I pulled my knees to my chest and hid my face, trying not to shake any more than I was, but it wasn't working.

"Eira, please. I saw that dream. I need you to communicate with me."

I couldn't say anything, even though I wanted to. I continued to shake, Tannek's lifeless eyes burned into my memory. Raikidan pulled me close and cradled me, rubbing my back in an attempt to help, but it didn't. The pain in my chest grew and I did one thing I thought I'd never do again. I cried. No tears rolled down my cheeks, but the memory of Tannek's death hurt too much to keep myself under control.

Raikidan stroked my head, murmuring calming words. It took a great deal of time for me to calm down, especially since a familiar incorporeal presence appeared in the room, making the pain worse.

Raikidan's words helped. None were insensitive, and all were easy to listen to; mostly him telling me he was there for me and to take calming breaths. After some time, I managed to get myself under control, but the pain still gripped my chest.

Raikidan rolled out of bed and lifted me into his arms. "We're going to take a bath."

I nodded and let him carry me into the other room. He slipped into the perpetually clean and warm water, holding me close and stroking my back. I leaned back into him, listening to his breathing—his heartbeat—I flinched when a ghostly image of Tannek flashed before my eyes in the room.

Raikidan tensed and then wrapped his arms around me. "What happened?"

I shook my head, unable to communicate. I wasn't sure whether I'd actually seen his lingering spirit, like before, or my mind was playing tricks on me in my worked-up state. Pain pulsed in my chest and I closed my eyes, only to open them again when Tannek's dying face haunted me. I started to shake, and Raikidan held me tighter, hushing me and murmuring more calming words, but this time, they didn't help. I couldn't escape that painful night.

"Will you be all right alone for a few minutes?" Raikidan asked.

I took a few calming breaths. "I think so. Why?"

"I need to request something of Shva'sika."

My eyes widened. "Raikidan, don't wake her because of this!"

Someone rapped on the door. "I'm actually awake. My brother woke me up. Said you were—"

"It's not for you to worry about," I said. "Go back to bed."

Raikidan climbed out of the bath. "You relax."

"Raikidan, please…"

My plea fell on deaf ears and he left me alone in the room, shutting the door behind him, so I wouldn't be tempted to follow or listen to what he had planned, though I did hear Shva'sika teasing him about his lack of clothes.

Minutes passed and Raikidan didn't return. The pain ebbed and flowed, each time it reached a peak, my mind was thrown back into that memory. I tried not to let myself be weak and sob more, but the memory had never clung to me like this. The other two times I relived it, I found ways to bury it away until it stayed gone. *I'd done so well…*

The door opened, and Raikidan re-entered the warm room. He

slipped in next to me and held his arms open in invitation. I accepted the gesture and snuggled deep into his embrace, hoping it would take the pain away.

"What did you do?" I asked.

"I spoke with him," Raikidan said.

Shock rippled through me. "You… what?"

"I saw how you reacted in here, Eira. You thought you saw him." He held me tighter. "I confronted him, but got a much different answer than I was expecting. He hasn't been in here. He hasn't checked on you in a few days, wanting to give us space. He's happy I'm here for you, and was glad I had such a strong need to confront him with my concerns. He just wants you to be happy, since he cannot be the one to give it to you anymore."

I tensed, the pain of his loss constricting me.

Raikidan kissed my head. "He can't move on until you let go, Eira. Let go of the pain." He rubbed his forehead to my head. "Let go of the guilt."

"It was my fault…" I whispered. "It will always be my fault."

"He made a choice, Eira. That isn't your fault." Raikidan kissed my head again. "You cannot hold yourself accountable for other's choices. Tannek knew what he was doing. He gave his life for you because he loved you. I would do the same."

I tensed, the image of Tannek's dying face replaced with Raikidan's. "Don't say that… please don't say that…"

"I know that's not what you want to hear." Raikidan tucked my hair behind my ear. "But it's the truth. I will not hide the truth from you. I would give my life if it meant you could live another day, just as you would for me."

Pain pulsed in my chest as what he was getting at sank in.

"If you did this for someone else, this same pain would fall on them. It hurts those left alive, but it doesn't make the sacrifice wrong. When you make such a sacrifice, you have to accept this. This is what love does to us."

I laid there in silence, processing everything. He was right; this would be the same consequence to the sacrifice I'd be willing to make for the others—for him. But letting go wasn't something I was good at.

Raikidan lifted my chin and kissed me on the lips. "This is why we are to make the most of every day. I don't know what will happen in these next few days. I don't know the outcome of this battle we fight. But I will live each day I'm given with you, to the fullest, in case one of these days will be our last. You may have been Tannek's mate in the past, but you're mine now, and I will make sure you are pleased to the fullest."

I stared at him. "He told you—"

Raikidan nodded. "He called you his mate, and told me to take good care of you."

I looked away. "He wouldn't stop calling me that after it slipped out of my mouth once…"

Raikidan chuckled. "I don't blame him. I'd have run with it, too, if I had been in his shoes."

He regarded me for a moment. "There aren't many races out there anymore that refer to their bonded partners as mates. Even the grekeleon refer to it as life-bonded."

My lips twisted as the truth caught on my tongue. "I need more time to talk about it."

"Then I guess my challenge is still in place." Raikidan grinned and caressed the corner of my mouth with his thumb. "But first—"

He claimed my lips with head-swimming passion, and the night faded away, taking all my pain with it.

CHAPTER 42

I slid my thumb over the name engraving on my panflute box. A week had passed since Raikidan and I had become mates. I woke up expecting he would want to extend our week-long time alone, since he really hated it when I was sent out on assignments, but to my surprise, he wasn't in the room waiting for me. A note had been left for me instead.

> *Eira,*
>
> *I will be back as soon as I can. Genesis needed me to go out on surveillance again. It's the same target I've been tailing for a while and we may have a breakthrough that will help us end this rebellion. Anything that will lead us to a day where I don't have to worry about you fighting anymore, is a day I will happily try to bring to fruition, no matter what is asked of me.*
>
> *I love you,*
> *Raikidan*

The loser had written any word I knew in draconic, forcing me to work hard to read it, but I wouldn't have expected anything less. I relished the challenge, really. I wanted to be able to communicate fully in his tongue one day. *Well, it's not really just* his *tongue, now is it, Eira?* I slid my thumb over the name on the box some more.

These past few days I wrangled with my desire to lay out the truth. I needed to do it, and I would be out of time once he returned. But I still struggled to get the words to my tongue.

He hadn't made any guesses himself, though I wasn't sure whether that was because he was waiting for me to say it, or if he was stumped.

Setting the box down, I slipped off my bed and grabbed a towel. I could use a nice bath to relax me. It'd help get my head right and maybe muster up the ability to tell Raikidan.

I stripped down and slid into the warm water, hanging my head back. *Just what I needed.*

My thoughts wandered to telling Raikidan, but I wasn't sure how to go about it. Just blurting it out would not be possible, or smart. And he was too dense for heavy hints to get him to guess, which also didn't go along with the deal I'd made. *I suppose I could go through my full metamorphosis.* I didn't exactly enjoy the idea, but it'd be effective. Of course, then I'd need to talk to Rylan, since the bond would force a change in him as well. *That would benefit Ryoko, too.* She deserved to understand the extent of what Rylan was.

"Hey, whoever you are, you've been quiet these past few days." I knew why. She told me she'd give me the privacy I deserved. *"What do you think?"*

"I think this bath feels wonderful," came from the voice, but not from within my mind.

I sat upright, and in front of me, a familiar sun-kissed woman with red and black hair, several locks braided together, lounged in the water. Large black wings growing out of her back draped into the water and revealing golden armor, looking more ceremonial than practical in nature, covered her sultry form. An ornate golden circlet with a gem-encrusted crescent moon centerpiece adorned her head.

Her golden eyes sparkled as she smiled. "Surprise."

I scrambled closer to the edge of the bath. What was going on?

The woman shook her head. "Don't be like that, dear. I finally manage to break out and you want to run? I thought you wanted to talk to me."

I licked my lips as I tried to formulate a sentence. "What the hell is going on?"

The woman laughed. "Just what I thought you'd say. I wish you'd use your head and think for once. All the answers have hung right in front of your face, and you've nipped at them all, but never latched on."

I tried to think but my brain wouldn't function.

She looked around. "I'm so glad you two finally consummated your mating. Your dancing around was such a tease, I thought I'd never feel the needed purification to lift my bonds."

My brow cocked. "Purification?"

Her lips twisted as if the words weren't allowed to come out. Then she sighed. "Still not enough. Dammit. I thought the bonds were unusually strong for what's been going on lately. What more must we do?"

The tension in my body eased. This was definitely her. Between the glimpses in the mirror and the clear match to her voice, this was the woman I'd been conversing with for so long. All my life. *Wait…*

My eyes widened. The answers were all there. Right in front of me, and I'd turned a blind eye to it all. "Rashta."

A wide grin spread up the side of her face. "About time you had some conviction behind that name. I couldn't respond to it until you did."

I turned when someone rapped on my bedroom door.

"Eira?" Mana called.

"Give me a second, Mana." I turned back to face Rashta, but she had vanished.

"Dammit!"

A chuckle escaped my lips as she continued to swear. *"We'll talk after."*

I left the bath, drying myself. When I entered the room I found Mana sitting on my bed.

"I could have come back," Mana said. "I didn't mean to disturb your alone time."

I chuckled and began dressing. "It's fine. I could use some female company for once."

"What am I, chopped liver?"

"You're a completely separate issue. Hold on."

Mana looked around. "I'm surprised Raikidan isn't here. I know Corliss said, due to the rebellion, he was only going to hold you to a week for now, but I didn't believe he could manage that. Corliss was awful all through our first year. I couldn't do *anything* on my own." Her face scrunched. "And I mean anything."

I chuckled and sat down next to her. "I don't think it's easy for

Raikidan, but he understands we can't be together in peace until this fight is over. He'll do anything to make this war end, including fighting his need to be with me at all hours of the day. Once this is over, I don't doubt he'll be as bad as Corliss for a while."

She leaned back. "I'm glad you take this strong bond so well. I'll be honest, as excited as I was for you two to be growing closer, I was worried."

I smiled. "You care about him, it's only natural for you to worry."

"I'm glad you're his mate. You're so good to him." She scrunched her nose. "Now hopefully he'll stop being mean to me."

I chuckled. "I'll work on that with him. You'll get an apology one of these days."

"I guess you know why he acts the way he does around me?"

I nodded.

"I figured you'd find out. As long as he stops blaming me, and is nice to me from now on, I'll take that as an apology. He's not good at giving them."

"He gave one to Corliss, so he'd better give one to you," I said.

Mana's eyes widened. "Really? Wow…" She then noticed my panflute box. "Is that yours? Can I look at it?"

I nodded and handed it to her.

Mana looked it over, careful not to drop it, her brow furrowing. "Eira, can I ask you something?"

"Does it have to do with why you're here?"

She blinked, her surprise clear.

"It's a little obvious you're using the box as a convenient segue to bring up a topic."

She gave me a demure smile. "Yeah, I need to work on being more assertive with my important questions. I can ask many types of questions no problem, but more personal ones are a bit harder."

"What is it that you'd like to ask me?"

She took a deep breath. "What exactly are you?"

I was taken aback by how she worded her question.

"I know a lot about history, even things that are thought forgotten, thanks to my grandfather. He knew everything! But anyway, I know that human mates can happen for dragons, as much as many dragons try to say otherwise. So, it's easy for me to accept you as Raikidan's mate, but I never once saw the way you held yourself as human. Not entirely, at least. And then our talk at that café confirmed it, but also posed a number of questions, too." She took a deep breath. "I won't judge you. I just want to know."

I analyzed her. "Interesting. Corliss knows. He figured it out on his own, though he gave me his word he'd keep quiet unless I gave the okay. I assumed he'd tell you, since secrets are a big issue."

Mana's eyes widened. "He's keeping a secret from me?"

My lips twisted at the look of utter betrayal in her eyes. It made me wonder just how quiet Ebon had been about discovering it as well. Had he told Nyoki, or was he breaking a mating rule as well for my sake? "I'm sorry. I don't tell anyone this secret of mine. Him knowing made me uncomfortable and because I didn't trust him at the time, I forced him to keep his word."

She nodded slowly. "That's right. You mentioned that during that late night talk. This is something not even Raikidan knows."

"Yes. I haven't mustered up the courage yet to tell him."

"You need to!"

"I'm well aware, thank you."

Mana took a moment and then peered up at me with pleading eyes. "So, can I know?"

Here was my big test. If I could tell Mana, I could tell Raikidan. Sure, I knew she'd accept what I was with more enthusiasm than anyone I knew at this rate, but that wasn't the issue anymore. Just uttering the words was going to be a chore.

I took a deep breath and the words stalled. *Fuck.* This was bad.

"Don't think, just speak."

"You already know. It's in the stories you hold close to you." Not the best way I could have done it, but it was a start, right?

"Could have been worse."

Her brow creased, Mana thought about my words. Then, her face relaxed and her eyes widened. "You're—"

Someone knocked on my window and the two of us jumped. Looking over, I found Sendara standing on the fire escape. She waved her fingers at me.

I slid off the bed to open the window. "Hey, Sendara. What can I help you with?"

"I have important information for you. A strange new development with Zarda," she said.

I motioned for her to come inside. "What do you have?"

"I'll cut directly to the chase. Zarda will be making an appearance in the city."

I laughed, thinking she was making a joke, but by the seriousness of her expression, I found myself wrong. "You can't be serious."

"Unlike my brother, you know I'm terrible at jokes when it comes to Zarda."

I crossed my arms. "Fair, but I'm struggling to believe he'd come out into the open. When he showed up at a party, it surprised everyone, and he didn't stay long."

"He's going by the cover of night, but we can't dig up any information for his visitation."

I held my chin, thinking. "That's even more out of character for him. If he was going to make an appearance, he'd want the whole city to know so he could make a spectacle of it. He likes the worship too much."

Sendara nodded. "Exactly. Shyden and the others are sending a report to your Council now on our findings. I don't doubt something will go down tonight. But due to the odd behavior, if you go, watch your back."

I placed a hand on her shoulder. "Thank you for this information. I'll use it well so we can formulate a plan of attack. We can't pass this opportunity up, but you're right. We're going to need to be careful. It's definitely fishy."

"I should be going. I have other things to attend to." She reached into a pouch and handed me a piece of folded paper. I opened it to find numbers scribbled down. "But if you want us there, contact Shyden. We want Zarda gone, and for everyone to remain as safe as possible."

I nodded. "Thank you. I'll keep it in mind."

She smiled at me and then left through my window. She poked her head back in a moment later. "Oh, um, thanks for the calling card... I'd worked with him for so long; I guess I never noticed the interest he had in me."

I grinned, noting the redness in her cheeks. "Happy to help."

She ran off. I let out an *oof* sound when Mana crashed into me and held on tight.

"Mana?"

"Be careful," she whispered. "I know you have to do this, but I don't want anything to happen to you."

I pried her hands from me and turned to face her, framing her face with my hands. "We're going to do everything we can to make it out of this alive and free."

Her fear-stricken eyes tightened. "Please do. I want to talk with you more about what you were telling me. But I know I'll have to wait. For now, know I support you, Eira. I'm happy to know what you really are."

"I'd appreciate that." I pulled away from her. "I should go speak with Genesis about the new developments."

Mana grabbed my wrist as I turned to leave. "Tell Raikidan. He'll accept you. I know he will."

"I hope so. But for now, I'll have to see if there's time to make the reveal. Otherwise, it'll have to wait until after this showdown with Zarda."

She nodded and let me go. "If that's your choice, I'll accept it."

I smiled my thanks and left my room. Ryoko, Rylan, and Mocha lounged on the couch watching TV, and Genesis sat at the far end, observing Shva'sika and Argus battle it out over a game of chess. Seda sat next to Argus, messing with his pieces from time to time.

"Hey, Gen," I called out. "A little birdie paid me a visit with some interesting info."

Genesis sat up straight. "Let's hear it."

Before I managed to open my mouth, footsteps thundered down the stairs leading to the roof. The door flung open and Raikidan ran out into the living room.

"Welcome back," I said. "And good timing. I have big news to share."

"Same here," he said. "But you go first."

"Zarda is going to be showing his ugly mug in the city tonight," I revealed.

Everyone stopped what they were doing and looked at me. But unlike everyone else, who appeared surprised, Raikidan threw up his hands. "I was going to say that. How did you find this out?"

My brow rose in inquiry. "Sendara paid me a visit just now. Said she and the other assassins she works with caught wind of it and did some investigating. How'd you find out?"

Raikidan jabbed his thumb in Genesis' direction. "She sent me out on a few surveillance assignments that led to me finding a lead about Zarda possibly showing up. I've been tracking leads for a few weeks now."

"He's been doing a great job," Genesis said. "Shifter abilities are far underused with us, and I regret not utilizing it sooner."

I nodded. "Well I hope you have more information to share with us than Sendara did. She only gave me a rough timeframe, which was tonight at some point."

Rylan's brow rose. "Seriously? Your trained assassins could only give you that much?"

"Yes, unfortunately. I suspect they only recently caught wind of the situation, so they didn't have time to learn more, like Raikidan has."

Raikidan nodded. "I don't have a lot more, since information leaks were hard, but I know of a rough path he'll take, so we could lie in ambush."

"But why is he going to be in the city?" Mocha asked. "That's not like him."

"I wasn't unable to uncover the purpose for his secret visit," Raikidan said. "Though, from bits and pieces I dug up, this isn't the first time he's been out in the city under the cover of night."

"Do we know at least how well guarded he'll be?" Ryoko asked. "We don't want to underprepare."

"As far as I uncovered, he won't have much security, and he'll be walking the city," Raikidan said.

Rylan narrowed his eyes. "This gets more suspect by the minute."

"Yes, but we can't pass up this opportunity," I said. "We're not making any headway with our normal tactics. We have to take a chance."

"I suppose you're right; I'm just concerned," Rylan said. "We don't want to walk right into a trap."

"You're right, it could be," Argus said. "But that's why we'll make a plan."

Genesis nodded. "I'll speak with the Council on the course of action they want to take. In the meantime, prepare yourselves. I'll bet that because Eira's contacts and Raikidan made the discovery, they'll choose us to go out on the front lines first. I should have information shortly."

She and Seda left the room, leaving me to deal with everything else.

"We should prepare for at least two scenarios: small-scaled assault and large scale. Shva'sika, I'll need you to get in contact with the shamans and dragons. If the Council goes with the large scale, we'll need them. Ryoko, get Zane and Blaze home so we can fill the two of them in; I don't want this information to go out through the communicators and risk a tap leak. Mocha, I'll need you for something specific, so meet me in my room once you've gotten yourself prepared." I turned to look at Mana. "Mana, if you could track down Corliss for me, I'll need him as well."

All four women nodded, and everyone but Raikidan dispersed. He followed me into my room. "What's up, Rai?"

"Are you okay?" he asked.

I rummaged through my dresser for my daggers. "I'm both nervous and excited. I started to think this opportunity would never present itself and we'd be stuck in an endless struggle. But now we have a chance, though there is a high possibility for casualties."

Raikidan walked over to me and lifted my chin so I'd look him in the eyes. "Whatever happens, I'll protect you to my dying breath."

I smiled. "And I you."

He let me go and I removed my necklace to store it away. I didn't want to risk damage coming to it in the scuffle.

"You look like you have something else on your mind," he said.

"I wanted to talk to you about the deal we made, the one about the truth, but this situation is far more pressing. We'll talk about it when this mess is over."

Raikidan stroked my cheek with the back of his hand. "Are you sure?"

I smiled, noting the mix of emotions on his face, and nodded. Just then, Corliss and Mocha showed up. "I need to speak to them, so you go get ready."

Raikidan nodded and left the room, closing the door behind him.

I addressed the other two. "All right, I need you two for something specific. While I don't doubt both Sendara's and Raikidan's information is correct, I can't shake the feel this could be a trap to lure us out. I want the two of you to stay in the shadows to watch, just in case. If we're captured, you two need to get back here ASAP and get everyone who stays behind out. Once our identities are known, they'll raid this place, and I don't want anyone else caught up in the crossfire."

"What about us getting help?" Mocha asked.

"If the Council is watching, they'll already know things went south. Your main priority is getting everyone to the Underground where it's safe. Then you can plan with the Council how to proceed."

"What will happen if you're caught?" Corliss asked.

"We'll be tried for treason," I said. "And unless the Council can figure a way to get us out, we'll be executed."

His brow furrowed with worry, but Mocha stopped him. "It's a risk we signed up for when we chose to defy Zarda. We're not afraid to die for something we believe in."

"I'd rather it not go that far," Corliss said, his eyes intent on me.

I knew his reason was more than the surface worry, but this was the risk I was willing to take to get my freedom—to free Lumaraeon from Zarda's vile existence.

Someone knocked on the door and then opened it. Ryoko poked her head inside. "The Council made their decision. Genesis is calling a meeting."

The three of us nodded and left my room to finish planning.

We snuck through the shadows of the street, keeping our eyes peeled and hearing open for any signs of Zarda or his goons. We had been doing this for some time, and I was starting to doubt the information Raikidan and my assassins picked up. If it was right, we should have found them by now.

Ryoko's ears twitched and Raikidan signaled for us to stop. We took in our surroundings and listened. We could hear people walking and speaking to one another, but it was hard to pinpoint where they were. When we saw a light, and shadows of people projecting on the walls coming down the street toward us, we had to act fast.

Raikidan pointed to an alley and we hid there. Keeping close to the wall, we waited. The group came closer, and as the shadows projected on the wall, it was obvious they were soldiers. Of course we couldn't be sure Zarda was among them, so we'd have to wait and see.

As we waited, a feeling of unease fell over me and I was sure I wasn't the only one feeling it by the way Rylan and Argus fidgeted. The sensation worsened when another light appeared. This time it was from the other direction. Either these two groups were separate patrols that had intersected, or—

"*Laz, it's a trap! Get out of there!*" Seda screamed at me telepathically when the patrols were nearly on us.

My eyes widened and I looked at everyone else, who were also aware of Seda's warning. But before we could react, we were jumped from above. Our attackers came at us quickly, and the men from the street appeared at the entrance of the alley. They shone a light in our eyes, making it harder to defend ourselves, and before we knew it, we were overpowered.

We all struggled as we were handcuffed and forced to kneel. Ryoko fought longest and hardest, but once the military enlisted a few brutes, she too was subdued. My eyes flicked back and forth, hoping to understand why we were being forced to stay still. Typically in these situations, we would have been dragged off somewhere so no civilian could possibly come across the situation. Zarda liked that kind of control over the city. He liked making them think the life they lived was better than it was.

The soldiers parted as someone approached, their boots clomping on the asphalt. I glowered when Zarda reared his disgusting face. He had his signature winning smirk and held himself high. Not that that was any different than any other day.

He chuckled. "You are so predictable, my dear. You made this game far too easy for me."

I spat on the ground at him, but that only made him smile more. "Of course you still have the spunk I so dearly love."

Someone we all knew too well drew up next to Zarda. I scowled. "Zo, you rat."

He grunted. "It's not my fault you got cocky and let me in on your little secrets so early. Of course, I can't take all the credit. I did have some inside help keeping you all distracted."

Zo glanced to Zarda, who grinned. "Yes. I thought you, Eira dear, were great at lying, but I think I found someone who may be just a little better than you."

He flicked his hand, and the soldiers holding Raikidan down let him go. Raikidan rubbed his wrists after his restraints were removed. My blood ran cold and my body numbed. *No, it can't be...*

"Raikidan, you scumbag, you sold us out!" Ryoko screamed.

"Of course I did." Raikidan caught a bag Zarda tossed at him, the contents jangling. The bag looked identical to the one I found in our vault and had confronted him about months ago. He lied to me. All this time…

Numbness fell over me. All the things I told him—what it was like living this life—what I wanted—letting go to trust, even if unwilling at first…

My chest tightened.

Doing the one thing I told myself I wouldn't be foolish enough to try again—falling in love. Believing every honey-laced word he spoke. *All of it, a lie.*

I bared my teeth. "You slimy, motherless cur! We trusted you!" *I trusted you…*

"That's your fault. You knew enough about us dragons, you should have been wary with a bounty on your head. You made it far too easy."

Zarda chuckled. "This is rather amusing. I honestly hadn't thought you'd be able to trick her so easily. Then again, I wasn't quite convinced with your resolve to turn on your own kind. Or, at least, half of it."

Raikidan gave him a puzzled look, and Zarda's mouth spread into a close-lipped smile. "Oh, my dear, you're still keeping secrets, even from him? I guess you didn't get her full trust after all, dragon. But no matter. Should I tell him our little secret, dearest Eira, or should I?"

I spat on the ground as I stared Raikidan down, all my past reservations holding me back from speaking the truth now gone. "I am Lazmira Eira Rysrin, daughter of General Amara Rysrin of Dalatrend, and Rizgar, leader of the North Hybria Mountain red dragon clan."

Raikidan's brow ticked up and he raised his voice. "Corliss, did you know this?"

All eyes peered up to his cousin as he sat on the roof above, chuckling. "I did, cousin, but I thought you figured it out, so never mentioned it. I found it quite obvious."

I tried not to be surprised. But I struggled with even that. I spat on the ground once again. "And what's your reason for helping? I doubt the bounty was enough for the two of you to share. Even with a promise of extra heads."

A grin on his face, he pulled up his sleeve, revealing a Crimson

Sanctuary tattoo. My blood ran cold. *How… how did he keep that hidden for so long?* "You see, little halfbreed, Kir doesn't want you and your little freak show friends running around. I knew his head-on assaults wouldn't work; you're too crafty for that. You always have been. So, when Raikidan mentioned you and his plan to collect your bounty, well, I knew of a better way to get you back in your chains."

Corliss chuckled. "And a few gold coins my way didn't hurt the incentive."

"And what of Mana?" Ryoko snarled.

He laughed. "Quite the little actress, isn't she? You all fell easy prey to her cute and nonthreatening demeanor. She'll be quite pleased she can go back to being the real her now."

All this time, Raikidan's expression remained neutral—uncaring. Even if he wasn't in league with the Crimson Sanctuary, gold called to him like it did all dragons. I was a fool to think one of them could ever be better than my father. *How could I have been so stupid… desperate…*

Zarda's eyes darted between all parties. For a moment I thought he was suspicious of something, though I couldn't place why. In the end, he was just bored.

"I grow tired of this." He snapped his fingers. "Take them away."

No way in hell. I refused to go quietly. The moment my knees came off the ground, I struggled and shoved my captors. They fought back, breaking rank and creating an opening to attack Zarda. I took it. I took a deep breath and went to exhale a breath of fire, but Zarda reacted far more quickly than I could have anticipated.

"Bind her!" he ordered.

A heavy cuff was thrown around my neck, and the flame in my throat caught. I choked on the flame and feared I'd swallow it and torch my insides, but Zarda motioned for them to release me and I spat the pathetic ember of a flame on the ground. I cursed under my breath.

I cringed when they used the restraint on my neck once again. It didn't take long for weakness to overcome me. I hated this restraint. Nickel-infused synthetic metal. It was my one debilitating weakness I'd done my best to keep secret, and one Zarda enjoyed using against me.

Zarda took several steps closer, reaching down and lifted my chin with a finger. "You know better than to fight, *Pet.*"

My lip curled and I forced all the energy I had left into my legs, colliding my forehead with his face. Zarda cried out in pain and stumbled back. A soldier punched me in the face, breaking something and causing me to bleed a little. *At least I got one shot in.*

Zarda pushed the soldier away, his seething eyes boring into me. "You'll regret your insolence."

I spat blood at him, a feat now difficult with these restraints.

"Take them away!"

My captors hauled me over to a transport truck, my weakened state preventing me from fighting back. *It doesn't matter…* I let my feelings get the better of me. I let them cloud my judgment and this is where it got me. A part of me always wanted to believe it had just been my father who was untrustworthy. I should have known, all dragons were cut from the same cloth. It was in their nature to look out for themselves. Even I had run away in hopes of gaining freedom for myself. But it was my human side that brought me back. *Not that it matters now…*

Just as we exited the alley, I removed the ring Raikidan had gifted me and let it fall to the ground. I didn't want it.

The soldiers threw us into the transport truck and slammed the door shut. The engine revved and before we knew it, we were on our way to the fortress to meet our demise.

43
CHAPTER

The soldier threw me into the cell when my restraints were removed, but I caught myself and headed to the back of the cell by the barred window. I took a moment to glance out. We were in one of the higher-up cells; I could see most of the city from the window. I sat in my corner to wait for the inevitable.

The others watched me after they settled down, but I couldn't look at them. This was my fault. I should have been more cautious. I shouldn't have trusted him; I should have stuck to my gut instincts to keep him at a distance. Had I done that, I would have seen this coming.

Several pairs of feet rushed toward our cell, piquing my interest. It was too soon and the feet were too quick for them to be taking us out for an interrogation. And there was no way the Council was breaking us out. At least, not this soon.

A group of soldiers appeared at the entrance of our cell, then opened it and threw two people in with us. It was Seda and Shva'sika, and only Seda's body fell as if it had any life in it.

"Shva'sika!" Ryoko screamed when Shva'sika's limp body hit the floor. She rushed over to Shva'sika as the soldiers chuckled and locked our cell back up.

"She's fine," Seda murmured as she pulled herself to her knees. She didn't look up. The military had put some sort of strange device on her head. I recognized it as one I'd seen on the two psychics Doppelganger and I had saved only days before. "They just knocked her out when we resisted."

"What is on your head?" Rylan asked.

"It's a device that suppresses my psychic abilities. And yes, it's painful, and it's not fully effective. I can communicate telepathically still, but only at short distances. But that's all I can really do."

"Is that why you're not looking at us?" Blaze asked. "Because you're in pain?"

Ryoko gasped. "They took your blindfold…"

The moment the words came out of her mouth, Argus sprang into action. He tore off a large strip from his shirt to tie over her eyes. Seda smiled at him gratefully and sat against the wall next to him.

"Is Genesis okay?" Ryoko asked as she went about moving Shva'sika into a better position.

Seda nodded. "Yes. Zane got her out while we held back the assault as long as we could."

I curled back up into my corner when the attention fell on me again. *"Eira, don't—"*

"Don't say it, Seda," I said. *"This is my fault. I don't deserve any sympathy."*

She sighed and left me alone. My mind went back to the missteps I made that led us here. I'd tried so hard to learn from my mother's mistake. I'd tried to remember what truly killed her. *In the end, apples don't fall from the tree…*

Not wanting to deal with this anymore, I forced my eyes closed and used my misery to will myself into unconsciousness.

She frowned. I hated it when she did that, but I wasn't going to lie to her. Not like my father had. I told her how I felt. I told her how I hate what I am, and my father, for all the lies and what it did to her.

"There's no way I'm going to change your mind, is there?" my mother asked.

I snorted. "He couldn't even change my mind if he magically showed up and tried to tell me he was sorry it took so long to come back. It's been too long."

"It hasn't been that long."

"I've been out of my tank for twenty years. And that means you've waited

seventeen extra. That's a long time. No sane person would keep waiting for that long and believe those words as truth."

"It hasn't been that long," she continued to insist.

I walked off. "Whatever. You can believe in a fairytale if you want. I won't."

My mother sighed but didn't follow. She had learned that when I walked off, I wasn't willing to discuss the topic anymore—not that I was willing to at any other point, either.

Just as I rounded the corner to head down one of the halls that led to the labs, I heard someone greet my mother. It wasn't someone I was familiar with. I backed up and peered around the corner to see a tall man with flaming red hair and green eyes standing in front of her.

"It's been some time, Amara," he said.

"Yes it has, Largren."

He frowned. "You seem troubled."

"Everyone is troubled in some way. What can I do for you?"

"You're unusually formal today. Are you sure you're okay?"

My mother took a deep breath. "Because I already know how this conversation is going to end. Because you're here and Rizgar isn't, you're going to tell me he sends his best, but can't come and get us as promised yet, because of complications. Am I right?"

Largren didn't reply right away, and I was becoming more curious by the minute. I had never met this Largren fellow, but my mother had, and it sounded as if they had met on more than one occasion.

"Yes, that's right," Largren finally said.

My mother sighed. "I thought so. I'd like for you to deliver a message for me."

Largren nodded. "Of course."

She took a deep breath. "Tell him… tell him to stop trying."

Largren took a step back, his eyes wide. I had to admit, I was also surprised. "B–but why?"

"I'm tired," she admitted. "I'm tired of waiting. I'm tired of being told the same words every year. I'm tired of fighting with my daughter over this."

She paused for a moment. "Tell him his daughter is lost to him. She despises him for all of this. She would have rather gone through life knowing he had just made a deal like all others do than be told lie after lie. She'd rather not know about him than be given false hope. She never wants to see him. She doesn't want to talk about him. And I can't blame her."

"Amara, please reconsider," Largren begged.

She shook her head. "I'm tired of hearing the same thing, and I'm tired of waiting. It's been twenty-five years since I last saw him. As my daughter has told me, no sane person waits that long."

My brow knitted. Twenty-five years? What was she talking about? It would have been thirty-seven, had the last time she'd seen him been the day my DNA had been placed in the tank for gestating.

Largren frowned. "I understand. I'll take your message to him."

"Thank you."

"Is there anything else you'd like me to do?"

My mother nodded and reached into a pouch on her belt and pulled out a folded piece of paper. "Give this to him. It's a photo of Eira. I know he'll want to know what she looks like now."

Largren smiled and took the paper. "I know he'll appreciate it. I'll take my leave now. Fare well, Amara."

"Goodbye, Largren."

I watched Largren leave for a moment before heading down to the lab again. I didn't want my mother to catch me eavesdropping. I needed to talk to Jasmine anyway. She may know why my mother mixed up the number of years she hadn't seen my father. I couldn't ask my mother directly, so Jasmine was the best bet.

44
CHAPTER

I opened my eyes and scanned the cell. Everyone was asleep. Well, everyone but Blaze. He was gone. I could only assume he had been taken away for an interrogation. It had been three days since Raikidan had sold us out and my dreams had finally caught up. I hoped they'd stay that way. I was tired of remembering—tired of being reminded of my mistake.

"Hey, Rashta?"

Silence.

"Hey, I don't know why you haven't been talking to me lately, but I know you can hear me. So… I just wanted you to know, I'm sorry for not listening to you and convincing you I was on the right path. I should know better than to make my own choices. I was made to do what others told me. Any other behavior is met with pain and misery. You'd think I would have learned that by now."

Still, silence. I accepted it. I didn't deserve answers from her. I wasn't worthy of kindness. I deserved this treatment.

My attention shifted to the entrance of the cell when I heard someone approaching. Normally I wouldn't have cared, but they sounded different from what I was used to.

I blinked when someone appeared at the door of the cell. "Yára?"

"I had to come see you," she said in a hushed voice.

I got up, wincing from pain, and met her at the bars. "How did you get here? I doubt Zarda would allow you up here."

She smiled. "Bone taught me how to sneak around without being detected."

"Will he be coming here as well?" I asked.

She shook her head. "No. As much as he wants to see you, he thinks they'll notice if he goes missing for even a few minutes, and doesn't want to cause issues."

I nodded. "What can I do you for then?"

Yára shrugged. "I just wanted to make sure you're doing okay. When I heard about the interrogation sessions, I became worried."

I chuckled. "It's nothing I can't handle. Even Shva'sika has enough energy to create lightning to deter soldiers from picking her."

"Are you sure? I have some decent pull here. I might be able to help in some way."

My eyes filled with sympathy, but before I could reply, the sound of a heavy door opening and boots stomping rang through the stone hallway. We listened. When a familiar, nasty smell wafted into my nose, I glowered. *I'll never forget that smell.* If I didn't act quick, Yára was going to get into a lot of trouble.

I glared at her. "You might as well stop wasting your breath."

Yára took the switch well and made herself look distressed. "Please, just listen to what I'm saying. If you repent, I can try to convince him to spare you. If you convince our brothers to come back and repent, I can do the same. We could be a family—a real one."

I spat on the ground. "I'd rather die than be his little pet."

"Sister…" Tears rimmed her eyes and it pained me. *She's a good actress!*

"Yára, what are you doing up here?" Zarda asked when he came out of the shadows of the hall. "You know you're not supposed to be here."

Her gaze fell to the ground. "I'm sorry. I just…"

I chuckled. "She was trying to appeal to my *humanity*."

Zarda stared at her. "Go back to your room."

Yára nodded and left. She tossed a glance over her shoulder at me, but I maintained my glare at her. I couldn't let my guard down. Not with Zarda around.

"You couldn't even be kind to your own sister?" Zarda said when he assumed she was out of earshot.

I snorted. "I have no sister."

"She's your clone. That makes her family."

"And what would you know about family?"

His eyes darkened and I grinned. He reached out for my face, but before he could get close enough to touch, I snapped my teeth at him and headed back to the far side of my cell.

Zarda chuckled. "Down, kitty."

I ignored him and closed my eyes.

"You know, she's right. If you just appeal to my better nature, you could spare yourself."

I opened my eyes, but he was gone. It was as if he had vanished into thin air. I grunted. *I won't sell out my friends. You'd never understand that.*

I closed my eyes again and let my body rest. In a few hours I'd have another beating to deal with.

45

CHAPTER

(RYOKO)

Laz slept in her corner; it pained me to look at her. A week had passed and she refused to speak to anyone or eat. It hurt to see her blame herself so much. I wished she wouldn't.

Raikidan's betrayal blindsided everyone. Everyone believed he was on our side. But per Laz's nature, she took all the blame onto herself.

I was also certain it wasn't just the betrayal that hurt her. He broke her heart. She let him in, and he'd turned on her. *Just as she feared he would… just as I'd ignored that fear and pushed for them to come together.* They'd been the perfect couple. He made her smile and laugh in a way I thought may have been lost. There was life in her again. *A reason to live…*

I feared for her now. It was all too obvious this had broken her. Now knowing she was part dragon, I was certain she had been seeking out acceptance from them, even if she wasn't willing to admit it. I was sure she wanted to believe her father's absence was a just a fluke, and there would be someone from that side of her who cared. She always searched for acceptance…

I was sure that was what she was thinking when she met Raikidan. *It had been her last hope, and…* I sighed.

Rylan draped his arm over my shoulder. "You need to sleep."

I shook my head. "I can't."

"Things will be okay. We'll get out of this. I have a good feeling about that."

"But at what cost?" I asked. "Laz won't be the same after all this."

"She'll be fine. Trust me."

I hope you're right. I leaned against him to sleep, when a shadow blocking the barred window caught my attention. I looked up to see a raven peering in at us. My brow furrowed. What was a raven doing awake at this time of night?

The bird hopped down from the window inside the cell and then shifted. My anger boiled. *Raikidan.*

"Ryoko, don't," Shva'sika said, grabbing me before I could think about throttling the overgrown snake.

"Why the hell not?" I bared my teeth. "He has no right to be here!"

Raikidan frowned. "I'm guessing things aren't going as planned if she's acting like that."

"What the hell are you spewing?" I spat.

Seda lifted her head. "No. Laz's memory still hasn't been restored."

Raikidan ran a hand through his hair. "It's been a week."

"I can only guess they're struggling with the restoration process," Seda said. "There are a lot of psychics here. Akama is going to need to be careful when she restores the memories, and can't have any interruptions."

I glanced between the two of them. "Are you saying this was planned?"

Blaze, Argus, and Rylan opened their eyes and we all waited.

Raikidan nodded. "It was a plan Eira and I came up together. Shortly before Shva'sika arrived, Zarda contacted me and tried to pay me to sell you out. I didn't give him any indication of my side on the matter, so he let me think it out. I didn't say anything for a while because I didn't want anyone to freak out."

His eyes darted about to each person in the room, as if making a head count or something. "The morning of the day I brought you the information about Zarda, I told Eira about the encounter and the two of us worked up a plan. We'd pretend I'd betray you all, and use the opportunity to attack Zarda from the inside once we had all the forces ready. We ran the idea by the Council, and they agreed to it, but only as long as Eira consented to having her memory temporarily erased. They figured because Zarda knew her so well, he'd see through her if she pretended to be surprised by it all. She agreed, and later that day I executed the plan."

I shook my head. "I can't… I can't believe this. You showed no signs of remorse when this was going on!"

Raikidan nodded and pulled a ring out of his pocket. It was the ring Laz had thrown away in her anger. "That wasn't as easy to do as it looked."

"He had help from me," Seda said. "He wouldn't have made it through all that had I not stepped in."

I shook my head. "You really expect me to buy your story?"

Blaze relaxed. "Why not? Sounds believable to me. And Seda says he's telling the truth."

Rylan and Argus nodded in agreement with him. I was the odd one out.

"Then, why doesn't Laz know now?" I demanded. "Why can't she remember yet?"

Seda let out a slow breath. "I've already given you the reason. We don't know why, but I'm assuming it's because they can't yet."

"She should have had it back within a day," Raikidan explained. "I figured things were going fine, and that's why I didn't come by until now." He pulled a backpack off his shoulders. "I brought you food. I assumed they'd be giving you slop, if anything at all."

He looked at Laz again. "From the looks of it, it's the latter."

"She hasn't been eating…" I admitted. "She refuses any food we offer and just sticks to that corner."

Raikidan's grip on the backpack tightened. "I knew I shouldn't have done this."

"Look at me."

He did, and I studied him for a moment. I searched for his sincerity in all this, and what I got hit me like a train. *So much pain…* I knew that look. He spoke the truth. He'd done this for her, even if it cost him more than it cost her.

"You should go," I said. "The guards will be doing the rounds soon. You don't need to be caught and end up messing up the plan."

He glanced at Laz and then nodded. I helped him take food out of the bag and divvied it up between everyone so we'd all have a fair share. While I did this, I watched Raikidan take an apple and place it next to her. It was a sweet gesture, knowing it was her preferred food when she wasn't feeling hungry.

Raikidan slung the empty backpack over his back before I was done handing out the food and he left. My senses picked up pain in the way he moved, and I hoped Laz would remember again soon. Even after finding about her deepest secret, he was still here for her. *He really does love her.*

She needed to know that, but it wouldn't be right for us to try and tell her. That would just add to the pain.

46
CHAPTER
(EIRA)

A fist collided with my gut and I choked, my hands clenching and my body swinging with the force. Another hit me. Then another. Over and over. I choked each time, the pain increasing, but I didn't cry out. I refused to give them that satisfaction.

The Brute assigned to my "punishment" frowned and hit me again, this time breaking a rib. Pain raked across my body and blood rushed into my throat, and still I refused. His eyes darkened and they flicked to a soldier standing by. She grinned and grabbed an iron rod sitting in a metal bucket. As she lifted it, the tip glowed red hot. *Awesome, this again.*

My torturers enjoyed this one. A touch of irony against the fire elementalist. The soldier pressed the hot iron against my arm, searing the flesh. I clenched my teeth and my hands fisted. Displeased with my resistance, she seared lower, closer to my armpit. She still didn't get the desired reaction.

"You know, we can do this all day," she cooed, heating up the rod again. "It'll be fun for us. But if you just did what we wanted, you could go back to your cell."

I didn't give her the satisfaction of a verbal response. They weren't worth my time.

Her displeasure spread into an ugly scowl and she jabbed the hot spike into my side. Pain seared through me and it took all my willpower to not cry out. The Brute followed up with another punch to my stomach and then to my face. Blood splattered onto the dirty floor. Splitting pain tore through me as teeth cracked and broke. I was quite sure my jaw wasn't left unaffected, either.

This action elicited a grunt, but not the desired scream, pissing the Brute off. His eyes snapped to the psychic in the corner of the room who watched on. "You, break her. Until her will is crushed, she isn't going to be a fun plaything."

Plaything. The last soldier who thought he could claim that of me and violate my body found himself dead of a broken neck. This one wouldn't get away with it, either.

I'd hidden my weakened state well. And now wasn't the time to hold back, else they'd find the weakness in my armor. With what little strength I had, I lifted my legs up and kicked the Brute in the face. It didn't do much, but it proved my will was far from broken. At least, not in the way they wanted.

The Brute growled and hit me three more times. My stubbornness won out. The psychic let out an exaggerated sigh, as if I'd inconvenienced him, and pushed away from the wall. An uncomfortable pressure slammed into the front of my head. I resisted, relying on my training to force him out.

The psychic scowled and pressed harder, finding resistance at every angle he tried. He came up to me and wrapped his hands around my head, the pressure increasing on all sides. It felt like a vice, taking all my will to resist.

The female soldier prodded me with the hot iron again, but the pain bolstered my resolve rather than weakening it.

"Don't do that!" the psychic hissed. "She finds strength in it."

The woman grumbled and put her toy back in the heating bucket. The psychic continued to force his way into my mind. I gritted my teeth, the wall in my mind starting to give.

"You will break!"

Never! But I could only do so much. The wall cracked, and he seized the moment to slip in. Excruciating pain assaulted my mind. And this time I couldn't fight.

An ear-shattering scream tore through my throat. A twisted grin spread across the psychic's face, but it disappeared when he realized I could handle this pain. I could allow myself to express the pain because this wouldn't break me. I wouldn't turn on those I cared about. *I'm not... him...*

I shouldn't have thought that. The psychic caught it and burrowed in deeper, grasping onto memories. Flashes. Sounds. Little bits here and there of my past. Some good, some not. He continued to push in deeper.

He found the memory of Raikidan betraying us, looping it twice before seeing I was now numb to this. I'd already run it through my mind enough on my own. I screwed up. No one could remind me of that more than me.

The psychic dug deeper, finding darker, more traumatizing memories. The first time I took a life—when I lost control in Zarda's gladiator arena—Tannek's death—my mother's death—me falling for a man who betrayed me; just like my mother had done with my father. Bits of conversations played, all with their own negative sensation attached.

Over and over they played. Sometimes on loop. Sometimes at a single crucial moment of emotional impact. And sometimes in an order that compounded the pain... loss... helplessness...

The emotions overwhelmed me, causing pain no physical torture could ever come close to. And then, something cracked. Images, and memories I didn't remember having. Conversations between individuals I'd never met. Names... Aria—Xetan—Nalia—Roan—the names and memories swarmed. I didn't know where they came from, or how to get it all to stop.

The psychic didn't either. I felt him trying to build up walls to push them back, but that effort was futile. He dislodged from my mind and backed up, heavy of breath. He wasn't the only one.

My body twitched and seized from his sudden and improper exit, the memories not stopping—mixing with the ones he'd intentionally pulled.

I barely heard the psychic ask, "What the hell was that, woman?"

I cringed and fought the wild mental pain of these overwhelming memories... images? There was no way all of this could be solely memories. It didn't make sense. *Nothing makes sense...*

Physical pain slammed into me, the Brute resuming his assault. Over and over he'd hit, the woman sticking me with her hot iron. The pain cleared my mind of the jumbled mess the psychic caused, but that didn't save me from the mental strain. And the psychic sensed it.

He invaded my mind again, this time at a distance. I couldn't fight him this time. This three-pronged assault was too much for me. I cried out in pain.

I didn't know how much time passed before they stopped. I felt so numb, I barely realized it.

I hung there against my restraints, my breath shallow. A barely audible whisper came from my lips.

The Brute sneered and leaned closer. "What was that, little assassin? You'll need to speak up."

"Deal…" I managed.

He chuckled and pulled away. "Go fetch Zarda. We broke her."

A pathetic grunt came from my throat when my body hit the floor. The soldier who threw me chuckled and slammed the cell door shut. Shva'sika rushed over and sent healing energy into me. Normally I'd refuse, my past transgressions not deserving of her sympathy, but this time, my body wouldn't move.

The moment my energy had been sufficiently restored, I pushed her away and pulled myself to my knees.

"Laz, please let me help you," Shva'sika begged.

I shook my head and slowly made my way to my corner. "Save your energy."

"You need healing. And you need to eat. You're going to kill yourself at this rate."

"We're dead anyway, so it doesn't matter how I go."

She sighed and sat back down. It didn't take long for her to succumb to sleep. She wasn't cut out for this kind of treatment. And yet, I didn't doubt she'd wake in a few hours and finish the job she'd started with me. She always capitalized on the moment I couldn't fend her off to heal me.

I gazed up at the moonlight filtering through the barred window. The deal I made today would end all this.

I touched my forehead when a small headache came on and I scanned the cell to distract myself. A normal reaction after what I'd gone through, coupled with my improper diet.

Everyone appeared to be asleep—except Seda. I could tell by the way she breathed that she was relaxing the best she could. She slept the least of all of us, due to the pain. The others had tried to get the device off her head, but as she had warned, it just shocked the others, and her, when they pulled on it. Only psychics could remove the device, and it took at least two of them to do so.

"Eira, it doesn't have to be this way."

My head swiveled. *Tannek?* A translucent figure appeared in front of me. It was him.

Tannek knelt and caressed my cheek with the back of his finger. "It doesn't have to be this way."

I shook my head. "I'll be joining you soon. There's no avoiding that."

"Your story isn't done yet."

"I never had one to begin with."

He chuckled. "Yes you do. You just can't see it yet."

"I die in three days. Nothing will change that."

"There is something, and it will happen." He stood back up and faded. "Fate is funny like that."

"Tannek, wait!" But I was too late. He was already gone. He was wrong, though. Nothing would change, and we'd be reunited. Just like I would be with my mother and aunt…

I held my head when my headache intensified. It felt like my brain was firing off pain signals everywhere. I shut my eyes when the pain peaked, and then something happened…

I opened my eyes slowly and yawned. The early morning sun filtered in through the skylight and I rolled over, reaching for Raikidan's form, only to find nothing. This caused me to awaken and I sat up. Quiet. No one was in the room with me. Where could he have gone? It wasn't like him to leave.

Then I thought about the date and realized our one week was up. Could he have… I took a deep breath so I wouldn't jump to any conclusions. He could be in the bathroom for all I knew.

My door opened then, and Raikidan strolled in, carrying a small tray. My mouth watered at the smell of breakfast wafting into the room. I should have known. He liked to bring me breakfast, he just usually waited until I woke up before leaving to get it.

"Ah, I timed this perfectly," he said. "Do I get points for that?"

"I'm tempted to say no, but I'm not in a particularly mean mood right now."

He grinned and placed the tray of food down on the bed. "I appreciate it."

I noticed he carried an empty leather bag in his hand. I chomped down on a strip of bacon. "What's with the bag?"

"I'll tell you after you eat."

I nodded and consumed my breakfast, sharing with him when he wanted something. I leaned back when I finished, and Raikidan moved the dirty dishes to the edge of the bed to be dealt with later.

He then took a deep breath, and it alarmed me. "What I'm about to talk to you about is important, but it's going to come off as horrible if you don't listen to me all the way through, okay? I don't want you jumping to the wrong conclusion."

I nodded. "I won't say a word until you tell me you're done."

He held up the bag I'd noticed earlier: a leather coin bag with fine embroidery. It looked a lot like the one we'd argued over when I found out he had left the city to grab money from his hoard. As I gazed at it, I realized it was that same bag.

"You remember this, right?" he asked. I nodded. He smiled when I kept my promise by not speaking, but it went away quickly. "You know how I told you I got the money from my hoard? Well... I lied. Or, more accurately, I let you believe it came from somewhere else so you wouldn't freak out more than you did."

He took a deep breath. "I received the money from Zarda."

My eyes widened and I nearly went into a panic, but resisted. Raikidan said it'd sound worse than it was, and I promised to hear him out. I took a deep breath. "Continue."

He nodded. "A few weeks before you found the money, Zarda contacted me. He seemed convinced that you were the real Eira he'd been searching for, instead of some immigrant, and figured if that was the case, that meant I was an outsider that could be persuaded to turn you in. He told me to meet him somewhere in the city. I was reluctant, but Seda told me to go ahead and meet him. She was sure nothing bad would come of it, so I humored them both. He tried to bribe me to turn you in, telling me the money he was giving me at the time would only be a down payment, and I'd get three times as much if I turned you in."

He rubbed the back of his neck. "I attempted to throw him off our trail and told him he had the wrong people, but he was persistent and told me to think about his offer. I didn't say anything to anyone because I figured everyone would come to the wrong conclusion. I didn't want any of you to hate me, even though I chose not turn you all in."

"So, why are you telling me now?" It was obvious he had no intention of turning us in, or betraying me after everything we'd gone through this past week, but I couldn't help but find it strange he'd tell me now after all this time.

"Well, there are two reasons. The first reason is that I've been feeling guilty about not telling you. It just… felt wrong to keep it a secret, because I don't want secrets between us. But because I was worried you'd freak out, I've dealt with it myself until now. The other reason is a bit more strange. I wondered if we might be able to use this to our advantage."

I took in this suggestion. "Like, make Zarda think you're taking him up on the offer?"

Raikidan nodded. "Exactly. I don't know what kind of plan we can come up with, but it's better than what we have working now, and it means this stupid fighting can finally end."

I pushed myself to my knees and threw my arms around his neck. "Raikidan, you're a genius!"

He stiffened, taken aback by my response. "Y—you're not mad?"

I pulled away and smiled. "No. I should be, since you kept this from me and could have easily done us in, but because you didn't and came clean instead, I'm grateful. Though, I have to know—why didn't you turn us in? At that time you didn't really know us that well, and he was offering up a lot of gold. I wouldn't expect a dragon to be able to pass that up. Frankly, I would have thought you'd use that as a means of revenge for your mother."

Raikidan scratched his head. "I didn't act on it because it was around the time I was realizing I couldn't take my revenge on you for my mother's death. Even though I was still learning about all of you and you were all still getting to know me, I felt like I belonged here. I didn't feel different, even though I'm a dragon—a half-color dragon at that. I've never felt that way before. And that feeling outweighed the urge to take the money. It was stronger than my drive to hoard, and stronger than my desire for revenge." He paused. "It's what got me to think about how wrong my path for revenge was."

I smiled more and rested my hand on his cheek. "Thank you."

He smiled back. "I'm glad I didn't act on it. I'm happy with you by my side."

I rubbed my thumb over his cheek.

"So, how are we going to use this?"

I pulled away and shrugged. "I'm not sure. We're going to need to inform the Council about the decision, so we may want to just go see them to find out if we can all come up with a good plan."

Just then someone knocked on my door.

"Yeah?" I called.

The door cracked open and Seda spoke. "Genesis and I are ready when you are."

"Geez, you two work fast."

She chuckled. "We knew what was going on. I just wanted to let you know we can see the Council at any time to discuss matters."

I nodded. "Well I just need to get dressed."

"That would be for the best."

Pain shot through my head. Or, I thought it was my head. Was it someone else's head? I couldn't be sure. My vision jumped around. I could see the stone flooring of a cell, and then I was walking with the others in the sewers. Then my vision flashed back to a cell, and then I was seeing the virtual training room of the Underground. Unbearable pain shot through my head again.

I waited as the Council members all gathered on the same platform as me in the discussion chamber.

"Seda already briefed us of the situation to save time," Eldenar said when they were all assembled. "Is it true you have had contact with Zarda?"

"Only once," Raikidan said. "He hasn't tried to contact me again since."

"Because he's playing games with us," Hanama hissed. "You should have never met with him."

"Why not?" I challenged. "Because it shows he's one step ahead of us? Or more likely, only running on hunches and relying on others to reveal the truth?"

Hanama growled, but Enrée nodded with agreement. "Eira is right. Zarda only worked on a hunch because of his obsessive nature. Raikidan never revealed to him the truth. He attempted to play on the lie that had been created."

"Zarda paid the outsider," Elkron said. "He knew."

"No, he didn't know," Akama argued. "He believed he did, and assumed if he paid Raikidan, then Raikidan would confess the truth. Zarda is waiting for Raikidan to contact him to prove him right. He has a big enough ego to be split into seven people."

"Genesis, you've been quiet," Eldenar observed. "What do you have to say in the matter?"

"I think you're all being stupid," she said. "Instead of focusing on how we can use this situation to our advantage, you're choosing to bicker about a decision that hasn't negatively impacted our cause in any way."

The Council members looked at each other and I held a clenched hand over my mouth as I bit it to stop myself from laughing at them. I took a deep breath when I got myself under control. "Now that Genesis has scolded all of you, I'm thinking a plan is in order."

Elkron nodded. "You're both right. The outcome of this situation is more important than how it began."

Akama nodded as well. "We should be thankful we have this opportunity. We may now be able to end this rebellion for good."

"The question is, what plan can we come up with that can utilize this information and minimize the risk of casualties?" Adina asked.

"Well, there's one thing that's obvious," I said. "Raikidan is to seemingly betray me, and maybe the rest of our housemates. This will get us into prison, and since we'd be held for treason, we'd be in high-level security towers in the fortress."

"We would need to utilize the moles," Genesis said.

I nodded. "Whether they sneak others into the castle or work independently is up for debate. But this will all have to take place at Zarda's castle."

"Why not in the city?" Hanama asked. "Why can't we draw him out where he's less protected?"

"The likelihood of me meeting him again is slim," Raikidan said. "When I spoke with him, he gave me a contact for when I was ready to hand Eira over. The way he held himself told me that dealing with me again was the last thing he wanted to waste his time on."

"We also need to worry about civilian casualties," I pointed out. "We can't get them caught up in this. Even if we plan an assassination, we can't rely on that working. With the alterations Zarda is making to his body, we need to prepare for a battle."

"We've had battles on the streets before," Hanama said.

"Not planned ones."

"I agree with Eira," Elkron said. "We can't risk it. We need the people to be on our side when this is over. Endangering them on purpose won't be good for our image."

Hanama crossed her arms. "Fine."

Enrée called for a vote. "Is it agreed we fight Zarda at the fortress?"

Each Council member agreed.

Elkron looked amongst us. "Now that we have that settled, we have the matter of implementing everything. The obvious is to have Raikidan meet with Zarda or his underlings, and agree to bring at least Eira to him. Somewhere secluded in the city will be the most likely agreement to be made."

"*We can meet him in an alley or a dead-end street, making it seem like he cornered us,*" I said. "*It'll satisfy his crave for coming out on top in situations like this. It might be best to involve some of my team as well, so he can feel like he's getting a bigger prize for his efforts.*"

Adina nodded. "That's a good idea. And while that is going on, we can work with the moles to get more of us inside the fortress."

"We can assign a group of rebels to break my team out once the perfect time comes, and lure Zarda out to the execution grounds," Genesis suggested. "He likes to deal with prison breaks himself, making it easier to bait him."

I nodded. "Sounds like a good idea to me. How long should we have this take? We all know how traitors are treated when they're in holding."

"I propose two weeks," Hanama said.

"That's a long time," Eldenar said. "Too long. We should aim for a much shorter turnaround. No longer than a week."

I shook my head. "No. Two weeks would be better."

"Are you sure?" Genesis asked, obviously worried. "They'll torture you."

I nodded. "I know. But we can handle it. If we don't take our time, we'll mess up and we cannot afford that."

Raikidan stared at me with a concern that was borderline fear. "I'm not consenting to that."

"It's going to be fine," I assured. "It's not as bad as everyone is making it out to be."

Raikidan eyed me skeptically but didn't voice an argument.

"So, it sounds as if we're all in agreement," Enrée said.

"There is one matter left to discuss." Akama said. "And that's to do with Zarda and Eira's relationship."

My brow rose. "What about it?"

"Zarda knows you well. It's possible he'll know something is up just by looking at you if you don't express yourself just right—"

"I hid things from him all the time. I have a secret he still doesn't know about."

"Yes, but that secret is also something you like to hide from yourself, correct?"

I frowned at her challenge. She was right on that. "What are you trying to get at, then?"

"I propose that none of your team is informed about this plan, and we remove this memory from your mind—at least temporarily."

I glowered. "You're not getting into my head."

Akama held up her hands. "Easy. It's only temporary. I'll be able to restore it within a day of your capture. Nothing bad will happen to your mind. I promise."

I chewed on my lip. I didn't like this idea.

Raikidan placed a hand on my shoulder. "Give us a minute to think it over."

Akama nodded. "Of course."

Raikidan lead me away. "How are you feeling about this?"

I shook my head. "I don't know. I don't want any psychics messing with my mind, and I don't like the idea of the others or myself not knowing about this. I don't want to think about how we'll treat you if we believe you've betrayed us."

"I can handle that," Raikidan insisted.

"I'm not sure I can, though. I take that stuff seriously. I don't want to think about how I'll treat you. And then having to remember it was planned…"

He placed his hands on both of my shoulders. "It'll be fine. I won't hold it against you. I'm more worried about the torture you mentioned."

"Rai, don't worry about that. It's really nothing we can't handle."

"I just don't want you to have to go through that…"

I held his gaze, my resolve unwavering. "It'll be the last time I'll ever have to go through it."

"Promise?"

I smiled and patted the side of his face. "I promise. Besides, I'm doing a total career change and advocating peace as Shaman Ambassador. If I'm in a situation of torture again while doing that, there's a problem."

He grunted. "Yeah, means I'm not doing my job."

I chuckled. "We should inform the Council of our decision."

Raikidan nodded. "All right."

As we rejoined the Council, pain shot through my head again. Or that other person's head. It hurt more to try and understand than to just accept the pain. My vision of Raikidan and me speaking with the Council switched to a view of a cell with people clustered in it. My head pulsed, and my vision showed me sitting down on a bed with Akama and Seda nearby. I wanted to cry out in pain but refrained.

"Raikidan, you'll be tasked with carrying her back to the house," Akama said. "While you do that, we'll work on putting your housemates to sleep to solidify the illusion we're creating. You'll have a short window to contact Zarda and get things set up."

"Understood," he said. "I had a thought just now. I want to loop Zo and Corliss into this."

I cocked my head. "Why?"

"To increase the believability. Zo is a new recruit for the rebellion. It'd be easy for

us to play off him worming his way in, and me using him as a liaison with Zarda. And Corliss, that's mostly backup in case I need extra manpower to ensure Zarda doesn't suspect anything." His lips twitched. "This may help convince you as well when the time comes. Who knows how you'll react to the betrayal in the moment."

"I believe this is a wise move," Seda said.

Akama nodded. "As do I. I've got my brother informing the rest, and he'll contact Zo so the two of you can meet in person before fetching Zarda." She turned her head to me. "Now, let's get this plan moving."

"Rai, you'll try to pack away my more valuable things, right?" I said. "I don't want Zarda's goons to destroy them when they raid the house."

He smiled at me. "Of course I will."

"I'll be assisting with that," Seda said. She smirked. "It'll also ensure he doesn't run off with my cat."

Raikidan grumbled and I laughed. His attachment to the feline, that acted more like a canine, amused me. I'd need to look into getting him a pet.

Akama patted the bed. "I need you to lie down and relax now, Eira."

I nodded and did as instructed. She hovered over me. A pressure built in my head and I squeezed my eyes shut.

My eyes snapped open and my breath came in shallow gasps. Seda had moved next to me and placed a hand on my shoulder. "Take it easy."

I took a deep breath. "Seda, was that—"

"Your memory returning?" She nodded. "Yes."

I ran my fingers through my disheveled hair. "I really had agreed to all of this?" She nodded again and my heart clenched. "Has Raikidan been the one bringing us food?"

"Yes. He stops by when you're asleep so as not to cause you any trouble with your blocked memory. He's been distraught over your memory not restoring when promised."

I stared at the floor. "I said and thought such nasty things about him…"

"He knew you would. He was willing to hear all that because he believed this plan would finally lead to the life he wanted you to have—a free life. You know this."

"Did you know all of this?" I asked Rashta.

"Yes. It's why I've stayed quiet the whole time. I didn't want to cause you more trouble. Though, we need to talk about the deal you made earlier."

I shook my head in an attempt to rid myself of the lingering pain.

"I was supposed to have my memory returned over a week ago. Why didn't that happen?"

"At first I assumed Akama was having difficulties restoring it. But as I've observed your behavior, I believe it's because of your emotional state. I think your anger and pain blocked your ability to remember."

I nodded. "I need to talk to him."

"He usually comes around midnight. He'll fly in through the window as a raven."

I nodded again and leaned against the wall to collect myself. Midnight wasn't too far away. I needed to prepare myself.

"Rashta?"

"If you're going to ask me questions to pass the time, I am limited on what I can tell you still."

"I just wanted to know why you did what you did in the bath. Especially knowing my mind had been altered."

She was quiet for a moment. *"I can't answer that in full—not yet. I can say it's because of timing, and because I knew you'd remember when your two realities combined."*

"That's all you can tell me, about any of that interaction? You can't tell me what's going on with you and me?"

"When this is over, you must go to the temple. Not the one in this city. One far to the northwest."

"That's not helpful…"

"It's all I can say right now."

I sighed and accepted it for what it was. The minutes ticked by slowly and I found my eyes growing heavy. I fought the urge to sleep; I needed to remain awake. My internal fighting caused small headaches to flare up, and it became increasingly difficult to rest. When I thought I couldn't stay awake any longer, I heard the flapping of wings. I curled up into my corner, pretending to be asleep, and kept one eye cracked open.

Just as Seda said, a raven landed on the window and squeezed itself between the bars. The bird jumped down into the cell and looked around before changing shape.

I sat up when Raikidan removed the backpack from his shoulders and set it on the floor. "Raikidan…"

He spun around. "Eira."

I frowned. "I'm… sorry."

His eyes widened. "You remember?"

I nodded. "This was all part of a plan we put together."

He closed the distance between us and embraced me in a tight hug. His musky ash scent overpowered me. "I'm so relieved. I was worried you'd never remember." He buried his face in my neck. "I thought I had made the biggest mistake of my life."

"I'm sorry for what I said to you…" I murmured into his shoulder, digging my fingers into his shirt. "I shouldn't have been so awful."

"Stop." He cupped my chin. "Don't you go apologizing on me."

"But I—"

"I knew what I was getting into when we agreed to this. I'm the one who should be sorry. I should have come up with a different way to do this."

"This was the only way."

"But you didn't get your memory back until now. That's far longer than we had agreed. Had I known this was going to happen, I would have come up with a different idea. Had I known Zarda was actually going to show up in that alley, I would have prepared for everyone to attack him then." His gaze lowered. "I was made to think I'd be paid second-hand."

I stroked his cheek. "Sometimes plans change and you have to be flexible. Which is something I—"

Raikidan kissed me with so much passion suddenly I thought my heart would stop. He pulled away a few moments later. "I'm going to make it up to you. When we get through this, I'll make it up to you with so much interest you'll hate me."

I was momentarily stunned. "Y–you still want to be with me?"

"Of course."

"Even after what you found out in my rage?"

He pressed his forehead against mine. "It was you this whole time. The voice. I was so surprised, and then guilty for not figuring it out sooner. I should have seen that."

Shock rippled through me, stealing my breath.

"I told you so," Rashta said.

I took a few moments to collect myself. "I wanted to tell you. I had planned to after the memory alteration. The time I spent alone allowed me to muster the ability, but then the plan came first, so—"

Raikidan pressed a finger against my lips. "You don't have to explain yourself. I knew why it was hard for you to tell me. I understand even more now." He stroked my cheek. The action sent a tingling sensation down my spine to my fingers. "I'm not your father. I will not be so foolish as to let you go. Dragon, human, you're Eira to me. My Lazmira."

My heart thumped in my chest. The way that name rolled off his tongue… I never wanted someone to call me by my given name more than I did now.

Raikidan kissed me again, and I rested my hand on his cheek, losing myself in the rush of passion flooding over me. But when the events from earlier today crept into my mind, I realized how wrong it was to embrace this.

I pulled away and he furrowed his brow. "What's wrong?"

I took a deep breath. "I need you to bring a message to the Council. The original plans have changed."

"Laz, you don't have to go through this," Seda said. I was surprised she had stayed quiet for so long. *"There are other ways."*

"She's right," Rashta said. *"There are many other ways than this."*

"Is this not the burden of the Dragon-Phoenix?" I said. *"Is it not my birthright to put my life before others?"*

"Do not allow stories of mortals to twist what you are," she said. *"You are more than a martyr."*

Concern flashed across Raikidan's face. "What's going on?"

I took a deep breath. "Because of my memory alteration, I made a deal with Zarda earlier today."

His jaw tensed, eye hardening. "What kind of deal?"

I hesitated for a moment. "In exchange for my life I will save hundreds."

Raikidan's eyes widened. "No! I am not bringing them that message to them. I'm not going along with that plan."

"You have to."

"I'm not going to let you die!"

"This will bring peace."

"Not to me."

My eyes softened. "I'm sorry, Rai. But there's no changing this. The execution is in three days."

"There has to be another way. I'm not going to lose you."

"It's too late, Rai. What's done is done."

His voice rose. "How can you be so calm about this?"

I hushed him so he wouldn't attract the attention of the guards or wake the others. "Because this is how it is. This is my fate. A fate not many could face."

"You deserve a good life! A better one than the one you've been living."

"And so do others." I stroked his cheek. "For the price of one life, my life, I will save hundreds, if not thousands, of other lives. Lives that are also ruined by Zarda's existence. If my life is really worth that much, then I'll give it up."

"For what? Lumaraeon doesn't owe you anything. Not with how you were treated by it. Why save it?"

I stayed calm. "Because it's the right thing to do."

"But is it what you want to do?"

An image of us two standing by a lake, hands entwined watching two children run about flashed through my mind. It made me pause, a longing setting in. I steeled myself. "Sometimes what we want, and what is right, are different."

"And what about me? Do you not care in the least about me and what I think about this?"

I grabbed the back of his head and pulled him closer for a rough kiss. Raikidan attempted to fight the separation when I pulled away a few moments later, but I couldn't allow it to last. "I do care. I do want you. I have accepted everything that came with caring about you so deeply, but I'm not meant to keep the things I want…"

My eyes flicked to the cell door when I heard footsteps. "You need to leave. The guards are doing their rounds."

"I don't care. I'm not leaving," Raikidan said.

"You will leave." My eyes burned into him with great intensity. "And you will deliver my message to the Council. Now go."

He frowned, his eyes pleading with me to reconsider. I held my ground and he reluctantly gave in. He emptied the contents of his backpack and stored the food in places the soldiers wouldn't notice before slinging the bag over his shoulder. His eyes lingered on me one last time before shifting and flying out the window.

A knot formed in my stomach, my thoughts turning inward. Was this right? Would this bring the desired result I hoped for?

I scrubbed my hands over my face and leaned against the wall. It didn't matter. This was how it had to be.

Footsteps echoed closer. The soldier who showed up took me by surprise. "Zo?"

He nodded and motioned for me to come closer. I did as he requested. "I heard from hushed whispers that you made a deal with Zarda earlier today. Is that true?"

I nodded. "Yeah."

"Do you know how upset your sister is?"

"I have a good guess. The others in this cell would be, too, if they knew."

"Why would you make a deal with him? We have a working plan."

"Because it benefits everyone but me. The plan we made together has the possibility for more casualties than mine."

"Are you sure you want to do this?"

I nodded. "Yes, and I need you to do me a favor. I just sent Raikidan to tell the Council about the change. Naturally, he doesn't want to go along with it, so I'm not sure if he's going to relay the message. I need you to make sure they know one way or another."

Zo exhaled. "You're sure you don't want to continue with the initial plan?"

"My execution is in three days. Unless someone can devise a strategy with fewer casualties, then I'm sure."

"Why would you do this?"

I pulled away from the bars, my voice dropping to a whisper. "Like I told Raikidan, it's the right thing to do."

Zo exhaled slowly. "Very well. I'll make sure the message is delivered, but I can't guarantee anyone will agree with it."

I sat down in my corner and closed my eyes. "We'll see."

47

CHAPTER

I peered around. Bright warm rays of the sun shone above me as the cool water of the lake lapped at my feet. The breeze carried the scent of wildflowers and my ears rang with the sounds of nature. The temple stood in the center as it always did, but without Raikidan here, I had no means of getting to it.

I turned around when something small running my way caught my ears. I was taken aback by the two children scampering through the grass toward me. One was a young boy and the other a young girl, and they both appeared to be around the same age. *They look… familiar.*

"Momma, come play with us!" the little girl yelled out.

I scanned my surroundings, hoping to find another woman standing somewhere, but it was just me. My confusion grew when the two children latched onto my legs.

The little girl had violet and red hair, fair skin, and freckles, and when she peered up to smile at me, my breath caught at the sight of her sapphire eyes with golden rings around her pupils. "C'mon, momma, play!"

I shifted my gaze to the little boy, and he shared many similarities with the girl, but had a few defining differences. He had violet and black hair, freckles and a bit darker skin, and his eyes were green with golden rings around the pupils.

The boy laughed as he tugged on me. "Yeah, momma, come play!"

I glanced between the two as I tried to figure things out. "I—I'm not your mother."

The girl giggled and ran away. "Don't be silly! Of course you are. Now come play with us and daddy!"

"Daddy?" My gaze followed the two children as they took off through the meadow that was between the lake and the forest that surrounded the lake. In the middle of the meadow stood a man who looked all too familiar. *Raikidan?*

"You can have this, you know."

I spun around at the sound of the new heavily accented voice and took a step back at the sight of the well-dressed, dark-skinned man behind me. "Raisu…"

Raisu smiled. "Hello again, Eira."

I glanced down at the children clinging to me. "Why are you showing me these kids again?"

"Because you rejected the dream before. I had hoped you'd embrace it this time."

My eyes narrowed. "Why? What is your angle?"

He frowned. "It's nothing dubious. I just want you to reconsider the choice you've made."

I shook my head. "There's nothing to reconsider."

"I disagree. There are many paths you can choose from. Ones that lead to your happiness and freedom all at once."

"There is no other way that will ensure so few casualties," I said.

"There are always other ways. You don't need to give up your life. You don't have to give up these dreams."

My eyes narrowed. "Why do you care? You gods don't care for one person. You think about the larger picture of this world, and that's it. One person's life is meaningless."

Raisu shook his head. "You're wrong. We do care about each individual, and we care about you."

"Right. And that's why I've had such a wonderful life, right? It's been so perfect I shouldn't be complaining in the least?"

He frowned. "Please don't do that."

"Don't do what? Prove a point? If I had actually mattered, things would have been a whole lot different."

"You weren't meant to have this life. Both Phyre and I have said as much on two occasions. This life wasn't planned for you. You have no idea how important you are, and I want you to see this dream as reality. I want you to take back this choice and make a new one. You must live."

I shook my head. "Not going to happen. Those I care about will be safe because of me."

"Why are you doing this?"

"Because no one else will."

He pointed to the children and the dream version of Raikidan. "But you want this."

"I would make for a horrible parent. The only reason Ryder came out so intact is because others helped me. I'd never dream to have more."

"But you want that choice!" He struggled to keep his frustration at bay now.

I shook my head. "It doesn't matter. I'm not allowed to have what I want. That's how it's always been."

He sucked air through his teeth but didn't say anything more. There wasn't a way for him to change my mind. Small hands grabbed onto mine and I looked down at the little girl.

"Momma, come play with us!" she begged. "Please?"

"Yeah, momma, come play," the little boy said as he grabbed onto my other hand.

I frowned and pulled away from the two.

"Momma?"

"I'm sorry," I whispered before turning and heading down the shore of the lake. It was best that I didn't indulge in this dream.

A strong hand grabbed my wrist, forcing me to stop. "Don't go."

I turned and faced Raikidan. "I'm sorry."

"Stay with us."

"I can't." I pulled away, my chest tightening. "I'm sorry, but this is how it has to be."

He tried to reach out to me again, but I turned and ran. I wished Raisu hadn't given me this dream. I didn't want to be reminded of what I was giving up—what I wasn't allowed to have.

Darkness fell over the lake; it was a thick fog I knew all too well. The fog rolled in around me, and in the darkness a hand reached out.

It wasn't an aggressive reach. No, it was a welcoming one and I took up the offer. I needed it to take me. I needed the feelings it gave, or lack thereof, to consume my heart so I could live with the choice I was making.

Take away the pain, one last time...

48
CHAPTER

I resisted cringing when the soldier holding me dug his fingers into my skin while another bound my wrists. Two days had come and gone, and no one had come to tell me we weren't going through with my new plan. No one came to bail us out. I knew the Council would go with my decision; it was logical. Now on the third day, I was going to face my end.

The soldiers pushed us forward once everyone was bound; I was surprised by their silence. I was used to them throwing insults at execution prisoners, so this was new. Sure, there were a few who were being rougher than necessary, but not all of them were. There were some who even carried a somber air to them, as if they didn't want this to happen. It made me wonder if they were part of the rebellion. It was possible, and it was also likely that not everyone had agreed with my plan, but it didn't matter.

We walked through the jail halls, and other prisoners made comments and strange sounds. Some even reached out to grab at us or at the soldiers. Once we were through all that, other soldiers joined our little doom-and-gloom parade and escorted us through the fortress until we reached the execution grounds. Hundreds of soldiers were already assembled in the courtyard.

Our group was pushed around until they had us in a line. Blaze fidgeted next to me, and a soldier hit him and he stopped. He should have known better. Any movement from prisoners that was more than breathing or the occasional weight shift was met with punishment. It was how we stayed controlled.

Rylan attempted to hold Ryoko's hand, but a soldier wasn't going to allow it. Unfortunately, Rylan wasn't going to be forced into submission, and he body-slammed the soldier. Ryoko gasped and I nearly growled. *He should know better.* Several soldiers tried to force him to calm down, but he was uncharacteristically unruly.

"Rylan." My voice was calm and assertive. He stopped his struggling and looked at me. "Show some dignity."

He let out a long sigh but stopped struggling. A soldier even pushed him, trying to provoke him, but he just took it. A group of soldiers parted to make way for someone who was coming through the crowd. *Zarda.* He confidently strolled into the center of the courtyard and barely gazed around; instead, his malicious gaze stayed fixed on me.

"Let's start this, shall we?" His grin made me sick.

He pointed at me and a soldier grabbed my shoulder. I didn't resist. I had accepted my fate. There was no changing it.

I had only taken two steps when soldiers began to panic and whisper. Moments later, large shadows flew over the ground. I gazed up and was taken aback by the enormous dragons flying over us. Most of them were red, but there were a few greens, blacks, and three half-colors I was certain I recognized. This was bad.

Zarda chuckled when three of the dragons landed in the courtyard. The black and red one was obviously Raikidan, and the green one was Corliss. But the full-red dragon was a mystery. It wasn't Zaith. I knew his features. This dragon was heavily plated down the neck and back, like armor, and had heavy plated scales covering his curved black horns. Black spines lined his chin and the top of his snout, while more spines framed the underside of his eyes until they merged with the large plated spines clustered on his cheeks. Under these spines was a large plate, in the shape of a frill with black-spined tips.

More spines trailed up the center of his snout, splitting and lining the top of his eyes until they merged with the plating on his horns. His body and bases of his wings were covered with heavy plating and black spines down to his spear-tipped tail.

But even though I didn't recognize him, there was an air of familiarity about him. I found out why when the three of them shifted. The man was tall, and more than just muscular. He was huge. He had green eyes with a golden ring around the pupil, a shaved head and red beard.

Anger boiled up in me at the sight of my father. *How dare he show his face here!* I watched as the three dragons advanced toward Zarda, who only grinned in response.

"Well, well, well, what do we have here?" Zarda looked them over. "Two betrayers, and a law breaker." Zarda turned his eyes to my father. "You have a lot of gall to show your face here, Rizgar."

"I have gall? You're the one readying the execution of my daughter." Rizgar bared his teeth. "Last I remember, that was against our agreement."

Zarda chuckled. "Coming from the one who snuck in for twelve years after the agreement was made."

Twelve years? I blinked slowly. What were they talking about? My mother never mentioned that, even when I first believed the lies he told us. *Wait, is that what she meant when I was wrong about how long he'd been gone?*

Rizgar growled. "I had a right to see them."

Zarda chuckled. "That's cute. If I remember correctly, you forfeited your right when you chose your kind over them. Is that right, dear Eira?"

My gaze remained impassive. "Can we just get this over with?"

Rizgar stared at me with surprise. "Eira, d—"

"Don't speak to me." My lip curled. "You have no right to be here. You should have just stayed on your mountain like you have for the past seven decades."

He stared at me, eyes filled with pain. I didn't care. He couldn't honestly think I'd just up and forgive him for what he did.

Raikidan took a step closer. "Don't do this, Eira."

I fixed an unwavering, stern expression on him before walking toward Zarda. A soldier ran to catch up with me, trying to maintain the appearance of an escort. As I was brought to my final place to stand, I watched Zarda load a three-barreled pistol. I noticed some kind of silvery-white liquid in the transparent bodies of the shells. It had to be nickel. It was the one true weakness of those with dragon blood—my one debilitating weakness that had been kept hidden away.

I was lucky that ordinary people could have allergies to nickel; I was able to use that as an excuse for me being careful with the jewelry I wore.

It would only make sense for Zarda to make my death painful. Any restraints he used on me always had it mixed in, keeping me under control, but not dead. It wasn't beneath him to make death any less of a release. If the bullet didn't kill me, the nickel would, but slowly and painfully. It was his style.

I opened my mouth to speak, but before I could, several portals opened in the courtyard. Cloaked figures rushed out of them. But that wasn't the only thing going on. A loud booming echoed through the air. The wall behind Zarda and the three shifted dragons cracked. Moments later, the wall broke away and a group of people rushed him. The two people leading them were my brothers, Rhaec and Trigon. These inner walls weren't made with synthetic metal. Zarda never saw a need for the resources to be wasted on this courtyard, so it would be easy for brutes to break them.

What is going on? The group my brothers led was small and the only psychics with them were Nioush, Saléna, and Nyra. Even with the shaman and dragon numbers, this couldn't be some sort of counter-plan the Council cooked up. What were they all up to?

Zarda gazed around with a grin. "Well, well, well. What do we have here? More party guests? Eira, dear, you're far more popular than I had expected."

"Let my sister go!" Trigon ordered.

"Or what? You'll rush over and attack me when I'm armed?" Zarda chuckled. "Not even your skin-hardening ability can save you from these bullets."

Trigon glowered and Zarda laughed. As much as I cared for my brother, he was more brawns than brain.

"You will let her go." I glanced over my shoulder to see Maka'shi advancing toward us from a portal with the other leaders and… *Valene? Why in Lumaraeon would they bring her here?*

"Or you will face the consequence for breaking our pact," Maka'shi continued.

Zarda laughed. "That's already been done by you."

Maka'shi frowned.

"What, did you really think I hadn't found out you had been hiding her away? Why do you think I had your pathetic village destroyed all those years ago? It wasn't about dear Eira. No. It was about teaching you a lesson." He let out an exaggerated sigh. "Sadly, those Hunters chose to chase after our precious lady instead of completing the task."

Maka'shi scowled. "We had done nothing wrong."

"You took in a fugitive."

"We took in a shaman. We will not turn our backs on our laws. That was part of our agreement with you."

Zarda snickered. "You expect me to believe you knew she was a shaman the moment you met her? I doubt you looked past her hardened expression before reluctantly taking her in. You aren't exactly the most trusting woman anymore, now are you, Maka'shi?"

I could see Maka'shi struggled to keep her composure but she wasn't the only one. They were just wasting time.

"Enough!" I shouted.

Everyone, including Zarda turned their attention to me.

"We have a deal, Zarda."

He chuckled. "That we do, my dear."

"So why don't you tell them? That way we can get this over with."

Zarda grinned. "Why would I want to do that?"

"Because them knowing is part of the deal, too, if you remember. Now tell them."

Zarda held up his hands. "Very well. At the cost of Eira's life, the rest of you and those who have allied with her are free. Free from all pacts, services, and any possible future persecution. I'm required to leave you all alone, at the expense of ending her life."

Gasps erupted all around us. Allies appeared surprised and confused, and my friends looked mortified.

"No, you can't…" Valene whispered, her hands covering her mouth.

"Laz, why?" Ryoko asked. Her eyes welled up with tears.

Rhaec looked nearly lost for words. "No… you can't go through with this…"

A tear rolled down Seda's cheek. I knew this was tough for her, more than anyone else. She had known this outcome was a great possibility, but kept it a secret from everyone. Such were the ways of psychics.

"This is my choice," I said. "This is how it will be. Now everyone is to stand down."

Most refused to listen—not that it surprised me. Why would they allow me to go through with this without a fuss? I was never allowed to make choices about my life. They were always wrong.

I couldn't be angry, though. I didn't want to die, but it was the only way to ensure the others lived. Even if Zarda wasn't trustworthy, I knew my sacrifice wouldn't be in vain. Any retaliation from him would be met with a force even he couldn't fight.

"I said stand down!" I ordered. "I will not say it again."

The others exchanged glances and tried to resist the command, but ultimately listened.

"Don't do this."

"It's the only way."

I glanced back at the soldier who had escorted me when he unlocked my chains. "What are you doing?"

"You don't need these. You don't go back on your word," he murmured.

I nodded my thanks as I rubbed my wrists before lifting my gaze to meet Zarda's, my resolve unwavering. "Let's get this over with."

Zarda grinned. "Oh, we will, my impatient little pet, but first"—he snapped his fingers—"I want to make sure someone is here to see this."

My eyes narrowed. *What is he up to?* I turned my gaze over my shoulder when I heard two sets of heavy boots advancing and what sound to be like… someone struggling. When I spied the people heading our way, my eyes widened and a quiet gasp escaped my lips. "Ryder…"

He was restrained and held onto by two soldiers. How had they gotten a hold of him?

"What is the meaning of this?" I demanded.

Zarda feigned innocence. "What do you mean, my dear? Don't you want him here? I thought you might want to say goodbye, just like I allowed for you and your lovely mother."

My anger boiled. "Fuck you, you motherless cur."

"Oh, now don't act like that, Eira," he chided. "I was just trying to do you a favor."

"You spineless snake!" Rizgar snarled.

Zarda pointed his pistol at Rizgar when he took a step closer in an attempt to come after him. "You have only yourself to blame. Had you not tainted her, it would have never happened."

My attention was pulled away from their confrontation when Ryder spoke quietly. "Mother, I was told you made a deal. Tell me it's not true."

My brow turned up as I gave him my best sympathetic gaze. "I'm sorry, Ryder, but I can't tell you that."

"You promised!" Ryder shouted. "You promised me…"

My heart clenched and yet I smiled despite the pain. "You're right. I did. And I never break my promises. I'll always be with you. Even if you can't see me."

Tears streamed down his face. "Please don't do this."

I continued to smile at him for a few more moments, even though it was difficult, and then turned my gaze toward Rylan. "Take good care of him."

Rylan gave me his best smile. "You know I will."

"No, don't do this!" Ryder shouted.

I looked back at him with sympathetic eyes. "Be good, Ryder."

He froze and I watched his tears roll down his cheeks before facing Zarda again. "Let's do this."

"You're still not running." He grinned. "Beautiful."

I clasped my hands behind my back. "Just shut up and get this over with."

Zarda chuckled and aimed the loaded pistol at me. "As you wish, my pet."

I took a deep, quiet breath. This was it. I was never meant to escape this fate. It's why I ran into *him*.

No matter how much I wanted to protect my heart, I still had people I cared about and would give my life for. I tried to keep that to a minimum, to maximize my chance at escaping my fate, but I couldn't run from it forever, and in the end more people came into my life that I just couldn't keep out, because deep down, I didn't want to. Even if it meant losing more in the end, it made me feel a little less alone.

Zarda pulled down the hammer of the pistol and I closed my eyes. I had always told myself I should live my life without regrets. I knew my fate, even if I didn't want to admit it, so it was best to live my life to the fullest. But I didn't listen. There were so many things I didn't do that I knew I should have.

I should have had Ryder come live with us. Even if it wasn't as safe, he could have had a home situation to live in. I should have smiled more. Even if I didn't feel like smiling, I had things to smile and laugh about. I had good friends and family in my life I should have spent more quality time with. I should have put the past behind me and told Raikidan how I felt sooner than I had.

Warmth welled up in my right eye and trailed down my cheek. *At least then I wouldn't have this regr—*

Something large crashed into me and the gun fired. But I felt no pain. My eyes snapped open as I fell to the ground. Turning as I fell, my eyes widened in horror.

"Eira, look out!"

Raikidan had pushed me out of the way but had been hit himself.

"Tannek, no!"

Raikidan hit the ground with a *thud* and didn't move much. I picked myself up immediately and rushed over to him. I flipped him onto his back and watched as he shook with half-closed eyes.

My mother told me all about the weakness I had inherited. Nickel was deadly to dragons, even a half-dragon like myself. But there was one major difference between full dragons and me—my human genes.

The human side of me had kept me protected on the outside. If my skin came into contact with the mineral, even for long periods of time, I'd only have what would seem like a severe allergic reaction that could also drain me of my energy, but not outright kill me. The only way for it to kill me was for it to get into my bloodstream, and even then it would be a slow process.

Dragons, on the other hand, weren't so lucky. Their scales could protect them for a little while, and even their skin while they were in human from, as Raikidan exhibited when the city fell under attack. But after a while it would start to kill them. And if the mineral got into their bloodstream, that was the end for them—they'd be dead in minutes.

Raikidan was dying, and fast. My chest ached and my one eye continued to tear as I shook him. "Raikidan? Raikidan, why? That was meant for me!"

"I promised... to protect... you," he managed. "Even... at the cost of... my life."

I shook my head. "You can't do this... You can't leave me, too."

He reached up with a shaky hand and wiped my tears away. "I told you… everyone can cry. I just never wanted to be… the reason you did… I'm sorry…"

His eyes closed and his hand dropped as if it were suddenly made of lead. "Raikidan?" I shook him. "Raikidan!"

Zarda laughed. "Well, that takes care of that problem. Saves me the trouble of having to track him down later and getting rid of him like that other one you cared for so much."

I froze. *Is he talking about Tannek?*

"Oops, did I let that slip? Oh well. It was bound to come out sooner or later. Yes, I'm the reason that medic died in your arms like this one is."

"Kill him," Rashta seethed.

"Well, it's your fault, really," he accused. "Had you just done what you were told, none of this would have had to happen."

My anger rose and my body began to feel strange.

"Make him pay."

"It's fitting, really, for this one, though. After what I did to his mother." He laughed some more. "He was so upset back then. But now they can be together."

I felt my body was on the cusp of a change, and I didn't fight it this time. My anger and pain numbed me to the fear of how others would react to seeing me. It numbed me to how I felt about it.

"Kill him!"

First Lord Taric and Xephrya, then my mother and Tannek, and now Raikidan. Zarda needed to pay—needed to die. My body convulsed and then discomfort ran through me as my body began changing. *He will die!*

49
CHAPTER

(RYOKO)

My heart stopped when Laz's body convulsed. I didn't know what was going on, but it looked like she was in a bit of pain. Rylan began choking next to me, gaining my attention. My pulse quickened and my mouth dried out when he fell to his knees and began shaking. I wasn't sure who was in more pain, Laz or him. *What's going on?*

"Someone needs to take those restraints off him," Seda warned. "If not, his arms are going to get ripped off. He can't fight the bond's pull."

I stared at her in horror. What was she talking about?

A soldier behind us rushed over to help Rylan, but another soldier grabbed him in attempt to stop him. I wasn't having it. No way was I going to allow Rylan to be hurt because of this stupid bond he and Laz were forced to share against their will.

I rammed into the soldier hindering Rylan's release, and he fell on his back and rolled with pain. The soldier attempting to help nodded his thanks and went to work releasing Rylan. The moment Rylan was free and his hands hit the ground, he began shifting—but this shift was different from his wolf shift. It was as if he were shifting into something larger—much larger.

I watched in amazement as his wolf-like body grew until his shoulders reached the height of the average human man and his canine teeth extended well past his jaw. The shackles around his neck and wrists, which he could never get rid of, expanded to accommodate his new size—and I wasn't sure how that was even possible. I honestly didn't know how he had gotten stuck in them to start with; he'd never told anyone. But from what Seda had revealed to me, it was a painful memory, and I respected him enough to not pry.

When Rylan seemed close to the end of his shift, the reality of it dawned on me. Rylan didn't have just any wolf DNA in him. He was Dire Wolf. I couldn't believe my eyes. They had been extinct for so long, I hadn't even thought it was possible to find remains with viable DNA for creation purposes.

Rylan tilted his head skyward when his transformation completed, and a deep, chest-rumbling howl came from his lips. Just then, the sound of a dragon's roar pierced the air, and as I gazed past Rylan, I spotted the source—*Laz*. My body locked up, shock coursing through me. She, too, had taken on a new form, but it was still somewhat human-like, unlike Rylan.

Large purple, red, and blue-colored scales covered her body. Well, not all of her was covered in scales. There were scales covering the center of her forehead in a V-shape, while more of the colored scales lined the underside of her eyes. Even more scales trailed her collarbone and onto her shoulders, and then trailed down her body, over the outsides and undersides of her breasts, and down the side of her body to her hips. The further down her body the scales grew, the larger they became.

Large plated scales covered her thighs, a small gap separating them from the scales on her hips, and somewhat large plated scales covered the sides of her forearms. Small and large scales spread across her back until they merged with the large plated scales on the long, whip-like tail growing out of her lower back. The rest of her tail was scaled as well, right down to the pointed tip with patches of heavy plating along the way.

Laz's canine teeth seemed to have grown longer, and her eyes were much larger and were now rather reptilian. Large black horns grew out of her head and curved backward, and her hands had distorted and were bonier than a human's. Talon-like nails added to her hands' deadly appearance.

Zarda looked between the two and appeared to be more surprised by this transformation than anyone. His surprise twisted to rage. "You bitch! You hid this from me. How dare you!"

Laz twitched her tail and stared him down. "Shut your mouth, you pathetic waste of space. You're going to pay for what you've done."

"The pact with us dragons has now been broken." Laz's father's fists clenched. "It's time you pay for your crimes, Zarda. Xephrya's son's sacrifice won't be for naught."

In an instant, he shifted into his stunning yet intimidating dragon form and went for Zarda. But Zarda wasn't afraid of the large teeth coming for his life. No, instead he grinned.

Standing still, an arm twitched and his muscles crawled unnaturally. My shoulders pulled back. I knew that change. A common and ever-so-subtle change for a number of Brutes. *Are we about to see what Zarda has done to himself?*

My eyes widened when Zarda flicked his wrist toward Laz's father and the large dragon went flying back. I braced myself as wind buffered us and Laz's father's large body crashed through the courtyard and took out a chunk of the fortress. *Fuck, we're in trouble.*

I prayed no one had been killed by that. We knew Zarda had been enhancing his body, but for him to send a dragon flying by the flick of his wrist, he was a lot more powerful than we were imagining. *Not even a Brute could do that.* What exactly had he done to himself?

My eyes cut to Laz, who appeared unphased by Zarda's action. She was probably too angry to be, not that I could blame her. Raikidan had run over to her before anyone could understand what was going on. Had I known, I would have tried to stop him. The pain of loss was not something I had ever wanted her to feel again. It was such a devastating thing for her, and this time had only been worse.

I watched as Laz stalked toward Zarda and Rylan began prowling closer. The moment Laz moved away from Raikidan's body, several shamans swooped in, attempting to heal him. *I don't think that's going to help…* He lay so still… *No.* I shook my head, banishing the negative thoughts. If there was any possibility of saving him, I needed to believe these shamans could achieve that. Laz needed him.

I glanced behind me when something messed with my shackles, spotting one of Laz's brothers picking the lock. The shackles clicked open. A soldier tried to stop us, but he was too late. I stomped on the ground and forced it to buckle, throwing him back. I was quick to turn back around and make a barrier around those attempting to help Raikidan, just in case someone tried to stop them.

Laz's brother advanced toward Zarda and I hoped their combined power would end this. Laz's choice of plan had failed, so now it was time for us to enact the original one. But if too many of us jumped in at once, we may end up creating more of a problem than helping.

I watched a mutiny transpire right in front of my eyes. Any soldiers attempting to help Zarda or stop Raikidan's healing process were taken down by rebels in uniform. At the same time, Laz's brothers attacked Zarda, but as I watched, Zarda overpowered them with ease. Even Trigon and Rhaec were thrown aside as if they were some weak civilians. *Zarda isn't breaking a sweat.*

Laz went to engage Zarda, but Nioush had other ideas. He lifted up a piece of broken wall and tossed it Zarda's way, but Zarda was too fast and dodged the attack. Rylan, though, was ready for a counterattack and lunged his huge shape at Zarda. However Zarda really wasn't going to go down easy.

He grabbed onto Rylan's large canine teeth and tossed him aside like a ragdoll. I saw Laz cringe when Rylan went through a wall, and I feared their bond was heightened in these new forms. But her pain didn't keep her from assaulting Zarda. She was fast, but he was faster somehow.

"Ryoko, we need your help."

I turned my attention away from the battle to Nyra and Saléna. The two knelt beside Seda and Argus. I hadn't even noticed them leave their place by the wall. Nioush must have acted as a distraction for them. His involvement in all this perplexed me, but maybe he was having a change of heart about Seda. Or maybe he did care more than he had been willing to admit and her capture had sent him over the edge.

"We're going to remove this stupid contraption from Seda's head," Nyra said. "But we need you and Argus to help keep her still so she isn't harmed."

I nodded and rushed over to them. Argus held onto one side of Seda while I braced her from the other. Nyra and Saléna held out their hands, focusing on the contraption.

Seda let out a sigh of relief when her sisters managed to remove the device. "So much better. Thank you."

Saléna smiled and held out the blindfold I had made. I was curious how she had obtained it. "You should wear this. As sweet as it was for your boyfriend to rip apart his shirt to make a new blindfold, this looks far better."

Seda giggled and gratefully took the gift.

My heart stopped when a heard a familiar female voice choke in excruciating pain. I turned and stared in horror at the sight of Zarda's distorted arm spearing Laz clean through, narrowly missing her spine. He laughed and then pulled his arm free. Laz fell to her knees, choking on blood.

"Did you really think you could stop me, dear?" he taunted. "Even this hideous form you take isn't enough."

Laz's head snapped up, and in a flash she assaulted him with her talon-like nails. Her speed caught him off guard, his clothes shredding. But his skin remained unharmed. *Did she miss?*

Zarda rounded a kick on her, sending her into the ground, and his hand distorted again. He brought it down on her, piercing her body. Laz cried out in pain. When he removed himself from her, she barely moved; only her hands twitched.

Zarda threw his head back as he laughed. "No one can stop me. Not even this strong halfling so many looked up to. Not even her disgusting mixed blood, was she close to a match for me. I will have what I want because I have been guaranteed what I want."

My horror burned into anger. *How dare he.* How dare he insult Laz like that! He had no idea how amazing she was. He could never understand her value.

My body tensed, the familiar pull of the wogron change cusping. I welcomed it. I was no different than Laz. We were both halflings, and there should be no reason for us to be ashamed of it. There was nothing wrong with us.

My body convulsed and changed, ignoring the pain that still came with it. I welcomed it, if my other form would give me the strength to take Zarda down. It was my control over my form that I hoped would keep up. I'd never been able to change at will. Peacekeeper Ryoko had attempted to show me, but I didn't quite get it. *Until now.*

My body distorted and a loud howl of pain and rage rang out of my throat. The moment my change was complete, I lunged at Zarda and slashed my claws at him. He dodged my attacks, but I wasn't the only one after him. Plants erupted out of the ground around him, lashing about his ankles, trying to trip him. I glanced over at the shamans and found Valene in a rage. Tears streamed down her face as she sent more plants Zarda's way. I couldn't imagine the pain coursing through her. First the loss of her biological mother and now Laz, the odd but perfect replacement she needed.

To my amazement, Zarda ripped the plants apart. I knew how durable these plants could be, and he was tearing them up as if they were made of paper. I continued with my attack until Zarda grabbed one of my arms and tossed me into the wall next to Rylan. He still hadn't been able to get up, but I was sure it was because of Laz's state. I wasn't even sure whether she was still alive from such an attack.

I laid there in a stunned state. Rylan whined. Could he speak in this form? The fact that he and Raid could speak in their dog forms was an unusual situation anyway, though the words were distorted as if the form fought against the phenomenon. This dire wolf form may not be capable of supporting such an unusual ability.

Rylan whined more, as if to make sure I was okay. He should know better. The impact had hurt, but I was a Brute. I could take a beating better than most, and this wogron shape was able to take even more. My body just needed a moment to recover.

Zarda's grating laugh echoed through the courtyard. "You waste your energy and delay the inevitable. I have been working for decades to perfect this body. I've created and destroyed more experiments for my perfection than any of you could possibly imagine. I tested on released experiments long before myself."

Those poor people… My gut twisted thinking of all the horrible things he'd put innocent people through for his own ambition. How so many of them never saw beyond the stone walls of their prison… never knew what it meant to live. *How many people did you create and never unleash so you wouldn't have competition, Zarda?*

Zarda chuckled, a deep, skin-crawling laugh. "I made deals to ensure my success and my rule. Nothing you do will stop me."

Made deals? What did he mean by that?

A ball of fire shot up from the ground, narrowly missing Zarda—the attack something like a statement to tell Zarda to shut his ugly mouth—and that he wasn't infallible. *Where did that attack come from? Was there another fire shaman or elementalist here? No—there.*

Laz struggled to her feet. I couldn't believe it. She was still alive, somehow. Blood poured out of her wounds. She was ready to fight to her dying breath. *How is she even conscious, let alone able to stand?*

Still hunched over, she breathed out a sizable blast of fire at Zarda and managed to land a hit on him this time. He had dodged most of it, but one of his legs had still gotten badly burned. Zarda looked at his leg and then went at her without spitting out an insult. The rage in his eyes was the only thing that gave away his emotional state.

Laz rolled away from his grab but was slow to get back up, and Zarda grabbed a hold of her by the hair. His hand distorted and he stabbed her in the abdomen again. Laz choked in pain. He did it again. And again. And again.

Each time she twitched and choked, her struggling ceasing. Her hands fell to her side, her eyes going blank. Pain gripped me. *No…*

Zarda let her go, backhanding her in the face. She landed with a *thud* and didn't move. *No. No. No.* It couldn't end like this. Not when we were so close. She couldn't die. *She can't…*

Laz's father roared, as did the other dragons in the courtyard. Her brothers, who were now getting back up on their feet, raged at the sight of their fallen sibling. But before they could mount an assault against Zarda, a large wave of water rushed across the courtyard. It consumed Zarda and then spun up into a cyclone, trapping him.

I was stunned. I had only known Amara to use water cyclones as an attack. Who else knew how to use them?

The cyclone destabilized, tossing Zarda away as it broke down. I watched as a small group of people stalked into my view, heading straight for Zarda. The group was the remaining number of brothers who hadn't left Zarda's service yet, except the person leading them. This person was a woman who looked so much like Laz. *Yára.*

She continued to stalk toward Zarda, who was now getting back up on his feet, as her brothers stopped for some reason. Had she been the one to use the water on him? She didn't have any formal war training, but maybe she'd gotten some in secret?

Zarda coughed. "You—"

She bared her teeth. "Shut your mouth."

I blinked. That wasn't the response I expected from her. She was such a sweet woman whenever I met her.

"First you caused my brothers to flee. Then you captured my sister and tortured her. Then you hurt my brothers and now you've killed my sister!" Fire burned in her eyes. "She was the only one who understood us. She was the only one who genuinely cared. She didn't fake a smile or force herself to be around us. She wanted us to part of her life, and you've taken her from me."

Zarda's eyes narrowed. "Go back to your room."

"No."

"That's not a request, Yára," he spat. "That's an order."

"I said no!" She ripped off the watch on her wrist and threw it on the ground. Her appearance changed. *A cloaking watch?*

She now no longer sported violet and blue hair. Instead her hair was a deep blue, similar to Danika's, and it was nowhere near as straight as Laz's and was held up into a messy bun.

"I'm not taking orders from you anymore. I'm not your precious little pet you can do whatever you want with. I'm my own person. I have real wants and feelings. I'm different than my sister, and I won't be made to be her. You don't own me, and I won't let you do any more damage to my family."

Zarda's lip curled. "You impudent wench. I gave you everything."

"No you didn't. You gave me what you wanted because you thought you owned me. Just because you created me, doesn't mean I'm an object for ownership."

"You'll regret going against me as well."

Yára snorted. "I won't go down easily. You may have not sanctioned any training for me, that doesn't mean I didn't get any when you weren't looking."

"What are you talking about?"

"My sister isn't the only one who can be visited by the dead."

My eyes widened. *She couldn't mean...* Yára didn't allow for any more conversation, beginning her rage-filled assault. She moved just like Amara, and there was no longer an ounce of doubt in my mind she had been trained by our former general—by her own mother.

She needs help. Even with secret training, Zarda was proving his modifications had been taken too lightly. I felt out my body's recovery state and found I was able to move. *Good.* I wasn't going to jump in right away. Even with the risk of this shape wearing off, I couldn't rush. I needed to be smart; else I'd be a hindrance.

Rylan stirred and finally managed to pull himself on his feet. He looked worn out, and I wondered how badly the bond affected him. There was no way Zarda's throw could have kept him down this long.

He flexed his muscles and I tried to stop him from joining the battle, but when he swiveled his head my way, I couldn't complete my reach out to him. The pained look in his eyes was just too much. Laz was dead. He would know before anyone else. An attack like that would kill anyone, but I had hoped…

Rylan traipsed over to Laz's body while Yára kept Zarda busy and on the defensive. She was doing a great job for someone who didn't have any battle experience. Yára and Laz's brothers appeared to all be getting ready to join in.

Especially Bone. He knelt by Laz, and despair gripped him over the loss of his elder sister. Even though they hadn't had a lot of time together, Laz had bonded rather quickly with her siblings and taught them what she could. Even when I was training Trigon and Rhaec, they couldn't stop talking about her.

My blood ran cold when a sorrow-filled howl came from Rylan. He now stood over our dead friend and cried to the sky. I watched as his pain surged into anger and he stared menacingly at Zarda.

As he did, his body radiated a cold aura and the tips of his fur froze. I found myself finding strength in his state and pulled to my feet. No matter what happened, I would avenge Laz. I would not let her and Raikidan's sacrifice be in vain.

Rylan howled again. A large wave of ice went crashing toward Zarda. Zarda dodged it, but was hit by Yára's counter move. He stumbled and recovered, only to be struck by ice when Rylan cried out another wave. This was when Laz's siblings jumped into the battle. They all went after Zarda at once. I thought we might actually win, but Zarda was able to dispose of them with ease.

I didn't understand. How could his modifications give him so much power? Even the best Brutes would be suffering from fatigue.

Zarda pulled his pistol and went to load it with the bullet rounds Laz's family were weak to, but Trigon rammed into him and the gun and ammunition scattered. Zarda recovered quickly, throwing Trigon aside with ease. Zarda hadn't been hurt at all by that attack—it was as if he had absorbed it.

Laz's siblings were up on their feet again and all attempted to attack him at once. Zarda sent out a wave of energy that resembled psychic energy and pushed them all back. This confused me. The Council had claimed he hadn't been able to use psychic DNA, so was this actually psychic power obtained later in his modification process, or what this a result of something else that was similar?

Most of Laz's siblings didn't get back up after that attack—and I wasn't the least bit surprised. Only Trigon and Rhaec were Brutes.

A large wall slab flew high above my head and headed straight for Zarda, but he pushed it away with another energy blast. I tilted my head up to see Seda hovering high above the courtyard with her two sisters and brother. It appeared she was doing much better now that she had time to recover from that suppressing device. The four of them appeared ready to fight together.

I was happy and excited they were joining in. We had more of a chance now. Zarda, on the other hand, wasn't unfazed. Instead, he sported a cocky grin. He then snapped his fingers and a large door opened on the opposite side of the courtyard. A band of psychics marched out of the door and took to the skies.

My heart sank. This was bad. Seda and Nioush were strong, but I didn't know if even they could take on this many.

Zarda seemed to be mirroring my thoughts. "You can't win."

"I beg to differ," someone called out.

I turned my large head and saw a band of psychics descending from the sky. Leading them were Akama and Enrée. My heart leaped. The group of psychics they led was still smaller than the military one, but Akama and Enrée were powerful. They had years of practice over any other psychic alive. The only ones who could rival them were Seda and Nioush. And with the addition of Nyra and Saléna to their power, the six of them alone would be able to take on half of the military battle psychics—at least, in theory.

Before my eyes, the psychics battled it out above us, but that still left

Zarda. Rylan howled loudly again, and another wave of ice shot out from him. Unfortunately, Zarda was ready and deflected the attack, sending it right for Yára.

Yára wasn't fast enough to move out of the way, and I was sure she was going to get hit until someone came out of nowhere and pushed her, taking the blow. *Corliss!* I couldn't believe what I had seen. I had been so wrapped up into the battle I had forgotten he was here. Even if I had remembered, that was the last thing I would have expected from him. He was nice and all, but to take a blow like that for someone he didn't really know, that was a bit out there.

Zarda chuckled as Corliss struggled to his feet. "I'm intrigued by this act. What drove you to do such an idiotic thing?"

"We dragons have different kinds of loyalties." He coughed up a bit of blood. "I made a vow of loyalty to Eira. And even in the wake of her death, I still honor that vow. I will not allow you to harm her sister."

Zarda laughed. "It's not my fault she got in the way."

Corliss growled and then spat at him. I watched as his spit disintegrated the ground when it landed near Zarda's feet. *Right, acidic saliva.* I was rather impressed with his expectorating skills—he had been able to spit that acid a good distance. Definitely didn't want to enter a spitting contest with any of them, that's for sure.

Zarda grinned. "You missed."

Corliss remained expressionless, as if Zarda's insult meant nothing. Instead he took a few steps forward and then took a deep breath and exhaled a plume of pale green smoke toward Zarda. I tried not to grin when Zarda seemed to feel no need to evade the smoke. He had no idea how poisonous that cloud was, and here he was just waiting for it to hit him.

I was taken by surprise when the poison engulfed him and it didn't affect him. *There's no way he could be immune to poison, too, right?*

Zarda laughed. "Did you really think your poison cloud could touch me?"

Corliss eyed him with caution and surprise.

"Yes, I'm aware of the abilities of green dragons. I had hoped to find DNA from one of you first, but settled for a red dragon since they were far easier to track down. I can't be stopped, not even by something so caustic."

"We'll see about that."

I turned at the sound of Zo's voice, finding him and other rebel soldiers with weapons in hand, standing at the ready.

"Just give up, Zarda," Zo said. "Even the most modified soldiers have a limit to their abilities. You're no different."

A wicked grin slipped up Zarda's face. "Why don't you test that theory?"

Zo made a motion and the platoon of soldiers opened fire. I watched as Zarda just stood there and took the blows. As the bullets fell to the ground around him without wounding him in the least I could see his body rippling. My eyes widened with realization. He was absorbing the impact. It was as if he had the organic ability of the armored cloth the scientists had developed.

The soldiers' magazines ran dry. Zarda threw his head back as he laughed. "You were saying? You fools don't know the extent of my power! But let me indulge you with the knowledge."

Zo glowered and reached for another magazine, but Zarda reacted faster. If it were possible for me to gasp in this form, I would have. Zarda punched his fist toward Zo and the platoon, and right before my eyes, his arm stretched and slammed into Zo. He then picked Zo up and swung him, at the end of his stretched arm, into the platoon.

Corliss tried to run and get Yára out of harm's way, but Zarda was fast and swung his fist over toward them, taking out his own men in the process without a care. His fist collided with Corliss the moment he reached Yára and the two were slammed into a wall.

Laz's father lunged forth and Zarda slammed his hand into the large dragon, sending him careening through a wall. Zarda then pulled his arm back, but only for a moment before sending it out again and knocking Rylan and Bone away from Laz.

My heart stopped when he raised his stretched arm into the air and sent it down toward Laz's body. I knew what he was about to do, and I couldn't allow him to do such a thing to her. I wouldn't let him crush her body in an attempt to cripple our spirits.

I put every ounce of energy into my muscles and leaped onto his arms. I dug my teeth and claws into his skin and held on for dear life when he screamed in agony and tried to throw me off. "Stupid bitch!"

He threw me into walls and slammed me onto the ground, but I refused to let go and dug my teeth into his arm until I finally managed to break skin and draw blood. His thrashing increased and I struggled to keep my hold.

Finally he slammed me into the ground harder than any other time before, and my body failed me. I let go and lay there, unable to move. My shifting failed then, sending me back into my nu-human form.

Zarda lifted his hand high above me and I closed my eyes, anticipating his plan to crush me, but a gun sounded instead. *That sounds like a shotgun.* I opened my eyes and nearly retched at the sight of Zarda's half-blown-off head. I weakly turned my head, to see Ryder panting with heavy breaths as if he had been running. In his hands he held a shotgun, and I smiled. He would be the one to actually do some damage to Zarda. It was fitting he get the last act of revenge for his mother's fall. Especially seeing the gun in his hands appeared to be one of his custom inventions. It would also explain why Ryder was the only one to put any damage on him. Or maybe it was Zarda's stretching that was the culprit. *I was able to draw blood after a while, so maybe…*

Zarda's arm retracted quickly back to his body, and he stumbled but didn't fall over dead like most normal people would have. Instead, his head twitched and then slowly regenerated. If the sight of his head half-missing wasn't gut churning enough for someone, the slow regenerating process was sure to do it. I had to look away in fear of retching up what little was in my stomach.

Zarda laughed, and I stole a glance to find him back to normal, his eyes crazed and wide. My heart sank. Not even a gunshot to the head could kill him. He really was unstoppable.

"I can't die!" Zarda gloated. "Your fight against me is pointless!"

"You're wrong, Zarda. All mortal lives end eventually. We may not like it, but that is the fact of life."

I weakly turned at the sound of Laz's voice. My eyes grew wide. *This can't be.* Flames engulfed Laz's body as she rose to her feet, eyes intent on Zarda.

CHAPTER 50

(EIRA)

I choked when Zarda stabbed me again—so much pain coursed through me. I had been too wounded to escape from this attack; I couldn't believe how fast and strong he was now.

Zarda let me go, and then the back of his hand smashed against my face and I fell to the ground. I was too weak to move; all of my senses dulled. *I'm dying.* There was no doubt about it. I hated knowing this. I hated not being able to get back up and take him out with me. I was too weak to avenge anyone—I was too weak to do anything right…

My vision darkened, and my other senses soon followed. A piercing dragon roar was the last sound to assault my ears before numbness took over. Moments that felt like forever passed and still nothing happened. Due to my shaman training, I'd be aware of my death, but this didn't feel like death at all. It felt more like I was… suspended.

A feminine voice chuckled. "Open your eyes, dear."

"Mom?" The voice sounded familiar—I was sure it was her. Even though it sounded a bit different than I remembered, it had to be because of my muted senses.

The woman chuckled again. "No, you're not dead, Eira, and I'm not your mother." Her voice lowered as if she were talking her herself. "Though I feel like it sometimes."

I'm not dead? That didn't make sense. Those had been mortal wounds.

"C'mon, stop being stubborn and open your eyes."

My eyes fluttered open and I peered around. I lay on my side on the marble floor of a large stone building. The building had huge columns and archways, and giant, intricately crafted statues of beautiful women and magnificent dragons. Exceptionally crafted tapestries covered the walls, and large braziers lit up with blue and red flames illuminated the building.

I rolled on my back and stared at the familiar woman hovering over me with a smile. My brow twisted. "Rashta?"

The corner of her eyes crinkled. "See, not your mother."

I sat up. "What's going on?"

She waved for me to follow. "Come. I'll explain what I can in the short window of time I have."

I did as requested, careful not to step on Rashta's wings as the tips dragged on the floor. Following her up some steps leading to a large dais, I peered around. "I'm in that temple, aren't I?"

"She caught on quick," a new female voice said, her words coming from the platform.

"Of course she did," another female voice said, this one sounding a bit familiar to me. "She's more intelligent than she gives herself credit for."

Rashta and I reached the top of the stairs, and before us, fifteen women lounged on pillows and blankets in a semi-circle. They all wore various styles of clothes, as if plucked from different moments in time and culture. I gazed around as Rashta seated herself in the midst of them all where two empty pillows lay.

She patted the vacant pillow next to her. "Come and sit, Eira. I know you want to take this in, but I'd rather explain as you do. I think you'll be able to accept this all better that way."

I glanced around once more before complying. Most were amused by my uncertainty. The pillow provided for me was comfortable, and after the harsh weeks in that cell, it was a welcomed relief.

"I have so many questions, I don't know where to begin," I said, still looking around at my audience.

"Let's start with this," Rashta began. "Yes, we're in your mind, and no, you're not dead."

My brow ticked up. "Um, were you not paying attention to the horrible job I'd done fighting Zarda?"

She frowned. "No, I'm quite aware of that situation, and for the record, you didn't do a horrible job. Your weakened state, on top of Zarda's unnatural modifications, set you up for a situation you'd struggle to win."

"Then how am I alive? How are you here? How are you *all* here?"

Rashta smiled. "Let's start from the beginning. A long time ago, Genesis and Zoltan thought up your existence, but hesitated to allow you to come into Lumaraeon because you were to be half-human and half-dragon—the first hybrid to ever exist. But I convinced them Lumaraeon was ready for hybrid beings. As the goddess of judgment, they listened to my council."

She gestured to the first woman on the left. She was tall and lean, with fair skin. Wavy copper hair flowed past her shoulders. Her brilliant green eyes crinkled at the corners as she smiled at me. I also noticed a golden ring surrounding her pupils. *Her eyes are like mine.* "Meet Isis."

Isis smiled and I nodded.

Rashta took a deep breath. "Unfortunately, I was wrong with my assessment. Creatures of Lumaraeon were split on their stance. Some accepted her, seeing her as a sign from us gods, while far too many saw her as a mistake. This split in ideals resulted in a devastating war over your fate."

She frowned. "It was then I realized my error, but none of us knew how to fix the problem. In our eyes, you deserved to live. You were perfect in so many ways, but we couldn't make the mortals see that. We couldn't force them to accept you."

Rashta's eyes darted to Isis. "Then, you did the unthinkable. You sacrificed your life so the fighting would stop. You wrongly believed your life was a mistake and thought Lumaraeon would be better off without you."

Isis shrugged. "I'll be honest. I still think that choice was the better one." Her eyes flicked to the other women. "Many of us believe that."

Rashta narrowed her eyes. "I disagree, which is why I stepped in." She shifted her gaze to me. "I deemed Isis worthy of living. So when she lay dying in her destined mate's arms, I judged her worthy in front of the warring mortals, and fused my life force with hers in order to save her."

I licked my lips as I processed this. "You've focused on me this whole time, though speaking of Isis as if she wasn't here. Does this mean… I was right? That *we* were right, about my soul?"

Rashta nodded, a smile on her lips. "Yes. You are more than just an old soul. You are an ancient soul—reincarnated now fourteen times because of the choice I made."

I stared down at my hands. *All this time…*

The third human woman in the lineup chuckled, pulling my attention. I took in her features, as well as the woman to her right—two psychic women. Both had sultry figures, fair skin, and white and red hair, but each styled theirs differently. One grew her hair long, while the other, the one who laughed, sported a mohawk-like style. "You were told the answer lay within."

Her sister elbowed her. "Lutha, be nice. It's not her fault things were more difficult than with the rest of us."

I turned back to Rashta. "So, how does this rebirth process work? Your immortal soul forces me into another life when I die or something?"

Rashta nodded. "Essentially, yes. It's not an instant rebirth, several hundred years tend to pass between each new life. The same goes for your champion."

There was that word again. "Champion?"

"Yes. In this life you called him Raikidan."

Isis rested her chin on her hand. "He's definitely a looker in this life." All of them chuckled, including her. "Not that he hasn't been every other time."

I looked to Rashta for clarification.

"Because your destined mate had been holding you when I saved your first life, a portion of my essence also fused with his soul, thus locking him into our eternal cycle of rebirth, binding the two of you together for all eternity."

"So, he and I have found each other over and over again?"

The short woman, tenth or eleventh in line—I wasn't quite clear how this lineup worked with the twins—dramatically threw herself over. She was tan and had short, curly black hair with green tips. Unlike the rest, who were all of average-to-tall height, she was short, but had a curvy shape that more than made up for it. Her green eyes sparkled. "It's the kind of love many mortals dream of. Like a fairy tale, but we get to live it."

The dark-skinned woman next her, apparently from a previous position in the timeline, snorted. "I wouldn't call some of our lives fairy tales."

My eyes shifted to her, her piercings catching my attention first, then her striking amber eyes. Most piercings were on her ears, though she did have a septum and lips piercing as well. Long, wavy dark brown hair with some red mixed in, draped over her mocha-tan skin. She too had a figure similar to mine, but with slightly more curve.

The tall, lithe, light-skinned elven woman, fourth in line, chuckled. Her braided, long dark green hair moved with the motion, and her green eyes sparkled. "Not all of it, but we all got our happily ever after, didn't we?"

I held up a finger. "Not to intentionally throw you all off, but can I get some names to match with faces? And I'd like to know why psychic number one here mentioned I wouldn't have an easier time knowing what's up than the rest of you? And I still haven't gotten an explanation on why I'm not dead."

Rashta chuckled. "Yes, there's quite a lot to explain to you. Let me give you names first." She gestured to Isis. "I've introduced Isis."

She gestured to the buxom, light-skinned elven woman beside Isis. Her violet hair and stunning silver eyes caught my attention quickly. She ran her fingers through a few tresses, red strands visible as they moved. A sparkle of energy flashed between her fingers as she made the motion. A few more questions added to my list. "Next we have Nisha. She is the reason you used memory magic on that mural."

My eyes went wide and Nisha winked. "Father was a violet dragon."

That explained a lot.

"Next, twins Lutha and Lina. They count as one life, which throws off our numerical ordering. We'll all understand if you don't get the matching right for a little bit. Your soul split into the two of them during this life. Quite the experience, really."

"I would imagine so," I mumbled as I nodded to the two psychics. "Next we have Raina."

My brow ticked up. *An elven woman named Raina?*

Raina smiled. "It's as you think. I am the first shaman Ambassador." I sat there, stunned. What were the odds?

Rashta chuckled. Either my shock amused her, or she knew something

I didn't yet. She gestured to the stocky, dark-skinned human woman relaxing next to Raina. Her amber eyes were pinned on me, though they didn't give off any hostility. Her long brown hair was braided on one side and pulled over the opposite shoulder with the free hair. "Nalia."

Rashta jumped immediately to the tall, olive-tan skinned woman with a curvaceous figure next to Nalia. This woman, I recognized. Her slightly wavy black-to-red ombre hair spilled over her shoulders. She waved her fingers at me, her sapphire eyes twinkling. *We were right. Something funny did happen when Doppelganger used his ability on me.* "And Atria."

Atria smirked. "We've met, of course, because of that odd friend of yours."

"How did that happen?" I asked.

"I just took over his ability when he tried to use it on you." Her lips twisted up the side of her face. "One of the perks of having Rashta's power at your disposal. It's how Nisha and Sylvia were able to speak to you."

I nodded, trying to take it all in, and Rashta continued with the women to our right, gesturing to a human woman with a sultry form. Her long black-to-violet ombre hair spilled over her tan skin. What caught me, though, were her kaleidoscopic eyes. Much like when looking at Chameleon, they were hard not to stare at. *How amazing...* "Zalia."

The dark-skinned woman next to her shifted, her black-to-aqua hair falling to one shoulder. Light warmth came from her silver eyes as she smiled at me. She had a build similar to mine, and also had hard-to-miss stunning silver eyes. "That's Aria."

Rashta continued. "Then we have Sylvia and Ayuma."

Sylvia nodded and Ayuma waved. Her personality reminded me much of Ryoko.

A light-skinned woman of average height with a curvaceous figure came next in the lineup. Long black and red hair flowed over her shoulders, her green eyes staring back at me. She, too, sported a few piercings. "Next we have Rinneth, your eleventh life. And then Pheydra."

The light tan woman with copper almond-shaped eyes nodded at me when I focused on her. Her long black and blue hair flowed with the motion. The most startling thing about about her, she had visible scars all over. Whatever she survived must have been horrific.

My eyes shifted to the next woman so I wouldn't be rude and stare, only to be met with a human of dark complexion with white and dark blue hair. Her one amber eye looked back at me. Her other eye was pure white, and a deep, long scar ran vertically down her face and eye. Either the eye was a prosthetic, or her injury caused the change. "That's Xenia."

Rashta took a deep breath and gestured to the last woman in line, who smiled at me, her striking green eyes shining. She had tan skin, and a hard to miss buxom figure. Her multi-shaded red hair flowed well past her shoulders, beaded and braided in many areas. But what struck me with her were her nu-human ears. "And lastly, we have Velsara, who also has had contact with you recently."

My eyes snapped to the last woman in the line. "Wait, Velsara, as in—"

"As in Pyralis' daughter, Zaith's adopted mother, and the previous Ambassador." Velsara smiled, her eyes squinting as she did. "Yes, that same one."

Her words were just as deeply accented as Zaith's.

By Satria! I wasn't sure how to take that bit of news. *No wonder Zaith…*

I took a deep breath. How was I supposed to process all this? "Okay. That's a lot to take in. But it explains some things that have happened recently." I looked around. "A lot, in fact."

Rashta frowned. "I'm sorry you had to find out this way. It was never meant to be this difficult."

My lips pressed into a thin line. "Why was it so hard?"

She took a deep breath. "Zarda's meddling."

Of course. I shouldn't have expected anything less.

"Not long after I first saved you, when you were Isis, her uncle, Kir, founded the Crimson Sanctuary."

My head whipped to Isis, whose gaze lowered. No wonder he was so hell-bent on killing me. *Wait, that's right. He called me Isis once.*

"Kir, despite perishing in the original war, was not at rest due to his hatred. He thought Isis had tricked us gods and forced us to side against him and his fellow brethren." Rashta shook her head. "This hatred allowed him to manifest into a physical form, creating the first revenant. He used this new form to build up an army against you in an attempt to break the cycle and destroy you for good."

Rashta's eyes ticked to Raina. "What he didn't anticipate was the power of the rebirth. Raina became one of many gifted individuals at the time that could communicate with spirits, and have the power to remove revenants from the living plane."

Raina frowned. "Sadly, even with all the work we'd done to remove revenants, Kir managed to slip through my grasp. Not even the two demons I had contracts with could track him down."

My brow ticked up. "Demons."

She grinned. "You've already met them. Rosa and Zaedrix."

I pinched my nose. "You've got to be kidding me."

She chuckled. "It's been quite comical seeing you weasel the same contract from them as I did."

I rubbed my face and then focused on Rashta. "So what does this all have to do with Zarda?"

Rashta took a breath. "After Kir was forced to regroup and rebuild his following, he found that some he'd brought to his cause had a different idea on how to deal with you. They believed his words that no halflings were worthy of life, but with the power you demonstrated because of my influence, they believed our power could be harnessed. Kir condemned such an idea, believing you should be eradicated like the rest, and as such, those followers broke off and created a group called the Crimson Wing."

Rashta's eyes scanned the women around us. "While they haven't been active in some time, because their numbers had been depleted over the years thanks to some of your previous lives' efforts, Zarda caught wind of your existence and their ideology. In his conquest for power, he researched your existence, finding out he was far too late to capture Velsara. But that posed a new opportunity."

Her eyes lowered. "By using the developed technology of human creation, he made you, destroying our original plan for your existence. He tried to twist you and me into a power only he could control. What he didn't know was the darkness he tried to force triggered the defensive side of our bond. This resulted in my absorbing the corruption."

I chewed my lips. "Corruption… it was the reason we couldn't communicate, yes?"

Rashta nodded. "It twisted the words I tried to speak. And it kept you from accessing your past lives."

"What changed?"

Rinneth snickered. "What, you can't put two and two together and figure out it was our favorite love-sick puppy?"

Aria narrowed her eyes at Rinneth. "Stop it. We all know that wasn't the sole reason."

"No, but it was the biggest one," Nalia said. "He's always the kink in the wheel."

I turned to Rashta for clarification. She smiled. "They're right. You did some of the work, but your champion is the main culprit. Because he has a piece of my essence with him, an uncorrupted one, your constant contact with him slowly purified me."

Zalia reclined and stretched out. "Oh, don't sugar-coat your words. It was a very specific type of contact that helped."

She winked and heat rushed to my face, making the others laugh. It didn't take a scientist to know what she meant. Rashta had reacted every time Raikidan kissed me in the past.

"So, now that I can see you, and the rest of my lives, is the corruption gone?" I asked.

Rashta shook her head. "No, what's left remaining requires the aid of the other gods. Once you recover, and Zarda is dealt with, I will ensure that happens."

"Yeah, about that." My brow twisted. "How is it that I'm not dead?"

She smiled. "I have a special ability that can be used on you once every life. It allows me to spare you if you sacrifice yourself for a just cause." She glanced at Isis. "This specific requirement exists due to how our merger came to be."

I thought about this. "That sounds like a noble reason, but I don't think that matches up to what I was doing."

Rashta chuckled. "You may have had selfish reasons for attacking Zarda, but deep down you also had noble ones. You are able to sense Zarda's corruption because of me, even if you can't identify it like I can. You seek out to stop him from causing any more unjustified pain to the world. This allows me to see your presumed death as a noble sacrifice and save you."

I nodded. "So, Zarda is corrupted."

Rashta's expression went grim. "Yes. He made a pact that sealed his fate."

I knew it. I got to my feet. "Well if that's the case, then I need to wake up and help the others."

My urgency amused the women around me for some reason. Rashta shook her head. "You need to be patient. This is a taxing process. Your friends can hold him off until then. Have faith in them."

I scowled. I didn't want to wait. "Then tell me, what's the key to dealing with him once I wake up?"

"Me." Rashta smiled and patted my pillow to encourage me to sit back down. "It will take the strength of a god to stop what he has become."

My hands clenched. I didn't like this. If a god was needed to stop him, then my friends were in trouble. "There has to be something I can do."

Rashta pinched her nose while sighing and Atria chuckled. "She's not going to calm down if you don't tell her."

My eyes darted between the two. "Tell me what?"

"If you concentrate hard enough, you'll be able to hear what's going on," Rashta said. "I didn't want you to know because it'd only make you more restless."

"I need to know what's happening."

She patted the pillow again. "Then come and sit. You don't want to fall over and embarrass yourself. To listen, you need to focus beyond yourself. The rest will come to you."

I sat next to her and closed my eyes, concentrating hard. Chaos assaulted my mind. Gun shots—Zarda's laughter—I didn't know what was going on out there. It made my head hurt. The longer I concentrated, the worse the feeling became.

I let out an exasperated sigh as I let go of what seemed to be a futile attempt. "How much longer do I have to wait here being useless?"

Rashta's eyes filled with sympathy. "Recovering. That is what you're doing. Zarda destroyed your body, Eira—lacerated your organs beyond normal repair. I may be a goddess, but I can only use special healing fire to save you. You know how slow that can work sometimes. Even infused with my power, I can't just spring your body back like nothing happened."

I gnashed my teeth tighter and clenched my hands, my shoulders tensing. "Still... the others..."

Sylvia leaned on her knees. "Why don't you ask some questions? You're bound to have them. And it'd keep you distracted."

I wanted to scream with frustration. My friends could be dying. Ryoko, Rylan… Ryder. I mentally shook myself—Sylvia was right. If I didn't do something to distract myself, I'd probably bust a gut. I let out a deep sigh and rested my cheek on my fist. "Okay, *fine*… how long does it take for us to be reborn?"

"A couple centuries," Rashta said. "Finding pairs that fill the necessary qualifications isn't easy. We need your father to be a dragon, and at least one of your parents to be carriers of the element of fire, though it doesn't have to be an active element. If your father is both, though, it helps to expedite the pairing process." She chuckled. "As long as we can find two souls that resonate. That is always a difficult thing to factor."

I tapped my finger on my lips. "If the rebirth isn't immediate, how does it work while I'm dead?"

"When you're alive, the energy used is yours. You can tap into mine when needed, but my power cannot sustain you. When you die, our energy is separated but still connected, with my energy sustaining us both. Your mortal soul feeds off my energy in death, draining me of my power. You must be given a new life before that power runs out."

I tilted my head. "What happens when it runs out?"

Rashta shrugged. "I'm not sure. It's never gotten to that point. But Lumaraeon herself warned us to not allow it to happen."

I nodded. "Okay. Now, this rebirth cycle. Did it cause a change in your position, or were you always responsible for a soul's rebirth?"

Rashta rocked her head back and forth. "I work with Arcadia when it comes to soul reincarnation, but mortals didn't know this. So upon my fusion with you, and the mortals finding out we are eternally reborn, they changed my title." She smiled. "This is also how you ended up with yours, Dragon-Phoenix."

I allowed myself to take this information in. Accepting I was the Dragon-Phoenix wasn't easy after all the time I'd spent denying it.

My thoughts turned inward. I didn't know what I wanted to do after Zarda was dealt with. With Raikidan gone… I didn't have a whole lot to look forward to. I'd lost my last chance at happiness. I couldn't see myself opening up to another, yet again, only to risk losing them, too.

But maybe I could find another purpose—one that focused on helping fellow halflings. Even if I couldn't be happy, that didn't mean others couldn't be given that chance.

Rashta smiled at me. "I can hear your thoughts. We are in your mind, after all. Your champion isn't dead."

My brow furrowed. "That can't be. Zarda shot him with liquid nickel."

"Your friends got him to a rejuvenation tank without Zarda even knowing he was moved." She chuckled. "His soul also found himself blocked from crossing over. You'll be reunited."

My heart fluttered. There was hope, then.

Lina smiled. "Don't worry. No matter what life he lives, he's not easy to escape."

Nalia grunted. "That's an understatement."

Everyone laughed, including myself. Though still anxious, I felt a little better. I narrowed an eye at Rashta. "How come the gods couldn't tell me any of this when I asked them questions?"

Rashta shrugged. "Because of a law set in place. I foresaw the events of Zarda obtaining his knowledge of your existence. There wasn't anything we could do to stop it, and I wanted to prevent you unneeded confusion and pain. So I enacted a law preventing any god from revealing the truth, except for me."

Her lips twisted. "Unfortunately, the corruption I absorbed caused a problem none of us could have predicted. Cosmic Law no longer saw me as Rashta, and thus I couldn't even tell you."

I grunted. "Well, that explains a lot."

She laughed. "Yes. Trust me; that was one folly I was not pleased to find out about in the moment."

A thought came to me, "So, wait… when I was in Hell with Arcadia, was that actually you who saved me?"

She nodded. "Yes. Arcadia just took the credit, for obvious reasons."

I knew something was off with that.

I peered around at the manifestations of my past lives. "Okay, so which ones of you have I had contact with? I know Atria and I have met, and Velsara has spoken to me, but some of the rest of you have also spoken to me."

Velsara raised her hand. "You received some of my memories. While disturbin', you needed to know what happened."

I nodded, remembering those bits quite well.

Sylvia nodded to me. "I was the one who spoke to you near that lighthouse. I wanted to test the rate of the purification—not only to see if you could hear me, but to see if I could impart some of my power to you. It's an ability that manifested later in the rebirth cycle, and one we used to help us gauge your purification process."

My brow twisted. "We can share abilities?"

Nisha giggled. "That's how I was able to impart you some of my magic."

I nodded. That made sense, with the violet dragon lineage. "This imparting of abilities… does this connect to our theory that a soul becomes stronger during rebirths?"

Nisha extended her finger up. "Bingo! And this life you live is the strongest yet."

I ran this through my head. "Knowing all this, is it safe for me to assume this verifies that souls and spirits are different?"

Raina spoke up. "That's correct. When our soul is in its death state, our individual lives separate and can interact as any spirit can, with the living and the dead. It's only in the living state we're fused."

I held my chin. *Fascinating.*

"Seven minutes and you're back on your feet." Rashta grinned. "Not to rush you or anything."

I chuckled, this time amused with her teasing of my impatience. I looked around at my manifestations. "Are all of you elementalists?"

All but Lutha and Lina nodded. Lina spoke. "We're not, for what we once thought were obvious reasons. But now that you've met those two psychic shaman children, we no longer know why we didn't receive elemental abilities."

"Kelen and Nisa are the first of their kind," Rashta said. "I do not know what Genesis and Zoltan have planned for them, but no one is a mistake, even down to their abilities."

I threw my thumb at her. "Our godly encyclopedia has spoken."

The temple filled with laughter.

I glanced around some more. "Raina and Velsara are shamans, and two of the past Ambassadors on top of that. Anyone else here a shaman?"

Nalia and Xenia raised their hands. Xenia spoke. "We're Ambassadors."

My mouth almost fell open. "You're pulling my leg." I looked around at everyone, each one of them grinning like cats. "Right?"

Their smiles only widened, and I threw my head back. "Seriously? I can't escape it!"

Laughter echoed through the temple again.

"Is that the secret to being a shaman, then?" I asked.

Rashta nodded. "Yes. The older the soul, the more likely it can touch the spiritual plane in life."

I leaned back. "Well, it'll be nice to strike that theory off as solved."

Rashta chuckled. "It's amusing. All any of you had to do was ask, and one of us gods would have answered. It wasn't like we were keeping the truth from you."

I grunted. "People these days get weird when it comes to talking to gods. Even shamans. I mean, remember that carnie who almost passed out after coming face to face with Phyre?"

She snickered. "Oh, I won't forget that for a while. Trust me."

My brow arched. *What was that supposed to mean?*

Rashta looked to the ceiling. "Two minutes. Any last minute questions?"

Deep lines formed on my brow as I thought. "Yeah, two. My *champion.* Is he ever aware of your presence?"

She shook her head. "No. My essence only ties him to the circle." Her brow creased. "Though, his most recent few lives, he's been more aware of his aged soul. It's quite possible he'll be able to access them in time, just as you can. Time will tell, though."

My mouth twitched as I took this in and thought about my possible last question. "Is there a way my soul couldn't be reborn?"

"If our bond is severed, it would end. The only way I am aware this could happen is if you ascend."

My fingers drummed on my leg. I wonder what I'd need to do to achieve that. I wasn't god material, but it'd be nice to break us from this cycle. And it'd help me understand what Kir was attempting for himself.

Rashta stood. "It's time."

My past lives murmured in excitement. I went to follow her action, but she motioned for me to stay where I was. "I need you to lie down and close your eyes. I'll do the rest. You'll know when you're back on the battlefield."

I nodded. "You'll help me fight him, right?"

Her grin slid up the side of her face. "I'm happy you asked. I'll do more than bestow my power to you again. I will judge him as my title requires. I will need to take control of you to do so."

Anyone else and I'd refuse. "I trust you."

She nodded, and gestured for me to lie down. I did so, and closed my eyes, taking calming breaths. My prior lives whispered words of encouragement.

Warmth filled my body, and soon my senses shifted. My skin no longer touched soft pillows, but instead, cold, hard ground. Voices became loud and less kind. A gunshot rang in my ears. *Ow… yep, I'm alive.*

My eyes opened just as Zarda laughed. "I can't die! Your fight against me is pointless!"

"He's wrong," Rashta said.

Strength returned to me, and a warmth like a strong fire built deep within me. It flooded through me until tendrils of flames licked my skin.

"You're wrong, Zarda." The words flowed out of my mouth as I pulled myself to my feet. "All mortal lives end eventually. We may not like it, but that is a fact of life."

Ryoko gasped. "Laz…"

Zarda took a step back. "How is this possible? I killed you."

My eyes narrowed at him. "No, you just delayed the inevitable."

"I can't die! I have a guarantee. I have been granted immortality!"

Rashta's knowledge merged with mine and her power grew inside me, fueling the fire engulfing my form. My body reverted back into its standard nu-human form, the bond's tug making me aware of Rylan's drained strength. "There are no guarantees in life. Not even being reborn again in time is a guarantee."

The fire around me swirled and then rose up. Rashta's presence drew out with the flames until she hovered behind me, her wings flowing about me in strong beats.

Zarda's eyes widened. "You were her. I had been successful in creating the Dragon-Phoenix. How, then? How is that I couldn't use your power for my own purposes?"

My eyes bore into him as Rashta spoke through my voice. "Zarda, you have broken Cosmic Law. You made a Pact of Life and Power with Nazir. You took the life of your mother, Lady Azura, and her unborn child in fear he would take leadership of this city instead of you. You slew your father, Lord Taric, for the sake of power, and placed the blame on his psychic consort."

Shock rippled through me. I knew Seda had cared about Lord Taric, but I never knew he had been the past lover she'd mentioned before. It did explain why she took his death so hard.

Rashta continued on. "You took false beliefs as truth and attempted the corruption of a god and my host for the purpose of unjust deeds. I, Rashta, the goddess of judgment and rebirth, hereby judge you now."

"No!" Zarda's hand clenched, his whole body seething in rage. "I am the rightful ruler of this city! My father didn't know how to rule properly and let others walk all over him. He was weak!"

Zarda's eyes widened, wild and crazed. "I'm stronger than he ever could be, and took leadership to make this city great. I have a guarantee from Nazir that I'm exempt from any cosmic judgment for actions that brought me to this point."

"I crossed my fingers."

Eyes fell behind Zarda. A giant of a man strode out of a dark portal. He wore black metal armor that matched the armor from ancient warriors found in library texts, with a large greatsword strapped to his back. His long ebon hair was pulled into a high ponytail drifting in an ethereal breeze. Confidence radiated off of him. His lavender eyes focused on Zarda. *Nazir.*

Zarda's lip curled. "You gave me your word."

Nazir chuckled. "I maybe have also been crossing my toes."

"You bastard." Zarda's eyes flashed. "We had a deal."

Nazir's lips twisted into a smirk. "I have a long list of deals you've gone back on." He gasped in mock amazement. "Oh, was that rule only supposed to apply to you?"

My brow twisted. I wasn't sure what to make of this god. He acted far differently than I ever imagined the god of death and corruption would conduct himself.

"Mortals tend to forget he's also the god of trickery and deceit," Rashta said in my mind.

Zarda's eyes darkened, his fist tightening. "I was guaranteed immunity to Cosmic Law and given immortality. I won't let anyone stand in my way—even the gods!"

I watched in stunned silence as he threw out his arm toward Nazir. It stretched as if he had no bones. *What has Zarda done to himself?*

Nazir drew his sword and sliced Zarda's hand when it came in range. Zarda howled in pain and retracted it immediately. The howling didn't last long, though—his hand healed up the moment his arm returned to its proper length. *No wonder everyone was having a hard time taking him down.*

I leveled a hard gaze at him. "You should know better than to attack a god."

Zarda threw his other hand at me. "Shut your mouth."

"Mother!"

I turned when Ryder called to me and caught the flying dagger he'd thrown to me. I grinned. It was my special dagger. Either he had gone searching for it when I was down, or, more realistically, this was the reason he had been captured in the first place.

I rolled out of the way of Zarda's attack and stabbed him. The blade didn't penetrate his skin as deeply as I would have liked, but I was going to use what I could.

I dragged the blade sideways and then tore it out as I ran toward him. Zarda cried out in pain and his eyes burned with rage.

"Eira, watch out behind you," Rashta warned.

I jumped over Zarda's arm as he retracted it and tried to take me out at the same time. I willed my weapon to change. I thought of a sword, but instead, it shifted into something heavier. I didn't have time to see what it became as Zarda attacked me again. I slid under his arm and swung the weapon into his body.

Crunch. I felt his bones break as the ornate hammer I held sent him flying. I gazed at the weapon—it looked more like a gavel than a typical war hammer.

"Do you like it?" Rashta asked.

"It's nice."

"It's my weapon. It's been some time since either of us wielded it."

"What do you mean?" I asked.

"I'll explain later. Right now we have to deal with Zarda. Please trap him in a ring of fire."

I took a deep breath. Zarda pulled himself to his feet, his livid eyes snapping to me. I breathed out a powerful flame. It rushed for him and then twisted and swirled, trapping him within.

"I'm going to temporarily take control of your body now."

"Go for it."

"Zarda, you have shown how deep your corruption runs," Rashta announced via my mouth. It was strange hearing my voice and seeing myself advance toward him without having any control. "You made a pact so you could gain power beyond anything natural. You attempted to corrupt my host for your own gain. You attacked a god, not out of anger, but out of spite. Your corruption runs—"

"I'm the only one who can rule this land!" Zarda's eyes grew more wild and he threw his hands out, emphasizing his derangement. I was pretty sure I saw him salivate as well. *Gross.* "No one else is powerful enough to keep order. No one else can go as far as what is needed to bring true peace in this world."

"At what cost?" A new voice spoke. "How many lives must be sacrificed for you to *unify* this world? How many species will have to die off for you to be happy?"

A raging flame burst from the ground behind Zarda, and Phyre stepped out. Then, to Zarda's right, the air distorted and two people seemingly appeared out of thin air. One was a man with ebon hair, dark skin, and blue eyes, and the other was a woman with blonde hair, light skin, and eyes that shimmered with all the colors imaginable. Both wore white tunics with elegant embroidery around the long collar and on the sleeves. *That's Zoltan and Genesis!*

The wind picked up, and on top of a crumbled building, a woman of light complexion appeared. Her long blonde hair flowed in the breeze, her crystal blue eyes intent on Zarda. The light blue dress she wore ruffled with the remaining wind she had stirred up. *Anila?*

More gods appeared. The number that had gathered astounded me. Solstice, the goddess of ice and snow, Lunaria, the goddess of the moon, and her partner, Solund, the god of the sun, all appeared in a whirlwind of snow that came in with Anila's wind. Valena, the goddess of earth and her partner Tarin, the god of nature, appeared out of a large oak tree that sprouted from the ground. Jin, the goddess of refined earth, and Le'carro, god of lightning, both appeared in an instant, black scorch marks sizzling on the ground beneath them as if they had been placed there by lightning. Even Arcadia, goddess of the spirits, Satria, the goddess of war, and Koseba, the god of shapeshifting, were here.

Rashta's commanding voice rang across the courtyard. "Zarda, you now stand trial before the gods. To witness your verdict, you stand in front of mortals to whom you have committed injustices. Zarda, for your transgressions—for the corruption you spread—I judge you as unworthy of the life given to you, and deem you further unworthy of eternal rest."

"No!" Zarda's eyes were wide and his hands trembled. I caught the quiver in his voice.

My arm brought the hammer up and then slammed it down onto the ground. The earth shook and fire sprung up from the impact point, rushing toward Zarda. It took the shape of a phoenix as it raced for him. It was so fast, he had no chance of escaping it. In less than a second, Zarda was engulfed in flames and screaming in agony. But before his body could burn to a crisp, Arcadia held up her hand and a strange portal opened behind him. Hundreds of black shapes moved excitedly inside the desolate wasteland that was quite obviously Hell. One reached out, and none of the gods stopped it. It took me a moment to realize it was reaching for Zarda.

As the being reached out, it took shape. What I saw took me by surprise. It was a dragon's head. *Anir.*

Anir clamped down on Zarda and pulled him toward the portal. Zarda, even in his weakened state, struggled against the toothy maw. Anir held fast, determination flickering in his eyes.

Rashta compelled my body to raise the hammer high into the air when Zarda and fire swirled around the head of the hammer. The fire that had trapped Zarda reacted and spun up, then collided with the portal to Hell. The force sent a shockwave through the courtyard, carrying the nauseating smell of sulfur and decay with it.

"It is done." Rashta turned my body, allowing me to take in the silenced courtyard. Mortals stared, awed and wide-eyed. Some even had fallen to their knees, overcome by the overwhelming presence of gods in their midst. And some even watched me, celestial-aura Eira who had just sentenced the most dangerous mortal alive.

Rashta continued, "Those forced into servitude of Zarda are now free. Your lives are yours to live, mortals. Live them wisely."

Her words melted the silence, loud cheers erupting throughout the space. This had been a long, hard-fought battle—one many believed would never end. The idea of being free was still surreal, even to me, but I was sure it'd hit me eventually.

I gazed up at Rashta, questions about the last few minutes buzzing in my head. "Rashta, why wasn't Zarda's soul separated from his body before his judgment?"

"To ensure a mortal can't use ancient forbidden magic to bring him back. Mortal forms break down in Hell in a matter of minutes. No body, no ritual component."

I had no idea that kind of magic was still known. "And why did Anir help?"

"Regret. Rage. Love. He regrets the pact he made with Nazir. He loved your life so much, your rejection compelled him to make a rash decision. And Zarda's treatment of you enraged him. To treat someone like you in such a cruel manner…" She sighed. "He knows this won't change his sentences, but didn't do it in hopes of that. He did it because his feelings remain, even after all this time. It's why he tried to warn you about Raikidan that one night."

The memory of me testing in the bath flashed through my mind. "That was him?"

She held my gaze. "Yes. Somehow he saw what your champion had planned, but didn't see the part where you'd both come up with it together as a ruse. He couldn't bear to think your destined mate could betray you like that, when he should feel so lucky to have you." Rashta snorted. "Of course, Arcadia thought he was trying to escape and cut off your communication with him."

Anir cared enough to do all this, even when so much time had passed. That was a long time to hold onto that feeling. It was a true emotion for him. "Why did I choose?"

She chuckled. "It's funny you ask, because later in that life you questioned the same thing. It came down to knowing neither male would agree to share you."

I touched my chin with my index finger and thumb. "I see…"

"Oh, um, you're going to want to sit down."

My brow ticked up, but before I could question, a sudden wave of weakness hit me—her power running through me earlier all but vanishing. My legs gave out, but before I could hit the ground, strong arms clad in dark armor caught me. I looked up at the god. "Nazir?"

He smirked and lowered me to the ground easier. "What kind of man would I be if I let a lady fall?"

I snorted. "I'm no lady."

Nazir chuckled and then turned his gaze up to Rashta. I glanced her way to find her arms crossed and looking elsewhere. She looked pissed.

"I'm retreating now," Rashta announced, not looking at either of us. "Your body can't accept my power anymore and you need rest."

She didn't give me a chance to argue. Nazir let out a quiet sigh and stepped away. My brow rose. *Okay…* I wasn't sure what this was all about.

"Don't ask," Rashta said.

"You know I will eventually. But for now, thank you for helping. I couldn't have done this without you."

"That's not true. You have great strength and even greater allies. Had you made different choices, things would have been different."

"Would I have not known about you if I'd taken those paths?"

She chuckled. *"No matter the life you live, you will always know my presence at some point. Had you chosen a different path, you would have found out another way. Now rest, and relish your victory of freedom."*

"Laz!" Ryoko called out.

I swiveled my head, finding her scrambling to her feet and rushing over to me. I prepared myself to endure a painful tackle, but she was surprisingly gentle when she latched onto me.

"I thought we lost you," she sobbed.

I smiled and stroked her head. "Nah, you can't get rid of me that easily."

Just then, a female body hugged me from behind; her blue hair hung over my shoulders. "I'm so glad you're okay, too."

"Hey, Yára." I turned to look at her and noticed what a mess she was. "What happened to you?"

Ryoko giggled. "She gave Zarda a thrashing."

"Yeah, but he got me back," Yára muttered.

I blinked slowly. "I'm lost."

Yára smiled. "I'll explain later."

"Yeah, good idea."

More of my friends and family came running over. I could tell my heroic attempt had really put them out of sorts and guilt gripped tight in my chest. I may have done what I thought was right in the moment, this emotional aftermath was the direct consequence of that choice, regardless if the outcome hadn't gone anywhere near how I'd planned.

My attention was pulled away from them when I heard someone running toward us from a far distance. My eyes fell on Ryder when he made it over to us and seemed out of breath. "You know I'm not going anywhere. I can't really stand."

"Yeah, that doesn't surprise me." He smiled. "I'm glad you're back. You had me worried."

I smiled back. "You all have such little faith in me."

"I doubt you had that all planned out," Rylan accused.

I chuckled. "Maybe I did."

He rolled his eyes and I took in Ryder's condition again. "Why are you out of breath?"

He pointed behind him. "Just checked on Raikidan for you. He's situated in a rejuv tank and stabilized.

I attempted to stand. "I need to see him."

Ryoko held onto me. "Easy. You need to rest. He's going to be fine now."

"I need to see him."

"Rest."

"No…"

Ryder knelt in front of me and pulled me into a tight hug. "It's okay. Everything is going to be okay."

I found myself unable to fight him. My body was just too tired. But it wasn't okay. It way my fault Raikidan had been hurt so badly.

"He did it to save you," Rashta said. "You gave him something to care about again. You can't blame yourself for his choice."

"Watch me."

She let out a sigh.

I looked up at Trigon when he approached. He had a big goofy grin on his face, and it was way too obvious he was up to something. Without saying a word, he scooped me up and walked toward the fortress.

"Trigon, where are we going?" I asked.

He smiled. "You said you wanted to see loverboy, yeah?"

My cheeks flushed. Everyone and their mother may have known about the two of us at this point, but it wasn't that easy to deal with the teasing just yet. "Shut up."

Trigon chuckled and carried me to the recovery lab.

51
CHAPTER

My fingers drummed on a computer station as I stared at the rejuvenation tank. Bubbles floated around Raikidan, the green fluid suspending him. The air mask strapped to his face was secure, and the computer read optimum oxygen flow. His vitals also exhibited ideal readings.

Physically, his wounds had healed, but he showed no other activity. Almen had assured me Raikidan just needed time, and not to worry, and I had done my best to stay calm in the last forty-eight hours, but each hour that passed without improvement further agitated my nerves. Ryoko and the others checked in every now and then, bringing me food and making sure I got some sleep, but otherwise left me alone in my vigil. I didn't know what else to do. It wasn't like I had the power to wake him up.

"He'll wake when he's ready," Rashta said.

"I know, I know." I paced. "This is just pushing my patience button a little too much."

"We could always call in your friends. They have all sorts of questions for you that could work as a prime distraction."

She wasn't wrong. Ryoko had been the most vocal about wanting to know what had happened to me during the fight with Zarda, but also didn't pressure me to explain so Raikidan could be my main focus. In truth, I didn't want to explain things without him there to hear it. He deserved to know the truth, too. I was done hiding it all from him.

"You could also take the time to get progress updates on the city."

From what I knew, the news hadn't been broken to the citizens yet. The Council was still deliberating the best way to go about it. It had to be in an impactful way that wouldn't also cause a revolt.

"Or, give Ryder some answers."

Ryder had paid me several visits. All to check up on me, though I could tell by the looks he gave, he had all sorts of questions. Every time I went to tell him, he'd run off to go help out with one thing or another. It was as if he knew and didn't want to hear the answers while I was dealing with Raikidan.

"I could give you more answers. Like how the dragons coined your title."

"It came about because of how they viewed me." It wasn't that hard to guess.

"Yes, that's true, but it came out of respect. Those who stood by you from the very beginning saw you as something special. They praised me for my sacrifice and you for the type of person you were—selfless, loving, the perfect vessel for a goddess." Rashta chuckled. *"And the perfect dragon. And that love for us grew when they found out about the rebirth process. They were more determined than ever to protect and honor us."*

Warmth spread through me, bringing on a small smile. It was nice knowing there were some out there that didn't hate us halflings.

"Okay, that topic died quicker than I'd hoped. How about you finally talk to your father? You could get some sort of proper closure at the very least."

Anger flared up, balling my hands into fists. During one of Ryder's visits, I found out my father still hadn't left. He insisted on speaking to me the moment I wasn't indisposed. My lips curled. He could rot in hell for all I cared. He had a lot of nerve showing up.

Rashta sighed. *"Or not."*

"Do not be so hard on her, Rashta," a masculine voice said. "There's a lot of resentment she has to work through."

I spun around to find Nazir leaning against the doorway of the laboratory. My brow rose. "Why are you here? And how do you know what she's saying to me?"

He played with a black feather in his hands. "I thought about being witty and telling you I'm the harbinger of death come to reap a soul"—he gestured to Raikidan—"but he'll be waking up soon, and it's in such poor taste I actually fear what you'd do to me. As for hearing what Rashta speaks, that's a secret."

A half-laugh came from my throat. "You're afraid of me?"

"I've seen your temper." He grinned. "It matches Rashta's quite nicely."

Rashta scoffed. *"Tell him to leave."*

My brow rose. This wasn't the first time she'd had a reaction like this to him. Yesterday I'd tried to find out why she wouldn't even look at him when he caught me mid-fall, but she refused to answer.

"Rashta, please talk to me. I swear to you, I didn't do what you think I did."

I sensed Rashta's annoyance, even as she refused to speak. I studied Nazir. His cocky attitude was nowhere to be seen. Instead, he just looked desperate. I was intrigued. "What does she think you did?"

His lavender eyes fixed on me for a moment. "She thinks the pact I made with Zarda was intentionally done to mess with your reincarnation. She's wrong."

"Liar!"

I cringed at her volume. "Can you, I don't know, come out and yell at him yourself, and not in my head?"

"Yes, please do, Rashta," Nazir said. "I'd much rather hear your voice than feel the essence of it."

"I'm not talking to that... fiend." I could almost picture her crossing her arms and turning away in a mini tantrum. The thought brought a half-smile to my lips.

"Um, can any past life hear me?" I wasn't sure how this all worked, but if one of them could assist, then I could put this to bed.

"Oh, me! Me! I got this!"

I chuckled. *"Thanks for answering my call, Ayuma. I could use assistance getting her to face him."*

"Oh, that's easy. Just fill your body with energy and force her out."

I doubted it was that easy, but I figured I might as well try.

"Don't you dare!" Rashta's tone was a mixture of anger and fear.

I ignored her and took a deep breath, building up a large store of energy. "Okay, eviction time."

"No, don—" She didn't get the chance to finish as I threw a

semi-corporeal form of her out next to me. She gave me a seething stare and then spun around, crossing her arms. Feathers fell from her wings, Nazir catching one, it taking a physical form on contact with his fingers. It looked identical to the one he already carried. *Interesting.*

Nazir waited for her to acknowledge him, but she refused. He sighed and walked up to her. "Rashta, please look at me."

"Go make a stupid pact or something. I don't want to hear it."

My brow rose. This behavior was so peculiar. I'd expected a goddess of her caliber to act—well, more goddess-like. Nazir reached for her arm, only for Rashta to yank herself away. Realization dawned on me. *Oh…*

I grinned. "Nazir, you could just give her a big passionate kiss. Up to this point, she's been a firm believer that those fix everything."

Nazir gave me a curious glance, his lips curling into a half-smile. Rashta, on the other hand, threw imaginary daggers at me with her eyes. "Don't you dare start."

I leaned back on the computer station. "Why not? You did it with me."

"That was *different.*"

"I disagree." I picked up an apple from a plate and bit into it before shifting my gaze to Nazir. "Why don't you explain your position, instead of begging for her to look at you? You'll make better progress that way."

His head tilted before giving a thoughtful nod. "Zarda called me to make a deal. In exchange for his soul, he wanted power. Enough power so that he could unify Lumaraeon. A noble goal to some, but I could see the darkness in his heart. That mattered not to me, so I gave him what he asked for. He received a great deal of knowledge lost during the War of End and before."

His gaze shifted to Rashta. "But I didn't tell him of you or the Dragon-Phoenix. I knew what this man was capable of. I would never have done that to you."

Rashta still refused to acknowledge him.

My head tilted as I gazed at Nazir. "Did you tell Zarda of the weapon strong enough to kill dragons?"

He shook his head vehemently. "No. I don't know where he found those plans."

Rashta's narrowed eyes pinned on him. "Why do you insist on lying?

You were opposed to my choice to save this soul, and have not been quiet about your displeasure. In fact, I've heard it after every life when the soul came to rest."

My brow rose. "You think he's being petty because of a choice you made?" A half-laugh escaped my throat. "I thought the goddess of judgment was more mature than that."

She stared at me, her face paling from my words. Even Nazir appeared taken aback.

I shook my head in disbelief. "You are unbelievable. Either some of my antics have worn off on you, or you're not as I imagined you to be."

Rashta's eyes narrowed dangerously. "You don't know our past."

"No, but I can tell when someone is being sincere. And really, what would he have gained from telling Zarda about us?"

"Nothing," Nazir said, his tone strong with conviction. "The gods would have had my head on a silver platter after they fixed the mess, which is another piece of proof it wasn't me. Had I given Zarda this knowledge, then Genesis and Zoltan could have stepped in. They could have fixed her birth outcome because of the laws put into place—laws you specifically set down to keep me in check, Rashta. You know this."

Doubt and turmoil flickered across her face. I understood her position. She'd been so sure. But even though the evidence pointed to the contrary, it was still hard to let go of her doubts.

Yet, some of his words made sense, even to me. The gods wouldn't have wanted a goddess like herself to go through this. Even if it was just her that they cared about—

"Don't go thinking that, little dragon girl," Nazir said, his eyes turning to me. "You matter as much as she does."

I threw my hands into the air. "How did you know?"

He smirked. "It's a god thing."

I shook my head. That was *such* an infuriating response.

He snickered. "It's why I do it."

"Stop that!" I pointed at him. "Or I'll force you to tell me what I want to know about you."

Nazir crossed his arms and shifted his weight to one side. "What do you want to know?"

His response gave me pause. I didn't expect him to be so open. *There's got to be a catch.*

"No catch."

I grunted. A stifled giggle slipped from Rashta; Nazir noticed it as well. "How did you become the god of your domains?"

His fingers drummed on his armor as he answered. "During my mortal life, I was a mercenary. There were few things I wouldn't do for coin—other than murder women and children, or go against a vow of loyalty. Even still, I was one of the best, and nearly outclassed all other warriors in battle."

I crossed my arms. "You had a moral and honor code once. What happened to it?"

His eyes shifted away from me for a moment. "I lost the most precious thing in my life. How it happened is what changed me. I hunted down those who stole it from me, and found my morals had shifted in the process. I went back on deals when they suited me, and became even more ruthless in battle. Still, my reputation kept coin flowing, even with the risks involved."

It didn't take much to know this precious thing was a person. I could only guess it had been a close family member or a lover. Either way, it wasn't my business to pry into something so personal. That kind of pain wasn't to be—

I straightened, my eyes going wide. *Wait.* How could I have not thought about this before?

Rashta's arms fell to her side as she watched me. "What is it, Eira? I'm unable to read your thoughts for some reason."

My eyes snapped to them both. "It's Kir. Kir told Zarda."

Nazir pursed his lips. "Why would he, though? He hates your very existence. He'd want to prevent your cycle from continuing, not encourage it."

"As much as I hate to agree with him, he's right," Rashta said. "He rejected the ideals of the Crimson Wing. He'd benefit nothing from encouraging your continued existence."

I shook my head. "Not true. You're viewing him as a single-minded individual—a rabid dog at best. This isn't what Kir is. He's methodical—he's cunning—he had a plan."

I paced. "Think about it. If he could force the rebirth, he'd have knowledge on how to make it work. If he and Zarda could successfully bend us to his will, then he'd be able to learn how to end the process even quicker. And if not, he'd have an easy time killing me."

I stopped and faced them. "He's also old enough to be capable of handing Zarda those weapon plans. Zarda's unstable mental state made him the perfect little pawn."

Nazir nodded thoughtfully. "Perfect, until he let you break away and escape. Then you threw his plans out the window and he had to resort to other tactics."

A grim smile crossed my lips. "Exactly."

Rashta had grown quiet, her skin reddening and body visibly trembling as conflict raged through her.

Compassion welled up in me for her. Goddess or not, this was obviously extremely difficult for her. I opened my mouth to express my concern, when the computer behind me beeped. I nearly jumped out of my skin, but then forgot everything else when I saw Raikidan's vitals moving.

"Ah, looks like our 'heroic' dragon is finally waking up," Nazir said. "I'll take my leave. We'll talk about this some more, Rashta. I hope by then you'll hear me out."

He looked to me. "Before I go, I've been instructed to let you know that in one year's time, we'll need to call on you to deal with an important matter."

Rashta's wings flexed. "They're going to wait that long?"

I glanced between them. What were they talking about?

Nazir nodded. "Yes. Gina claims the corruption that still clings to you is minimal enough to be dealt with at a later date."

Oh, that. Nazir's eyes ticked to me. "So long as the Dragon-Phoenix and her Champion do not part for long periods, it will not spread."

"It'd be prudent to deal with this now," Rashta argued.

"I agree with you, dear, but they've deemed some mortal issues to be of more importance."

Rashta's eyes narrowed as if she didn't believe him. He released a strained exhale, his eyes pleading with her to trust him for once, and then he strolled off, disappearing into the darkness of the hall beyond. Rashta gazed after him for a moment before giving me a sidelong glance. "Can I go back now?"

I grunted. "Sure, but we'll be talking about your secret little love-affair with the former mercenary."

She narrowed her eyes dangerously for a moment, then winked out of existence. The computer beeped again and then the lights above the rejuvenation tank danced as they reacted to something. Raikidan's hands twitched, and then his face. A wide smile spread across my face as I ran up to the glass and placed my hands upon it.

Raikidan stirred a bit more and his eyes fluttered open. The water wouldn't hurt them, but it would blur his vision.

"Experiment in the rejuvenation tank," a computer voice read out. "Do not panic. You will be released momentarily."

Raikidan flicked back and forth, his eyes attempting to adjust and take in his confusing situation. When I moved, his attention zeroed in on me. For a moment, I thought he may not be able to see it was me, but then his hand slammed against the glass where my own hands rested. Startled, I jumped back.

His hand remained on the glass and I realized he had just misjudged the distance between the clear surface and him. I motioned to him to wait, hoping he'd see and understand, then ran over to the computer station. I punched in the release codes I had seen Jasmine use in the past.

The tank buzzed twice and then the computerized voice spoke again. "Code orders received. Tank draining. Experiment inside, do not remove breathing mask until glass unit is removed."

I snatched a towel as the tank drained. When the tank finished, clean water poured in to wash Raikidan of the chemical water and then drained once more. Raikidan removed his breathing mask the moment the glass pulled up.

He grinned as he stepped down from the tank. "Hey, Butterfly."

Words escaped me. I knew he'd make it, but to see him like this, as if he hadn't almost died...

Raikidan reached for the towel. "Am I allowed to dry off a little?" He looked down at himself. "And put on some clothes so that you don't yell at me for being indecent?"

His words barely penetrated the fog in my head. I reached for his face and then a loud *smack* echoed through the room when my hand collided with his cheek. Shocked as I was for my sudden action, Raikidan took a moment to register the sting. When he did, he touched the red mark on his face and mouthed a silent, "Ow."

"Don't you ever do anything like that again, you hear?"

He rubbed his face some more. "I'm not going to apologize. I know that's how you lost Tannek, but there was no way I'd just stand there and watch you take those bullets. I'd do it over again if it meant saving you."

"You'd better apologize!" My shoulders tensed. "You're not allowed to—"

I sucked in a sharp breath when his lips crashed into mine. The towel dropped to the floor and I threaded my fingers into his wet hair. My back hit the wall, Raikidan's hard body pressing against me. His hands firm on my thighs, he lifted me up, his kiss growing demanding. The familiar aroma of his ashen musk, now tainted with the scent of tank water enveloped my senses. My heart thundered in my chest.

Then, when I thought I'd be unable to keep breathing, the kiss ended and Raikidan rested his forehead on mine. "That good enough?"

I took a few breaths. "Yes…"

He brushed my cheek with the back of his hand and grinned. "That didn't take long to get out of you."

Confused, I touched my face to find it rough, almost scaly. "You make it hard to keep it at bay. I've never had such a hard time until you came along."

His fingers slid across my skin some more. "I want to see the whole transition. No holding back like you've done in the past." He chuckled. "Pretending it's back pain and all."

My face flushed hot as my eyes darted away. "To be fair, it does cause me pain since I don't change regularly."

He frowned. "I want to know all sides of you, but if it's going to cause you pain…"

I took a deep breath. "I can handle that. My major block is Rylan and the artificial bond. If I change, he will be forced into his direwolf form, and vice versa. I need his permission before doing this."

Raikidan lifted my chin. "Do you? Or could you just ask for forgiveness later?"

I pushed his hand away. "Don't be like that. I'm not about—"

"*Laz,*" Seda messaged. "*Apologies for interrupting, but Rylan gives permission. When I informed everyone Raikidan had finally awakened, Ryoko went back to pestering him about seeing his direwolf form.*"

"*Well if they both want to see our freak side—*"

She giggled. *"Sorry, but that term has a vastly different meaning to me."*

I pinched my nose and groaned. *"Really? Must you?"*

She laughed some more. *"Oh, don't be like that. There's nothing wrong in a little exploration. But, we're getting off topic. I'll leave you to your…* freak *show."*

I did not miss the meaning behind her tone, sending a wave of heat through me. Raikidan tilted his head. "What's with all the strange reactions?"

I shook my head. "Sorry. Seda said some weird things."

"I see." He moved in closer and planted a light kiss on my temple, murmuring against my skin, "So, do I have permission to help you show me, or am I going to have to teach Rylan a thing or two about secrets?"

He kissed just under my jaw, sending a wave of weakness through me. The bond tugged hard, telling me this was going to get interesting for both parties, more so than it normally did when either chose to be intimate with their partner. "I… wouldn't mind a little help."

Raikidan grinned against my neck and then my back met the wall again. His teeth grazed my skin and various sensations assaulted me at once—lust—the bond's pull—the cusp of transformation.

Then it all disappeared when someone cleared their throat. Raikidan's lips curled as an inhuman hiss escaped his throat. We turned to see who had interrupted, and I scowled at the sight of my father.

"What do you want?" Raikidan muttered.

My father remained calm. "I wish to speak to my daughter."

"You want to talk?" I pushed away from Raikidan and stalked over toward him. "After eighty-plus years, you now have the gall to tell me you want to talk? After all the broken promises, you think you can just show up and talk?"

I stopped directly in front of him and stared him down. He didn't attempt to say anything. He just gazed at me, his eyes pleading. Then, without having to think about it, my hand flew up and slapped him across the face. My father held the area I had hit but he didn't grow angry. He didn't yell. It was as if he merely accepted my anger.

"You hit like your mother." A small chuckle escaped his lips as he caressed his cheek. "That was honestly refreshing. I miss when she used to hit me like that."

"Shut up." My hands clenched, my shoulders tensing. "Don't you dare talk as if you still care."

His eyes widened as if something clicked in his head. "You don't know…"

"Know what? Know that you weren't there? That you never intended to keep those promises you made us? That you're the reason my mother is dead!" I slammed my fists into his chest. "I hate you! This is all your fault. She'd still be alive if it weren't for you. None of this would have ever happened. You're the one who killed her."

My chest pulsed with pain as I was unable to keep my emotions in check and tears welled up in my eyes. "You made empty promises. You made her believe you'd be coming back. You weren't around when she needed you! You weren't there when I needed you… You weren't there…"

Unable to control myself, I sobbed into his chest. Instead of talking, my father just held me. I felt so pathetic, but I couldn't stop. I was angry and sad and confused. I couldn't pinpoint a single emotion to feel. This whole not-bottling-up-my-emotions-and-pretending-I-didn't-have-them thing was outright frustrating.

"I'm sorry," my father murmured. "It was never my intention for it to end up this way. I meant it when I said I loved your mother. She meant everything to me. Which is why I continued to see her, even when I was forbidden to."

I pulled away from him. "What?"

He sighed, his shoulders sagging as he held my gaze. "You really don't know… though I guess I shouldn't be surprised, since you hate me. I doubt you wanted to hear what she had to say."

"What are you talking about?"

He held my shoulders. "I spent a year in this city before completing the agreement with Zarda. I used that time to get to know your mother and choose her as my mate. That was part of the agreement, though Zarda wasn't happy I had chosen her."

I grunted. "Naturally."

"He sought to change the agreement and make it so I couldn't see her or you. For the sake of the clans, I had to agree, but had no intention of upholding the agreement. After the year passed and Zarda forced me to leave, I continued to sneak in and see your mother since I couldn't up and take her without you. I couldn't bear the thought of leaving you behind."

My breath caught in my throat, my mind racing as I struggled to take all this in. *Could it be true? Was it just more lies?*

"Listen to him, Eira," Rashta's voice echoed through my mind.

My father took a deep breath before continuing. "For twelve years I did this. For twelve years, your mother and I snuck around under Zarda's nose. I watched you grow, Lazmira. I watched the amazing transformation your body underwent." His voice grew quieter—filled with sadness. My heart clenched at what he said next. "I thought about all the things I wanted you to experience about our world—what it meant to be a dragon. I spoke to you... your mother said you could hear me. The computer monitoring you showed you could..."

"Mrymy ivxy fel e zummzy knewiv wunz." The words rolled off my tongue flawlessly as if I had been capable of speaking the language all along.

My father stared at me. "Do you know what that means?"

I shook my head. "Raikidan taught me *knewiv*. It means *dragon*. And he taught me *mrymy*, which means *there*, but that's all I know." A grimace crossed my face. "I'm quite terrible at speaking the language."

Raikidan reached out and touched my elbow. "You're not terrible."

My father stared down at me, his eyes brimming with moisture. *"Lry fel lmnivw evk pyeomudoz."*

"Evk rek ev yay din lruva mruvwl," the words tumbled from my mouth.

A bittersweet smile spread across his lips. "You did hear, then... I told you a story in pieces every night I came to see the two of you. I made it just for you and spoke to you in our tongue in hopes to make it easier for you to learn it one day. Jasmine also tried to program the computer to teach you how to write our words."

"That explains why the symbolic writing you use is so close to ours, Eira." Raikidan's voice was filled with wonder. "It's probably why you can't read common either. The computer could have given you conflicting messages and you merged the two languages in the written form. That's why you were able to pick up on our tongue so quickly. Even with dragon blood, you'd have to be raised around us to catch on as quickly as you have."

A sudden chill went up my spine. I backed away from my father. This was getting a bit too weird. And I didn't quite like how Raikidan agreed with all this.

"Lazmira, please," my father pleaded. "I don't want you to hate me. I honestly didn't want it to end this way."

"Give him a chance, Laz," Rashta encouraged.

I didn't answer her. In truth, conflict raged inside me. There was one more thing I needed to hear before considering anything more. My voice caught in my throat as the words spilled out in barely controlled anger. "W–why… why did you stop showing up? Why… did you send someone else with an empty message?"

My father's face fell, his entire frame sagging. "Zarda found out. He caught your mother and me in the lab. He… threatened to kill you both if I didn't leave that very moment and never come back."

He grew silent for a moment, moisture brimming in his eyes once more.

I held my breath, willing myself to be still—to not react just yet.

He cleared his throat, and continued. "I… didn't want either of you to suffer because I had chosen to go against the pact… so I left and had Largren deliver the message to your mother. It was a promise to find a way to get you both out. I was determined to do so at any cost, short of your lives. But…"

My eyes narrowed as he paused. "But *what?*"

He hesitated a moment more as if wrestling with himself, then set his jaw and plunged on. The words spilled from his mouth in a vast rush as if he had been holding onto them for an eternity. "But your mother had a condition to my promise. I had to come up with a way that wouldn't endanger the lives of the clans or make it so we'd have to live on the run. I agreed to her terms, not realizing how hard it would be."

I wrapped my arms around myself and stared at him, not knowing what to think. *Is he really telling the truth? Or is it just another lie?* It sounded like the truth. So many things pointed to it, but lies also sounded so much like truths.

My father took a step closer, but I stepped back. His moisture-filled eyes pleaded with me. That look made it hard for me to hate him. Yet, I wanted to hate him. I wanted him to pay for what he had done. *But, do I really?* Suddenly, I wasn't sure what I wanted.

"It's okay to forgive someone."

"That's not—"

"And it's okay to admit you're wrong. It doesn't invalidate how you felt over the years. But it does allow you to move on. You know this."

I knew all of that. That wasn't my issue. I just wasn't sure of the truth anymore…

"It's buried deep within, dear. Under all the pain."

Rashta's words washed over me like a cold bucket of ice. I thought about all the information that had been laid at my feet. I went over the story again and again in my mind. Why was I remembering it? I didn't understand it, but I still… heard it… in my head…

"I wish we could just take her out now."

"Rizgar, you know we can't do that."

He sighed. "I know, but I just want her to have a better life than the one she'll get. I want her to have the chance to grow up slowly and experience life the way she's supposed to."

"You're not the only one…"

My vision clouded, and before I knew it the lab was gone and I was surrounded by green liquid. Everything was blurry, but I could make out two people in front of me. They were standing close together and I was sure they were looking at me. Based on their shapes and voices, I assumed one was a man and the other a woman.

Then suddenly, more people showed up and someone started shouting.

"Grab her!"

Someone grabbed one of the people who had been standing in front of me, but the other person tried to save her. "Don't touch her."

The woman was forcefully taken away and they held something up to her head. "Come any closer and she pays the price."

"You wouldn't dare."

"Actually, I would. You've tainted her, so I should destroy her regardless. But I can be merciful. Leave now and I'll spare her and the girl. Come back, and she and your daughter pay the price."

"Rizgar, go. I'll be fine."

"But—"

"Go!"

"You will regret this, Zarda."

I watched the man run off and I wanted to stop him. I didn't want him to go…

I jerked with surprise when someone touched my arm. I spun to see Raikidan holding up his hands. He hushed me softly. "Easy. Just me. You left us for a moment and I was concerned."

I shook my head as a wan smile split my face. "Sorry. Another episode."

"That's the first in a while."

I nodded as I tried to process what I'd seen. He'd really been here. I was old enough to have that memory stored. *I would have been twelve…*

"What did you see?" my father asked, his voice tentative.

I locked eyes with him and held his gaze, the anger suddenly leaving me. My voice shook as I responded softly. "You… Dad."

He stared at me, his face paling with shock from my my chosen word. But I was done being angry. I couldn't blame him anymore. I never thought I'd call him that, but I now knew the truth.

Tears openly streamed down his face as he rushed over and threw his arms around me. I returned the gesture, holding him in a tight embrace.

"I'm sorry," I whispered as I held onto him. "I'm so sorry for being angry…"

"Don't be," he hushed me. "You had every right to be angry. The truth doesn't change anything. I wasn't around when I should have been. But I'm going to make it up to you. If you let me, that is."

I pulled away and gazed into his pleading eyes, the side of my mouth curving slightly. "You have a lot of time to make up for."

A grin crossed his tear-streaked face. "Then I'd better get started." He glanced at Raikidan. "But first, I'll let you two get back to whatever it is you were up to."

Raikidan snorted. "Thanks to you, that's not going to happen."

My brow ticked up in puzzlement. "What's going on?"

"According to Seda, the Council wishes to speak to you immediately." He shrugged. "For some reason, they want some answers to something that happened during the fight with Zarda that I missed. And they want your input on a matter because of it."

Oh, right. Raikidan needed to be told a few things—and before everyone else. I looked to my father. "Can you give us a few minutes? I need to speak to Raikidan about something in private."

My father's face twisted in slight confusion, but let it be and nodded. "I'll be down the hall."

My father left, casting one last glance over his shoulder, as if worried I'd disappear or something. This left me and Raikidan alone—sort of. Rashta remained present in the front of my mind, ready to help if needed with this.

"So, what do you have to talk to me about?" Raikidan asked. "Is it about what I missed after taking that bullet?"

I nodded and retrieved a towel for him to finally dry off. "You're going to want to sit. It's quite a bit to take in."

He did as I asked, and I went to telling him what he missed. Raikidan's face and body twisted and jerked with all sorts of emotions and reactions as he listened. But it all stopped when I got to the part about the two of us and our connection to Rashta. By the end, his eyes were wide and he sat stiller than I'd ever seen him be capable of.

I dipped my head when a good five minutes of silence passed, and kept my eyes soft. "Rai?"

He blinked and then shook his head, coming back. "Yeah, sorry. Just… processing. I know we had theories, but for it to go to this extent…"

I stroked his cheek. "Take your time. If you have questions, I'll answer them as best I can."

"I will help as well," Rashta said.

"I don't know where to start, really." Raikidan pressed his lips into a line. "I guess I should be sure I'm not dreaming. Or really dead."

I leaned in and pecked him on the lips. "Well, if you're dead, so am I. And I'm quite sure Rashta stopped that from happening, so you're certainly alive."

He nodded. "Okay… Is there… is there a way I can see this for myself?"

"Rashta?"

"Push me out again."

I concentrated and did it. Raikidan jumped to his feet and took several startled steps back. This made Rashta laugh. Raikidan stared at the two of us, his eyes wide and bewildered. "Oh… okay… give me a moment."

The two of us were patient, giving him several more minutes to calm himself and accept this.

Raikidan took a deep breath when he was ready to talk. "So, you've been here this whole time?"

Rashta nodded. "It's a bit complicated, but yes."

He turned his attention to me. "And you knew, all along?"

My face twisted and I rocked my head back and forth. "Not exactly. I'd heard her voice, and we'd started to communicate more and more over the past year, but I didn't know the extent of her importance until recently."

He frowned. "But you knew enough to keep it from me."

I let out a long sigh. "Really? You're going to do this? I would have told you if I'd understood her presence better at the time. But as it stood, before the stuff with Zarda went down, I didn't know who she was. So instead of sounding crazy, I decided not to tell you until I figured out more."

"If you had told him, it would have helped with the purification," Rashta said in a sing-song *I told you so* voice.

My eyes narrowed. "I'll banish you back into my mind."

Raikidan reached out to us. "Please don't yet. I have another question."

Rashta and I exchanged a glance. She spoke. "What is it, dear?"

"Eira, you said you can hear these past lives of yours every now and then. Even communicate with them. Why can't I do that?"

Rashta nodded. "That's an excellent question. It has to do with the fact that you are not my host, and only affected by my essence. Though..." She tapped her lips. "I wonder..."

Raikidan took several steps back when she approached. "What are you doing?"

The winged goddess reached out and tapped his forehead, her eyes flashing an orange light. Warmth pulsed in my chest and both Raikidan and I gasped at the same time. Rashta stepped away while Raikidan supported himself on a computer station, his eyes wide.

My eyes snapped to Rashta. "What did you do?"

"Eira, they won't shut up," Raikidan said.

My shoulders slumped and I threw my head back. "Really? Why would you do that to him?"

Rashta shrugged. "I wanted to see if it'd work. Your champion has never interacted with his past lives before. It'll only last a day, from my best guess."

My brow ticked up. "You're only guessing, though?"

She shrugged again. "Yeah. Have fun with that."

Rashta then winked out of existence, her energy returning to me. I muttered an insult under my breath and then worked on helping out Raikidan.

"I get it." He held his head. "I get it. If I had any doubts, it's gone now. Please just make them shut up."

I popped up on my toes and pressed my lips against his forehead, murmuring against his skin. "Boys, please behave. This is a lot to take in."

"Only a few stopped," Raikidan reported.

"If you don't all stop, I'll have to punish you."

Raikidan grunted. "One just said that sounds fun and promising."

I pulled away. "Oh, it's not the fun kind of punishment, I can guarantee that."

Raikidan grinned and snickered. "That shut them up. Thank you."

I kissed him on the nose. "I'm sorry Rashta did that to you. I didn't know she could."

"I'm not sorry in the least," Rashta said.

Raikidan shook his head. "It's fine. It did help remove any possible doubt, that's for sure."

"See. I know what I'm doing."

"A little warning would have probably helped me handle that better, though."

Rashta let out a *humph* and a few of my own past lives' giggling made it through.

Raikidan cocked his head, as if he were listening to something. "Seda says we can't stall much more. The Council is getting antsy, as well as a few of our friends."

My brow ticked up. "Ryoko?"

He nodded. "She's no longer focused on seeing Rylan's form. Expect hysteria."

I snorted and retrieved some clothes for Raikidan.

52
CHAPTER

As soon as Raikidan was dressed, I led him and Rizgar through the maze of halls. A slight sickening sensation hit me because of how ingrained these halls were to me. I had to squint when we walked down to the corridor leading to the courtyard.

"Raikidan!" Ryoko shrieked when we appeared in the courtyard.

"Laz!" Valene squealed.

The two ran over and crashed into us. Valene was being gentle for once, but Ryoko's air-lifting hug to Raikidan was a different story, from the face he was making. My father looked impressed by her strength.

"I'm so glad you're okay," Ryoko said.

Raikidan chuckled. "Good to see you too, Ryoko. But do you mind letting up just a bit?"

She set him down and ducked her head. "Oops, sorry."

Her excitable, short attention span kicked in, and she jumped to focusing on me. "Okay, you. Spill. What was with all the mumbo-jumbo magicky flaming-glory stuff the other day?"

My father chuckled. "She doesn't waste any time."

Ryoko gave him a quick assessment. "I see you're not dead." Her eyes darted to me. "That's a good thing, yes?"

I nodded. "We've come to an understanding and are working things out."

Rylan, who stood off a little ways, scratched his head. "Well, then, I think I've seen everything now."

"Oh, child, you have no idea."

I snickered but didn't reveal anything yet. "Before I explain, I need to introduce my father to a few people. It's well overdue."

Ryoko tossed her thumb behind her. "Bone and the others are waiting for you over there."

Seda approached, and bent close to my ear. "Just so you know, the Council isn't going to be patient much longer."

"And I'm supposed to care what they think?" I said, loud enough for them to hear. "Last I remember, only two of them actually risked their lives fighting Zarda, and another one would have worked with them to come up with an alternate plan to my newly forced one since she wouldn't be useful in a fight against him. I could really care less what type of timeframe they want to work on."

Seda smirked. "Well, I'm just the messenger. You do you."

She then walked off to Argus, who mingled with her two sisters and her brother. From the looks of it, they were all getting along, surprisingly. It seemed Argus had proven his loyalty to Seda, thus proving himself to Nioush. *He may be a jerk, but deep down I knew he cared about his sisters.*

My siblings' approach caught my attention, and I grabbed my father's wrist, pulling him along to meet them halfway. "C'mon, time for you to meet the rest of your kids."

"Wait, they're really—"

I chuckled. "Yep."

"But the agreement said you could be the only one," my father said.

I gave him a long look. "Did you really think Zarda would keep his word? He executed Mom, for Satria's sake."

"I had hoped that wasn't the case." His frame sagged. "I'm sorry. Had I known it was going to happen, I would have tried to save her."

I shook my head. "No, I am. I can't blame you. It took us all by surprise. Even some of Zarda's most loyal soldiers couldn't believe he had chosen to do it. If I had known how to contact you, I would have. Even if it would have been a futile attempt, I would have tried anything to save her."

My father squeezed my hand. "Let's not linger in the past. Best to look to the future instead."

I gave him a genuine smile and nodded. "But first, the present."

I held out my arm just as Yára made it to me and I embraced her in a hug. Trigon was the next to approach, and he had a shit-eating grin on his face. "Hey, you give Loverboy a good *I'm glad you're not dead* smooch?"

My ears and face burned. "Butt out."

He chuckled and then turned to our father. "So, is he really—"

"Yes, this is our father, Rizgar," I said. "Father, meet your ten sons and other daughter."

Rizgar stared, wide-eyed, taking in their presence one by one. "There are so many of you."

Rhaec crossed his arms. "There used to be more."

"Amara spent time with all of you?"

Bone frowned. "No. Only Eira and Ryder got to meet her. We were only released a year ago, and hadn't had contact with Eira until more recently."

"Yára says she's met her, but can't prove it," Trigon said.

Yára stomped her foot. "I did!"

Our father's brow furrowed. "Who is Ryder?"

"I am." My brothers parted and Ryder walked up to us. "And before you ask, no, I'm not your son. I'm your grandson."

My father looked like he was about to have a heart attack. I chuckled softly as he took it all in. When the blood returned to his face, he set his gaze on me. "I thought Largren was pulling my leg."

"I told you I wasn't."

I nodded to a tall, red-haired man as he approached. "Largren."

"You're so civil with me now." A teasing smirk crossed his lips.

"Bite me."

He laughed heartily. "There we go."

"So, why were you picked to bring my mother and me messages?" I asked. "You had to have some special quality that made you immune to the pact."

He smirked and turned his head to reveal a small patch of black hair. "Besides being your father's lieutenant, I come from a line of diluted mixed-color heritage."

I nodded in understanding. "Making you an exception to the pact rules."

"Can we go back to this whole grandson bit?" my father asked. "I thought you and the whelp—"

I shook my head. "Father, think about it. I'm an experiment. When Largren told you about Ryder, I was still in service. Do you really think I up and had a kid?"

"Well… uh… no, I guess…"

The entire family laughed, as did I. *And I thought Raikidan could be thick.*

Largren cleared his throat. "Rizgar, I should inform you, I had the clan head home, based on some discussions we overheard. As much as they would like to meet Lazmira—"

"Please, call me Eira," I said. "It's my preferred name."

He nodded. "I apologize. I'll try to remember that."

My father peered at me with a hurt expression. "You don't like the name I gave you?"

"I hated you. Why would I like the name you gave me?"

He sighed, his shoulders slumping. "Right."

"I've come to prefer my human middle name, but I've allowed select people to call me by a shortened version of my dragon name."

"So, I can call you by your name then, yes?" my father asked tentatively.

I exhaled in resignation. "I'd expect you to, regardless of what I would prefer."

My father grinned. "I'll take that as a yes."

I turned my focus to Largren. "You said something about the others leaving?"

He nodded. "Yes. As I was saying, although they'd like to meet you and your siblings, we thought it best to choose another day for that to happen."

I nodded. That was probably for the best. Taking slow steps to integrate into the clan would help all of us. I never thought it would ever happen, and it'd be a major change for my siblings if they chose to do so as well.

My head tilted when claws scraping stone caught my ears. Then a familiar female voice called out, "Eira, incoming!"

I reacted in an instant, moving away from my family and turning to prepare for Rimu's approach. The, small-horse-sized red-and-black whelpling barreled through the courtyard, eyes focused on me. When he tried to jump into my arms, as if he were still small, I moved away. He chirped with a cocked head and jumped for me again. I dodged and turned it into a quick little game. It entertained everyone as Xaneth bounded over, her gorgeous red hair bouncing around her freckled shoulders.

"Rizgar," she greeted with a dip of her head.

He nodded back. "It's good to see you again, Xaneth."

Apparently these two were familiar with each other. Xaneth look to me and opened her arms for a hug. I gave it to her, allowing Rimu to finally catch me. He gazed up at me with big eyes and chirped. *"Happy to see Eira."*

My jaw went slack and I snapped my attention to Xaneth. She smiled. "He's been practicing." Her eyes drifted to Raikidan. "Thanks to someone's lessons while babysitting, he ended up with an extra push over his siblings."

Raikidan grunted. "I didn't babysit. She did."

Xaneth and I passed each other a quick glance of amusement and knowing. "Anywho, I came here, Eira, to let you know the clan will remain here for a little while longer if you need us. Your Council has us keeping an eye on the citizens while they deliberate on how to break the news to them, but if you need us during that, we're here."

I smiled. "Thank you. I appreciate that help. Also…" I rubbed the back of my neck. "I need to talk to Zaith at some point. It appears I've given him some incorrect information about me that I wasn't aware of until recently."

Xaneth's eyes sparkled as a wide grin spread across her face. "Don't worry. We don't fault you. We suspected there was an issue that left you in the dark."

"You have no idea."

The older female dragon chuckled. "But if you insist on apologizing, it can wait a year or so."

A year? What was with everyone making things wait a year?

Rashta chuckled. *"Have you already forgotten Raikidan will expect mating rites to be upheld?"*

Oh… right… That was bound to get interesting.

"Oh, oh! Tell Xaneth I say hello," Velsara said.

I smiled at Xaneth. "Velsara says hello."

Xaneth's eyes widened, and a bit of moisture bubbled up in them. She then kissed me on the forehead. "That's for you both."

My father cleared his throat. "So, it's true then? She's really—"

Xaneth nodded. "Yes. You're very lucky, Rizgar."

My father's whole body relaxed as various emotions flashed over him. Largren found amusement in the reaction.

"Uh, can we be looped in now?" Ryoko called out. "We've been waiting rather patiently—more than you should expect from me at this point—and it's not fair the dragons know what's up! How did you die, but not die, and come back in a flaming kick-ass of glory, summon a bunch of gods, and pop out some badass winged lady from your butt?"

I laughed. "All the *magic* you witnessed the other day is due to the fact that my soul is bonded to the goddess Rashta."

Silence permeated the air—only the occasional shuffling of feet and the roaring city in the background could be heard. Ryoko stared at me. "Come again?"

It would be easier to show them.

"When you're ready, you can push me out again."

"Not enjoying your freedom?"

She laughed. *"Quite the opposite."*

I encouraged Rimu to sit down and took a few steps back to give myself room. I mustered up the energy and forced Rashta out again. Her wings unfurled and she flew up into the sky. This received a mix of reactions. *A little over the top...*

Ayuma giggled in my mind. *"She gets it from her father."*

"And who is that?"

"You'll find out one day."

Man, I hated that.

Rashta descended and stood next to me. My audience was left speechless. Except Rimu. He spun in a circle. *"Rashta! Rashta!"*

Xaneth stared at her son, her eyes wide. "I didn't tell him what you looked like."

Both my and Xaneth's eyes snapped to Rashta when she chuckled and crouched to give Rimu attention. "You didn't need to. His soul is always able to sense me out. It's why he was so curious about Eira to start with. Her personality kept him coming back to bond with her, of course. But I'd expect nothing less from my most devoted follower."

Any ability to process left the older female dragon. My father wasn't the only parent here with a special child.

Rashta stood and addressed everyone. "What Eira tells you is truth. I am Rashta, the goddess of judgment and rebirth. And the two of us are bound due to an event that transpired long ago."

She continued on, detailing many events, including how Zarda's meddling made it difficult for the two of us to communicate for such a long time. Once done, silence surrounded us, those out of this loop battling to process all this. Even the dragons found themselves struggling with certain bits of information. The only person who took this well was Seda. Being a demi-god psychic, it made sense, but it also made me wonder how much she knew and never told me.

"I didn't know," she messaged. *"It just doesn't surprise me. The moment I met you, I knew you were different. And when you mentioned that voice you heard was a separate entity, my speculation began."*

"But you never told me?"

"You and I both know you don't work well on speculation. It's why I never said anything about you being Raikidan's voice. I didn't have proof, just a suspicion."

That explained a lot.

Ryoko stepped closer to Rashta, her eyes wide with wonder. This made the goddess smile. "I was hoping you'd get curious. It's nice to finally meet you in this life, Ryoko."

This life? The words rolled off my friend as she reached out to touch Rashta. The winged goddess met her halfway, their fingertips touching.

Ryoko's eyes shone, a large smile spreading across her face. "You're real."

Rashta nodded. "Yes, child."

My friend's eyes snapped to me and before I could react, she threw her arms around me. "I have the most amazing friend in all of Lumaraeon!"

I laughed. "I'm not that great."

"Yes, you are," she muttered.

Ryoko's reaction helped everyone around us relax. Rashta watched with amused eyes for a moment before breaking us up. "I'm afraid I have to go back now. Eira hasn't worked up the energy to sustain this for a long period of time." She smiled. "But there will be more time later for any questions you may have."

"Wait, Rashta." Mana stepped forward. "I have one question."

Rashta smiled at her. "I know what you're going to ask, dear, but that is not a question I can answer."

Mana frowned. "Who can?"

"There is an ancient text in the hands of someone you know. All the answers lie within there."

Rashta glanced at me and I knew exactly which book she meant. Raikidan and I had talked about it before. My eyes darted to Mana and I nodded. It wouldn't be easy, but we could figure something out to get Raikidan's father to cooperate.

Rashta then winked out, her energy filling me again. Ryoko squealed. "You're a goddess!"

I chuckled and pried her off. "No, I'm just a host."

"Goddess, or a mere host, that may help us," someone said.

I turned to see Adina and the rest of the Council approaching.

I crossed my arms. "Sounds like you have a plan in mind."

Eldenar nodded. "We need the citizens to accept this change as easily as possible. We believe you and Rashta may be able to help us the best with this."

My brow ticked up, curious what plan they'd concocted. "I'm listening."

53
CHAPTER

I fussed with the band of my shaman outfit top. Two weeks of not eating properly didn't do well for the figure. Raikidan slipped his arms around me and worked against my efforts to dress.

I huffed. "Raikidan, we need to get ready. We're already late."

He kissed my neck. "Are you sure we need to go? They can handle this themselves. That's part of the responsibility they want to take on, governing this city."

I chuckled and tried to shoulder him away, to no avail. "What, didn't get enough in the shower?"

After our discussion with the Council on the plan of action, I suggested we take a shower and get some food in our bellies before dressing for the occasion. Eating wasn't an issue, but Raikidan had other plans once it came to showering, not that I complained. He also received his request to see my hybrid appearance. That positive response was overwhelming, as was his promise to work on his between-metamorphosis shifting to take the same shape when I did.

He grinned in my ear. "I'll never get enough of you."

An enticing chill ran down my spine. "Well, that's good, because you're stuck with me for a *long* time."

Raikidan kissed my ear. "I'm not complaining." He pulled away and shook his head. "Though, I will complain about these voices."

"Rashta, are you sure that'll go away?"

"No, but it should."

"And if it doesn't?"

"Then he'll be just like you, and we'll have to teach our men to behave," Zalia said. She chuckled. *"I'm not opposed to retraining them."*

While amusing, her comment had another meaning to it. *"Care to elaborate on that?"*

"Oh, nothing major. Just that you're able to use your energy to allow one of us to take your place for a little while. It comes in handy sometimes."

My brow ticked up. *"How does that work?"*

"Think of it like a shapeshift. But instead of an animal or difference race, you change into a life you once lived."

"What happens to the current me?"

"You're tucked into the mind like the rest of us, and watch what the past life does."

I rubbed my chin. *"Interesting. And Raikidan and his lives?"*

"Well, in the past that wasn't possible for him, just like communicating with them. But if what Rashta did was any hint at what could happen with this life, things might change. We'll play it by ear."

"I really hope he can," Aria said. *"Would be a nice change of pace."*

"But how would it work for the twins?" I asked.

"Uh, we're not entirely sure," Lina said. *"We've never tried to come out this way. We were too nervous to."*

I'd have to look into that conundrum at some point. Well, all of this. But now wasn't the time.

Raikidan tilted his head. "You done with your private conversation?"

I smirked. "Jealous?"

"Feeling a bit left out."

I lifted up on my toes and kissed him on the forehead. "I was just talking to Rashta and my lives about this situation you're in. Now, boys, I expect you to behave. I need Raikidan in his best form to help me with this plan. It's going to be tough on me as it is, so him being my steady rock will keep me composed. I promise, you'll be rewarded later."

Raikidan grinned. "That shut them up."

I pecked him on the lips. "Good. Now we need to finish up here."

He sighed. "Fine."

The city flashed past the moving vehicle. Citizens walked the streets in the same direction, all heading to the area where I'd be giving my speech. I clutched a part of my cloak. The idea of standing in front of so many people turned my stomach. *I don't know if I can do this.*"

"*You're going to do fine,*" Rashta said. "*I'll be helping you, too. Don't worry. The speech we created will work.*"

Raikidan grasped my hand and gave me a reassuring smile. He, too, would be by my side the whole time, as well as all my friends and family. The dragons and shamans would also be there, unhidden from the world. It was going to be a major shock to these people, but I hoped they'd quickly come to terms with their freedom and our plan for peace.

"*Eira, I must confess something,*" Rashta said. "*I am nervous about the governing plan set in place.*"

My brow ticked up. "*Why?*"

"*The idea is sound and as long as the citizens accept it, which I believe they will, it will work. My concern comes with some of these Council members you've had to deal with all these years. Many will make great leaders. But there are some I don't trust.*"

I almost chuckled. "*Well, if they try to pull anything funny to become the next Zarda, we could always kill them. Or set them before the gods to be judged.*"

She laughed. "*Your dark humor amuses me. Thank you. I needed that to calm myself.*"

"*You may be a god, but I'm learning quickly that not even gods are perfect.*"

"*No. Not even Lumaraeon herself is. But just like any kind-souled mortal, we do our best for the world.*" She grunted. "*Well, most of us.*"

"*Look, if you just batted your pretty eyes enough, and flashed what you rock under that armor, I'm sure you'd persuade Nazir to change in no time.*"

Our bond allowed me to feel the heat coursing through her. "*Stop it.*"

I laughed and everyone in the vehicle looked at me, confused. I ducked my head. "Sorry. Conversation with Rashta."

Ryoko tilted her head. "It's going to be strange seeing you interact with someone we can't see."

"Trust me, it's not easy. I'm just glad you all know. I like looking slightly less crazy."

Rylan snickered. "But not by much."

Chuckles echoed in the car and in my head.

The vehicle came to a stop and I peered outside. The largest crowd of people I'd seen in one place had gathered within a designated area set up by soldiers. They clustered before an empty podium on a stage, the looming inner wall behind it.

I took a deep breath. There wasn't any going back now. Ryoko grasped my hand. "We're with you."

"Are you sure you don't want to be with my brothers, enacting the fun part of the plan?"

She shook her head. "I'd rather be here, giving you my support."

I smiled and nodded. They'd be there with me every step of the way. I pulled my hood up and we all exited the vehicle.

Soldiers patrolled around, keeping the area secure. Shamans gathered near the the stage, their hoods down. They'd come to this agreement earlier. They'd only adapted to hiding their faces because of Zarda. With him out of the picture, there was no need. It felt a bit bizarre, though. All I'd ever known was for their faces to be obscured in public. *But it's all part of change, I guess.*

"Change is hard sometimes. But these changes are a good thing."

"I know…"

It made me quite aware of how different life was going to be for everyone. We'd all start moving on with our lives. It was going to be strange, getting used to it all. But we'd all have each other still in the end, and that was what mattered.

We made it to the set-up stage. I was greeted by friendly smiles from allies, and curious glances from citizens who were close enough to peer over.

Shva'sika placed her hands on my shoulders. "You're going to do great. Just remember the goal and speak from your heart."

I nodded and headed to the podium. Raikidan remained close, but gave me the distance we discussed earlier, as to not put off the citizens with his behavior.

I adjusted the microphone, and then pulled down my hood to reveal my face.

"Who is this woman?" "Where is Zarda?" "What's going on?" and various other questions were heard amongst the crowd. My shoulders tightened as I scanned them.

"It's okay, Eira. We're all with you. Just tell them."

I swallowed hard. "Zarda won't be addressing you all today."

"Why not?" "What's going on?" "Where is he?" were all thrown at me.

My nerves got the better of me, and my mind shut down just long enough for me to awkwardly blurt out, "Zarda is dead."

Shit! People buzzed, their fear radiating out in one giant wave. "He's dead?" "No he can't be." "It's a trick!" "Well, good riddance to him." "Don't say that! He was a great leader." "He had no heir, what will we do now?" "It's those rebels. They had something to do with it." "Is she one of them?" "Her outfit is strange. Maybe outsiders are the issue."

I held up my hands as I spoke to calm them. "Everyone, please. Please, listen to me. Please, don't panic."

They ignored my words, and the soldiers monitoring the crowd looked about, wondering if they weren't going to have to use force. *No. That isn't our way. Not anymore.*

"Remember what Del'karo taught you. Humans have one defining weakness."

That's right. I tipped my head back and exhaled a large breath of fire. No heat burst from the flame, as I quickly turned it into harmless show fire. But the display caught my audience's attention. Humans were so easily captivated by fire.

I manipulated the fire into a phoenix, and flew it over them. Some "ooh'd" and "ahh'd" while others cowered. The bird swooped down to hover just above them. The bravest of the civilians reached out to touch it. Some I didn't doubt were those we'd instructed to blend into the crowd to help push the reactions and energy we wanted from this.

This action from the brave worked to calm the fearful. I expected as much, hoping it'd work in my favor.

"People of Dalatrend. Please listen to what I have to say." I pulled the bird back and had it rest next to me. "Many of you may recognize my face. Most of you won't. My name is Lazmira Eira Rysrin. I am a former soldier. I am the current Shaman Ambassador. I am a halfling." I scanned the area. "And I am the Dragon-Phoenix, the mortal host of the goddess of judgment and rebirth, Rashta."

Gasps and loud murmurs filled the air. I had much of their attention, though I could see most didn't believe me. We anticipated this, and with my blunder earlier, I was going to need to enact her help more than ever.

I held out my arm and Rashta's energy shot out, her form coalescing next to me. More gasps, and those who didn't believe, changed their tunes quickly. Heads and bodies bowed.

Rashta flexed her wings before stepping up, her voice carrying far like you'd expect of any god. "Good people of Dalatrend, I ask you not to bow, but to gaze upon us and listen. My host speaks the truth. Zarda is dead, but not by the means many of you may think. Over the years, Zarda has mistreated others for the sake of power, going as far as to sell his soul to gain what he wanted. We gods watched as he slipped away from the light and into madness. I myself watched this treatment and deterioration firsthand, thanks to my host here."

She peered around, and even looked right at the camera equipment. "Zarda fell at the hands of us gods, his corruption too deep for him to be saved."

The crowd reacted again, showing many mixed reactions.

"Please do not mourn his loss. As a leader, he treated you poorly. These walls you see around your city were not constructed to keep you safe, but to keep you locked inside."

"It doesn't have to remain this way, though," I said, finding courage to speak from somewhere. I made a motion to Zo, and he spoke into his communicator. Not long after, the ground rumbled and the people looked around, frightened. "Please, do not be afraid of what we're about to show you."

The wall behind me cracked and then fell. A domino effect occurred with the inner wall, as shamans and Brute soldiers tore the structure down from all sides of the city. The plantations beyond the outer wall sprawled before the citizens, as did the outer wall, but only briefly.

As we'd planned, the second wall came down as quickly as the first. Citizens gasped at the sight of what lay beyond the wall, the majority of them having never seen it before.

I addressed them again. "Lumaraeon is a great and wondrous place that all should be free to experience. This includes all of you. You are free to come and go as you please. No paperwork."

I nodded to Valene, and she ran off to execute the rest of the plan. "I want to stress that this freedom is for everyone. Zarda pushed into our minds that nu-humans were superior in every way. He lied."

The crowd grew restless. I knew this part would not go over easy.

But I had to stick to it. This course was for the best. It'd be the only way we'd find peace.

"We nu-humans are no better or worse than any other race out there. We have our strengths, and we have our weaknesses. Zarda sequestered this knowledge to push his agenda. But if we wish to be free, we cannot allow ourselves to believe this lie."

"And how do we know you're not lying?" someone shouted. Others agreed.

I smiled. "Because I am a halfling who should not exist, by Zarda's claim. He wanted us to believe that dragons do not exist anymore, that he championed a war that wiped them out because they were evil monstrosities hellbent on subjugating those they believed inferior. He lied. My title, Dragon-Phoenix, is not just a title. It is my halfling origin. I am half-dragon, and my full-dragon kin are alive and well."

The wind picked up, and a thunder of dragons descended from high above us. People screamed, and the soldiers had to act quickly to keep them from bolting. Rashta waved her hand, and a bright light flashed over the people in a huge wave. They calmed immediately.

"Do not be afraid," she said. "Dragons are not evil creatures. On the contrary, they are intellectuals who prefer a good chat rather than a fight."

"At least, the majority of us are that way," Raikidan said.

I gave him a hard stare that screamed, "not helping!" He ducked his head, and to my surprise, people found this amusing. It relaxed them and allowed my kin to find purchase in areas we'd deemed okay prior to this event. A few landed behind me in a shifted state, two of them being Zaith and my father.

I scanned the crowd. Their attention was now firmly on me. "You see the truth before you. I hope this will help you listen to what I say next. As I said, nu-humans are not superior, but equal to all races out there. Dalatrend is one of the only nu-humans cities left to believe this farce. If we are to move on, and be a better, freer people, we must be willing to change."

Valene stepped forward, her cloak hood down, and with her she guided a young human woman, dirty and weary from her years of servitude and hard labor. I extended my hand to the woman, and she gulped before reaching out with a shaky hand, her chains rattling.

Her hand in mine, I pulled her closer, keeping my posture warm and inviting. I wasn't sure how much it'd help her; I doubted she'd ever felt a kind nu-human hand, if any kindness at all.

Rashta moved to stand behind us. The human woman shook, but with one gentle touch on the shoulder from Rashta, the fear ceased. She gazed up at the goddess with wide eyes.

I turned to the crowd. "It is time we move past our prejudices. It's time we become better than what Zarda turned us into."

Rashta reached out and touched the woman's bindings. They glowed bright, as well as the ownership brand on her arm, and then broke apart, clattering on the ground. Her brand disappeared, leaving clean skin.

I held the woman's hand up, her eyes bewildered. "Dalatrend will no longer be seen as a place of subjugation, but a city of free people, regardless of their race or gender."

The people gasped and murmured. The human woman's eyes went wide. "I'm… free?"

I nodded, as did Rashta. Tears welled up into the young woman's eyes. "Thank you. Thank you."

Valene gestured to the hundreds of human slaves gathered. I pulled my dagger from my arm and handed it to Rashta, pulsing energy into it. Rashta grasped the handle, and changed it to her favored hammer. She rose it above her head, but before she could do anything, a nu-human pushed his way through the soldiers and shamans.

"Wait! Hold on. You can't just take my slaves."

Rashta's eyes flashed, and she lowered her arm. My bond to her made me aware of just how much she despised his words. She took several steps toward the man. "I'm sorry, I don't think I heard you. Can you repeat yourself, a little louder?"

The man's knees trembled, and he hesitated for a moment, but spoke again. "I… I said you can't take my slaves. They work my fields."

"And why do you think they belong to you?"

He swallowed. "Because I paid for them."

Rashta's eyes flashed again. "You can't own people."

"They're just humans!"

"As are you!" Even I was taken aback by her sudden flash of rage. "You are also human. You can dress yourself up with a new name all you wish, but at the core of your existence, you are also human."

She raised her gavel once again, and fiery light swirled around her before springing out to the humans. This frightened many of them, but others accepted whatever may come. The light hit them, and their shackles and brands glowed in a light just like it had for the first woman. Then they broke apart, and their brandings disappeared.

Each one of them took in this surprising new freedom in their own way before gazing up at Rashta and then, strangely me.

"You all stand as my witnesses," Rashta announced. "Henceforth, Dalatrend shall be a haven for the free, of all walks of life."

I stepped up. "It will be the center of peace for Lumaraeon. We will usher in an era of peace not seen since the War of End. We will do so not by subjugation, but by acceptance."

The humans dropped to their knees and thanked us. Praised us. *Both* of us. I wasn't sure how to handle that.

The plantation owner's face reddened watching all this. "And what am I supposed to do without my slaves? I have a plantation to run. Food to provide to this city."

I set neutral eyes on him, as hard as it was to do, but it was Valene who spoke. "You hire people."

All eyes fell on her. She raised her arms and petals blew out from her hands, surrounding the man and the citizens. She received some gasps, as well as some *oohs* and *ahhs*. "We all have gifts. Some more unique than others. But just because we're born different doesn't mean we can't get along. I come from a place where it's safe to be me. I can walk around and be like everyone else, not someone's property. This place can be just like where I grew up. You just have to open your eyes. Hire people and treat them like they matter."

She smiled at the plantation owner. "And if you don't want to do that, you can do the work yourself and find out just what hard work these people did to keep your gold flowing."

"She took my lines," I semi-complained.

I got a number of laughs from that. I took the moment to get a feel for the reception of what we were bringing to this city. *The reception is… mixed.* Some were like this plantation owner, but more looked as though they were seeing what we were aiming at. If not totally on board, they were either considering or fighting what they'd known all these years. And it wasn't based on what quadrant these people originated from. Yes, I saw more Quadrant One citizens accepting this change, but even wealthy Quadrant Four citizens were getting behind this.

"And if I don't choose those options?" the man said.

I chuckled and pointed out of the city. "Then you can pack up and leave to find a place you think will support your ideals. But I can tell you with certainty, you're not going to find it."

The man scowled but backed down. He knew when he'd been beat. He didn't have a choice in the matter anyway.

"Can I ask a question?" a hesitant voice called out.

I scanned the crowd. "Who spoke?"

A mousey woman minced forward in the front of the crowd. "Um, I did."

I smiled at her. "What's your question?"

"Well, what are we going to do without Zarda? Dalatrend has always been led by one family. Zarda had no children of his own. And with all these changes you and Rashta have enacted without a leading government's approval, what will be come of us without order?"

I continued to smile. "Don't worry. There will still be order. Just a different type."

I motion for the Council to step forward. "We already have a governing system thought up that we'd like to propose. This system will have to be agreed on by the majority." I glanced at Rashta. "And to keep everything fair, a god has offered to oversee this process. This city has their favor. They believe, like Rashta and I do, this city can be great."

I expected Eldenar to step forward. He had a tendency to lead the Council. It was part of his experience commanding soldiers. But to my surprise, Genesis stepped up. I gave her the microphone spot and stood close to Rashta.

Raikidan drew up to me and placed his hand on my lower back, murmuring in my ear. "You're doing well."

"I'm doing the best I can after I nearly screwed this all up."

"No, I think how you handled it is exactly what they needed."

Genesis adjusted the microphone. "My name is Genesis. I am the first nu-human."

The citizens reacted to her as I figured they would. No one would believe the first nu-human was still alive. But with a goddess standing by, no one would be able to get away with lying.

"The others with me are also experiments. We've seen many things in our lives, both good and bad. We know this city because this has been our home for a long time, much like it had been for so many of you. We want to see it thrive, be better than what Zarda had made it. Bring it past the glory of Lord Taric's reign."

She took a deep breath. "We believe that allowing one single individual to rule is giving that person too much power. It's too tempting to abuse. So, we propose to everyone that Dalatrend run on a council. This council would consist of an equal number of individuals that represent the makeup of this city; nu-human, human, halflings, men, women, experiments, and natural-born citizens. With this system, we believe we can have fair governing for everyone."

Citizens murmured amongst themselves, a majority agreeing to this plan—more than I expected. Actually, these people were accepting this new life far better than I'd anticipated. It made me hopeful.

Rashta stepped forward. "As my host mentioned before, I have appointed a god to oversee the voting of this proposed governing system. We will also allow for others to offer ideas of their own. Their plan must be detailed, and must meet the guidelines we've set. After the system is decided on, based on a majority vote, we will oversee implementation. We also encourage you all, once the city has come back to order, to consider an embassy. Strengthening connections outside this city will be vital."

Shva'sika stepped up onto the platform. "My apologies for interrupting, Rashta, but Lord Taric just spoke to me. He requests to oversee this new government implementation. And, he also wants to offer guidance to the new government afterward, to ensure the city thrives."

The crowd grew excited and confused. Rashta held up a hand. "Shva'sika here is a shaman. She speaks with the departed." Rashta faced Shva'sika. "If that is what he wishes."

She nodded. "We're already working on a long-term crystal for him to use. A small group of shamans will be tasked with caring for and protecting it."

Rashta addressed the people. "I believe having a favored leader guiding you into a new path is an agreeable compromise to all of this, yes?"

She received many agreements. Some were still not okay with the new arrangement, but the majority spoke louder in support.

Rashta and Genesis, as well as a few others, continued to speak to the citizens, allowing me some much-needed rest from their eyes. Though, for some reason, many continued to look over to me. I wasn't sure why, and was unable to read them well enough to guess.

Raikidan rested his hand on my lower back and kissed me on the top of the head. I looked up at him and smiled before leaning into him.

The young human woman I'd freed peered over to us. "Um, may I ask you something?"

I nodded and straightened. "Of course."

"Is this man always with you?"

An odd question, but as I processed it, I also noticed that the looks I'd received a moment ago from the citizens were far more intent all of a sudden. It was as if Raikidan's presence had added to their curiosity.

I glanced up at Raikidan, a smile creeping up my face. "He's been by my side for many millennia."

Her eyes widened. "Millenia? How... how old are you?"

I chuckled. "This life, only in my eighties. But the many lives we've lived, it's been a long time together."

She tilted her head. "Is that part of what makes you so special?"

"I suppose so." I rocked my head back and forth. "But I think what truly makes me special, is that I understand everyone because I've just about been them all. I've known what it means to live as a human, as nu-human, and even an elf. I've always been a halfling, and have seen the good and the ugly that comes of it. I've lived prosperously and lived in squalor. I've been to hell and back, many times. I'm not perfect, but that's okay. It doesn't mean I can't hope and try for the best for everyone."

I prayed that reasoning satisfied her. I wasn't entirely assured of it myself, but if it convinced her, then maybe that could be part of what made me special.

"It is. Among other things," Rashta said in my mind, not taking herself fully away from the matter at hand.

The young woman smiled wide and then hugged me tight. "I think there's more to it, but I can accept that answer. Thank you. Thank you giving someone like me a chance."

I lifted her chin and wiped a stray tear from her cheek. "Live your life to the fullest. That is all the thanks I need."

She nodded. "I promise I will, goddess Lazmira."

She then ran off.

"Wait, I'm not—" I sighed when she disappeared from sight. Raikidan and Rashta both chuckled. "It's not funny."

Raikidan kissed me on the forehead. "I'm laughing at your reaction. You should accept what she called you. It is what you are."

I elbowed him. "I am not a goddess."

He pulled me closer and murmured into my ear, his tone husky. "You're a goddess to me."

The hair on the back of my neck rose, a shiver running down my spine and sending a wave of desire through me. I swallowed hard. *Something about the way he said that—*

"Whoa, cool it down there, loverboy," Rashta said as she headed our way. "You're in public still."

He grunted, and it was my turn to laugh. When I calmed, I smiled at her. "Press conference over?"

She nodded. "I'll be retreating now. You're free to go about your business. The Council will handle things from here."

Rashta winked out and her energy returned to my body. Raikidan held me closer. "So I can finally steal you away now and have you all to myself, right?"

"No, no!" Ryoko yelled to him. "We still need to party our freedom up! Then you two disappear for a night."

Raikidan narrowed his eyes at her, and I snickered, encouraging him to walk with me over to our friends. "But only one night?"

She rested her hands on her hips. "Well, yeah. He can't steal my best friend from me."

"I wasn't going to steal her," he muttered. "Just take her for a year or two for myself."

"Uh, yeah, no. Not acceptable."

"Dragon mating rites."

"Mating rites, my butt. You're not taking my best friend away from me over some stupid make-believe rites. This is what you agreed to when you chose my best friend…"

The two bickered back and forth. It was amusing. But it wasn't long before I noticed the staring again. While many of the citizens dispersed, there were a large number still hanging around, watching me.

I left Raikidan's side and jumped down off the stage to go right up to them at the security gate. A few stepped back, nervous about my approach, but others appeared excited.

I grinned. "I am real."

One of the girls in front of me giggled. "We weren't sure. It's all so surreal, ya know. Being free to do what we want. Meeting someone who is a host for a goddess. Seeing a goddess with our own two eyes. It's like… a dream or something."

I held out my hand. "See for yourself."

The woman hesitated then touched my hand with hers. Her face lit up on contact, and we manipulated our hands together.

I smiled. "See?"

The others clustered closer, all wanting to know for themselves. I allowed it. I didn't want these people to fear me. And the more they understood, the more likely I could bring them on my side and keep them from falling to the hands of people like Kir.

"How is it you became a host?" someone asked.

I chose my words carefully. "A few choices, both good and bad, we found ourselves bound together. For better or for worse."

Rashta snorted.

A woman giggled. "What's it like sharing a body with a god?"

I rocked my head back and forth. "Interesting. Sometimes fun. Sometimes annoying."

"How long have you been bound to her?" a man asked.

"Many lifetimes."

"What do you mean by that?"

"I mean, I've lived many lives. Gone by many names, and come from many types of backgrounds."

Wonder crossed their faces.

"I've never even seen a statue of this goddess before, and yet I know her somehow," another person said.

I nodded. "There is a god out there on my list to reprimand for stealing her statues for fun."

"It's Phyre."

"And now I know who it is. I just have to wait until he shows up."

The people around me jumped back, and I suddenly felt heat on my back. I turned to see Phyre standing there. "Ah, speak of the devil."

"I've returned all the statues to their rightful places." He grinned. "I even returned duplicates, because why not."

I reached out and cropped him in the back of the head. He complained and rubbed the "injured" spot with a small pout. "That wasn't nice. I said I returned them."

"A reminder to not do it again."

He huffed. "Fine, fine. Ruin my fun."

"He's already moved on to other statues."

I narrowed my eyes. "You stole your sister's statues, didn't you? That's why she was mad at you that one day."

His gaze flicked elsewhere, his hand behind his back. "I don't know what you're talking about."

"Right, that's why Rashta has informed me she's about to show up."

"What?" Panic flashed across his face and he took a few steps back. "I have to go."

He then disappeared in a puff of smoke. Rashta and my lives lost it. I shook my head. "That was way too easy."

I faced my audience again and they looked star-struck. My attention pulled away when a firm hand rested on my back. I smiled at Raikidan. "All done losing to Ryoko?"

His nose scrunched. "We're not going to talk about that right now."

Which meant he lost.

"She is however, being her impatient self and wants to know when you're ready. It sounds like a big party is planned."

I glanced at the citizens gathering, and the first woman to have spoken with me smiled. "It's okay. We're just glad you were willing to take the time to talk with us. Thank you."

I nodded. "It was a pleasure to meet you all."

Raikidan then whisked me away. As he did, Rashta chuckled.

"What?"

"They bowed to you two as you left."

"You mean, they bowed to you."

"Nope. It seems you both have left an interesting impression on these mortals. I'm curious to see how this plays out."

I wasn't. I wanted a quiet life. One with Raikidan and my friends and family. Of course, I'd need to survive this party first.

Raikidan's wings beat strong as we zipped through the open sky, the setting sun before us casting orange streaks over the forest below. I nestled into Raikidan's grip, protective as always, utilizing the time to recoup my energy.

That party had been crazy. Everyone I knew and everyone they knew had gathered in the North Tribe for one heck of a celebration. Food, music, merriment—it was everything I'd expect from people celebrating their freedom. People talked about future plans. Shamans invited elementalists to stay longer to train and learn. My siblings and I, as well as Ryder and my friends, met our clan. They received us better than I'd ever expected—eager and accepting, even to Ryder and the concept that I had a mate who wasn't my son's father. They took the time to teach me about them, and fill in missing information about our kind where they could. We also received an open invitation to stop in at any time to learn more, or even live there if we so pleased.

The others talked about their plans. Some didn't know, while others had some well-thought-out plans. When Ryoko and the rest of them wanted to know what I was planning to do, I didn't know what to tell her. Raikidan and I hadn't discussed where we'd live. He had his territory, but I also had obligations with the shamans. Shva'sika made it clear I was getting a house built there now, whether I wanted it or not.

Ryoko also insisted I had to live with her still. This amused everyone, even me.

There wasn't any pressure for us to choose right away.

Raikidan now set a course for his territory, wanting to show it all to me before we figured it out. Of course, Ryoko assumed he was just trying to steal me away, though he didn't exactly deny it, either, and they went back to their "ownership" bickering. It was amusing how much they acted like siblings.

Raikidan's altitude shifted, and I peered out between his claws. The expansive forest sprawled out below, but a clearing caught my eye. A river flowed through it, crashing down a cliff, before continuing on. I knew this area. We'd arrived.

I swiveled my head, trying to take in this view, but everything appeared the same from up here. *How does he navigate like this?*

"You can always ask him."

"You know, can't I have a moment to internalize questions before you tell me what to do?"

"No."

"Rashta, leave Eira alone," Isis said.

Rashta started complaining, and my brow ticked up when she suddenly went quiet. *"Um?"*

"Don't worry. We'll keep her away for a bit. Enjoy your time."

"Uh, thanks?"

Raikidan swooped down for the clearing far faster than I'd anticipated. I clung on as best I could and his grip tightened, realizing his mistake. I didn't blame him. It wasn't as if he was in the habit of carrying humans around.

He landed at the top of the waterfall and set me down. I gazed about as the sun set behind the Larkian Mountains. *So beautiful.* And I could see this every day for the rest of my life, if I wanted.

Raikidan shifted and came up behind me, helping me remove my cloak before resting his forehead on the back of my head. "Farther than you can see, it's all yours now."

I grinned. "It's *ours*."

He wrapped his arms around me and pulled me close, kissing my ear. "I like how nice that sounds. And since it's ours, I'm going to have to teach you some of the rules."

"Rules? Like where the boundary is?"

"Yes, and no. As a female, you get special lenience on boundary crossing."

"Even as a half-breed?"

He kissed my ear again. "None of my neighbors care about that. Not even the red to the south of us. His mate is black-red too."

"Sounds like we have good neighbors."

"For the most part. He'll push the lines every now and then, but it's nothing I can't handle."

"Okay, so if that's not a rule I need to worry about right now, what is?"

He grinned, and the front of my top popped open, my breasts spilling out into his ready hands. "Clothing is optional here."

I stifled my sharp inhale. He was going to play that angle, was he? I pressed against him, making him believe he was going to get what he wanted, only to slip out of his grasp and clip my top back together. I was going to need the support.

I grinned as I backed up to the forest. "I can't let it be that easy for you."

Raikidan's eyes glowed. "You're going to have me chase you? After I already claimed you?"

I took a few more steps back. "Xaneth told me it was a step I missed with you. I was supposed to let you chase me to prove yourself."

Raikidan advanced, his eyes intent. "I'd count the last year of padding after you the chase. I had to do a lot to get you to trust and accept me."

"Normally I'd agree, but this promises to be fun." I spun on my heels and took off into the woods.

Raikidan chuckled. "Be quick as you want, little butterfly. When I get you, you're mine."

I ducked behind a tree and threw my voice. "I thought I was your goddess now?"

I didn't receive a response. I listened and I couldn't even hear him. Then, it was too late.

Raikidan's hot breath hit my ear. "Oh, that comes after I catch you."

Instinct told me to bolt, and I tried to listen, but he grabbed me with his strong arms and pulled me into his hard body. My top popped back open, and this time I didn't fight him as he slipped it off me.

He nipped my neck, his hands roaming all over my front. "I'll show you where the hoard is. I've got the perfect spot for you there."

I took a deep breath, the hairs on the back of my neck rising. "So your goal was to steal me away."

"Don't worry. I'll take good care of you. I'll even let you outside at least once a day."

I sputtered a laugh, and then two of us fell into a laughing fit. I didn't mean to kill the mood, but it was his fault.

Our laughter calmed when a luna moth fluttered into view. I held out my hand and it landed, the little creature pulsating with strange energy. This wasn't a real moth. I held one of Lunaria's messengers. But it didn't deliver a message. It fluttered away into the darkening sky. *Maybe that is the message. That everything is as it should be now, and they'll be watching.*

"Graced by luna moths, and now a true messenger of Lunaria?" His hands went back to roaming my body. "You really are blessed. I'm more convinced than ever you're a goddess." He pressed harder into me. "My goddess."

I grinned. "Does that make you a god?"

"Hmm." He kissed my neck. "I was thinking favored worshiper and lover, but I don't hate the sound of being your god, either."

I turned to face him. "Well, we have a long lifetime to figure it out."

Raikidan pushed me up against the tree, careful of the rough bark. "Starting now."

EPILOGUE

Warmth surrounded me, a cocoon of comfort and a shield to the morning sun invading my dreams. A muffled voice and a tiny hand pushed against my dull senses. I curled up, fighting against the call to wake. I failed.

"Momma Eira? Momma Eira, wake up," a young girl said. "Momma, wake up."

I groaned and peeked out from under my covers. My groggy green eyes were met with big brown ones belonging to a young girl with russet skin.

The young girl smiled wide. "Morning, Momma."

I yawned and croaked out, "Morning, Stella."

She climbed up into the bed and I took her into my arms for a cuddle. "Papa Raikidan is making brunch."

"Hmm, is that so?" I glazed over at the window, the heavy curtains still drawn. "Is it that late in the day already?"

She nodded. "We also have guests. That's why Papa had me wake you."

This woke me up quickly. "Guests? What kind of guests?"

"I've never met them before, but Papa says they work for you or something. One is a pretty lady and the other a guy. They don't wear much for clothes."

My brow furrowed. "When you don't look at them directly, do their features change?"

She nodded enthusiastically. "Yes!"

What were Rosa and Zaedrix doing here? "Stella, go let Papa know I'll be down in a moment, would you?"

"Okay!"

She rolled off the king-sized bed and ran out of the room.

Rashta chuckled in my mind. *"I can't get over how adorable she is."*

She wasn't wrong.

With Stella now gone, this gave me a moment to wake up fully. As I did, I gazed around the room.

It'd been a whole year since Dalatrend's liberation. The processes set in place to make Dalatrend great were working well, and the city was prospering for the first time since Lord Taric.

Raikidan and I had chosen to keep our territory in the mountains, as well as live in the West Tribe. As promised, Shva'sika had her family build us this house. It was too big for my liking, but she claimed to have done it to accommodate for Raikidan's dragon form, if he so wished to take it inside. Only some of the rooms were big enough for that, and there were far too many rooms for me to believe it to be her sole motive.

"She's expecting you'll be having a big family, with how needy Raikidan is," Rashta teased. *"Not that you're much better than him."*

I ignored her and got ready, entering my large closet. My sex life would not be discussed.

Shva'sika also didn't stop at one house. After this one was finished, they went to work building us a house in our territory. It wasn't done yet, but it wouldn't be much smaller than this home. And Shva'sika insisted she had a way to connect the two homes somehow, so we wouldn't have to fly back and forth all the time. Or use portals when I remembered that was a possibility.

Raikidan didn't get the quiet one-year honeymoon he wanted with me, but I did my best to make it up to him. He never complained about that part, and I always had to remind him we'd be together for a long time. I also needed interaction with more than *just* him every now and then.

About six months ago, when we officially moved into this house,

Stella moved in. She'd refused every family Ken'ichi had picked for her, insisting she wanted to live with Raikidan. So, live with him she did.

Allowing her into our lives unnerved me at first. I didn't know the first thing about raising a girl, not that my parenting skills raising boys was any better. But, so far I'd managed, and Raikidan blew the parenting thing out of the water. For a dragon, he was wonderful at being an adoptive parent. You would have never known there would be any apprehension to the concept with him.

I left the bedroom and headed downstairs for the kitchen, the delicious smells already wafting through the hall. There, Raikidan cooked away, having become quite the chef over the past year. Worked out well for us, since I still couldn't make much that was edible, even if Raikidan still disagreed.

Stella sat at the island counter on a stool, kicking her legs and humming as she stared at the food already prepared. To the far side of the kitchen, at our table, sat Rosa and Zaedrix. Nothing had changed about them.

Rosa swirled a tea cup in her hand. I'd learned they could consume ordinary food if they desired. It didn't sustain them, but they enjoyed partaking in feasts and drink now and then. She tipped her head up and grinned. "Ah, sleeping beauty has finally joined us."

Raikidan looked up from his task and smiled. "Food is almost ready."

I came up behind him and gave him a hug. "Thanks for cooking. Smells great."

"If you ask our little mouse, who is trying to steal yet another piece of bacon, I'm sure she can tell you how great it tastes."

I glanced over to Stella, who pulled her hand away from the prepared meat, giving me a cute and innocent look. I snickered and kissed her on the forehead before sitting down at the table across from the two demons in our house. "So, what has you visiting us at this hour? Something to do with Kir, I hope."

He'd disappeared without a trace. No demon, god, or shaman had spotted him or found any trail. With his latest pawn out of the picture, I knew he'd gone into hiding to figure out his next plan. But the silence killed me. I didn't know if he was recruiting or planning to go at this alone.

Rosa frowned. "Afraid not. Even his followers have vanished."

"Literally," Zaedrix said. "We'll catch a trail and then suddenly, nothing. Quite annoying, really."

I scowled. That wasn't a good sign. "Alright, well, if you don't bring news about Kir, why are you here?"

Zaedrix reclined in his seat, passing Rosa a look before speaking. "We've been sent to fetch you."

Rashta stirred in my mind, and my back straightened up. A year had gone by, and that meant only one thing.

A plate was set down in front of me. I glanced at Raikidan. "We're not leaving until you eat."

I sputtered out a laugh and ate.

Once Stella had eaten her fill, Rashta popped out and played with her. It was an idyllic scene, considering what might lay ahead. Still, whatever the gods had planned for us, we'd be ready.

GLOSSARY CHARACTER

DALATREND

LEADERS

Taric – Former ruler of Dalatrend, nu-human, father to Zarda, deceased

Zarda – Ruler of Dalatrend, nu-human, son to Taric

MILITARY

Rana (*RAH-nah*) – Nu-human experiment, assassin, trained under Eira, vendetta against Eira, reformed ways, deceased

Rick – Nu-human experiment, general, deceased

Verra – Nu-human experiment, general, vendetta against Eira and Amara, deceased

Zo – Nu-human experiment, general, interested in Eira

REBELLION

COUNCIL

Adina (*ah-DEE-nah*) – Oversees Team 7, nu-human experiment, first Dalatrend shapeshifter experiment

Akama (*ah-KAH-mah*) – Oversees Team 5, nu-human experiment, first Dalatrend Seer experiment (not planned), twin to Enrée

Eldenar – Oversees Team 4, nu-human experiment, first Dalatrend war experiment

Elkron – Oversees Team 6, nu-human experiment, first Dalatrend elementalist experiment

Enrée (*EN-ree-ay*) – Oversees Team 2, nu-human experiment,
first Dalatrend Battle Psychic experiment (not planned), twin
to Akama

Genesis – Oversees Team 3, first nu-human, necromantic
abilities

Hanama (*HAH-nah-mah*) – Oversees Team 1, nu-human experiment, first Dalatrend anthropomorphic experiment

TEAM 1
Assassin based

Evynne (*Ev-een*) – Nu-human experiment

TEAM 2
Recruitment based

Dan – Nu-human experiment, former Lieutenant to Eira

Innon (*EYE-nin*) – Battle leader, nu-human experiment, former
commander

TEAM 3
Income based, former Brute and foot soldier mostly

Andariel – Nu-human experiment, double ear prototype,
brother to Azriel, former medic, strip club owner: Midnight

Argus – Nu-human experiment, inventor, partner to Seda

Aurora – Nu-human experiment, experimental shapeshifter:
vampire bat, Underground computer tech

Azriel – Nu-human experiment, double ear prototype, brother
to Andariel, former medic, night club owner: Twilight

Blaze – Nu-human experiment

Eira (*AIR-uh*) – Nu-human dragon hybrid experiment, battle
leader, former commander, assassin, sister to Bone, Rhaec,
Trigon, Yára, Elgren, and thirty other brothers, mother to
Ryder, host to Rashta, Dragon-Phoenix: fifteenth life, Shaman
of the Rising Sun. Alt names: Laz, Laz'shika (*laz-SHEE-kah*).
Mate to Raikidan

Lena – Nu-human, partner to Zenmar

Orchon (*OR-con*) – Nu-human, bouncer at Twilight

Raid – Nu-human experiment, brother to Rylan, experimental shapeshifter: dog, interested in Ryoko

Raikidan (*RYE-ki-DAN*) – Black and red dragon, brother to Ebon, cousin to Corliss, son to Xephrya and Raiden, Dragon-Phoenix Champion: fifteenth life, Guard. Mate to Eira

Rylan (*RYE-lan*) – Nu-human direwolf hybrid experiment, brother to Raid, experimental shapeshifter: wolf, former captain, partner to Ryoko, artificial mental bond with Eira, ice elementalist

Ryoko (*Ree-OH-koh*) – Half-wogron experiment, clone of Peacekeeper Ryoko, Brute, former lieutenant, partner to Rylan, best friend to Eira

Seda (*SAY-duh*) – Nu-human demi-god, psychic: Seer, twin to Nioush, sister to Saléna and Nyra, granddaughter to Sela, partner to Argus

Xantar (*ZAN-tar*) – Nu-human experiment

Zane – Nu-human experiment, uncle to Eira, Bone, Rhaec, Trigon, Yára, Elgren, and thirty other nephews, brother to Jasmine and Amara, former soldier, mechanic, interested in Shva'sika

Zenmar – Nu-human experiment, crippled in a skirmish, partner to Lena

TEAM 4

Reconnaissance based

Alex – Nu-human experiment, Run competition participant, interested in Eira

Lara – Nu-human, mother to Lexi, Run competition help for Alex

TEAM 5

Psychic based

Avila (*ah-VEE-luh*) – Nu-human experiment, psychic: Seer, twin to Telar

Telar (*tell-ARE*) – Nu-human experiment, psychic: Battle Psychic, twin to Avila. Interested in Eira

Vek – Nu-human experiment, psychic: Battle Psychic, registered

TEAM 6
Research and development based

TEAM 7
Reconnaissance based
 Chameleon – Nu-human experiment, molecular fusion ability, former assassin

 Doppelganger – Nu-human experiment, temporary cloning ability

 Ezhno (*EZ-no*) – Nu-human experiment, Underground computer tech

 Mocha – Nu-human experiment, anthropomorphic: cat

 Nioush (*NEE-oosh*) – Nu-human demi-god, psychic: Battle Psychic, twin to Seda, brother to Saléna and Nyra, grandson to Sela

 Raynn (*rain*) – Nu-human experiment, former general, former battle leader, former general, clone of Peacekeeper Raynn, deceased

MOLES
 Arlon – Nu-human experiment, recent tank release, fan of Eira's reputation

 Bone – Nu-human dragon hybrid experiment, assassin, clone of Eira

 Elgren – Nu-human dragon hybrid experiment, assassin, clone of Eira

 Rhaec (*RAY-ek*) – Nu-human dragon hybrid experiment, brute class, clone of Eira

 Nyra – Nu-human experiment demi-god, psychic: Battle Psychic, twin to Saléna, sister to Seda and Nioush, granddaughter to Sela

 Ryder – Nu-human wolf dragon hybrid experiment, son to Eira and Rylan, ice and fire elementalist

 Saléna (*sah-LEY-nah*) – Nu-human experiment demi-god, psychic: Seer, twin to Nyra, sister to Seda and Nioush, granddaughter to Sela

Talon – Nu-human experiment, bone spike ability

Trigon – Nu-human dragon hybrid experiment, brute class, clone of Eira

Yára – Nu-human dragon hybrid, experiment, clone of Eira

MERCENARIES

Arnia (*ARE-nee-ah*) – Nu-human experiment, twin to Jaybird, metal elementalist, former mole. Interested in Ven'lar

Greeve – Nu-human experiment, assassin, shadow blind ability, codename: Shadow

Helkin – Nu-human experiment, assassin, molecular breakdown ability, codename: Mist

Jaybird – Nu-human experiment, twin to Arnia, air elementalist, former mole

Salis – Nu-human experiment, assassin

Sendara – Nu-human experiment, assassin, codename: Death Angel

Shyden (*SHAY-den*) – Nu-human experiment, assassin, Eira's mentor and father figure, shadow manipulation ability

Zelmen – Nu-human experiment, assassin, codename: Reaper

SHAMANS

NORTH TRIBE

Es'tla (*ess-teh-LAH*) – Half-elf, Shaman of the Rising Sun

Fe'teline (*fey-TELL-een*) – Nu-human, Shaman of the Rising Sun

Sha'hiri (*sha-HEER-ee*) – Leader, nu-human, Shaman of the Frozen Waste

Ven'lar (*ven-LAR*) – Nu-human, Shaman of the Cleansing Spirit, interested in Arnia

SOUTH TRIBE

Ir'esh (*EAR-esh*) – Chief, elf, father to Tla'lli, Shaman of the Fractured Crystal

Kelen – Shaman of the Rising Sun and Shaman of th Rising Tides, Psychic: type unknown, Twin to Nisa

Ne'kall (*nay-CALL*) – Elf, son to Del'karo and Alena, father of four, Shaman of the Rising Sun

Tla'lli (*teh-LAH-lee*) – Elf, daughter to Ir'esh, Shaman of the Whispering Winds, interested in Talon

EAST TRIBE

Nela – Nu-human, Shaman of the Dancing Lights

Se'lata (*say-LAH-tah*) – Elf, spice merchant, Shaman of the Fractured Crystal

Xa'vian (*ZAH-vee-an*) – Leader, elf, Shaman of the Dancing Lights

WEST TRIBE

Alena – Elf, wife to Del'karo, mother figure to Eira, mother of Vanya, Ne'kall and eleven other sons, Shaman of the Cleansing Spirit

Daren – Human, Valene's adopted father, inn keeper, former partner to Valessa

Del'karo (*del-CAR-oh*) – Elf, mentor and father figure to Eira, husband to Alena, father of Vanya, Ne'kall and eleven other sons, Shaman of the Rising Sun

Ken'ichi (*ken-EE-chee*) – Nu-human, friend to Eira, Guard and Shaman of the Cleansing Spirit

Maka'shi (*mah-KAH-shee*) – Leader, half-elf, Shaman of the Frozen Waste, widow

Me'kunar (*may-COON-are*) – Elf, scholar

Mel'ka (*mel-KAH*) – Elf, elder, storyteller, Shaman of the Fractured Crystal

Shva'sika (*sh-VAH-see-KAH*) – Elf, sister to Xye, mentor and adopted family to Eira, Shaman of the Dancing Lights, interested in Zane. Alt names: Elarinya (*ell-are-IN-yah*), Danika

Valene (*Vah-LEEN*) – Human, daughter to Valessa, Eira's and Daren's adopted daughter, plant-based Shaman of the Fractured Crystal

Valessa – Human, mother to Valene, former partner to Daren, Shaman of the Fractured Crystal, deceased

Vanya – Elf, daughter to Del'karo and Alena, sister to Ne'kall and eleven other brothers, godchild to Eira

Xye (*zeye*) – Half-elf, brother to Shva'sika, attempted to court
Eira, Shaman of the Cleansing Spirit, deceased.

Ral'ko (*ral-KOH*) – Human, Guard

Ren – Elf, Shaman of the Cleansing Spirit

Va'len (*VAH-len*) – Former leader, elf, former husband to
Maka'shi, Shaman of the Fractured Crystal, deceased

DRAGONS

Ambrose – Black dragon, mate to Salir, father to Rennek,
grandfather to Corliss, Raikidan, and Ebon, great-grandfather
to Anahak

Corliss – Green and black dragon, cousin to Raikidan, mate
to Mana

Ebon – Black and red dragon, mate to Nyoki, brother to Raikidan, cousin to Corliss, son to Xephrya and Raiden, grandson
to Salir and Ambrose

Enrek – Green and black dragon, brother to Corliss, cousin
to Raikidan and Ebon, infatuated with Mana

Mana – Green dragon, mate to Corliss

Nyoki (*NEE-oh-key*) – Black dragon, mate to Ebon

Rennek – Black dragon, adopted son to Salir and Ambrose,
uncle to Raikidan and Corliss

Salir (*sah-LEER*) – Black dragon, mate to Ambrose, mother to
Rennek and Raiden, grandmother to Corliss, Raikidan, and
Ebon, great-grandmother to Anahak

Xephrya (*zef-RYE-ah*) – Red dragon, mate to Raiden, mother
to Raikidan and Ebon, deceased

VELSARA WILDS CLAN

Anahak (*an-ah-HAWK*) – Black dragon, mate to Xaneth, father
to Rimu and six other offspring

Rimu – Black and red dragon, son to Anahak and Xaneth

Xaneth (*zan-ETH*) – Red dragon, mate to Anahak, mother to
Rimu and six other offspring

Zaith – Clan leader, red dragon

Rizgar – Clan leader, red dragon, mate to Amara, father to Eira, Bone, Rhaec, Trigon, Yára, Elgren, and thirty other sons, grandfather to Ryder

Largren – Clan lieutenant, red dragon with black dragon ancestry

DRAGON-PHOENIX

Isis – Human red dragon hybrid, fire elementalist, first life

Nisha (*NEE-shah*) – Elf violet dragon hybrid, fire elementalist, arcane user, second life

Lutha – Human white dragon hybrid, psychic: Battle Psychic, twin to Lina, third life

Lina – Human white dragon hybrid, psychic: Seer, twin to Lutha, third life

Raina – Elf green dragon hybrid, plant-based Shaman of the Fractured Earth, first Ambassador, fourth life

Nalia (*nal-EE-ah*) – Human brown dragon hybrid, Shaman of the Fractured Earth, Ambassador, fifth life

Atria (*ah-TREE-ah*) – Human black dragon hybrid, fire elementalist, sixth life

Zalia (*ZAL-ee-ah*) – Human black-chromatic dragon hybrid, lightning elementalist, seventh life

Aria – Human blue dragon hybrid, water elementalist, eighth life

Sylvia (*SILL-vee-ah*) – Human brown dragon hybrid, metal-based earth elementalist, ninth life

Ayuma (*EYE-yoo-mah*) – Human black-green dragon hybrid, fire healer, lightning elementalist, dream walker, tenth life

Rinneth – Human black dragon hybrid, lightning elementalist, eleventh life

Pheydra (*FAY-drah*) – Human black-blue dragon hybrid, water elementalist, twelfth life

Xenia (*ZEN-ee-ah*) – Human brown-red dragon hybrid, sand-based Shaman of the Fractured Earth and Shaman of the Frozen Waste, Ambassador, thirteenth life

Velsara – Nu-human dragon hybrid, Shaman of the Rising Sun, Ambassador, fourteenth life

GODS

Anila (*ah-NEE-lah*) – Goddess of air

Arcadia (*are-KAY-dee-ah*) – Goddess of spirits, daughter to Solund and Lunaria, sister to Phyre

Genesis – Goddess of time, partner to Zoltan

Gina – Goddess of health and healing

Halcyon (*hall-SEE-on*) – Goddess of the sea

Imera (*eye-MEER-ah*) – Goddess of literature and knowledge

Jin – Goddess of refined earth

Kendaria – Goddess of water

Koseba (*koh-SAY-bah*) – God of shapeshifting

Le'carro (*ley-CAR-oh*) – God of lightning

Lunaria – Goddess of the moon, partner to Solund, mother to Phyre and Arcadia

Nazir (*nah-ZEER*) – God of death, corruption, deals, trickery and deceit, interested in Rashta

Phyre (*fire*) – God of fire, son to Solund and Lunaria, brother to Arcadia

Raisu (*RAY-sue*) – God of dreams

Rashta (*RAH-sh-tah*) – Goddess of judgement and rebirth, bound to the first halfling soul. Interested in… complicated

Rasmus – God of love and fertility, partner to Savada

Satria (*sah-TREE-ah*) – Goddess of war

Savada (*sah-VAH-dah*) – Goddess of sex and seduction, partner to Rasmus

Sela – Goddess of psychics, sister of Tyro, grandmother to Seda, Nioush, Saléna, and Nyra

Solstice – Goddess of ice and winter

Solund – God of the sun, partner to Lunaria, father to Phyre and Arcadia

Tarin – God of Nature, partner to Valena

Tyro (*TIE-roh*) – God of psychics, brother of Sela, great uncle to Seda, Nioush, Saléna, and Nyra

Valena – Goddess of earth, partner to Tarin

Zion – God of dragons

Zoltan – God of matter, partner to Genesis

MISCELLANEOUS

Alyra (*all-EYE-rah*) – Nu-human experiment, former soldier, partner to Lakon, mother to Eyri, musician

Ayluin (*eye-LOO-en*) – Elf, grandfather to Sumala, tries to find Eira suitors

Carlos – Nu-human, Run competition competitor help

Den – Nu-human, Run competition commentator

Devon – Nu-human experiment, former assassin, musician

Eyri (*EYE-ree*) – Nu-human, Lakon and Alyra's daughter, musician

Lakon (*LAY-con*) – Nu-human experiment, former assassin, partner to Alyra, father to Eyri, musician

Lucas – Nu-human, Run competition competitor

Nordec – Dwarf, tavern owner

Reynor (*RAY-nor*) – Nu-human, Run competition commentator

Rosa (*ROH-sah*) – Succubus, mated to Zaedrix

Sumala (*sue-MALL-ah*) – Elf, granddaughter to Ayluin

Vorn – Dwarf, old friend to Eira

Zaedrix (*ZAY-driks*) – Incubus, mated to Rosa

SPIRITS

Amara (*ah-MAR-ah*) – Nu-human experiment, general, mother to Eira, grandmother to Ryder, sister to Jasmine and Zane, water elementalist, deceased

Anir (*ah-NEER*) – Black dragon, claims to know Eira, deceased

Jade – Nu-human experiment, former soldier under Amara, deceased

Jasmine – Nu-human experiment, aunt to Eira, sister to Amara and Zane, geneticist, deceased

Lazei (*LAH-zay*) – Human, ancient swordsman, protector of the Eternal Library, deceased but active by use of spiritual crystal

Tannek – Nu-human experiment, double ear prototype, brother to Andariel and Azriel, medic, former partner to Eira, deceased

Zeek – Nu human, Brute, former soldier under Amara, former partner to Ryoko, deceased

PEACEKEEPERS

    Assar – Dwarf, deceased
    Pyralis (*PIE-ral-iss*) – Red dragon, former Valsara Wild Clan
        leader, father of Velsara, deceased
    Raynn (*rain*) – Human, deceased
    Reiki (*Ray-KEY*) – Green dragon, deceased
    Ryoko (*Ree-OH-koh*) – Half-wogron, Shaman of the Fractured
        Crystal, mate to Varro, deceased
    Varro – Elf, healer, mate to Ryoko, deceased

ORPHANAGE

    Lyra (*LIE-ruh*) – Matron, Nu-human
    Myra (*MEER-uh*) – Nu-human, attached to Raid
    Orphans (Elara (*el-ARE-ah*), Jakcel (*JACK-sell*), Elsa, Levi,
        Panga, Nari, Kelcen (*Kell-SEN*), Alson, Ellie)

GLOSSARY LANGUAGE

ELVISH

Elvish is an eloquent language, light on the tongue with an airy sound. Even the usual consonants of common don't hold the same harshness in Elvish. Many elves and other humanoids raised with Elvish as their mother tongue carry this light speech over in their common.

While not the easiest language to learn, Elvish is a favorite among the linguistically gifted. Those who seek to learn this language seek out elves before any other race and are taught by full immersion. Some elves will provide a few words for the humanoid to start with but it's not common to do so. The elves believe this technique is the best way to learn and creates a better understanding of the language for everyday use.

Written Elvish is just as elegant as spoken, usually written in script by native speakers. Non-natives tend to forgo the script, which is accepted by native speakers, though the handwriting is still expected to be neat, and flourished on important documents. Sloppy writing is considered an insult.

Phrases used in the series:

Éan ag eitilt – Flying bird

Go dtí go gcomhlíonfaimid arís – Until we meet again
Nuair a ardaíonn an ghrian arís – When the sun rises once more

DRACONIC

Draconic is a guttural language made up most of grunts and growls with the occasional tongue flick, exhales, or teeth clatter. It's difficult for a non-dragon to learn, as the formation of these words are foreign to most humanoids. Some sounds are impossible for non-dragons to create so other sounds are substituted as an alternative. Even dragons taking a humanoid form must make these changes. Rarely is a humanoid able to perfect the speech, even when raised among dragons.

Those attempting to learn are always taught single words before attempting sentence structures. Draconic sentence structure is similar to Common, but with a possessive edge due to the mindset of dragons. There are no contracted words in Draconic, as such, dragons who don't speak common often, tend to use the same sentence structures of their mother tongue when they do speak common.

It's not common for dragons to write in the current age but there is a basic written form of the language that was used more extensively in the past. This written form is comprised of glyphs easily created with dragon claws and easy to decipher for most dragons no matter the cleanliness of the script. Non-dragons find this writing easier to learn than the spoken language and most of the time will stop learning after they've master it.

Words Raikidan has taught Eira in the series:

Aio – You	*Diik* – Food
Aion – Your	*Dnyy* – Free
Aionl – Yours	*Duny* – Fire
Ayl – Yes	*Din* – For
Cull – Kiss	*Dinytyn* – Forever
Cyyg – Keep	*Dnis* – From

Dnuyvk – Friend
Eny – Are
Eun – Air
Ev – An
Evk – And
Ezfeal – Always
Femyn – Water
Finna – Worry
Frem – What
Fryzg – Whelp
Fulkis – Wisdom
Fuzz – Will
Gyexy – Peace
Gyelevm – Peasant
Gzyely – Please
Id – Of
Iddlgnuvw – Offspring
Ion – Our
Iv – On
Ki – Do
Keowrmyn – Daughter
Knewiv – Dragon
Lgunum – Spirit
Lisymruvw – Something
Liv – Son
Livw – Song
Lmneuwrm – Straight
Lmnyvwmr – Strength
Lreny – Share
Lry – She
Luny – Sire
Lulmyn – Sister
Lupzuvw – Sibling
Lxezy – Scale
Lynyvuma – Serenity
Lyy – See
Mi – To

Mii – Too
Mioxr – Touch
Mrevc – Thank
Mruvc – Think
Mryny – There
Mnyelony – Treasure
Ol – Us
Pnimryn – Brother
Pnyemry – Breathe
Pumy – Bite
Py – Be
Regguvyll – Happiness
Rel – Has
Rety – Have
Rl – He
Rosev – Human
Rovwyn – Hunger
Rul – His
Rus – Him
Ryn – Her
Ryzzi – Hello
Sa – My
Simryn – Mother
Siny – More
Suvy – Mine
Sy – Me
Semy – Mate
U – I
Ud – If
Ul – Is
Um – It
Vi – No
Vim – Not
Vyyk – Need
Wiikpay – Goodbye
Wik – God
Wikkyll – Goddess

Wym – Get
Xifenkza – Cowardly
Xivvexmyk – Connected
Yem – Eat
Yenmr – Earth
Ytyv – Even

Ziaeza – Loyalty
Zity – Love
Zoxca – Lucky
Zudy – Life
Zulmyv – Listen
Zutyl – Lives

Phrases spoken in the series:

Ion cuvk – Our kind

Lazmira, sa xruzk – Lazmira, my child

Zity, gyexy, lgunum, ziaeza, lynyvuma, lmnyvwmr, fulkis – Love, peace, spirit, loyalty, serenity, strength, wisdom

Sa mnyelony – My treasure

Aio xevvim rety – You cannot have

U gnimyxm ryn – I protect her

Lry ul suvy – She is mine

Sevugozemuty pumxr – Manipulative bitch

Aio rety vi nyez gongily – You have no real purpose

Aio eny synyza ev enmuduxuez xnyemuiv – You are merely an artificial creation

Aio gilmony mi ruky aoin finmrzyllvyll – You posture to hide your worthlessness

Mrul finmrzyll xnyemuiv rel mry detin id Zion – This worthless creation has favor of Zion

Frem pzylluvw kiyl aoin dunyzyll lxezyl rety – What blessing does your fireless scales have

U mii pyzuyty lry fuzz lety ol – I too believe she will save us

Evk Raikidan ul zoxca mi py wutyv ryn – And Raikidan is lucky to be given her

Ud ivza ry fuzz zulmyv evk wym rul gnuinumuyl lmneuwrm – If only he will listen and get his priorities straight

U ki vim mruvc fy fuzz rety mi finna epiom mrem – I do not think we will have to worry about that

U fuzz py pexc – I will be back

Py wiik din Eira – Be good for Eira

Lry ul suvy, fryzg – She is mine, whelp

Lry vim pyzivw mi aio – She not belong to you
Lry sa mnyelony – She my treasure
U myzz ryn ud xiozk – I tell her if could
Aio vim – You not
Aoi vim xeny yviowr – You not care enough
Aoi elresyk – You ashamed
U vim – I not
Muvk nyekuvw dnyec – Mind reading freak
Aio pimr cyyg ryn ledy – You both keep her safe
Lry ul usginmevm – She is important
Mryny ul lisymruvw lgyxuez epiom ryn – There is something special about her
Ytyv ry lyyl um – Even he sees it
Aio xvyw epiom mrul dylmutex? – You knew about this festival?
Mrymy ivxy fel e zummzy knewiv wunz – There once was a little dragon girl
Lry fel lmnivw evk pyeomudoz – She was strong and beautiful
Evk rek ev yay din lruva mruvwl – And had an eye for shiny things
Regga mi lyy Eira – Happy to see Eira

LOST LANGUAGES

Thought the history of Lumaraeon, language has developed and died, but some have left a more notable impact on the races. These forgotten languages hold important information lost during the millennia of turmoil making them important topics for scholars.

OLD TONGUE

Old Tongue, also known as God speech, is the most ancient form of speech that was replaced by the various languages of Lumaraeon, ultimately dying out among the mortal races. Much of the language was lost during the War of End and with no one but the gods around to remember, the language was thought dead. Until a large find of books in the Eternal Library turned up after a new entryway was found, eight hundred years ago.

Scholars have done their best to decipher the old language and have since found new discovery sites all over Lumaraeon to help with their research. But while the tongue is researched, it is not know if the translations are quite right, and no one has thought to ask the gods, not even Imera, the goddess of literature and knowledge.

Words used in the series:

Mukarna – Makers
Spekta – Spectral

ANCIENT DRACONIC

Ancient Draconic is the most ancient form of dragon speech. Most of its knowledge has been lost to the ages, not even ancient tomes contain information about it. It's said this tongue powered magic lost to the mortals during the War of End, and what little remains, allows the dragons to speak with the elements of their scales. What speech remains is passed between dragons of the same color, never to outsiders, and none is written for others to see.

ABOUT
THE
AUTHOR

Shannon Pemrick, is a full-time USA Today bestselling author, and fuller-time geek and dragon obsessed. She also has too many novelty mugs, not enough chocolate, and a forbidden love-affair with all things shiny.

Shannon resides in Southern New Hampshire with her overly sarcastic husband and one too many pets who steal all her bed space. When she's not burning her fingers across a keyboard or trying to squeeze into a spot on the couch for movie night, she's rolling dice and getting lost in RPGs or searching for brides for her dragon overlords.

You can learn more about Shannon by visiting her website at:
Shannonpemrick.com

www.ingramcontent.com/pod-product-compliance
Lightning Source LLC
Chambersburg PA
CBHW031923110726
47902CB00001B/20